To Light a Candle

The Obsidian Trilogy, Book Two

Mercedes Lackey and James Mallory

TOR®
fantasy

A TOM DOHERTY ASSOCIATES BOOK
NEW YORK

This is a work of fiction. All the characters and events portrayed in this book are either products of the author's imagination or are used fictitiously.

TO LIGHT A CANDLE: THE OBSIDIAN TRILOGY, BOOK TWO

Copyright © 2004 Mercedes Lackey and James Mallory

All rights reserved, including the right to reproduce this book, or portions thereof, in any form.

A Tor Book
Published by Tom Doherty Associates, LLC
175 Fifth Avenue
New York, NY 10010

www.tor.com

TOR® is a registered trademark of Tom Doherty Associates, LLC.

ISBN 0-765-34142-5
EAN 978-0-765-34142-6

First edition: October 2004
First mass market edition: January 2006

Printed in the United States of America

0 9 8 7 6 5 4 3 2 1

To Light a Candle

"Lackey and Mallory combine their talents for storytelling and world crafting into a panoramic effort. . . filled with magic, dragons, elves, and other mythical creatures."

—Library Journal

"Wide-ranging viewpoints and interwoven plots suggest an action thriller. It's a rich world with an ingenious system of interlocking magics." *—Amazing Stories*

The Outstretched Shadow
VOYA Best Science Fiction, Fantasy, and Horror

"Once Kellen realizes there is a world full of wonders, diversity, and people who think and live differently, he cannot return to the oppressive sameness of City life. When he refuses to give up the books, his father banishes him forever from the City and to a horrific death prearranged by the mages. The Wild Magic has another agenda for him, however, involving an acerbic unicorn and a woman—heavens!—to learn the Wild (but not sex) Magic from. Delightful." *—Booklist*

"Kellen sets down a road he never expected to take, on a journey of dire importance to both humans and nonhumans (the latter including elves, unicorns, and other enchanting creatures). The narrative speeds to the end, avoiding a jarring halt while leaving the reader satisfied and wanting to know more."

—Publishers Weekly

"Lackey and Mallory join forces to create an epic fantasy filled with sorcery and swordplay set in a world on the verge of a Demon war." *—Library Journal*

"Their skill in weaving a story will leave readers eager for the next installment. Lackey and Mallory create a wide variety of multidimensional characters, especially Kellen who grows to manhood in realistic starts and stops, recognizing and accepting both his heritage and the consequences of his actions." *—VOYA*

To my amazing editor at Tor, Melissa Singer

To Natasha Panza at Tor for the details

To Russ Galen, the best agent a writer could have

And to the "Bad Boys" (1st Platoon), "Charlie" Company,
1-16 Infantry Regiment: good fortune and safe home.

Contents

One

In the Forest of Flowers

Kellen Tavadon could never have imagined fighting a battle so one-sided as this, but he no longer had the energy to spare for despair.

Up and around the circumference of the Black Cairn he went, and as he did, the icy wind slowly increased. It seemed to Kellen as if the source of the wind was the obelisk itself, as if it blew from someplace not of this world. As if from a great distance, he could hear inhuman yelping and the sounds of battle. If he looked, he knew he would be able to watch his friends die.

But he refused to look. He could not afford to be distracted from his battle. It took all his concentration to keep his footing on the stairs. Kellen's teeth chattered uncontrollably in the cold; tears that owed nothing to grief streamed from his eyes and froze along his cheeks and lashes. He gripped Idalia's keystone hard against his stomach and prayed that it would hold together.

If he had been able to think, he would have been certain that his situation could not be any worse, and then, as a further torment, grit mixed with the frigid wind began to pelt him. Fine sand at first, that left him blinking and half-blind, but soon good-sized pieces of gravel and small rocks that hammered his skin and even drew blood. He could taste grit between his teeth, on his tongue, feel it in his nose, in his lungs, choking him. He pulled his undertunic up over his head. It was hard to breathe through the heavy quilted leather, but as he heard the wind-driven sand hiss over its surface, Kellen was glad he'd buried his head in its folds.

Better to be half-stifled than blind. Slowly his tears washed his eyes clean.

Soon it was not just gravel that the wind carried, but rocks the size of a fist. At this rate, he'd be dodging boulders soon. And one direct hit from anything really large and he'd be dead—and the fate of Sentarshadeen, and perhaps of all of the Elves, would be sealed.

He needed to protect the keystone as well as his eyes and lungs. Kellen quickly shoved the keystone up under his shirt, and turned toward the wall so it was protected by his body as well. The keystone was as icy against his skin as it had once been warm against his hands. He turned his face against the wall, and crept even more slowly, up the stairs. The sand made them slippery, and he knew Something was hoping he'd fall and break the fragile keystone.

At least the howling of the wind and the booming of the rocks against the stone shut out all sound of the battle below. If it was still going on. If all his friends weren't dead already.

I won't look back, *Kellen promised himself.* Whatever happens, I won't look back.

It was so unfair for the enemy he faced to be throwing rocks at him! Unfair—no, it wasn't so much that it was unfair. It was humiliating. The Enemy wasn't even going to bother wasting its Demon warriors on stopping him; he wasn't an Elven Knight, after all. He wasn't any sort of a real *threat. He meant so little to the Enemy that the Enemy thought it was enough to batter him with a few rocks, certain that he was so cowardly, so worthless, that he would turn tail and run.*

That, as much as all the pain and despair, nearly broke Kellen's spirit.

Only his anger saved him.

Anger is a weapon, as much as your sword.

"I'll—show—you!" he snarled through clenched teeth. *And went on. Slowly, agonizingly slowly, blind, aching, terrified, but now, above all else, furious, he drove onward.*

Then came the worst part—when the wind and rocks be-

gan hitting him from all sides. Kellen realized that must
mean he was near the top of the cairn. Groping blindly, his
head still muffled in his tunic, he slid his hand along the wall
in front of his face, until he touched emptiness. The wind
pushed at his fingertips with the force of a river in flood. If
he tried to simply walk up to where the obelisk was, the wind
would pluck him off and hurl him to the ground.

Very well. Then he would crawl.

Kellen got down on his hands and knees and crawled up
the rest of the stairs, brushing the sand away carefully from
each step before him. It caked on his abraded hands, and
every time he wiped them clean on his tunic, fresh blood
welled up from a thousand tiny scratches. And the wind still
blew, cold enough now to steal all sensation from his flesh.

He reached a flat place, and crawled out onto it, pushing
against the wind.

Suddenly, without warning, the wind stopped. The silence
rang in his ears.

"Well, you make a fine sight," a man said from somewhere
above him, sounding amused.

The voice was elusively familiar.

Kellen dragged his tunic down around his neck and
stared, blinking, into the watery green light.

He was facing . . . himself?

Another Kellen stood on the other side of the obelisk, grinning down at him nastily. The point of the obelisk came just to
his heart level. This Kellen was sleek and manicured—no one
would ever call his smooth brown curls unruly!—and dressed
in the height of Armethaliehan finery, from his shining half-
boots of tooled and gilded leather to his fur-lined half-cape
and the pair of jeweled and embroidered silk gloves tucked
negligently through his gleaming gilded belt. The cape and
gloves were in House Tavadon colors, of course. No one would
ever forget which Mageborn City House this young man belonged to, not for an instant.

Slowly, Kellen got to his feet, though his cramped and
aching muscles protested. Instantly, Other-Kellen clapped

his bare hands over the point of the obelisk, blocking Kellen's access to it.

"Think about what you're doing," Other-Kellen urged him. "Really think about it. Now, before it's too late. You've had a chance to taste freedom, and you've found it's a bitter wine. Only power can make it sweet, but you already know the responsibilities that power brings. Even the powerful aren't really free. The only real freedom we have is of choosing our master, and most people don't get even that. But you can choose."

"I don't serve anyone!" Kellen said angrily.

"Oh? And you a Wildmage," Other-Kellen said mockingly. "I should think you would have learned better the moment you opened the Books."

Kellen snapped his mouth shut abruptly. If this was a fight, he'd just lost the first battle. He did serve the Wild Magic, and so far he'd done exactly what it told him to do. How free did that make him?

"You've made some bad choices in the past," Other-Kellen continued smoothly. "Even you're willing to admit that. Wouldn't you like the chance to undo them? To start over, knowing what you know now? You can have that. Few people get that opportunity."

Other-Kellen smiled, and for the first time, Kellen could see his father's face mirrored in this stranger's that was his own. The sight shocked and distracted him, even in this moment and in this place. Assurance . . . competence . . . or just corruption?

"You left Armethalieh because you rebelled against your father's plans for you, but you know better now, don't you? Arch-Mage Lycaelon only wants for you what he has always enjoyed himself! And that's not so bad, now, is it? What does it matter if it takes a bit of groveling and scraping, and a lot of boring make-work to get there? Think about how you used to live—and how you live now. The life of a High Mage has its compensations—and the High Mages were right, back when they walled themselves off in their city. They were right *to want to build safeguards against the prices and bargains the Wild Magic required," his doppelganger said, his voice as silken and sweet as honey, reasonable and logical. Kellen himself had never sounded like that. "What's so wrong with trying to improve something? They still practice magic, and they do so without the prices that the Wild Magic demands. They give their citizens a good life—and if life in the Golden City is too restrictive, well, when you're Arch-Mage, Kellen, you'll be able to make all the changes you've dreamed of."*

That shocked Kellen so much that he almost dropped the keystone. Of all of the things he had imagined and fantasized about, that was never one that had occurred to him!

"And you can be Arch-Mage," the double said, persuasively. "You have the gift and the talent; your father isn't wrong about that! If everyone must serve, then choose your service. Serve the City. Go back now, beg your father's forgiveness—it won't be that hard. Give up the Wild Magic. That won't be hard, either, will it? Step back into the life you should have had, and work for the good of Armethalieh. You'll have everything you wanted. Just think of all you can do for the City when you return . . ."

Kellen stared in horrified fascination at his doppelganger. Was this really him? The person he could have been—or could still be?

If he did this, could he even turn the City to help the Elves, and forge a new Alliance as in the old days?

But Jermayan would know what had happened—

Shalkan surely would—

Vestakia—

"Your companions are already dead. You have no one to consider but yourself. No one will know what happened here but you. Isn't it time you did what you want, for a change? Here is your future, Kellen." His doppelganger leaned forward, his face wearing a mask of pleasantry, his voice eager, urging. "You have but to reach out and seize it. And you will receive nothing but praise for your actions."

Now Kellen looked away, down toward the plain below,

but everything below the top of the cairn was covered with a thick layer of yellow-green fog. It was as if the rest of the world had vanished. Quickly he looked back at his doppelganger, suspecting a trick, but Other-Kellen had not moved. His doppelganger smiled at Kellen sympathetically, as if guessing the direction of Kellen's thoughts.

"But if you go through with this foolish adventure, your future will be set. If you think you have troubles now, you can't even begin to imagine what your life is going to be like afterward—assuming you don't die right here. Think of the Demons. They know your name, Kellen. The Queen and Prince of the Endarkened know who you are. They know all about you, and they'll find you wherever you go. You won't have an easy death, or a quick one. Torment—oh, for them, it is the highest form of Art, and they have had millennia to perfect it. You won't die, but you will long for death with all of your being. For years, Kellen, for years . . . "

Other-Kellen shuddered in mock-sympathy, his eyes never leaving Kellen's face. Kellen's face. Kellen trembled, remembering his nightmares, knowing they must have fallen far short of the truth.

"Oh, you might survive triggering the keystone. You might even manage to get back to Sentarshadeen alive. And I'm sure your friends the Elves will do their best for you. But it hasn't really been much of a best so far, has it? They couldn't even manage to save themselves without a Wildmage or two to help. And when it comes right down to it, they're going to take care of themselves and their families first once the trouble starts, aren't they?

"I wouldn't say we're friends, exactly, but I would say I'm the closest thing to a friend you've got. Right here. Right now. Think about it, Kellen. This is your last chance. After this, you have no choices left. Think. Use what you've learned. They've all tried to keep the truth from you so you wouldn't know what the stakes are. Think how hard you've had to work to find out what little you have. Why is that? So you wouldn't know enough to make a fair choice," Other-Kellen said.

Fair, *Kellen thought bitterly.* Nothing about this is fair. *Nothing had ever been fair and out in the open, from the moment he'd found the three Books in the Low Market, and hearing all his secret fears and unworthy hopes in the mouth of this manicured popinjay was the least fair thing of all.*

He remembered Jermayan telling him about The Seven— how when they'd faced down the Endarkened army at the pass of Vel-al-Amion and first beaten them back, the Endarkened had tried to seduce them to the Dark.

As one of the Endarkened was trying to seduce him now. This, then, was their last line of defense, and the most compelling of all.

"Well . . . " Kellen said, walking closer and lifting the keystone in his hands as if he were about to hand it over. "I guess I really ought to be smart and do what you say."

The Other-Kellen smiled triumphantly and relaxed, certain of its victory.

"But I'm not going to!" Kellen shouted.

He brought the keystone down—hard—on the doppelganger's hands. It howled and recoiled as if it had been burned, jerking its hands back from the point of the obelisk.

And in that moment, it . . . changed.

The Other-Kellen was gone. In its place stood a Demon.

It—she!—towered over Kellen, her wings spread wide. He caught a confused glimpse of blood-red skin, of horns and claws, but she was barely there for an instant, for in the moment that the Demon had released her hold on the obelisk, Kellen slammed the keystone down over the tip of the stone.

The instant the keystone touched the obelisk, the Demon howled in fury and vanished, her cheated rage a whiplash across his senses. For a moment he was blind and deaf in a paroxysm of pain. He cringed, but kept his hands on the stone.

They had not counted on his experience with being lied to. And perhaps that was the greatest weapon Lycaelon Tavadon had given to him.

I know a lie when I hear it, you bastards! His father had

lied to him so smoothly, so convincingly, and so often, that Kellen had learned every guise that a lie could wear.

Kellen trembled all over, realizing in that moment how close the Demon had come to winning. But it hadn't.

Now it was up to him. Despite everything he had already gone through, the hardest part was still to come. Hardest— and yet, in its way, the easiest. All he had to do was surrender—surrender his will, surrender his power, and put it all in the service of something far outside himself.

He took a deep breath and reached down into the keystone with his Wildmage senses, touching the power waiting within. The power leaped toward him eagerly, but Kellen knew that he was not to be its destination. Gently he turned it toward the obelisk.

He felt the obelisk's resistance, and pushed harder, adding the last of his strength and all of his will to the keystone's power, forcing the link into being.

One by one, the obelisk's defenses gave way. Kellen felt the triggering force begin to rush through him and into the obelisk. He kept his palms pressed against the keystone's sides; without him to maintain the link, the spell would be broken before the Barrier was breached. And all of it—the journey, the others' sacrifice—would all have been for nothing.

Then, breakthrough.

And his body spasmed, convulsed, his mouth going open in a silent scream.

This was worse than anything he could have imagined. He felt as if he were being struck by bolt after bolt of lightning, a torrent of energy that somehow went on and on and on, searing its way through him.

His hands were burning. Holding the keystone was like clutching red-hot metal fresh from the forge, and there was no respite, no mercy. He could smell the pork-like scent of his cooking flesh, could feel blood running down his wrists as blisters swelled up and burst, and then, in a thunderclap of agony, the fire was everywhere, coursing through his veins with every beat of his heart.

Kellen howled unashamedly, great wracking sobs of hopeless agony. And he held on. Perhaps it was stubbornness, but he had always been stubborn. And he would not give the Demons this victory.

Then came a single thought, emerging through the fire and the pain.

I'm going to die.

He realized at that moment that this was the price of the spell, the rest of the cost. It must be. A Wildmage's life. Idalia must have known when she created the spell that the price of casting it would be the life of the one who triggered it. His life. Kellen felt a flash of pride in his sister at keeping the painful secret so well.

But he would have to consent. No Wildmage could give up that which belonged to another—not without turning to the Dark.

She had known the price of the magic, but she could only have hoped he would pay it. Well, he wasn't going to let her down. He would be everything she had hoped. And if he had been an uncouth barbarian to the Elves of Sentarshadeen, at least he would be an uncouth barbarian whose name would live on in their legends forever.

If that's the price, he shouted silently *to the Powers,* then I will pay it! I wish I didn't have to, but I swear I pay it willingly and without reservation!

But more than ever, having surrendered his life, he yearned to keep it. To see the sun again, to feel the gentle summer wind, to walk through the forest or drink a cup of morning tea. But all those things had their price, and so did keeping them. And some prices were too high to pay. The price of his life would be the destruction of all those things, soon or late. The price of keeping his life would be victory for the Endarkened.

No. Never!

My life for the destruction of the Barrier. A fair bargain. Done. Done!

Then the pain was too great for thought.

Abruptly the obelisk began to swell, its stark lines distort-

*ing as if the malign power it contained was backing up in-
side it, filling it beyond its capacity. Its swelling carried him
upward; he collapsed against its surface, clinging to the keystone, and still it swelled. Now the stone was a baneful pus-
yellow color, nearly spherical. Kellen lay upon its surface,
unable to preserve the thought of anything beyond the need
to maintain the link.*

The whole cairn shook like a tree in a windstorm.

The toxic light flared lightning-bright.

*And for Kellen, there was sudden darkness and a release
from all pain.*

⟜

THEN, of course, there was a return to life, and pain. And
since the latter meant that he still had the former, it was less
unwelcome than it might have been. And through the pain,
the faces of Vestakia and Jermayan—so they had survived!

It had all been worth it then. Only afterward did it occur
to him that the compounded trouble he had fallen back into
might make him begin to regret that return to life . . .

⟜

IT had taken them only a sennight to travel from
Sentarshadeen—easternmost of the Nine Cities—into the
heart of the Lost Lands to face the power of Shadow
Mountain.

The return trip took longer, though at least nobody was trying to kill them this time. That did not mean, however, that the
journey was less trying. If anything, it was physically harder.

To begin with, it was raining—although rain, Kellen reflected grimly, wearily, was a mild word to apply to the water that had been falling from the sky nonstop for the last
moonturn.

It was just a good thing that Elven armor didn't—couldn't—
rust.

Jermayan, of course, didn't mind the rain at all. But the Elven lands had been suffering under the effects of a deadly spell-inflicted drought for almost a year. Kellen had only spent a few days in Sentarshadeen before heading north toward the Barrier, and even what little he'd seen of the Elves' desperate attempts to save their city and the forest surrounding it had been enough to daunt him. How much more terrifying must it have been for an Elven Knight, one of the land's protectors, to watch every-thing he loved wither and die for sennight upon sennight, know-ing there was nothing he could do about it?

No wonder Jermayan welcomed the rain.

Vestakia didn't seem to mind the weather all that much ei-ther. But then, Vestakia had spent her entire life living nearly alone in a little shepherd's hut in the wildest part of the Lost Lands, with only a few goats for company. A little rain—or even a lot of rain—probably didn't bother her too much.

But it felt increasingly like torture to Kellen. For one thing, he still wasn't all that used to uncontrolled weather. He'd grown up in the Mage-City of Armethalieh, where everything—including the weather—was governed by the rule of the High Mages. He'd never actually *seen* rain until he'd been Banished by the High Council for his possession of the three Books of Wildmagery—and his Banishment hadn't been that long ago. He'd never had to stand out in the rain in his life.

But now . . . well, there wasn't anything like a roof for leagues and leagues, probably. Even when they stopped to rest, they never really got out of the rain. The most they could manage was to drape some canvas over themselves, or, if they were lucky, find a half-cave, or shelter under a tree.

To add to his misery, he was still suffering from the in-juries he had gotten in his battle to break the Barrier-spell. He'd been so sure that his life would be the price of the spell that awakening afterward had been a shock. After all, every kind of magic required payment, and the first lesson the Wildmage learned was that each spell of the Wild Magic came with a cost, both in the personal energy of the caster, and in the form of a task the Wildmage must perform.

But in this case, it seemed his willingness to sacrifice his life had been enough. Or perhaps, just perhaps, the cost had been his willingness to live and endure.

If you can call this living, he thought, as he rode along behind the others in the direction of home. His injuries had been so severe that it had been a sennight before he'd been able to ride at all, and his burned hands were so heavily bandaged that he couldn't possibly wear his armored gauntlets, much less hold a sword. Any protecting that was going to be done was going to have to be done by Jermayan, and maybe Shalkan, and possibly Vestakia; he was strictly along as baggage.

He had become so used to pain that now he could hardly remember a time when he had lived without it as a constant presence. And underneath the pain was fear, fear he never openly expressed, but was constantly with him. The fear of what was underneath those bandages.

He would much rather dwell on the minor misery of the rain.

His heavy hooded oiled-wool cloak was soaked through. His heavy silk surcoat was wet. The unending rain had managed to make it through both of those layers and even through the tiny joins and chinks in the delicately-jointed Elven armor that he wore, soaking the padding beneath.

It wasn't that he was cold—he wasn't, even with winter coming on. All the layers he wore saw to that. But he'd never felt so soggy in his life.

He rested the heels of his hands—wrapped in goatskin mittens to keep the bandages dry, and medicated to the point where the pain was only a dull nagging—against the front of his saddle, gazing around himself at the transformed landscape. Everything looked so different now! On the outward trip, they'd been navigating mostly by his Wildmage intuition to find the direction of the Barrier; his sister Idalia, who was a much stronger Wildmage, hadn't been able to locate it by scrying, and until he and Jermayan had linked up with Vestakia, they'd had no way of sensing it directly. So for the first part of the trip, they'd been traveling mostly by guess . . . and through a far different countryside than this.

The rain had changed everything about the landscape that had once been so parched and barren. There were lakes where none had been before, meadows had become impassable swamps, trickling streams had become rivers, and all the landmarks he'd memorized on the outward trip were gone. On their return passage, they'd had to rely on Jermayan's familiarity with the Elven lands and Valdien's and Shalkan's instincts to find them a route that wasn't underwater or under mud.

"Are we there yet?" he muttered under his breath.

"Sooner than you think," Shalkan answered.

Kellen sighed. He hadn't thought Shalkan would be able to hear him over the sound of the rain. But by now, he should know better than to underestimate the keenness of the unicorn's hearing.

"How long?" he asked.

"Less than an hour. We've already passed the first scouts from Sentarshadeen. They've probably gone back to warn the welcoming party to be ready to greet us." The unicorn's voice was bland, but Kellen's stomach clenched in a tight knot of tension. He'd lost all track of how long they'd been traveling, and hadn't had any idea they were so close. Now the aching of his body was joined by the clenching of his gut. They had gone out a party of three. They were returning a party of four. And one of the four was not going to be welcomed with open arms by the Elves.

"Does he know?" Kellen asked. He nodded to where Jermayan rode on Valdien, with Vestakia—thoroughly bundled up, of course—sitting behind him on the destrier's saddle. At the end of a long tether, the cream-colored pack mule ambled along behind Valdien, every inch of her covered with the black mud splashed up from the road. At least once they were back in Sentarshadeen it would be someone else's job to try to get her—and Valdien—clean.

"He saw them, I imagine," Shalkan said, without adding

the obvious: that naturally Jermayan would recognize exactly where he was, even if Kellen didn't. And that Elven senses were much keener than Kellen's. Especially now, when most of Kellen's awareness was wrapped in pain.

Almost home—at least, as much home as Sentarshadeen was. Dry, out of the rain, and a chance to sleep in a proper bed again. And most of all, a proper Healer to deal with his hands and anything else that was wrong with him. Kellen tried to look forward to those things.

Unfortunately, there were a lot of things about their welcome home that he wasn't looking forward to. And unfortunately, he was not really certain that a Healer *would* be able to set his hands right again.

⌐

EVEN at the beginning of winter, the Elven valley bloomed. The silver sheen of the unicorn meadow had turned to deep emerald when the rains came, and the parched city had come back to life.

Released from their desperate hopeless task of attempting to irrigate the forest lands surrounding their canyon home, the Elves had resumed their patrols of the deep woods and the extended borders of their homeland, for now, more than ever, it was vitally necessary, with their ancient Enemy roused to life once more. And only a short time ago, one of those scout-pairs—a unicorn and his rider—had brought word to Queen Ashaniel that Kellen and Jermayan had been sighted upon the road.

Idalia had been about to scry for news of them when the Queen's message was brought to her. She had immediately gone to the House of Leaf and Star, both to thank the Queen for the news and to hear more of it than the scouts had brought to her.

Though the House of Leaf and Star was—in every sense that humans understood the word—the palace of the King and Queen of the Elves, it was not even as grand as the house Idalia had grown up in. Elven buildings were not meant to be imposing, but to be *suitable,* and although the House of Leaf and Star was one of the largest structures in all the Elven Lands, it still managed to look welcoming and homelike. It was a low, deep-eaved house built of silvery wood and pale stone, and age and strength radiated from it as from an ancient living tree.

By the time she had crossed the long roofed portico, her cloak and wide-brimmed Mountain Trader hat had shed most of their burden of water, and her boots had dried themselves upon the intricate design of slatted wood with which the portico floor was inlaid—crafted for just that purpose, as all the works of the Elves managed to combine beauty and practicality with flawless ease.

She was not surprised to see the door open before she reached it.

"I See you, Idalia Wildmage," the Elven doorkeeper said politely.

"I See you, Sakathirin," Idalia answered with equal politeness. Elvenkind was both an ancient and a long-lived race, and except under extraordinary circumstances, its members were unfailingly courteous and unhurried. Part of the courtesy was the assumption that a person might not wish to be noticed; the greeting *I See you* was meant to convey acknowledgment of one's presence, with the implicit right being that one did not have to respond if one wished to be left alone. "I have come to share news with the Lady Ashaniel, if she would See me as well."

"The Lady Ashaniel awaits you with joy," Sakathirin said gravely. "Be welcome at our hearth." He stepped back to allow Idalia to enter.

The rain pattering down on the skylight echoed through the tall entry-hall, its music a counterpoint to the splashing of the fountain that once more bubbled and sang beneath it. Idalia smiled, seeing that reflecting pool was once again filled with fish, their living forms mirroring the mosaic they swam above, that of fish swimming in a river. The Elves delighted in this form of shadowplay, combining living things with their copies so expertly that it was often hard for mere humans to tell where Nature ended and Elven artistry began.

By the time Sakathirin had disposed of her cloak and hat, one of Ashaniel's ladies-in-waiting had appeared to conduct Idalia to the Queen's day-room.

In Armethalieh, such a room would have been called a "solar," but that was hardly an appropriate word for this room today. The walls were made of glass—hundreds of tiny panes, all held together in a bronze latticework—and the room seemed to hang in space, surrounded by a lacework made of light and air.

And water.

Raindrops starred the palm-sized windows, and streaks of rain ran down the outside of the glass like a thousand miniature rivers. The effect might have been chilly, despite the warmth of the lamps and braziers that filled the room, save for the fact that the room's colors were so warm. The ceiling had been canopied in heavy velvet—not pink, which would only have been garish—but a deep warm taupe, rich as fur. The pillows and carpets picked up those colors and added more: deep violets, ember-orange, a dark clear blue shot through with threads of silver . . . autumn colors, and those of winter, concentrated and intensified until they kindled the room.

The Queen herself was dressed in shades of amber, every hue from clear pale candle-flame yellow to the deep ruddy glow of sunset's heart. Her hair was caught back in a net of gold and fire opals, and she wore a collar of the same stones about her throat.

"Idalia," she said, smiling and setting aside her writing desk as she indicated a place beside her on the low couch upon which she sat. "Come and sit beside me, and we will talk. Your brother and Jermayan will not reach the edge of the city for some time yet, and there is much to do in preparation. They seem well enough, so Imriban said," she added, answering the question Idalia could not, in politeness, ask.

"Though Imriban said that the Wildmage rides as one lately injured."

Idalia came and seated herself, taking care that her damp buckskins didn't touch Ashaniel's elaborate velvet gown.

"It would be good to hear all of what Imriban had to say," she offered carefully.

Learning to speak in accordance with the dictates of Elven politeness was one of the hardest lessons for the humans who came to live among them to learn. The closest it was possible to get to asking a question was to announce your desire to know something, and hope your hearer took pity on you.

"Imriban said . . . " Ashaniel paused, and for the first time seemed to be choosing her words with great care. "Imriban said that they do not travel alone."

"Not alone—" It was a struggle to keep from turning her words into a question, but Idalia managed. "It puzzles me to hear that," she finally said.

"It puzzles me as well," Ashaniel admitted. "The one who rides with them rides cloaked and hooded beyond all seeing. And it occurs to me to wish that perhaps Imriban had been less . . . impetuous."

And maybe stopped and spoken to them, instead of just tearing back to Sentarshadeen to bring the news that they were on the way. Idalia finished the Queen's unspoken thought silently. It was hard to imagine who Kellen and Jermayan could have run into on their quest, and why they'd bring whoever it was back to Sentarshadeen.

"I suppose we'll know soon enough," she offered reluctantly.

"Indeed," Ashaniel said with a sigh. "And yet . . . it will be well should we meet them as close upon the road as we may, so Andoreniel has said. Even now, a place is being prepared at the edge of the Flower Forest, where we may receive them in all honor."

"LOOKS like they couldn't wait to meet us," Shalkan said dryly, dipping his head to indicate the flash of yellow in the distance with his horn.

"What's that?" Kellen said superfluously.

Jermayan cleared his throat warningly before answering. "A pavilion."

Kellen took the hint. On the road, their manners had been free and easy—War Manners, Jermayan had called it. The Elven Knight had set aside the elaborate code of Elven formality; he'd asked Kellen direct questions, and Kellen had been allowed, even encouraged, to question Jermayan directly in return.

But they were back in Civilization now, and he guessed he'd have to get used to it all over again. It hardly seemed fair. He'd gone through so much—and why must he be burdened with this stifling formality now, when it was all he could do to pretend that he was certain he would be all right?

Well, he'd better warn Vestakia.

He was trying to figure out the best way to phrase it when Jermayan beat him to it.

"In Elven lands, except in time of war, or dire need, to question another directly is considered to be unmannerly. I do not say that this is good or bad, merely that this is our custom, and perhaps we are fonder of our customs than we ought to be," Jermayan observed, as if speaking to Valdien. "Perhaps it is a failing in us. Perhaps it is merely that when one lives as long as an Elf, custom becomes habit, and habit is often so difficult to break that one gives over the attempt."

Kellen heard Vestakia's muffled snort of nervous laughter. "I don't think I'm going to be asking anyone any questions anytime soon, Jermayan. I'll count myself lucky if they don't fill me full of arrows on sight."

"That they will not," Jermayan said, his voice filled with grim promise now.

As they rode closer, Kellen could see the yellow pavilion more clearly.

It was rectangular, and quite large—large enough for

them to ride right inside, as Kellen suspected they were meant to. Colored pennants flew from the centerpost and from all four corners—and whether from the artfulness of their construction, or from a touch of the "small magics" the Elves still commanded—they *did* fly, and were not simply sodden rain-soaked rags wrapped around the gilded tent posts. The tent was trimmed in scarlet, and the tent ropes that held it firm against the buffeting winds were scarlet as well.

In the grey gloom of the day, the lamps inside the walls of yellow silk made it glow like the lanterns the Elves hung outside their homes at dusk, casting shadows of tables and moving bodies against the fabric.

As they came closer, a flap in the near side of the pavilion began to rise. Kellen saw two Elves in full armor walk it out and peg it into place with tall gilded poles, so that it formed a sort of canopy entrance. Now he could see into the pavilion, and see that there was some kind of flooring as well. Trust the Elves to do everything . . . thoroughly.

They rode forward, into the tent.

The sudden cessation of the rain drumming on his head felt wonderful. Kellen glanced quickly around as he kicked his feet free of Shalkan's stirrups and swung his leg over the back of the saddle. It was awkward not being able to use his hands, but he managed.

Idalia was there, and it looked like all the cream of the nobility had turned out to meet them as well, all wearing their finest robes and jewels. There were a few Elves wearing armor like Jermayan's, but even their colors blended into the harmonious whole: nothing clashed, nothing was out of place.

Both Ashaniel and Andoreniel were present, dressed in what Kellen thought of as full Court robes—Ashaniel in gold, Andoreniel in bronze—along with several of their counselors, and—

"Kellen!"

He'd barely steadied himself on his feet when a small bundle of energy detached himself from his nurse's skirts and ran forward, flinging his arms about Kellen's waist.

"You came back! I told them all you'd come back!" Sandalon said defiantly.

"Of course I came back," Kellen said, patting the young Elven prince's back awkwardly with one of his goatskin mitts. "And I brought Jermayan back, too."

"He's got someone with him," Sandalon said, with a young child's directness.

Kellen turned, to see that Jermayan had dismounted from Valdien, and was lifting Vestakia down from the saddle. As he did, her hooded cloak fell back, and her face was exposed.

She grabbed for the hood, but it was too late. Everyone there had seen.

"A Demon! Jermayan brings a Demon here!" Tyendimarquen gasped. All around him, the pavilion was filled with frightened whispers as the Elves drew back.

Lairamo rushed forward and grabbed Sandalon, the Elven nurse snatching the boy up into her arms and hurrying back behind Andoreniel and Ashaniel.

"Jermayan, you will explain yourself," Andoreniel demanded, his voice harsh.

Before he answered, Jermayan made sure that Vestakia was steady on her feet—and then, very deliberately, drew the hood of the cloak back so that all could see her face.

Her skin was the rosy-red of ripe cherries; her short curly hair a darker shade of the same red, and her ears were as pointed as an Elf's. Pale gold horns sprouted from just above her slanting eyebrows and curved back over her head. Her eyes were the same yellow-gold as a cat's, with the same narrow slitted pupils. All these things, everyone knew, were the marks of the Endarkened, the evil race that was the enemy to all that lived and walked in sunlight. But despite her appearance, Vestakia was no Demon. And had anyone bothered to look past the mask of her face, they would have seen her expression—frightened, pleading, open, and desperately hoping for some kind of acceptance.

"Lord Andoreniel, Lady Ashaniel, I bring before you Vestakia, an ally, without whose help the Barrier would not have fallen," Jermayan said evenly, turning to face the other Elves. "She is without Taint, a fellow-victim of *Them*, and I have promised her refuge here."

Shalkan took a step backward, toward Vestakia. Knowing what was expected of her, Vestakia placed a hand on his neck, her scarlet fingers sinking into his soft silvery fur. At this, the murmurings from the gathered Elves broke out anew. Everyone knew that the touch of a unicorn was death to Demonkind. If Vestakia were truly what she seemed, she should not be able to touch Shalkan.

But it wasn't enough. Andoreniel was shaking his head.

"No. You have promised that which you cannot fulfill, Jermayan son of Malkirinath. She will not enter the city."

"Then we're leaving."

For a moment Kellen wondered who'd spoken, then realized it was him. But the words felt right. The decision felt right. And—all right, he needed a Healer, but surely Idalia would follow them and fix him, even if they left. Surely—

He glanced at Shalkan.

"I'm with you," the unicorn said.

"And I," Jermayan said firmly.

"We won't stay where *all* of us aren't wanted," Kellen said, locking eyes with Andoreniel. "Without Vestakia's help, the Barrier would still be standing. She's the one who found it for us. She—and Jermayan, and Shalkan— protected me while I destroyed it. No matter what she looks like, she *isn't* one of *Them*. She's as human as I am. So—"

"There's a simple way to solve all of this."

Idalia stepped forward, into the open space between the new arrivals and the Elves of Sentarshadeen.

"If you won't take the word of an Elven Knight, a unicorn, and a . . . Knight-Mage . . . for the fact that Vestakia bears no Taint, it would be good to hear that *my* word will suffice. There are simple tests I can perform, right here in the Flower Forest, to determine beyond a shadow of a doubt whether she can bring any harm to Sentarshadeen—if you will trust

me and accept my judgment in this matter," Idalia announced matter-of-factly.

Kellen felt a wave of relief wash over him, and saw the
tension ease in Andoreniel's face as well.

"Of course we will trust you, Idalia," Andoreniel said,
bowing slightly. "We are in your debt."

Andoreniel might feel that way, but Kellen doubted everyone there shared his feelings. Elven expressions were notoriously difficult for mere humans to decipher, but the tension
in the pavilion was thick enough to cut with a sword.

"Kellen?" Idalia went on, turning to Kellen and Jermayan.
"Will you abide by my judgment as well?"

Though Kellen was the one she asked—for the sake of
politeness—the question included both of them, and it was
Jermayan who answered first.

"I have no doubt of what you will find, Wildmage," Jermayan said austerely.

"Well, I, uh . . . yeah," Kellen said. He knew Idalia
wouldn't lie, and he knew Vestakia wasn't Demon-tainted.
So how could she be a danger to Sentarshadeen?

"Go with her, child," Jermayan said softly to Vestakia.
"She will do you no harm."

THIS was not the grand reunion she had envisioned between
herself and Jermayan, Idalia thought with a flash of irritation, as she settled her hat more firmly upon her head and led
Vestakia out of the pavilion and into the rain once more.

Trust Kellen to manage to work a few surprises into a simple homecoming—and to come home a Knight-Mage, as well!

He was thinner than he'd been when he'd left. There were
shadows and hollows in his face that hadn't been there even
a scant few sennights before. And he'd found his way into
his magic—his own magic. What he had become was unmistakable in the sight of any Wildmage.

A Knight-Mage. The rarest kind of Wildmage, only appearing in a time of direst need. If they'd needed any more proof that they were all in deep trouble, Kellen's manifestation of Knight-Mage powers should provide it. But despite that, she found it in her heart to be happy for him, because for the first time since her little brother had been dropped back on her doorstep through the auspices of an Outlaw Hunt, she sensed that Kellen had a real sense of his place in the world, of who he was and what his purpose was.

It was just too bad it was so very dangerous . . .

She and Vestakia reached the edge of the Flower Forest, and Idalia led Vestakia beneath its leafy canopy. The force of the rain was muted almost at once, to a gentle patterning on the dense canopy of leaves.

Though it was late autumn, the Flower Forest was in full leaf. Since the destruction of the great Elven forests in the Great War, many of the trees that grew in the Elven Flower Forests no longer grew anywhere else in the world, and the Flower Forests—as had the great Elven forests of which they were the only survivals—paid little heed to the turning of the seasons.

Thick moss cushioned the ground beneath their feet, and the air was appreciably warmer within the forest than it had been outside. The air was filled with the spicy scent of the trees and the rich fragrance of their flowers.

"It's so beautiful," Vestakia breathed in wonder, staring about herself in awe. "I never . . . I was raised in the Wild Hills, you see. I saw forests when we rode south, and Kellen said that there were even larger forests further south, but . . . "

"Well, nothing could really prepare you for the Flower Forest," Idalia said kindly. "There isn't really anything anywhere like a Flower Forest . . . except maybe another Flower Forest."

Vestakia giggled nervously. "Are there many of those?"

"Well, there are nine Elven cities, and every Elven city has a Flower Forest, so there are probably at least nine," Idalia said gravely. "I've only seen two of the Elven cities—counting this one—so I can't say for sure."

"It must be wonderful to be able to travel and see things," Vestakia said, sounding very young. Idalia wondered just how old she was. It was hard to tell, given the girl's rather *exotic* appearance, but she didn't seem to be much older than Kellen was.

They stopped in a little clearing, where the rain had made a small pool. Tiny white and purple flowers starred the deep green moss about its verge. The forest canopy stretched overhead, protecting them from the rain.

"We didn't actually have to come all the way in here," Idalia said, "but I thought you'd like a little privacy. Elves can be rather *daunting* when you meet a lot of them for the first time. Although you and Jermayan seem to get on well enough."

"Oh." Abruptly recalled to the reason they'd come to the forest, Vestakia regarded Idalia nervously with wide golden eyes.

Idalia reached into her bag and pulled out a small flask, offering it to the girl. "Here. Have a drink. It's just brandy and hard cider. My name's Idalia, by the way, if you didn't catch it back there in the tent. I'm Kellen's sister."

"Yes," Vestakia said, unstoppering the flask and drinking gratefully before returning it to Idalia. "He told me about you—a little. You're a Wildmage. My mother was a Wildmage, too."

Idalia's eyes widened a little at that, but she said nothing. So Vestakia's mother was a Wildmage, was she? Even more reason for Kellen and Jermayan to trust her.

"And how did you come to find my brother?" Idalia asked. She drank in turn, and as she slipped the flask back into her bag, she closed her fingers about a charged keystone.

Show me truth, she commanded.

"Oh, I didn't find Kellen," Vestakia said simply. "He found me. He rescued me from a bandit who was stealing my goats—and then I went with him and Jermayan to the Barrier, just as they said. They never would have found it without me," she added proudly.

All at once her shoulders seemed to droop with more than weariness.

"Jermayan told me his people would accept me here. But . . . I do not think they will. No one will, when I look the way I do!"

The keystone spell had told Idalia nothing, which was in itself an answer. The truth was already here for her to see.

"They're afraid," Idalia said neutrally. "But tell me the rest—if you've known my brother for any length of time at all, you'll know he's miserably bad at telling a story, and if I wait to hear the rest of your tale from him I might very well wait forever!"

It took very little prodding to get the rest of Vestakia's story out of her, of how her mother, a Wildmage, had been seduced unawares by the Prince of Shadow Mountain; how discovering that she was pregnant with a half-Demon child, she called upon the Wild Magic to help her . . . and been offered a choice.

The unborn child could be completely hers in spirit, and its Demon-father's in body; or its father's in spirit, yet human in body. Vestakia's mother had made the harder choice; Vestakia had a human spirit, but a Demon's body. To keep her unborn child from being slain at birth, Vestakia's mother had fled with her sister deep into the Lost Lands, where Vestakia had been born. There Vestakia had lived alone after both women had died, until Kellen had found and rescued her.

Her Demon-father, of course, continued to hunt for her, but Vestakia had one great gift that kept her safe, though it came at a price. She could sense the presence of Demons, because they made her ill. The closer they were, the greater her distress, and she learned quickly to hide whenever she felt a hint of their presence.

"And then I found—when Kellen asked me to try—that my gift worked just the same way with the Demon magic, if the spell is strong enough. So we found the Barrier," Vestakia said, her voice a mixture of triumph and remembered horror.

"Jermayan saved my life there. And Kellen . . . Kellen saved all of us," she said softly.

⌒

THERE was a moment of awkward silence after Idalia and Vestakia left, and Kellen wasn't quite sure what to do next. At least he was sure that everything was going to turn out all right. Of course Idalia would find that there was nothing wrong with Vestakia, and they could all stay. Of course. Idalia could do anything she set her mind to.

And if he had to—well, wait until Jermayan told them the whole story of destroying the Barrier. Elven custom would *force* them into such overwhelming obligation to him that they would probably do anything he asked of them. For once, the intricate dance of Elven custom would work in his favor, for by the time Vestakia got enough accustomed to the Elves that she would be able to tell when welcome was forced and when it was not, it would be too late, for they would have discovered for themselves just how worthy of their trust she was, and the welcome would be real.

Jermayan settled the matter, removing his cloak and handing it to another Elf who seemed to appear out of nowhere. Another arrived to take his sword and shield, then Jermayan removed his helmet and gauntlets, handing them off in turn before moving to Kellen's side.

It was a little embarrassing—okay, a *lot* embarrassing—to have to just stand there while Jermayan removed his cloak, helmet, shield, and sword for him, but Kellen couldn't really do any of those things for himself with his hands in the goatskin mitts. And he knew that only nervous tension was keeping him on his feet now.

"Come and sit," Jermayan said softly, taking him by the elbow.

When they stepped forward, the waiting Elves settled gracefully into their places, just as if they'd rehearsed every motion for years. There was a long table draped in heavy damask set along the right side of the pavilion—the left side apparently being reserved for the comfort of the animals—with simple wooden chairs clustered around it.

"You must be weary after your long journey," Ashaniel said when they had seated themselves.

Looking across the pavilion, Kellen could see that servants—if there were servants among the Elves, something he still wasn't completely sure of—were unsaddling Valdien and removing Lily's packsaddle, and even helping Shalkan off with his armor and saddle. That wouldn't make it easy for them to leave in a hurry, if they had to, but Elves did not hurry. Even if they were angry, Kellen supposed.

"It was a journey I did not think we would live to complete," Jermayan answered somberly. "But Leaf and Star favored us, and brought us safely home again."

"And you, Kellen Knight-Mage. I trust that you also fare well," Ashaniel said, pouring cups of wine with her own hands and setting one in front of each of them.

"Well enough, Lady Ashaniel," Kellen said, though "well" was nothing like what he felt. Elven custom, Elven courtesy; he was surrounded by them, and pulled along as if by a strong current he could not hope to swim against. He pulled the goatskin mitts off and carefully set them in his lap before reaching for the cup with both hands. It was awkward, but he managed. His hands were still numb, but now that he wasn't soaked to the bone, the pain was getting worse, and he was beginning to long for something to take the edge off, at least. "I do wish things weren't quite so . . . damp . . . though," he said ruefully. He took a sip of the wine. It would probably help.

"Idalia says that soon the rain will turn to snow," Ashaniel said, smiling, "which will not be quite as—damp. And by the spring the weather will perhaps have returned to its accustomed ways. It gladdens my heart that you have returned to see our city as it should be seen—and soon you will be healed of the hurts you have taken in our service."

Kellen glanced down at his hands. Only the very tips of

his fingers were visible in the thick cocoon of bandage, and Vestakia and Jermayan had made sure he never got a good look at them on the infrequent occasions they changed the bandages. He wondered just how badly his hands had been burned, back there at the obelisk. Very badly, if the pain he felt whenever the salve started to wear off was any indication. So badly his mind itself flinched away from thinking about it.

"I'm certain that is so," he said politely. It was hard, very hard, to sit here making polite conversation when what he wanted was to down another of those pain-killing potions, soak in a hot bath, then sleep for, oh, a year or so . . .

Shalkan came wandering over, and stuck his head over Kellen's shoulder. "Those little iced cakes look delicious," he said pointedly. Shalkan had a notorious sweet-tooth, one that the unicorn indulged at every opportunity. This time, however, he was going to have to wait. Kellen couldn't manage anything as small as a cake with his bandaged hands, and everyone else was too busy making polite noises at each other while they listened for Idalia's return to favor him with a treat.

"If the snow is to be heavy this year, then the Winter Running Dance should be exceptionally fine," Jermayan observed.

All this politeness was enough to make Kellen want to scream. Except that he hadn't enough energy to do more than sit there, look solemn, and nod. Even his nervous energy was beginning to flag.

"Indeed it should," Ainalundore said, from her position behind the Queen. From her tone, the Counselor greeted the introduction of such an innocuous subject with great relief.

To Kellen's faint disbelief, the Elves, Jermayan included, embarked upon a lively discussion of forthcoming entertainments to be held in Sentarshadeen—just as if the threat of Shadow Mountain wasn't still hanging over all of their heads. Just as if they weren't all dying for Idalia and Vestakia to come back. Just as if they were totally oblivious to the fact that Kellen himself was about to fall over from exhaustion.

"Cake," said Shalkan, "is very nice. One could spear a cake with a fork, if one was so inclined, and place it on a saucer, and I could eat it."

Shameless. But it made him smile, and he did exactly what Shalkan wanted, now that he knew how he could manage to maneuver things. And out of politeness, he ate a cake himself, and discovered that the sugary thing gave him a little more energy. He sat and listened, carefully feeding Shalkan most of the plate of little iced cakes—and taking one or two for himself—as he finished his cup of wine. The wine did help; he would have liked more, but he was afraid in his current state he could slip from pleasantly numb to clearly intoxicated with very little warning, and that would probably horrify the Elves. Sandalon was still safe in Lairamo's clutches, somewhere out of sight at the back of the pavilion.

What was taking Idalia so long? Surely she just had to *look* at Vestakia to know that she was Good?

But there was no point in starting an argument here and now, particularly one Kellen was pretty sure he'd already won. Andoreniel and Ashaniel had promised to abide by whatever Idalia said, and their word was Law here.

"They're coming." Shalkan's breath tickled Kellen's ear.

Kellen glanced up. A few moments later, Idalia and Vestakia appeared in the doorway of the pavilion.

All conversation stopped.

Idalia approached the table with Vestakia, her arm around the girl's shoulders. Kellen had the feeling that without that support, Vestakia might have run.

"I have searched thoroughly with the Wild Magic," Idalia said without preamble. "Vestakia is not one of the Endarkened, nor does she bear Demon-taint."

Jermayan half-rose from his seat. Idalia held up her free hand, indicating that she had more to say.

"Yet, by her heritage, the Endarkened do have a kind of link to her. They can affect her physically by sympathetic magic, though she will sense anything they attempt, through the gift passed to her by her Wildmage mother. And for this reason, anyone who has been in intimate contact with her is similarly at risk."

Here Idalia broke off, eyeing Kellen sharply. She didn't have to say what he knew perfectly well: if Shalkan hadn't demanded a vow of celibacy and chastity from him in exchange for his aid in helping Kellen escape from Armethalieh, they might all be in very deep trouble right now.

"But the bad is balanced—and exceeded—by the good. By her gift at locating Demons and piercing their illusions, Vestakia can aid us to track the Endarkened, just as she found the Black Cairn for Kellen. Though her range is not great, nor can she see into the future, with her aid, should she choose to give it, we can know when something is just an accident and when it's the work of the Endarkened. And if there are Demons around, however disguised, Vestakia will know."

There was a long pause, while Andoreniel weighed Idalia's words. "This is a great gift," he said at last, getting to his feet. "It would make good hearing to know that you will use your power for the good of the Nine Cities, Vestakia."

Idalia must have coached her back in the forest, because Vestakia seemed to have no difficulty understanding what Andoreniel meant.

"Yes," Vestakia said, her voice very soft. "Yes, I will. It would be my honor to help you, however I can. How could— I mean, anyone who has any sort of gift that could be used to oppose such evil would do just the same."

"Then be welcome in Sentarshadeen," Andoreniel said gravely. "Jermayan and Abrinath will see you to your hearth."

That seemed to settle it. No matter who had doubts about this—and there were probably plenty who did—there could be no arguing with the King. At least, not in public.

And in private—well, that didn't matter. Kellen felt almost dizzy with relief, and was very glad he hadn't drunk that second cup of wine.

Jermayan and Abrinath weren't the only ones leaving with

Vestakia. Quite a number of those present made preparations to leave as well, including a couple of grooms leading Valdien and Lily away, presumably to their stables. Kellen watched, fascinated, as they unfurled large parasols at the door of the pavilion—only, unlike the ones he'd seen in Armethalieh, these were apparently designed to keep off rain, not sun.

"You'll be fine," Kellen told Vestakia, under the cover of the preparations for the departure. "You'll like it here. I'll see you soon."

"Do you promise?" Vestakia asked, sounding a little desperate.

"I promise," Kellen said. "Ah, they'll be giving you your own little house, by the way, one of the guest-houses. Just be sure to invite Jermayan to come inside when you get there. I don't think he can come in otherwise."

Vestakia smiled, a fleeting nervous smile. "I'll remember," she said.

And then Jermayan offered her his arm, and the two of them walked away.

Kellen glanced back at Idalia, to see her watching the two of them go. The expression on her face caught him by surprise.

Something's changed here.

When they'd left, Idalia had been holding Jermayan at arm's length. Kellen knew that she loved Jermayan as much as he loved her, but the fact that Elves bonded once, and for life, and that Idalia was inevitably going to die centuries before Jermayan did, had made her refuse to acknowledge that love, hoping that Jermayan would find someone else.

But now Idalia's attitude seemed to have changed, if the expression on her face was any indication.

It isn't any of my business, Kellen told himself firmly. He got to his feet, glancing from Shalkan to Idalia uncertainly. He wasn't quite certain what to do now. And then, he started to sway, just a little, as exhaustion caught him by surprise.

"Oh, no, brother mine," Idalia said firmly. "You're not going anywhere until I see what's under those bandages."

Kellen stared around in alarm. Here? Now?

"I'd take you home first, but if it's something I need to call in extra help for, I'd just have to bring you back through the city again. Might as well deal with it here," Idalia said, leaning close and speaking softly, for Kellen's ears alone.

Ashaniel gathered up most of the remaining courtiers—and all of the women, including Lairamo, who was still clutching Sandalon tightly—and prepared to leave. Andoreniel and Morusil stayed, along with several others whose names Kellen didn't know.

"We look forward to celebrating your triumph before all Sentarshadeen once you are properly healed and rested, Kellen Tavadon," Ashaniel said gravely.

"Thank you," Kellen said simply. Somehow this didn't seem like the time to complain that he hated parties.

Ashaniel turned and swept away, reaching out to take Sandalon's hand in hers. The young Elven Prince was gazing back at Kellen forlornly over Lairamo's shoulder.

"I'll see you again soon," Kellen called to the child, and saw Sandalon's face light up with pleasure. Then the Queen and her court were gone, and two attendants were closing the pavilion awning behind them.

"Why don't we get you out of that armor?" Idalia said pragmatically. "Better now than later."

As deftly as if she'd done this a hundred times—and Kellen didn't know she hadn't—she unbelted his surcoat and lifted it off, then pulled out the locking-pins that held the armored collar in place and slipped it free, then lifted off the armored breast-and-backplate. Next came the multi-jointed armored sleeves, then the boots, then the leggings, then Kellen stood wearing nothing more than the thin quilted leather undersuit that went beneath the Elven armor.

It was damp from the rain, and had shiny worn scars on its surface where the armor had rubbed it.

Kellen felt peculiarly light and unfinished without his armor. In the short time since he'd first donned it, it had grown to be an extension of his self, as much as his sword was.

One of the attendants handed Idalia a thick belted robe—

in the same shade of soft green as Kellen's surcoat—and she helped him into it and tied the sash. Heavy soft over-the-knee boots of green-dyed sheepskin, woolly side in, completed the outfit. The Elves did nothing by halves.

"Comfy now?" Idalia asked.

"So far," Kellen said cautiously.

Idalia snorted eloquently, and opened a large box that someone had placed on the table while Kellen hadn't been paying attention. The box was large but not deep—though still too big for one person to carry comfortably—and made of a satiny golden wood, so beautifully crafted that Kellen couldn't make out where the pieces were joined. When Idalia opened it, Kellen could see that it was lined in padded leather, and filled with small glass flasks. Idalia inspected the contents critically for a moment before choosing one.

The liquid inside was a lurid violet color. She picked up the goblet Kellen had used before and poured a generous portion of the violet liquid into it—it was thick and syrupy—before filling the cup the rest of the way with wine.

She lifted the cup to his lips. "Drink it all, as fast as you can," she ordered.

"I suppose it tastes terrible," Kellen said resignedly, having some experience with healing potions.

"Not this one," Idalia said, sounding amused. "But it needs to start working before *I* can start working."

Steadying the cup with his bandaged hands, Kellen complied. She'd been right; it didn't taste that bad—particularly in comparison with other potions he'd had to drink—but the violet syrup gave the wine an odd sweetish undertaste that he didn't actually care for, like eating candied flowers.

Idalia took the cup back and set it carefully on the table, then reached for his hand. Reflexively, Kellen drew back.

"I have to see what's under there," Idalia said gently. "It won't hurt. Not once what I put in the wine takes effect anyway. Tell me what happened."

"I burned them," Kellen said simply. He knew he ought to tell her more, but somehow he really couldn't bring himself to talk about what had happened at the top of the cairn. Not to Jermayan. Not to Shalkan. Not to anyone. "It was the key-stone," he finally added reluctantly.

"Do they hurt now?" Idalia asked, as impersonal as any physician.

"No. Not much, anyway. Jermayan had some kind of salve in his pack."

"Night's Daughter," Shalkan supplied. "Mixed with all-heal."

"Well." Idalia seemed surprised, and Kellen wondered what "Night's Daughter" was. "Just as well he came pre-pared for every occasion."

"And he gave me something horrible and brown to drink every night so I could sleep," Kellen added. "It tasted like moldy hay."

Idalia raised her eyebrow. Evidently she recognized what it was without Shalkan telling her. "It's just as well you came back to us so soon, then."

She knelt in front of him and unwrapped his hands slowly, alternating hands so that both would be exposed at the same time. Shalkan stood close, his cheek nearly touching Kellen's. Kellen could tell that whatever was in the wine was starting to work. He felt sleepy, and it was hard to concentrate. As the outer layers of bandage came away, he could see the inner layers, sticky and glistening with greenish ointment.

And the more layers Idalia peeled away, the more Kellen could see that his hands looked *wrong*.

They just looked *wrong*.

Jermayan and Vestakia had never let him watch when they tended his dressings on the trail. He'd gone along with it then. He didn't remember why just now, but he had. Maybe he'd been asleep when they'd done it. Maybe it was that brown stuff.

But he wasn't asleep now.

"Don't look," Shalkan suggested, as Idalia lifted away the last layer of bandage, but Kellen couldn't manage to take that good advice.

He looked. And wished he hadn't.

His hands were warped and charred, caricatures of themselves. All the flesh was burned away from the palms, and Kellen thought he could see bone showing. Toward the edges of the burn, puffy moist colorless flesh hung in sloughing rags. His fingers were crooked into claws, the tendons pulled tight by the burns. He tried to flex his fingers and couldn't. There was only pain—dull and distant, but there.

He made a strangled sound, and would have risen from his seat if not for Andoreniel's hands on his shoulders, pressing him firmly down. Even through the effects of the draught Idalia had given him, Kellen could feel a rising tide of panic.

I'll never hold a sword again!

Idalia made a hissing sound of dismay, and somehow that turned Kellen's panic into anger.

"Well, what did you expect?" he said harshly, struggling with his feelings. He'd known he was burned. He'd known the burns were bad—very bad. But to *see* them . . . !

"I expected you to die," Idalia said, all the grief she hadn't shown before thick in her voice. "Oh, little brother, I'm so glad you came back alive!" She put her hand over his arm—above the burns—and squeezed gently, then sat back, looking over his shoulder.

"Kellen. Don't look at your hands. Look at me," Shalkan demanded. *"Now."*

With a great effort, Kellen pulled his gaze away from his hands and met Shalkan's gaze. The unicorn had beautiful eyes—deep green, and fringed by the longest silver lashes Kellen had ever seen.

"It will be all right," the unicorn said softly. "You've seen Idalia heal worse injuries. Remember the unicorn colt? Just look at me and keep breathing. Let the potion do its work."

Kellen took a deep breath. Anger was a tool of the Knight-Mage, but panic was his enemy. He wasn't going to panic. He concentrated on Shalkan.

As if from a great distance, he heard Idalia's voice:

"Will anyone here share in the price of this healing?"

"I will," he heard Andoreniel say. "For what Kellen has done for my city, I stand in his debt forever."

"And I," Morusil added. "It is a small repayment for the refreshment Kellen has brought to my garden, and the saving of the forest."

"And I—"

"And I—"

In a few moments, all the Elves who had remained behind had pledged themselves to share in the price of Kellen's healing.

Two

A Healing and a Homecoming

That will make *things easier,* Idalia thought absently. She reached out with her small knife and cut a few strands of Kellen's hair, then a few of her own.

Bless the boy, he didn't even notice. He was staring into Shalkan's eyes as if he'd found his one true love, breathing slowly and deeply, doing all he could to aid her in her spell. For a moment there, when he'd first seen his hands, she'd thought she was going to have to waste valuable energy putting him into Sleep, but he'd pulled out of his panic admirably.

Morusil had already gathered strands of hair from everyone else there. She added her own and Kellen's hairs to the bundle, then pricked the ball of her thumb with her knife, and squeezed out a drop of her own blood, holding the now-bloody bundle of hairs under her hand so that the drop of blood fell on it and bound them all together.

Power flared up in the yellow pavilion, encircling them all and settling into a dome of protection. Once it had steadied, Idalia tossed the hair and the herbs necessary to her spell into the brazier that Morusil had also prepared, and whispered her spell.

Normally she would not need to do so much work to prepare a Healing. But Kellen was very badly injured. And Idalia was already laboring under the shadow of an unpaid Mageprice, incurred when she had cast the spell to bring the rains safely to Sentarshadeen. Though Andoreniel, Morusil, and the others would bear much of the cost of Kellen's healing, there was always Magedebt to be paid: this was the law of the Wild Magic.

The weight of the Presence filled her, and she waited to hear the price. But instead, a voice seemed to speak within her: *You have already paid your price in full.*

No! Her denial was automatic. There was no magic without a cost—that was the first and most basic tenet of the Wild Magic. What price she had paid was for gifts she had already received, not for this.

But Kellen needed healing, and it would be foolishness to argue with the Presence. *I accept,* she said, and felt the Presence depart, just as if she had accepted a normal *geas.*

Green fire filled her hands, as thick and rich as wild honey. She tilted her hands and it spilled over, splashing onto Kellen's hands and clinging, and where it touched, ruined flesh began to heal and re-knit as if it had never been burned. Once that damage had been repaired, the green fire spread—up Kellen's arms, across his torso, down his legs—repairing all the lesser damage he'd sustained at the Barrier.

In moments the Healing was over. After a moment, Idalia dismissed the sphere of protection. She got stiffly to her feet.

At least she felt just as tired as if this had been a normal Healing, and judging from the faces of the Elves, they all felt the same.

Kellen met her eyes, his expression dazed and unfocused with exhaustion. He looked down at his hands, his eyes opening wide in delight and wonder at the sight of them whole and unmarred. He opened his hands wide, and then closed them into fists.

"They're all right," he said, his voice blurry with the after-effects of the potion. "They're all right!"

"Of course they are," Idalia said, with an assurance she hadn't felt until that moment, and with affection and love flowing over into her voice. "And *now* we'll go home."

"I'll help," Shalkan said. "I'm not sure Kellen remembers where it is. And even if he does, I'm not sure he could get there without deciding to lie down on the path for a nap. Which would severely inconvenience anyone else who needed to walk there."

Kellen grinned tiredly, but did not contradict his friend.

Idalia brought Kellen's cloak, then Kellen swung his leg over Shalkan's bare back, and the three of them made their way to the small house Kellen shared with Idalia. Morusil accompanied them for part of the distance, until his path diverged from their own.

This time, Kellen didn't even mind the rain.

No one seemed to take any particular notice of them. Elves were tactful in that way.

⇒

"HERE we are."

Kellen was nearly asleep by the time they reached their door. He blinked at it in surprise.

Everything looked different—familiar and strange at the same time. While he'd been gone, Sentarshadeen had taken on something of the aspect of a dreamworld in his mind; something too good to be true. But here it was again, as real as the rocks in the road. He took a deep breath and swung his leg over Shalkan's back.

"I'll see you later," Shalkan said. "Get some sleep." When the unicorn was sure Kellen was steady on his feet, he turned neatly on the path before the door and trotted delicately away.

Idalia opened the door, and Kellen hurried to get in out of the rain.

"Rain. It's been raining since we started back. It's raining now. Doesn't it *ever* stop?" he asked, yawning as he walked inside. Everything was just as he'd left it, with the addition of a cloak-tree and drip-pan just inside the door. Kellen hung his sodden cloak on the highest peg, stretching and yawning again.

"Eventually," Idalia promised. "Normally I'd suggest a hot bath before bed, but frankly, I don't think you'll stay awake through it—and I'd hate for you to drown after all my hard work. Why don't you get out of those damp leathers and into your nice dry bed? You'll need to sleep off that Healing. And then we can talk."

Kellen nodded, heading toward his room. Bed! His *own* bed! And it would be dry, and warm, and he would not have to drag himself out of it at first light for sword practice, or another long day in the saddle . . .

With a mumbled thanks to Idalia, he slid back the door and walked inside.

The bed was turned down and waiting for him. Everything had been changed to autumn colors; there was a new bed-robe laid out, and—Kellen grinned to himself—towels as well. He sat down on the bench beneath the window and pulled off his clothes, toweling himself thoroughly dry afterward.

Even in the exhaustion that was the aftermath of the Healing spell, every time he used his hands he felt an enormous pang of relief. Just to pick something up, to close his hands, to look down and see, not numb bandage-covered lumps, but ten healthy responsive pink fingers was almost enough to rouse him to wakefulness again—almost. He'd lived with the fear for so long, that—because of the way they'd been burned, by magic—there'd be nothing Idalia would be able to do to Heal him.

But now that was all over. He was fine. Better than fine. Healed.

Time to move on to the next crisis, Kellen told himself, stumbling toward the bed.

He was asleep before he'd pulled the covers up over himself.

⌐

A few minutes after Kellen disappeared into his room, Idalia looked in. She found Kellen's clothing strewn all over the floor, and Kellen asleep like a hibernating bear. She smiled faintly to herself and went to brew tea.

She was tired, but not tired enough to seek her own bed. There had been several present to share the cost of the Healing, and so the physical cost to her had been minimal. Normally, she would have also had a price to pay . . .

But not this time, apparently.

Idalia frowned. She'd never heard of such a thing before, but Wildmages didn't run to libraries of books setting down the accumulated lore of Wildmages past. For one thing, the Wild Magic itself was fluid and ever-changing, and the way things had happened in the past wasn't the way things would necessarily happen in the future.

As it seems I've just proven. Ah, well, if there are explanations to be had, I suppose I'll find them in the Books of the Wild Magic.

Once the water was hot and her tea was steeping, she went to her room and got out her three Books.

The Book of Moon, The Book of Sun, and *The Book of Stars* were the three Books every Wildmage possessed. The Books were magical in themselves, and once they had found their Wildmage, they could not be separated from him or her by any means save the death of the Wildmage. Nor could they be destroyed. In them was everything a Wildmage needed to know in order to set their feet on the path of the Wild Magic, and a lifetime was not enough time to master their contents.

Idalia sat in the front room and read, drinking tea and listening to the rain. Though she found comfort in the familiar pages, she found very little in the way of enlightenment about what had happened when she'd healed Kellen. There was no gift—no magic—without payment. That was the way the world worked. All magic—whether the Wild Magic, the High Magick of Armethalieh, or the Shadow Magic of the Endarkened—had to be paid for, either in advance, with stored personal energy, or afterward, with a Mageprice—or sometimes both. Any attempt to subvert that Balance led to disastrous consequences: it was just such a temptation that the Endarkened had offered to the Wildmages during the Great War—a temptation to which some of them had succumbed, that of power without price.

So why had she not been asked for payment?

If the question bothers you enough, ask, she told herself, putting down *The Book of Stars.* She picked up her cup of now-cold tea, frowning down into its bowl.

Subconsciously, she realized she had been waiting for something.

No, not something.

Someone.

Jermayan.

Surely he ought to have been here by now?

"Fool," Idalia muttered under her breath. She'd been sitting here like a maiden in a wondertale, expecting Jermayan to come to her just because she'd changed her mind—but after the thorough job she'd done of driving him away when she and Kellen had first come to Sentarshadeen, if there was to be a reconciliation, the first move in that dance would have to be hers.

She retreated to her room again, opened her desk, and penned a brief message.

There were times when it was distinctly advantageous to be a Wildmage, and this was one of them. She went out into her garden, and sent out a silent call.

She'd expected a bird to come to her call, but it was raining, and birds did not fly in the rain unless they must. To her surprise, a sleek white hound appeared, cocking his head alertly and regarding her curiously, tail wagging slowly.

He was no masterless animal—his smooth coat and the collar about his neck told her that much—but was apparently willing to take time from his own pursuits to do her a favor. And his price was easy enough to meet: a slice of meat-pie from her larder satisfied him. She tucked her note into his collar and secured it with a ribbon. And then, she sat down to wait.

JERMAYAN arrived with admirable promptness. He was dressed in blue and silver, his waist-length hair elaborately braided with long silver cords that had a tiny teardrop of midnight-blue lapis at the end of each. They matched the larger drops of lapis that hung from each ear, his cloak-brooches, his rings, and the lustrous bloom of the deep-piled silk-velvet breeches tucked into butter-soft high-heeled boots that swept extravagantly all the way to mid-thigh.

His tunic was a pale grey heavy silk brocade oversewn with thousands of beads of crystal and moonstone in a seemingly-random pattern meant to mimic a shower of raindrops. The latest fashion among the Elves was clothing that looked as if it was wet when it wasn't. Idalia was impressed—the man had barely been here half a day and was already leading the style.

"Be welcome in my home and at my hearth," she said, meaning the words as she had never meant them before.

Jermayan shook out his cloak—wet with real raindrops—and hung it on the cloak-tree, and set his rainshade—blue and silver, of course—beside it.

"Well met, Idalia. It is good to be welcome in the home of friends."

"Kellen is asleep," Idalia said, decoding the unspoken question with the ease of long practice. "The Healing went well, and he is restored to complete health; a good, long sleep and a few decent meals will complete the Healing, leaving him as hale as when he left here."

"That makes good hearing," Jermayan said. "Then he will be ready to resume his lessons soon. There is much yet for him to learn in the ways of a Knight-Mage."

And so little time for any of us!

"I would offer you tea," Idalia said in a faintly-strangled voice, turning toward the stove that stood tucked neatly into one corner of the room. "And it would be interesting to know how Vestakia finds Sentarshadeen as well."

But Jermayan did not answer, and the silence stretched as Idalia set the kettle on the stove to heat, and rinsed and filled the Elvenware teapot with several measures of Autumn Rain tea.

Why didn't he say anything? If he were angry with her for any reason, he would not have come, so that could not be the reason. Could something have happened to Vestakia?

Darkness damn all notions of Elven propriety! If he didn't explain himself soon she was going to break down and *ask* him.

Idalia turned around—why was it so hard to face him, now of all times?—and found that Jermayan had not moved away from his position near the door. He was standing, watching her with that utter Elven stillness, his face expressionless. She forced herself to meet his eyes.

"Idalia, you once played our courtly games far better than this. Now you are as awkward in our ways as Kellen is," Jermayan said, very gently. "You have changed your mind. Perhaps you would show kindness to one who is your brother's friend and who has always . . . meant you well."

She forced herself to take one step away from the table, then another, noting with a distant measuring part of herself that her legs trembled. Why was this so hard? There was no place in a Wildmage's life for dishonesty and false pride. She had abandoned those things—she thought she had—years before.

And because that was true, she knew the reason now. She'd taken risks that mattered before. She'd hazarded her life and her safety. But not her heart. Before, she'd only offered up her life, or a Wildmage's honor . . . not something that, if everything went wrong, would leave her whole in body, able to mourn and suffer, without even the chill consolation that she'd done it all in the name of Service.

Because she was doing this for herself.

"Idalia?" Jermayan asked. A question. She felt her face quirk in an uncertain smile. She held out her hand.

His fingers closed over hers. Warm, when his touch had always been so cool before.

"Because—when you were gone—I realized that we're all going to die."

Jermayan's fingers tightened over hers.

"No, it isn't magic, not a vision, don't worry. Just common sense. You're an Elven Knight—"

She felt him relax. Looking up, Idalia could see that he smiled. She let him draw her closer.

"My heart, I have been an Elven Knight since before your grandparents met," Jermayan said.

"And I am a Wildmage," Idalia agreed. "And never in either of our lifetimes has Shadow Mountain begun moving so actively against our peoples. You know, and I know, we're going to war. Kellen destroyed the Barrier. Shadow Mountain won't stop because of that; if anything, it will speed their plans. Of all of the creatures of Light that the Shadow hates the most, the Wildmages and Elven Knights are at the top of the list of those first to be destroyed."

"Yes," Jermayan said, meeting her gaze steadily, "I fear that you are correct. And so you think I will die before you, and for this reason you are at last willing to hear the counsel of my heart."

No, Idalia thought, closing her eyes for a moment. *But I think you will not survive me long enough to grieve overmuch.*

"I think I have been foolish to throw away the chance for joy," Idalia said softly. "And I thank the Gods that I have been given a second chance."

She went into his arms willingly, as she had not since the day she had first realized he loved her, and such felt a sense of peace and joy well up as she had never experienced out-side of the Wild Magic.

"Then let it be so, Idalia," Jermayan said. "And if I do not share your optimism at the length of my life, it is no matter—I shall surrender upon any terms you set. Now be merciful in your victory, and grant one concession more: name the day upon which we may be wed."

⌐

IDALIA only barely managed to keep from recoiling in hor-ror from Jermayan's words. Taking Jermayan as her lover was one thing. But marriage . . . ?

Elves had given up their share in the greater Magics long ago in exchange for peace and long lives. But they had had many, many years in which to learn to use the small magics they yet possessed in the most effective way possible, and some of them were very potent. Elves mated for life. None of the Elvenkind would offer marriage to someone that they did not recognize a soul-bond with, and when they wed, one of the purposes of the ceremony was to strengthen that soul-bond with those small magics, binding the partners together body, mind, heart, and soul.

If she married him—perhaps if she did so much as accept his betrothal pendant—they would be linked. It was not im-possible that Jermayan would have a certain amount of ac-cess to her thoughts—including, possibly, knowledge of the price she had accepted to bring the weather down safely to Sentarshadeen.

And that was something she didn't dare allow.

"Not yet," Idalia said firmly. "A proper wedding takes *time* to plan, Jermayan!" she added, making her voice light. "You are no lowly herb-tender, to expect to leap a broom with your chosen goose-girl and call it done! You have an obligation to Sentarshadeen and to your liege to create an occasion that all may treasure in memory!"

This time she blessed Elven custom for its intricacies. Jermayan would have to ask permission of the King and Queen, who would in turn have to debate this—for Idalia was human, and while such marriages were not unknown, they were rare. He would have to arrange for the *appropriate* sort of wedding, and it would have to be a very public occasion. And by the time even half of that was accomplished—

Sentarshadeen might well be a city under siege, and such considerations as weddings would be forgotten.

"Time—and perhaps fair weather and dry," Jermayan teased. "And I do not doubt that we will find other things to beguile us during the moonturns of waiting . . . "

HE'D thought he'd heard voices.

Kellen awoke, disoriented by the unfamiliar sensation of sleeping in a warm dry bed. For a moment he couldn't remember where he was, or how he'd gotten here, but then the memories slipped into place. Sentarshadeen. Home. He felt better than he had in sennights. No bruises, no torn half-healed muscles. And his hands—his hands. He stretched, luxuriating in the feeling that there was nothing whatsoever wrong.

He'd definitely heard voices.

And he was hungry. Hungry enough to eat—if not Valdien, then something of approximately the same size as Jermayan's warhorse, and he wouldn't really care how thoroughly it was cooked, either. He knew it was the aftereffect of the healing Idalia had performed on him, but that didn't make him any less hungry. He only hoped the larder was well stocked.

He belted on the heavy overtunic he'd worn home, too hungry to stop and look for the bedrobe he remembered seeing, and slid back the door into the common room.

Jermayan and Idalia were there.

Both of them.

Together.

And from the look of things, they had definitely settled their differences.

Kellen retreated quickly, feeling his cheeks flush, and slid the door shut a shade too forcefully, leaning against it. His hunger was momentarily forgotten.

He felt himself growing hot with embarrassment. He stared around the room, and as he did, he saw a bowl of fruit and a carafe on the bedside table. He walked over to it, discovering that there was not only fruit, but a plate of cheese pastries covered by a cloth. The carafe contained cider.

See? Kellen told himself, sitting down on the edge of the bed and biting into a pastry. *There's food in here. You don't need to go out there.*

In fact, he thought he might not ever go out there again . . .

There was a faint rattle as the door slid open again.

"You can come out now," Idalia said, stifled laughter in her voice. "It's safe. I promise. And we wouldn't want you to starve to death in here."

Kellen got to his feet, setting the remaining half of the second pastry back on the plate and brushing crumbs from the front of his robe. He thought of all the things he could possibly say, and decided not to say any of them. They were all simply too horribly embarrassing, especially with Idalia looking at him that way and obviously trying so hard not to laugh.

"I wish both of you all happiness," Kellen said instead. He was surprised—both to find that he meant it, and that it was exactly the right thing to say.

THE following evening a formal banquet was held to officially welcome Kellen and Jermayan home to Sentarshadeen.

Kellen spent the day preceding it indoors. He had a choice, or so Idalia told him that morning. He could stay inside. By Elven standards of etiquette, that would mean he was not officially "here," and no one would bother him.

Or he could go out. But once he crossed his doorstep, he'd be fair game, and though the Elves were notoriously—and unfailingly—polite, they also lived to gossip, and he would probably be the center of more attention than he liked.

"What about Vestakia?" Kellen asked. He'd just as soon avoid the attention, but he didn't want to abandon Vestakia on her first day in Sentarshadeen.

"Vestakia," Idalia had answered with a wicked smirk, "will be spending the morning—the entire morning, and possibly most of the afternoon—receiving a new wardrobe from Tengitir, who announced that she has waited her entire life for such a challenge as Vestakia represents. You know, I do believe that if the Prince of Shadow Mountain were to appear before her, Tengitir would demand that he take off his clothes and step into the light so that she could best determine what colors and fabrics suited his skin," Idalia added bemusedly.

Kellen laughed. Having been dressed by the Elven seamstress himself—Tengitir's specialty was in designing clothing for the non-Elven—he thought that was almost possible.

"Afterward—if there's time before the banquet—Jermayan and I will take her around Sentarshadeen a little. To show her the city—and to show her *to* the city as well, of course. The sooner everyone sees that there is nothing to fear from her, the better," Idalia added.

"And if there is anything *wrong* in the city, she'll find it," Kellen said.

"Yes," Idalia said. "I'd thought of that, as well."

So with one thing and another, Kellen spent the day at home, mostly by himself. Idalia seemed to have a great many errands to run, going in and out all day, returning more often than not with mysterious parcels which she wouldn't let him unwrap.

"Time enough for that later, little brother," was all she would say. She seemed cheerful enough, and Kellen was glad of that. When they'd first arrived in Sentarshadeen, she'd seemed so . . . grave. He preferred this Idalia better. It made it easier to pretend that in destroying the Barrier they'd solved all their problems, though Kellen knew they hadn't. They'd only bought themselves and the Elves some time— though how much time, and what form the next attack would take, was something he doubted even Idalia could guess.

To distract himself from the unavoidable banquet— though the son of the Arch-Mage of Armethalieh had a certain amount of experience with formal banquets, this would be the first such event Kellen had attended among the Elves—Kellen spent the day cleaning and polishing his sword and armor, having found that his gear had been delivered to the house the previous day. Not that it really needed doing—someone had obviously been at it before him—but it gave his hands something to do, and settled his mind.

When he'd finished that, he got out his Books, and turned to *The Book of Stars.*

The Book of Stars was the most esoteric and puzzling of the three books. *The Book of Moon* was the simplest, containing basic cantrips and the building blocks of spells. A budding Wildmage could begin working Wildmagery within minutes of opening *The Book of Moon.*

The Book of Sun contained some information about spells as well, but was more occupied with *why* spells should be cast than how, and often with whether they should be cast at all, since the Wild Magic was a magic of Balance, and often things tended to slip back into balance without the Wildmage's help.

The Book of Stars seemed to be about the underlying principles of the Wild Magic. Idalia had once told Kellen that studying it helped the Wildmage become a better Wildmage, although Kellen had never been able to see how, as nothing he'd read in it had ever really made a lot of sense to him. She'd said he should study it anyway, so Kellen had.

It seemed to make a lot more sense now that Kellen knew he was a Knight-Mage instead of a regular Wildmage.

The Book of Stars said that *"The Knight-Mage is the active agent of the principle of the Wild Magic, the Wildmage who chooses to become a warrior or who is born with the instinct for the Way of the Sword, who acts in battle without mindful thought and thus brings primary causative forces into manifestation by direct action."*

When they had discovered that this was what Kellen was, Jermayan had told him that a Wildmage and a Knight-Mage's gifts lay in opposite directions; that while a Wildmage reached out to all the world, a Knight-Mage's gifts turned inward, so that he could not be turned away from his course once he had chosen it. Because of that, Kellen's abilities in Wildmagery would never be as strong as Idalia's, but Jermayan also said that a Knight-Mage could withstand forces that would destroy a regular Wildmage, for the Knight-Mage's true power lay in endurance and the alliance of his knightly skills with his Wildmagery.

It all sounded very fine, but kind of unsettling, and while Kellen had a lot more confidence in his Wildmage skills—especially now that he wasn't measuring them against Idalia's—he knew he still had a lot to learn about this knight business. And he'd better learn fast.

Fortunately, he had Jermayan to teach him.

He wasn't surprised to find that *The Book of Stars* seemed to make a lot more sense now that he knew what he really was. For the first time, the words in the tiny handwritten book seemed to be speaking directly *to* him, as if the long-gone Wildmage who had copied it out from his or her own Books—why? Kellen still sometimes wondered, and as part of what Mageprice?—were here, and speaking directly *to* him.

"Only when you cease to try, will you achieve. Only when you cease to seek, will you find. Only when you are emptied, will you be filled."

If that wasn't exactly what finding the Way of the Knight-Mage was like, he'd eat his boots. It gave him a kind of comfort, to know that whatever might come to pass, it was somehow within the sphere of the Wild Magic.

And for the first time, he wondered if all copies of the three Books were the same. Oh, probably *The Book of Moon* was, and maybe *The Book of Sun*—but what about *The Book of Stars*? Because what was in his Book certainly wouldn't apply to Idalia, would it? Was every copy of *The Book of Stars* suited only to the Wildmage who was supposed to read it?

"Kellen? Come back to the world, little brother."

Kellen startled at the sound of Idalia's voice, disturbing Greymalkin, who had insinuated herself into his lap as he read. The cat yawned and stretched, stalking slowly from his lap.

Kellen blinked up at his sister, surprised to see how far the light had failed. He'd been sure he was still reading, but now he saw that it was too dark to make out the words on the page.

"Which Book?" she asked.

Kellen closed the worn leather volume and brandished it in explanation. The small gold star glinted faintly on the spine. Idalia raised an eyebrow and smiled, saying nothing.

"Time to have a bath and get dressed. It's going to take you a while to climb into all your finery," she said teasingly.

Kellen sighed, getting reluctantly to his feet. His experiences with formal dress when he had lived in his father's house had not been pleasant ones, and he doubted he'd show to advantage in a roomful of costume-obsessed Elves. One of the oldest Histories in Armethalieh said that "the Elves have elevated mere living into a form of Art," and that included clothing, of course. Even if his own outfit for tonight had been designed to take into account the shortcomings of clumsy short-lived humans—and since Tengitir had certainly made it, it undoubtedly had—among the Elves, he'd look like a turnip in a rose garden.

Just as out of place as he had back in Armethalieh.

"Bath," Idalia said firmly, taking him by the shoulders and turning him in that direction. "I'll lay out your clothes while you do that. And hurry up, because I still have to wash and change myself."

Kellen headed for the bathroom—he could get his robe

while the tub filled. He felt a little better, knowing that Idalia was going to be there, and just as overdressed as he was. He could hardly imagine what she'd look like in high Elven finery.

~

AND by dusk, he knew.

Idalia was wearing a dress—Kellen's first reaction was to laugh, but he didn't; she would have slain him on the spot— whose main color was the same violet as her eyes.

On second look, there was no reason to laugh. He'd never seen Idalia in a dress before. In fact, after what little she'd told him about her childhood, he'd thought she wouldn't be caught dead in one, but somehow, it didn't look . . . unsuitable. There was nothing ornate or frivolous about it, just clean simple practical lines, as businesslike as a good sword.

But it wasn't plain, any more than an Elvenware bowl was plain. The shimmering violet silk glowed like glass, as if it were somehow lit from within, and was accented by insets of dark bark-brown velvet almost the color of her hair, velvet that somehow had a furtive, iridescent glimmer of the same violet rippling along the surface of it wherever the light struck it. There were insets along the collar, at the shoulders, and inside the full outer sleeves. She looked—elegant. He hadn't known she could look elegant.

"I'll be tripping over my skirts all night," Idalia muttered, stalking across the room to glare into a mirror, but Kellen knew she wouldn't. They only seemed to touch the floor, but that was a clever illusion. The hem was actually uneven; it didn't touch the floor at all, and was several inches shorter in front than in back.

"You'll be fine," Kellen said soothingly. "And you look"—he sought for a word that would convey what he thought—"dignified. Amazing, actually."

"So do you," Idalia said. She slid a pair of ebony and Elvensilver combs into her hair—her only jewelry—and turned to regard Kellen critically.

He'd been relieved to find that he hadn't needed help dressing after all. His costume (he really couldn't think of it any other way) was not very much more elaborate than Idalia's—and fortunately, the sheer, body-hugging styles that the Elves favored for themselves were nowhere in evidence in Kellen's own garb.

There were a few notes of the same sea-green that was the accent color for his armor—he guessed he'd better get used to the idea that the Elves thought of it as his official color now—in the very plain heavy silk trousers and long-sleeved tunic that were the bottom layer of his outfit. But over those went a long sleeveless vest that fell to mid-thigh, closed all the way to its high neck by a double row of tiny silver buttons that had taken him ages to do up. It was made of a sheered velvet in a leaf-pattern—parts were sheer, and parts were thick velvet, and Kellen couldn't quite decide what the color was. Silver? Gold? Brown? All of them?

Eventually he gave up. It looked okay over the green, anyway, making the silk undertunic (where it showed through) shimmer in a silvery—definitely silvery—way.

Over that came a long full-sleeved robe that fell to mid-calf, in a green so dark it was almost black. It was a kind of cloth he'd never seen before, soft like wool, and smooth, but faintly iridescent. It was lined in dull gold satin, and belted with a wide—and very long—sash in a slightly brighter shade of green than the overrobe. That had nearly been his undoing, until Idalia had taken pity on him and showed him how to wrap and tie the sash properly.

Low boots, of a reassuringly normal-looking pale gold calfskin, completed his outfit.

"I don't look bad," Kellen agreed. *And I don't feel silly,* he realized with relief. Nobody was asking him to wear earrings, braid jewels into his hair, paint his face, or do any of the other things the Elves did when they got themselves done up for some festive occasion. Now, just as long as no-body asked him to make a speech . . .

"Except for your hair," Idalia agreed. "Come over here."

A few minutes with a comb, and Idalia had pulled Kellen's mop of light-brown curls back into a short twisted braid at the nape of his neck. It felt reassuringly normal—it was the way he wore his hair under his helmet, after all.

"There. Presentable." She craned around and kissed him lightly on the forehead. "You'll definitely do. I'll just get our raincapes and rainshades, and we can be off. Don't worry—they're bespelled to keep the rain off—and I actually think it's slackening a bit this evening. Not stopping, of course, which is just as well," Idalia said.

"Where are we going?" Kellen asked, thinking to ask for the first time.

"The gardens at the House of Leaf and Star. There's no other place large enough to accommodate the guest list—and the unicorns will want to be able to listen—from a distance, of course."

"Outside? In the rain?"

Idalia snickered at Kellen's expression.

"Under canvas—or silk, actually. Relax. Everything that should be dry, will be dry. You look like you're being sent to an execution, not to a banquet."

All things considered, Kellen would rather have gone to an execution.

THE formal gardens of the House of Leaf and Star were subtly beautiful, like all the creations of the Elves: the natural world raised to an impossible pitch of perfection.

He'd never seen the gardens, but then, he hadn't been in Sentarshadeen long, and had gotten most of his tour of it courtesy of Sandalon, who'd shown him the things that Sandalon thought would interest a human stranger . . . which had not, obviously, included his parents' gardens.

Kellen looked down, realizing that at some point, without noticing, he and Idalia had gone from the streets of Sentarshadeen to a wide-slatted wooden path laid across the meadow to a path of white gravel.

This must be the garden, then.

Tonight it was filled with more lanterns than Kellen would once have been willing to bet were in the entire city of Sentarshadeen. Before the rains came, it had been necessary to keep the lights of evening from starting any accidental fires in a city made tinder-dry by drought. Now it was only necessary to keep the flames from being drowned by the rain. But the Elves—who accomplished far more through clever engineering than humans had ever done through magic—made it look effortless.

Some of the lanterns shone through tall gauzy windbreaks set up to blunt the force of the blustering, rain-heavy winds, turning them into tall, softly-gleaming rectangles of color. Though they seemed as insubstantial as kites, Kellen doubted they'd fall if the wind blew ten times as hard, though they quivered when the wind struck them. Kellen suspected they were meant to.

Inside the curving walls of windbreaks, the air was nearly still, and the flames inside the artfully-scattered lanterns— some suspended on tall posts, some nearer the ground— burned steadily. But the towering windbreaks were walls only, not roofs, and Kellen was still glad to have his rainshade and cloak for protection. He'd gotten his fill of being wet on his return from the Barrier.

But the other purpose for the windbreaks, besides sheltering the lanterns, was obviously to protect the dining pavilions.

Unlike the place in which he, Jermayan, and Vestakia had first been received—if not entirely welcomed—these were little more than canopies suspended on poles. Even in the rain, the entire garden was lit as brightly as the common room of Kellen's house, and very little of it was really open to the falling rain. Their cloaks were taken from them as they arrived at the edge of the garden, leaving them their light and elegant rainshades. The garden was already filled with Elves, their rainshades making them look like fabulous flowers.

"Like it?" Idalia said, gesturing around.

"Everyone's already here," Kellen said uneasily. "Are we late?"

"No. The honored guests arrive last. And of course, having spent all day putting this together, they certainly expect you to take some time to admire it before the banquet begins. Let's look around."

Idalia put her free hand on his arm and led Kellen forward. He didn't see much of the garden as it normally was—but he *did* see a lot of dining pavilions, and oiled-paper lanterns, and people he knew. All of Sentarshadeen was here tonight indeed, and he and Idalia stopped several times to speak politely to people that Kellen knew from the time he'd spent on the work crews watering the forest, and to several of Idalia's friends as well.

All the time his sense of dread grew. Everything seemed so quiet, so . . . formal. He wouldn't be able to get through this evening without making some terrible error. He knew it.

"We'll be sitting over there, under that green awning," Idalia said, when their slow meander finally brought them within range of the canopies.

In the back of his mind, Kellen had been wondering where everyone was going to sit. Under the tents, obviously, but surely there weren't enough tables and chairs—not to mention plates and cups—in the city to host a banquet for its entire populace? Unless the Elves had built them all—but in two days? He sort of thought that would take greater magic than they claimed to possess.

He glanced around.

He was surprised to see that what was under the awnings wasn't large, long banquet tables—such as he would have seen in Armethalieh—but instead an assortment of tables in various shapes, sizes, and woods. All harmonious, of course, in the Elven fashion, but certainly not giving the impression they'd all been built for the occasion. In fact . . .

He was sure he recognized some of the furnishings. Surely that table under the rose-colored canopy was from the House of Leaf and Star? Yes, he was sure of it. He'd eaten dinner at it his first night in Sentarshadeen, alone with Ashaniel, Lairamo, and Sandalon.

Suddenly Kellen realized why the tables and chairs—and the tableware as well—were a harmonious assortment instead of an harmonious whole. It might be held in the gardens of the House of Leaf and Star, but the tables and chairs were from nearly every home in Sentarshadeen.

Andoreniel and Ashaniel weren't giving this banquet. The entire city was.

Kellen felt himself relax at last. He realized he'd been thinking of tonight in Armethaliehan terms—of this banquet as an event meant to crush spectators and participants with its magnificence and to inspire them with thoughts of their own unworthiness to attend it. But if Elves thought that way, the House of Leaf and Star would be a cold and forbidding palace, terrible in its majesty.

No.

When the Elves said that this was a welcoming banquet, that was exactly what it was. Their ways might be strange, and their code of etiquette difficult for a human to understand or to follow, but that was what they meant. For all the garden's daunting and ethereal beauty, tonight had far more in common with the party the Centaurs and farmers had held back in the Wildwood to bid him and Idalia farewell than it did with *anything* that might ever occur in the Golden City!

"The Elves are like no other people in the world," Idalia said quietly, watching his face. "You read the Histories, back in the City? Where they talk about the Other Races? Do you remember what they say about the Elves?"

"That they make living into Art?" Kellen asked.

"Oh, there's that," Idalia said, shrugging. "But it also says they lie."

Kellen turned to face her, outraged.

"I was surprised," Idalia said, "so I went to an older, unexpurgated version—the one in the locked case in Father's library. There, it says that Elves never lie—and never tell the truth."

"Not much better," Kellen muttered, but then he thought about it. "Never lied"—he couldn't remember Jermayan, or any of the other Elves he'd met ever lying to him. But told him the truth? The whole truth, the way he thought he wanted it, as fast as he wanted it?

He had to admit he hadn't gotten that, either. And maybe still didn't have it, even from Jermayan, who was his friend and teacher.

"Maybe fairer," Kellen said grudgingly. *Not much though.*

"Elves are different from humans," Idalia said. "Very different. They live much longer, they have a different way of looking at the world than humans do. I am *not* saying you shouldn't trust them—you'd say I'd gone crazy, and you'd be right. But don't expect them to think like humans, because they just won't." She stared off into nothing for a moment. "When you live as long as they do, you take your time about everything, and you wait for everything to come in its proper time. So, for instance, an Elf will never tell you the whole truth all at once; he'll wait for the right time to tell you bits of it, until, in the end, you've come to see the shape of it for yourself. Which is the point, for them—that you should come to see and understand a truth for yourself, and not have to be told what it is. Now, give that a lot of thought, and you'll begin to see how they live their entire lives."

"Why didn't you tell me all this when we first came here?" Kellen asked curiously. Surely all this good advice would have been a lot more useful then?

Idalia smiled crookedly. "You wouldn't have listened. We weren't going to a formal banquet then. And you weren't meeting the entire city population on more-or-less equal terms. Oh, there's Jermayan and Vestakia."

She pointed.

Kellen turned, spotting Jermayan and Vestakia coming up behind them.

Jermayan was dressed pretty much as Kellen was—the long belted robe seemed to be a standard sort of evening fashion—though Jermayan's robe was practically transparent, and so were both undertunics. Kellen felt his face get a little flushed. Not that Jermayan didn't have the body for such an audacious outfit, but still!

But Vestakia . . . !

There was no possible way to conceal the fact that she looked like a Demon, so Tengitir had obviously decided to make a virtue of what could not be ignored.

Her gown left her neck and shoulders bare, and her deep rose skin sparkled as if it had been dusted with gold. It probably had been, in fact, because there had been subtle patterns painted on her forehead in gold, in imitation of some of the filigree diadems worn by some of the Elven ladies. Her eyes had been accentuated with lines of black and gold on the lids, making them look bigger and somehow more innocent.

A wide band of gold and red embroidery held her cherry-black hair away from her pointed ears, exposing both them and her tiny golden horns, and a band of the same material decorated the neckline—if you could call it a neckline—of her long-sleeved dress, holding in the folds of shimmering gold brocade that were gathered into a tightly-pleated waist before sweeping out into a full skirt that was gathered up at the sides to reveal an underskirt the exact shade of her skin.

"You look amazing," Kellen said.

Vestakia smiled shyly, ducking her head.

"Come on," Idalia said, looking at him oddly. "I'll escort Vestakia around. You and Jermayan . . . mingle."

~

"IS she—I mean, it would please me to know that Vestakia is going to be all right," Kellen said, catching himself just in time. He barely avoided hitting Jermayan with his rainshade, but Jermayan handled his own with as much grace as if it were a sword.

"Idalia will see to her comfort," Jermayan said. "And certainly no harm nor insult has come to her yet."

"Good," Kellen said. About then, his brain caught up with the rest of him and he realized why Idalia and Jermayan had gotten him away from Vestakia so quickly.

He'd been so stunned at the sight of her in that dress that he'd just stared, but now, thinking back . . .

No. No thinking. Not about that, or anything like that. Not for a year.

He'd sworn a vow of chastity and celibacy to Shalkan in exchange for the unicorn's help in getting away from Armethalieh and the Outlaw Hunt. And it didn't matter whether or not Shalkan was his friend. If Kellen broke that vow, Shalkan would have no choice but to exact the penalty for breaking it.

And Kellen didn't *want* to break his vow.

But Vestakia—

No.

Kellen tipped back his rainshade—Jermayan ducked gracefully out of the way—and took a deep breath of the cool moist air. It had been easier when he'd been sick and drugged. A lot easier.

"I need a great favor from you. You have to explain for me, Jermayan," Kellen said, though it was the last thing in the world he wanted to say. "You have to let her know why I can't—spend as much time with her as I want to. I don't want her to think I'm avoiding her."

Although that was exactly what he was going to be doing, at least for a while, at least until he could get all this straightened out in his own mind. Maybe Shalkan would have some good advice for him—not that he'd be seeing Shalkan here tonight, of course. Unicorns were notoriously uninterested in the company of the non-chaste, and even Shalkan's tolerance had limits.

"I will," Jermayan promised. "And remember—she is not

unfamiliar with the obligations a Wildmage must undertake. As for you, you will be far too busy to worry about the matter. After the Council meeting tomorrow morning, come to the House of Sword and Shield, where we will continue your training—"

"That will be—" *Wait a minute. Council meeting? There's a Council meeting? And I'm supposed to go?* Without success, Kellen attempted to come up with a polite way to indicate he wanted to know more about that. "It would be most gratifying to hit you now, Jermayan," he finally said.

The Elven Knight smiled. "You may attempt the exercise tomorrow afternoon. In the morning I believe you will be accompanying Idalia, to advise Andoreniel and Ashaniel upon the best way to deal with . . . the problem."

The Elves almost never spoke the words "Shadow Mountain" or "Demon" aloud, as if to say them might be to summon the Endarkened—and from the very little Kellen knew of Shadow Magic, that might even be true.

So he was going to the Council meeting . . . and Jermayan was not.

"Idalia goes because she's a Wildmage . . . and I think she's the only Wildmage anywhere around near here. And I guess I go because I'm a Knight-Mage," Kellen finally said.

"Tomorrow, perhaps we may know if you are correct," Jermayan said. "But these are grim subjects for a night of celebration! Come, and I will bring you to that which will lift your spirits."

They passed among the canopies and among the lanterns. Jermayan moved purposefully, but not so swiftly that Kellen did not have opportunities to appreciate the beauty that surrounded him. There was probably no "best time" to see the garden; like every work of the Elves, it was undoubtedly designed to present a different aspect at every hour and season, and even at night and in the rain, it caught and held Kellen's attention.

But the garden was not what Jermayan had brought him to see.

In a corner of the garden—not quiet, precisely, because there was a rowdy game of chase-and-catch going on, but secluded—there seemed to be a party-within-a-party going on.

"Children," Kellen said quietly, stopping at the edge of the smaller garden.

"The children of Sentarshadeen," Jermayan agreed.

They were not alone, of course. There were other Elves there—servants (assuming the Elves had servants), companions, older brothers and sisters, perhaps even their parents. Kellen recognized Sandalon, and a moment later the young Prince spotted him and came running over.

"Kellen!" he shouted happily.

The game stopped instantly—Kellen had the sense that the others had been entertaining Sandalon—and everyone looked at him.

Oh, this is awkward. If dealing with adult Elves could be embarrassing, the potential problems in dealing with Elven children—far more direct than their elders—could be mind-boggling.

"Uh . . . hi," Kellen said.

"We've been waiting for you! Everybody wants to meet you! This is Alkandoran," Sandalon said, pulling Kellen firmly into the midst of the group. "He's nearly as old as *you* are, Kellen!"

Kellen found himself face-to-face with a boy who—and he saw no reason to assume Sandalon was mistaken—must be about his own age. Alkandoran was dressed in a tunic and leggings and sleeveless vest, but without the long robe and belt of his elders. He was willowy and slender, androgynously pretty, and almost painfully determined not to gawk at the human stranger.

"I See you, Alkandoran," Kellen said, bowing slightly. He was pretty sure he knew just how Alkandoran felt.

"I See you, Kellen Knight-Mage," Alkandoran said, bowing in return.

"And this is Tredianala," Sandalon continued.

Tredianala didn't just look uncomfortable. She looked terrified, as only the very shy could be in the presence of strangers. She was much younger than Alkandoran—maybe ten? Twelve?—and dressed in a knee-length tunic over full trousers. Kellen was reminded of some of the shyest Other-folk, the ones you might share a forest with for years, but never see.

"I See you, Tredianala," Kellen said softly, carefully not looking directly at her. "It pleases me to meet a friend of my friend."

"I See you, Kellen Knight-Mage," another girl boldly said, without waiting for Sandalon to make the introduction.

"I See you—"

"Merisashendiel," Sandalon supplied cheerfully. Kellen turned toward the child, feeling as much as seeing Tredianala make her escape back behind the adults.

Merisashendiel looked enough like Tredianala to be her twin sister—they were dressed in similar costumes—but there all resemblance ended. Merisashendiel regarded him with frank interest, as if she was bursting with questions that she intended to ask then and there.

But she was enough older than Sandalon to know better than to do that, at least in front of strangers.

"I See you, Merisashendiel," Kellen said, bowing *very* low. She giggled, regarding him with speculative approval, then swept into a full low curtsy, watching him all the time.

Kellen grinned. *That* one was going to provide her parents with more than a few sleepless nights in a few years, at least if Elven ways were anything like human ones.

The byplay was entirely lost on Sandalon, of course. And would be for some years yet.

"And here is Vendalton."

When Kellen had first arrived in Sentarshadeen, he'd found Sandalon playing alone along the dry riverbed. And Ashaniel had said that Sandalon was often lonely. Kellen had assumed, at the time, that that was because Sandalon was the only child in Sentarshadeen, but it made just as much sense if these were *all* the children in Sentarshadeen. He wasn't all that good at judging the ages of Elven children, but Vendalton seemed to be easily twice Sandalon's age. A five-year difference in age might not matter later, but it was a huge gap now.

"I See you, Vendalton," Kellen said.

"I See you, Kellen Knight-Mage," Vendalton said. "Sandalon said that you slew a . . . something evil."

"With the help of my friends, I destroyed the Barrier that was keeping the rain from falling on Sentarshadeen," Kellen said, choosing his words with care. "Everyone helped, and even so, it was very hard. It also could not have been done without the magic of my sister, in which all of Sentarshadeen participated. So you see, it was all of us together, as a whole, and not any one individual that broke the bonds of evil. I was only the channel through which all of our effort flowed."

Sandalon and Vendalton stared hard at each other, and Kellen wondered what long-running argument he'd just resolved—or made worse.

Jermayan cleared his throat significantly, regarding Sandalon.

"But she can't talk!" Sandalon protested.

"Nevertheless, I am sure she will wish to meet Kellen, if her nurse will permit," Jermayan said gravely.

"Of course I shall, Jermayan," a new voice said.

A woman stepped into the light, holding a bundle in her arms. She stopped a few feet away from Kellen and set it down on the grass.

A lady.

A very young lady.

Quite the most enchanting young lady Kellen had ever seen in his life. He fell instantly under her spell, and went down on one knee to greet her properly.

Adult Elves were stunningly beautiful. Elven children had all their elders' beauty, plus the natural appeal of the young of any species.

The combination was enchanting.

"And this is Kalania," Jermayan said, a smile in his voice.

Kellen didn't know how old Kalania was, but it was obvious that walking was a skill she had only lately begun to master. The tiny Elven child regarded him out of grave dark eyes, firmly clutching the hand of the slender woman dressed in rose velvet who knelt behind her.

"Come to me, sweeting," he coaxed. "You can do it." In the City he'd seen few children—but still far more than any of his peers had, for Kellen had spent as much of his time as he could on the streets of the Low City. The youngsters he'd seen playing in the streets there had never known how much he'd wished he could change his life for theirs. Now he wondered what it would be like to grow up in Sentarshadeen, with unicorns for playfellows. He held out his hand to the baby.

Kalania seemed to study him carefully before making up her mind. She released her nurse's hand and came staggering toward him, her chubby arms flailing.

The other children—even Sandalon—watched in fascination as Kalania made her uncertain way across the few feet of space toward Kellen. If she showed any sign of falling, he was prepared to swoop her up before she did, but she made it, grabbing his outstretched hand in a surprisingly strong grip to steady herself.

"Oh, well done, Bright Heart!" Kellen said, scooping the baby up into his arms and getting to his feet. Kalania crowed with delight at the ride into the sky.

Kellen crossed the little distance and returned her to her nurse, knowing he'd been given a great gift tonight. Jermayan had been right. Seeing the Elven children *had* made him stop brooding.

After a few minutes more—Kellen found himself answering quite a number of artfully indirect not-questions about his journey to the Barrier and about Vestakia—they left the little garden again. He was very careful to edit his answers, too. There were things that these children did not need to know. It was enough to tell them that the man he had rescued

Vestakia from was trying to steal her goats, and not any of
the rest of it. Telling them that she was Shalkan's great and
good friend now told them that no matter what she looked
like, she was not to be feared.

Once they were away from the others, he found Jermayan
regarding him curiously. "Idalia told me you didn't know the
Old Tongue."

"I don't," Kellen said, puzzled. There were days when he
felt that getting along in the Common Speech of the City—
which the Elves now used as well—was enough trouble.

He knew that there were other languages in the world—
spoken over the sea, and therefore anathema in the City.
Probably there had once been other languages spoken on
this side of the ocean as well, before the Great War had destroyed most of civilization. The Elves had probably learned
the commonest human language in order to communicate
with their allies, and then never abandoned it.

"Yet you knew what Kalania's name meant," Jermayan
pointed out reasonably. "You called her 'Bright Heart.' *Kala*
means 'heart,' and *Ania* means 'bright' in the Old Tongue."

"Coincidence. My nurse used to call me that," Kellen said
uncomfortably. Only he'd never *had* a nurse. He remembered
a nurse—quite a succession of them, in fact—but those
memories were at least partially false, implanted through
magic by his father, the Arch-Mage Lycaelon, to conceal the
fact that he'd been cared for as a child by his sister Idalia,
Banished from the City as a Wildmage when Kellen was six.

And whom Lycaelon had not wanted Kellen to remember.

But it was far too pleasant an evening to think of old
troubles.

"Undoubtedly a coincidence," Jermayan said, sounding
unconvinced.

"Really," Kellen said. "If I'd suddenly developed the ability to understand Old Elvish, I'd tell you."

Jermayan said something liquid and incomprehensible.
Kellen gazed at him expectantly.

"I said that all Elven names come from the Old Tongue."

Jermayan, Kellen suddenly realized, positively enjoyed making leading remarks—of the sort that, in any human society, would cause the hearer to respond with a question. And knowing perfectly well that Kellen's first impulse would be to ask that question.

I am almost sure I didn't need to find out what passes for a sense of humor among the Elves.

"I am very nearly certain that Idalia knows what your name means, and will tell me if I ask her," Kellen said with a wicked grin.

Jermayan smiled faintly, acknowledging that Kellen had won this round. "It means 'strong shield,' " he said. "A *mayn* is a shield. And now, I believe we are bidden to take our places, for the banquet is about to begin."

Suddenly Kellen realized that for the last few minutes he'd been hearing music—a music that blended into the rain-chimes and rain-drums, but music nonetheless. He bowed elaborately to Jermayan.

"Be my guide, O Elven Knight."

Three

The Banquet in the Garden of Leaf and Star

After Jermayan and Kellen left, Idalia tucked her arm reassuringly through Vestakia's and drew her firmly along beside her. From what Vestakia had told her about her childhood, the poor girl probably had never seen so many people gathered together in one place in her entire life.

"Kellen certainly left us very quickly," Vestakia said. "I'd been hoping to talk to him," she added wistfully.

"Maybe later," Idalia said. She wondered how much to tell Vestakia. From the way Kellen had looked at her when she'd showed up in the festive—and very flattering—gown, some-one should, and it was a good bet Vestakia didn't know the details of Kellen's vow, or possibly even that it existed.

Well, no time like the present. And one advantage to es-corting Vestakia around was that it gave Idalia rather more privacy than she'd have otherwise. While everyone in Sen-tarshadeen knew that Vestakia wouldn't be here at all if she were Tainted, she still *looked* like a Demon. And Elven memories were long. Even if none of the Elves now living had fought on the battlefields of the Great War, the fathers and grandfathers of many of those here tonight had.

"You know that Kellen is a Wildmage—as your mother was," Idalia began slowly. "And you know the price we pay for our magic—the vows and obligations we offer up to the Gods . . . "

"Oh, Blessed Lady!" Vestakia gasped, stopping dead and clutching Idalia's arm. "He's not going to *die*?"

"No, no—nothing like that," Idalia said hastily, remem-bering suddenly that Idalia's mother had given up twenty years of her lifespan in exchange for Vestakia's human spirit. Quickly she explained Kellen's obligation—and the reason why Kellen was able to spend so very much time in the company of a unicorn.

"Not many people know," she finished. "Most of the time it doesn't . . . impinge."

To her surprise—and secret delight—Vestakia gave a great whoop of laughter, startling the Elves walking nearby.

"Oh! Oh, my," the girl said. She sobered quickly, glancing around, then looked back at Idalia. "Does that mean I—he and I—won't see each other at all?"

"I don't know," Idalia said honestly. "But if you don't see him, try not to mind too much. It won't be because he doesn't like you, or care about you. Rather too much the re-verse, perhaps. I know he wants you to be happy here; he is very, very concerned that you are comfortable."

"With water—and *hot* water, too—available for the turn-ing of a handle? And every kind of food—fruit, too!—there when I reach out my hand? And such a warm soft bed that I don't think I shall ever be cold again? How can he wonder?" Vestakia asked in bafflement.

"I think he is worried that the people may be unkind," Idalia said gently, trying not to smile.

Vestakia sniffed, shaking her head. "It isn't important, now that they know in their heads that I want to help, and I know that eventually their hearts will understand. Yes, they stare—and point at me when they think I am not looking. But no one will try to kill me here for what I am, and . . . there are goats here, too. I can herd them, and milk them, and make curds and cheese. I can deliver a kid if the nanny has trouble. I can be useful, even beyond making sure that *They* do not come here. The Elves will see that, too, with time." She smiled shyly. "You know, and they surely know, that you cannot lie to an animal. They know when someone is good or bad. Sooner or later most people here will understand in their hearts. And until then, there are so many wonderful things to see, and to do—and not everyone turns and runs, you know. Some talk to me, and—" Vestakia's eyes grew wide, and she lowered her voice, as if about to confide a great wonder. "There are *books* here, Idalia! Oh, hundreds of them! I do not read very well—we only had one or two that Mama traded for—beyond her three Books, and those of course I could not read—so I learned my letters out of them and memorized them long ago. But with all the books here to practice on, soon I shall read so much better than before . . . "

Vestakia was quite right about being able to make a place for herself in Sentarshadeen, Idalia thought. She'd probably been a very good goatherd back in the Lost Lands—calm, cheerful, and patient, all qualities one needed when dealing with goats. Idalia tried to imagine one of the spoiled daughters of the City in Vestakia's situation—wrenched away from everything she knew, and dropped among a strange people who despised her. No matter how luxurious the surroundings, Idalia knew that the Armethaliehan girl would be weeping and complaining, demanding that things be adjusted to her liking.

But Vestakia had not complained once. She sounded so happy—and so determined to *be* happy—that Idalia kept her fears of the future to herself. If war came—*when* war came—there would be no room in it for the quiet, gentle future Vestakia spoke of so easily.

And yet—

And yet Vestakia surely knew that too. Or guessed it, at least. She was the daughter of a Demon. She knew what the Endarkened did, and wanted. So the quiet, gentle future she was envisioning was one she must know could not last for long.

She and Idalia were very much more alike than Idalia had thought, for Vestakia was seizing her own chance for peace and joy while it was there, and would live every moment that had been granted her to the fullest.

And when trouble came, as it would—well, Idalia had the feeling that Vestakia would meet it head-on.

ONE thing about the evening did match Kellen's expectations of how a formal banquet would go, and that was that he was seated at the same table as the King and Queen. Idalia and Jermayan were there as well, and Vestakia, and Sandalon with Lairamo.

He was glad to see both Vestakia and Sandalon, and surprised to see both of them together, though Sandalon was next to him, and Vestakia was at the far end of the table. He supposed that Andoreniel and Ashaniel were making a point. And Vestakia deserved to be here as much as he and Jermayan did.

Sandalon was gleefully delighted to be among the adults, and painfully conscious of his manners.

"You won't go away again, will you, Kellen—I mean, it would be interesting to know if you contemplated a journey soon, wouldn't it?" he said, looking up at Lairamo for approval.

"I don't know if I'll have to go away again, Sandalon," Kellen said gently. "I hope I won't. I'll tell you as soon as I know. I can promise that."

"Good!" the boy said. "I hope you won't have to go away either. Idalia was sad while you were gone. She stayed in her house and wouldn't talk to anyone."

⌒

THE banquet went on until quite late. There were more—and more elaborate—dishes offered than Kellen had yet seen, but fortunately he quickly realized he didn't have to try everything offered, and stuck to the things he could identify.

Or so he thought. The Elven love of illusion extended even to their culinary arts—the slice of venison in sauce he took turned out to be made of mushrooms, and the "roast goose" was not fowl, but fish. Still, both were perfectly edible, even delicious. And a roast turnip could look like few other things—though he was a little surprised to find it had been hollowed out and stuffed with apple.

At one point Kellen looked up to find Vestakia gone, and realized that she must have slipped out sometime after the main courses were served—at least, he didn't see her again during the evening.

He wished he could do the same. Though the banquet was entertaining in an exotic fashion, it was tiring, and Kellen couldn't help feeling that there were more important things to be doing than throwing a big party right now. While he tried to keep from worrying about tomorrow's Council meeting, he was a human, not an Elf, and he didn't have their seeming ability to let tomorrow take care of itself.

And he did know what was proper good manners in this situation, having checked with Jermayan to make sure. So despite the fact that he'd rather have been out in the meadow with the unicorns—despite the rain—or back in his own home, he stayed at the banquet through the long dessert course—iced cakes, candied fruits, flavored ices, custards, and even *xocalatl*—did his best to make polite conversation with dozens of people whose names he was sure he wouldn't remember in the morning, and entertained himself with thinking how horrified his peers back in Armethalieh would be if they could only see him now.

Eventually the last round of fruit cordials had been poured and drunk. Fortunately there didn't seem to be very much alcohol at all in Elven wines and cordials, but since custom required everyone to change tables for every course of the desserts—and there were a lot of courses—Kellen was just about as confused as to just *where* in the garden he was as if he'd been drinking strong Armathaliehan ale.

"But now the hour grows late, and we do not wish to weary those whom we also honor," Ashaniel said, rising gracefully to her feet. "And so we give grace to the night and to the season, and bid you all fair rest and refreshment in the name of Leaf and Star!"

At that signal, the guests began to prepare to depart. Kellen was already on his feet. He looked around, but couldn't see Jermayan or Idalia anywhere. It didn't matter. He could catch up with Idalia at home.

⇌

BUT when he reached the house once more, Idalia wasn't there.

No reason to wait up for her, Kellen told himself, hanging up his cloak and shaking out his rainshade before setting it in its tray to finish drying. She'd probably stopped to talk to friends. He'd just make sure to leave a few lamps burning for her, and make sure the stove had plenty of fuel.

All in all, his first Elven banquet hadn't been all that bad, he decided, folding his new finery neatly and climbing into bed.

⇌

SINCE the rains had returned—with a vengeance—the brooks and streams that criss-crossed Sentarshadeen had refilled, and in some cases done more than that. It was not the ruinous flooding that could have occurred if the rains had been let to reach the Elven Lands unchecked, but it could have been messy and inconvenient, so the banks of some of the shallower tributaries had been shored up and reinforced. Since the work had been done by Elves, it had been done beautifully, with walls of brick and stone and tile edging the rivulets, until they took on much the look of canals.

Whoever had been looking after Jermayan's house while he was gone was apparently someone with a lot of free time to make certain that Jermayan never be inconvenienced by the flooding of his home. This highly industrious individual had built the restraining walls especially high. Higher, in fact, than the footbridge to the front door, which fitted as neatly into it as if they had always been meant to be together.

In one way, that was a good thing, because the little stream that flowed around the cottage was running very high. However, this conscientious person had not been particularly good at imagining what would happen if the stream actually *did* get that high, because that little footbridge should have been raised along with the walls.

When he and Idalia reached it, Jermayan cleared his throat uncomfortably, regarding the bridge.

"Generally it is, ah—"

"Drier?" Idalia suggested mischievously.

"Yes. Drier. In the sense that the bridge is not quite so wet."

"It would, of course, be drier if it were not raining," Idalia said agreeably, watching the river foam over the planks of the bridge. To be fair, the bridge was not so *very* much underwater.

"It would be churlish of me to expect an honored guest to ruin her dancing shoes because of my unruly stream," Jermayan said decisively. He advanced upon Idalia and swooped her up into his arms before she could protest.

Idalia was not a small woman, but she'd felt in no danger of being dropped as Jermayan carried her across the bridge and up the walk, managing both their rainshades with elegant ease. In fact, it was a remarkably pleasant experience; there was something significant in allowing someone else to take charge of her safety for once. Even in so small a thing as keeping her feet from being soaked. As Jermayan carried her over the stream, she had the rather light-headed sensation of crossing something more important than just a bit of running water.

The bridge was hung with pale blue lanterns, and there were more at the door. The ones at the door were in the shape of seashells, a watery motif particularly suited to the weather, and their surfaces were starred and speckled with flecks of green.

Jermayan thrust the door open and set her down inside.

"We arrive without incident," he observed. "Be welcome, Idalia, in my home and at my hearth."

"I am welcome," Idalia said, removing her raincape and furling her rainshade. "And it's quite . . . dry."

"And perhaps the stream will subside by morning, though I do doubt it. There is tea, of course, or if you prefer, I might warm some cordial."

"Tea, I think," Idalia said. "There has been quite enough cordial this evening."

Jermayan went off to prepare the tea, after setting his cloak aside. The cottage was larger than the guesthouses, and had a separate kitchen. While he was gone, she looked around.

It much resembled his home in Ondoladeshiron, where she had once been a frequent guest. There were several familiar tapestries hung upon the walls, and between them, on small shelves, exquisite pieces of Elvenware, meant for display and not for use.

A low table was pulled up to one of the long padded benches that lined the room. It was heaped with books—both conventional bound books, and the older scrolls that some Elves still preferred. A *xaqiue* board with a half-finished game took up about half the table.

In an open case on the bench was Jermayan's harp.

It was a small instrument that could be held in the crook of one arm, suitable for carrying into the field. The wood was black with age, and polished smooth by the caress of countless hands over the centuries, and it was strung with silver.

An Elven Knight was expected to learn to master at least one of the "gentler arts" as well as those of war and warfare; most chose something like carving, mosaic-setting, or gardening, all things where beauty could be achieved in the laying out of mathematical designs according to established rules. A slightly smaller number became musicians, but were players rather than composers. Very few chose the more challenging realms of music composition, poetry, or the creative visual arts.

But Jermayan, being Jermayan, could never do anything by halves. He had taken up and mastered several instruments, the harp becoming his favorite—and he wrote music for it. Or at least, he had done so when Idalia had last known him.

She did not touch the harp herself, for she was feeling unwontedly sensitive, and was afraid she might pick up far more than she wanted or he intended if she did so. Instead, she settled herself beside the fire to wait.

He came in with tea set out on a footed tray; the ones like it in her home were of carved wood, but this one was actually more practical if you were going to carry liquid about, being made of sculpted metal with an inlay of glass mosaic. She made a mental note to commission one like it, but knew better than to admire it—because Jermayan would immediately try to give it to her.

Instead, when he put it down carefully between them and settled himself, she poured tea for both of them and nodded toward the harp. "I'd been wondering if you still played," she'd said, in order to keep the stillness from deepening into the uncomfortable. "I was hoping nothing had happened to make you lose interest—" Then she smiled. "Or worse, decide that the harp wasn't challenging enough and move on to the pandehorn!"

"Ah, the ill woodwind that never blows good," he replied with a rare chuckle. "No indeed. I have found a great deal of comfort in music. And I have continued to compose as well." And without waiting for her to ask, he set down his tea and reached for the harp and began to play.

It was not a piece with which she was familiar, and within moments, she fell under the spell of it. If this was one of Jermayan's own works, he had improved out of all expectation as a composer, and he had been good to begin with.

But it was not a *comfortable* piece, nor could it be described as "pretty," though it was so very powerful that before long Idalia had found her eyes stinging with unshed tears. It was full of a deep sadness and inarticulate longing. There was a sense of things left unfinished, not because they had been abandoned willingly, but because abandonment had been forced.

Even the ending cried out with emptiness that yearned to be filled.

Idalia swallowed down the lump in her throat, and said, thickly, "It's very—beautiful."

Jermayan set the harp aside, and replied, almost casually, "I wrote it about you. And for you. After you left Ondoladeshiron."

But then, before she could manage to stammer *anything* in reply to that astonishing statement, he turned, and the gentle smile he graced her with took her breath away.

"I shall have to write something happier now."

THE next thing Kellen knew was that someone was shaking him, and watery morning light was streaming through his windows.

"Sometimes I think you'd sleep through a unicorn stampede! Wake *up,* slug-a-bed!"

"Idalia?"

Groggily, Kellen sat up and stared at his sister.

She was still wearing the dress she'd worn last night. Hadn't she been home?

"Council meeting in less than an hour. You've barely got time to get up and dressed—and I've got to change, too."

Kellen abandoned the question of where Idalia had spent the night in favor of more pressing issues. He *really* didn't want to go to the meeting.

"Why do I—?" he began.

But Idalia, seeing him awake, was already leaving the room.

If he wanted to argue his point, Kellen realized, he was going to have to be up and dressed to do it. He flung back the covers, shuddering at the chill of the air, and grabbed for his bedrobe. Wrapping it firmly around him—and wondering where his house boots had gotten to *this* time—he hurried over to the clothespress. Grabbing the first things that came to hand—it really didn't matter much, since *all* his Elven clothing was suitable and becoming—he dressed quickly, dragged a comb through his now almost shoulder-length hair (thankful that he'd taken the time to unbraid it last night before going to bed), and hurried into the outer room, boots in hand.

When he came out of the bathroom, Idalia was ready. She was wearing Elven clothing today instead of her usual Wildwood buckskins: boots and tunic and a knee-length coat in several shades of violet.

"Ready? Good," she said.

"But I haven't had breakfast," Kellen complained.

"Then you should have gotten up earlier," Idalia said implacably.

"And I don't really see why I have to go at all," Kellen added mutinously. "I don't know anything about . . . whatever the Council is going to talk about."

"Then it's time you learned," Idalia said, reaching into the cupboard and handing him a chunk of yellow cheese, a small loaf of bread, and an apple. "The Council will be discussing its plans. Attending meetings like this is something Knight-Mages do, so you'd better get used to it. Besides, you might even be helpful." She reached up and patted him on the shoulder.

Kellen made a rude noise, and bit into the cheese. Since he could hardly say he wasn't a Knight-Mage, he supposed he'd better go along to the Council meeting. At least the afternoon promised to be more interesting. He'd be meeting Jermayan for his first formal lessons in knightly practice then.

Jermayan had taught Kellen all he could on the way to the Barrier, and the fact that Kellen's Wildmage gifts lay in that direction helped a great deal. But that was no substitute for training and practice—a lot of practice—under conditions that Jermayan simply hadn't been able to reproduce on the trail. Kellen was looking forward to continuing his education.

And meanwhile, he guessed he was pretty sure he knew where Idalia had been last night, and he was happy for both her and Jermayan. He just hoped that neither one of them would start quoting poetry at him.

ONE concession that had been made to the eternal rain was that a slatted wooden pathway had now been laid across the meadow to the door of the House, so that one arrived on the doorstep, if not quite dry-shod, at least not covered in mud.

Just as on the previous occasion on which Kellen had been brought to a meeting of the Council, he and Idalia were met on the doorstep and conducted deep within the House, to a windowless circular chamber deep within the center of the Palace.

Hanging from its walls were thirteen narrow banners of brightly colored silk, each bearing a single elaborate symbol worked upon it in shining silver. The last time, they'd been a complete mystery to Kellen, but he knew a little more about the Elves now.

Nine for the Nine Cities, probably, but that leaves four. That one symbol almost looks like the Great Seal of Armethalieh: could the other four be for the Other Races?

*Men, Centaurs, and . . . but that doesn't work either, because
there are more other races than four, aren't there? Fauns,
and selkies, and dryads, and unicorns, and . . .*

Despite Idalia's insistence that they were going to be late,
she and Kellen had been the first to arrive. Now his musings
were interrupted by the arrival of the others: Ashaniel and
Andoreniel, Morusil, Ainalundore, Tyendimarquen, and two
others he'd met and learned the names of the night before:
Dargainon and Sorvare.

Six of the seven Elves took their seats around the large
round table of gleaming pale wood—Tyendimarquen remained standing. In the table's center, the inlay of the symbol of the royal house gleamed as brightly as if it were
aflame, reflecting the illumination of the mirrored lamps
which hung above it.

Though Kellen and Idalia were by far the most plainly-
dressed of the group, Kellen found he felt no sense of awkwardness, and Idalia obviously felt perfectly at ease. He
supposed that though the Elves *could* make someone feel
uncomfortable and out-of-place if they chose, they obviously weren't choosing to do so on this occasion.

Or perhaps what he was wearing was perfectly suitable
for the situation.

As before, the doors swung shut behind them, seemingly
of their own volition, and Tyendimarquen slid several bolts
into place, locking it securely. As she slid the last of the bolts
home, Andoreniel raised his hand and sketched a small shape
in the air, and once again Kellen felt a brief sense of *pressure,* as the room was magically sealed against all manner of
intrusion and eavesdropping, both magical and mundane.

"Now we may begin," Andoreniel said, when Tyendimarquen had taken her seat. "We call this meeting to discuss
what provision we have made thus far in dealing with the
Enemy, and what provision we have yet to make."

Ainalundore was the first to speak. He rose gracefully to
his feet—as if the Elves ever did anything awkwardly—and
began to speak in measured tones.

Kellen discovered that a report on the drought had been sent to the Viceroys of the other eight Elven cities: Ondoladeshiron, Lerkalpoldara, Windalorianan, Deskethomaynel, Thultafoniseen, Valwendigorean, Realthataladon, and Ysterialpoerin, to explain that it had been discovered to be the work of the Enemy. A further report had been sent when the Barrier had fallen, explaining that with the destruction of the Enemy's first ploy, further attacks could be expected. Response from the other cities, according to Ainalundore, had been gratifying; Andoreniel could be assured of their vigilance, and could expect regular reports.

That's it? Kellen thought in disbelief. *That's all? Shadow Mountain is waking up again—the biggest threat in a thousand years—and all the Elves are going to do about it is WRITE REPORTS?*

Dargainon was next to speak. And before he did so, he glanced aside at Kellen and Idalia. Particularly at Kellen.

"The Enemy is long-lived, as are we; it is my assumption, which I know is shared by others on this Council, that as this last attack upon Sentarshadeen was a subtle one, long in the planning and execution, so is the next move in this campaign likely to be. The Enemy has learned from his mistakes; we believe that he is unlikely to make any sudden or overt attacks; rather, this war is likely to be a slow and drawn-out campaign of attrition. This would have had a great likelihood of success; had it not been for the efforts of Idalia Wildmage, we probably would not have known it for an attack until it was too late." He bowed a little to Idalia, who in her turn bowed back.

"Nevertheless, there are other considerations. We cannot be sure of what the next move may be. It has been suggested, since Idalia Wildmage is unable to advise us from what direction the next attack of the Enemy may come, nor are the woman Vestakia's abilities reliable in that regard, it is an important consideration to look to the safety of our children. Therefore, a plan is presented for the approval of the Council to secure their safety by conveying all of our children to the Crowned Horns of the Moon."

Kellen looked questioningly at Idalia.

"A fortress high in the Mystral Mountains, that was never taken during the War. A good choice," she said in an undertone.

A good choice it might be, but that hardly prevented a number of comments from being made on it, even though Kellen got the impression that this was old business that had been hashed out pretty thoroughly before the Council met today. At last it was decided by Andoreniel that the plan would go forward as it stood. Convoys from each of the Nine Cities would begin stocking the fortress immediately. In a few weeks, once winter had made travel in the higher elevations a bit dryer, parties of Elven Knights would begin taking groups of children to the fortress a few at a time, where they would remain with their protectors and guardians until the situation with the Enemy had changed.

Or until they've all grown up, Kellen thought wryly. He didn't know how long that would take, but if Demons were immortal, and Elves were very long-lived, neither side might be in a real hurry about going to war, inevitable as it might seem.

Sandalon, of course, being the Heir, would be the greatest prize for any enemy to capture, and for that reason, the young Prince would be sent at some point in the middle of this migration—as neither the first nor the last—to avoid drawing attention to him.

He'll hate that, Kellen thought ruefully. *But maybe, among all those kids from the other cities, he'll find some his own age to play with.* He hoped something like that would happen, for the boy's sake. And he was just as glad not to be the one to have to tell Sandalon he was being sent away from the people and things he'd known all his life.

"Let it be done," Andoreniel said, ending the discussion.

"And now," Ashaniel said, sounding almost reluctant,

"there is the matter of the Others. If the Enemy walks again, in the end, its foe is all the children of the Light, not merely the Children of Leaf and Star."

There was a moment of silence around the Council table.

"Certainly they must be told," Tyendimarquen said unwillingly. "Yet to waste good counsel on those who would not believe it, when such telling might make matters worse, is the action of a fool."

"The High Hills will listen," Idalia said. "They, too, have felt some of the effect of the Barrier and its fall. You still trade with the High Hills, after all. And as for the Otherfolk, the creatures of forest and woodland—the unicorns can carry your warning there, and be believed."

Tyendimarquen seemed relieved. "Yes. There is a good solution, Idalia. We will warn the High Hills, and the Other Folk, and let both of them spread the warning as they will."

"The Out Islands may well listen," said Ashaniel, thoughtfully. "Let the unicorns also take word to the People of the Water, for the merfolk and the Out Islanders are allies still."

"But what about Armethalieh?" Kellen said, asking the question before he could stop himself. "I mean . . . the Mountain Traders don't trade with Armethalieh, not directly, and not at this season. They won't pass a warning on, or if they do, the City won't believe it. The City needs to be warned about the Endarkened."

There was another long moment of silence, as all the Elves looked at each other, seeming to share a moment of unspoken communication.

"Surely it would grieve us to see any of the Children of the Light fall to the Great Enemy, even those who inhabit the Golden City, Kellen Knight-Mage," Sorvare said slowly. "But as one who has lately lived within her walls, you more than most will understand that it is no light matter for one of the Children of Leaf and Star to attempt to carry a warning there. Perhaps such a warning *would* be believed. Perhaps—and you may search your own heart for the truth of my conjecture—it would be seen as a form of attack, and gain us, instead of an ally, a new enemy at a time when we can ill afford one. And so I must counsel caution in any attempt to deal with Armethalieh directly, lest intended good become unimagined harm."

"It is not impossible that we will find an ally of the proper sort to carry our message to Armethalieh, Kellen," Morusil added kindly. "Perhaps an Out Island captain, for instance. But neither you nor Idalia can return there under pain of death, and our kind is now similarly barred from setting foot upon City lands. Still, knowing the Enemy's ways, we will do what we can."

"The proper sort" being human, Kellen thought in dismayed realization. Both Morusil and Sorvare were right— neither he nor Idalia could act as the Elves' envoy, and if the Elves couldn't go themselves, what did that leave? And if the High Mages saw the Elves' warning not as a help, but as an attack . . .

He couldn't fault their logic. But all the same, his mind did go back to the words the Demon had taunted him with back at the Barrier: that when war came, the Elves would look to their own first.

Wasn't that just what they were doing now?

And if someone did manage to warn Armethalieh now, would it do any good? Was there *anyone* who would be believed?

The meeting ended, with plans having been made to remove the Elven children to the Fortress of the Crowned Horns and to send a message—soon—to those lands bordering on those of the Elves that Shadow Mountain was once more spreading its blight across the face of the land. Once more Andoreniel dismissed the seal that sequestered the Council chamber, and the Elves departed to their tasks.

Ashaniel stopped Kellen as he was about to leave.

"Perhaps you do not think we act with sufficient haste, Kellen Knight-Mage," Ashaniel suggested, placing her hand upon his arm.

Kellen glanced wildly around for Idalia, trying to locate her without seeming rude. But she was nowhere to be seen.

"Lady Ashaniel, I'm really sorry if I offended anybody today," Kellen said. "It's just that I . . . " He tried to think of how to phrase his thought politely, and gave up. "If there's going to be a war, we should be preparing for it. That's all."

"Yet to say what form our preparations must take, when the Enemy has not yet declared the shape of his own intention, might be to doom us all," Ashaniel said gently. "We have met the Enemy upon the battlefield twice before, and by the grace of Leaf and Star, we prevailed. Fear not for your friends. They will be warned in good time." She turned away.

They're not my friends, Kellen thought with a sigh. He couldn't think of one person back in Armethalieh that he could reasonably call a friend . . . but that hardly meant he wanted the City to fall to a Demon attack. There were hundreds, thousands of perfectly innocent people there, people who were harming no one, leading contented lives, trying to be good to each other, and if they were unreasonably prejudiced about outsiders, well, those prejudices had been carefully taught and carefully nurtured . . .

He left the Council chamber. An Elf was waiting for him in the hallway, to conduct him back down the labyrinth of passageways that led to the front door of the House of Leaf and Star. Kellen was fairly good at not getting lost, but he was glad of the guide; he was willing to bet that he hadn't taken the same route to or from the Council chamber twice.

Idalia was waiting for him on the portico.

"Ready to head over to the House of Sword and Shield? You look like you could stand to hit something," she said.

Kellen groaned faintly. "Ashaniel was just telling me not to worry, because the Elves have everything under control, and the moment *They* make a move, the Elves will make the appropriate response. But what if it's something else like the Barrier? They already know that *They* are a threat, and out there: why don't they just gather up the biggest army they can and go get them?"

Idalia pulled up the hood of her raincape and stepped off the portico, unfurling her rainshade as she did. Kellen followed, copying her gestures. For a minute or two they walked down the wooden path through the rain in silence.

"Those are reasonable questions, considering how little you actually know about the Enemy—and the Elves don't really know all that much more. For instance, they don't really know how strong the Enemy is, either in terms of numbers or magic—but they do know that if *They* can call in as many allies and slaves as *They* could in the Last War, *They* can probably put a larger army into the field than the Nine Cities can, and this time the Elves can't count on having much in the way of human allies. Next, the Elves don't have any magic, while the Enemy are the strongest Mages there are. I'm not even sure that if we got all the Wildmages, and all the High Mages, and all the Good Otherfolk to work together there'd be as much magic on our side as there is on the Enemy side. Not after the Great War and the death of the dragons."

"That's comforting—I don't think," Kellen said uneasily. "Especially since the High Mages *won't* fight on the same side as Wildmages. Or Elves."

Idalia shrugged. "They might, eventually. But it doesn't really matter. Because you can't attack what you can't find, and no one's exactly sure where Shadow Mountain is. It might not even be entirely in this world. North of here, that's all I know. That's all anyone knows. And well-enough shielded that all the Seeking spells in the world aren't going to find it. So . . . we can't find the Enemy stronghold, and if we could find it, we don't have the strength to attack it and win."

"So what are we going to do?" Kellen asked.

"What Ashaniel said. Wait . . . and hope," Idalia said. "I know it sounds like a recipe for disaster, but the Elves have fought the Enemy before, and won. And once we see what *They* are going to do, we might be able to think of something creative." Now she smiled a little. "That is one of the strongest weapons we have, actually. No creature of the Enemy can match our creativity and imagination—the ancient saying is, 'The Endarkened cannot make, they can only mar.' No matter what else has happened to the Endarkened, I doubt that has changed."

THE World Without Sun was changeless and eternal. Not for its inhabitants the ceaseless erosion and decay of the seasons of the Bright World: theirs was a world of stone and darkness, utterly suited to their nature.

The Endarkened did not change. Let the Elves dwindle and fade, becoming a mockery of what they once were. Let the humans pass from savagery to senescence without ever reaching true civilization. The Endarkened would remain just as they had been at the moment that *He Who Is* had first created them, an unchanging tribute to His foresight and wisdom.

And in the end, they would triumph, because of their unchanging nature. Because in all the millennia of their existence, they had never forgotten that they had one goal, and one goal only.

The utter destruction of all who walked in the Light.

UPON her Rising—for though adult Endarkened did not sleep, they regularly entered a sort of deep trance—Queen Savilla summoned her slaves, and as they groomed her, she heard, as was her custom, the Petitions of the Grooming Chamber. These were usually—though not always—trivial matters of a personal nature, suited to the surroundings.

But today, though she was careful to give no sign of it to her courtiers and attendants, her thoughts were not upon the endless details of her Court, but elsewhere, for the news from the Bright World was good.

Things were going especially well in Armethalieh. Conditions were deteriorating in the City, even as her human agent moved upward in influence and position, and soon—very soon, as the Endarkened reckoned things—he would be in a position to influence, if not dictate, policy on the High Council itself. Then she could move on to the next step in her plans: to bring the Golden City over to the Endarkened side, its resources intact, its people ripe to feed the Endarkened need for ever more power.

Savilla smiled inwardly. In a thousand generations of the Endarkened, such an audacious coup had never been attempted. The single largest enclave of humans in the land; an inexhaustible supply of power, slaves, and food—allying itself with the Endarkened willingly because they would have convinced themselves that all the rest of the Brightworlders were their implacable foes and only the Endarkened—the poor, misunderstood, Endarkened!—could save them.

With Armethalieh as their vassal, the Endarkened would be invincible. And all it would require would be the subjugation of the High Council—a handful of foolish humans. The High Council had turned everyone else in the Golden City into witless sheep long ago. The Armethaliehans would do whatever their Mage-masters told them to, and ask no questions.

Once the business of the Grooming Chamber had been dealt with, Savilla dismissed her attendants and headed for her Stone Garden, a lovely private monument to her past triumphs in the Endarkened's greatest art, that of torture. The Stone Garden belonged to her alone, and her subjects knew that she was never to be disturbed there.

But today was different.

Prince Zyperis stood at the gateway to the garden, obviously waiting for her.

"I wondered if I might walk with you today," he said deferentially, furling his great scarlet wings tight to his body submissively.

"Of course," Savilla said graciously. So her son and lover wanted something, did he? She was not entirely displeased. It was the way of their kind. He was a promising youngster. But the greater the promise, the greater the threat.

She offered him her arm. He took it, and the two of them

passed into the garden. For a while Zyperis made idle conversation, speaking with knowledgeable pleasure about the history of her trophies, for he had been present at the collection of some of them.

Within each colored crystal, Savilla had trapped some moment of agony of one of her special victims, so that she could treasure it forever. As she and Zyperis strolled along the paths where nothing grew, she would stop occasionally to waken a stone into life with a touch of her power.

—Here, the death of the last of the bearwards. They had been formidable enemies to many of Uralesse's slave-races; strong as giants, and utterly committed to the Light. Their inroads had weakened Uralesse to the point where it had been possible for her to destroy him and take the Shadow Throne. Yet flay them of their bearskins, strip them of their magic, and they were as weak and vulnerable as any human. She had killed his mate and his cubs before his eyes, savoring their blended agony. . . .

—There, the death of a nest of firesprites. They were difficult to torture; it had required all her creativity. But water, or better yet *ice* . . . oh, yes, that had served her very well.

The minds and souls represented here were long expended, gone to fuel her magic. But the trophies of her past triumphs remained.

Zyperis was silent for some time, conscious of the honor of being invited into Savilla's private garden. But at last, as she had known he would, he raised the true reason for his visit.

"How goes the war, my sweet Crown of Pain? I know the destruction of the Barrier was only the merest and most minor of setbacks, but since the moment when it fell, you have told me nothing," he said, pouting prettily. "I languish in ignorance that only you can remove."

"You will be pleased," Savilla said, allowing her long ivory fangs to gleam in a smile of pleasure. "Our agent in Armethalieh rises higher in the confidence of the Arch-Mage, and will soon gain a seat on the High Council itself. From there it should be a simple task for him to convince

Lycaelon and the rest that we are not the true enemy, and that someone else—it hardly matters who!—has misled them all these centuries for his own fell purposes. I suspect they will pounce upon some long-dead Arch-Mage whose progeny they wish to discredit as the source of their misinformation, and proceed to purge their own histories of anything they believe to be tainted by his hand and thoughts."

Zyperis preened with delight. "Then they shall—so they think—become our allies, when in fact they will become our slaves. I have an idea, my Liege-Mother. You must convince them that there is a vast conspiracy of Wildmages ready to destroy their city, allied with the Elves. They already loathe both the Elves and the Wild Magic, and the Arch-Mage will not soon forget that his own son was Banished for dabbling in it. The combination should drive them absolutely wild. That way, we can save them from the two things they hate and fear the most—Elves and Wildmages."

"I do not think my agent will find that very difficult," Savilla said, reluctant approval in her voice.

It was a good idea—a clever idea—one more proof, if she needed it, that inevitably Zyperis would someday make a try for the Shadow Throne. So the longer she could keep him off-balance, uncertain of his ability, the longer it would take for that day to come.

"But it will take time to get him onto the Council, and time for him to eliminate his rivals," she said, as if the idea had just occurred to her. "Until his position is secure, we have to keep the Elves securely occupied with their own problems. We must keep them from managing to warn Armethalieh. How do you propose to do that?"

She stopped strolling and gazed demandingly into his eyes.

Zyperis's wings unfurled and drooped slightly, and Savilla felt a hot spark of triumph. Obviously the boy hadn't thought that far ahead.

"We could carry off their messengers," he suggested doubtfully.

"But we don't want to act openly . . . yet," Savilla said.

"And direct opposition only strengthens the foe's will to resist. No. The Elves have no real interest in warning Armethalieh, so we will make it easy for them to avoid it. We will provide a diversion that will occupy all their energy . . . the sacrifice of a pawn."

"Oh, don't tease me so!" Zyperis begged. "You've had a plan all along—you know you have. Tell me what it is!"

"No," Savilla said archly. "I don't think I shall. You have not yet impressed me with your . . . sufficiently sincere desire to know."

THE House of Shield and Sword was located on the southern edge of the city. From his rambles with Sandalon, Kellen had gotten the impression he knew the city fairly well, but somehow this was one of the places that had never been included on their walks.

It was out beyond the firing kilns, separated from the city proper by a dense plantation of balsam-bough trees. There was no pathway through the forest; nothing to indicate that anything lay beyond the evergreens but more woodland. If Idalia had not been with him, Kellen might well have turned back at the forest's edge.

"Here you are," Idalia said, stopping at the far side of the trees. "Think you can find your way from here?"

"I . . . oh."

A whole pocket canyon spread out before him, its floor rich with tall grass. The forest, he realized, had been planted— and carefully tended—to screen its opening. Horses grazed loose in the meadow, their coats shiny with rain.

About halfway down the canyon floor was the House of Sword and Shield.

Like all Elven architecture, it blended in to its surroundings so harmoniously it seemed to have grown there instead of being built. Unlike the House of Leaf and Star, it was all of simple golden stone except for the roof; one story, and with the high-peaked roof making it look even lower and wider.

"Why is it out here in the middle of nowhere?" Kellen asked.

"You'll have to ask Jermayan," Idalia said, amused. "I think he's coming now."

She pointed. A rider was coming toward them. Jermayan, and Valdien.

Today the Elven Knight wore no armor at all, merely a simple tunic and leggings in green beneath his raincape, with soft boots to match, and Valdien wore only a simple halter. Elf and destrier moved as one being, and Kellen wondered absently if he could learn to ride a horse, and if he could ever manage to equal Jermayan's easy grace.

"The student approaches," Jermayan observed. "I promise, Idalia, that he will be returned to you . . . reasonably unscathed."

"Oh, don't bother on my account," Idalia said cheerfully. "As *The Book of Stars* tells us, *'There is nothing worth knowing that is not bought without effort or pain.'* I'll see you later." She turned away, walking back through the pines.

Jermayan dismounted from Valdien and slipped the halter from Valdien's head.

"Come," Jermayan said to Kellen, beginning to walk back toward the House of Sword and Shield. "It is time for your proper training to begin."

Valdien followed Kellen and Jermayan like a hopeful pet, occasionally nudging Jermayan in the back.

Kellen felt a flutter of nervousness at the pit of his stomach. It wasn't that he doubted his own skill—he didn't; he was a Knight-Mage after all. But all of his experience with formal training of any kind had been disastrous, and all of a sudden he was afraid that this was going to turn out the same way.

"Jermayan—" he said, stopping.

His friend looked at him questioningly.

"I'm . . . well, I'm not very good at some things," Kellen said awkwardly.

"That," said Jermayan, "is why you are here. The House of Sword and Shield has trained Knight-Mages in the past. The House remembers."

"But I . . . " There just wasn't any good way to say this! "I don't want to make trouble." *Or get into trouble.* "I just don't . . . I asked the Council a question this morning," he admitted dolefully.

That surprised a startled laugh from Jermayan.

"No doubt certain members of the Council were surprised by your boldness, and were instantly forthcoming," he commented.

"Not really," Kellen said with a sigh.

"But to allay your fears, there will be times within the House when questions will be encouraged, for War Manners are taught here, along with all the other arts of War. You will learn all that we can teach you, my word on that, Kellen."

By now they had reached the doors of the House. Jermayan turned to Valdien and dismissed the stallion firmly with a pat on the shoulder. The stallion lingered for a moment, for all the world as if hoping to be invited inside, then turned and trotted off with a reluctant sigh.

Kellen realized that the building was taller than he'd thought, the height of the indoor riding rings back in Armethalieh. The doors added to that impression; they were tall enough to admit two mounted knights riding side-by-side.

But they were not constructed like the doors back home. These seemed designed to fold back in four panels rather than just open. Jermayan opened one tall narrow panel, and the two of them stepped inside.

"Be welcome in the House of Sword and Shield, home to all who bear the sword for the Nine Cities," Jermayan said formally.

Kellen looked around.

The first thing that caught his attention was the ring of

steel on steel. In the center of the room, four armored Knights whirled and danced around one another, swords flashing in a deadly pattern of light and motion. Kellen studied them, his attention caught. Were three attacking the one? Was it two against two? It was impossible for him to tell; they moved so fast . . .

Then a fifth man, unarmored, wearing dark green robes, his hair the silver-blue of great age, walked into the midst of them. All four immediately put up their swords. The man began talking, too low for Kellen to hear.

"Belesharon is one of our greatest teachers of the sword," Jermayan said quietly. "His father once trained a Knight-Mage. He looks forward to meeting you."

Kellen blinked, slowly reasoning it out. If Belesharon's father had trained a Knight-Mage, that meant that Belesharon's father had fought in the Great War, since that was the last time there'd *been* any Knight-Mages. He looked away from the armored Knights, unwilling to draw Belesharon's attention to him any earlier than he had to.

Although, if he could actually ask Belesharon questions . . .

Kellen looked around as he pulled off his sopping raincape and hung it next to Jermayan's on one of the row of hooks beside the door. Having seen on the night of the banquet how few Elven children there were, he didn't expect this place to be actually crowded, even if, as Jermayan implied, all the Elven Knights from all the Nine Cities were trained here, so he wasn't terribly surprised.

But if we're going to war . . . and this is all we can put into the field . . .

Including the four in armor, there were about twenty Knights in the room. Some of them, to Kellen's vague surprise, seemed to be female, though he supposed there was no reason they shouldn't be. He didn't really know enough about the way Elves did things to know whether they cared about things like that or not. Armethalieh certainly did, but the way Armethalieh did things wasn't the way Kellen wanted to run his life.

None of the other groups of Elves were in armor. They were all dressed just as Jermayan was—loose tunics, pants, and soft boots, though the colors varied from pale green to deep yellow to red. The ones in pale green were sitting in a corner, apparently listening to a lecture—Kellen recognized Alkandoran in that group.

Pale green for the youngest students, then.

Those in yellow were practicing simple forms and stances—as Kellen remembered doing a few times himself— with wooden practice blades under the guidance of a few of the red-tunic'd students. The few remaining red-tunics were sparring against each other, also with wooden swords, under the watchful eyes of other Elven Knights, all of whom seemed to be wearing some shade of darker green, though none was wearing quite the same shade that Belesharon was.

Kellen already knew that the Elves could distinguish a much wider range of colors than humans could, and he imagined all those colors meant something very particular. He only hoped he wouldn't be expected to be able to tell what it was—he suspected that in comparison to the Elves, humans were practically color-blind.

Kellen turned his attention from the students to the building itself. The interior was the largest single room he'd ever seen. The ceiling was high—the building was actually closer to two stories in height than one—and a gallery ran around three walls of the room, with open stone staircases leading up to them on the two long sides of the building. Long windows without glass pierced the walls at regular intervals. They could be closed with heavy wooden shutters, but today the shutters were folded back.

Despite that, Kellen wasn't in the least cold, and after a moment he realized why. Heat radiated up through the brick floor of the room, a gentle pervasive warmth that filled the air.

"There is a furnace in the chamber below this, that heats a network of pipes that warms the floor. It is one of the apprentices' duties to keep it stoked—a duty that you will be spared," Jermayan said with a faint smile.

Kellen grinned back. He'd chopped enough wood in the Wildwood not to be afraid of chopping more.

"It is a marvelous thing," he said teasingly, "to have seen the Elven armies in their flower."

"You think we are few," Jermayan said shrewdly. "But most are in the field, and winter—especially this winter—is not a time when you will see the House heavily frequented. You worry too much, Kellen."

"You worry too little," Kellen said, stung to sudden honesty. *You didn't see her—the Demon Queen—you didn't talk to her. The Endarkened mean to kill you all, and you sit here worrying about your clothes, and the proper time to let everybody else know they've got a problem . . .*

"Then teach us to worry," Jermayan said gently. "And meanwhile, hone the skills you will need when the battle comes, as we both know it must. And learn what I could not teach you alone."

He took Kellen's arm and led him out of the entryway, onto the stone floor of the hall. Belesharon had concluded his instructions to the armored Knights, and turned to face Jermayan.

"I See you, Jermayan," he said, bowing.

"I See you, Belesharon," Jermayan said, bowing in return. "I bring you Kellen Knight-Mage, who comes from the lands of Men to learn what you can teach him."

"I See you, Kellen Knight-Mage," Belesharon said. He did not bow, but studied Kellen with cold black eyes.

What's going on? But this wasn't the time to wonder about it. Kellen bowed deeply. "I See you, Belesharon." He rose from his bow and studied the Elven swordmaster in return.

He'd thought Morusil was old, and until this moment, Morusil had been the oldest Elf Kellen had ever seen. But next to Belesharon, Morusil was a mere child. Up close, Belesharon's bone-pale skin was spiderwebbed with the fine lines of age; his eyebrows nearly white. Perhaps Elves had run shorter centuries ago, or perhaps age had shrunk him; Belesharon was as small as a child, making Kellen feel lumpish and ungainly as he had not since his days in Armethalieh.

But no matter how old he was, there was nothing of infirmity about the ancient swordmaster. His eyes sparkled with alert intelligence, and his movements—as Kellen had seen previously—were lithe and swift.

"Well," Belesharon said after a moment. "Staring gains only so much. Bring practice swords, Ciradhel."

One of the green-tunic'd teachers hurried off.

"I don't understand," Kellen said. Always a safe enough statement when dealing with Elves.

Belesharon snorted. "When one undertakes to teach a student, young Kellen, one begins by judging his quality. We will spar. You will attempt to strike me, holding nothing back. If you fail in this, I will know. And you will no longer be welcome in my House."

"But—" Kellen glanced at Jermayan with indecision bordering on agony, but Jermayan's face was unreadable.

He remembered facing Jermayan at their streambed camp, and nearly killing his mentor and friend by accident simply because neither of them had been prepared for the scope of Kellen's newly-awakened Knight-Mage powers. And Kellen still didn't know their full extent.

If Jermayan had expected this, he would have warned Kellen—if that was allowed by the strict rules of etiquette that governed every aspect of Elven daily life. Kellen bit his lip, thinking very hard. He did not doubt for a minute that Belesharon was speaking the simple truth.

But killing—or injuring—the Master wouldn't be a very good start either.

He bowed.

"Master Belesharon."

"The fool speaks. Come, take your weapon and face me. Choose either."

Ciradhel had returned, carrying two practice swords similar to the ones he'd seen the yellow-garbed students working out with. They were the length and shape of Kellen's own sword, but made entirely of wood.

But even a length of wood could be deadly in the hands of a Knight-Mage.

Kellen bowed again.

"If you like, I am a fool. And you have trained fools and children for a very long time, so you will understand when I say that there is a saying among my people that nothing is foolproof, because fools have too much ingenuity. I do not wish to hurt you."

He waited, holding his breath.

Now Belesharon bowed, his eyes twinkling with amusement.

"Such courtesy! Such respect for age! You rascals would do well to heed it, and have more consideration for an old man who is nearly on his deathbed. Young Kellen, your honesty and thoughtfulness do you credit, and I honor the truth of your words. Therefore, our contest will be closely watched, and if I am in danger, my students will intervene. You, however, must look to yourself."

Kellen bowed again, and reluctantly took the sword that Ciradhel held out to him. He'd hoped to avoid the match altogether, but it was a good compromise.

He hoped.

Belesharon took up his own practice sword and strode to a practice circle marked out on the stone floor. Kellen recognized the dimensions as being equal to the ones Jermayan had marked out on the ground when his training was just beginning. The rules were simple: stay inside the circle at all costs.

For a moment Kellen considered simply letting Belesharon push him outside the circle, then dismissed the notion. If he didn't do his best, the swordmaster would know. He had no doubt of that. The only thing he could do was to pull his blows as much as possible. Surely there'd be no objection to that?

Reluctantly, he took his own place in the circle. The four armored knights, swords drawn, took their places just outside it. They didn't seem at all worried. Jermayan was the only one who seemed concerned—but then, Jermayan was the only one who'd seen him fight.

Kellen realized with resigned dismay that all other activity in the hall had stopped. Everyone was watching.

Grand. Either I end up looking like an uncouth barbarian, or else I do something like I did to Jermayan. And either way, I'm in trouble.

"Now we shall begin your education," Belesharon said. He raised the wooden practice sword in a fluid salute.

Kellen copied the gesture, at the same time summoning up his spell-sight. At once there were two separate Belesharons: the living man, overlaid with a web of glowing red showing Kellen how he must strike, and a glowing ghost, indicating how Belesharon might move.

That's never happened befo—

WHACK!

Kellen yelped and jumped back, jarred entirely out of battled-mind in time to see Belesharon step back into ready position. There was a stinging welt on his upper thigh.

"Too slow, Knight-Mage," the swordmaster commented mildly "Perhaps you still think to spare my old bones."

Not any more, old man.

Resolving to ignore the peculiar doubling of his spell-sight, Kellen summoned it once again. No matter what else it showed him, it still showed him where to hit.

This time he struck without warning—the match was already begun, after all—but somehow, instead of a clean hit, he missed entirely. Belesharon swayed out of the way at the last moment.

Kellen paid no attention, moving on to the next target, and the next. But instead of one clear possibility, his spell-sight showed him a dozen, forcing him to think, to choose—

Forcing him out of battle-mind. Forcing him to be only Kellen.

Each time he summoned it anew, only to have it stolen away again. He realized as the match wore on that Belesharon could have hit him a dozen times. He realized everyone in the hall knew it too. The best he'd been able to manage had been to stay in the circle.

He began to feel a dull desperate anger. *I'm better than this! I have to be!*

Because if he couldn't be good enough, people were going to die.

Focus!

He fed his anger into his magic, making it his tool. The enemy's confidence was also a weapon he could use. Once more he summoned up his spell-sight.

Once again the patterns before his eyes were as confusing as before. Kellen ignored them. He reached beyond them, to their source, to the Gods that made the patterns, the Gods who sent both Knight-Mage and Wildmage into the world.

And struck.

There was a gasp and a hiss of steel from outside the practice ring. Kellen realized he had closed his eyes. He opened them.

His wooden blade was pressed against Belesharon's ribs.

The swordmaster's blade rested gently against the side of his neck.

The swordmaster withdrew his practice blade.

Kellen stepped back shakily, lowering his own blade. He only hoped he hadn't struck very hard.

"A most instructive bout, young Kellen," Belesharon said, bowing with no evidence of discomfort. "Of course, you would have been dead as well, but I think time and practice will remedy that defect. And now, if you will be so good as to don your armor, we shall see how you fare against multiple attackers."

Belesharon handed his sword to the nearest Master, and turned to go.

Kellen barely remembered in time to bow. He felt as if he'd been running for several leagues. Uphill. Carrying Shalkan.

"This way." Jermayan stepped into the circle and led him out through the gathered crowd. Half of them were staring at him as if he were a Demon Incarnate, and the other half were talking among themselves in excited whispers, too low for him to catch.

"How did I do? What did I do?" Kellen asked when they were away from the others. "I mean—"

"Never mind," Jermayan said, waving away Kellen's apologies. "I am merely grateful to have seen such an exhibition of technique. And . . . you *hit* Master Belesharon."

"I didn't mean to," Kellen said. "I mean, I *did,* but—"

Jermayan slid open a panel in the back wall and ushered Kellen inside.

The room was much smaller than the one outside, its walls of wood, not stone, shallowly carved in an intricate geometric pattern. A moment later Kellen realized why, as Jermayan went over to a part of the wall and pulled it out, revealing it to be a drawer.

"Here is your armor and sword," Jermayan said, lifting out the familiar pieces and handing them to Kellen. *Here? What if I hadn't passed Belesharon's test?* Arms full, Kellen headed toward one of the benches in the center of the room.

"If it had somehow happened that you were not found suitable for the House of Sword and Shield, it would simply have been returned to your home. But you will find it is easier to keep it here during your training."

Kellen began removing his clothes, surprised to find they were sodden with sweat.

"I hope I didn't hurt him," he said, pulling on the leather underpadding for his armor.

Jermayan had opened another drawer and was removing his own armor. He stopped and looked at Kellen quizzically.

"You have no cause for concern. But it was . . . startling."

Four

In Training at the House of
Sword and Shield

When both of them were armored, they returned to the main hall. Everyone ignored him so thoroughly that Kellen thought he'd rather have been stared at. The story of the bout was probably going to be all over Sentarshadeen by nightfall—in fact, given the Elves' penchant for gossip, it was probably already making the rounds.

Jermayan led Kellen back to the teaching circle, where Belesharon was waiting with the four armored knights. Belesharon glanced up when he saw them, and his face crumpled into an almost comical frown of disapproval.

"This armor is a disgrace to the House of Sword and Shield," Belesharon said. "I see no enamelwork, no gilding, no jewels. It is the armor of a brigand or a hill bandit, not a knight."

Jermayan had said that direct speech, even questions, were permitted in the House of Shield and Sword, but this was rude speech even for a human.

And once again, it seemed to Kellen that the Elves were obsessed with something that didn't matter. It was true that his armor wasn't as ornate as Jermayan's, but it was still beautiful in its own way.

"Forgive him, Master Belesharon, but it is the only armor he possesses. It was made in a day, and there was no time to finish it properly," Jermayan said.

"Then let another suit be made, one more suitable," Belesharon said irritably.

Kellen winced inwardly. Jermayan looked great in gleaming sapphire-colored armor that looked like expensive jewelry. But he didn't think he would.

"Suitable perhaps, for an Elven Knight, Master Belesharon," Kellen said. "But I am human; my people are simple, as am I. Please forgive my presumption, but as Elvenware is simple, yet a perfect blend of form and function, it seems to me that for a human, and for me in particular, there should be no more adornments than there are upon a perfect bowl. I am—my people call it a 'virgin knight,' one who is untested in battle. If one wears the map of one's experiences upon the metal he is clad in, then mine should be unadorned. And—forgive me again, but I have an emotional attachment to speak of as well. This is the armor I was wearing when I found out I was a Knight-Mage. I should like to keep it just as it is."

"The human child is bold and stubborn," Belesharon observed to no one in particular. "He contradicts me in my own house. Well! Perhaps it is for the best."

Kellen had the oddest feeling he'd just passed another test.

"Now. Dainelel, Kayir, Naeret, Emessade, and Jermayan will attempt to kill you, just as in a real battle. All swords will be in practice sheathes. I will award injuries. It is not necessary to remain within the circle."

Ciradhel brought Kellen and Jermayan practice-sheathes—the others already had them. Jermayan showed Kellen how to fit the heavy leather sheath over his blade and bind it over the guard so there was no possibility of its coming loose during a practice bout. With these in place, even the lethally-sharp Elven swords were safe to use.

What does he mean, "award injuries"? Kellen wondered.

Then there was no more time to wonder, as the bout had begun.

His main advantage was that—having just seen him fight Master Belesharon—Dainelel, Kayir, Naeret, and Emessade were cautious about engaging. But the Elves knew how to work together as a team, not getting in one another's way.

Quickly they spread out, encircling Kellen, forcing him to defend himself from every side at once.

But unlike Belesharon, the images they presented to his spell-sight were clear and precise . . .

"Dainelel, Naeret, you are both dead. Retire from the field, if you please." Master Belesharon's voice came to Kellen distantly as he whirled to block an attack from behind, and turned about—too late!—to respond to an attack from Jermayan.

"Kellen, you have taken a disabling cut to the thigh. Drop to your knees, if you please."

"What?" Kellen shook his head, not understanding. The other three had withdrawn, swords at rest, waiting.

"Kayir's blow got through. I judge it was quite strong enough to have severed the tendons of the leg. You cannot stand, but you can still fight. Drop to your knees, if you please," Master Belesharon repeated.

Feeling rather foolish, Kellen did so. Fortunately, the Elven armor was flexible enough to permit the move.

On his knees, unable to maneuver much, Kellen was easy prey, though to his secret delight he was able to "kill" one more of his attackers before receiving a "fatal wound."

If this had been real, I'd be dead now, Kellen thought soberly.

Jermayan helped him to his feet.

"Perhaps you would share what wisdom you have gained this day in The House of Sword and Shield," Belesharon said when Kellen was standing before him once more.

Despite aches and pains and the fact he was dripping with the sweat of exhaustion, Kellen grinned beneath his helmet. From the way his head hurt, some of his opponents had managed to land more than a few blows, though he hadn't felt them at the time. Kellen's adversaries had used their feet, fists, and shields, as well as every part of their swords against him. Only the protection of his armor had kept Kellen from collecting a spectacular set of bruises this afternoon, but his muscles were certainly convinced he'd given them a splendid workout.

"I have learned that I need to learn a very great deal, Master," Kellen said honestly.

Belesharon smiled. "Good. Jermayan, take this callow youth to pick out a horse. And come early tomorrow, Knight-Mage. You have much to learn."

⸻

"IT would be interesting to know why it is that I am going to pick out a horse," Kellen said when he and Jermayan had left the House, managing to wrestle the question into the proper form with only a little effort.

"Naturally you expect to ride Shalkan for a year at least," Jermayan agreed. "But after that, circumstances may change. And learning to understand the mind of a destrier is part of the training of an Elven Knight. I myself chose Valdien's parents and saw him foaled. But Master Belesharon does not expect that of you. It is enough that you learn to ride properly, and to fight from horseback. You may need those skills. And if the Enemy moves into direct conflict slowly—perhaps it will be that you have ample time to pick your foal and train him before you see true war."

The rain had settled into a gentle mist; not really unpleasant, and Kellen was quite dry inside his hooded cloak. Before they'd gone out, Kellen had followed Jermayan's example and kilted his surcoat high above the knee, so it didn't take on water from the grass.

As they rounded the side of the House, they passed the wooden buildings he'd seen before. Jermayan told him they were bathhouses, where students could soak away the pains of the day.

"It's all beautiful, Jermayan, but it still doesn't seem very . . . large," Kellen said, trying to sound tactful.

Jermayan smiled. "The impatience of humans! Come, then, and see the rest."

Jermayan led him past the bathhouses, through a stand of birches, standing stark and leafless now that the winter rains had come. Just beyond them, the ground sloped gently away.

"This is what you wished to see," Jermayan told him.

What Kellen had thought was a small pocket canyon was anything but. It spread out before him, its farthest edges lost in the mist. From the top of the rise, he could look down on a whole complex of buildings, almost a second city, hidden in plain sight.

"The stables and the blacksmith's forge," Jermayan said. "The practice ring."

There was a wide oval of white sand in the middle of the green, flanked by a complex of low buildings that somehow managed to give the impression of *belonging*. There were two bare fixed posts set at opposite ends of the oval; a lone horseman moved between them in a figure-eight pattern, his mount moving with slow deliberate grace. Beyond the stables and the outbuildings, Kellen could see more horses scattered across the meadow, indifferent to the rain.

"I wouldn't have thought the House of Sword and Shield would have a lot of spare time to keep horse herds," Kellen said, congratulating himself on making a question seem like an idle observation.

"The breeding of warhorses is the business of others," Jermayan said absently, "and that place is not in Sentarshadeen. The animals here belong to Knights. Some keep mounts too old to ride beneath arms with them here, out of affection and to honor an aged comrade, instead of sending them back to the Fields of Vardirvoshan. And some of them are bred and trained as teachers; it is such a one I have in mind for you, for I think it would be just as well if neither one of you grew too fond of the other. Later, perhaps, you will come to Vardirvoshan and choose a proper mount."

"Maybe," Kellen said doubtfully. A time when that might be possible seemed unimaginably far away.

They walked past the riding ring. Jermayan saluted the mounted knight, but did not speak to him. Kellen could see that the knight was not using reins at all; in fact, the reins were tied up to the pommel of the saddle. Nevertheless, as the destrier cantered, he was doing changes of lead and of direction without the knight using the reins to direct him. Kellen could not for a moment imagine how the knight and horse were communicating. Surely they could not be speaking mind to mind . . .

No, that couldn't be it. In a battle, the knight would have every bit of his attention concentrated on fighting. No, there was some secret there . . .

He began to wonder how far they were going to walk, but when they had gone only a little distance past the riding ring, Jermayan stopped and looked around. Apparently he saw what he was looking for, because he stopped, raising his arm over his head in a purposeful gesture.

A few moments later Valdien appeared, three mares at his heels. The four animals stopped a few feet away, all of them regarding Kellen calmly.

"Ah." Jermayan sounded oddly satisfied. "You keep exalted company these days, my friend," he said, addressing his mount. "Now, Kellen, choose the lady who will be your companion and teacher while you are here at the House. This is our way; the experienced mounts teach the young riders, and the experienced riders teach the young destriers."

Kellen sighed inwardly. He supposed this was like choosing his sword—any would do, but one was best. Only the sword had been a piece of metal, and the horses were, well, *alive*. And seemed to be regarding him with the same doubtfully assessing expressions as Master Belesharon had.

All three of them were soaking wet, and muddy besides, so it was hard to tell their true colors. One was grey, with a darker mane and tail. One was a strange pale red, a color Kellen had never seen before in horse, Centaur, or unicorn. The third was a dark brown with a brown-flecked saddle of white over her rump, long white socks, and a wide white blaze.

All of them were beautiful, of course. The ladies might be past their prime, but Kellen suspected they could still run any horse of human breeding into the ground and not raise much of a sweat. He was tempted to choose one at random, but he knew that would almost be cheating. Perhaps the Wild Magic could help him? He wasn't sure how, since he certainly wasn't planning to *hit* any of them.

"It is easier, of course, if one approaches the animals more closely," Jermayan observed in neutral tones.

Kellen gritted his teeth. He suspected Jermayan was laughing at him. And he knew the horses were. Cautiously he walked toward them, hoping they weren't just going to take this as an excuse to run off. The only real experience he had with horses was with Idalia's mare Prettyfoot and with Valdien. Valdien followed Jermayan around like a large dog, but Prettyfoot would take any excuse to go larking off, and if Shalkan wasn't around, she could take hours to catch. He knew these were Elven warhorses, but they didn't know him from Great Queen Vielissiar Farcarinon, and if they were anything like Prettyfoot, they could decide to lead him a chase just for the sheer mischief of it.

Valdien stepped delicately aside as he approached. Kellen approached the grey, reaching out his armored glove and placing his hand gently on her shoulder. She lowered her head and sniffed at him gently. Kellen smelled grass and wet horse; strong, but not unpleasant.

As if that were a signal, the red mare and the spotted one crowded in, nudging and sniffing at him. Kellen wished suddenly that he'd brought treats for them, and stooped carefully to tear up handfuls of the grass at his feet, feeding each of them in turn. They took the morsels neatly and delicately.

Behind him, Jermayan cleared his throat meaningfully.

Oh.

It was time to stop entertaining himself and get to work. He summoned up his spell-sight, wondering what—if anything—it would show him.

As always, the world seemed oddly simplified, though Kellen could never quite put his finger on just how that was. It was almost as if everything that didn't immediately *matter* disappeared, though everything he needed to see was there. He could feel Jermayan and Valdien behind him. He could tell that Jermayan was leaning against Valdien's shoulder, and knew he would sense instantly if either of them changed position. He ought to find "seeing" things he couldn't see unsettling, but somehow he didn't. He guessed it was all part of settling in to being a Knight-Mage.

Now he focused his attention on the Elven mares.

The spell-sight overlay was subtle, but present. He could see the ghosts of old injuries and the faint symbolic presences of things he had no words for. *Help me to make the right choice*, Kellen said, without quite knowing who—or what—he asked.

At last, as he waited, a sense of *rightness* filled him. He reached out and placed his hand against one of the mares' shoulders, blinking the spell-sight away. "This one," he said, looking to see that he'd chosen the tawny red mare.

"A good choice," Jermayan said. "Deyishene will serve you well. She has trained many a knight. Come, then."

"Come, my lady," Kellen said, a little self-consciously. Deyishene shook herself like a wet dog—a very large wet dog—and took a step forward.

"Come," Jermayan said. "She will follow."

⟶

JERMAYAN led Kellen down to one of the stable blocks that flanked the riding ring. There, Kellen brushed and toweled his new charge dry—or at least merely damp—before going to help Jermayan select saddle and armor from the tack room.

"It will not be in your colors, of course," Jermayan said, "and the colors here are . . . unfortunate." He regarded a large shelf of neatly folded caparisons, the knee-length saddlecloths worn over or under equestrian armor, and the fancy rein decorations that matched.

Kellen saw red, gold, and two shades of green. The pale green wasn't appropriate for him—he wasn't *that* much of a beginner. He wasn't sure whether Master Belesharon thought he ought to be wearing the gold or not, and he didn't think it went *that* badly with the shade of green of his cloak and surcoat.

"But perhaps Master Belesharon will be inclined to be merciful," Jermayan continued, real concern in his voice.

"Honestly, Jermayan, whatever you think is best," Kellen said. "Maybe I could just skip this part."

"It is necessary," Jermayan said, in tones that brooked no argument. He sighed, and dug through the stacks of folded barding, obviously searching for something. "Ah. I had thought these might be here." He pulled out a heavy bundle of white fabric, and handed it to Kellen. "Unexceptionable. A bit daring, but no one can quarrel with such a choice."

Whatever that's supposed to mean, Kellen thought. Oh, well. It must be just another example of the Elven passion for detail and protocol.

Fortunately Jermayan was with him, for Kellen would have had no idea of how to choose the right sizes of everything from *shanfron* and *peytrel* to *flanchard* and *crinet*, though he had saddled and unsaddled Valdien enough times to know exactly what items made up an Elven destrier's armor, and how to put them on. Though the pieces were surprisingly light, they were bulky, and it took both of them—and two trips—to carry them back to Deyishene's stall.

"Now let us see if you remember your lessons, and afterward, a turn about the ring," Jermayan said implacably.

While Kellen worked his way—slowly—through saddling and armoring Deyishene, Jermayan made a far brisker job of preparing Valdien, rubbing the stallion dry, saddling him, and armoring him, long before Kellen had the straps and buckles adjusted and the complicated pieces of armor locked into place. He knew better than to hurry, though. Haste now could lead to a variety of disasters later, from saddle sores, to armor that fell to pieces, to a loose saddle-girth which could dump its rider from his mount's back—

which could be humiliating or downright disastrous, depending on when it happened. As he worked, Kellen talked to Deyishene, much as he would have talked to Shalkan, explaining who he was and why he was here. He knew she couldn't understand as much as Shalkan would, but talking made him feel better. She kept one ear on him at all times, and occasionally uttered a snort that sounded as if she was satisfied with what he was saying.

At last the job was completed to his satisfaction. Kellen led his warhorse out into the daylight again.

Jermayan was already mounted, waiting in the middle of the ring. The other rider was long gone, but Kellen discovered he was not to be without an audience. Shalkan had arrived, standing nonchalantly at the edge of the stable block.

"Decided to replace me, have you?" the unicorn said blandly.

"Oh, uh, hello," Kellen said uneasily. Shalkan had an unpredictable sense of humor. "This is Deyishene. Master Belesharon said I needed a horse. And Jermayan says I need to learn how to ride a destrier."

Shalkan switched his tail. "Well," he said after a moment, "maybe she'll teach you to ride better than a sack of turnips afflicted with the gout. There's a mounting block over there."

"Thanks," Kellen said glumly. He'd been reasonably proud of his riding skills, considering the fact that Shalkan moved more like a deer than like a horse—including covering ground with great bounding leaps when moving at top speed.

He walked Deyishene over to the mounting block.

It wasn't that difficult getting into the saddle, but once he had, the ground seemed awfully far away. Shalkan was only the size of a small pony; Kellen had forgotten how far away the ground was when you were sitting on a horse's back.

Deyishene took a few shifting uncertain steps, as if something worried her. Automatically, Kellen leaned forward, clutching at the front of the saddle to steady himself. Deyishene stopped dead.

"Sit up straight," Jermayan called.

"And tuck in your knees," Shalkan added. "And your behind. Rest your weight forward more. Pretend there's a silk scarf between your leg and her, and you daren't let it drop."

So began Kellen's first riding lesson.

Riding did not come as instinctively to him as swordplay had, but his experience with Shalkan, though very different, had built a good foundation (no matter what the unicorn said to the contrary), and at the end of a couple of hours' practice, Kellen felt a lot more confident in the saddle. He was still a long way from mastering the intricate partnership of horse and rider that was ultimately required of knight and destrier, and as yet was unable to ask Deyishene to perform the more sophisticated maneuvers in her repertoire—or to be certain of staying in the saddle if she did.

After his lesson was over, Jermayan and Valdien demonstrated the things Kellen would learn in the future. Kellen and Shalkan watched as Jermayan and Valdien cantered to the end of the riding ring, then galloped back. Suddenly Valdien stopped dead and lashed out with his heels, then jumped, spun, and kicked out hard in the opposite direction. He reared up, lashing out with gleaming metal-shod forehooves, then sprang off his hindquarters, lithe as a cat, vaulting over an imaginary fallen enemy. He trotted around in a tight circle, then sprang forward, again leaping an imaginary obstacle from a standing start.

"I hope you don't expect me to do that," Shalkan said.

"Oh, do it if you like," Kellen said magnanimously. "Just don't expect me to be on your back when you do." The unicorn could jump like a frog and climb like a mountain goat, but the display Kellen had just seen was mind-bogglingly impressive for a horse—and it certainly explained why the equestrian armor was as flexible and intricate as that of the knights. He wondered how long it had taken Jermayan to train Valdien to do that.

Through all Valdien's acrobatics Jermayan had remained perfectly composed, sitting as comfortably in the saddle as if Valdien moved at a gentle walk. He cantered Valdien around the oval twice and then returned to Kellen and Shalkan.

"Of course," Jermayan said casually, "it does take a certain amount of practice to manage lance and sword while one's mount is engaged in such activity." His tone was so dry that even Kellen recognized he was being ironic. "But as I do not think the Flower Wars will concern you overmuch, perhaps you will not need to concern yourself with the lance. Now it is time to see to your horse, then to your armor, then to soak the stiffness from your limbs. By then, it will be close upon lamp-lighting time, and you will wish to rest yourself in preparation for the numerous exertions of the morrow."

And maybe when I get home, I can ask Idalia if anybody's going to actually DO anything about Shadow Mountain, Kellen thought, suddenly remembering what all this training was for.

⌒

THE walls of the Mage City of Armethalieh, called the Golden City, the City of a Thousand Bells, had stood for a thousand years. High Magick had built it, High Magick ruled every detail of its daily life, and the High Council labored tirelessly to make sure that for its citizens, every day was much like every other—and that no one could imagine a time when that would not be so.

Except for a tiny minority among the ruling council of High Mages, their memories hedged about with wards and spells, no one knew the history of Armethalieh. None of her citizens could imagine a time before her walls had risen, a time before wealth poured into her coffers from carefully-controlled trade with all the world—a world which was nevertheless barred from walking her streets, for Armethalieh was, first and foremost, a city for Armethaliehans, and outsiders were not tolerated. Her wealth, her privileges, and her magick were for her citizens alone . . . and, in judicious moderation, for the Home Farms, those lands just outside the Western Gate that provided the crops that fed the Golden City's teeming multitudes.

Or so matters had stood until recently.

Change had come to the Golden City.

The City was ruled by her Mages, and the Mages were ruled by the High Council. The High Council was ruled by the Arch-Mage, but the twelve High Mages who shared the dignity of a seat on the Council all looked to the day when one of them might supplant him, and now that Arch-Mage Lycaelon Tavadon's son and heir had been Banished for practicing the forbidden Wild Magic, Lycaelon's control over his fellows was less than absolute. Each of them looked to consolidate his own power, to make himself the next Arch-Mage of Armethalieh . . . and soon. Usually the Arch-Mage had to die before the power passed to another—but not always.

And there were those who thought that it might be no bad thing for Lycaelon Tavadon to be . . . persuaded . . . to retire.

Of the twelve, High Mage Volpiril was the most ambitious. When Lycaelon's bid to annex the Western Hills collapsed in disaster, Volpiril had suggested—in a direct, though veiled, attack upon Lycaelon—that the Council withdraw its borders to the walls of Armethalieh herself, abandoning their claim on not only the Western Lands, but the Home Farms.

The Council, rattled by its mysterious defeat and swayed by Volpiril's speechmaking, had voted its assent. Lycaelon could not overrule them, though he had taken a grim pleasure in casting the lone dissenting vote.

Some of the villagers greeted the news that they were no longer the property of the City—and might set what prices they liked for what had once been Armethalieh's by right—with cheers of delight. Others, more perceptive, were quick to see that if Armethalieh's control was withdrawn, so was her magick. There would be no more healing for the villagers, no pest control or destruction of blight, no preservation for their grain storage, no certainty of favorable weather for planting and harvest.

The petitions piled higher on Lycaelon's desk each day, arriving with each cart of overpriced produce and gaggle of hysterical rustics until, with a malicious sense of justice, Lycaelon had set Volpiril to deal with the matter, reminding the High Mage that it was a violation of Armethaliehan law to expend her magick for the benefit of anyone but her citizens or subject peoples. And so, if the Delfier Valley farmers no longer belonged to Armethalieh, it was Volpiril's duty to explain to them why Armethaliehan magick would no longer be employed in their service . . .

And in the marketplace, the prices rose. And kept rising.

It could not be helped. Through Volpiril's vicious bungling, the farmers must now be paid for their produce. The City could absorb some of the cost, but not all, and not forever. So the prices rose, for everything from turnips to sugar biscuits. No one knew why, of course. It was not in the Council's interest that they should.

And this year of all years, Lycaelon thought with a sigh, sliding the latest summary of reports into a drawer in his desk and locking it. The winter rains promised to be exceptionally heavy. It wouldn't matter within the City itself, of course, where the Mages ensured that rain only fell late at night, and only in sufficient quantity to water the gardens and keep the cisterns filled. But there would be flooding in the valley this year. Undoubtedly that would mean a poor crop in the spring.

He got to his feet, cursing the stiffness in his muscles. He glanced toward the small office just off his own, but no light showed beneath the door. As it should be. He had stayed late, reading—and had sent Anigrel home bells ago. As he left his office, waving the Mage-lights to darkness behind him, Lycaelon could feel the faint hum of power from the Council chamber, where Mages worked tirelessly, as they did every night, weaving the elaborate and beautiful spells of the High Magick for the good of the City. He shook his head. *Light grant a spell to preserve us from the maddened ambition of fools like Lord Volpiril, Darkness take him!*

⌒

MASTER Undermage Chired Anigrel—his abrupt increase in rank a sign of the signal favor in which Lycaelon Tavadon held him—regarded his new accommodations with a satisfaction he was careful not to display before witnesses.

The suite of rooms on the third floor of House Tavadon had had every trace of their former occupant ruthlessly expunged. Every stick of furniture had been sent into storage in the house's vast attics. The walls had been scrubbed down and repainted to an even more marmoreal shade of white. Suitable furnishings had been acquired to outfit one of the two rooms as a comfortable—but not over-luxurious—bedroom, the other—the one with the excellent view of the gardens and the Council House—as a workroom and small study, and all carefully coordinated to be in the House colors of black and white. When the renovations were finished, no trace of the former occupancy of Lycaelon Tavadon's Banished Outlaw son remained, and the suite appeared to be another perfectly fitted extension of Lycaelon's taste. There was no sign of Anigrel's own personality here. This was exactly as Anigrel wanted it. He wished for Lycaelon to think of Anigrel as an extension of himself.

Anigrel retained his rooms at the Mage-Courts on the College grounds, of course. It would not do to flaunt openly what everyone knew—that he now lived at Tavadon House, Lycaelon's adopted son in all but name.

And perhaps, someday, in name as well, Anigrel thought, settling back in his chair. Lycaelon had no one else. Both his children had given themselves to the Wild Magic and been Banished from the City. And Anigrel had taken pains to make himself so very indispensable to the Arch-Mage over the past moonturns, though he was certain that Lycaelon—so innocent in his way!—did not know the half of what Anigrel did for him.

The Mageborn were greedy for power, and ruthless in their unending quest for rank and position. As Lycaelon's private secretary, Anigrel saw many Mageborn every day, yet was nearly invisible himself; one more grey-robed underling doing the work of the City. It had been a simple thing to shape the opinion of the Mageborn with an innocent comment here, a casual observation there, and turn it inexorably against Lord Volpiril, so that the Mages now saw disaster in the High Mage's ever-more-desperate makeshifts and pronouncements before the Council, and they saw it before the trouble actually appeared. As the situation in the City worsened, Volpiril's position would become even more unstable. It was not impossible that he would be voted off the Council, though such a thing hadn't happened in centuries.

And if actual shortages began to appear, then Lord Volpiril's reign on the Council could be numbered in moonturns.

That would leave a vacancy.

Anigrel meant to have it for himself.

He was already a Master Undermage, elevated to that rank years ahead of time, and there was already talk—for once he hadn't needed to start the rumors himself—that Lord Lycaelon would soon sponsor Anigrel for the tests to the rank of Magister-Practimus, if not Magister-Regnant. Either rank would be sufficient to allow Anigrel to take a seat on the Council.

Anigrel had no doubt of his ability to pass the tests. The difficulty all these years had been in concealing the extent of his power, not passing the tests his Mageborn teachers set.

For Anigrel's power stemmed from a far different source, and his true teachers were far more powerful, and far, far more dangerous than any High Mage could imagine being.

It was the other reason he retained his rooms in the Mage-Courts, for there were things he did there that could not be done within the walls of the house of the Arch-Mage of Armethalieh.

There was a faint scratching at the door panel. With a gesture, Anigrel caused the door to dissolve. A servant stood in the doorway.

"Lord Anigrel. The Arch-Mage arrives," the servant said, bowing.

Anigrel nodded, dismissing the servant as he got to his feet. The servant bowed again, and backed away the prescribed three steps before turning to go.

The servants might have treated Kellen Tavadon with indifference and contempt, but it had taken little effort for Anigrel to teach them proper manners in his presence. And just as he wished them to show him every courtesy, so it would not do for him to be remiss in showing Lycaelon every evidence of humility, deference, and respect.

Until the Arch-Mage no longer mattered.

AND just now, a touch of appropriate distress was in order. "Lord Arch-Mage. You are weary." Anigrel arrived in the reception room just as Lycaelon entered.

"Anigrel. I sent you to your bed hours ago," Lycaelon said, looking—yes—gratified to see Anigrel.

"Some trifling matters occupied my attention," the younger man said. "And I was . . . concerned by the burdens you bear for us all, Lord Lycaelon," he added softly.

Lycaelon smiled faintly. "I am accustomed to them, my young friend. But perhaps, of your kindness, you will take a glass of wine with me in the library? After so many years of laboring in the Circle for the good of the City while the common folk dream, it still seems odd to sleep at night."

Anigrel followed Lycaelon through the panel that led into the large formal library. Lycaelon seated himself in a chair beside the window—the long sapphire-blue drapes were drawn now, since it was night—and Anigrel went to the sideboard and collected a decanter and two glasses. The decanter shimmered faintly with the Preservation Spell that kept its contents fresh and unchanged, no matter how long it stood untasted and unopened. Ostentatious, and yet frugal; ostentatious to use a spell on something like a decanted bottle of wine, yet frugal to have the spell to keep the wine from spoiling after it had been opened, when one only wanted a glass or two at a time.

He set the glasses on the small table between the two chairs and poured them both full, handing one to Lycaelon before taking his own seat. He waited for Lycaelon to drink, then sipped his own wine appreciatively. A rare moment and a rare vintage, brought by Selken ships from Ividion Isle, the only place in the world where the salt-marsh grapes could grow. At least the Out Islands were not affected by Volpiril's policies. This would not be the last such bottle obtainable.

Lycaelon laughed, his thoughts on a private joke. "Ah, if only the Commons could see us now, Anigrel—they *would* be shocked! They think we live on light and air and pure well water—and we do our part to keep them thinking that way, don't we?" He drained his glass and filled it again, before Anigrel could do it for him.

"Of course, Lord Lycaelon. It's unthinkable that the common clay should have any reason to criticize their masters. They're happier that way," Anigrel said. "Far better that they believe there is nothing to envy us for."

"Of course they are," Lycaelon said. "Everything we do is for them . . . and for the good of the City. Envy is a bitter thing, and would only disturb their peace."

"Oh, yes. Of course," Anigrel said, making sure his words rang obviously hollow. He sipped his wine and waited.

"You must tell me if there is something concerning you, Anigrel," Lycaelon said. "It is not only the Commons that I serve, but my fellow Mages."

"I can conceal nothing from you, Lord Lycaelon," Anigrel said with a rueful smile. "But . . . you know it better than I, and I do not wish to add to your burden. And yet . . . you

know that I hear what you do not, simply because there are
those who will say in front of me what they will not say to
the Arch-Mage?"

"I depend upon it," Lycaelon said. "I do not think you can
surprise me, Anigrel, and your words may serve the City.
Tell me what worries you. Do not fear to offend me, for I already know that you love the City as much as I."

"You know that Lord Volpiril has—perhaps!—not acted
entirely in the City's best interests in a certain recent instance. At present, the circumstances are known only to
those of our own class, but the effect of that action cannot be
concealed. Many believe that soon these circumstances will
become known outside the Mageborn. The effects of that
knowledge could be . . . unfortunate."

"Unfortunate? Disastrous!" Lycaelon nearly groaned.
"There will be famine in the Delfier Valley in the spring—
and no food available for sale to the City at any price. Yet
that fool blocks any attempt to reverse his policies, saying
they will bear fruit with time. Fruit! Oh, yes, and the fruit
will be a bitter and withered harvest!"

Anigrel leaned forward. "Lord Lycaelon, do not let your
merciful and charitable nature keep you from doing what
must be done. To discredit Volpiril's policies, discredit
Volpiril first. Without him to goad them on, the Council will
gladly abandon something so worthless—"

But Lycaelon had raised his hand, silencing Anigrel.

"To force him from the Council without the support of my
fellow Mages would be a greater disaster than riots in the
streets of the City. I shall seek that support, and pray to the
Light that I find it in time. And now, I find I am weary, Anigrel. I give you good night."

"Rest well, Lord Arch-Mage." Anigrel got to his feet,
bowing, and left the library.

He was not wholly dissatisfied with the evening's work.
He had planted the ideas in Lycaelon's mind that he'd
wanted to. Now Lycaelon was thinking about eliminating
Volpiril before the City was in open rebellion against the

Mageborn. All Anigrel had to do was give Lycaelon a good excuse.

And just as Lycaelon once had, Volpiril had a son.

A most malleable son . . .

⌐

CILARNEN Volpiril was a perfect example of Mageborn breeding. All the Mageborn were slender and fine-boned, their bodies shaped by no physical labor more arduous than lifting a wand or a pen. Their coloration was vivid: black, blond, or red hair running strongly in particular Mage families; in this they stood out sharply from the Common-born, whose hair color was muddied with brown, and whose bodies were stockier than those of the pure-blooded Mages. Oh, from time to time one with Mage talents arose in a common family, but such were marked by their very appearance as Commons-born, and though it would never be *openly* acknowledged, that appearance would keep them from rising far within the ranks. Perhaps, such a Commons-born Mage could find a pure-blooded daughter of an insignificant family to marry, and his descendants would be of an acceptable appearance. But for such a one—well, there were limits, and properly so.

The Volpiril line had auburn hair; Cilarnen could inspect the portraits of noteworthy Mage ancestors that graced the walls of House Volpiril and see his own russet hair and pale blue eyes depicted there with the precision of his bathing-room mirror. Only the styles changed, and that not by a great deal, except in the very oldest portraits, for was it not Armethalieh's greatest boast that she was as unchanging as her walls?

His family's history had been one of privilege, service, and High Magick for uncounted generations, and the niches in the walls of the family Chapel in House Volpiril were filled with golden alabaster urns containing the ashes of great Mages who had brought luster to the family name. Until last winter, Cilarnen had been serenely certain that he would follow in their footsteps just as his father had, rising quickly and pleasantly through the ranks of Adeptship—for his studies in the High Magick had always come easily to him—and seeing no other possible future for himself than one spent as a Mage of the Mage-City. A privileged post in one of the more important City Councils, inevitably, just as soon as he attained sufficient rank. A seat on the High Council, not impossible. And perhaps the Arch-Mageship itself, for Volpirils had held that post in the past, nearly as often as the Tavadons, and Lord Lycaelon Tavadon could not live forever . . .

But all that had been—before. Before his mistake; before his disgrace.

Cilarnen had two sisters, much younger, who were being carefully groomed to someday take their places as the pliant dutiful wives of his peers, but they scarcely mattered to his carefully-ordered life, his sisters having been placed under the care of nurses and governesses—and Cilarnen's distant, well-bred, Mageborn mother—from the time they could walk. Dialee had been born when he was six, and Eshavi when he was eight, and Cilarnen, encouraged by his father, had already been looking toward the future, toward the day when he could pledge himself as a citizen of Armethalieh and begin his studies in High Magick.

Women had no place in the life of a young Mage. Students did not marry, did not court, did not admit the existence of women. Nor did Apprentices. A Journeyman might, but only after he had reached his thirtieth year, if his patron gave him permission, and only if he had decided he did not wish to advance further in the ranks of the Art Magickal. Only if one advanced so swiftly that a higher rank than Journeyman was in one's grasp, did a young Mage have cause to think of women before the age of thirty.

And even then, marriage among the Mageborn was not a matter of love, but of consolidating one's position, of repaying past favors or of buying future ones, of choosing the best possible mother for future Mageborn sons. Cilarnen knew all that. Love was a madness that afflicted the unGifted, a sickness of the magickless Commons who thronged the streets of the City outside the Mage Quarter. His kind were above such things.

Then he saw Lady Amintia.

It was quite by accident. He'd come home unexpectedly in the middle of the day—a spell had gone awry during the morning lessons, and his tutor had fallen ill and been unable to see him for his afternoon's private lesson. On a rare whim, he'd decided to go riding instead, and gone home to change.

His rooms overlooked the gardens of House Volpiril. He'd gone to the windows and opened them, stepping out onto the small balcony, and as he did, he stepped through the Silence spell that shielded his rooms, and heard peals of laughter coming from the garden below.

He looked down.

The garden was filled with females.

He recognized none of them—though logically, two of them must be his sisters. There were perhaps two dozen of them, all running about in a fashion Cilarnen himself had given up a dozen years before, playing some sort of elaborate game of touch-and-run, crying out and laughing as they scored off one another. Their faces were flushed and shiny with exertion, their hair tumbled down around their shoulders, their City-Talismans—the golden rectangle of citizenship that every citizen of Armethalieh wore—flying to the ends of golden throat-chains and colored neck-ribbons as they played. Shawls and scarves were scattered about the grass like strange drifts of brightly-colored mist. Along one wall of the garden, a long table stood, severe and correct in white linen, its burden of refreshments awaiting the moment when the ladies tired of their fun.

Cilarnen blinked, feeling almost as if he had opened one of the Forbidden Books and read something he was not meant to see. He looked away from the others and saw . . . her.

She did not join in the jostling games of the others, but stood watching them, her back to the base of the enormous magnolia tree that dominated the Volpiril garden. Her raven hair was bound neatly and suitably at the base of her neck, and just as Cilarnen looked down, she looked up. Her eyes were such an intense shade of blue he could see their color clearly, even across the garden.

He did not know what he expected her to do. Like all proper young Mageborn youths, Cilarnen had barely even seen a woman of his own class. But she simply regarded him, saying nothing, and doing nothing to draw unwelcome attention to him.

"Amintia! Come join us!"

One of the others called her name, and she looked away, shaking her head and smiling gently. Cilarnen backed into his room, blushing in hot confusion as the blessed silence of the Shielding Spells enfolded him once more. He touched his own City-Talisman on its jeweled chain, pressing the cool metal against his skin.

What had just happened?

He didn't know. But he liked it. He went to the window again, taking care to stay well within the spells. Here he could see out without being seen. He stood at the window, watching, until the garden was empty, his plans for the afternoon forgotten.

⌒

IT was easy enough to find out who she was. His father kept a comprehensive genealogy of the Mageborn families in his library, and the Mageborn did not repeat names within generations. She was Lady Amintia of House Amaubale. Lord Amaubale was a Mage who served on the Council of Public Safety; she had two brothers, Nathuren and Pretarkol, who were several years behind Cilarnen at the Mage College.

She was someone House Volpiril might ally itself with— someone he might have. But not for years—an unimaginable number of years, more years than he had already lived. And what if her father bestowed her elsewhere in the interim?

It was an unbearable thought, and one that began to obsess him as the sennights passed. His studies suffered—if only a little—by his distraction. He even disgraced himself so far as to seek out the Amaubale residence and walk past it. Once.

And at last, he came up with a plan.

He would seek his father's agreement to a betrothal. That would solve all his problems. No one else would marry Amintia. She would be his, waiting for him until the day when he was prepared to claim her. It was the perfect solution to his problem—his obsession.

Unfortunately, his father did not agree.

Once each sennight, Cilarnen was accustomed to receive a private audience with his father, so that he could make an informal account to Lord Volpiril of his progress with his studies—though of course his father received detailed reports from his tutors—and give Lord Volpiril his own assessment of his current, and perhaps future, rivals. Generally these occasions had been relatively pleasant affairs, with Lord Volpiril taking the opportunity to make some small gift to Cilarnen—of pocket money, a book, or some newly-fashionable accessory—to indicate his pleasure with Cilarnen's diligence. That audience seemed the perfect time to make his plea, and he approached his father's study fully confident that he would emerge from it with all his troubles smoothed away.

He opened the door, and bowed. "My Lord Father."

As always, Cilarnen entered his father's private study precisely at the Second Afternoon Bell of Light-Day. So it had been since he had begun his studies in the Art Magickal, and Cilarnen could not imagine a time when it would not be so. His interview invariably lasted precisely two chimes.

He stopped before his father's desk and bowed a second time. As always, his father was working, even at home and on Light's Day. Lord Volpiril was a High Mage and a member of the High Council. His duty to the City was never-ending; this was a credo he had drummed into his son from the day Cilarnen could walk, talk, and perhaps, make demands on his father's time. So from that time, it had been made very clear to him that the City came first, and Cilarnen a very distant second.

"Ah, Cilarnen." His father looked up as he approached the desk. "So it is Light's Day once again. What news do you have to bring me?"

For most of a chime Cilarnen spoke of ordinary things; his progress in his Magickal studies and his relationships with his fellow students. Then, quickly, he presented the matter nearest to his heart.

"There is another matter, sir, a matter of a young woman, my Lord Father—a daughter of House Amaubale. Her name is Amintia; I am sure Mother knows her. I believe—subject to your approval, of course, sir—that this would be an excellent alliance for us when the time comes. I know that it is far too soon for me to consider marriage—far too soon; I had not thought of such a thing before I saw this young woman—but she is—I find her—it *is* a good match. I have consulted the genealogy, and House Volpiril has married into House Amaubale in the past. So I thought, if you would consider it, perhaps a pre-contract—"

Intent upon convincing his father of the logic and worth of this plan, Cilarnen was not watching Lord Volpiril's face. Then, with a scrape of his chair that startled his son, the High Mage rose to his feet, his expression furious.

" 'A *pre-contract*'? To think that I would hear such words upon the lips of my own son! Are we merchants or nobles? We are Mageborn! Magick flows in our blood! It is a sacred calling, one that requires the utmost dedication." Volpiril's face was flushed scarlet, and Cilarnen shrank back involuntarily before his wrath. "There can be *no* room in the thoughts of the Student or the Apprentice for anything but dedication to his Art. Have you gone utterly mad?"

"But—" Cilarnen stammered.

Volpiril's jaw clenched. "Your tutors had mentioned you were strangely unwilling to apply yourself of late I had meant to ask you the reason today! And now, now you flaunt it proudly, and dare to demand that I aid you in your foolish descent into emotionality. Where did you come by such a notion? Why, I would have expected this sort of nonsense out of a silly girl, not out of a well-educated son! Shall I remove you from school and dress you in a gown, next?"

Cilarnen flushed, his face and neck growing uncomfortably hot. He said nothing. He could not bring a single word up out of his constricted throat.

His father snorted. "It is fortunate you did not forget yourself entirely, and brought this to my attention before you made yourself a public scandal." Lord Volpiril's tone was harsh.

"I—But—It has been done in the past . . . " Cilarnen protested weakly. "Great-grandfather—"

"If you need no other lesson in why the companionship of females is forbidden to young Mageborn, consider your own actions today! Look what this has brought you to!" Volpiril stormed. "Open rebellion, daring to contradict me beneath this very roof! I will not have it! You, sir, may consider yourself on notice. And be sure that I will speak to Lord Amaubale and make quite certain his daughter never sets foot in this house again."

Cilarnen felt himself grow as cold as he had been heated a moment before. Never to see her again! But—

"You have displeased me greatly today, Cilarnen." Volpiril took a deep breath, and stared down at his son. "Very greatly. But you still have a chance to make amends. Apply yourself strictly to your studies. Reclaim your pride of place in your classes. Forget this cozening creature—no doubt she merely thought to entrap the son of a High Council Mage for her own advancement. Women are manipulative, secretive, and no matter how sweetly innocent they may seem, even the youngest of them is as adept at spinning webs to ensnare an unwary young man as any spider. When I speak to her father, I shall advise him to see her quickly married. *That* will put an end to her foolishness!" Volpiril said darkly.

Cilarnen stood, frozen in shock. Amintia—*his* Amintia—married to someone else?

"You may go, Cilarnen," Lord Volpiril said brusquely, sitting down once more and returning his attention to the papers before him. From his demeanor, his son might as well have ceased to exist. All that Cilarnen could do was to bow, and take himself out.

⟶

HIS father's displeasure was bad enough, but far worse was the terrible inevitability that Amintia was going to be lost to him forever. Once Lord Volpiril put his mind to something, it was as good as accomplished. Cilarnen knew that if he was to get back in his father's good graces, he must do as his father instructed and put her from his mind, but somehow he did not think that he could manage to do that without telling her—just once—how much she had meant to him.

He thought of writing her a letter, but after several attempts, Cilarnen gave up. He couldn't find the proper words, and anyway, if he sent a letter to her house, her parents would read it first. His father read all of *his* infrequent correspondence, and Cilarnen had no doubt the custom was universal.

But he could write her a poem. An *anonymous* poem. That would be best, and safest, too. Poetry was one of the classes taught at the Mage-College, and Cilarnen was fairly confident of his ability to write something suitable, something that would move her heart, and perhaps make her pity him. Besides, ever since he'd seen Amintia, somehow poetry had made so much more sense to him than it ever had before.

He labored over his work for sennights, as winter passed into early spring, copying the final result out onto a slender scroll, which he tied with a silver ribbon. After moonturns of watching the house, he knew all of the Amaubale servants by sight. He would simply arrange to be in the Garden Market at the same time that one of them was there, and give the creature a few coins to pass the scroll on to Lady Amintia.

Then she would know that someone had loved her—not for her family or her position, but for her incomparable eyes, rare as blue roses, for her grace, for her quiet beauty, for all that made her the Lady Amintia.

The scroll had vanished before he could deliver it, and the next time Cilarnen had seen it, to his utter horror and humiliation, it had been in the hands of Mage Hendassar, in his History of the City class. Mage Hendassar had read it out loud to the entire room of students.

They had laughed. Laughed at him, at his weakness, at his foolishness.

Cilarnen would gladly have died. He hated Mage Hendassar, hated his classmates, hated his father—there was no doubt of how the scroll had come into Mage Hendassar's hands—and most of all, perversely enough, he hated the Lady Amintia as much as he had heretofore loved her.

This was her fault. If he had never seen her, none of this would have happened. No female was worth such agony.

His father had been right.

Life might have been utterly unbearable if his father had ever made any reference to the matter, but Lord Volpiril did nothing of the sort. Of course, he had not needed to. The tale spread all over the Mage-College, of course, and might have hounded him for the rest of his years, if not for the fact that only a fortnight later, the Arch-Mage's only son Kellen Tavadon was summoned before the High Council, and after that none of them ever saw Kellen Tavadon again.

This was a far more interesting scandal than a simple love poem, since not one of the students had the least idea of what Farmer Kellen might have done, and none of them was ever able to find out. Some swore they had seen Kellen working as a laborer down in the Low Quarter—as if that were possible. Others said he had fought with the Arch-

Mage and been sent to live in one of the farming villages as a punishment.

All Cilarnen knew was that if people were talking about Kellen, they weren't talking about him, and he was profoundly grateful. He had learned his lesson, and he would work harder than ever before to be the son his father wanted.

But somehow it did not seem to be possible. Because from that moment on, nothing, *nothing* that he did was ever good enough.

Spring became summer. Lord Volpiril's temper was always short these days. No matter what Cilarnen did, his father only told him he must do better, in ever-harsher words of criticism. And all of it was so unjust! He *was* trying! He was at the top of several of his classes! His tutors all voiced themselves satisfied with him! Yet his father acted as if he was putting forth no effort whatsoever. Cilarnen seethed with resentment under the unjust critique. And he began to wonder if it was not he who was at fault, somehow failing, but his father.

The sons of the other Council Mages whispered fantastic gossip of unrest on the High Council, of great plans afoot.

Cilarnen did not know what they were, of course. Volpiril did not speak of them, and the days when Cilarnen might bring the rumors to his father and ask for more information were long gone now. If Cilarnen had taken second place in his father's concerns before, he now felt as if he had descended to last in priorities. He felt oddly lost, and somehow cheated.

If not for his tutors, he would have been utterly alone.

Like most young Mageborn, Cilarnen's lessons included practice in dance and swordplay as well as in the Art Magickal. He had little practical use for either, but both were good exercise, and the practice of the Art Magickal was an arduous business, requiring great stamina, both mental and physical.

Three times a sennight he went to Master Kalos's salon at the edge of the Mage Quarter for his lessons in reed-blade.

The sword he studied there was nothing like the ponderous steel weapons the Militia carried, and certainly nothing like the wide heavy blades used in High Magick. The reed-blade was an elegant thing, smaller than his little finger at its base and tapering to a blunt, squared-off point. It was used to touch one's opponent, elegantly, and in the proper style. Special Talismans worn by each of the combatants ensured that the blades could not go awry and accidentally strike outside the permitted target zones.

It was incredibly hard to score according to Master Kalos's exacting specifications, and at the end of each bell-and-a-half lesson, Cilarnen was as exhausted as if he'd spent the entire time running around the inside of the enormous hall, instead of standing nearly still attempting to hit a man with a length of metal he could balance on two fingers. But Master Kalos praised lavishly for each improvement, and told Cilarnen he could have made a fine swordsman, if he had not had the misfortune to be born a Mage.

A joke, of course, and Cilarnen had smiled dutifully. Master Kalos's odd sense of humor was well known.

For one of the sennightly lessons he saw Master Kalos alone, for the other two, he was part of a class of about twenty other young Mageborn. Since the classes were grouped by skill, not age, Cilarnen soon found himself among not only some of his fellow students, but grouped with some older Mageborn as well. They treated Cilarnen with casual good-fellowship, as if he were one of them. He found it an odd and interesting experience to be in a place where rank very nearly didn't matter.

It did, of course. Lord Volpiril's only son would be a fool to believe otherwise. Bur the illusion was comforting, and for a little while, he could pretend that he actually had people around him he could call "friend."

⟳

HIS dancing teacher was Lord Nendimos, a Mage who specialized not only in teaching dance, but in the history of dance, and the magic of dance, a series of lectures that one must be a Journeyman-Apprentice to sit for.

Lord Nendimos was a Journeyman-Undermage. He had been a Journeyman-Undermage since long before Cilarnen had been born, and would never rise higher in the ranks, though his power and his knowledge outstripped many of his betters, and if he could only have gained the sponsorship to do so, he could have passed a dozen of the qualifying tests with no difficulty whatever. Gaining such sponsorship might even have been possible, though difficult, for the same reason that Lord Nendimos was still a Journeyman after four decades.

Lord Nendimos liked women. He liked them as people. He enjoyed their company, their fellowship, and even claimed that some of them were his friends. He made no secret of it. When he was not putting the students of the MageCollege through their paces, he was dancing master to half the Mage Houses of Armethalieh, and there he was welcomed by the Mageborn women with—if he was to be believed—as much warmth as if he were a family member.

His fellow Mages regarded his eccentricity with dismay, and with resignation. But once they were satisfied that he would not pass on his bizarre tastes to their sons, they decided to tolerate his peculiarities. His family was old and well connected. His brothers were perfectly normal—and highly-placed. His sisters were married into some of the best families.

And his talents were too valuable to lose.

The dances of Armethalieh were slow, stately . . . and very complicated. It took time to learn them well—even more so since it was not to be considered that Mageborn sons and Mageborn daughters should learn them together. That sort of foolishness could be left to the Tradesmen, the Nobles, the Laborers, and all the rest who lived lives of foolish self-indulgence.

Dancing practice was held in the auditorium at the northern end of the quadrangle. Students were grouped by age, not academic rank, and drilled, endlessly, in the set figures of Armethaliehan dance, taking the roles of the "sun" or the "moon" in turn.

Once a Student reached his fifteenth year, attendance was no longer mandatory, but Cilarnen had chosen to continue because he found the class interesting and even pleasurable. At this point, his class was made up of the older students and Apprentices and even a few Tutors. He enjoyed the stately movement, like a slower form of swordplay, and Nendimos drilled this oldest class hardest of all, for having had years to master the steps, he told them, he now looked for perfection of form.

When the music played, and Cilarnen concentrated on mirroring his partner's moves, his mind on nothing beyond the moment, sometimes he felt almost as if he were a sort of living wand, tracing through the glyphs of a spell. He'd said as much to Lord Nendimos one day after practice.

The old man had regarded him shrewdly. "I trust you will come to my lectures when you are old enough, Lord Cilarnen. I shall save a place for you."

But of all his teachers, Cilarnen's most important was his private tutor in Magick. Master Tocsel had been his tutor in Magick since he had been a small child. The venerable Master Undermage knew everything there was to know about the practicalities of High Magick, from the simplest spell to the most abstruse conjuration. He had trained Cilarnen's father, and his grandfather. He was certainly not a kindly man, but if Cilarnen was truly making an effort, Tocsel was endlessly patient. His one concern was to see his pupil do well. His feelings had been quite hurt during that period when Cilarnen had been unable to pay attention to his lessons, but to Cilarnen's intense relief, his renewed efforts had been rewarded with praise and encouragement, and Master Tocsel had been willing to forgive Cilarnen's dereliction, even when it seemed his own father would not.

"Mark my words, young Cilarnen," Tocsel said one day as Cilarnen's lesson drew to a close. "You will soon be a mere

Apprentice no longer. It is in my mind to recommend you for the tests for Entered Apprentice the next time the Board sits. No more blue robe for you!"

There were three ranks of Apprentice: Student Apprentice (which Cilarnen had passed long ago), Apprentice, and Entered Apprentice. Of the three, only the last was entitled to wear the grey robe of Magecraft and cast spells for any purpose other than practice. Entered Apprentices still pursued their studies at the College, but they also worked elsewhere in the City, assisting Mages at their work.

"Thank you, sir! I—" He nearly asked if Master Tocsel thought he was ready, and bit back the question. Master Tocsel would not have made the comment if he did not think Cilarnen was ready. "I only hope my lord father will be pleased," he said instead.

Tocsel made a rude noise, the privilege of age. "And why should he not be? You've come along splendidly. Not like the Arch-Mage's son. Bad blood there. Oh, everyone knew it, but Lycaelon wouldn't be told; once he set eyes on that ridiculous barbarian woman, nothing would do but that he marry her. And look what happened! Learn from his mistake, boy, and let your father pick your bride when the time comes. Emotion should never play a part in marriage."

A bride! Cilarnen winced inwardly, though he was careful to let nothing of his feelings show on his face. He hoped he never *saw* another woman until he was as old as Master Tocsel!

Five

Secrets in the City of Golden Bells

When the Board sat, he passed its tests easily, and advanced in rank to Entered Apprentice. Lord Volpiril seemed to think it was no more than the consideration that House Volpiril deserved and was not due to any effort on Cilarnen's part. This hurt, but Cilarnen was careful not to show it; the traditional celebration was held—House Volpiril's consequence demanded no less—but to Cilarnen's mind, the festivities seemed rather perfunctory, and he knew for a fact that every aspect of the event had been handled by Volpiril's secretary, including the gift presented to him in Volpiril's name: a fine silver-and-ebony Wand-case. Once he would have cherished such an item, thinking it had come from his father. Now he could barely bear to look at it, though of course he had said everything that was proper at the time. Whatever his private feelings, he would do nothing to diminish the consequence of House Volpiril in the world. All this would someday be his, after all.

As an Entered Apprentice, in grey robe and soft cap (to distinguish him plainly from Journeymen, who also wore grey robes, but hooded ones), Cilarnen saw far more of the City than he ever had before. He worked with—or more precisely, *for*—Mages in every aspect of their tending of the City, reporting back to the Master of Apprentices each time a Mage released him to be set to a new task.

Cilarnen also began to make friends among his fellow Entered Apprentices, knowing that these would be his colleagues and confederates for the rest of a life spent in service to the City. Perhaps "friend" was not the right word; emotion didn't enter into the choices he made for his associates. "Allies" would be more accurate. And the associations felt hollow. Unsatisfying as one of the puff pastries that looked so delicious and were nothing more than a dusting of sugar over a thin crust that fell to insubstantial bits at the first bite.

He could not name the day on which he realized that he would never again be readmitted to his father's favor, no matter how hard he worked and what honors he achieved, but surely it was a blessing sent by the Light, for at about this same time, rumors began filtering down from the highest levels of Mageborn society that Lord Volpiril had caused the High Council to repudiate the City's ancient contracts with the Home Farms, withdrawing the City's boundaries to the walls themselves.

At first Cilarnen gave the matter little thought—what did the farms have to do with the City, after all?

But soon he began to learn. No one paid any attention to an Apprentice. His seniors spoke freely in front of him. Before long, Cilarnen soon knew what "everyone" knew about Lord Volpiril.

And none of it was good.

"THE Light-forgotten fool will be the ruin of us all. Wand."

Cilarnen lifted the instrument from the insulating cloth and placed it carefully into Juvalira's hand. The Senior Journeyman began tracing the complicated pattern of a Preservation spell in the air as his assistant—another Journeyman; Cilarnen was far from being allowed to actually assist in a Casting as yet—drew a complementary pattern on the stone floor of the warehouse with a sword. Both patterns flared and settled.

They were working in one of the cereals warehouses near the Market District. The building's spells needed to be constantly reinforced, for there were a great many of them—not only spells against vermin of all kinds, but spells against fire, damp, and leaks. Not only were there spells upon the building itself, but there were also a host of spells upon the building's contents—a separate matter, each needing to be worked separately, and in a precise order. Spells against spoilage, against rot, and against the destruction of any of the myriad containers of the grain, for since it had all been brought from the farms or from Selken ships, it came stored in sacks and barrels, some as milled flour, some as whole grains.

This was Cilarnen's first visit to this particular warehouse, but even he could see that it was emptier than it ought to be. There were empty spaces upon the shelves, stacks of barrels that weren't quite even, a sense of vacancy that made him faintly uneasy.

"More incense, boy," Thekinalo said curtly.

Cilarnen hurried to dip several carefully-measured spoon- fuls of powder onto the glowing coals, chanting the appro- priate spell under his breath.

"It's hardly a surprise," Thekinalo said, continuing the conversation. "They see a chance for profit now that they are free, and so our warehouses empty, and the farmers' pockets fill with Golden Suns. And the price of a baker's loaf has doubled in the last moonturn, may the Light defend us."

"From Lord Volpiril and his policies," Juvalira agreed, raising his wand again. "And from the Commons, should they ever discover the reason bread is so dear."

His partner simply laughed, and lowered the sword to the floor once more.

⌐

"SOMEONE must do something," young Lord Gillain said earnestly.

At the end of their daily duties, many of the Apprentices gathered at a tea-house at the edge of the College. The Golden Bells sold nothing stronger than *kaffeyeh*, teas, and fruit juice, of course, but it was a place where Apprentices and the younger Journeymen could gather together and socialize, free of the constraints of their elders. And providing their elders approved, of course.

Cilarnen shook his head minutely, saying nothing. Gillain was a fool. His rash speech would get him into trouble someday—and soon, no matter that his grandfather sat on the High Council.

"What do you suggest?" Flohan asked, with a touch of sarcasm. "Do we petition the High Council? My cousin says that half the farmers in the valley are already doing that. The Council won't change its mind and take them back."

"Its tiny mind," Gillain said, and there was laughter from the young men gathered around the table—some genuine, some merely nervous.

Only two didn't join in the general amusement. Cilarnen, and a Journeyman named Raellan.

Raellan had been coming to the Golden Bells for several sennights now. He was a quiet man, having little to say, but when he did speak, it was always sensible and to the point.

"I think that if someone wanted to change the Council's mind about its policies," Raellan said now, looking straight at Cilarnen, "he would have to be very brave, and very dedicated to the good of the City."

"This is getting too deep for me," another Entered Apprentice named Viance said hastily. "Let us talk of pleasant things. Who has tried the Phastan Silvertip that has just come in?"

The talk quickly turned to tea, and the moment passed.

⌐

CHIRED Anigrel—known in the Golden Bells, and in a few other select establishments in the City as Master Raellan—left the teashop a few chimes later, well pleased with the evening's work.

Few would recognize his face there and elsewhere, and to baffle those who might, the smallest and most subtle Cantrip of Misdirection cast over his features before he left his rooms ensured that he would not be recognized.

If Lord Lycaelon needed a reason to dispense with Volpiril's services, Anigrel would give him one.

As well as the opportunity to rid himself of all other Mages who might prove to be—inconvenient.

IF the specter of Shadow Mountain hadn't been hovering over events, Kellen would undoubtedly have been happier than he'd ever been in his entire life.

He got up each morning while the dawn mists still filled the valley of Sentarshadeen, dressed, and, carrying his breakfast with him, walked to the House of Sword and Shield, eating as he walked. Sometimes Shalkan came with him, and the two friends talked of nothing in particular. The weather—it continued to rain, but Kellen was getting used to it. How Vestakia was settling in.

When Kellen arrived at the House, he would either change to his working clothes (he wore a distinct shade of green—not his signature color, either—a hue which had been arrived at after a great deal of debate, apparently) or into his armor, depending on what he was to work at that day.

Kellen was learning things that Jermayan had lacked the resources to teach him. To attack, and to defend himself against multiple attackers. And more—he was learning to keep the choices in every combat in his own hands, so that he could kill or not as he chose. Under Master Belesharon's guidance, he was learning to trick an attacker, to stun or disarm him, to simply be elsewhere when the blow fell.

It was more than simple misdirection, far more than the feints and dodges that Jermayan had tried to show him. It was—well, if he had to put a name to it, it was a new state of mind. Part of the battle-mind, to be sure, but a state in which he could choose to be like a fish in the water. He could see where the fight was going, the way a fish could sense a rock in the stream ahead of him, and he could move with the fight, or around it. When he finally got the trick of it, it had all come at once; suddenly, the sense was *there,* and he'd slipped aside from every blow that the four other knights were trying to land on him, without needing to counter any of them. And the state of mind he had been in was so uncannily *peaceful*—as if it was a kind of meditation! It was only when Master Belesharon had called a halt to the fight and he dropped automatically out of that mental state that the exhaustion hit him.

"I would not toy with that, if I were you," Master Belesharon said, neutrally. And Kellen had readily agreed. Useful that might be, if he were surrounded by attackers that he dared not strike at, but the effort this state took was greater than actually defending himself.

With his Knight-Mage gifts to guide him, Kellen learned fast; but there was always more to learn. There was the theory of war itself, not of knight against knight, but of armies in the field.

And so he was introduced to the two great Elven strategy games, *gan* and *xaqiue.*

Gan was played on a square board divided into 864 tiny squares. There were 144 counters, divided into six suits, and up to six players could play, though usually only two or three did. The simple object of the game was to be the last person with counters on the board. The complex object of the game was to win beautifully and with style. An opponent's counters could be removed from play either by surrounding them, or by forcing them to the edge of the board.

So far Kellen had lost every *gan* match he'd played. But he was starting to lose more slowly.

Xaqiue bore a faint resemblance to *shamat*, which was played in Armethalieh. In *shamat*, there were two armies of playing pieces, each of which could move only a certain way, and the object was to capture the other player's City.

Xaqiue was similar—in that one of the points of the game was to capture the opposing player's pieces. But in *xaqiue,* captured pieces remained on the board, in the service of whoever captured them last, and the moves each piece could make changed depending on how many moves it had already made and what other pieces were nearby.

Kellen found *xaqiue* fiendishly complicated.

"It is no more complicated than a battle," Naeret would say, when Kellen had been forced to resign yet another game in the middle, hopelessly tangled in a welter of moves and countermoves, and having managed to forget which pieces still belonged to him. "Yet you would remember that well enough."

"I could get killed in a battle," Kellen muttered.

"Yet all life is war," Naeret said, setting the pieces out once again. "Perhaps it is all worth considering equally seriously."

⌒

BETWEEN sword exercises and games—though Kellen suspected that the Elves did not think of "games" in quite the same way he did—there were the lectures (though he supposed "instructions" might be a better word). Seen simply, these were tales of ancient battles—and just what he'd wanted to hear ever since he'd realized there *had* been ancient battles.

Seen another way, they were histories, or chronicles, or even guidebooks of a sort, filled with instructions and warnings.

Kellen shared these lectures with the novices, of course, for he had never had the opportunity to hear these stories before. He was fascinated to discover that they were not only stories of the Great War—what the Elves called among themselves the Second War—but the First War as well, fought so long ago that humans had not yet been civilized. It was oddly sobering to realize that the gentle, supremely cultivated Elves—so polite that they considered a direct question to be the height of barbarian rudeness—had been a warrior people since before his own folk had discovered fire.

But perhaps that was the very reason why they placed so high a value on peace and civilization.

Most afternoons were spent with Deyishene, and Kellen was already a much better rider than he had been when he began. He'd ended up being introduced to the Elven lance after all. Though there was little likelihood Kellen would ever use it under combat conditions, learning to handle it—without breaking it—taught grace, balance, and concentration. Kellen had already broken half a dozen.

When he wasn't actually busy at the House of Sword and Shield, Kellen was mindful of the promise he had made to Sandalon, and spent as many hours with the young Prince as he could. He even brought him to visit at the House of Sword and Shield—after obtaining Master Belesharon's permission, of course—and showed him all around. There was no reason, according to Jermayan, that Sandalon should not someday train as an Elven Knight if he chose to.

Someday. If he ever gets out of that fortress before he's got a long grey beard. If Elves grow beards, that is.

Ashaniel had broken the news to Sandalon that he would be going away to the Crowned Horns with the rest of the Elven children not long after the meeting at which the plan was decided, and for a few days the boy had been upset and unhappy. But Sandalon was very young, and as the leave-taking didn't happen immediately, after a sennight or two the young Prince seemed to forget the matter entirely.

But today, when Kellen went out to the stables to Deyishene, he found Sandalon and Shalkan both there, waiting outside her stall.

The young Prince had obviously been crying, though his tears were under control now, and he smiled dolefully when he saw Kellen.

"I am to go—the day after tomorrow!" Sandalon blurted out, obviously unable to contain the unhappy news one moment longer than necessary.

"Oh." There didn't seem to be very much to say, but Kellen tried. "But there will be children from all the Nine

Cities there—perhaps you will make new friends. I am sure that there will be at least one person who is almost exactly your age, and there may be more. Think, Sandalon, how good it will be when there are several others around you who want to do the same things that you do, and play the same games that you like!"

Sandalon was too well mannered, even at five, to contradict Kellen, but his face plainly said that he found the possibility highly unlikely.

"Will you . . . there will be a great many Knights riding with us. And unicorns, too! Maybe—"

But Kellen was already shaking his head. "I'm sorry, Sandalon. I'm just starting to learn all the things a proper Knight has to know. I still have a lot more to learn before I get to do something that important."

Oddly enough his answer—meant in all honesty—sent Sandalon off into a fit of the giggles, and even Shalkan swiveled his ears and coughed, indicating the unicorn was trying very hard not to laugh out loud.

After a moment, Kellen realized why, and grinned sheepishly.

A short time ago he'd destroyed the Black Cairn, just about single-handedly, and now he was saying that something as simple as convoying a bunch of kids through peaceful territory to a well-defended stronghold was too difficult for him. And put that way, it did sound ridiculous, but a job like that *was* a lot more complicated than just riding off with Jermayan and Shalkan into the unknown. And Kellen couldn't afford to spend the time away from his lessons.

"Go ahead, laugh at me, both of you," Kellen said good-naturedly. "But Master Belesharon would not think I was a very good student if I asked to be released from my lessons just because something more interesting came along. I have a lot to learn right here. But I don't think he would mind too much if we took tomorrow off to go exploring, just the four of us."

"The four of us?" Sandalon asked doubtfully.

"You, and me, and Shalkan, and Vestakia. I thought I'd ask Vestakia to come with us—if you didn't mind, of course."

He'd seen very little of Vestakia since he'd begun training at the House of Sword and Shield—of course, Kellen had seen very little of anyone but his fellow students. Idalia had assured him that Vestakia was doing perfectly well, and understood the reason for Kellen's absence.

But he missed the easy comradeship they'd shared on the road, and wanted to see for himself that she was okay. A picnic should be the perfect opportunity. And nothing could go wrong with Shalkan there to play chaperon.

"Oh, no," Sandalon said happily. "Vestakia's nice. And she isn't nearly as bossy as Lairamo is."

"Then it's settled, providing your nurse and my Master both agree," Kellen said, though he doubted Master Belesharon would have any objections to Kellen spending a day making Sandalon feel a little better about being sent away. "Now, want to come watch me practice? You might be doing this yourself someday, after all."

"I will!" Sandalon said enthusiastically. "I'm going to become a Knight just like you and Jermayan, and win *all* the Flower Wars, just like he does!"

LATER Kellen would look back at the day he spent roaming through the hills beyond Sentarshadeen with Shalkan, Vestakia, and Sandalon as the last truly serene day he was to spend for a very long time, but at the time he only thought of it as his farewell to Sandalon, and a way of making the child's departure less painful. Though Idalia had told him that there was to be "a break in the weather," in fact it had rained most of the day, but none of them had minded. When Vestakia had left him at the end of the day, Kellen had been unsettled by more than the strain of the thoughts forbidden by his *geas*, though Shalkan had kept him from getting into any real difficulty.

As he took Deyishene back to the stables, he found himself wondering if—and hoping he was going to have—a future that included Vestakia. He found himself simply wanting her company, quite apart from anything else. She was simply the best *friend* he had ever had: she was clever, she was kind, she knew how to have fun, and how to make it too.

But with the storm clouds of Shadow Mountain gathering on the horizon, he couldn't quite make himself believe that any kind of future, much less a peaceful one with Vestakia in it, was ever going to exist. He wasn't used to thinking that far ahead and he wasn't used to feeling this—grim—about things. Idalia was the dour introspective one—and all Kellen's attempts to try and get a grip on the situation only left him feeling troubled for no reason that he could put his finger on.

Fortunately Shalkan interrupted his thoughts before he sank too deeply into depression.

"The caravan will be leaving from the House of Leaf and Star tomorrow before dawn. You'll want to be there."

"I don't know," Kellen said, surprised at the suggestion. "Elves aren't much on big going-away ceremonies, I thought."

"No," Shalkan agreed. "But you'll want to see it, just the same. Don't worry. I'll make sure you're here in plenty of time."

———

THE next morning the unicorn routed Kellen out of his cozy bed in what seemed to be the middle of the night. It was still dark when the two of them made their way through the sleeping city back to the House of Leaf and Star, but the convoy was already gathered.

Most of the supplies that the evacuees would need at the Fortress of the Crowned Horns had already been sent on ahead. These wagons would only carry supplies for the journey, and the people themselves.

There were two wagons for the children and their attendants to sleep and travel in. They looked like houses on wheels, down to the softly-glowing colored lanterns hung from each corner, and were drawn by four mules each. Four more wagons carried what Kellen supposed must be supplies and camping gear for the rest of the party, and each of those had six mules hitched to it.

Kellen assessed the caravan with a newly practiced eye, seeming to feel Master Belesharon standing over his shoulder. It was true that a herd of thirty-two mules was a lot to take care of—and carry feed for—and certainly both the carts and the wagons could be drawn by fewer. But if some went lame on the road, there would be no place to get replacements. Better, Kellen supposed, to start with more animals than you needed than have to turn back.

Then there was a sudden drumming of hooves, and Kellen saw the real reason Shalkan had brought him here.

The Elven Knights had arrived.

And only some of them were riding horses.

The unicorns danced—there was no other word for it—as if the earth could not hold them down. They sprang forward, ahead of the horses, circling the wagons once as if to make sure all was well, then trotting off to stand in an easy formation a little ways off in the meadow while the equestrian Knights distributed themselves closely around the wagons.

"I thought you'd like to see that," Shalkan commented.

The doors of the House of Leaf and Star opened. Kellen was too far away to hear what was said—he'd come only to see, not to intrude—but he saw Andoreniel and Ashaniel standing there, bidding a last farewell . . . not as Sandalon's parents, Kellen realized, but as the rulers of the Elves.

Slowly the little party exited the portico and climbed into the wagons. The drivers climbed onto their seats, and the train began to move off. The Unicorn Knights stood watching it for a moment, the horns of their mounts gleaming faintly in the first pale rays of dawn, then trotted briskly after it, quickly passing the wagons and forging on ahead.

"Well," Kellen said with a sigh, "I guess it's time to go to work."

AT the end of her seventh Rising following that walk in the Stone Garden, Savilla was pleased to see that Zyperis had been driven half-mad with curiosity. He had wooed her favor with every gift and attention he could think of, including the gift of several of his own personal slaves to do with as she wished.

All this was most satisfactory, and in addition, proved two things. One, that he was still submissive enough to be malleable, and two, that his clandestine sources of information within her personal household were not as well-developed as he might wish, for if there had been some way for Zyperis to discover her intentions on his own, he would certainly have done it.

But having made her point, she was prepared to relent before he turned sullen. Besides, it was such a lovely plan that it would be a shame to have no one to share it with . . .

THAT Rising, she commanded Zyperis's attendance, and after the business of her courtiers had been dealt with, she drew him aside.

"I have a lovely surprise for you, my dear," she said, her voice husky and playful. "Come with me."

She took him to a small chamber nestled among her private rooms. Its walls, ceiling, and floor were made of ivory, intricately joined and carved. The walls were golden with age, for the room was very old; a place to summon visions and see what must be seen.

The floor should, perhaps, have been the same warm golden hue, but it was not. Instead, it was a deep brown, like old leather, for centuries of shed blood had permanently darkened it.

A small ebony table stood in the center of the room, and on it was a large shallow bowl carved from one piece of

black obsidian. It gleamed in the light of the shining golden
orbs burning overhead.

A naked human girl knelt beside the table, waiting with
utter stillness. Her long blonde hair was elaborately jeweled
and coiled on top of her head, and every inch of her pale
skin had been intricately painted. When the two Endarkened
entered the room, she did not move. She had been very well
trained; one of those humans was taken captive so young she
remembered no other world than this, and no other way of
life than service to her Demon masters. She had been
Zyperis's most recent gift to his mother.

"Fill the bowl," Queen Savilla said, holding out a small
ebony and crystal knife to her son.

He did not hesitate a moment; if anything, his eyes lit with
avidity. "Come here, precious," Zyperis said to the girl. He
took the knife as the human slave got to her feet and stood as
he directed her. He positioned her so she was standing in
front of the obsidian bowl and he was standing behind her.

With quick precise movements, he bent her forward,
turned her head to the side, and cut into the pulsing vein in
the side of her neck. The bowl rang faintly as the girl's hot
blood spurted into it, and she gasped and at last began to
struggle. Zyperis held her firmly until she quieted, and then
lifted her body off the floor so that it would drain more easily.

"It does seem something of a waste," he observed, watching
the blood fill the bowl. "For it to be over so quickly, you know."

"There's very little sport in the tame ones," Savilla said
consideringly. "And we can enjoy her later. Filendek does
thrive upon a challenge, and he has been complaining that I
do not tax his culinary skills enough of late. But come. Now
I will satisfy your wanton curiosity, my son."

The bowl was full, and Zyperis tossed the girl's body
aside, leaning eagerly over the bowl of steaming blood. Savilla joined him.

"Show me what I wish to see," the Queen commanded,
staring into the bowl of shimmering blood.

The surface of the bowl shimmered, going from dark to pale. Faint shadows began to swirl mistily beneath its surface, then grew brighter as the images in the bowl steadied into mirror sharpness.

Zyperis looked into the bowl and saw a caravan of Elves moving through a wintry landscape. Six wagons—four obviously carrying nothing but provisions—and perhaps twenty outriders, at least a third of them mounted on unicorns.

"More Elves, Mother!" Zyperis protested. "But why show me this, when you have decreed that we must let the caravans pass unharmed, no matter how tempting the opportunity? And *Elves,* Mother—it has been so long since we have had Elves to play with!"

"Oh, yes, it is true that I have allowed the previous caravans to make their way to that annoying fortress of theirs unmolested. But unfortunately—for the Elves and their little Prince—nothing lasts forever . . . "

THE party from Sentarshadeen had been on the road for nearly two sennights, and by now they were deep into the mountains. Although back in Sentarshadeen it was no more than early autumn, here the hand of winter rested implacably on the land.

The snowfall had already been heavy—only the unicorns found it easy going—and at the village of Girizethiel the party had transferred from wheeled wagons to sledges. Fortunately, the trail had been well-broken by the previous convoys.

The day was overcast, and it was snowing lightly but steadily, though the wagonmaster, who had made this trip several times before, said that the snow would grow thicker throughout the day. Visibility was already bad, with the prankish wind whipping up veils of powdered snow and carrying them through the air to cloud the sight.

If they had not been where they were, Ciradhel would have

been more concerned about a possible ambush, but the Fortress of the Crowned Horns was well within the borders of the Elven Lands, and all patrols had reported the land secure for moonturns. Ciradhel was more worried about keeping his young charges from getting into trouble along the way.

Kalania was no more than a babe in arms, and Hieretsur kept her young charge well under wraps. And Tredianala was a shy girl, who stayed close to her nurse and rarely ventured away from the wagons at any time.

But her cousin Merisashendiel was her opposite in every way, always underfoot and into everything, wanting to explore at every stop, no matter how brief it was. She and Vendalton were partners in every kind of innocent mischief, and wherever the two of them led, Prince Sandalon would inevitably follow. Ciradhel found it hard to begrudge the youngsters their youthful high spirits, for it was hard for them, he knew, to travel such a long distance to live in a strange place when you were so very young.

As for Alkandoran, he had already begun his training as a Knight, and had argued long and hard that he should be allowed to remain to defend Sentarshadeen against possible attack. But he was far too young—little though he thought it—so over his protests he had joined the others. He continued to let his unhappiness be felt, despite Ciradhel's assurances that his knightly training could continue at the fortress.

Ciradhel clucked to Jilka, and the Elven mare trotted forward over the snow to where Rhavelmo sat upon Calmeren, waiting for the convoy to make its slow way past.

The unicorn's white coat was a perfect match for the snow. Where it was not covered by the saddle and armor, it was fluffed out against the cold, giving the little creature a downy appearance that almost made the unicorn seem insubstantial. Her horn glistened like ice.

"Another day, and we'll be rid of them," Rhavelmo said, looking up at him. Her rose-colored armor and cloak were already powdered with a fresh fall of snow. "We should reach the Crowned Horns by midday. Evening at the latest. Look. You can already see it—or you could if not for this blasted weather."

She pointed.

Automatically, Ciradhel looked. All that was to be seen was white, and more white, but he had been here many years before, and let imagination show him what his eyes could not.

The Fortress of the Crowned Horns did not occupy the highest peak in the Mystral Range, but as Idalia had told Kellen, it had never been taken by an enemy, nor could it be.

The fortress had been carved out of the living rock thousands of years past, in the days when the Elves had faced the Endarkened for the very first time. The surface of the mountain had been made too steep and smooth for a dragon to land upon it, and the very top of the fortress—the only level place—was too small and too well-defended to be accessible by Dark-tainted dragons. The only access to the fortress was up a long narrow causeway that led to the outer gates. The causeway was so narrow that only one cart could travel up it at a time, and at need, the defenders had a hundred ways of rendering it completely impassable.

"It will be faster going back, too, if we don't have to wait for the wagons," Calmeren said hopefully, switching her tail to shake it free of snow.

"Faster even with the wagons," Ciradhel pointed out. "Since they'll be all but empty. And we can't leave them unprotected. Even if there aren't—"

"Wait," Calmeren said. The unicorn shifted, raising her head and turning into the wind. Her nostrils flared as she inhaled deeply.

Suddenly there was a faint howl in the distance, a single eerie ululating wail. It hung alone on the air for a moment, and then was joined by others, a chilling wolflike chorus.

But all three of them knew that whatever creature had made that sound, it wasn't a wolf.

"We have to run," Calmeren said. *"Now."*

Neither of the Knights considered doubting the unicorn's word. There would be time for questions and incredulity later, when—if—they were all safe. Ciradhel cast one despairing glance at the wagons. They could not possibly move any faster, especially in this weather.

"Bring in the unicorns—quickly. We'll put the children on them," he said.

Calmeren and Rhavelmo sprang away, and Ciradhel turned Jilka back to the wagons.

"Stop the wagons. Everyone out. Bring your cloaks. Tuika—Henele—unhitch the teams as fast as you can. Cut the harness if you have to. Naeret—Emessade—get the children onto the unicorns. We have to run for it."

He swung down off Jilka's back and strode forward, running tallies in his head. Seven unicorns—six children. Each of the unicorn-mounted Knights could take one of the children—Kalania could go in her nurse's arms—and they would send Sandalon's nurse on the last of them. That left thirteen warhorses, seven of which would have to carry an extra passenger, but no one would be left behind for whatever was making that howling noise.

"This is most unexpected," Hieretsur protested, coming down the steps of the wagon with Kalania in her arms.

"There is no time to explain," Ciradhel snapped. Calmeren had returned with the others, and he seized the nurse and deposited her on the unicorn's back.

"Run," he said.

"Like the wind," Calmeren agreed, and bounded off.

There was another chorus of howls—closer—and this time everyone heard it.

"One presumes that is what we are running from," Naeret said, her nervousness showing in her stone-like expression. She settled Vendalton in front of Vikaet's rider and the black unicorn took off after the others.

"Yes," Ciradhel said briefly.

Now only Sandalon and Lairamo were left.

"I will see you again soon," Lairamo said firmly, setting

Sandalon into the saddle in front of Dainelel. His unicorn sprang into motion the moment the boy was settled, following the others.

Lairamo looked at Ciradhel. "Perhaps—" she began.

"He will need you. Go."

Lairamo climbed carefully up behind the last of the Unicorn Knights, and it followed the rest.

Getting the children onto the unicorns had been the work of moments, and it had taken easily as long to finish unhitching the mules and to get the wagon drivers and the rest of the children's companions onto horseback. Now Ciradhel sent those carrying double off after the others.

The mules had caught the scent carried upon the wind, and though normally the most docile and well-mannered of creatures, they had been terrified. The moment they were free, they had fled across the ice, slipping and skidding in their haste to be away. Tuika and Henele had not been able to properly unhitch the last teams, and had simply cut the main traces as the mules fought to be free. Even the Elven destriers were agitated, looking to their riders for reassurance.

"What about the rest of us?" Naeret asked, falling easily into War Manners.

Ciradhel smiled at her, swinging up onto Jilka's back and loosening his sword in its sheath. He looked around at his four remaining companions.

"I thought we might go see what is making that infernal racket, were you all so inclined," he answered politely.

THEY were barely a hundred meters from the wagons when the pack appeared in the distance, a shimmering patch of darker silver in the snow. Beyond it, the five could see a small army of moving upright figures. The sunlight glittered off their armor and weapons, and the Elves could see the faint shimmer of the magic protecting those of them for whom sunlight was lethal.

"Frost-giants—ice-trolls—and a pack of coldwarg," Ciradhel said grimly. "All ancient allies of the Enemy."

"How could they come here without our knowing?" Naeret demanded, her voice high with outrage and anger.

"The cold is their element," Abrodiel, eldest of them all, said.

"Come," Ciradhel said, spurring Jilka forward. "We must buy the others as much time as we can."

COLDWARG had been created by Endarkened sorcery during the Great War. They were nearly the size of a unicorn, with enormous jaws capable of ripping out the throat of a horse—or a man—in one bite. In the last war, the Enemy had needed to spell-shield them on the battlefield, for coldwarg suffered in the heat, and died when the temperature grew too warm.

But here in the mountains, they were in their element.

Ciradhel knew that he and his companions were doomed. It was a small pack—not much more than a dozen beasts—but five Knights could not hope to kill them all and the creatures that followed. All they could hope for was to kill some of them, and to buy the rest of the party precious time to escape.

And because they were trying to stop the pack, not save themselves, they could not use the one maneuver that would give them any hope of survival: grouping into a tight pack to protect one another.

"Bows first, then swords," Ciradhel said.

Spread out into a line, the five Elves charged down the slope directly into the coldwarg pack.

The frost-giants cheered when they saw the Elves, and their shambling turned into a trot, and then into an eager run.

The battle cries of the Elven Knights mingled with the howls of the coldwarg. They shot until their quivers were empty, but the arrows had little effect on the monsters, though every shaft found its mark. Then they drew their swords, and the battle was joined. The Elven destriers fought viciously, with teeth and steel-shod hooves, but one after another, they went down beneath the tide of dappled silver bodies.

Then it was the turn of their riders.

Ciradhel saw Naeret stagger to her feet over Ashtes's fallen body. The crippled stallion was screaming and thrashing, trying to rise as a coldwarg ripped at his belly. Blood fountained from the stump of Naeret's sword-arm, and as she fumbled in the snow for her sword, another coldwarg leaped for her throat. She went down.

One of the beasts leaped at Jilka's throat. Jilka danced back, and Ciradhel struck at the coldwarg with his sword, feeling a hot flash of pleasure to see the blade bite deep into the hellbeast's shoulder. The coldwarg sprang back, jaws gaping wide and pink tongue lolling. Its yellow eyes danced with a feral amusement. *It's only a matter of time,* the beast's gaze seemed to say. It turned and loped off in the direction of the caravan.

Ashtes had stopped screaming.

Henele was trapped beneath his fallen horse. Its head was gone. Two coldwarg were on him, one with its jaws clamped around each arm. They were pulling, shaking their heads and growling, like puppies with a toy. Henele should have been screaming, but he made no sound, and from that Ciradhel knew he was already dead.

They were all dead.

All but him.

Why?

He looked around.

The surviving coldwarg had broken off their attack to take up the pursuit of the others again.

And the marauders that had followed the pack had arrived.

"Nice puppies, to save one for Dalak," the frost-giant said, giggling nastily, a high-pitched sound that sat ill with the giant's size and bulk. "You go on," he said to the others. "This one's mine."

Ciradhel used those precious moments to assess the enemy, on the faint chance he would ever be able to make a report.

There were a full dozen ice-trolls, all wearing Talismans to protect them against the sun, for they were creatures of night and caves. Their skin was the pale blue of pack ice, and they wore nothing more than a narrow loincloth, whether male or female, for they needed—nor wanted—no protection from the cold. Around their necks they wore elaborate collars of bones taken from their dead enemies, and carried bags which contained their hunting implements. Their main weapon was a bone atlatl, a notched rod with which they could launch polished bone shafts with deadly force and skill.

There were twice their number of frost-giants in the band, and they were formidable foes. The shortest of them was twice Ciradhel's height. They had hair the color of frost, and pale eyes, and—unlike some of their cousins—no need of protection from the sun. Frost-giants were notable smiths and metalworkers, and all the giants wore articulated plate armor, well-padded with fur against the cold. But despite their ability at crafting swords, the frost-giants' preferred weapon was the club, and it was a club that Dalak unlimbered now, swinging it back and forth as he smiled at Ciradhel.

The others grumbled at being denied a chance to watch the fun, but Dalak seemed to be their leader, and after a few moments of indecision they complied, lumbering off after the coldwarg with stupefying speed.

"Come, little Elf. I promise I'll be gentle," Dalak rumbled. "And you will reach the Cold Hells long before most of your friends."

"And I shall wish the same for you," Ciradhel said politely. He urged Jilka forward.

Dalak had superior reach, but Ciradhel and Jilka were faster. They were equally matched, and Ciradhel began to hope he might win. At the very least, every moment he could delay Dalak left the marauders without their leader.

But suddenly he felt a rushing *presence* above him, and a

burning pain in his shoulders as great talons seized him, shearing through his armor as if it were silk.

Something lifted him from his saddle.

He cried out.

Dalak stepped forward, swinging his club with all his strength. It hit the side of Jilka's head, and Ciradhel heard her neck snap.

Then Dalak reached up and grabbed him by the ankle. There was a tearing pain, a shrill soundless cry that lanced through Ciradhel's head, and suddenly he lay upon the ground, looking up at the frost-giant.

Dalak put his boot on Ciradhel's chest.

"Say good-bye to the Light, little Elf," Dalak said, raising his club again.

And then Ciradhel knew nothing more.

⟳

THE seven double-burdened warhorses ran over the snow in the direction of the Crowned Horns. None of the Knights knew what they fled from, but no one was foolish enough to disregard Calmeren's warning, and all of them had heard the howling.

The unicorns were far ahead, springing over the snow at their fastest pace, one that no horse could match. Athonere hoped they and their precious cargo could reach the safety of the fortress. He cursed the fell weather. If the day had been clear, the sentries would have been able to see them. They might even have been able to see what lay behind the fleeing party.

But even if that had been true, none of them could have expected assistance from those within the citadel. The defenders would not have dared to come out, lest this be a trap, a ruse to lure them away from the children they guarded.

Just then Athonere saw a flash of movement through the veils of blowing snow, as a sinuous rill of silver fur flowed over the snow, easily passing the galloping horses.

They seemed to be monstrous misshapen wolves. Some of them were bleeding from fresh sword cuts, and several had the stumps of Elven arrows protruding from their necks and shoulders, but despite the blood that starred the snow in their wake, they moved with terrifying fleetness.

No. Not wolves. *Coldwarg.*

Athonere risked a glance behind him—and saw, over his passenger's shoulder, a host of squat bluish creatures running toward them, moving nearly as fast as the galloping horses. Without slowing, they began to hurl objects toward the mounted Knights.

The woman clinging to Athonere's back screamed. She thrashed frantically for a moment, then fell from the saddle before he could catch her.

One of the horses beside Athonere grunted heavily and went down, its hind legs tangled in a contraption of stones and leather cord. The force of its fall spilled both the Knight and his passenger into the snow with stunning force.

Athonere reined in, turning back. His passenger was lying in the snow, three shafts protruding from her back, dead. Screams—Elven and animal—told him that more ice-troll shafts were finding their mark. Their only safety lay in attack, lest more of their charges be slaughtered as they fled.

He drew his sword and charged into the mob of ice-trolls.

"To me! To me!" he shouted.

But the ice-trolls refused to stand and fight. They scampered back and forth across the hard-packed snow, calling mocking taunts in an unknown tongue, trying to lure the knights off the trail and into the drifts. And always came the deadly volleys of hard-flung arrows. Though the Knights returned fire with their own bows—those who had not given them to arm the surviving caravan drivers—they missed more often than not, for the ice-trolls were fast-moving and hard to see, and to stand still long enough to take aim was to become an attractive target.

"They're waiting for something," Luamzir said grimly.

She'd recovered from her fall, though Perta had not been as fortunate. Merisashendiel's nurse had had no armor to protect her, and lay dead in the snow. And though Luamzir had cut the leathern cords from Panorak's legs, the animal was dead lame, barely able to stand, much less run.

"We dare not run—and they will not fight," Athonere said grimly. If only it would stop snowing . . .

Suddenly the ground began to shake. A moment more and the frost-giants were upon them.

At least the children are safe, Athonere thought. Neither trolls nor giants could outrun a unicorn.

⌐

THE seven unicorns ran steadily through the blowing snow, Calmeren in the lead.

Suddenly there was a high shrill wailing that made her head hurt. She sprang sideways, crouching and staggering as something swooped down out of the sky and passed low above her head. She heard the sound of claws grate against Rhavelmo's armor, and Hieretsur screamed.

"They're here!" Calmeren cried, the stench of the Enemy in her nostrils, and the other unicorns wheeled and stood, searching for the foe. There were shadowy shapes in the sky, difficult to see through the blowing snow, wheeling over them like a flock of carrion birds.

"No!" Rhavelmo vaulted down from the saddle and pushed Hieretsur forward. "Go! Run!"

Calmeren gave Rhavelmo one agonized glance, and sprang forward again.

Rhavelmo unlimbered her bow and shot a dozen arrows into the sky. It was a difficult mark, but her aim was true. One of the creatures fell to earth—a monstrous bat, its body as large as a man's, its fur and its wings as white as the snow itself. It thrashed in its death agonies, red eyes gleaming with mad hatred.

All around her, the Knights were quickly dismounting. It

was the best chance they could give the unicorns carrying the children and Lairamo, because the children must be saved at all costs.

"YOU must be strong now, Prince Sandalon. Hold tight to Queverian's saddle and don't let go, whatever you do," Dainelel said quickly.

The boy nodded, too frightened to speak.

"Take care of him, my love," he said to Queverian, a tremor in his voice.

"I will," the unicorn said, and Sandalon had no time to say anything more, for she was off, speeding across the snow, with death flying ever nearer overhead.

CALMEREN had barely hit her stride again when more of the bat-things began to dive upon her, slashing at her face, and, worse, at the precious burden she carried. They stank of Taint and carrion, and try as she might, she could not escape them. She found herself turning away from the Crowned Horns, fighting to keep from being driven into the deep snow away from the trail.

None of the others fared any better. The younger children cried out in fear as the monstrous bats swooped down through the storm, snatching at them.

She had nearly made up her mind to make a dash back the way she had come when the coldwarg pack arrived.

And they were not alone.

Appearing out of the storm like ghosts were a host of cloaked and hooded figures, their white garb rendering them nearly invisible against the snow. At first she thought they were Elves come to their rescue, then she knew they were not. All carried long spears.

"Do what you must!" she cried to the others. "But run!"

A coldwarg leaped at her. She reared to meet its charge, praying that Hieretsur could hold on. She thrust her horn into the wolf-thing's belly and shook her head savagely, flinging its dying body aside.

Teeth raked her unarmored flank, and she spun and kicked at the new foe. A yelp told her that her sharp hooves had connected.

Then leathery wings enfolded her head, blinding her. Enormous wings battered at her with punishing force, and she felt Hieretsur's weight leave her saddle. She could hear baby Kalania wailing in terror and pain. She felt sharp claws scrabbling at her throat and chest, shearing through her armored collar, and raking into the flesh beneath. She shook her head savagely, and felt her horn slide into the leather of its wing, but these were not creatures of Dark Magic to die at the touch of a unicorn's horn.

Blindly and desperately she fought, hearing screams all around her, and the yelps and howls of the coldwarg.

At last she managed to drag the monster beneath her hooves to trample it.

The children—where are the children?

She heard faint screams overhead. Looking up, she saw two of the bat-creatures soaring away, bodies struggling in their claws.

The snow was red with blood. The other unicorns, some dead, some mortally wounded, lay on the snow. The coldwarg were quarreling over the bodies.

The cloaked figures moved through the carnage, checking for survivors and gathering up fallen weapons.

At the moment, no one was looking at her.

Calmeren moved, silently as only a unicorn could, away from the battlefield. When she was sure she was concealed by the storm she began to run with utter determination, agony lancing through her with every step.

Sentarshadeen must be warned. Whatever the cost.

WHEN Idalia had brought the rains safely to the Elven Lands with the Wild Magic, there had been, as always, a price. It had been a high one, and a hard one to accept, but she had weighed the cost in lives and pain if she did not, and made her bargain.

The price for the power to save the Nine Cities had been her life—but it seemed that the Gods were slow to collect.

She had been surprised to awaken from her working trance at all, and had spent a sennight in the House of Leaf and Star, recovering from the heavy demands the magic had placed upon her body. Each day had been a gift, and an odd surprise, but she had come to realize that Gods' time was not the same as mortals'. They had accepted her bargain, and would collect upon it in Their own good time. But she knew that every hour she lived now was borrowed.

When Kellen had returned from the Barrier, and she had healed him, Idalia had almost grown used to that, but then she received another unsettling reminder of how much things had changed. When she summoned up the power to heal her brother, no personal price was asked of her . . . and there was always a price to the Wildmage over and above the personal power expended.

But no longer. Wildmagery still drained her personal energy, just as it always had, but now no additional obligation was set upon her when she did her work, as if all prices had already been paid.

Perhaps they had. Perhaps accepting the greatest price she could pay had negated the need to pay any other. Ever.

As much as possible, she tried to forget the choice she had made, trying to live in the present moment, as the Elves did. When she was not with Jermayan, she went where she was needed in Sentarshadeen, or worked steadily at creating a store of items that would be useful later, when Shadow Mountain showed its hand at last. *Tarnkappa* were the most obvious of these; cloaks that would conceal all sight, sound, and scent of the wearer from enemy detection. Such things would be useful for spies and scouts.

But each one took sennights to complete, and she had other things to do as well; the distillation of medicines that only a Wildmage could make. The Elves were master herbalists, and she had learned many of the recipes she used from them, but even their most potent cures for Taint and Shadowed poison were stronger when infused with a Wildmage's power.

No one questioned the obsessive haste with which she worked. The Elves thought all humans rushed around anyway. Only Kellen would have noticed anything out of the ordinary in her behavior, and he was away from dawn until well after dusk these days, engrossed in learning all that his Elven Masters could teach him about the Way of the Sword.

Gone was the gawky unsure boy who had ridden into her forest clearing half a year ago on Shalkan's back, half-dead of his wounds. Gone even was the uncertain half-trained young Wildmage who had set out with Jermayan to destroy the Barrier. No one would ever call Kellen Tavadon clumsy again, in or out of armor. And now that he had accepted his Knight-Mage gifts, there was an assurance, a maturity to him that simply hadn't been there before.

And had he stayed in Armethalieh, there never would have been that assurance. *Not with the way Lycaelon Tavadon tried to break his spirit!* Idalia thought with a rare flash of spitefulness.

Idalia's happiest hours of all were spent with Jermayan in his home. Every hour—every moment—was a gift that might not come again.

And certainly would not last.

⟶

THE temperature had been dropping for the last sennight, and the morning frosts and fogs had been growing heavier. To complicate matters, though the rain had lessened recently, it had never really stopped. It had turned to sleet instead, so that everything became covered with an increasingly-thick shell of ice. Beautiful, but treacherous.

Even the simplest journey became fraught with unexpected peril, and the newest article of outdoor wear was cleat-bottomed sabatons to strap over one's boots for the navigation of the ice-covered streets. Crews went out at intervals, day and night, to use simple, minor magics to break the ice from the tree branches, lest the branches themselves snap under the weight of the ice.

With all the ice, it was no longer possible for Kellen to work with Deyishene in the afternoons, as the practice-ground had become a solid sheet of ice, too slippery to use. Master Belesharon said he would be able to resume his practice once the snows came, for snow provided a less treacherous footing than ice, but at the moment, Kellen's afternoons were spent with extra sword practice.

It had also become necessary to begin laying out fodder for the horses, since the meadow grass was fast being covered by the ice. But neither activity took as much of his time as working with Deyishene had.

It gave him a lot of time to think about other things.

ONE afternoon he left the House of Sword and Shield early, and went home to change into his best clothes. He intended to go to the House of Leaf and Star and ask a favor of Ashaniel—if she would see him. And since he was going to ask a favor, it only made sense to look as if he really meant to approach the Queen with the greatest of respect.

When he opened the door—having stopped on the porch to shake frozen sludge from his heavy hooded cloak—he saw Idalia leaning over a large bowl on the table, peering into it intently. She glanced up when she saw him, startled.

"Kellen! I wasn't expecting you this early."

"I've got an errand to run, and I thought I'd change first. What are you doing?" he asked, coming over and peering down at the bowl. It was a large blue-glazed bowl of heavy pottery, filled to the brim with water.

"Scrying—or trying to. Normally I'd try this at one of the springs, but I'd rather not freeze solid. And I haven't been having any luck anyway." She sighed. "I've been trying to see what's been going on back in the Wildwood after the Scouring Hunt went through there. I've been trying to find out for moonturns, actually, but my scrying won't show me anything reliable."

"It's supposed to show you what you need to see, not what you want to see," Kellen reminded her.

"Yes," Idalia agreed. "And nothing I've seen makes any sense from that point of view either, really. Just a lot of flowers."

"Want me to try?" Kellen offered.

"Well, a change is as good as a rest, so they say," Idalia said. "If you wouldn't mind, I would be glad of your help." She sighed. "Perhaps I'm just trying too hard."

The ingredients—fern leaf (dried, at this time of year) and wine—were ready beside the bowl. Kellen cast four drops of the wine into the bowl and then floated a bit of the fern leaf on the water.

" 'You who travel between Earth and Sky, show me what you see,' " he said.

He remembered the first time he'd scryed, in the spring behind Idalia's cabin in the Wildwood. How reluctant and resentful he'd been at having to try, and how sure he'd been it wouldn't work. Now it seemed an obvious and natural thing to do.

The vision came immediately. The water in the bowl turned white.

"Snowstorm," Idalia said, since she could see what Kellen saw.

"Not really helpful," Kellen said, peering into the bowl. "Unless this just means there's a really, really big blizzard going on somewhere—or coming straight at us. Which it is, I can't tell. Even if there's something there I ought to see, I can't see it."

As if taking exception to his comments, the snowstorm faded, and was replaced with the image of a face.

It was a young man, about Kellen's age. His face bore the unmistakable stamp of Mage-breeding. He had auburn hair and pale blue eyes, and looked angry—or possibly scared. Or both. Kellen knew that feeling only too well. He was wearing the pale grey cap-robe-and-tabard of the Entered Apprentice. Wherever he was, it was dark, for Kellen and Idalia could see nothing more than his head and shoulders.

Then that image, too, faded, and the bowl held nothing but water once more.

Kellen frowned. "I think I know him—or knew him. But I don't remember his name. Why show me that, though? It's not as if I'm going back to Armethalieh—or an Apprentice is ever going to leave it."

"Who knows?" Idalia asked. "What I *do* know is that if I can't get any sense out of this pesky bowl of water, I think I'm going to have to take a trip over the Border to see for myself how things are in the Wild Lands. That will serve a double purpose, as I can warn the crofters and the High Hills that the Enemy is on the move again. Maybe I can convince Jermayan to go with me."

"I don't think you'll have much of a problem there," Kellen said, grinning. "I think you'd have a lot harder time keeping him from coming with you." He picked up the heavy bowl carefully and walked over to the sink to pour out its contents.

Six

The Room of Fire and Water

An hour later, suitably dressed, Kellen presented himself at the House of Leaf and Star.

Ice had turned the entire building into something magical, and the Elves, connoisseurs of natural beauty, had left it as it was. Every surface was covered with a thick sheet of nearly transparent ice, so that the House took on the unreality of a structure cast out of colored glass. Long icicles hung down from the eaves, and each one was filled with rainbows from the watery sunlight.

Kellen knocked at the front door, and, when it was opened, asked if the Lady Ashaniel would receive him—or to be more precise, he suggested to the august personage who answered his knock that it would give him very great pleasure to attend upon the Lady Ashaniel, if she happened to be at home, and was willing to take time from her busy day to allow him to do so.

"Be welcome within our house, Kellen Wildmage," the august personage told him, bowing.

Kellen bowed back—his bows were much improved, after a few fortnights under Master Belesharon's tutelage—and he followed the Elf into a small side parlor.

"I will see to your refreshment," the august personage said, closing the doors behind him as he departed.

It was only after he'd left that Kellen realized the man hadn't said he'd tell Ashaniel that Kellen was here, but he supposed she'd find out eventually. He doubted there was much that went on beneath her roof that the Lady Ashaniel didn't know about.

Even if he had to wait a long time, there was much here to keep his attention. At one end of the room was an enormous fireplace, its elaborate hearth stretching all the way to the ceiling. It was designed after the fashion of a dragon—the hearth being in the belly—and the outswept wings were carried out in tiles that covered the entire wall of the room. A cheerful fire leaped and crackled on the hearth. It was an astonishingly cheerful-looking dragon. Quite friendly, in fact. More like a winged cat with scales than a dragon; the artist had managed to convey the impression that this dragon not only did not mind that its belly was being used to warm the room, but positively welcomed the idea.

At the opposite end of the room, a fountain played. A column of water bubbled high into the air, falling back into itself and down into its catch-basin. There were glittering motes of color caught within the water; coming closer and inspecting it, Kellen realized they were tiny shapes of colored glass, but they were moving too fast for him to be able to tell quite what they were meant to represent . . .

"I see that the fire-and-water room pleases you," Ashaniel observed from behind him.

Kellen turned around. While he'd been studying the fountain, Ashaniel had entered the room, Morusil with her. A servant entered behind them, bringing a wheeled cart with tea-things.

"Yes, it does. Very much," Kellen answered honestly. Looking around—now that he was not so thoroughly distracted by the fountain—he could see that the end of the room with the dragon fireplace was decorated in reds and oranges and fire motifs, while the other end, where the fountain was, ran to greens and violets, and the walls were covered, not with tiles, but with seashells in every shape and size. It should have looked garish or busy, but somehow it managed to be a harmonious whole.

"And Morusil," he said, bowing. "I am happy to see you again."

"And I to see you, and to have the opportunity to thank

you for bringing me such an eager student," Morusil replied.

"I am glad that Vestakia has found a friend in you," Kellen said, as sincerely as he could manage. "Your wisdom inspires her, and your encouragement heartens her."

"It is always a privilege to hear the words of the young," Morusil said. "But you will have come to visit with Ashaniel, and I do not wish to intrude."

"I don't wish to interfere with your plans, but I would welcome your company as well," Kellen said hopefully.

"Then we shall all take tea," Ashaniel said decisively.

They settled themselves around the fire, and the servant set out the teapot, the cups, and a plate of assorted cakes on a small table between them. When she had left, Ashaniel and Morusil began discussing the weather, and the prospects for the Winter Running Dance, which would be held on the first Full Moon after the first snowfall, which was expected any day now.

"Perhaps you will not wish to participate in the Dance, young Kellen—not everyone does, you know—but it is quite beautiful, and few humans have seen it," Morusil said.

"I am quite certain it is worthy of seeing," Kellen agreed politely. *Elves do not rush,* he reminded himself. And it *would* be nice to finally know what a "Winter Running Dance" was, since people had been mentioning it, one way and another, since he'd gotten here.

"But though we find your company agreeable, of course, and it has been too long since you visited the House of Leaf and Star, I think perhaps you did not come to talk upon these subjects," Ashaniel said with a teasing smile.

Kellen found himself smiling in return, half-dazzled, as always, by her beauty. "I am afraid I've come for something else, and perhaps to raise a subject that you will find tiresome, for I have probably spoken of it far too much for your comfort."

Morusil and Ashaniel exchanged a look, one that Kellen was unable to interpret.

"It is to be hoped that you will always feel free to speak your heart here in the House of Leaf and Star," Morusil said, after a pause. "Even if the ways of humans are not our ways, there is often much wisdom to be gained from listening to the words of those who are unlike ourselves."

The two Elves regarded Kellen expectantly.

Kellen took a deep breath, trying to get everything he was about to say organized in his mind.

"I know I'm not going to get this all right, but . . . at the Council meeting, I know you really didn't want to send someone to tell Armethalieh about the—the Enemy. Because, well, you didn't think it would do any good. And you thought it might make matters worse. And you might be right. But, well, what if—I mean, that might not be true. And they *need* to know. They *hate* De—the Enemy there. Really, they do! The reason I was cast out was that they believe that the Wildmages are allied with—the other side. If they knew the Enemy were active again, they might not help us—they probably wouldn't—but they'd at least protect themselves. And that's important, too. So is there—Maybe there's some way to get a message to Armethalieh that they'd listen to. Because I think it's important to try, at least." He swallowed, his mouth gone dry despite his tea, feeling as if he must have sounded as clumsy as an untutored bumpkin. "And I think we ought to try as soon as possible; I can't tell you why I feel this way, because I don't know, and even though I've tried scrying, it hasn't told me anything. But I still do. That's all."

Kellen sat back in his seat, trying not to look as agitated and anxious as he felt. Some diplomat he turned out to be!

But maybe he hadn't been as persuasive as he could have been? Maybe, secretly, he *didn't* want Armethalieh to be warned, because he still resented the Golden City, but he wanted to be able to say—assuming anyone ever asked—that he'd done everything he could to save it.

Maybe he should go himself. Or try to. Perhaps with a suitable disguise . . .

"I think perhaps that you are right, Kellen Knight-Mage,"

Ashaniel said after a very long pause. "Perhaps we have been overhasty in dismissing the threat the Enemy poses in human lands. Certainly a timely word of warning would not go amiss, could the Golden City be persuaded to accept it. Yet the selection of a proper envoy is a delicate matter."

"I would say that it must be either Bevar or Hyandur," Morusil said consideringly. "Both have been to the Golden City in the past—though not for many years, of course—and both are familiar with the ways of humans. I shall speak to each of them within the moonturn to see if he is willing to go. I believe that one of them will be, and if he is, he will leave before the heavy snows. Rest assured, young Kellen, warning of the Enemy's intentions will be carried to the human city in a timely fashion, though whether it may be successfully delivered is something which only the Gods Themselves may say."

"Thank you both," Kellen said feelingly. "I know it doesn't seem like a very important matter to you—"

Ashaniel raised her hand, silencing him.

"In the tapestry of the weaving of the Gods of Leaf and Star, none who are living may see the whole pattern and know its completion," Ashaniel said gently. "Perhaps the threads of your spinning are as important as the rest."

Perhaps so. Kellen only hoped the Gods thought so—and that they could make someone in Armethalieh listen to whoever Ashaniel and Morusil sent.

ABOUT a sennight and a half after the caravan left, the first snowfall came to Sentarshadeen, and a few days after he went to the House of Leaf and Star, Kellen awoke to find Sentarshadeen transformed once more. Snow had begun to fall during the night, making the whole city silent and white. As a result, he slept later than usual, only to be awakened by a messenger from the House of Sword and Shield, who had come to tell him that Master Belesharon had decreed that

there would be no classes today, so that all could honor the
first fall of snow.

Kellen stood in the doorway, wrapped in his house robe,
watching the messenger leave. He stared up at the sky, then
looked away quickly, blinking and shaking his head.

Snow was *dusty*. And cold.

He brushed his face clean and stepped back inside, closing the door and frowning suspiciously.

Idalia had described snow, of course. It was fluffy frozen
water that fell from the sky in winter whenever it felt like it.
But they'd barely had rain in the City, and the only snow
Kellen had ever seen was either already on the ground in
the City parks—since the Mages in charge of the weather
made sure it fell only on the parks, and only at night—or
sold in the City markets in Preservation-spelled containers.
It had not been coming down from the sky as if it would fall
forever.

He wasn't sure he liked it.

"Was there someone at the door?" Idalia slid open the
door of her sleeping room and poked her head out, her
sleeping-braids hanging loose about her face. "It's snowing,"
she added unnecessarily.

"Vinshan came to tell me that there are no classes today.
We're to honor the snow," Kellen said, hoping he didn't
sound too grumpy about it. He didn't know why, but the
snow made him feel uneasy. As if there were something bad
about it.

"Then I guess you should do that. At least it will be
warmer now that it's started snowing," Idalia said, which
certainly didn't make any sense.

She retreated back into her room and came out a few moments later, her braids secured on top of her head with a few
bone pins, and wrapped in her favorite winter house robe.
She moved immediately to the stove and began building up
the fire.

Kellen went over to the window and stared gloomily out at
the snow. It sifted down steadily, making everything white.

Even the pines in the forest opposite had turned a pale silvery grey. The only spot of color in the landscape was the surface of the swiftly-moving river below.

"Will you stop pacing, please?" Idalia said a few minutes later. "You're acting like a caged bear."

Kellen came to himself with a start, realizing he'd been doing exactly that.

"The tea's ready. Go get dressed. Have something to eat. Maybe that will settle you down."

Sheepishly, Kellen retreated to his room, dressing in warm working clothes, a half-formed notion brewing in his mind. Master Belesharon had said it would be safe to ride again once the snow had started, after all. And Vinshan hadn't said Kellen *couldn't* go down to the House of Sword and Shield, only that there were going to be no lessons today. Maybe a workout with Deyishene was just what he needed to take the fidgets out. And that would be honoring the snow, wouldn't it?

He came back out and accepted a cup of tea from Idalia, but when she offered him the plate of breakfast pastries, Kellen found that he wasn't really hungry. He tucked a couple of the dried fruit ones into his pockets for later—if he didn't want them, Deyishene would relish the treat.

"Are you feeling all right?" Idalia asked, sounding worried.

"I'm fine," Kellen said, forcing himself to sound as if her question didn't make him want to scream. "It's just . . . well, snow takes some getting used to, you know. It doesn't seem natural; maybe that's what's getting on my nerves."

Idalia smiled. "I keep forgetting you haven't seen very much wild weather. And the snow's going to be especially heavy this winter because the weather patterns are still settling back to normal. But you'll soon get used to it. And it's quite beautiful really."

"And warmer," Kellen said sardonically.

"Warmer than bright clear days where everything's covered in ice. Really. You'll see," Idalia said. "Not a *lot* warmer, I'll grant you that, but even a little can seem like a lot in winter. And snow is easier to walk in—and over—than ice. Now that it's finally come, we can trade our sabatons for snowshoes, and the going will be a lot easier."

"If you say so," Kellen said doubtfully. He set down his empty teacup. "I think I'll get going." He rubbed his head.

"Headache?" Idalia asked.

"Not really. Everything just feels . . . tight. I'll feel better with a little fresh air and exercise."

But the feeling didn't go away on the walk down to the stables, and by the time Kellen reached them, he felt definitely unsettled. It wasn't anything like the feeling he'd had when he'd faced the Endarkened Barrier—nothing in the world could compare to that!—but it was almost like *remembering* that feeling. He felt touchy and out-of-sorts, and was glad there was no one around to see him but the horses. The stable was fuller than he'd ever seen it, with a number of the animals having come in to seek shelter from the snow. An equal number, of course, were reveling in it, romping and rolling in the icy stuff, kicking up great plumes of white. All of them were in full winter coat by now, their heavy coats making them look round and shaggy, not at all the sleek gleaming creatures they were at high summer.

Deyishene was glad to see him, of course, but the Elven mare seemed to catch some of his mood as soon as Kellen put his hands on her. Though she'd let him groom her, and was happy to eat both his breakfast pastries, every time he tried to put a saddle on her back she made it clear in no uncertain terms that she wasn't having any, and at last he gave up. Not only the weather, but his lady was playing him false today.

When he finally put the tack away, she followed him to the tack room, nuzzling at his neck and shoulder as if to try to apologize for something she couldn't explain. Kellen patted her shoulder resignedly.

"Never mind, Deyishene. I guess I'm just not having any luck today. I'd better go find some place quiet to drown myself," he said with a halfhearted grin. "That is, if I don't have to break the ice to do it!" *Someplace where I won't make trouble for myself that I just have to clean up later when I'm feeling better.*

The unicorn meadow and the Flower Forest beyond was the obvious destination. If he was lucky, he might run into Shalkan, who might be able to talk him out of this peculiar mood, or at least provide a counter-irritant—since Shalkan could be *very* irritating when he tried. And the Flower Forest was beautiful enough to make anyone feel better, and it was always warm in there.

Maybe he just missed Sandalon more than he thought he would. Even though sending the Elven children to the Crowned Horns had been a sensible decision, their leaving had cast a pall over all of Sentarshadeen.

Yes, the unicorn meadow was a good choice. But he needed to stop at home first—for a dry cloak and boots, a cup of tea, and to see if there was anything in the pantry that might serve as unicorn-bribes. If he was lucky, Idalia might be out (honoring the snow herself, he had no doubt) and he wouldn't inflict his sour mood on her.

But when he got home, not only was Idalia there, Vestakia was with her.

IDALIA had been relieved to see Kellen leave that morning. He was radiating distress like a beacon—finally strong enough to notice it himself, though Idalia had known there was something not-quite-right for a sennight.

But that wasn't really it. It wasn't that something was not-quite-right. It was that *Kellen* felt there was something not-quite-right, and that even he didn't feel it strongly enough to notice it consciously. She only sensed him sensing it because she knew him so well. And finally it was starting to come toward the surface of his conscious attention.

She didn't want to say anything, lest she disrupt the fragile process of his magic—assuming it was Knight-Magery at work, and not just growing pains—and cause him to lose the intuition completely. So she kept quiet, although if there were going to be many more days like today, she might just settle for burying him in the nearest snowbank and see if he'd figured the matter out by spring thaw.

She'd spent a soothing and solitary morning preparing a batch of Drawing Salve—a similar sort to the one Jermayan had used on Kellen's hands, and a delicate process because many of the herbs and oils involved were poisonous in the wrong quantities—and was just preparing to charge it when there was a knock at the door.

She opened the door to find Vestakia standing there, bundled in a violet and mulberry cloak crusted with snow, looking as bedraggled and woebegone as a half-drowned kitten.

"Vestakia!" Idalia said, surprised. "What's wrong?"

"Oh, *I* don't know," Vestakia burst out, sounding frustrated, irritable, and apologetic all at the same time. "I just . . . I . . . there's just something not *right,* is all, I didn't want to be alone, and I wasn't quite sure where else to go."

"Well, come in and have some tea. You look half-frozen. And tell me what seems to be the problem," Idalia said, resigning herself to the fact that no more work would get done today. But friends came first, and the poor child looked half out of her mind with worry.

"It isn't—the Enemy," Vestakia said immediately, stepping inside and hanging up her cloak to dry. "You know I would have warned everyone if I'd felt anything like that. I just woke up with the worst headache, and nothing I can do will make it go away! I even tried snowpacks, the way I did in the mountains. I was hoping there was something you could do to help?"

"Perhaps a little willowbark syrup?" Idalia suggested.

"But I *tried* that!" Vestakia cried pettishly. "Nothing works. I just feel as if I'm about to fly into a thousand pieces."

"Well come and sit down and have a cup of tea. I'll see if I can make something up that will help," Idalia said soothingly.

Now this was puzzling. First Kellen, now Vestakia—and Vestakia was normally the most well grounded of people, with no particular magical Gift, other than her ability to sense the nearness of Demons or strong Demonic Taint. Yet Idalia felt nothing at all.

Vestakia said that her headache had nothing to do with Demonic activity, and she should know if anyone did, yet if willowbark syrup hadn't had any effect on it, Idalia hesitated to offer her anything stronger. Still, a little something to calm her nerves wouldn't come amiss, and do no harm. While the tea was brewing, she went to her shelf of tinctures and syrups—it was much easier to work with a number of medicinal herbs when they had been refined this way—took down an Elvenware cup from the shelf, and prepared a quick mixture, including a healthy dose of strong syrup of chamomile. She diluted it with a measure of white brandy, and stirred it thoroughly, then brought it over to Vestakia.

"Here. Drink this. It should help."

Vestakia took a deep breath and gulped it down quickly— herbal medicines were not noted for tasting good. She choked only slightly, and took a deep breath afterward. "Thank you. I hate to be so much trouble—"

Idalia smiled. "Oh, don't be silly! It's a positive relief to have someone come in and ask me straight out for what they want, for a change, you know. I do love the Elves, but even when they think they're being direct, every conversation always starts with half an hour's prattle about clothing and the weather—the weather is obvious, and I'm not that interested in clothes, you know!"

She was relieved to see that she'd won a faint smile from Vestakia. Though it was impossible to tell whether Vestakia was looking pale—since her skin was always a deep cherry-red—Idalia could tell that the lines of tension were starting to fade from around her eyes and mouth, though the girl was still very keyed-up. "And now, I think the tea is ready."

They were just finishing their first cup—Idalia had had little success in getting any more information out of Vestakia about her unsettled condition—when Kellen showed up again.

If anything, he looked even more rattled than when he'd left several hours before. He'd obviously been out in the snow for most of that time, because his cloak and boots were crusted heavily with snow in the process of turning to ice. He looked sheepish and disgruntled, and not very pleased to find people there.

"Oh . . . hi," he said ungraciously.

"Hi yourself," Idalia said. "You look like a soggy, half-frozen snow-rat. Go change into some dry things, then come say hello to Vestakia. She's got the same headache you have."

Kellen looked rather thunderstruck by the idea that he had a headache at all, but meekly went and did as he was bidden. He went off to his room, coming back a few minutes later in fresh clothes, his other cloak bundled under his arm. He managed to smile at both of them, though Idalia could see he was making a real effort to do so.

"I'm not really fit company for anyone today—human or otherwise, so Deyishene tells me—so I thought I'd take a walk up to the unicorn meadow and let Shalkan tell me off. I thought I'd stop back here and see if I could find any suitable bribes, first, though."

"As luck would have it, I have a few things," Idalia said, smiling, "though with the drought, the sugaring certainly isn't what it ought to be this year. Have some tea while I make you up a package. Have you eaten?"

Kellen winced, shaking his head. "I'll eat later." He poured himself a large mug of tea, though, and dropped in several of the crystallized honey-disks that were the usual form of sweetening.

"Why don't you take Vestakia with you?" Idalia said suddenly. "I'm sure she'd like to see Shalkan again." And if the source of Vestakia's unease was the same as Kellen's, maybe throwing the two of them together would bring it to light more quickly.

She saw Kellen frown, then his face abruptly cleared as if the notion suddenly struck him as a good one as well.

"Oh, no," Vestakia said quickly. "You said you wanted to be alone—"

"I said I was horrible company," Kellen corrected her. "If you don't mind that, you're more than welcome to come along—if you don't mind a hike through a blizzard. And maybe Shalkan won't beat me up as much if he has an audience, though I doubt it."

"Blizzard!" Vestakia scoffed. "This little bit of snow? In the Lost Lands, we call this autumn! I'd love to go with you, if you don't mind."

"Then it's settled," Idalia said quickly. "Only you'd better take my cloak, Vestakia. I don't think yours is dry yet. I'll spread it out in front of the stove while you're gone, and it should be dry by the time you get back."

KELLEN found he was actually glad of Vestakia's company as they walked through Sentarshadeen in the direction of the unicorn meadow.

Everyone seemed to be taking a holiday from their regular tasks today. Kellen saw a number of Elves with brooms out in front of their houses, sweeping the paths clear of snow—a fruitless task, it seemed to him, as the stuff was still falling. Larger, horse-drawn brooms were going through the streets, making sure that only an inch or two of snow stayed atop the ice. Everyone worked to clear the snow away, but—this being Sentarshadeen—it was not simply being left in piles at the edges of the road. Certainly not. Everywhere there was space and raw material, fantastic shapes were rising—half sculpture, half structure—so that a second city, marmoreal and evanescent, seemed to be rising in the interstices of the true Sentarshadeen. Kellen and Vestakia moved slowly through the streets, admiring the display. It was strange and beautiful, and it made him feel better than he had all morning.

"I just hate all this waiting," he said to Vestakia, as they reached the edge of the city and left the snow sculptures behind. "I know that it isn't really waiting—I'm training to be a Knight, and learning so much I need to know—but at the same time, we're all just waiting to see what They're going to do next, and that just doesn't feel right. When I think about it too much, it starts to drive me crazy. But it's not that I want there to be a war . . . "

"I know," Vestakia said mournfully. "It's stupid, but I keep having this horrible feeling that something's happening—or has happened—that I ought to know about, that I just can't sense. But I wouldn't be able to sense it, would I, unless it was *Them*, or *Their* magic, and that can't happen anywhere near here, can it?"

"So Andoreniel and Ashaniel say," Kellen said broodingly, his dark mood returning full force. "But they didn't know about the Barrier, either, until Idalia found it. So I just don't know. You didn't always have the ability to sense *Them*. Maybe you're developing new abilities now."

"Oh, I hope not!" Vestakia burst out feelingly. "Not if it means I'm going to be sick all the time and not know why!" She rubbed her head and heaved a deep sigh.

"Well, maybe Shalkan will be able to give you some good advice. Look, there's Songmairie. He should be around here somewhere. We'll just—"

But suddenly Vestakia sank to her knees, groaning. She pointed wordlessly off in the direction of the hills, shaking her head in pain.

Kellen didn't stop to question. He drew his sword—he wore it everywhere these days as a matter of habit—and took off running in the direction she'd pointed.

The snow gave him good traction. It was deep, but not so deep that it slowed him down very much—not a Knight who had survived the worst Master Belesharon had managed to throw at him so far. As he ran, he summoned up his spell-sight. The world shifted subtly. He could see exactly where he must go, though he couldn't see his destination yet. His magic lent strength and speed to his muscles, and Kellen fled over the snow with the speed of a running hare.

He topped the rise that led to the road out of Sentarshadeen and stopped, his battle-trance broken by the sight he saw before him.

The snow was dappled with blood. Lying in the snow was a unicorn mare. Her fur had been white once. Now it was streaked with blood, some old and brown, some red and fresh. All hers. Kneeling beside her were an Elven border guard and his unicorn mount. The fallen unicorn's ribs heaved as she gasped for breath.

Kellen ran down to join them.

"Get Idalia. *Now!*" he ordered.

The Elf stared at him for a moment in shock, as if he could not imagine where Kellen had sprung from, then swayed to his feet—almost ungracefully—and mounted his unicorn. The two of them sprang off in the direction of Sentarshadeen.

Kellen knelt down beside the fallen unicorn, set his sword within easy reach, and gently eased her head into his lap. "Easy, girl, easy," he said soothingly. "Help is coming."

He only hoped she could hear him. He wished he could heal her himself, but healing didn't come easily to him—not like it did to Idalia. He needed herbs and tools that he didn't have with him to summon that particular aspect of the Wild Magic.

Her body was painfully thin and wasted, as if she hadn't eaten for days, and there were deep claw marks covering her shoulders and haunches. Kellen wasn't sure what kind of animal could leave those marks. Maybe a bear? But bears should all be asleep at this season, and most animals in Nature wouldn't attack a unicorn to begin with. At least her horn was intact.

Shalkan arrived, leaning down to nuzzle gently at her face. The unicorn whimpered painfully, but did not open her eyes.

"Hush, darling, hush," Shalkan said, in a voice unlike any

Kellen had ever heard him use before. "It will be better soon. I promise."

"I sent for Idalia," Kellen said.

"Yes," Shalkan said. "I passed Sharmet on the way into the city." He seemed to gather himself to impart bad news, and gazed steadily into Kellen's eyes. "Her name is Calmeren. She was with the party sent to the Crowned Horns with Sandalon."

Kellen had the sense, all at once, of a pattern. No, more than a pattern, a *picture,* or perhaps a diagram, or—well, whatever it was, he knew, he *knew* what this meant, and why he'd been feeling ready to kill something and why Vestakia was feeling the same way! It formed like a crystal exploding into place around him, all of its lattice forming a whole he could, at long last, read.

"They were attacked by the Enemy," Kellen said. "Vestakia sensed it somehow. She was feeling awful today, and when Calmeren got close enough, she got sick."

"Taint," Shalkan said calmly. "It will be gone once Calmeren's been healed."

The two of them stayed with the wounded unicorn, Kellen gently brushing snow from her head. Others of the herd arrived, forming a protective circle around them, all gazing down at Calmeren in worried silence. It seemed a very long time until Idalia arrived, though Kellen knew she would have come as fast as she could.

She arrived on horseback, Sharmet and his rider running ahead. Idalia rode one of the horses that Kellen had seen plowing the city streets—obviously the quickest form of transportation she could grab. The unicorns scattered as she approached, bunching up into a small herd several yards distant.

"See if you can get her to drink this," Idalia said, handing Kellen a waterskin. "And you," she said to Sharmet's rider, "go and see if Vestakia's all right. She's back by the spring."

Kellen gently eased Calmeren's mouth open and squeezed some of the contents of the waterskin onto her tongue as

Idalia began to unpack her equipment. Even in the cold, he could smell a green minty scent. It wasn't just water, then.

Calmeren swallowed convulsively as the liquid trickled over her tongue, and then began to suck greedily at the waterskin. Her eyelids flickered, but she still didn't rouse.

Kellen smelled a whiff of burning as Idalia called the charcoal to light. She handed Kellen a large pot of salve.

"Put this on her injuries, but don't try to turn her. Just slop it on. It's sovereign for Taint, and will make it easier to heal her."

Kellen pulled off his gauntlets and scooped up large handfuls of the stuff. It was a bright violet color, and even in the cold it was as thin and drippy as honey. He wiped it on as gently as he could—Calmeren seemed to sigh with relief as soon as it touched her—emptying the jar, and then scrubbed his hands clean in the snow.

By then, Idalia was ready to begin. "Who will share the price of this healing?" she asked.

"We will—all of us." A black unicorn mare, who seemed to be the little group's leader, stepped forward and spoke.

Shalkan shook his head mutely, stepping back from Calmeren. "I'm sorry," he whispered, so low that only Kellen could hear.

"Me, too. I'll share," Kellen said. If Shalkan couldn't help Calmeren—he didn't understand but this was no time to ask questions—he'd take his friend's place.

"That should be more than enough to make this easy," Idalia said. She handed Kellen a knife, and at her direction, he gathered strands of hair from each of the waiting unicorns' manes, then presented the bundle to Idalia. She reached out and cut a few blood-soaked hairs from Calmeren's mane, added a few strands of her own hair, and pricked her finger to add her own blood to the mix, then tossed the little knot of hair onto the brazier.

Once again, Kellen felt the sheltering weight of Presence reach out to enfold them all—him, Idalia, Calmeren, all the other unicorns except Shalkan. But this time, there was a difference. Calmeren's body sizzled and smoked when the protective dome came down over it, as if there were something about her that could not survive within it. A dark oily smoke seemed to rise out of her coat, and especially out of her wounds. In a few moments, it was gone. Kellen felt light-headed, as if there had been a cost to do that much. But Calmeren's wounds still remained, stark and ugly against her matted fur.

"Now I can begin," Idalia said. She reached her hands out and held them over the unicorn, and green fire spilled out of them like water, striking the unicorn's coat and making it glow as if Calmeren were filled with the sun.

In a few moments—Kellen was always surprised at how quickly something so miraculous could run its course—Calmeren's wounds were healed. It was as if they simply melted away, sinking back beneath the surface of her coat as the flesh knitted together, though the salve and the streaks and clots of blood remained, matting the white fur.

Kellen didn't hear the Mageprice that the Powers asked of Idalia, of course—that was between her and her magic, though she might tell him if she chose. Whatever it was, he hoped it was something small and easy to pay; she was doing so much for Sentarshadeen these days that it hardly seemed fair that much more should be asked of her.

Kellen felt the protective shield disperse and the Presence depart once the healing Spell had run its course. Idalia was already dousing the brazier, scattering the coals in the snow, and packing her things away in her bag, then moving back, because her nearness would be uncomfortable for Calmeren and the rest of the herd.

"Is she going to be all right?" Vestakia asked, coming up behind Kellen. Her cloak was covered in snow where she'd fallen to the ground, but the pain in her voice was gone.

"Yes . . . now," Kellen said. "Idalia healed her."

The unicorn mare was already struggling toward consciousness. She opened her eyes—they were as green as Shalkan's—and gazed wildly around, breathing a shaky snort of relief at the sight of the unicorns.

"Home!" she gasped. She rolled onto her stomach, trying to get her legs under her to stand, but was obviously still very weak. Kellen and Vestakia hurried over to her, lifting and steadying her. She leaned heavily against Kellen, and he could feel that she was nothing more than skin and bones.

"Thank you," Calmeren said huskily. "I must see Andoreniel and Ashaniel at once! Coldwarg—others I have no name for—they attacked us within sight of the Crowned Horns. They carried off the children. All the rest are dead." Her head drooped in despair.

Ciradhel? Naeret? Dainelel? Emessade? Kayir? He'd trained with all of them in the House of Sword and Shield. Naeret had taught him *xaqiue*. Ciradhel had helped to teach him to ride. He'd practiced with Dainelel a hundred times. They'd all gone with the convoy.

And Calmeren said they were all dead, killed by Shadow Mountain.

"I fought and fought—but they took the children and killed the rest. All the rest—all gone—all gone." Her head hung down to her knees, and her sides heaved. Unicorns couldn't weep, or at least, if they could, Kellen had never seen it happen, but the sorrow and despair in her voice was enough to bring tears to *his* eyes. "There was nothing I could do."

"You brought us warning," Shalkan said quietly. "That is a very great deal."

"I should have known!" Vestakia burst out. "I should have known that was why I felt so strange!"

"We should all have known that *They* wouldn't just leave us in peace," Kellen said bitterly. "But we didn't."

"Do you think you can walk as far as the House of Leaf and Star?" Idalia asked. "I've healed you, but you're still very weak. You'll need rest, and care, and food."

But the unicorn's head came up again at that. "I have to go

back," Calmeren said, sounding frantic. "I have to save the children!"

"No," Kellen said, his voice hard. "You have done your duty, and more than your duty, Calmeren. You aren't strong enough, even healed; now your duty is to pass the task on to someone else. You only have to tell me where to go. I'll save them. That's my job."

⇌

LESS than an hour later, the Elven Council had gathered again. This time Vestakia was present as well, so that they could hear what she could tell them about what she had sensed that morning.

On the way to the House of Leaf and Star, Kellen had heard the rest of what Calmeren had to tell him.

"Not the Enemy—" Calmeren shuddered. "And not Elves. But enemies!" She shook her head so hard she staggered, and Shalkan, walking beside her, leaned into her to steady her.

She'd managed to slip away as the hooded ones moved among the wounded Knights and unicorns, finishing off any who still lived. She knew—she *knew* that she was only one wounded unicorn, and that to stay would be to die, but to run would be to bring help. So she had run, as hard as she could, stopping for nothing, back along her trail to bring warning to Sentarshadeen. Along the way, she'd seen the slain bodies of the rest of her friends—every Knight, every servant, every destrier that had ridden out from Sentarshadeen a fortnight ago was dead.

"But they did not die alone," Calmeren said with grim satisfaction. "They were able to take some of their attackers with them, and so I could see what else had been hunting us. Ice-trolls and frost-giants. A small war-band, but enough."

"Both creatures of the Dark, long-time allies of Shadow Mountain," Shalkan said.

"And they knew exactly where to strike, and when," Kellen said. "And how to sneak right up on the caravan without being seen. How?"

"With help," Shalkan answered. "The question is . . . whose?"

—

NOW Kellen stood before the Elven Council and told them everything that Calmeren had told him.

"Calmeren said they were careful to take Sandalon and the other children alive," he finished. "That isn't good, but it's better than it could be. It means we have a chance of getting them back. First, we need to find them, and I think we have a way of doing that."

"Tell us," Andoreniel said simply.

"Vestakia can track them. You know she can sense when *They* are nearby, or when *They*'re working strong magic." He glanced at Vestakia.

She bowed her head a little. "Yes. I could sense the presence of the Demontaint on Calmeren when she came close enough—I think my powers are growing stronger. If there is Demontaint near the Crowned Horns, I should be able to follow the trail it leaves." She brought her head up again, and now her eyes shone with tears, and with anger, as well as justifiable fear. "I will gladly do all I can to rescue the children."

Kellen patted her shoulder, knowing what those brave words had cost her. If Vestakia fell into Demonic clutches, her fate would be too terrible to contemplate.

"While of course we all appreciate Vestakia's kind offer in the light in which it has been extended," Councilor Sorvare said, "it might be in the best interests of the children to consider matters carefully at this delicate pass. Certainly, as no one will deny, our ancient Enemy seeks to weaken us by striking at our most vulnerable point. We must analyze the situation carefully from all possible aspects before moving forward, lest we overlook an avenue of possible threat."

Kellen wasn't sure what Sorvare was getting at, but from the looks on Andoreniel's and Ashaniel's faces, they'd had no trouble at all unraveling his little speech.

"I say again—and for the last time—that I repose all trust in Vestakia," Andoreniel said, an edge of true anger in his voice. "She is a citizen of Sentarshadeen, as much as any of us here, and gladly and willingly do I place the life of my son in her hands."

Oh. *Oh.* Now that he'd had it translated for him, Kellen felt angry as well. Sorvare had as good as called Vestakia a traitor, saying she'd probably lead the rest of them into a Demon-trap.

"There is going to be a rescue party," Kellen said, cutting off Dargainon as he began to speak. "And you might as well resign yourselves to the fact that it is going whether or not you like it; debate all you want in our absence, but we are going, and going *now.* I am not going to leave the children in Enemy hands for a single moment longer than it takes to reach them. Idalia, Jermayan, Shalkan, Vestakia, and I have already agreed. You can send anyone else you like, but it leaves at first light tomorrow morning, and anyone who goes had better be able to keep up."

⚬

"I would say that you handed some of the Counselors a rather stinging rebuke," Idalia said, sounding surprisingly calm, as the three of them walked back toward the house a little while later. "I think you shocked them."

"How could he say something like that about Vestakia?" Kellen burst out.

"It's all right," Vestakia said. "I do know what I look like, Kellen."

"It's the Council's business to be cautious," Idalia added. "Not just to agree with everything Andoreniel and Ashaniel want to do."

"But not to be idiots," Kellen countered angrily. "For the Light's sake, Idalia, the Enemy has the *children!* And one of them is Sandalon! How could they stand there and even *think* about debating when every moment that passes could mean—"

"Well, you won," Idalia said, "and I don't think half the Council will ever get over the shock." Now she smiled, though grimly. "That's the price of having Wildmages around, and I think that they'd forgotten that. Now, Vestakia and I both have a lot of packing to do before morning—and shouldn't you get over to the House of Sword and Shield and see what knights you want to take with you for tomorrow?"

"Me?" Kellen said, stopping and staring at her in confusion.

"You," Idalia said, giving him a little push in the right direction. "You're the only Knight-Mage we've got—and unless I'm very much mistaken, you've just appointed yourself the leader of this rescue party."

THE cellar was damp and cold, located at the edge of the Low Quarter of Armethalieh. It was, however, well lit. Balls of Mage-light hovered near the ceiling, illuminating every corner with a spectral azure glow.

Before he'd become an Entered Apprentice, Cilarnen would not have been able to imagine that such a place could exist. That he had come to enter it at all, however, had little to do with that, and much to do with his new friend, Master Raellan.

In Master Raellan, Cilarnen had found an ally and confidant who did much to fill the aching void left by his father's continuing displeasure. Master Raellan shared Cilarnen's love for the City—and more, his fear that all was not as it should be.

Now that his eyes had been opened, Cilarnen could see the signs. Oh, not everywhere. There was no change in the lives of the Mageborn. But among the people they served, there were subtle indications everywhere he looked. Not of unrest, of course. But of confusion. All was not as it had always been in the Golden City, and the change was not for the better.

Despite the best efforts of the Provenders Councils,

prices were rising, and wages were not rising to match. Some foodstuffs had simply disappeared from the regular markets. And all because the High Council—pushed by Lord Volpiril—had removed Armethaliehan protection from the Home Farms. So far as Cilarnen knew, there was not actual *hunger* in the City yet, but the day was not far off when there would be. The sellers of small luxuries that did not happen to be edible were looking anxious; when bread cost twice what it had in the summer, people had to stop buying other things to afford it.

Something must be done. And if the High Council would not—or could not—set things right, then the Mageborn themselves must act. For the good of the City.

It was a terrifying thought, one that would have paralyzed him completely without Master Raellan's support. But Master Raellan seemed to know his thoughts almost before he voiced them. It was Master Raellan who assured him that many of the High Council felt just as he did. They merely needed to be brought to see that it was safe—in fact, vital—that they speak openly. Someone had to be brave enough to make the first move, to begin saying aloud what others only thought. Someone young, but known for his good sense and devotion to the City and his duty. Someone charismatic enough to lead.

Someone like Cilarnen . . .

Thus supported, Cilarnen began making cautious overtures among his fellow Entered Apprentices, to see which—if any of them—might have the wit and the stomach to do more than grumble around a table in the Golden Bells.

Gillain he dismissed at once. The young lord was far too reckless, and could not keep his mouth shut to save his life. Besides, he was notoriously scatterbrained—he'd actually managed to *lose* his City Talisman on more than one occasion! Viance and Flohan were too timid—while they were more sensible than Gillain, neither of them would be willing to do what it would take to save the City.

He would certainly have despaired had not Master Raellan

steered him gently toward a different group of Mageborn.

Jorade Isas was the great-great-grandnephew of the Isas who sat upon the Council.

Geont Pentres was the youngest son of House Pentres, a minor Mageborn House which was distantly allied to the Breulin line, and thus much at odds with the Volpirils at the moment.

Kermis Lalkmair's family had the rare and odd distinction of never having held a City office or a Council seat. The Lalkmair line produced scholars exclusively, and it was said that Lord Lalkmair would rather Burn the Gift out of one of his sons than see him hold a seat on any of the City Councils.

Tiedor Rolfort was the son of a tradesman. His Gift had appeared early, and he had been fostered with House Arcable. He had repaid the House's kindness with utter loyalty, and complete devotion to his new class.

Margon Ogregance was the son of High Mage Epalin Ogregance, who oversaw the Merchant's and Provender's Council. More than any of the others, he knew exactly what was going on with the City's food supply, and knew just how bad things were.

"We shall starve by spring," he said bluntly.

The other five stared at him in shock, unused to such plain speaking.

"Well?" Margon said impatiently. "Isn't that what you wanted to know? Isn't that why we're all here? Jorade—Cilarnen—Tiedor—Kermis—Geont—we didn't all slip away from our families and hide out in this drafty cellar to take tea."

"But . . . " Tiedor began.

"Starve," Margon repeated flatly. "The Home Farms can't—or won't—supply us with what we need at any price. I suspect the answer is that they can't; without us to control the weather and the pests, they have only enough to feed themselves. The Council has already authorized Father to contract with the Selkens for grain, but that's not to say it will get here in time. And one can't depend on foreigners, you know."

"Besides," Jorade said slowly, working it out, "to ask them to bring in food—and so much food—that tells them we're weak, doesn't it?"

"They'll attack us, not help us," Geont said, looking at Cilarnen. "And it's all *your* father's fault."

"The Peace of the Light be between you," Kermis said firmly, raising his hand. "If not for Lord Cilarnen, none of us would have the least idea how bad things really were, let alone that there might be something we could do about it."

"But what?" Tiedor asked.

And that, indeed, was the question.

The six young men looked at each other. Finding one another and daring to meet—and openly criticize the High Mages—had been hard enough, both to imagine and to do. To actually go from words to deeds . . .

"Master Raellan will know," Cilarnen said firmly. "We must try to come up with a plan, and I'm sure he will have an idea of how to implement it."

But though they talked until Second Night Bells rang out, none of them was able to come up with any practical notion of how they might cause the High Council to realize the gravity of the situation, or to avert the danger to Armethalieh that they all saw so clearly. They did manage to agree to meet here again in three days' time, with Cilarnen to bring Master Raellan if he could.

Seven

Discord in the City of a Thousand Bells

A girls' sewing-circle would make more efficient conspira-tors, Anigrel decided, entering the now-deserted cellar a chime later and triggering the spell that would release the stored memory of the boys' conversation into his consciousness. An evening's worth of pretty speeches, and not one sensible—or useful, from his point of view—suggestion among them. The young idiots could talk from now until the City walls crumbled around them, and do nothing more treasonous than flout curfew!

That would hardly be enough for Anigrel's purposes.

With a sigh, he dismissed the globes of Mage-light that the boys had forgetfully left burning. It would hardly do for anyone to wonder why Mageborn had been lurking here. Not just yet, anyway.

And it seemed he would have to take a more active hand in this "conspiracy" than he had first intended. It was just as his late father had said. *"If you wanted something done right, you had best do it yourself."*

⟵

IN the sennights that followed, Cilarnen found himself split into three people, and none of them got much sleep. There was Cilarnen the dutiful son and student, who attended lectures at the Mage College and ate his meals at House Volpiril. That role was easy to play: he'd been doing it all his life. And if it was harder now, it was only because he now knew there was so much more to Life than he had once thought. But he dutifully went through the motions, studying hard—for the High Magick obsessed him now more than ever—and being all that was polite to the father he saw ever more infrequently.

Then there was Cilarnen the Entered Apprentice, who went about his tasks throughout the City with ears open wide, listening closely for any scrap of gossip or careless word from the Mages he served, for anything he heard might come in useful later. In this role he practiced effacing himself completely. Gone were the lordly airs and mannerisms suitable to a son of House Volpiril; this Cilarnen made himself meek, and humble, and as invisible as the lowliest Entered Apprentice from the lowest-ranked House in all Armethalieh. He was no one of importance. He was only Cilarnen, a pair of hands to be called upon at need, and ignored when not actually being ordered about.

Last of all there was Cilarnen the Conspirator, who had learned a hundred ways of slipping out of House Volpiril by night, of stealing a few chimes here, half-a-bell there, for errands that served the City in ways that would horrify the City if it knew.

But all would come right in the end. He was sure of it.

⌒

"ARE you sure this works?" Jorade asked curiously, looking down at the small lump of silvery-grey stone in his palm.

"Of course it works. Haven't you ever seen umbrastone before? Here, I'll show you," Kermis said.

He took the lump of stone from Jorade's hand and set it down on the table. "Who's got a lantern?"

Several of them did—the back streets were dark at night, and it wouldn't do to advertise their Mageborn status by walking the streets lit by balls of Mage-light, after all. Margon produced his, and Kermis set it on the table beside the lump of umbrastone.

"Now light it. A Fire Spell's simple, right?"

Jorade simply glared at him. The spell to summon fire was the first one every student of the High Magick learned. He concentrated on the lantern.

Nothing happened.

"You've warded it," he accused.

"I swear by the Light—I haven't," Kermis said. "Try any spell you know. It won't work. Umbrastone eats magic. The only reason the Mage-lights are still glowing is because they were already lit when I brought this piece in. We couldn't cast them now, and if this were a bigger piece of umbrastone, it would put them out."

"How much magic can it eat?" Tiedor asked with interest.

"I'm not sure," Kermis admitted. "A lot. When it gets full, it crumbles away, though. I know that much from the books in my father's library."

"So we'll need a lot more," Cilarnen said thoughtfully. "For the guards, for the Stone Golems . . . enough to absorb all the spells the High Council will throw at us."

"Where are we going to get that much?" Geont demanded. "You're talking *pounds* of this stuff, and it took all our allowances together to bribe that Selken to bring in this much!"

"If I might make a suggestion . . . ?" Master Raellan said.

The boys turned and looked at him hopefully.

"Now that we have a sample to work with—and have proven that it will meet our needs—wouldn't it just be simpler to make it here? I grant you that it's a delicate process, and proscribed, of course, but I am not without certain resources myself, and among you, certainly you have the knowledge to oversee the work? Surely the recipe is to be found in one of your fathers' libraries?"

Anigrel waited with barely-concealed impatience, wondering if he was going to have to bring them the book from Lycaelon's library himself. He took care to stay well away from the small piece of umbrastone on the table, for if it touched him it would dispel the small glamouries of misdirection that disguised his true self. And even if Rolfort, Isas, Pentres, and Lalkmair weren't close enough to the seats of power to recognize him, both the Volpiril brat and young Ogregance would certainly recognize Arch-Mage Lycaelon's so-effacing private secretary.

At last Kermis spoke. "I think I can find it in my father's library. He never notices when I go in there, or what I do."

Anigrel breathed a faint inward sigh of relief. Once the manufactory for the umbrastone was in place—well, *that* was treason, pure and simple. And easy enough to hang High Mage Volpiril himself with it: yes, and any other members of the High Council he chose to implicate . . .

"How long will it take?" Geont asked. "To make enough, I mean?"

"Does it matter?" Margon answered. "The problem isn't going to go away. Or get better. White flour's being rationed in the Market now, and even the Commons are starting to wonder why. Father's been in meetings every day for the past moonturn, trying to figure out what to do about it. And the only thing possible is to get the Council to reverse its decree, and take the Home Farms back."

"But why can't they just *see* that?" Jorade said miserably.

"The High Council will never reverse itself," Cilarnen said bitterly. "Not when it means doing so publicly. By now everyone"—he meant, as his listeners knew, all the Mageborn—"knows about the decree to draw back the Borders to the City Walls. Lycaelon Tavadon was the only one who voted against the decree. That means that reversing the decree is endorsing the Arch-Mage, so they'll never do it."

"So the City suffers . . . for petty politics," Kermis said grimly.

"Unless young men like yourselves—who love the City, and who set themselves above such things—will save her," "Master Raellan" said.

The six young Entered Apprentices regarded each other. What they'd done so far was serious, but if it came to light, they could expect no worse than a severe scolding—at the worst, a censure from the Council. What they were contemplating now, each of them knew, had far graver consequences.

"We'll meet here again on Light's Day," Kermis said. "I should be able to get the book we need by then. We can study it to figure out what materials and equipment we need to buy—or steal." He looked at Cilarnen.

"If anyone wants to back out, do it now," Cilarnen warned. "Because once we start making umbrastone . . . well, there's no going back."

"I'm in," Jorade said.

"You know I am," Kermis said. "Light blast all politicians."

"And I," Tiedor said. "For the City—and the Mages."

"I know what the stakes are better than any of you," Margon said. "I won't back out now."

"If you're in, House Volpiril, so am I," Geont said gruffly. "You're twice the man your Light-damned father is."

"Thank you all," Cilarnen said warmly. "Then we'll meet back here on the day. And the Light go with you all."

⟿

ALL was proceeding perfectly, Anigrel thought to himself as he walked back toward House Tavadon. He was careful to take a more circuitous route than the boys, for they believed that "Master Raellan" was a younger son of a minor Mage House, and it would not do to have their illusions shattered. He might well wish to play this game again someday soon, with new players.

And what a splendid game it was! Lycaelon would certainly be furious to discover additional plots against him among the Mages, and the foiling of this one would provide him with all the leverage he needed to take back control of the Council from that eternal pest Volpiril.

And to further Anigrel's ambitions as well . . .

He reached the Mage Quarter, where no one would think it odd to find Undermage Anigrel upon the streets, even at this late hour, and a wave of his hand dispelled the glamourie, restoring his own natural appearance and that of his clothing. At length he achieved his own—or rather Lord

Lycaelon's—doorstep, passing between the stone mastiffs without incident, and a waiting servant hurried to open the door for him.

"Good evening, Undermage Anigrel," the butler said, bowing deferentially as he hastened to receive Anigrel's cloak.

"Good evening. Is the Arch-Mage at home?"

"Arch-Mage Lycaelon is still at the Council House, Undermage Anigrel," the butler said, bowing again.

"In that case, have a tray with a light supper brought up to my rooms in two chimes. See that I am not disturbed until then."

Anigrel passed through the panel and ascended the staircase, his immediate thoughts on a hot bath and one of the exquisite meals served up by Lycaelon's talented cook. Beyond that, there was much to do to ensure that the plot against the High Mages—such as it was—turned out satisfactorily.

For some people, at least.

TO create a measure of umbrastone took approximately three moonturns, once all conditions were right. And for all conditions to be right, as Cilarnen had discovered that Lightday, was one of the reasons that umbrastone was expensive, in addition to being proscribed.

There were a lot of ingredients that went into its manufacture. Some of them were rare and difficult to acquire—certain herbs and flowers—while others, such as gold and sea-pearls, were merely expensive. And some were just peculiar, like fresh chicken eggs. It seemed a lot more like *cooking* than like any branch of the Art Magickal than Cilarnen had yet studied.

Strangest of all, no spells seemed to be involved at any stage of the stone's manufacture.

"That's because this is the Art Khemitic," Kermis had explained when Cilarnen had questioned him. "It's Proscribed, of course, but its essential doctrine holds that the objects of the natural world have an elemental nature possessed of innate qualities, which, when combined in specific amounts, can create objects with certain powers."

"Sounds dangerous," Geont had said, with a look of distaste.

"It is," Kermis answered with a thin smile. "There are more warnings in this book than spells. Looks like fun, though, if you don't mind getting blown up."

"What do we do after we put all the things together?" Cilarnen had asked, trying to head off what had promised to be a lengthy debate.

"They have to be kept in total darkness at a constant temperature for three moonturns in a sealed container inside a special brazier. The Khemiticists call it an *athanor*."

"An *athanor*?" Margon had said in surprise. "*That's* a magickal tool? It's just an oven. The Baker's Guild uses them to extract oils from spicebark and finish delicate pastry. I can get one. They're kind of big, though."

"How big?" Cilarnen had asked warily.

Margon sketched a shape in the air with his hands.

"Not too bad," Tiedor said with relief. "My birth-father is a carter. He'll let me borrow one of the carts and teams, and he won't ask any questions if I tell him it's Mage-business. I can drive a cart and team, too." He regarded the rest of them, a faint smirk on his features, and Cilarnen felt a faint pang of . . . guilt? Relief?

He'd always looked down on Tiedor—who hadn't?—because of his Common blood. But it was just that—the fact that he came from the Commons and remembered what he'd learned there—that would make their plan work now.

"That's good then. And, Tiedor—thank you. I don't think this would work without you." He turned to the others. "We seem to have a plan. Margon will get us the *athanor*, Tiedor will get the cart to transport it here, Kermis will write out the list of materials that we need to make the umbrastone, and we'll all work on getting them. We can work out the rest of our plan while we're actually making the umbrastone."

IT was a good plan—Cilarnen had discovered, over the last several moonturns, that he had a talent for planning—and the first part of it went exactly as he intended. The *athanor* was acquired, installed, tested, and seasoned—both Margon and Kermis agreed on the necessity for that.

Obtaining the ingredients for the recipe took far more ingenuity, though the six of them were wealthy by any standards but those of the Mageborn.

But finally, almost two moonturns later, they were ready to begin.

It had not been an easy time for Cilarnen. He had the disturbing feeling that his father was watching him more closely than he had for a long time, and the gossip he overheard in his work as an Entered Apprentice was not encouraging. Though the City was protected from inclement weather, the Delfier Valley was not. And outside the City, the autumn storms had been ferociously hard; Cilarnen did not precisely understand the details or the logic, but apparently because of the bad weather, the farmers were withholding the rest of their food, just as Margon had warned would happen.

And what was the Council doing? Engaging in screaming debates (so it was rumored) as to whether—and if so, *how*—to continue its trade with the High Hills, now that it no longer had a Trading Outpost available in Nerendale. Would the caravans even be willing to come into Armethalieh as they had a generation ago? And if they were, would the Council be willing to allow them in?

Well, they won't have to. By spring, this will all be settled. I hope, Cilarnen told himself uneasily. He still wasn't sure what they were going to do once they *had* the umbrastone. The making of the stuff had turned out to be so complicated that none of them had even begun to discuss the next phase. Deep down in his heart, he just hoped that the Council would see how serious things were, and understand that they *had* to take the Home Farms back.

Perhaps he was going about this all wrong. Maybe he should just petition for a private audience with the Arch-Mage Lycaelon. It was every Mageborn's right—a right rarely invoked, but still the law of the City. He could ask the Arch-Mage what to do.

Tonight he'd been the first to arrive at their secret meeting place, and his train of thought was interrupted by the arrival of the others.

"I've brought wine," Geont said. "I think we'll need it."

Kermis shuddered faintly. "Well, I've brought tea—and decent water." He flourished a packet and a large flask. "Phastan Silvertip. I hope the pot's clean."

"And I've brought the mixing bowl," Jorade said, lifting a huge shallow container of pure gold from beneath his cloak and setting it on the shabby wooden table with a grunt. The rickety table creaked and shifted beneath the weight. "I borrowed it from the family chapel. Nobody will miss it—so long as it's back before Morning Devotions, of course."

"It will be," Kermis said. "And Tiedor?"

"One dozen hen's eggs, fresh from the hen and this morning's market," the young Entered Apprentice said. "The ways of Mages are mysterious," he added with a grin. "The silly woman had no idea why I'd want to be down in the Fowl Market buying my own eggs. She fluttered as much as one of her own geese!"

"Women!" Cilarnen agreed, dropping his own contribution into the bowl—eight ounces of white roses (heads only). The recipe had specified that they had to be cut precisely at sunrise without the use of metal, so Cilarnen had been unable to simply buy them in the Flower Market. Rather, he'd had to slip out of bed at an unspeakably early hour, make his way across the City to the Park, charm his way into one of the greenhouses with a tale of a youthful dare, and bribe one of the gardeners heavily to allow him to cut them with an ivory letter opener he'd sharpened for the purpose. And hope that nobody—like his father, or his tutors—checked up on his story, because it would be a little awkward to explain.

Though not nearly as awkward as the truth.

The eggs and the roses were the only fresh ingredients. The others they had been able to gather and store here over the last several sennights. As Tiedor carefully broke the eggs into the bowl—they weren't sure from the recipe whether to break them or not, but as Kermis pointed out, if they *didn't* break them, what they would have would be chickens—the others added the rest of the ingredients. Last of all, Kermis added several ounces of fluid—and rather poisonous—quicksilver, and then dropped in the original piece of umbrastone. It would form the raw materials in its own image, making the creation of new umbrastone more certain. It instantly sank to the bottom.

All of them stared down at the golden bowl full of peculiar and unappetizing varicolored slime. The quicksilver floated on the top, eddying around the broken eggshells and the rose-heads. It smelled . . . odd.

"Well it isn't going to do anything yet!" Kermis said, sounding irritable and nervous. "Help me pour it into the containment vessel. Then we'll light the *athanor.* Then we wait."

It took four of them to pick up the bowl now that it was full, and it hadn't been light to start with. The room was dark, lit only by entirely mundane lanterns, for Kermis was worried that any use of the Art Magickal would interfere with the delicate operation of the Art Khemitic. They would be using ordinary wood and coal to heat the oven, which meant that one of them would have to be here every day to make sure it stayed at the proper temperature.

Cilarnen locked eyes with Master Raellan across the lip of the bowl as the four of them lifted it in unison. Master Raellan gave him a small smile of triumph.

"Halt in the name of the High Council!"

Suddenly the cellar blazed bright with Mage-light. Cilarnen heard the clatter of Stone Golem feet on the steps leading down into the cellar. He didn't know who dropped the bowl first, only that it slipped from his hands to strike the floor with a ringing clang, spattering its noisome contents everywhere.

Spell-fed panic gripped him, and despite the Mage-light glare, it was suddenly hard to see. Cilarnen backed away from the mess on the floor until the wall jarred hard against his back.

"Run!" someone shouted, but there was nowhere to run to. There was only one entrance to the cellar, and it was filled with Stone Golems and grey-clad Journeyman Mages, their wands tracing glowing Glyphs of Containment in the air.

This has all gone terribly wrong. It was a ridiculously understated thing to think, and it was the last conscious thought Cilarnen had before one of the floating glyphs touched his face. It seemed to burst, stealing his senses from him.

⟞⟝

ANIGREL watched with grave approval as the Stone Golems carried the last of the unconscious conspirators from the cellar. It had been the work of an instant for Master Raellan to vanish, and Undermage Anigrel, here on the Arch-Mage's orders, to take his place. And though the children might speak of Master Raellan all they liked, no one would ever be able to locate the fellow, no matter how hard they searched—which would only add to the High Mages' paranoia once the full extent of this night's work was disclosed. It would be obvious that the children were merely the spearhead of a conspiracy to destroy the very fabric of life as the City knew it.

At least, it would be once he was through explaining things to Lycaelon.

⟞⟝

"THE conspirators have been secured, my lord."

Anigrel stepped into Lycaelon's private office in the

Council House. Outside, the single carillon of Midnight Bells rang through the night air.

"Good." A flame of triumph kindled in Lycaelon's grey eyes. "And their fathers?"

"Remain—so far—in ignorance that their activities have been discovered," Anigrel said smoothly.

"You feel they were involved as well?" Lycaelon said sharply.

"My lord, how could they not be?" Anigrel said, feigning surprise. "Young men of good families . . . how could they mount a conspiracy of this magnitude without assistance from their families? Could young Lalkmair have gained access to the information he needed to create umbrastone without his father's assistance, for example? And I'm sure you will find, when you question them, that there are others involved as well. Assuming their memories have not already been erased by magick to protect their fellow conspirators, of course." There! That should do much to explain the inconvenient fact that Cilarnen and the others would insist they were alone in their plans.

He watched as Lycaelon contemplated the prospect.

"There must be trials," he said at last. "There can be no accusations without evidence of guilt. But it is a time for the testing of fealty, Anigrel. Yes, and a time to reward loyalty."

"Trials, of course," Anigrel said smoothly, "but you will wish to proceed with the utmost caution, naturally. It seems obvious that this is yet another attempt by the Wildmages to subvert our ranks, for who else would need to weaken our magick in order to replace it with their own? Further, it now seems clear that Lord Volpiril has been involved all along, and that his insistence on reducing the borders of our influence is in fact another aspect of this very conspiracy. He will have to resign his Council seat at the very least—and as for Cilarnen, I imagine the Council will recommend Banishment, don't you?"

Lycaelon smiled. "Indeed. Banishment for Cilarnen and for the tradesman's whelp—and that means the re-enlargement of our Borders to make that punishment more than a meaningless reprimand. Volpiril, Isas, and Breulin—at the very least—will lose their Council seats over this night's work."

Anigrel merely nodded, and schooled his face into an expression of humility.

"And that leaves vacancies on the Council," Lycaelon continued. "And I know precisely whom I intend to appoint to one of those places. Oh, it hasn't been done for centuries, but there is precedent for it. I have the power. I shall raise you, my *loyal* aide, to the rank of High Mage at once, and you shall take Volpiril's place, to serve me loyally as he never did."

Anigrel waited a beat, as if the news had not actually penetrated, then assumed a look of mingled pleasure and surprise. Not shock; shock would be a little too much. "My Lord!" he said, gazing at the Arch-Mage. "I—I hardly know what to say!"

"And I do not think I shall fill the other vacancies at all," Lycaelon went on, with grim satisfaction. "Let those seats stand empty, rather than being occupied with those who would only become my enemies."

The next few bells were full of feverish activity; messages sent and received, certain Mageborn notified, certain of them kept in ignorance. And through it all, Anigrel worked quietly at Lycaelon's elbow, as if nothing had changed. Which was exactly what Lycaelon wanted, of course.

So now he would be a member of the High Council, Anigrel thought to himself. And afterward—little though Lycaelon might suspect it at the moment—they would go on winnowing the ranks of the Council of those who were not perfectly loyal to the Arch-Mage.

The Arch-Mage and his so-devoted acolyte.

THEY were somewhere underground, that much Lairamo knew for certain. Despite her best intentions, she had lost consciousness several times during that frightful aerial journey, when she had dangled far above the surface of the ground, half-frozen and battered by the winds of the storm.

When she had regained consciousness, it was dark. She could smell damp stone, and knew by the stillness of the air that she was somewhere far beneath the earth's surface, in a tunnel or a cave. She was being carried in some kind of sling by beings who did not need light to see by, and had not known whether to pray that the children were with her, or not. She knew that if they were not with her, they were surely dead, but perhaps death was better than her own eventual fate.

But as they traveled, each step making her sway nauseatingly back and forth in her sling, faint sobs and whimpers told her that at least some of the children still lived.

At last their journey ended. There was a break in the darkness; a patch of eldritch purple light, almost blinding after the unrelieved darkness. Having a point of reference in the blackness made Lairamo feel even more ill. She had no choice but to close her eyes tightly.

She opened them again as the sling was being set down. The source of the violet light was now visible: a thick encrustation of luminous lichen high on the walls of the small grotto.

Her captors' forms were concealed in deep hooded cloaks. They moved with silent efficiency, and even though she knew she ought to try to find out why they had been brought here, Lairamo was afraid to speak to them. There was something about these silent creatures that horrified her: somehow—even though they were completely muffled in shapeless cloaks—Lairamo could tell that there was something about them that was so deeply, poisonously *wrong* that it revolted her very nature.

They quickly deposited their burdens and departed, as silently as they had done everything else. The moment they were gone, she raised her head and counted the slings.

Six. She got to her feet, pushing the enveloping folds of her sling aside, and hurried among the bundles. She began unfurling them, wrinkling her nose at the odd, fusty odor they exuded. All the children were there, and safe—some unconscious, some merely terrified into unblinking immobility. She caught up Sandalon and Kalania in her arms, unable to think of what to do next. The children were groggy from cold and shock. Sandalon clung to her wordlessly and tiny Kalania trembled, too terrified to cry.

Lairamo looked around, clutching the youngest children to her. Apparently they were to be kept alive for a while, for the edges of the cavern were piled with boxes and bundles, some bearing the marks of great age.

"Alkandoran!" she said, calling out his name until the boy roused. The teenager sat up slowly, looking around groggily and then with increasing apprehension.

"Look through those bundles. Get the others to help you. We need to find a brazier or something that will serve as one, and some way to start a fire. It is cold in here. We need light—and heat."

"Yes, Nurse Lairamo." Alkandoran was not so many years away from having had a nurse of his own, and from his expression, Lairamo could see that it was far easier for him at the moment to take orders than to think about where he was.

Tredianala, Merisashendiel, and Vendalton had freed themselves from their hammocks at the sound of familiar voices, and were looking around with a growing curiosity. Lairamo didn't think it had occurred to the younger children yet that the others were dead, and if the Gods of Leaf and Star were kind, it might not occur to them for a long time to come.

"Come on," Alkandoran said sturdily. "We need to look for useful things."

Merisashendiel and Vendalton were eager to help. Tredianala, the more timid of the cousins, came and curled up next to Lairamo.

"Will we be going home soon?" she asked trustingly, leaning her head against Lairamo's shoulder.

"Soon, I hope," Lairamo said, since it would hardly do to tell the child the truth: that they might be going home to the

Gods, but they would almost certainly never see Sentarshadeen again.

She doubted anyone at all had survived the massacre.
Creatures that could outrun unicorns—and kill them, as she
had seen, to her horror—must certainly have destroyed
everyone else in the caravan first. There would be no one left
to warn Sentarshadeen that they had been taken, and though
the Fortress of the Crowned Horns would know they had not
arrived on schedule, it would be sennights before they could
send word to Sentarshadeen to warn Ashaniel and Andoreniel of the disaster.

And by then . . . whatever fate was planned for them
would surely have befallen them. And where could their rescuers begin to look for them?

"I found a brazier!" Alkandoran cried delightedly, tipping
the pieces out of their bag with a clatter and peering at them in
the dimness. Further discoveries followed: lanterns, and oil,
some odd amber-colored, waxy cylinders that Lairamo identified as candles—something the Elves did not use—and
thankfully enough charcoal to keep the two braziers Alkandoran had found burning for quite some time, though they would
have to be careful of the toxic fumes. Still, the air seemed
fresh enough now that Lairamo thought they probably had
more to worry about from the cold than from suffocating.
Down here the air was always cold, and there was the danger
of falling into a body-chilled lethargy that could end in death.

Though perhaps that might not be a bad end . . .

Most of the looted goods that had been left for them were
of Elven manufacture, but there was enough of peculiar and
unfamiliar design—and therefore probably of human
origin—to suggest that their captors had plundered human
trade-caravans as well as Elven ones.

There were no blankets—at least they'd found none so
far, though there were many more bundles to search through,
and searching should keep the children occupied for at least
a while. Lairamo sighed. Perhaps the peculiar slings could
be used as blankets.

"Light two of the lanterns first, Alkandoran. We'll feel better with some light."

The boy hurried to comply—his hands shook only a little—and the shadows rushed back as the welcoming golden light blossomed. In the stronger illumination, the fungal glow disappeared, the lichen becoming merely a greyish encrustation on the cavern walls.

"The walls glitter!" Merisashendiel cried, pointing.

It was true. Beyond the reach of the lichen, the pale walls and ceiling of the cave glittered in the lantern light like a snowfield in the sun.

"Crystals," Vendalton said. "Sometimes they grow a lot bigger than that."

"They look like eyes," Tredianala whispered, burrowing in closer to Lairamo.

"They are *not* eyes," the nurse said firmly. "As Vendalton said, they are crystals, which are often found in caves. Now, Merisashendiel, you may light one of the braziers, after which it will be a great deal more comfortable in here. And Tredianala, you may fold up those . . . slings. Tidily, now, and be sure not to tangle them."

"I don't want to touch them, Nurse Lairamo," the girl whimpered.

"We all do a great many things we do not wish to do in life," Lairamo said firmly. The child was all set for a nasty bout of hysterics, and if she gave vent to them she would certainly set the others off. And they could not afford that. "You will oblige me now."

Her firmness worked. Tredianala gave her a look equally compounded of hurt and resentment, and went off to fold up the peculiar hammocklike slings.

"The rest of you: go through all the bundles and sort the contents neatly. I wish to know everything that is here, and how much there is of everything. Tredianala may help you, when she has finished her task."

A ragged chorus of "Yes, Nurse Lairamo," greeted her latest order, and the children—all but Kalania and Sandalon—set to work.

Once some of the lanterns were filled and lit, and the lit brazier began radiating heat, everything seemed less nightmarish, but no less terrifying. Lairamo only hoped the children didn't really realize the extent of their danger, though she suspected, from the look on Alkandoran's face, that the youngster knew perfectly well that they were in deep trouble. He said nothing, though, simply taking charge of the others in sorting out the stockpiles.

Lairamo tucked her cloak more tightly around Kalania and Sandalon. At the movement, Sandalon raised his head.

"It's my fault," he whispered, so low that only she could hear. "We're here because of me." There was an unchildlike bitterness in his voice.

"My heart—no!" Lairamo said, hugging him tightly.

But he shook his head, for the first time contradicting her. "Yes. I am the Prince. And my father is King. We are here because of me."

⌒

THE rescue party from Sentarshadeen left at first light the following morning: Kellen, Shalkan, Jermayan, Vestakia, Idalia, and six Elven knights, all that could be gathered at such short notice. A second party was being assembled, which would follow with additional supplies and as many knights as Andoreniel could call up quickly; Calmeren would be able to lead them as far as the place from which the children had been taken. But it would be at least a sennight before the larger rescue party was ready, and it would only be able to travel at wagon-speed. Kellen had no intention of waiting for anything or anyone.

Elven palfreys had been found for Idalia and Vestakia. Though the two women could certainly have ridden pillion with Jermayan and Kellen, Shalkan and Valdien might need to be able to carry other passengers later, and every rider was burdened with their own supplies: journey-food, of course, but they must also carry supplies and medicines for those they hoped to rescue.

The caravan had taken nearly two sennights to reach the ice-meadows below the Crowned Horns, and die. Calmeren, wounded, running flat-out at a unicorn's top speed, had covered the same distance—in the opposite direction—in a little over two days, though it had cost her dearly.

It was five days before Kellen's party reached the spot, rising before dawn and riding long after sunset, and pausing only when neither man nor beast could place one foot in front of the other.

The first thing they encountered was the place where the guard of Elven knights had faced the coldwarg pack. The remains of the dismembered bodies of Elves and horses still remained after a sennight, half-buried in new snow, and strangely undisturbed by the natural predators known to inhabit these mountains.

"No natural beast will feed from a coldwarg kill," Jermayan said, rising to his feet and brushing his gauntlets free of snow. They had stopped long enough to uncover one or two of the bodies, for as important as it was to rescue the captive children, they dared not rush to that rescue blindly. "We cannot tarry now to send you to your final rest, my friends," he said, looking around at the snow. "But do not fear. We shall return for you. You will not lie in the dark earth, but return to the wind, and the stars."

"The caravan road lies in that direction," Idalia said, pointing. "I flew over it often enough when I was a Silver Eagle. They must have heard the 'wargs coming and split the party, half of them riding toward the pack, the rest fleeing toward the Crowned Horns, and safety . . . or so they hoped."

"They wanted to slow the pack, to give the unicorns as much of a head start as they could," Shalkan said. He put his head down, sniffing at a drift of snow and then beginning to paw at it. "But the coldwarg weren't hunting alone." He nudged his prize free.

"What's that?" Kellen asked, walking over and picking it up. He stood it on end and regarded it curiously. It was a club—he could see that much—black and polished with use, and very nearly as tall as he was. But that really didn't answer the question of *what* it was.

"Frost-giants—just as Calmeren said." A knight named Artaliar spoke up. "The pack was traveling with frost-giants." His voice was a mixture of disgust and despair.

Jermayan sighed, shaking his head. "It should not have been possible."

"Vestakia?" Kellen asked.

She shook her head. "Nothing here."

"Then let's go on."

THEY stopped at the wagons only long enough to make certain that no survivors had taken refuge there—a slim hope, but one they had to make sure of. Something had been at them after the party had abandoned them; they had been looted—or vandalized, or searched; by now it wasn't quite clear; and whatever had done it had left traces that made Shalkan and the other two unicorns wrinkle their muzzles in disgust, and made Vestakia look distinctly uncomfortable.

But there was no one alive, and no clues that would help them in their search, so the party rode on.

FINALLY they reached the killing ground where all but Calmeren had died. Some freak of weather had swept the area free of new snow, and the bodies of the Elven knights and the unicorns in their armor glittered starkly against the field of ice like savagely disjointed dolls.

They smelled the battlefield before they saw it. Even in

the cold, something here was decaying, and the smell was worse than anything Kellen had ever encountered—worse than cleaning out Perulan's cesspit back in Armethalieh, worse than the sensory derangement at the Black Cairn. The Elven destriers, well-trained and battle-tried as they were, balked at approaching it, and rather than force them, the party left them with the unicorns to guard them, and approached the site on foot.

Today the air was still, the weather was clear and bright. The harsh mountain light showed every detail clearly. The dryness of the air had leached all moisture from the bodies, and not even birds had come to despoil what little the cold-warg and their allies had left behind. Every detail was starkly, terribly, clear.

The source of the stench was quickly apparent. Kellen gazed down at the gruesome remains of something that lay entangled with the remains of one of the unicorns. Long delicate wings covered with greyish membrane were spread across the snow—it had the proportions of a bat, but a bat the size of a small sailing ship, and its head was shaped more like a wolf's than a bat's, with a long muzzle and yellow carnivorous teeth. Its body, rotting swiftly even in this cold, was covered in a thick white fur.

He looked around, then off into the distance. The Fortress of the Crowned Horns was clearly visible, a tiny doll's castle a few hours' ride away. So very near to safety, and then, to be taken by Demons on their very doorstep, within sight of their greatest stronghold . . .

Their Enemy was mocking them. Telling them how helpless they were. Telling them that they could be struck down anywhere, at any time, by the forces that Shadow Mountain could deploy against them.

But how? Kellen frowned. Andoreniel was no fool, and Idalia had certainly warned him that Shadow Mountain was active once more. The Barrier had been ample proof of that. And Kellen knew that Elven Knights were patrolling all the Elven Lands, even more thoroughly than before. And half a dozen parties before Sandalon's had come this way—all well guarded—and none of them had reported anything suspicious.

Yet coldwarg, and frost-giants—and Idalia had said it looked like ice-trolls as well—all creatures of Darkness, all predators of the High Cold—had slipped into the heart of Elven lands undetected to mount a raid and kidnap the young Prince.

How?

He looked back down at the remains of Death on the wing.

"It stinks of Taint," Shalkan said, coming up behind him.

"Well, it stinks, anyway," Kellen said gloomily. "You'd think someone would have noticed."

"You would," the unicorn said noncommittally. "In the sky, these things would be visible for leagues, and frost-giants don't move all that fast on the ground. It would take them some time to get here."

"Which means that *They* knew our plans all along—and picked this caravan to attack. Specifically," Kellen said.

"Not that we'd leave any child in the hands of Demons," Shalkan observed, "or anyone else for that matter. But you know what the basis of Endarkened magic is. And Sandalon is the Heir."

Kellen took a deep breath. Endarkened magic drew its power from blood and pain and death—from torture. And the death by torture of the Royal Heir would undoubtedly be a source of greater power than any other sacrifice the Demons could marshal, as well as being a great blow to the Elves.

Kellen gazed around the battlefield again. The others were walking among the dead—saying prayers, Kellen supposed, or trying to identify fallen friends. He glanced over his shoulder. Vestakia had stayed with the horses. She was standing beside her mare, leaning against the saddle, the hood of her cloak pulled well up over her face.

Kellen turned back to the battlefield. It was almost as if the bodies—where they lay, how they'd fallen—told a story, and it was one he needed to disentangle. None of the children were here. Calmeren had said they'd been taken, by things that flew, but the only reason she'd survived was because she'd fled before the battle was over. He needed to know more than she could tell him.

Could his magic help him here?

It was worth a try.

Tell me what I need to know, Kellen said silently, summoning up his battle-sight.

There was a shimmer, a faint doubling of vision as the battle-sight rose up, peopling the icy battlefield with the silent silvery ghosts of the dead. He watched as the battle replayed itself before his eyes: the moment when the unicorns realized that flight would not save their precious charges, when they turned, desperately, to fight. They'd been facing the coldwarg pack—the ice-giants would not have been fast enough to keep up with the pack—and . . . something?

Kellen glanced up at the sky, empty now.

Yes. When the unicorns had turned to face the coldwarg, the flying creatures had attacked as well, forcing the unicorns back into the lethal jaws of the pack, and then carrying off the children and Lairamo. He watched the Deathwings as they attacked, agile and deadly, the long razor-sharp talons on their feet clawing and grasping at the unicorn's heads and shoulders, snatching Knights into the air with a fell swoop only to drop them to the ground once more with a stunning impact.

But the coldwarg had possessed other allies as well.

Kellen watched as the last of the unicorns and their riders were pulled down, and saw, with distant surprise, a party of cloaked figures move onto the field. Calmeren had said it had been snowing heavily that day. The cloaked figures would have been concealed by the snow until the last instant.

The silvery vision-ghosts moved among the dead and dying without fear of the feeding coldwarg. Allies, then, and too heavily cowled for Kellen to be sure of what they might be. Perhaps even men.

The vision faded, and Kellen blinked, seeing only the battlefield once more.

"What did you see?" Shalkan asked quietly.

"The battle," Kellen said simply. "Calmeren was right. Those bat-things—Deathwings—carried the children off . . . somewhere."

"But where?" Jermayan's voice was tight with frustration.

"I don't know," Kellen said, feeling a moment of utter despair. To come so far, and to fall just short of success . . .

"I can find them," Vestakia said.

She'd come up behind him while Kellen was watching the past unfold. She'd pushed the hood of her cloak back, and Kellen could see that her face was set with a mixture of horror and determination. If her skin hadn't been the color of ripe cherries, Kellen would have bet she would have been pale. As it was, she looked as if she might be sick at any moment, and not just from the ugliness of the sight before her. Shalkan said the killing ground reeked of Taint as much as the stench Kellen's physical senses could perceive, and Vestakia's gift and curse was that she was peculiarly able to perceive Demonic Taint. And more than any other creature of the Light, she found it debilitating, sickening, perhaps even painful. Kellen didn't know for certain; she had never elaborated, and he could only guess.

Shalkan took a step sideways to press his shoulder against her hip.

"They were taken by Demons—or for Demons," Vestakia said in a small, determined voice. "They were taken by things like *that*." She indicated the Deathwing with a shudder. "I think I can track them."

Jermayan regarded Vestakia with warm approval.

By now the others had gathered around as well.

"There's something more you need to know," Kellen said. "When I saw the battle"—he shrugged, not sure how else to say it—"there were others, helping the coldwarg and the Deathwings. Not giants, and not Endarkened. Figures in cloaks, man-sized. I don't think I could have seen them clearly even if I'd been there in the flesh. But that means we have another enemy to worry about."

"Not Elves!" Trotaliath exclaimed. "Elves would never betray their own to the Enemy!"

"Men. Yet it would be desirable to know how Men could come so far into our lands without our knowing," Debarniekel said, eyeing Kellen with disfavor.

"As well wonder how came the frost-giants, or the ice-trolls, or any of our misfortunes," Jermayan said grimly. "And we do not know yet that they were Men, Debarniekel."

"I guess we'll find out when we catch them," Kellen said. He knew from what Vestakia had told him that Demons could change their shape, and appear in almost any form, but he couldn't imagine why they'd bother to disguise themselves to come here. They couldn't have expected to be seen, after all.

And hadn't the whole point been to have the caravan disappear without a trace? A few more sennights—another big blizzard or two—and there wouldn't have been any traces at all left for them to find. Only the charred remains of the wagons, if that. The Deathwing would have been completely rotted away.

"Come on," he said, turning and walking back toward the waiting mounts. "Vestakia, what do you need us to do?"

It felt odd to be taking charge and giving orders like this—especially since he was pretty sure he was the youngest one here, Vestakia included—but Idalia had been right. This was his rescue party. He was the leader, and even while it felt odd, it felt right.

The wind rose while they walked, and the air cleared. All of them breathed easier.

Vestakia had obviously been thinking as they moved.

"I think we need to get away from here, to where I can't feel that . . . thing. Kellen, you said you 'saw' the battle. Which way did the creatures fly?"

Kellen thought for a moment, then pointed into the sky. "But you know that doesn't mean anything," he added conscientiously. "Once they were in the air, they might have circled around, gone in any direction."

"I know," Vestakia said. "But it gives us a place to start, doesn't it? We'll get out of range of this, and then I'll see what I can sense, and we'll follow it. I know I'll be able to pick up the trail when we're clear of that dead *thing*," she said, determination in her voice. "They thought going by air would leave no traces to track, but they were wrong. I even think I feel it now, but I want to be sure."

They mounted up again and rode away from the battlefield.

A few minutes later they stopped. The destriers were calm again, and even Kellen felt better, as if an annoying sound just below the threshold of audibility had stopped.

Vestakia dismounted and walked away from the animals. She paced back and forth for a few minutes. Kellen could see the steam of her breath being whipped away by the wind, and hear the crunch her boots made as they broke through the crust of the hard-frozen snow.

It all depended on her, and on her using her gifts in a way she'd never used them before. Jermayan was a fine tracker, but there was no physical trail to follow. Idalia might cast a Finding Spell with the Wild Magic, or Kellen might, but for either of them to do that would be to incur Magedebt, and there would be no guarantee that it would work. The Endarkened were powerful magicians, easily able to cast greater spells than any either he or Idalia could summon. They could certainly shield their stronghold, just as they must have shielded the presence of the attackers within the Elven Borders. The one thing they could not conceal was the presence of their magic, and that was what Vestakia could follow.

After a nerve-wracking interval, Vestakia returned.

"That way," she said with certainty. "I'm sorry . . . I don't know if it's the children. But it's Taint . . . "

"And it's within Elven Borders," Jermayan finished grimly. "So we must investigate it, and pray that it leads to what we hope to find."

SEVERAL times Vestakia stopped to reassure herself they were continuing in the right direction. Kellen was relieved to see that though she seemed to be uncomfortable at sensing the presence of Demon-taint, it was not draining her as badly as it had when she had approached the Black Cairn.

The trail led them deeper into the mountains, back below the edge of the tree line, where there was more shelter from the wind. Soon, as Vestakia became more assured in following the trail, they became able to move at the fastest prudent speed over the snow, with the unicorns breaking the trail for the heavier destriers.

It had been noon when they had left the battlefield. The short winter day was drawing to a close by the time they reached their destination.

And their destination looked exactly like everywhere they had already been; the granite mountain rising up out of the pine forest, cold and silent and forbidding. It was silent here; it had been silent in most of the forest as they had backtracked the trail of the mysterious flyers. Evidently it wasn't only Vestakia who could sense the Taint; the birds, at least, did not want to be anywhere near where the Deathwings had passed. There should at least be crows, sparrows, something—and there was nothing. Not a sign, not a call. Empty sky, empty trees.

The snow—waist-deep in some places—had impeded every step. It would have shown the signs of any life, and there were none.

"There," Vestakia said, pointing to a cave opening in the rock. "The trail leads in there."

It was impossible to tell in the reddish sunset light whether the opening was natural or man-made. The riders had stopped down the slope, near the edge of the trees, and watched it warily, alert for sentries, though there didn't seem to be any. There were no tracks in the smooth mantle of snow that led up to the narrow dark opening in the stone wall, but it had been snowing heavily and almost steadily in these mountains for the past sennight, and even the meanest outlaws knew enough to use brooms on the snow to conceal their tracks.

Vestakia looked tired—far wearier than even a day's hard riding could account for—and pressed her hand to her forehead as if trying to rub away a pounding headache. This close to the source of the Taint, it was obvious she was feeling its draining effects.

"We'll set up camp here," Kellen decided, gesturing toward the pines. It was closer to the cavern mouth than he liked—and too close for Vestakia's comfort, he knew—but they were losing the light, and to travel through snow this deep by night would be a bad idea. Besides, they were all cold and tired. They needed hot tea, hot food, and a breathing space to plan their next move.

The Elves moved beneath the trees, found a clearing, and began setting up camp with quiet efficiency, clearing a space for the braziers and setting snow to melt for tea and soup. Kellen unsaddled Shalkan and gave him a quick rubdown— sweat would quickly turn to ice at this temperature—and then saw to Vestakia's mount as well. She'd already done more than her share of work today.

By the time he was finished, the tea was ready. He collected two cups and brought one over to her. She was leaning against a tree at the edge of the clearing, staring broodingly back the way they'd come.

"How bad is it?" he asked.

"Not too," Vestakia said bravely. "More like a sore tooth than anything else. So it isn't Demons in there. Just something they've touched." She shuddered. "As if that isn't bad enough."

Kellen held out the steaming cup of tea. Vestakia took it, and sipped.

"Do you want some of that stuff? I know Idalia brought

some. You know, the thing that shuts down your magical senses? That way you wouldn't be able to feel it," Kellen offered.

Vestakia opened her eyes very wide. "Oh, Good Goddess, no!" she exclaimed, almost sputtering. "Kellen, I'd rather feel something a thousand times worse than this than have *Them* be able to sneak up on me and not know!" She reached out and patted his arm awkwardly. "I'll be fine. Well, not fine, exactly, but I'll be all right. It's those children you should be worrying about. What are you going to do now?"

"I'm not—" Kellen began.

"And by Leaf and Star, I say you will not!" Jermayan declared.

He had not shouted—not quite—but he had certainly spoken loudly enough to catch Kellen's attention. Kellen's head whipped around.

Jermayan and Idalia were facing each other in the center of the clearing. Idalia held a small bundle in her arms.

"I will," Idalia said quietly. "It's the best chance they have. And you know it, Jermayan."

Kellen hurried over.

"Um . . . what's going on?" he asked.

"Your sister has this foolish notion—" Jermayan began.

"Jermayan thinks—" Idalia shot back.

"No." Kellen held up his hand. Both of them stopped, looking at him in surprise. "You're arguing. I can see that. Arguing wastes time and energy. Let's find another way." It was one of Master Belesharon's favorite sayings. "Idalia, what are you holding?"

"A . . . a *tarnkappa*," she said reluctantly.

"And what were you going to do with it?" He had a sinking feeling he already knew, but Master Belesharon always said it was better to know than to guess.

"I'm going to put it on and go in after the children. I'll be safe," she said, sounding defiant.

"Madness!" Jermayan protested vehemently.

"It will work! Nothing in there will be able to sense me

while I'm wearing it—and I've added a spell to this one to give me darksight. I'll be able to see even if there's no light. We can't just go rushing in there—it might be a trap—"

"Of course it's a trap!" Jermayan and Kellen said, almost in chorus.

"Then you see why I have to be the one to spring it," Idalia said inexorably. "And—with luck and skill—come away with the bait—or at the very least, find out that it isn't there, so Vestakia can cast about for a fresh trail."

"No!" Jermayan said again, a note of desperation in his voice.

"It's my *tarnkappa*," Idalia said. "I am not only the most expendable member of the party, I'm the logical one to go. If there are any traps of Dark Magic down there, I can sense them and avoid them—can you, Jermayan? And I'm a much better tracker than you are, Kellen. If there's a trail to be found, I'll find it."

She was right. Kellen realized it even as he hated the fact. It *was* a trap, so the safest, the most logical thing to do was to send one person to spring it. And the person in the party with the best combination of skills to get into—and out of—the trap alive was Idalia.

Both Idalia and Jermayan were looking at him. She might go no matter what he said. But they were waiting for his decision.

"So you can find your way in," he said. "But how are you going to find your way back?"

Idalia opened one hand to reveal a thick stick of chalk. "Why, I'll blazon my way, brother dear, just as I would in an unfamiliar forest. And I'll use the marks to lead me home again."

She'd answered every objection.

"All right," he said, feeling suddenly old and weary. "But—" What was he going to say? Be careful? "Don't take too many chances. If it's a trap, they might not be there at all."

Idalia laughed. "Don't worry, brother dear. I'm in no hurry to die." She hugged him quickly, the *tarnkappa* a bulky softness between them, then turned back to Jermayan.

Kellen moved quickly away to give the two of them a little privacy.

"You did well," Shalkan said, moving up to stand beside him. Even through his armor, Kellen could feel the heat of the unicorn's body, as if Shalkan carried his own private summer with him.

Kellen grinned without mirth. "I just pretended I was Master Belesharon. Besides, I knew she'd go anyway, and there was no point to wasting the time that would be spent as she and Jermayan shouted at each other."

"Ah," Shalkan said dryly. "The beginning of wisdom."

IDALIA moved over the snow in the direction of the cavern mouth, the *tarnkappa* wrapped tightly around her. Only the footprints she left in the snow betrayed any hint that someone moved here; while wearing the magical cloak she could not be seen, or heard, or scented.

She hoped it would be enough to keep her safe once she entered the darkness—both figurative and literal—ahead.

She was not quite as confident as she had let on to Jermayan and Kellen. Everything that she'd told them was true—she *was* the logical candidate to explore the trap—but she wasn't sure that getting in and out again would be as simple as she'd made it sound, especially if that was a natural cave. Idalia had a little bit of experience with natural caves, and knew that they could stretch on for leagues, twisting and turning more elaborately than any Elven-crafted labyrinth. Despite her tracking skills, she might well get lost, and if she needed to cast a spell of the Wild Magic to find her way out . . .

It might very well bring the enemy right down on top of her.

Idalia shrugged beneath the *tarnkappa*. There was no use borrowing trouble before it came to call. Her life was already forfeit to the Greater Powers. When They chose to claim Their price was Their business.

Hers was getting the children out of danger. If they were even there.

When she reached the mouth of the cavern, Idalia pulled the hood of the *tarnkappa* well forward. She could see through the fabric as if it wasn't there at all, and through the magic's aid, everything became sharp and clear, the dim twilight vanishing to be replaced by a bright, clear—though monochromatic—landscape.

She took a deep breath, touching the long knife at her belt, and stepped inside.

She walked a few feet down the passage—it was narrow, and except for the levelness of the floor, looked very much like a natural cave—moving carefully and listening intently for sounds from within. Except for the sound of the wind whistling over the cavern opening, she heard nothing, and as she moved deeper into the mountain, even that sound stopped.

At first the path was simple to follow, for there was only one possible way to go. But soon the passageway opened out. She quickly took the chalk and made a small arrow, low on the stone, pointing back the way she'd come.

She stood for a long moment, gazing out into the day-bright darkness. Passages opened out to the left and the right, both bearing recent marks of use. The one to the right seemed to have been more heavily trafficked, though, and taking a few steps along it, Idalia could see traces of scrape-marks along the walls, as if something large and heavy had been brought this way fairly recently.

Good enough. She went to the right, making another mark on the wall to indicate her choice.

At one point she stopped and lifted her hood. Utter blackness enveloped her, and she could smell no trace of lamp-oil torch-smoke in the air of the cave. Whatever lived here did not need light to move through the darkness. She lowered her hood, relieved to be able to see once more.

At intervals she paused to mark her way, for if the signs were too far apart there was a danger of missing one. As she moved deeper into the caves, she saw signs that Nature's work had been improved upon—stone had been crudely cut away, paths had been widened and leveled. All these things were signs, not of a temporary hiding place, or even a carefully-constructed trap, but of a place where something made its home.

And that should not be—not if what lived here was Dark-tainted enough for Vestakia to be able to track it.

By now she had penetrated quite far into the cave system, and though she was on the trail of whatever lived here, she wasn't sure she was any closer to finding the children.

Suddenly she became aware that there were faint sounds, coming from somewhere ahead—though the direction of sounds could be misleading underground. They were barely louder than her own breathing, but she wasn't making them.

Idalia moved faster.

The path led to the edge of a cliff. Here the cave opened out into the largest space Idalia had yet encountered. Crude stairs were cut into the cliff face, leading down to the space below.

Below lay a sort of village, and Idalia got her first good look at what must be the mysterious hooded figures that Kellen had described.

From where she stood, she counted about twenty of them. They were gathered around a central cooking fire, where some indeterminate carcass smoked and sizzled over a bed of coals. When Idalia risked another peek without the *tarnkappa*, she could see it was a bed of carefully banked charcoal, giving as little light as possible, and none of them looked at it directly. She pulled her hood back down and continued watching.

Their garments were primitive, consisting of little more than a crude loin-wrap for males and females both. The half-dozen children that she could see wore no clothing at all.

They were no race that Idalia knew, or had ever heard described. Their skin was a dull fish-belly white, save for a long dark stripe down their spines, and a matching one that covered their lower face and extended down their stomachs. Their hands and feet seemed to be a darker color as well, though whether that was natural pigmentation, or just dirt and callus, Idalia wasn't sure. Their bodies were entirely hairless, but shaggy dark hair, left long and untended, grew from their scalps. From everything she could see, they existed at the most primitive tribal level.

Their faces were the most unsettling, as if someone had taken something familiar and cruelly distorted it. Their eyes were large, round, and bulging. They were practically chinless, upper and lower jaws pushed forward in a muzzle-like fashion, and when one of them opened his mouth to speak a few words in a curious low barking language, Idalia could see that the mouth was filled with long discolored fangs.

And their ears were pointed.

When she saw that, the nagging sense of almost-familiarity Idalia had felt when she'd seen the creatures settled into place with a sense of almost physical force. It was as if . . . it was as if someone, somehow, had managed to breed Elves and Goblins together, and this was the result.

Oh, that isn't possible, Idalia thought with a wave of nauseated faintness. But she knew it was. The Endarkened delighted in perverting any of the creatures of the Light that fell into their hands, and they were masters of Dark Magic. The creatures they had created to fight their battles in the Great War still plagued the world today—the coldwarg were just one sample. Why not these . . . Shadowed Elves?

And it would explain how they could be here undetected, she told herself with brutal pragmatism. If these debased creatures possessed Elven blood, it was more than likely they could circumvent the ancient wards against intruders placed upon the Elven lands. They would, after all, *be* Elves, in a sense, able to come and go within Andoreniel's domain as they wished. The could have brought the ice-trolls and the frost-giants over the border through their own caves. No wonder no one had seen them until it was too late!

Idalia stared down into the Shadowed Elf village with cold horror. How many of them were there? It had been centuries since the Endarkened had possessed Elven captives to experiment upon. And more important—*where* were they? This couldn't be the only encampment of them.

She hesitated, on the verge of turning back right now to warn the others. This was a greater threat than the missing children—a Dark-Shadowed race living undetected within the borders of the Elven realm itself.

Suddenly a chorus of furious barking down below drew her attention back to the village. An argument had broken out at the central firepit.

Several of the Shadowed Elves were standing in front of it. One had a large basket at his feet, filled with what looked, from this distance, like large mushroom caps or flat loaves of bread. He was gesturing at the roasting carcass, and speaking urgently.

The other, facing him—the chief?—was speaking equally imperatively, underscoring his words with gestures that Idalia had no trouble in interpreting as a refusal. No meat, then. But for who?

The argument concluded, and the first Shadowed Elf picked up the basket and walked away. His companion—a female—followed.

Idalia watched as they paused to don long hooded cloaks that covered them all the way to the ankles, and for the female to pick up a large jar of the sort that might contain wine or water. From the way she moved, it was heavy.

That was curious. They obviously weren't going outside—they hadn't put on boots, or gloves, or any undergarments. The cloaks were plainly for concealment.

Feeding prisoners on "bread and water"? Prisoners that they didn't want to see them?

Idalia's heart began to beat faster.

Once they were cloaked and provisioned, the two Shadowed Elves began ascending the steps. Idalia moved quickly back along the rim, looking frantically around for a niche to hide in. They couldn't see or hear her, but nothing would save her from discovery if they walked right into her.

She found nothing, and was forced to retreat back the way she came, hoping that wouldn't be the direction they ended up coming. But luck was with her, and when the two Shadowed Elves reached the top of the steps, they headed away from her. Idalia chalked a quick trail-sign and followed them.

Fortunately—because the water-jug was heavy and fragile—they moved slowly, and Idalia was able to follow them at a prudent distance, making marks along the way. The only danger was that they might hear the sound of the chalk against the stone, but she was well behind them, and apparently it did not occur to the Shadowed Elves that there might be any interlopers within their stronghold.

Without them to follow, Idalia wasn't sure she would ever have found the prisoners, for the path they took involved a number of twists and turns. But at last they reached their goal, a pocket cavern deep within the bowels of the mountain.

The doorway to the cave stood open. The Shadowed Elves had trusted—and rightly so—to the darkness outside to serve as a more perfect jailer than any doors or locks. Only the truly desperate would try to find their way through that blackness, and if the captives did not fall to their deaths over an unseen precipice, they would be easily recaptured before they ever found their way to the surface.

Eight

Prisoners of Darkness

Lairamo did not know how long they had been here. It was hard to measure time even by sleeping and waking. Their cloaked captors had fed them seven times since they had arrived—baskets of flat tasteless fungus, and jars of stale water—and so she had scratched seven marks upon the wall. But the meals, such as they were, might not be coming at regular intervals, or if they were, those intervals might not be the same as a day.

She kept her thoughts to herself. There was no point in adding fresh terrors to a situation that had already grown beyond horror.

At first she had been grateful that they were left together. That no atrocities were visited upon her charges. It had been peculiar that the door to the cavern was left unbarred and unguarded, and it had been Alkandoran who had first suggested that they must try to escape. He had persuaded her to let him take one of the lanterns and see if he could find the way out, and at last, reluctantly, she had let him have his way.

He was gone a very long time.

At last he had returned—in the hands of two of their hooded captors. His face was white and strained, and the lantern was gone. They had shoved him back into the cavern, then entered, selecting one of the remaining lanterns and smashing it carefully. The lamp oil had kindled in a bright brief flare as it burned away into darkness.

The silent message was clear. Escape was impossible. Further attempts would be punished by the removal of more of the lanterns.

Lairamo did not think any of them could stand this captivity in the darkness. And the hooded ones might take one or both of the braziers as well, and the children surely could not survive the cold.

So they huddled together in the wan light of the two remaining lanterns, keeping their spirits up as best they could. All of them were cold and filthy—especially the baby—and slept huddled together beneath a pile of their cloaks and the strange hammocks in which they'd been carried here. Lairamo encouraged the children to sleep as much as they could, and did everything she could think of to keep them from talking or thinking of what the future might hold. Among the items left behind here by their captors had been a *gan* set. Alkandoran had taught the younger children to play, and bullied them into it constantly. No one was very good at it, but it kept their minds off where they were, at least a little.

The only thing they could do was wait. Alkandoran had told her of what little he'd managed to see before he'd been recaptured—he'd wandered for what seemed like hours through cave passages that all looked alike, and he'd been pretty sure he'd been going in circles. The hooded ones had waited until his lantern ran out of oil before taking him, so he was fairly sure they'd been following him the whole time.

A faint scuffling in the outer darkness heralded the return of their captors once more. Reflexively, Lairamo drew the children to her and scuttled back against the farthest wall of the cave. They huddled against her skirts, and she put her arms around as many of them as she could.

A few moments later, the two cloaked and hooded figures appeared, faint ghosts in the dimness. As always, one carried a wide shallow basket and the other carried a water jar. They set their burdens down just inside the doorway, where the shadows were thickest, then one of them moved to collect the empty jar. In moments the two were gone again.

Lairamo made them all wait for several minutes before they approached the food and water, though they were hungry all the time these days, and thirsty as well. She rationed their supplies as best she could, but they were entirely at the mercy of their jailers, and without constant supplies, they would die of thirst long before they starved.

Just as she was getting stiffly to her feet, Kalania balanced on her hip, there was a sudden blur of motion, and a figure appeared out of nowhere, standing in the middle of the chamber. Tredianala gave a hoarse cry of alarm, and Alkandoran jerked the slender girl behind him.

But after a moment's pang of terror, Lairamo recognized the intruder.

"Idalia! Praise to the Gods of Leaf and Star!"

"I've come to get you out of here. There's a rescue party waiting nearby."

⟶

IDALIA had followed the two Shadowed Elves to their destination. She waited until they were well out of sight before advancing on the cave. She didn't know what prisoners it might contain, but she meant to rescue them whoever they were—she would leave no one in the hands of these creatures.

She edged closer, wrinkling her nose. The cavern smelled of long—and unsanitary—occupancy. When she rounded the corner and looked inside, her heart leaped. Lairamo and the children—and as far as she could see, they were all alive and whole, though filthy and haggard.

She stepped into the cave and flung off her *tarnkappa*.

Instantly the world became dim—though by some whim, the Shadowed Elves had left their Elven prisoners a lantern or two to see by.

"They will catch you," the oldest boy said grimly. "I tried to get away once. They followed me for a long time, then they brought me back here."

"Ah," Idalia said lightly, hoping to rally their spirits. "But I have magic. This cloak conceals me from sight and sound—and anything I have under it as well. I've marked the way to the surface, and with the hood down, I can see in the dark as well as they can. I can carry you all to safety, and no one will suspect a thing."

But it will take several trips.

"Sandalon and Kalania will go first," Lairamo said calmly. "They are the youngest, and the smallest. The rest of us will wait here."

⟶

"THERE'S something moving out there."

The unicorns had excellent night-sight—better even than the Elves'—and the three unicorns in the party had volunteered to keep watch on the cave mouth from the edge of the trees. Shalkan had the first watch.

Kellen was standing with him—not because he could be at all useful; the darkness was nothing but dark to him, and the moon was too new to give any proper light, the merest fingernail crescent in the sky, sennights from full—but because this was, in a sense, his plan, or at least his responsibility. He was too keyed-up to sit at the warmth of the brazier with the others, waiting for Idalia to come back. His fidgeting would do more harm than good to their spirits. He was wise enough to know that much.

"What is it? What do you see?" Kellen fought to keep his voice low and level.

"Footprints in the snow," Shalkan said. "Coming this way."

Kellen loosened his sword in its scabbard. He hoped it was Idalia in the *tarnkappa,* but other beings possessed the secret of invisibility as well. Or someone might have taken it from her. But Vestakia had given no warning, so Kellen was merely alert, not preparing for battle.

A few yards away from where Shalkan stood, the air seemed to shimmer. Suddenly Kellen could see Idalia clearly. She was holding a bundle in her arms. There was a wriggle of movement, and Sandalon dropped from her back and ran to Kellen. Kellen dropped to one knee to receive the Elven Prince, who buried his face in Kellen's shoulder. The boy was trembling, but did not make a sound.

"I've got to go back," Idalia said without preamble. "The rest of them are still there—alive and safe, for now, but I'm the only one who can get them out, and it has to be done quickly. There's more news, and worse—that cavern is home to a whole race of Dark-tainted creatures that seem to be some kind of Elven-Goblin hybrid."

She thrust the bundle—the baby Kalania—at Kellen, swirled the *tarnkappa* around herself again, and vanished.

"Come on," Kellen said, picking up Sandalon and trying not to drop the toddler. "Let's go back and find the others. Jermayan and Vestakia are here. They'll be glad to see you, you know. You're safe now."

Sandalon began to tremble even harder, and Kellen felt the warmth of soundless tears against his cheek.

⟷

KELLEN was able to hand Kalania to Vestakia when he reached the others; Sandalon flatly refused to let go of him. Everyone had leaped to their feet when he approached, taking in the sight of the two children and understanding what it meant.

"Where is Idalia?" Jermayan demanded, the normal courtly speech of Elvenkind subsumed beneath War Manners.

"Gone back for the others," Kellen answered briefly. "She says they're all alive and well, and that she can get them all out."

"Everyone on your guard and ready to ride," Jermayan said. "We need to move as soon as everyone has been recovered."

The knights moved briskly about the campsite, saddling horses and unicorns and checking equipment. Evanor, the Elven Healer, took Kalania from Vestakia and laid her down on a blanket near the brazier, and peeled off the layers of sodden foul garments to examine her. Though the toddler was thin and filthy, and obviously stunned with terror, Evanor was able to apply soothing salves to the worst of her rashes, swaddle her in clean cloths, and get her to drink a little broth with a soothing potion mixed in, after which the child fell immediately asleep.

"It would be well if I were to examine young Sandalon as well," Evanor said, when he was finished with Kalania.

"I'm fine," Sandalon said sharply, his voice high with fear. His hands were wrapped around a cup of broth, and he was sitting on Kellen's lap. At Evanor's words, he recoiled.

"Of course you are," Vestakia said, coming to kneel beside Kellen. She smoothed back Sandalon's hair; it was greasy and matted after so long without washing or combing. "*I* can tell that. I know about these things. We found you because I can sense *Them*, you know. That's the trail we followed. But I couldn't sense any of you at all. We didn't even know for sure you were in there until Idalia went in to look. So that's how I know you're all right."

"You're sure?" Sandalon asked, his voice torn between pleading and suspicion.

Poor little fellow! Kellen well remembered his own agonized fears of being Demon-tainted—and he hadn't been a five-year-old child who'd seen all his friends horribly slaughtered, then been held prisoner by monsters down in the dark. No wonder the boy didn't want to be examined too closely!

"I'm sure," Vestakia said firmly.

Sandalon looked at Kellen.

"She'd know," Kellen assured him. "And you should let Evanor make sure you're not hurt, or going to become ill, and give you clean dry clothes to change to. We're going to have a long way to ride tonight." *If Idalia gets the others out safely. And what if she doesn't? What are we going to do then?*

Reluctantly, Sandalon allowed himself to be examined by Evanor, who pronounced him to be in better shape than Kalania, and dosed him with a strengthening cordial.

Just then, two of the unicorns trotted off, as if summoned

by a voice only they could hear. And Shalkan walked into the clearing with Tredianala clinging to his mane.

The girl was crying and quivering with terror—Kellen recalled that she had been particularly timid—and Evanor quickly took charge of her, speaking soothingly to her and leading her over to the brazier.

"Four more to go," Shalkan said, coming over to Kellen. "Four more trips."

Kellen didn't ask the question that was uppermost in all of their minds: *How long can Idalia's luck hold out?*

⟶

LAIRAMO had sent the oldest girl on the second trip because Tredianala was the most fearful of the remaining children, and Idalia had blessed the sound-cloaking properties of the *tarnkappa* with every step she took, as the child had cried the entire way, just as if she were not on her way to rescue and safety. The second in-and-out went much faster than the first, and she was able to deposit Tredianala within sight of Shalkan, and turn back to the cavern.

By now her tracks were a deep rut in the snow. The sight of them gave her a sinking feeling in the pit of her stomach, but there wasn't much she could do about them. If the Shadowed Elves came outside, the proverbial goose was cooked anyway; they just had to hope they could get the captives out and make it to the Fortress of the Crowned Horns with them before the Enemy could come up with any more Deathwings or coldwarg.

Down into the dark again, and the caverns began to seem like an old friend. This time she took Vendalton. Now only Alkandoran, Merisashendiel, and Lairamo were left. The boy rode piggyback, his arms clutched about her throat. Her back was starting to hurt; this was different from carrying a pack all day in the Wildwood. A pack didn't squirm around trying to get comfortable, and occasionally kick you in the stomach by accident.

She reached the cave opening and stepped outside. She looked around, wary of ambush.

"I will take the child, Idalia."

Coethare materialized silently out of nowhere. With a grateful sigh, Idalia set Vendalton into the unicorn's saddle and turned back into the cave.

Merisashendiel was next. The girl regarded her with big-eyed fear, suddenly unwilling to leave the others. Lairamo had to scold and bully her before she would take her place on Idalia's shoulders.

"But what if they die?" Merisashendiel said. "What if the others come while you're gone and take them?"

"Hush," Idalia said brusquely. "Talking can't change what will be. And if they haven't come yet, they probably won't come at all." *I hope.* Did the Shadowed Elves check on their captives between feedings? There'd be no real reason to. And they'd just been fed. She tried to put from her mind what Alkandoran had said about how he'd been tracked and tormented on his one escape attempt. As she'd told the child, talking couldn't change what would be.

Up through the twisting maze of tunnels that led to the village cavern. Along the rim. Back through the maze of tunnels that led to the surface and safety. She could no longer remember for how many hours she'd been doing this, how far she'd walked through this underground world.

The surface once again, and another waiting unicorn. Merisashendiel wanted to argue with her, to suggest that *she* should be the one to go back down. Idalia dumped her rudely into the unicorn's saddle and turned away.

⟶

"LAIRAMO should go first," Alkandoran said when Idalia arrived.

"Certainly not," Lairamo said calmly. "You will heed me in this, child. Go with Idalia."

Lairamo looked up at Idalia. Their eyes met, and Idalia

knew that they were both thinking the same thing. She couldn't carry Alkandoran, but he was small and slender. She could fit him under the *tarnkappa* with her, if he put his arms around her waist and pressed very close to her, and they moved slowly.

She could not fit Lairamo under the *tarnkappa* with her at all.

I will find a way, Idalia vowed silently.

"But—" Alkandoran began.

"We'll do it her way," Idalia said. "Now this is going to be awkward and slow. I'll need your help, and your full cooperation if we are to get out of here alive."

Alkandoran swallowed hard, doing his best not to look as frightened as Idalia knew he felt.

"The sooner I have you out of here, the sooner I can come back for Lairamo," Idalia said calmly.

Alkandoran nodded.

This trip to the surface was agonizingly slow, as the two of them shuffled along beneath Idalia's cloak. Over and over Idalia blessed Lairamo's practical no-nonsense calmness—after a sennight in the hands of the Shadowed Elves, the captives could all have been completely hysterical, too terrified to cooperate in their own rescue. She wasn't sure what she would have done if that had been the case—the younger ones she could have bespelled into unconsciousness, perhaps (and hope that using the Wild Magic didn't draw their captors to them immediately) but she would never have gotten Alkandoran to the surface without his intelligent cooperation.

Shalkan was waiting at the cave mouth.

"You were gone a long time, this time."

"Slow going," Idalia said, untangling the cloak from herself and Alkandoran. The youngster stepped away from her, drawing a shaky breath. "Just Lairamo, now."

"We'll be waiting for you. Come, lad," Shalkan said.

Idalia took a moment to stretch, wrapping the cloak firmly around her, before stepping back into the cave once more. She'd already made up her mind what to do about getting Lairamo out. She suspected that Shalkan had guessed her plan.

Lairamo wasn't going to like it. But it was the only way. And she only hoped she'd be around so that Jermayan could scold her for it later.

⌒

"NO," Lairamo said, when Idalia told her.

"Yes," Idalia said, just as firmly. "I've been over the route several times by now, and besides, I'll be right behind you. I know how to move silently. Just follow the marks I've left, and they'll lead you straight to the surface."

"I will not buy my life at the expense of yours."

"And what of the Prince?" Idalia was fighting dirty and she knew it, but she intended to win this argument, and swiftly. "He has seen his friends killed, and goes now to live among strangers at the Fortress of the Crowned Horns. Do I tell him I have left you behind to die? He needs you, and the Nine Cities need him. You will take the *tarnkappa*."

Lairamo's shoulders slumped as Idalia's arguments hit home. "Best done quickly then," the Elven nursemaid muttered. "But I do not forgive you this debt you place upon me, Idalia Wildmage."

"I do not expect it." *I carry too many unpaid debts these days.* She quickly flung the cloak over Lairamo's shoulders and pulled the hood down over her face, showing her—by touch, since Lairamo was now invisible—how to hold the cloak to keep herself concealed. Then, with her hand on the shoulder of the now-invisible presence before her, Idalia and Lairamo made their way out of the cave.

They moved more slowly than Idalia would have liked, for Lairamo had to stop and look for the marks that Idalia had left, but they gradually made their way toward the surface, and freedom.

All along Idalia worried more for those waiting than for herself. They were pressing their luck every moment the party waited outside the cavern mouth—if this were *her* home, she would certainly post a watch over its entrance. But perhaps the Shadowed Elves did not think like Elves, or like Men. Or perhaps letting the captives escape was just another aspect of the trap.

All went smoothly—though with agonizing slowness— until they reached the path around the underground "village." Idalia recognized it by the feeling of space, and by the faint glow of the firepit below—not enough for human eyes to see by, but enough to mark the place, since she had passed it so many times already this evening. She only hoped the creatures were all asleep, but thought that was too much to hope for—the meat she had seen roasting earlier argued that they were hunters, and probably hunted at night. She strained her ears for sounds from below.

Suddenly she heard what she had feared and dreaded— the stealthy approach of bare feet on rock. There was a faint click—as of a spear butt hitting rock—and a flurry of muttered whispers.

She felt invisible hands plucking at her frantically. Perhaps Lairamo had tried to shout a warning, not realizing that the *tarnkappa* would muffle all sounds.

"Go, Lairamo!" Idalia shouted. "Go on for Sandalon's sake!" Praying the woman would heed her, she turned and fled back in the opposite direction, her eyes tightly shut, hoping desperately that she remembered the tunnels as well as she'd claimed.

A chorus of guttural cries greeted her flight—no more need for silence now that the prey was wise to the hunt—and Idalia heard the sound of bare feet slapping against stone as the creatures ran after her.

LAIRAMO stood frozen in horror as five creatures out of nightmare ran after Idalia. None of them so much as paused to glance at her, so strong was the Wildmagery of Idalia's cloak. A choking sensation rose in Lairamo's throat as she realized that Idalia had given up her life to draw the hunters away, so that Lairamo could gain the surface alive.

For the young Prince, Lairamo thought, her heart stone-heavy. Grimly, she turned away to look for the marks that would lead her to the surface.

"PACING won't get them here any faster," Kellen said to Jermayan.

The Elven knight shot him a dark look, and did not reply.

Everyone was standing to saddle, ready to ride the moment Idalia and Lairamo appeared. It was better than tempting fortune by lingering here a moment longer than they had to. Vestakia was standing watch now at the edge of the trees, adding her own magical senses to that of the unicorns, alert for trouble. If the creatures Idalia had named Shadowed Elves came near to the surface, Vestakia would know.

Kellen had been dearly tempted to send the others on ahead, but he did not want to split the party into two small groups. If there were an ambush laid along the way, they needed to be at their full strength.

So they waited.

Suddenly Sandalon gave a high scream of terror, and a moment later, Lairamo appeared, kneeling beside him and clutching him to her chest, stroking his hair and gabbling apologies for having frightened him. The *tarnkappa* was pooled at her feet.

"It was the cloak, my heart, I forgot the cloak, oh, forgive me, my darling—"

Sandalon clung to her, sobbing in relief.

Jermayan snatched up the cloak and shook it, as if its empty folds might somehow produce Idalia.

"Idalia," was all he said.

Lairamo looked up at him, her face filled with grief and misery. She looked at the *tarnkappa* as if she wished to burn it on the spot.

"Only one could wear it. She was seen. She ran . . . deeper into the cavern, lest—Lest I be discovered."

"Come on." Kellen barely recognized the voice as his own. "We've got to get you out of here."

"I'm staying," Jermayan said, wadding the *tarnkappa* in his hands.

And probably charging right in there after her, if no one stops you, Kellen thought.

"Vestakia, you go with them," Kellen said, continuing as if Jermayan hadn't spoken. "You'll need to keep watch along the road, to let them know if there are any traps along the way. Jermayan and I will keep watch here, and bring Idalia along when she comes."

The way he said it, it almost seemed as if it were possible. And if he were to think of it logically, they should all leave now, together. But Idalia was a Wildmage of great power, and Kellen wasn't ready to give up on her quite yet. As for Jermayan, well, the world would fall apart around him before anyone could make him leave.

"Leaf and Star be with you," Evanor said quietly.

Vestakia and the knights quickly mounted, taking Lairamo and the children up with them, and rode off in the direction of the Crowned Horns, the unicorns leading the way. In moments the clearing was deserted except for Jermayan, Valdien, Kellen, Shalkan, and Idalia's palfrey.

"I'm going in after her," Jermayan said.

"No, you're not," Kellen said, snatching the *tarnkappa* out of the Elven Knight's hands. "Not if I have to knock you senseless to keep you from doing it."

"As if you could, Knight-Mage," Jermayan said. But there was a grudging willingness to listen in his voice. Kellen might be able to convince his friend, if he spoke quickly.

"One, we both know Idalia can take care of herself. Two, neither of us knows where she is. Three, she hasn't been gone that long—not if she's leading pursuit away deeper into the mountain. What we're going to do is wait for her—here, where she knows to find us. If she hasn't come back in a reasonable time, then I'll do a Finding Spell, and based on what that tells us, we'll come up with a plan. But I don't know whether those things can sense Wild Magic, so I don't want to do one before it's absolutely necessary."

"Very well," Jermayan said grudgingly. "I will wait. For a while. But do not try my patience for long."

IDALIA ran through the darkness, her hands outstretched in front of her to keep herself from running full-tilt into a wall. She dared not slow her headlong pace, for she could hear the sounds of pursuit close behind. She no longer knew where she was in the cave system.

A flung spear made her flinch aside, then another, and suddenly there was no rock beneath her feet, only air.

Idalia fell.

CILARNEN awoke lying on the floor in a tiny room that could only be described as a cell. It was a cubicle a bit less than eight feet square—though at least three times that in height—with a stone bench at one end. The only light came through a small grille set in the door. When he ran to the door and looked out, he could see that the corridor was as featureless as his cell, though it was lit to blinding brightness by globes of hovering Magelight.

He wrapped his arms around himself and shivered, gulping several times to try to banish his fear. When they had begun this adventure—and he now realized, with the clarity of despair, that in some sense it had been an adventure for all of them—it had never occurred to any of them that it could end like this.

He had no idea of where he might be, though he knew he was in the hands of the High Council. Somehow they had discovered what they were doing, and arrested them all.

He hoped the others were all right.

All right? Cilarnen's mouth twisted in a bitter smile. He wasn't sure what was going to happen to them, but he doubted any of them was going to be "all right."

He walked stiffly over to the bench and sat down, leaning back against the wall. Whatever the Council decided, he knew his own fate. His father would burn the Magegift from his mind and disinherit him.

What in the name of the Light was he supposed to do with the rest of his life? He was a Mage. That was all he was. That was all he'd ever wanted to be. To study the intricacies of the High Art—to use his power for the good of the City—to perhaps, someday, create a refinement of one of the spells in the Great Book and to gain his father's seat on the High Council or even to serve beside him.

And now it was all over.

He wasn't even nineteen yet.

What in the name of the Light did you think you were DOING?

It was like awakening from a beautiful dream only to discover that it had been a nightmare all along. Everything had seemed so plausible: with the umbrastone, they could convince the High Council to listen to them before the City was in ruins.

Idiot. Idiot. Whatever made you think they'd listen to you when they wouldn't listen to half the Mages in the City? All you've done is bring disgrace on House Volpiril and ruination on your friends! Farmer Kellen couldn't have done better. With the thought of Kellen Tavadon, a new thought struck him. *If the High Council made Lycaelon Tavadon's son disappear, maybe they'll send me to the same place.*

Strangely, the thought brought comfort.

AT the same time Cilarnen was awakening in his cell below the Council House, Setarion Volpiril was being escorted into Lycaelon's private offices as the chorus of Second Night Bells echoed through the City.

He had not, of course, been asleep. The High Mages were, by necessity, creatures of the hours of darkness, since the quiet night hours were best for the elaborate workings of the High Magick. He had been called from the Grand Circle—which was by day the Council chamber—by the Arch-Mage's personal authority, and escorted to Lycaelon's office by six stone golems and the Arch-Mage's personal private secretary.

Anigrel stood aside to let him pass, then followed Lord Volpiril into the office. He kept his face carefully neutral, betraying no hint of the exultation he felt. Tonight was the culmination of plans carefully-nurtured for years—plans that would deliver such a blow to the Golden City that would weaken it past all ability to defend itself.

He had seen Lord Volpiril before—almost daily, in fact—but for the first time, it struck Anigrel how very much Cilarnen resembled his father—the same russet hair, the same pale blue eyes. Proper Mageborn breeding saw to that, of course. Among the sons of the Mageborn, only Kellen Outlaw had not taken after his father . . . in more ways than one.

"What is the meaning of this?" Volpiril demanded before Lycaelon had a chance to speak. "You interrupt the Working upon the City-Wards—we shall have to begin again from the beginning—all that time, all that preparation—wasted! This had better be worth my time."

"Another will take your place," Lycaelon said calmly. "Be seated, Lord Volpiril, and calm yourself. Because of your long service to the City—however misguided—I have brought you here tonight to offer you a choice."

Whatever Volpiril might have been expecting to hear, obviously it was not this. He turned sideways, glancing back at Anigrel, who was still standing beside the door.

"I repose all confidence and trust in Anigrel. And what you will hear from him has every bearing on the decision you will make here," Lycaelon said.

"Decision? What decision?" Volpiril demanded, sweeping his robes about himself and settling into the seat opposite the Arch-Mage's desk. His pale eyes glittered with exasperation.

"Whether to give up your seat on the Council and retire utterly into private life. I am willing, in that case, to accept your oath and parole, providing you do nothing to interfere with Cilarnen's trial and Banishment."

"Cilarnen?" Lord Volpiril half-rose from his seat, thought better of it, and settled slowly back again. "What has the boy to do with anything? He is at home asleep in his bed."

"He was arrested not two bells ago—for treason," Lycaelon said. He smiled, gazing fully into his enemy's eyes.

"Treason!" Volpiril leaned back in the low chair, visibly shaken. "I do not believe it. I *will* not believe it!"

"A dozen Mages saw him—and the cabal he had formed—preparing to make umbrastone," Anigrel said, speaking for the first time. "There can be no doubt."

"Where would he have gotten such a notion?" Lycaelon demanded, his grey eyes hard. "Where would he have gotten the materials—the information? There is only one place. Oh, he has not been questioned yet. Whether he is questioned . . . that is up to you."

"But I am innocent! I knew nothing of this! Question me under Truthspell, and by the Light, I will give you your proof!" Volpiril demanded, his face the ashy grey of shock.

"My dear Setarion," Lycaelon said, shaking his head ruefully. "I am certain that you no longer remember your part in this. No Truthspell would implicate you, as you well know. And I doubt young Cilarnen remembers who it was that set his foot upon the path to treason. But your recent actions in Council speak for themselves about your oft-professed love for the City."

"My—recent—actions—" Suddenly Volpiril grew even paler, if that had been possible. Seen in the light of *this*, his

demands to remove the protection of the City from the farm-
lands outside it, and the subsequent results, would look like
the beginning of a plan to destroy Armethalieh.

"No. There is no profit to be had from this, Setarion, and
the best you can hope for is to escape with your own skin intact," said Lycaelon. "Either resign your seat, and retire utterly from public affairs, or I shall see you tried for treason
beside your son. And when you are Banished with him—as
you shall be—I shall see House Volpiril brought down to
ruin, and all who bear your name shall live out their days in
poverty and shame."

Anigrel's face was impassive. Lycaelon's was *almost* as
expressionless, but there was, perhaps, the trace of a gleam
in his eye.

"Choose."

Lord Volpiril got to his feet, trembling with rage, and
perhaps—at last—even with fear.

"This is a plot," he said, his voice hoarse with anger.

"Indeed," Lycaelon said. "And your son was its instigator."

"You leave me no choice."

"There is always a choice," the Arch-Mage said dispassionately.

There was a moment of tension, then Volpiril bowed his
head.

"Very well," he said in a low voice. "I resign."

"And I have your oath that you will work no further treason?" Lycaelon asked silkily.

Volpiril's head snapped up, and he took a quick step toward Lycaelon, fists clenched. For a moment Anigrel, watching, thought that Volpiril might actually attempt to strike the
Arch-Mage, and regretted leaving the stone golems outside
the door, but Lycaelon had judged the character of his enemy well.

"You have my oath," Volpiril said, his voice a groan. "I
shall work no treason—against the High Council, against the
City . . . or against the Arch-Mage."

As he spoke the words, Lycaelon lifted his wand from his

desk and sketched a glyph in the air, keying the prepared spells. Each one drifted outward from the walls and settled over Volpiril's body, binding him more firmly and eternally than golden chains.

"Very good, Lord Volpiril," Lycaelon said, a note of patronizing approval in his voice. "Now go home."

Anigrel opened the door for Lord Volpiril, and closed it quietly behind him. He wondered, in a disinterested fashion, if the man would still be alive by morning, or would contrive to end his life in some spectacular fashion. Certainly he no longer had anything to live for.

"Come, sit," Lycaelon said to Anigrel, indicating the chair beside him. "Now we have made a place for you on the Council, but I am not finished yet. Breulin and Isas must go—they are implicated as well, are they not?"

"Jorade Isas is the great-great-grandnephew of Lord Isas; his heir, I believe, as Lord Isas has never married. Geont Pentres is the youngest son of House Pentres, which is allied to House Breulin. I believe a case can be made for both lords' involvement," Anigrel said smoothly.

"You're certain Cilarnen was the ringleader—at Lord Volpiril's instigation?" Lycaelon demanded eagerly.

"Absolutely. His magickal abilities were rated by his teachers at the Mage College as exceptional. I would not be at all surprised to learn that there were spells of compulsion involved on at least some of the others."

Lycaelon smiled. "Very good. A little judicious mind-healing, and Pentres and young Isas won't remember their parts in this terrible matter. I will offer that to Lord Breulin and Lord Isas as an inducement to see reason. If they will not, of course, there is no reason to believe that their dependents have the proper character to wield the High Magick, now is there, Anigrel?"

"Certainly not, Lord Lycaelon," Anigrel said gravely.

"And the other three?" Lycaelon asked, moving on.

"One is Tradeborn. With your permission, we can burn the Gift out of him tomorrow and Banish him tomorrow evening or the day after, once the boundaries have been extended over the Central Valley once again. He is being fostered by House Arcable. Fines and restrictions there, I'd suggest."

"Very good. I'll see a proposed schedule for that on my desk by the end of the sennight. Ah, I must remember to stop giving you such orders, Anigrel. You must instruct my new secretary to be as efficient as you have been."

"I will see to it, Lord Lycaelon," Anigrel said with a smile.

"The last two conspirators present unique difficulties, each in his own way. One is Kermis Lalkmair—you will recall the family?"

Lycaelon sighed. "An eternal thorn in my side!"

Anigrel permitted himself another smile. Dyren Lalkmair was an eccentric scholar devoted to study and research. The family shunned politics utterly. "It is said that Lord Lalkmair would rather Burn the Gift out of one of his sons than see him hold a seat on a City council. He would view treason even more harshly. You will be seen as both merciful and just if you simply hand Kermis Lalkmair over to his family for judgment . . . and I do not think he will ever be a problem to us again."

"An excellent notion, Anigrel," Lycaelon said warmly. "You will be a formidable asset to the High Council. And the last? You said there were two problems."

"Margon Ogregance. He is the son of the High Mage Epalin Ogregance, who oversees the Merchants and Provender's Council."

Lycaelon sighed. "And Lord Ogregance has been telling me since before the rains came that Volpiril's decree would be the ruin of us all—as if I didn't know it!" He frowned.

Anigrel regarded the Arch-Mage with faint curiosity. He'd never thought that either charity or disinterested kindness were a part of Lycaelon's emotional makeup. Such hesitancy over young Margon's fate was most unlike him.

Or perhaps this was the considered rumination of a consummate political game-player, weighing all the possibilities before coming to a decision. The High Mage

Ogregance was an important figure in the City—especially now—and to alienate him at this delicate juncture could be disastrous. It was Ogregance who dealt most directly with the Home Farms, and kept the skittish and quarrelsome merchants in line.

"It is, of course, a transgression worth Banishment," Lycaelon said at last. "Or at the very least, the removal of young Margon's Magegift. But—as I will make plain to Lord Ogregance—House Volpiril has been at the root of all of this, from the attempt to starve the City by the ruinous and ill-considered reduction of our borders, to this latest attempt to overthrow us utterly. His son was but a pawn.

"There will be punishment, of course. Margon Ogregance's advancement in rank will not be as swift as it might have otherwise been. We must be certain that this . . . cankerous growth was entirely of House Volpiril's instigation. But once these inconvenient memories have been pruned from his mind—I shall do that myself—perhaps the young tree will grow straight once more."

And Mage Ogregance will be your devoted partisan and supporter for as long as he lives, lest you suddenly discover "evidence" that Margon was, in fact, a willing participant in Cilarnen Volpiril's plot, Anigrel thought admiringly. Lycaelon Tavadon might be foolish in many ways, but the man was a master manipulator of his fellow Mages, and even Anigrel stood in awe of his grasp of politics.

All for the good of the City, of course. As defined by the Arch-Mage Lycaelon Tavadon.

"An excellent solution, Arch-Mage," Anigrel said, allowing his voice to fill with the warmth of admiration. "And, if you will permit, I will take care of the preparations for Rolfort and young Cilarnen. After all "—he smiled coldly—"it need not be elegant."

"Indeed." An answering wolf-light kindled in Lycaelon's eyes. "But I know that your work could never be anything less than perfection, Anigrel. You are . . . you are the son I *should* have had."

Anigrel bowed his pale head modestly, casting his eyes downward.

"Lord Arch-Mage, I—"

"And why should you not be?" Lycaelon said, struck by a sudden inspiration. "I have no children—you have no family. You have been my son in all but body. It is not right that the name of Tavadon, which has served this great City so well and so long, should die with me. I shall adopt you—make you my heir—and you will serve the City after me, in the name of Tavadon!"

"My lord, I—" This was going even better than he had dreamed. As the Arch-Mage's heir, Anigrel would be in an unassailable position of power and influence. No one would dare speak against him. Such adoptions were not common, but they weren't entirely unheard-of, either. Especially in the light of Lycaelon's personal history. Both his children Banished, and both half-breeds; he'd never actually *had* a true Mageborn son. "I shall serve you more faithfully than you can imagine."

"My son." Lycaelon seemed to savor the words as if they were some rare delicacy. "My *true* son. Come Light's Day I shall have you entered on the rolls of the Temple of the Light as my true son and heir. You shall take Volpiril's seat in Council, and I shall see you raised from Master Undermage to the ranks of the High Mages themselves!"

"My lord," Anigrel said, a faint modest note of protest in his voice. His present rank was Master Undermage; his elevation to that rank from Journeyman Undermage had been unwontedly swift, and a signal mark of Lycaelon's favor. To go from there to High Mage was normally the work of decades of study: many Mageborn never reached the higher ranks of Magery at all.

"What? Do you not think *my son* is worthy of such an honor?" Lycaelon demanded with heavy-handed humor. "I know you are more than capable in the Art."

"I think, my lord," Anigrel said practically, "that it will cause jealously and bad feeling among your fellows." *And that will work to my advantage, in time.*

"Bah! The petty quibbles of petty fools! I swore I would bring the Council to heel when Volpiril forced his madness upon me, and so I shall. This is but the beginning. We shall do great things together, Anigrel."

"Indeed we shall, Lord Arch-Mage. Indeed we shall."

⟳

HE must have slept—though Cilarnen had no memory of dozing off—but the hard click of stone-on-stone roused Cilarnen to heart-pounding wakefulness.

Footsteps in the corridor outside. Stone golem footsteps.

He was on his feet before he realized he'd moved, his back pressed against the wall of his cell as if he could somehow transport himself through the unyielding stone.

They were coming for him.

His hands clenched and unclenched without his conscious volition. He made a hundred plans and discarded them in an instant—not for escape; he knew that was impossible; but to somehow save the others. Surely the High Council would give him a chance to explain, to tell them that this had all been his idea . . .

The cell door opened. Cilarnen blinked as light flooded the cell. A globe of Mage-light floated in over the man's head and rose toward the ceiling, and in the new brightness, Cilarnen could see that his visitor was a blond man who wore the plain grey robes and tabard of a Master Undermage. Behind him stood a pair of Stone Golems.

"Cilarnen Volpiril. You are in a great deal of trouble," the stranger said pleasantly. "I am Undermage Anigrel. I am here to explain matters to you."

Anigrel? But . . . the Arch-Mage's private secretary? Here?

One of the stone golems stepped into the cell and set down a large basket beside the door.

"The necessities of your imprisonment," Undermage Anigrel said.

Cilarnen did not bother to glance toward the basket. His

whole being was focused on the Undermage. Imprisonment? For how long? Forever?

"What . . . what about the others?" It was the hardest thing Cilarnen had ever done to get the sentence out. His mouth was dry, and his tongue seemed to have grown unbearably clumsy. He stumbled over the words as if he had forgotten how to speak.

Undermage Anigrel raised his eyebrows in mild reproof. "The other traitors? They will be dealt with appropriately. You should consider your own fate."

"They—It was my idea. All of it." Words came easier now, and it seemed terribly important to make Undermage Anigrel believe him.

"Oh, we know that. All a plot of House Volpiril to seize power in the City for itself. But you have failed."

Cilarnen stared at the Undermage in dawning horror. It had never occurred to him—never!—that no matter what he did, anyone would think his father was involved in it.

"No! He— my father— Lord Volpiril— No—" He took a step forward, though he had no idea why. The ingrained habit of submission to lawful authority held, even now.

Undermage Anigrel raised a slender hand. "Do not try to protect him. He has already confessed everything, and resigned his seat on the High Council, preparing to await his fate. Now there is only your fate to consider."

Cilarnen staggered backward again, leaning now against the wall of the cell for support. The cell seemed suddenly airless, its atmosphere stifling. His father had confessed?

To what?

"I don't understand," Cilarnen whispered. "I told him nothing."

"But it was he who first planted these ideas in your mind, then erased the memory of the conversation—though not the seeds of treason—by Magecraft," Undermage Anigrel said kindly. "How else could you have come by such foolish notions? What could you have been thinking of?"

"I don't know—I don't know—" Cilarnen moaned. He

staggered the few steps to the stone bench and flung himself down, covering his face with his hands. Could that truly be what had happened?

He didn't know. He didn't remember.

"I want to talk to my father," Cilarnen said, raising his face from his hands. He would confront Lord Volpiril, demand an explanation—or at least the truth.

"Alas, that is no longer possible," Undermage Anigrel said. He did not sound sorry at all. "It will never be possible again. And now you must pay for your part in these events as well, for even if your father *planted* the compulsions in your mind, had you been a true son of the City and loyal first to her welfare, you would have thrown off those compulsions, recognizing them as treasonable." He shook his head, sadly. "No, I fear that the fruit does not fall far from the tree, and treasonous blood breeds treasonous blood."

Cilarnen simply stared at Anigrel, stunned now to numbness. He'd thought the plan was all his own idea. Now the Undermage was saying that it wasn't—but he was saying that Cilarnen was still to be punished for it.

"Oh, come, Master Cilarnen," Anigrel said chidingly, sounding in that moment so much like one of Cilarnen's Mage-College tutors that for a moment he had the surreal feeling he was back in school. But Anigrel's next words returned him to reality with a chilling jolt. "It does not matter *where* the foul notion of overthrowing the High Council came from. You were still free to reject it—,to go about the lawful business of serving the City. But you did not."

"But we—but I—but we never . . . we only wanted the Council to listen to us," Cilarnen said in a very small voice.

"And so you chose to create a weapon that destroys magick. What an odd way to make someone listen, to be sure," Undermage Anigrel answered caustically. "You dabbled in the Proscribed Arts, Master Cilarnen, and for that crime you are to be stripped of your Gift and Banished from the City, just as soon as her Bounds are restored. At sunset three days hence you will be set outside the Delfier Gate, garbed in the saffron cloak of Felony. From that moment, you are Outlaw, forbidden sanctuary anywhere within Armethaliehan lands. You will be provided with a day's supply of bread and water; after that is gone you must find sustenance on your own. At dawn, the Outlaw Hunt will pass through those same gates, and if you are still within the bounds of Armethaliehan lands, they will rend you limb from limb, so you would be well advised to spend the night getting as far away from the City as you can. You may not go to the villages. By tomorrow's dawn they will once more belong to the City. Do you understand?"

"Banished?" Cilarnen stared at Undermage Anigrel, stunned. "From the City? But . . . no one is Banished. Not any more. Not for centuries."

It was a tale to frighten children with—like Demons. Surely . . .

Anigrel smiled. "Believe what you wish for as long as you can. In two days' time, Rolfort will know the truth. In three, so will you."

"But . . . where will I go?" Cilarnen asked blankly.

Undermage Anigrel shook his head in exasperation. "Boy, it does not matter to us. From the moment you don the Felon's Cloak—from the moment you are set outside the City gates—you are no longer a citizen of Armethalieh. You are dead to the City and to everyone you ever knew, just as your father is. You will never return here. You are Banished. *Now* do you understand?"

⌐

EVEN in the azure Magelight, Anigrel could see that the boy was deathly pale, his face sheened with the sweat of terror and growing despair. Anigrel felt a warm glow of satisfaction. Let the pampered highborn brat think his father was dead—he would never know otherwise.

"I understand," Cilarnen said at last. His voice trembled.

"Very good. And since we cannot have Mages wandering

around outside the City—especially rebellious, half-trained Mages—*you would do well to heed me now.*"

The key-phrase triggered the prepared spell, and Cilarnen's eyelids fluttered closed as he slipped quickly into the spell-fed trance. He barely struggled: the stronger the Gift, the more susceptible the subject to certain forms of Magick.

Anigrel moved closer, catching Cilarnen as he slumped and laying him out on the stone bench. He felt the pulse of Cilarnen's Magick, hot and strong, and when he entered Cilarnen's mind, he could see that the parts of the boy's brain that sensed and handled Mage-energy glowed as bright as a furnace. Cilarnen was a strong Mage, with a strong, well-trained Gift.

IT took Anigrel nearly two bells to do what needed to be done—Lycaelon was quite right; his work was never less than perfection—and there were few other Mages in the City, of any rank, who could have equaled it.

And none who could have detected it.

When he had finished, Anigrel felt the weight of weariness pulling at him. Perhaps he should sleep and rest himself before dealing with young Rolfort, though the work he would do there would be much simpler. He considered the matter for a moment, and decided against it. No, to wait might raise questions—he could pass off the length of time he'd spent here by saying he was questioning the boys, but not the need to rest between Excisions. And if his work on Rolfort was less than elegant, well, the boy wasn't going to live long enough to show evidence of the fact, now, was he?

Unlike young Lord Cilarnen.

Anigrel had plans for Cilarnen.

He gazed down at the sleeping Mageborn with the fondness of a craftsman for a tool that would yet give good service.

To anyone who might think to look, it would seem that Cilarnen's Gift had been burned from his mind, just as was proper for any of the higher ranks of Magery who were Banished. It would seem that way to Cilarnen himself, for a time.

But Anigrel had other plans. Cilarnen Volpiril was far too valuable a pawn to cast away simply because he had been useful once. And if he were to be useful again, Anigrel wanted him intact and at the height of his powers.

It was possible, for the first time in recent memory, to survive the Hunt—enlarging the City's boundaries to their old limits would be the work of moonturns, and when Cilarnen was turned out of the Delfier Gate, the City Lands would only extend over the Central Valley. A determined man—a man who had the wit to steal a horse—might actually escape the City lands in a night.

Rolfort, of course, would not be so fortunate. Anigrel would make certain of that.

But when Cilarnen escaped—and a desire to escape was only one of the compulsions Anigrel had laid upon him in his long Working—there was only one place he could go.

To the Wild Lands, where the Outlaw Kellen lived.

Like would surely call to like. Fellow Outlaws, fellow victims of misfortune, surely they would become as brothers?

And then Anigrel would spring his trap.

Taking a deep breath, and marshaling his strength, Anigrel summoned the globe of Mage-light and walked from the cell, preparing to pay a call upon his other victim.

AT Dawn Bells, Lycaelon was given the exquisite pleasure of entertaining Lords Isas and Breulin in his Council chambers.

Both Mages, of course, already knew most of the details of the plot and the arrests that had occurred at Midnight Bells. If servants' gossip ran swiftly in the City of a Thousand Bells, then gossip among the Mageborn ran swifter, and Lycaelon had seen no reason to stifle it. He had known that within a bell at most, the Undermages who had arrested the boys would have seen to it that the details of the matter would reach their families, whether out of spite or from a hope of currying later favor. He had entertained himself with imagining the petitions that must be flying back and forth between the families involved and their High Mage heads—Isas and Breulin—as everyone scrabbled for information that simply wasn't available.

Isas had always been something of an ally to him, but even Isas had not voted with him against Volpiril in the end, and he would pay for that now. And Breulin had always opposed his policies. It would be well to be rid of both of them.

He saw Isas first. The aged High Mage was escorted into Lycaelon's chambers by the same Stone Golems who had summoned him from his house. The old man was quivering with such indignation that for a moment Lycaelon was sure Isas was going to drop dead on the spot and save him a great deal of trouble.

"Lord Isas," he said cordially, "do sit down. You really don't look well." Light forgive him, but he *was* enjoying this!

"Lord Lycaelon—what is the meaning of this?" Isas demanded.

"Oh, I think you already know," Lycaelon said, almost purring. "The question is, what are you prepared to do about it?"

THE meeting went very much as Lycaelon intended it to. Jorade was Lord Isas's only possible heir; to keep the boy whole and unmarred Isas was willing to give up his seat on the Council and take the same oath Lord Volpiril had.

He was, in fact, absurdly grateful to do so.

"My dear Lord Lycaelon—I had no idea—no idea . . ." he quavered.

The elderly Lord Isas seemed to have aged a decade from the moment he had entered Lycaelon's chambers. His skin had taken on a greyish tinge and his breathing was harsh.

"Did I not warn you—all of you—what Volpiril was, time

and again?" Lycaelon's voice was stern. "Yet none of you listened—even you, Lawell, and I thought you my friend."

"I was—I meant to be—" Isas protested. "But—after Kellen—all of us thought . . . "

Lycaelon's face froze at the mention of the forbidden name. Yet, he consoled himself, he had a new son now. A better son. A son who would be all to him that The Outlaw had never been.

"You thought I had let my emotions overmaster me," Lycaelon said heavily. "And now you see that I acted—then, as always—for the good of the City."

"Yes," Lord Isas said, bowing his head humbly. "I see that now, Lycaelon."

"Go home, Lawell," Lycaelon said, almost kindly. "I will send Jorade to you when the mindhealers have finished with him. Treat him well. A true son is a precious gift." He reached for the bellpull. "Let me summon a servant to escort you home. You really don't look at all well."

THE meeting with Lord Breulin went a bit more awkwardly. Breulin had always been his opponent in Council; he was a man in the vigor of his prime, ambitious enough to wish to become Arch-Mage himself someday.

But Lycaelon was firm.

"My lord, if you wish to see the matter come to a public trial before the Council, that is, of course, your right. But I and many others find it very difficult to imagine how a handful of children conceived of a plan of this nature by themselves. The question that must be asked—and will be asked, frequently, in the moonturns to come, should you force me to put the matter of young Geont before the Council—is not only where they came by their peculiar notions and the means to carry them out, but who would benefit from a, shall we say, radical rearrangement of the Council?" Lycaelon said.

Lord Breulin regarded him warily, obviously not liking the note of confidence he heard in Lord Lycaelon's voice.

"May I direct your attention to the names of the conspirators?" the Arch-Mage continued. "Isas—Pentres—Lalkmair—Rolfort—Ogregance—Volpiril. Isas, Lalkmair, Rolfort, and Ogregance we can dismiss at once. Three of them have no Council ties, and all the world knows that Isas is—*was*—my supporter. He could hardly be expected to see benefit from the overthrow of the Council. This leaves Volpiril and Pentres, and House Pentres is a Breulin supporter, its fortunes tied to those of your House, my lord Breulin.

"How odd. The world believes Volpiril and Breulin to be at odds. Certainly the two of you seemed to be in opposition in Council—except when you were opposing me. How singular to find Volpiril's heir and Breulin's dependent so closely linked. Perhaps you believed you could share the spoils. Or perhaps you intended a further betrayal of one another?"

Lord Breulin's face had turned a deep shade of maroon, making his stiff silver beard stand out even more brightly against his skin.

"You have no proof of that," he said through gritted teeth.

"I have Lord Volpiril's resignation from the Council," Lycaelon said simply. "Lord Isas has also resigned."

Breulin's eyes narrowed. Resignation—for a man as ambitious as Lord Volpiril—was as good as a confession of guilt, yet how could it be otherwise, when Volpiril's heir was the acknowledged ringleader of the young conspirators? Lycaelon needed no spell of Mindhearing to know Lord Breulin's thoughts. They were plain upon the man's face, as at last he awoke to his own peril.

"What will be done with the boys?" Breulin asked, after a long pause.

"For some, Banishment," Lycaelon said. "As soon as the Hunt has space to run free once more."

"And Geont?" Breulin said when Lycaelon said nothing further.

"In the end, his fate is in your hands, Lord Breulin," Lycaelon answered. "As is my understanding of the degree of your involvement."

THOUGH the matter was an open secret, it was not yet a public scandal—and perhaps Lord Breulin's conscience was not quite as clear as he wished it to be. Certainly, if he allowed Geont Pentres's Gift to be taken from him, Lord Breulin would make enemies of those who had been his allies and supporters. And in the end, whether the hearings proved him culpable or innocent, he would still be tainted by the shadow of conspiracy.

So to avoid the shame and publicity of a Council inquiry—and incidentally to save himself from the humiliation of giving up a kinsman to the Excision of his Magegift—Lord Breulin, too, resigned his position on the Council and gave his binding oath before the second bells of day rang out through the City.

Nine

The Council of Fear

At First Morning Bells, the High Council convened in special session.

The Council chamber was one of the most imposing rooms in all the Golden City, though few but Mages and Outlanders ever saw it. It had been built by Magecraft, as had been the whole of the Council House, and its unadorned walls of white marble gleamed, polished to mirror-perfection, their flawless curves unrelieved by any ornament save two golden doors opposite sides of the circular chamber. Each door was wrought with the symbol of the Eternal Light in gleaming high relief, so that the planes and angles of their exquisite surfaces glittered as if they were aflame.

If the walls were stark and unornamented, the floor was their opposite. It held a complex pattern of black and white marble. Though it might seem to be nothing more than an overelaborate decorative pattern, it was in fact a series of keys that allowed Adepts to keep their proper places during the nighttime Workings, for the Council chamber was also the Temple where the Great Circles were held for the Mage's nighttime Workings.

At one end of the Council chamber stood a curved judicial bench twice the height of a tall man, as black as the wall behind it was white. It was here that the High Council sat to pass judgment upon every aspect of life in Armethalieh. The room had been designed by the ancient Mages who had wrought it to overawe the mind and numb the spirit. Even the Mages who worked here daily were not immune to its effects, and that was as it should be. Let all who entered here know that the individual was as nothing, and the City was all.

The Arch-Mage's thronelike chair was in the center of the bench, with six lesser seats on either side. Until today, every seat had always been filled.

The remaining Mages—Meron, Perizel, Lorins, Arance, Ganaret, Nagid, Vilmos, Dagan, and Harith—entered the chamber where Lycaelon was already seated. When the nine of them had taken their places, they looked with various degrees of consternation at the three empty seats.

"Breulin, Isas, and Volpiril have resigned from the Council, for reasons of which I think all of you are aware," Lycaelon said. His voice filled the chamber, resonating from the polished marble walls. "This special session will be devoted to dealing with the matter of the traitors, discovering the extent of the corruption, and repairing the harm that they have done to the City. But first, there is the matter of filling the vacancies created."

There was a stir of anticipation in the room. Vacancies on

the High Council were rare. For there to be three at once was unprecedented, and every man in the room had his own candidates to fill the vacant chairs.

But Lycaelon was not finished speaking.

"I propose to you my own candidate, Chired Anigrel, who is to become my son and the heir of my House this Light's Day. Many of you will know him as my private secretary, but in these past moonturns he has done far more for the good of the City than scribing mere paperwork. It was through Undermage Anigrel's tireless work that the traitors were uncovered and the conspiracy disarmed before the threat could grow. He has demonstrated an uncommon devotion and loyalty to the City, as well as a mastery of the Art that much exceeds his rank. I open the matter now for discussion before I call the vote."

"Discussion . . . ? But Arch-Mage, surely you do not expect us to vote upon the matter today?" Lord Dagan asked, almost timidly.

"My lords," Lycaelon said ponderously, "I wish from the bottom of my heart that we had the leisure to consider the matter in our usual deliberate fashion. But the empty seats among us are proof enough that this cannot be. For the other vacancies, yes, of course, we shall take as much time as you like. But in light of the service he has already rendered to the City, I do not wish to deprive us of Anigrel's sapient counsel for another moment. Providing, always, that we are all in agreement."

"My lord Lycaelon, may I be the first to offer you congratulations upon your heir? May the Light defend him in all his works. It is heartening to hear good news when the shadows seem to gather on every side," Lord Harith said.

"I shall convey your congratulations to my son," Lycaelon said, bowing his head. "We are both gratified." He smiled inwardly. Harith had obviously decided which way the hare would jump and was anxious to assure Lycaelon that he would continue to support him.

Perizel leaned forward, signaling his intention to speak

next. The man was a consummate political animal, and cloaked his ambition in a punctilious insistence on the observance of proper form. If Lord Perizel disliked an idea, he could delay it for sennights by debating every detail of the form of its presentation.

"My lord Arch-Mage. Without in any way speaking to Undermage Anigrel's character or other qualifications to join our Council, I must raise a point of order regarding his possible appointment. As you yourself have remarked, his rank is but that of Undermage. Yet one must be of the rank of High Mage to serve upon the Council. Is that not so?"

There was a murmur of agreement—not unmixed with relief in a few cases—as the remaining members of the Council conferred among themselves, whispering and nodding their heads. Lycaelon allowed it to continue for a few moments before speaking again.

"My lords, I believe you will find there is precedent for a Mage of lesser rank serving upon the High Council, should his other qualifications be exceptional. I direct your attention to the case of Undermage Camorin in the 427th year of the City—and your ancestor, Lord Arance, who served with distinction upon the Council beginning in Year 719, though he had not yet attained the distinction of High Mage. And should Lord Anigrel be permitted to test for advancement upon an accelerated schedule, then this consideration would certainly be set at rest."

Lord Perizel regarded the Arch-Mage for a moment, then smiled faintly and nodded, settling back in his chair. "You are correct, Lord Arch-Mage. There is precedent. I withdraw my objection."

Lycaelon glanced around at the other Mages. Their faces were studiously blank, but there was no way they could argue with facts. Both Mage Camorin and Arance's ancestor *had* been of lesser rank when they served upon the Council—not only had Anigrel found the citations for him to strengthen his argument, but every man here should recall the cases from History of the City under Mage Hendassar.

THOUGH the Mages continued to debate—with Lycaelon and with each other—Lycaelon could tell that their words were merely a cloak for the furious debate each Mage was having with himself.

What was Lycaelon's *real* motive in proposing Anigrel for the Council? Was there more to be gained by supporting Anigrel's nomination or by blocking it?

Every Mage here knew about the arrests and the resignations that had followed them, of course. All of them were shocked—as Lycaelon had been—that such a thing could happen, and fearful of how far the treasonous taint might have spread. If Mageborn could conspire against Mageborn, then no one was safe.

Further, each one of them—none better, in all the City— had seen what disaster their ill-considered support of Lord Volpiril's plans had led them into. Now it seemed that Lycaelon—and Anigrel—were poised to lead them out of it, to undo as much of the damage as *could* be repaired, and take steps to ensure that the rest was handled suitably.

"How did Lord Anigrel discover the traitors?" Lord Ganaret asked, after a full bell of debate.

Lycaelon smiled sadly, and spread his hands wide. "My lord, it is with regret that I cannot disclose Lord Anigrel's methods as yet. You see, I am not entirely certain that the entire cabal has been uprooted."

That got their attention! Nine pairs of eyes focused on Lycaelon's face, and the Council chamber was suddenly silent.

"But . . . they were arrested . . . " Lord Ganaret gasped.

"Boys making umbrastone," Lycaelon said, scoffing. "Terrible in itself—but my lords, who told them to make it? Who put that idea into their unformed minds? Who nurtured them in rebellion and then covered his tracks so flawlessly? Could mere boys have come up with such notions on their own? Could they have known where to find the proscribed instructions so easily, had they not had experienced help? I

have prayed—I have hoped—there was another answer. But
I can find none."

"Because there is none." Ancient Lord Vilmos spoke, his
quavering voice cracking with certainty. "Lord Lycaelon,
you are right. This conspiracy touches us all. We must have
Lord Anigrel on the Council."

"Yes—appoint Anigrel to the Council and make the City
safe again," Harith said. "Discover the traitors and Banish
them!"

Lycaelon allowed himself a small nod of approval. Clever
of Harith not to be the first to suggest Anigrel's appointment.
That would look too pointed.

"My lords, do you wish time for further discussion?" Lycaelon asked. "Or will you vote now?"

One by one, the assembled High Mages placed both
hands, palm down, upon the table before them, each signify-
ing his readiness to vote.

"Then I call the vote," Lycaelon said. "Admission of Undermage Anigrel to the High Council." He raised his hand,
palm out. Assent.

One by one, the nine remaining High Mages copied his
gesture.

The vote was unanimous.

Anigrel was to be admitted to the High Council.

IN the antechamber, Anigrel waited. It took all of his skill at
concealing his true nature to disguise his nervousness now.
Lycaelon was a master of manipulation, and after the events
of the night before, the Council was a pack of nervous
frightened old men begging for decisive leadership, whether
they knew it or not. But it was still far from certain which
way the vote would go.

Either way would serve his—and his Dark Lady's—
ultimate goal, of course.

If the Council accepted him, he would have a direct voice

in the ruling of Armethalieh. He would be able to put forward his ideas himself, and not have to manipulate Lycaelon into coming up with them.

If the Council rejected him, it would enrage Lycaelon, and make the Arch-Mage that much easier for Anigrel to manipulate. But the son of Torbet Anigrel, himself the son of a tradesman—Torbet Anigrel, who had died in obscurity, spurned with contempt by the highborn, pure-blooded Mageborn—would burn with hatred and humiliation at the rejection. Not even his adoption into House Tavadon would salve that wound.

And either way, he must go before the Council and hear their verdict to his face.

At last—it seemed as if eons had passed, though Noon Bells had not yet rung—a Journeyman came to conduct him to the chamber.

Anigrel passed through the golden door and crossed the vast expanse of black and white floor. He reached the white marble square that marked the center of the chamber, turned to face the judicial bench, and bowed. The ten men looking down upon him might have been carved of the same material as the walls and floor, and for a moment Anigrel's heart beat faster. Had it gone as badly as that?

Then Lycaelon smiled.

"Welcome. Welcome, Lord Anigrel, to the High Council of Armethalieh. May you serve the City long and well."

Anigrel bowed—more deeply this time, and for once, he did not have to disguise his expression as he rose. An expression of joy was not at all amiss on such an occasion. What Mage worth his robes would *not* be overjoyed to hear such a pronouncement?

And if his voice trembled with emotion, well, that was not amiss either. "My lord Arch-Mage—my lord Mages. I vow to you that I shall render to Armethalieh such service as she has never seen in all her long and glorious history. This I do swear, from the bottom of my heart."

"Then come, join us. There is much to do," Lycaelon said.

Anigrel came forward and mounted the three steps he had ascended so often in the past on some errand for the Arch-Mage. But this time, he was not an errand-boy. He was a member of the High Council.

He glanced around quickly, found Volpiril's chair, and seated himself.

"OUR first order of business: the boundaries of the City Lands," Lycaelon said.

"I think we can safely agree that we must take the Home Farms back at least," Lord Meron said smoothly.

"Certainly we must do more than that," Anigrel said promptly, "but Lord Meron is quite right to remind us that we have a number of calls upon our resources at the moment. We must begin with the Delfier Valley, of course, so that the Banishings on our calendar proceed as scheduled."

"No difficulty in outrunning a Hunt if the bounds extend no further than the City walls, eh, Meron?" Lord Nagid pointed out, and there was general, if slightly nervous, laughter from the assembled Mages.

"And meanwhile, in the light of the current emergency—though I understand this is only a formality—I propose that we immediately sever all ties, both explicit and implicit, with all Lesser Races," Anigrel added. "In my work for the Arch-Mage, I noted that there were still active trade agreements in our records with the Elves, which is an intolerable threat to our security. Need I remind any of you that the Elven-born have long maintained cordial relations with the Wildmages? I do not say that they are the source of the umbrastone that lately plagued us . . . but now, more than ever, we must be strong in our loyalties to our blood and our race."

He knew from his contacts with the Dark Lady that the Elves might attempt to warn the City that the Endarkened were active once again. Though there was little chance that the Mages would pay any attention to the words of one of the Lesser Races—or even allow them within the City walls—why take the chance?

"These matters must be voted upon as separate items," Lord Perizel pointed out irritably. "First we must vote upon remaking the boundaries, then we must vote to sever all agreements with the Lesser Races. And what of the Mountain Traders? *They* trade with the Elves as well."

"You are an example to us all, Lord Perizel," Lycaelon said gravely. "Very well. Let us first settle the matter of the boundaries. The debate—and the vote—is upon the matter of extending them once more over the Central Valley. Discussion?"

But no man there wished to be seen as supporting Lord Volpiril's policies. There was no discussion, and the vote was unanimous in favor of extending the boundaries back over the entire valley once more.

"So voted," Lycaelon said, his voice rich with satisfaction. "Tonight we will Work to extend the Borders once more, and at tomorrow dusk we will begin to cleanse Armethalieh of her traitors. We will resume at First Afternoon Bell to debate the second matter upon our agenda."

WHEN the Council resumed after luncheon, at first it seemed that the matter that Anigrel had raised would occupy the Mages for the rest of the day. No one was in favor of trading with the Elves, of course, but the question of precisely what to do about it seemed—with Lord Perizel's help—to become more tangled the longer it was debated. Were Elven-made goods also to be excluded? What of those humans known to deal with Elves, such as the Mountain Traders, even though they no longer traded directly with the City? And should the ban be extended to those, such as the Selken Traders, who might be trading without any regard to proscriptions—who, in fact, might well be trading with anyone and anything that approached them?

Lycaelon might have been forced to table the debate—in

the name of getting other necessary work done—if Auronwy hadn't chosen that opportune moment to enter with a message.

"Your pardon, Arch-Mage," the young Journeyman said, leaning over to place a single sheet of velum in front of Lycaelon, "but there is a . . . person outside the gates, requesting an audience with the High Council."

Lycaelon glanced up at the odd note in the Council page's voice. The boy looked positively terrified.

"What sort of person, Auronwy?" he said gently.

"A . . . an . . . Arch-Mage, it is an *Elf!*" Auronwy whispered. "He—it—he asked for an audience with the High Council . . . "

Lycaelon glanced down at the paper in front of him. It was the standard report from the guard tower on any who approached the Delfier Gate unexpectedly, listing the numbers of the party and the general description. The creature had come alone.

"Very good, Auronwy. Now go. Rest. We will deal with this."

He waited until the Journeyman had left the chamber.

"My lords," he said, raising his voice to cut across the discussion. "We no longer have the leisure for debate. At this very moment, one of the proud and haughty Elven-born stands outside the Delfier Gate, demanding admission to this very chamber. By our ancient laws and treaties, we must admit him . . . but what purpose can he have here? Is it not suspicious that he chooses this moment to arrive?"

"Yes!" Lord Vilmos shouted. "It is the Elves—the Elves are behind it all! They must be! Send the creature away! Send it away at once!"

Lord Vilmos, Lycaelon thought, would definitely be the next to go. He had obviously reached that time of life at which the stress of Council business was proving far too much for him. But for now, the man's willingness to jump at shadows was proving useful. His hysteria stampeded the Council as nothing else could. Perizel suggested that they call the vote at once, but confine it entirely to the matter of the Elves and the Lesser Races; Lycaelon graciously acceded.

It was unanimous. Ties with the Lesser Races would be severed immediately.

Lycaelon summoned another Page. He scribbled a few lines on the Gate-captain's report and sealed it with his Council ring.

"Take this to the head of the City Guard. Tell him that the creature waiting outside the Delfier Gate is to be turned away. Tell him he is authorized to use supreme force if necessary."

—

CILARNEN had no idea how long he spent in the gloomy cell. When he awoke, Lord Anigrel was gone, and his head ached terribly. He felt dull and ill. This must be the way the unGifted felt all the time; he knew he had been stripped of his Magegift: the thing that made him a member of the ruling classes of Armethalieh, City of Mages.

Eventually, hunger and thirst drove him to investigate the basket the stone golems had left. It proved to contain several loaves of penance-bread, a large jug of water, a small tin cup, and a larger tin utensil whose purpose was not hard to guess. Though the water was flat and warm, thirst made it bearable, but he hadn't the stomach to try the bread just yet. He still felt too sick.

Drinking cleared his head—enough to worry about his friends and his family. What would happen to his mother and his sisters now that Lord Volpiril was dead? Would his mother's family take her back, with such an awful disgrace hovering over her? He vaguely recalled that his elder sister Dialee had been betrothed, but could not remember to whom—would her suitor call off the match? Undoubtedly. And poor Eshavi would certainly never find a husband now at all. Unless some common-born fellow deigned to take either of them. He groaned at the thought.

But such matters could not occupy him for long when he

had his friends to worry about. Were they all to be Banished as well? Or was there some more terrible fate in store for them? He shuddered. What could be more terrible than being stripped of one's Gift and being turned out of the Golden City to face an unknown future?

Or—were the rest of them to be spared, and only he to be Banished?

He would never know. Unless, somehow, by the mercy of the Light—and Cilarnen wasn't entirely sure it would *be* a mercy—he managed to evade the Outlaw Hunt, and they did too, and he met them upon the road.

Cilarnen's conception of the world outside the City walls was hazy at best, and his mind rebelled from contemplating it now. He would know soon enough, whether he wanted to or not.

Eventually hunger drove him to try the penance-bread. It was like no food he had ever encountered in his life. The bread was coarse and unpalatable, very strong-tasting, and required a great deal of chewing before he could choke it down. He supposed, dourly, that he should be grateful that an Outlaw-to-be was given any bread at all, considering the state of food supplies in the City.

He ate it all, but no one came to bring him any more.

In fact, no one came back at all, for a very long time.

The water in the jug—by now sour and brackish—was nearly gone when Cilarnen heard footsteps in the hall again. Not Stone Golems this time. The softer footsteps of leather boots on stone.

When the cell door opened, he could almost have cried with relief—he had nearly convinced himself that Undermage Anigrel had lied: that he was not to be Banished at all, but left in this tiny cell to starve and die of thirst. But he caught his breath in dismay at the sight of two City Constables in the deep scarlet uniform of the City Watch.

They were fully armed with truncheon and halberd, and regarded Cilarnen with expressions of disgust and contempt.

"Time to leave, Outlaw," one of them said. He tossed a

bundle to the floor. It skidded across the stone and stopped at Cilarnen's feet.

He reached down and picked it up. Some kind of a pack. And a Felon's Cloak.

He had seen Felons paraded in the City Square, of course: social unfortunates condemned to wear the lurid yellow Cloak with its black Felon's Mark for a sennight or a moonturn for some infraction of the City's laws. But never— never!—had he thought that the day would come when he, a Volpiril, would be forced to handle such an object. Though the cloak was thick and warm—made of heavy felt—the fabric was harsh to the touch, and stank of cheap dye. He wondered who had worn it last.

"Put it on, Outlaw. And give me your Talisman. You don't belong to the City any longer," the Constable said.

Cilarnen touched the Talisman he wore around his neck. Though they might wear it on a leather cord or a cotton string or a silver chain or one of gold and jewels, every citizen of Armethalieh wore the same gold rectangle, marking them as a citizen of Armethalieh.

Now it was to be stripped from him.

With shaking fingers—feeling more light-headed than either hunger or panic could account for—Cilarnen unlaced his tunic and drew out his Talisman on its jeweled golden chain. The sapphires were colorless in the dimness.

It took him a long time to undo the catch, to work the Talisman to the end of the chain and slip it off, and when he got to his feet and walked over to the Constable, golden rectangle in hand, the man wouldn't take it. Cilarnen stood there for a long moment before realizing that the man would not touch him, then bent and set the Talisman carefully on the floor. He'd thought nothing could make him feel worse than waking up and knowing he'd been stripped of his Gift, but losing his Talisman—his last tie to the City—was somehow worse. He clasped the chain again carefully and tucked it back into his tunic.

"Now put on the Cloak, pick up your pack, and let's go,"

the Constable said, drumming his halberd-butt on the floor of the cell to emphasize his point.

Quickly Cilarnen picked up the Cloak. As he did, the Constable picked up his discarded Talisman and put it into the pouch on his belt.

"Put it on, Outlaw!" the man barked, apparently having used up what little patience he possessed.

Thoroughly cowed, Cilarnen quickly put on the Cloak and pulled the hood up over his face. It tied at the throat with a drawstring, but his hands were shaking too hard for him to manage that, and he settled for wrapping it around himself. He picked up the leather pack and held it in his arms, uncertain of what to do with it.

One of the Constables stepped outside the door. The other—the one who had done all the speaking—gestured with his halberd for Cilarnen to follow. Cilarnen staggered after him, wincing at the brightness of the corridor after so long in the dimness of his cell.

He wanted to cry, to scream, to run. But there was nowhere to run to.

He followed the Constable up a flight of stairs, wishing now only that the nightmare would end as swiftly as possible. As he neared the top of the stairs, he heard the first notes of Evensong begin, and discovered, with sick surprise, that he was in the Western Courtyard. Ahead lay the Delfier Gate, with the lesser gates within the Great Gate standing open. Waiting for him.

It was sunset—of what day? a foolish part of his mind wondered—and the day had been bright and clear. He hesitated, shivering as he breathed in the cold winter air, and was rewarded with a sharp poke in the back from the Constable's halberd. It registered only dimly through the thick fabric of the Cloak, but that the man had dared to do it was shock enough.

"Keep moving, Outlaw."

The golden bell of the Council House joined the Evensong, its booming ring so close that Cilarnen winced as he staggered forward. Constant proddings in the back urged him to quicken his pace, and soon he was almost running toward the open gate.

He stopped in shock the moment his feet touched dirt. He was *outside the walls.*

Behind him the Lesser Gates boomed shut. Cilarnen stood there in numb shock as Evensong slowly faded into silence. He clutched the Cloak around himself, shivering with cold—back in the cell he would never have thought he'd be happy to have it, and it was not nearly as warm as any of his own warm winter cloaks, but it was far better than nothing at all. He took the time, now, to tie the draw-strings at the throat closed, but the cold made him clumsy, and he dropped the bag he'd been holding. It hit the ground at his feet.

As he picked it up, he remembered Undermage Anigrel's words. The bag contained bread and water. Food!

He tore open the sack, revealing another penance-loaf and a full waterskin. He tossed the sack away and drained half the waterskin in a few gulps, then tore into the loaf, wolfing it down hungrily. It did much to still the growling in his belly, but when it was gone he was still outside the gates of the City.

It was dark—twilight—and growing darker quickly. He was colder than he'd ever been in his life—as much because he knew there was no welcoming hearth and hot cider at the end of his journey as because of the temperature. He ought to just sit down right here and wait for dawn. But some strange impulse of restlessness made him head down the rutted cart track that led away from the City.

ONCE he might have summoned Mage-light to light his way, Cilarnen thought bitterly, as he stumbled along in the dark. Or at the very least, he might have Called Fire to warm him. Now all he could do was grope his way from tree to tree, unable to understand why he didn't simply lie down in the middle of the road and wait for it all to be over.

But something deep inside wouldn't let him.

He startled at every unfamiliar sound—and there were many. The very bushes seemed to be alive with unnameable creatures, and moonturns of neglect had left the road crusted with ice and hard-packed snow. Cilarnen fell several times before he learned to walk upon the treacherous surface.

At least—once the moon rose—the whiteness of the snow made it a little easier to see where he was going.

How far was it to Nerendale? That was the nearest village to Armethalieh—he knew that much of the world beyond the City walls. He would reach it—somehow—before dawn— force them to give him food, shelter . . .

No. He would take a horse. They must have horses. With a horse he could outpace the Outlaw Hunt, and be beyond the bounds of the City Lands before it reached him.

He could not quite remember when it had become so important to outrun the Hunt. It hadn't been anything like a conscious decision. If he'd had anything approaching a plan for his future, it had been to face the Hunt: surely there would be a Mage with it, to control it? Perhaps he could ask for more time to make his way out of City lands? Or perhaps the Hunt would escort him the rest of the way? That must be it. All that talk of Undermage Anigrel's about the Hunt tearing him to bits had only been to frighten him. It must have been. How was he supposed to know where the boundaries of City Lands lay? It wasn't a subject studied at the Mage College, after all. The night spent outside the walls must only be a punishment, and the Hunt sent to escort the Outlaw to the boundaries of the City Lands in the morning. The more he thought about it, the more sense it made.

But now he'd abandoned all notion of awaiting the Hunt. The only thing that mattered was getting as far away as he could as fast as possible.

Then he saw the light.

Here in the darkness, among the winter-bare trees, it was

easy to see: a bright spark, burning steadily. For a moment Cilarnen wondered if his eyes deceived him. He blinked hard, but it was still there, somewhere tauntingly ahead.

With renewed purpose, he moved toward it.

—

"I See you, human child."

The cool voice came out of the darkness when Cilarnen was still too distant from the light to make out anything but that it burned. He stifled a yelp and froze where he stood. Though he strained his eyes against the darkness, he could not see the speaker, though from the voice, whoever had spoken must be very near.

"You have seen my lantern."

This time the voice came from nearer yet, though he'd seen no sign of movement. Cilarnen ground his teeth shut on a moan of terror.

"I see by your raiment that you have been cast out by the Golden City."

This time the disembodied voice actually seemed to expect some reply. Cilarnen took a deep breath, mustered all his courage, and answered.

"I—Yes. I was cast out. Banished." His voice was hoarse, but steady. Speaking reminded him of how thirsty he was, and he wished he hadn't thrown away his waterskin when it was empty. But what good had it been to him then?

"Come. Warm yourself at my fire. The night is cold."

Cilarnen took a shaky step forward, and immediately tripped over a stone. An iron grip just under his left elbow steadied him. He yelped aloud at the contact.

"Forgive me. I had forgotten what poor vision you humans have. I will conduct you, if you will permit."

Cilarnen nodded, not trusting himself to speak. Even this close, his rescuer was still no more than a shadowy cloaked and hooded figure to him, although he was standing right next to him. And could apparently see quite well, for at

Cilarnen's nod, he began to move forward, leading the young Outlaw through the darkness toward the unwavering light.

As they approached, Cilarnen could see that it was a small lantern. By the light it gave, he could make out a tidy campsite. There was a brazier such as the Mages used in making Magick, and beside it a bedroll spread out upon the ground, with a pack set at its head. Some sort of traveling merchant, then. A horse and a pack-mule were tethered nearby, and regarded him incuriously. Even in Cilarnen's distracted state, he could see that they were animals of great quality.

The brazier radiated a surprising amount of heat. Cilarnen moved toward it gratefully, holding out his icy hands toward its warmth. Only then did he turn and look back toward his companion.

The man was wearing a dark grey cloak with a deep hood lined in silver fur. As Cilarnen watched, he raised gloved hands and pushed the hood back, affording Cilarnen his most profound shock of the last several days.

It was not a man at all, but a—well, it wasn't a human creature.

Skin nearly as pale as snow, dark slanted eyes, long pointed ears that rose up through the sleek black hair elaborately coiled at the base of the neck. With a jarring sense of unreality, Cilarnen realized he was gazing upon a member of one of the Lesser Races. An Elf.

An Elf, within City Lands! For a moment he felt a spasm of indignation and righteous wrath, before he realized it simply didn't matter to him anymore. He'd been Banished.

His momentary fury vanished, to be replaced by numb weariness. He simply stared at the Elf, unable to think of anything else to do.

"So. You have been Banished. And I—have been barred from your gates. It seems we have something in common, then; and I suspect that it would be best if we took ourselves elsewhere. We will drink tea, and then we will prepare for the journey. I think it would be well if we were both out of the lands claimed by the Golden City before dawn," the Elf said, regarding Cilarnen calmly.

The Elf was going to take him outside the City Lands ahead of the Hunt. At the moment that was all Cilarnen cared about. With a sigh of exhaustion, he sat down next to the brazier.

⟶

ANIGREL'S formal investiture as a member of the High Council took place at the Chapel of the Light at the Mage College that Light's Day. It directly followed his formal adoption into House Tavadon, and it was hard to say which ceremony was the more significant of the two, though one had been overseen by as many people as could cram themselves into the Great Temple in Armethalieh's Central Square, and the other was attended by only a select group of the highest-ranked Mages of the City.

In the first ceremony, Anigrel (now and forever Anigrel Tavadon, having chosen that as his new name) knelt before Lycaelon and the Arch-Priest of the Light as he swore his Oath of Adoption. He rose, was divested of his plain grey tabard and given a new one embroidered in the Tavadon colors—black and white—making his new status plain for all to read. He then gave his new father a formal son's kiss.

Then the City Rolls were brought out—the great record in which every citizen's birth and occupation, marriage and death, were recorded. And with the whole City to witness, the Arch-Priest altered them, adding Anigrel's name beneath Lycaelon's own.

And so it was done.

The Chapel of the Light was smaller, and the oath he swore there was more complicated than the one he had sworn in the Great Temple, but Anigrel meant it as little—and as much—as he had the other. It was that which kept the Mages who administered it from detecting any deception on his part, he suspected. Anigrel sincerely intended to serve the City. And bringing it under the rule of the Endarkened would surely be best for all, in the end.'

There he exchanged his new tabard for yet another—this one with additional embroideries marking him as a member of the High Council, this time in his own, newly-chosen colors: red and gold. He received his staff and his ring of office, and the second ceremony was complete.

Normally the day would end with festivities at Lycaelon's house, a party such as had marked his first son's Naming, or Lycaelon's own ascension to the dignity of Arch-Mage. But these were troubled times, and there was much work to be done. Instead, after a brief flurry of congratulations to the newest member of the High Council, the Mages returned to the Council House—even though it was Light's Day—to debate Anigrel's latest proposal.

—

AS this was a more complicated matter than either of the others, Anigrel had gone to the trouble of drafting a formal written proposal, which had been circulated to the Council earlier in the Day. He was fairly confident it would be accepted, at least eventually. After all, there was still the matter of the other conspirators to run to earth—and with Jorade Isas's, Margon Ogregance's, Kermis Lalkmair's, and Geont Pentres's memories thoroughly edited, and Tiedor Rolfort and Cilarnen Volpiril Banished—and Rolfort certainly dead—the Council had destroyed any possibility of tracing the true genesis and scope of the problem.

He wondered if any of them realized that.

He'd had to move fast to get his hands on Kermis Lalkmair before the boy was returned to his father—not wanting to risk the possibility that Lord Lalkmair might choose to be merciful, Anigrel had wished to remove all memory of "Master Raellan" from the boy's mind—but the man had reacted entirely as expected. Young Kermis was now living upon the charity of distant relatives while he recovered from the Excision of his Magegift and the destruction of all memories related to his Mage-training and to the conspiracy. Frankly, Anigrel did not expect the boy to live very long.

But though the actual "conspiracy" was quite dead, Anigrel had no intention of allowing it to seem so. Its success had not been his purpose for starting it in the first place. Even his seat on the Council had only been a welcome dividend.

No. His intention had been to create a climate of fear among the Mageborn. Fearful men were easy to manipulate.

━

IN the Council chamber, Lord Lycaelon called the Council to order.

"We are gathered in this special session of the High Council of Armethalieh to consider Lord Anigrel's proposal for the good of the City. You have all had an opportunity to review a copy of his proposal, as is our custom. Now Lord Anigrel will make his formal presentation."

Anigrel allowed the silence to gather for a moment before speaking. He knew that the members of the Council would already have discussed the matter among themselves. But this was his chance to sway them further.

Harith would back him, of course, once he saw that the Arch-Mage approved. Vilmos was ready to start at shadows, and would vote in favor of anything that held out the faintest hope of security. Four sure votes out of eleven—only two more would give him a sufficient majority to pass his measure. Fear: that was his best ally now. Fear killed thought, and the more fearful men were, the more they were ready to give up in exchange for the promise that the source of their fears would be dealt with.

"Lord Arch-Mage—my fellow Councilors—in this past sennight we have been led to the shocking and unwelcome revelation that our fellow Mageborn—whom we thought above corruption, above reproach—can be led to conspire against their fellow Mages and against the City. Let me assure you all that I will not rest until I have rooted out every last tendril of corruption and exposed it to the healing fire of the Light."

There was a murmur of reluctant approval from the men seated around him.

"But—as we are all unfortunately aware—that is not enough. We face a time of great trial. Where there was one assault upon our security and the safety of our City, there may be more, and as you, my august brethren, have pointed out so many times, our enemies are many.

"And so I propose to you that we be vigilant inwardly as well as out. I propose a Council of Magewardens, its members to be drawn from the ranks of both Journeymen and High Mages, who can move freely among the Mageborn, seeking out trouble before it starts. No longer will we be forced to bear the burden of such tragedies as have so recently befallen us. We can be warned against them before they have a chance to happen—and more. We will know the names and the faces of our enemies, whether within or without, before they have the opportunity to steal the hearts and minds of our innocent children as they slumber peacefully in their beds."

So far, there was no sign that any of the Council members found this to be an outrageous notion. That was good. He pitched his voice to sound reasonable, reasoning, and calm. "Such a vast undertaking is not without its mundane costs, and I know as well as you all what a heavy burden our precious City labors under at this moment—a burden that it will be the work, not of moonturns, but perhaps of years, to redress. And so I propose two further measures—not only that there be an organization similar in nature to the Magewardens to move among the common people of the City, actively seeking out those who might wish to change things for the worse, but also I propose a tax upon magick, to fund both Wardencies."

Some puzzled looks, perhaps, but no outright objection. "The second Wardency upon the Commons I can understand," said Harith, sounding as puzzled as he looked. "And it is more than reasonable—the commons are so easily led and manipulated, after all, that I am surprised we had not instituted such a thing before. But why a tax upon Magick?"

Anigrel gave him a look of empathy, as if to say that there was every reason to be puzzled. "My lords, Magick is a great gift. We Mages tirelessly labor for the good of the City, expending our lives and our Art like water poured out upon the sand—and our work is as little regarded by the average Armethaliehan, I assure you! They take the privileges we exhaust ourselves to provide as no more than their rightful due. This must change. If the common people wish to profit from the wisdom we have spent so many painful years laboring to acquire, they should pay a price for the benefits we bestow. And if they doubt those benefits, well, it would be no bad thing to permit the farmers from the Delfier Valley to be allowed some free gossip, so that our own citizens understand the calamities that can befall when those benefits are withdrawn."

He sat back, indicating he had finished.

"This is, as you well know, Lord Anigrel, three separate matters," Perizel said, sounding bored. "Let us settle the matter of how—and if—you are to fund your grand plan before deciding whether it is to go forward, shall we?"

"Very well," Lord Lycaelon said, with a faint sigh. "We will consider the matter of the tax first—and separately. Continue."

"But . . . the Commons already pay for our services," Lord Lorins pointed out, after a moment.

"They pay for the spell, yes," Anigrel said. "But do they pay for the privilege of being allowed to have the spell at all? And so many spells are not actually *paid* for—those that control the weather, for instance. Or those that keep buildings in repair. I am suggesting a tax, not an increase in fees."

"They'll never accept it," Lord Arance said dryly.

"Then let them do without," Lycaelon suggested. "Naturally this would not apply to matters affecting the City as a whole—at least, not at first. Simply to private, individual matters—the ones we all find so tiresome. Or simple things that do not truly affect much except minor comfort. Weather Spells for instance. Those that prevent snow from falling within the walls; those that keep rain from falling except at night. A few days of slogging through wet streets might change some minds."

"But . . . a new tax?" Lord Lorins asked hesitantly.

To Anigrel's surprise and delight, here he had an ally, and an entirely unexpected one. "Actually," Lord Perizel drawled, "it is a very old tax. It merely has not been assessed in the last few hundred years. But you will find it still on the tax rolls, Lorins, if you take the trouble to look. I see no reason we should not reinstate it. We can always use the money for something, and Light knows we have spent enough Golden Suns on the Selkens this past quarter to leave the Treasury in need of replenishment."

Anigrel should have known that Perizel, that peruser of ancient records, would know there had once been such a tax! That made things much simpler. Something new—well, that would be resisted. But something old—oh, that was to be embraced.

After a bit more discussion, the measure to institute—or reinstitute—the tax on the privilege of calling upon the Mages for Magick was passed.

The discussion over the formation of the Magewardens and the Commons Wardens took far longer. Everyone was in favor of keeping a closer eye on the Commons, of course, but no one was completely comfortable with the idea of spying—for that was what it amounted to—upon their own kind. Only when Anigrel promised that he would head the Magewardens Council himself, and make full and detailed reports of everything it discovered, was Lycaelon able to at last call the vote.

The measure passed, nine to two. Perizel and Arance abstained.

"YOU take too much work upon yourself, Anigrel," Lycaelon said afterward, as the two of them walked toward Tavadon House through the winter evening. "You will burn yourself out, and end up a doddering friendless old man—like me."

Spirits of Darkness, the Arch-Mage was making a joke. Anigrel smiled. "Dear Arch-Mage, that will never happen—not while I am alive. But you must see, it was the only way to gain a majority in Council. I confess, I was surprised at how the vote went, at the end."

Who would have thought that so many of the witless sheep could be stampeded so easily? He'd have to keep an eye on Perizel and Arance, though.

"As am I." For a moment the Arch-Mage's expression went hard and distant, then it softened again. "But we shall soon bring those doubters to heel. And now we shall go . . . home, my son." Lycaelon's voice was fond.

Was it at all possible that the Arch-Mage was growing senile? It was too much to hope for—though Anigrel knew spells that could help the process along—and certainly the man had received enough shocks recently to drive a lesser man to a state of catatonia.

" 'Home.' It has a good sound, Lord Arch-Mage. But I think—if you will permit—that I will keep my rooms at the College as well." He smiled. "There are those whom in my capacity as Chief Magewarden, I should not like to bring into our house."

Besides which, those heavily-warded rooms were where he made his communion with his Dark lady, something Anigrel did not think he could manage unnoticed within the walls of Tavadon House.

"Of course, my son. You must do just as you think is best. And, Anigrel . . . you must call me 'Father.' "

"Yes . . . Father."

He would serve the City with as much devotion as Ly-

caelon could wish. And if he served it to a different purpose
and a different end, it was entirely possible that Lycaelon
Tavadon would die without ever knowing.

IDALIA did not know how long she lay unconscious before
the pain roused her. She was disoriented and terribly thirsty,
and lay in darkness so absolute that for a moment she
thought she must be blind.

Her head spinning, her mind blank, at first she wasn't quite
sure what was going on. Where was she? Where were the
children? Then, unwarily, she tried to move, and savage pain
shocked her, hammering her senses with nausea and vertigo,
and the agony brought her fully to consciousness. She relaxed as far as she could, waiting for the pain to subside.

She was deep within the caves, and safe. Well, safer than
she would be if she were in the hands of the Shadowed
Elves, anyway. The children and Lairamo—Gods grant—
were also safe and far away from here with the rescue
party. She knew she could count on that much: Kellen was
in charge, and he would make *sure* that the children were
safe away.

She wondered how far she'd fallen, knowing even as she
wondered that her mind was wandering—a symptom of
concussion. How peculiar that she was alive to be wondering that at all. Her life had been forfeit to the Gods from the
moment she had done the weather-working that saved the
Elven Lands from flood. Her life had been the cost of that
spell, and Idalia had paid it, if not gladly, then willingly and
freely.

But though the Gods of the Wild Magic might ask for her
life, suicide was no part of her Mageprice. She had the right
and duty to preserve her life for as long as possible.

Even now.

Escape on her own—well, *that* was impossible, for certain. No walking out with two broken legs, a shattered col-

larbone, and worse. She could not Heal herself—the pain and her injuries made her magic too hard to control.

But she could call for help. She had control enough for that, she thought. *Call for help . . . call for help . . . oh, fool, you should have agreed to marry Jermayan when he asked . . . he'd know right where you were, now . . . yes, and come charging right into a trap against any odds to save you . . . and then you could be dead together, your lives just the same length, just as you came to realize in the end . . .*

She came to with a start and realized she'd been drifting, only half-aware. She must do what she could now, before her strength ebbed any further.

She shifted position slightly—kindling a new bright flare of pain that brought tears of furious pain to her eyes—and closed her eyes tightly, though closed or open made no difference here in the stygian darkness of the cave. With all her remaining strength, Idalia focused her will on *Calling.*

A friend—an ally—someone to carry my message to anyone who can hear and will help—

So long a time passed that Idalia began to wonder if there was anything at all within range of her call, or if perhaps the power of the Wild Magic had deserted her utterly. But at last she felt a faint disturbance in the air, and a substantial weight landed on her chest, making her gasp and cough. With her uninjured hand, she reached out toward it.

She could feel the heat of its body, and her fingertips brushed leathery wings as it moved suspiciously away from her touch.

A snow-bat.

White-furred, nocturnal, the size of chickens, they fed on mice, small birds, even fish, and were dormant through deepest winter. There was a certain justice in her aid coming from the distant—very distant—cousin of the creatures that had carried off the Elves in the first place. She extended her magical senses, and felt the spark of the bat's life; a small consciousness, occupied mostly with thoughts of food and flight. But there was room there to imprint the snow-bat's mind with her cry for help, and with the last of her strength, Idalia added her Call, giving the little creature a new desire, stronger than any natural desire it possessed: *Find an ally. Deliver the message.*

She felt the Wild Magic well up in her and flow through her and into the snow-bat, and when the power had crested and ebbed away, Idalia's consciousness ebbed with it.

⟢

THE pulse of magic washed over the bat like a pulse of the strongest moonlight it had ever imagined, sending it hopping awkwardly away from the *strangewarmthing*, scurrying and flapping across the floor of the canyon until it could manage to take flight. Its new need was strong, sending it soaring through familiar territory, toward the opening that led to its hunting fields. Its keen predator's senses told it that the weather outside was still and clear: perfect for hunting.

But as it neared the outer tunnels, the light drove it back. *Too bright! Too bright! Now is a time for sleep, not flight!* It veered back, into the welcoming darkness, and would have resumed its interrupted slumbers if it could have, but the need planted in it by *strangewarmthing* drove it onward.

It would have approached the *cavernothers* if it could— even though they often hunted its kind for food—but the Need told it that they were not the allies it sought, and so it flew onward, deeper into the darkness, singing the high-pitched song that created the world around it in pulses of form.

Deeper it flew, far from the sleeping places of its sept, into territory unknown. Its wings grew tired, and many times it stopped to rest, but each time the Need drove it on again.

At last—there! below!—the Need touched a suitable mind.

⟢

ANCALADAR dozed, dreaming of centuries past. They weren't terribly pleasant dreams, but they were his.

They were all he had left.

Something landed on his nose with a thud.

Ancaladar went from half-sleep to wakefulness in an eye-blink. He reared back, dislodging the small weight, which flittered around his head, crying out in a high irritating voice.

A snow-bat.

Ancaladar relaxed. For a moment he'd thought . . .

But for some reason, the bat wouldn't go away. It circled his head like a maddened wasp, landing on his head again, and this time Ancaladar caught the scent of magic.

His nostrils flared, nearly sucking the bat inside.

Magic—Wild Magic! It was a scent Ancaladar had fled from all his life, for it posed a unique danger to his kind.

But . . .

The bat was a messenger. Someone—some Wildmage—needed something. Very badly, if the sense of urgency Ancaladar could read coming off the little creature was any guide. He sniffed—more gently this time—but could detect no more to the message. Apparently the bat had been sent to guide whoever found it back to the Wildmage.

Ancaladar sat back with a sigh.

If he had any sense, he'd stay right here. He could ignore the bat. Or eat it. He was safe where he was.

But a Wildmage?

Here?

It was an odd place for a Wildmage. These caverns were overrun with stinking Tainted mock-Elves. They'd come burrowing in to Ancaladar's nice safe retreat—oh, he couldn't really remember how long ago. Sometime after the Great War, anyway. They'd started overrunning the caverns, scaring off the local game, and generally making a mess of things.

Maybe the Wildmage had come to fix things.

And Ancaladar didn't have to get involved, not really. He could go give the Wildmage whatever he—she—it wanted, and then go back to sleep. So long as what it wanted was something small and insignificant.

He'd be careful.

With a grunt, he levered himself to his feet, careful not to dislodge his furry guest.

"Show me," he rumbled softly.

THE pain pulled her toward consciousness and pushed her away from it at the same time, until Idalia floated in a dazed state, only half-aware of her surroundings, knowing that Death was only days—perhaps hours—away. Her pain-fevered body was wracked by shivers—it was cold here in the cave—and the cold and shivering stole what little strength she had left.

Sometimes she forgot entirely where she was. Sometimes she thought she was back in Ondoladeshiron, where she had first met Jermayan, walking with him beneath cloudless skies. Sometimes she was still a Silver Eagle, soaring through those same skies.

Sometimes—those fantasies were the worst—she was a girl in Armethalieh again, living in her father's house, her horizons no wider than the walls of Tavadon House and the short walk to the Ladies' Academy where the daughters of the Mageborn received their lessons in dancing and painting and other ornamental arts suitable to ornamental females. Prison and torment all in one, knowing she was scorned and shunned by the other girls as a half-breed, knowing there was so much more in the world than she, a mere girl, was allowed to see and be, and knowing that nothing, bar a miracle, was going to give her access to that wider world.

Suddenly she was conscious. The nightmare vision of the Ladies' Academy dissolved, and the tinkling laughter of the other girls—how she'd always hated it!—became a scraping sound, as of something—something *heavy*—being dragged over the rock. Her heart beat wildly, and she strained her eyes in the darkness, turning her head cautiously as she tried to locate the source of the sound.

Two glowing lights hung somewhere in the darkness, their size and distance impossible to judge. Eyes? Lanterns? Idalia didn't know: she only knew that the sudden strength she felt came from the presence of another's magic, not her own strength. It was a brief gift, she could tell that much, and she dared not waste it.

"Wildmage. You called for me," a deep soft voice said.

"Help me," Idalia whispered. "The Endarkened rise against the Elves."

To speak aloud had taken all the strength the stranger's magic had lent her, and Idalia fell into a deep and final unconsciousness.

＿

ANCALADAR regarded the Wildmage. He wondered what her name was, not that it mattered to him.

The Endarkened, now, that was another matter. He'd known they were active again—they'd been hunting dragons lately, which was one of the reasons he'd taken such pains to hide himself so carefully. But if they were going to war against the Elves . . .

Then the Wildmages would want the dragons to fight for them.

Again.

He reached out one taloned claw toward the woman, and drew back. He could not help her himself. He was a creature of magic, but he could not use his magic himself—only his Bondmate could. And Ancaladar had no Bondmate.

Oh, yes, he'd been so clever, Ancaladar thought in disgust. He'd watched his brothers and friends die in the Great War—not only in battle, but from linking their immortal span of years to the brief mortal span of their Bondmate's lives, for a Bonded dragon died when his Bondmate did.

He hadn't been able to bear the thought of that, and so he'd hidden, making himself safe from meeting the one Mage—whoever he or she might be—who could be his

Bondmate. What could one dragon do to tip the balance, anyway?

But there were worse horrors, he discovered, than dying in service to the Light. Dragons had fallen to the Dark when their Bondmates had been corrupted by the Endarkened with the promise of immortality.

Now he was safe. One of the last of the dragons. He ought to congratulate himself on his prudence at surviving this long, but more and more these days, it felt as if he'd cheated, or been cheated, or both at the same time. It certainly felt as if he hadn't been clever at all, that he'd shirked his duty. He was a creature of the Light, wasn't he? He was bound to help the cause of the Light. Except that he hadn't. He'd been a coward, done as little as he could, and run away as soon as possible.

Maybe what he felt like was a failure.

Maybe this was a chance to make things right. He regarded the Wildmage with faint suspicion. At least he felt no hint of a possible Bond with *her*.

Ancaladar made up his mind. He'd help the Wildmage. And perhaps the Elves would be willing to provide him with something in the way of steady meals in return. In the Old Days, his kind had been able to bargain for nice, tasty domestic cattle or sheep, and having to hunt for himself—and hide while he did it—just was getting to be too hard. Was this what *getting old* felt like? Or was it only that he was *becoming less?*

He raised his head and looked around, extending his senses as far as they would go. He didn't sense any of the mock-Elves anywhere around. It was daytime, anyway— even far underground Ancaladar could sense the position of the sun—they'd all be securely asleep for some time yet. She'd be safe enough while he went to look for her friends.

He didn't really want to expose himself in daylight, but if he actually intended to help, he had no choice.

Humans were fragile things, and this one looked badly broken. If she was going to be fixed, it would have to be soon.

Ten

The Return of the Dragons

Kellen had managed to convince Jermayan not to go charging in after Idalia during the night—though it took every bit of diplomacy that he had—but when dawn came, and Idalia still hadn't come back—he was starting to run out of ideas.

He *knew* she wasn't dead. But what if she was a prisoner? Or trapped somewhere? Or hurt? Or just lost somewhere down in the cave system? Jermayan had suggested all those possibilities and more in the past hours.

Any of those things might be true. The one thing Kellen knew for sure was that there was only one *tarnkappa*, and that if anybody was going down into the caves after Idalia, it had better be him.

The question was, how to convince Jermayan of that.

There's no way. There's absolutely no way.

"Look. I agree. You're right," Kellen said, about two hours past dawn, two hours of intermittent, polite, Elven "arguing." "We've got to go after her."

"Finally—!" Jermayan said, making a grab for the *tarnkappa*.

"But we have to do this right," Kellen said, holding on to the bundle of fabric firmly. "We need to find a more secure place to leave the horses than right in front of the cave, and I'd kind of like to know if there's anything out there looking for us before we go in. If Idalia . . . if she's hurt, we're going to have to spend the night right here, and it's going to have to be a place we can defend if we have to. Also, maybe you can find another way in. They might be watching this one."

Please, please, let him decide he's the best one to do this because his woods skills are better than mine . . .

Jermayan studied him for a long moment, then nodded.

"Very well. You can break camp. Be ready to ride out the moment I get back. I won't be long."

Just be long enough, Kellen thought.

He watched as Jermayan saddled Valdien and rode away over the snow.

He hated running out on Jermayan this way—not that the Elven Knight would hesitate to do the same if their positions were reversed—but one man alone had a better chance than two down there in the caverns. Between the *tarnkappa*, and the fact that Kellen was going to risk a Finding Spell, Kellen was pretty sure he could get to Idalia wherever she was.

He shook out the *tarnkappa* and looked at Shalkan.

"I hope you can—" Kellen began.

Shalkan cleared his throat. The unicorn was looking over Kellen's shoulder with a very odd expression on his long equine face.

Kellen whirled, dropping the *tarnkappa* to the snow, his hand going to his sword.

And stared.

He was face-to-face with a dragon.

A very large, very black dragon. Its head shimmered iridescently in the strong sunlight, the blackness of its armored plates sparkling with all the shades of a midnight opal: blue and gold and fire-red.

He'd seen dragons before, but only in visions, and then only from a distance. They had seemed vaguely lizardlike, but bore as much resemblance to the lizards of the forest as Shalkan did to a horse, and as little. Long sinuous necks, tails twice the length of their bodies, ending in a broad flat barb to help the creatures steer in the currents of the upper air—for most of all, dragons had *wings*.

This one was only a few feet away. Its head alone was the size of a boat, and took up so much of Kellen's field of vision that he couldn't see any of the details he remembered from his visions. It blinked golden pupilless eyes the size of large melons at him.

How had it gotten so close without him knowing? Why hadn't he at least *heard* it? The thing was the size of a building—and not a little cottage, either—it should make *some* noise!

And now what was he going to do? He certainly didn't dare attack it . . .

"Wildmage. You are a friend to the other Wildmage."

It was not a question. Its voice was deep, and surprisingly soft for its size.

He hadn't known they could talk.

"Idalia! Do you know where she is?" Kellen demanded eagerly.

"Yes. She is hurt, and needs help." The eyes blinked. "I will take you to her. The way will not be easy: the Tainted mock-Elves that infest the caverns were roused by my exit, and search for me now. To reach your Wildmage, we must return the way I came. They may discover us, and they are eager to take me prisoner."

"Leave them to me," Kellen said, touching his sword.

For a moment, he would have been willing to swear the dragon smiled. It hesitated for a moment. "My name is Ancaladar."

"I'm Kellen. Idalia's my sister. We'd better go quickly."

He glanced at Shalkan.

"I'll wait here," the unicorn said. "Somebody needs to explain things to Jermayan—and sit on him if necessary."

Kellen nodded, and scooped up the *tarnkappa*. He'd need its spells to see once they got into the caves—he'd have to explain the cloak to Ancaladar, so the dragon didn't worry that Kellen had deserted him.

A dragon . . .

"Come, then," Ancaladar said. The dragon spread his wings—blotting out the sun for a moment—and launched himself into the sky in an eerie silence. He flew low, obviously intending Kellen to follow.

"Better wear that," Shalkan said, nodding at the *tarnkappa*. "Just in case you run into Jermayan on the way."

Kellen nodded, swirled the cloak around himself, and took off after Ancaladar at a run.

His training under Master Belesharon served him well—before he had entered The House of Sword and Shield, Kellen would never have been able to run almost half a league uphill over snow to the foot of a cliff without falling flat on his face at the end of it. But though he wasn't able to keep pace with the dragon—even though he could tell that Ancaladar was gliding very slowly—he reached the spot where the dragon circled very quickly, and flung back the *tarnkappa* as Ancaladar dropped down to a neat—and silent—landing.

"Here I am," Kellen said, looking up at Ancaladar. "Idalia made this so she could sneak around in the caverns."

"I could see you quite clearly," the dragon said.

Now that was interesting. Ancaladar could see through the *tarnkappa*'s spells?

"I'll need it to see underground," Kellen said, wrapping it around himself again.

"Then it is good that you should wear it," Ancaladar said. "Humans find these caverns very dark."

The dragon turned his attention to the cliff face. Several yards up the icy rock wall, Kellen could see a wide slit in the stone. Ancaladar stuck his head into the gap and squirmed in, furling his enormous ribbed wings tightly against his sides. And that was possibly the strangest thing that Kellen had seen in—well, a long time. The dragon shouldn't have been able to fit in there. What could it do, disjoint all its bones?

My turn. Kellen flexed his gauntleted hands, and began to climb.

Elven armor, it was said by its makers, was flexible enough that its wearer could dance in it, and certainly the combat form practiced by the Elven Knights was very much like dance. Kellen also knew, from previous experience, that you could climb in Elven armor, but he'd never tried climbing a vertical ice-covered wall in it.

He managed to get halfway up, though, before a long black-scaled arm tipped in golden talons appeared out of the darkness and plucked him into the cave.

"You take too long," Ancaladar said.

Oh.

"Um. Sorry. I'm a lot smaller than you are. It takes me longer to get places." Kellen squirmed past the dragon's body—fortunately this entrance to the cave system was fairly wide—and moved forward until he was in front of Ancaladar's head. Even though he was technically in front, the dragon was so enormous that it was still in the lead—it had only to stretch out its long sinuous neck to put its head several yards in front of Kellen.

The passage here was fairly straight, without any side passages, and the *tarnkappa*'s darksight spell ensured that it was as bright as day, even though Ancaladar's body blocked all the light from the outside. Kellen started forward confidently.

Soon the passage opened out into a cavern. It was so large that he could not see the far side of it, even with the aid of the *tarnkappa*'s magical sight. He could feel a faint steady breeze blowing over him—from deep in the earth toward the outside air.

The path ended in a drop-off, but fortunately it wasn't a sheer drop. There was a slope—steep, but manageable. Kellen gritted his teeth and started down it.

It was steeper than he'd thought, and he ended up making most of the journey to the bottom on his rump. Behind him, he saw Ancaladar step neatly to the cave floor—the dragon's size made the drop-off no more than a single step for him.

Kellen was about to ask which way they went now, when Ancaladar's head suddenly shot up. He saw the dragon's nostrils flare—*just like Shalkan's when he smells something bad*—and then, without a word or a sound, Ancaladar gave a great bound and launched himself at the nearest cave wall, climbing quickly and silently until he'd vanished into the shadows.

That was good enough for Kellen, even though he heard nothing. He scrambled quickly to his feet and looked around for a place to get out of the way. He saw a niche between the edge of the cliff and the cave wall—not much, but it would have to do. He quickly moved toward it and pressed himself back into the corner.

Just in time, it turned out. He'd barely settled himself when he began to hear faint noises, as of a large group of people moving quietly, but not entirely silently. A few moments later they came into view.

There were eight of them. Six were male, the two bringing up the rear were female. It was easy to tell, because none of them was wearing much more than a hip wrap. All were barefoot as well.

The two females were both carrying large bundles of netting. The nets were made of some substance Kellen had never seen before—a shiny, silvery-grey substance that looked something like silk.

All of the males were armed, both with long spears balanced for throwing—Kellen's Knight-Mage gifts told him that—but also with a variety of looted weapons. Kellen recognized swords and daggers that had belonged to his friends from the House of Sword and Shield, and felt a dull surge of anger.

These must be the Shadowed Elves Idalia mentioned—what Ancaladar calls "Tainted mock-Elves."

They were horrible in their own right, but to anyone who counted Elves as friends, they were especially horrible. There was no doubt of their Elven blood, but just as Idalia had said, somehow it had been mixed with Goblins to produce those fanged muzzles, receding jaws, and pale bulging eyes. Their hands and feet had talons, not nails, as well.

No wonder Vestakia had been able to find this place. And Idalia had said there was a whole colony of these creatures here.

They were obviously searching for Ancaladar. Every few feet the one in the lead would squat down and sniff the ground, then speak to the others in a strange guttural barking language. He was not the leader, apparently, for the leader urged him onward with blows, causing a dispute to break out among the hunting party. During all of this, the females cowered back, hissing.

At last they moved on. They passed right by Kellen's hiding place without stopping to look, and Kellen blessed the Wild Magic that had gone into the *tarnkappa*'s making. Even when he could no longer see them, he stayed where he was, waiting for Ancaladar to return.

At last the dragon reappeared, gliding down to the floor of the cavern to land soundlessly. Even now it did not speak, merely swiveled its great head and pointed in the direction they should go.

Ancaladar had told the truth when he said that the Shadowed Elves were desperate to capture him at any cost. They encountered three more patrols as they went. Each time Ancaladar quickly hid, giving Kellen plenty of advance warning to conceal himself as well.

They moved through a series of interconnected caverns. All of them weren't as large as the first one, but Kellen quickly realized that since they were following Ancaladar's preferred route in and out of the caves there weren't going to be any small passages. The only real problem that Kellen encountered—other than having to hide from the Shadowed Elves—was that terrain that Ancaladar could cross with ease presented towering obstacles for Kellen to climb over or detour around. Occasionally Ancaladar would grow impatient with the delay and pluck him into the air, setting him down somewhere several hundred yards distant. Kellen hadn't quite made up his mind yet, but he thought he preferred scrabbling over slabs of basalt to being whisked through the air in the claws of an impatient dragon.

Not that he was feeling terribly patient himself, with Idalia somewhere ahead, trapped and hurt. He didn't know, of course, but he had the sense that Ancaladar was being forced to detour by the Shadowed Elf patrols. That wasn't good.

Finally Ancaladar stopped. He lowered his head, so it was right beside Kellen's.

"This is the last of the ways we can go to reach your sister," the dragon said, in a whisper so low that Kellen barely heard it. "It could be the safest of the ways we can go, or the most dangerous—it's very narrow, and there's nowhere to hide, but they may not have thought to look this way yet."

Narrow. Terrific, Kellen thought, following the dragon as he moved forward again.

But "narrow" was a relative term. The passage was narrow for Ancaladar—the dragon had to fold his wings tightly and crouch down on his belly—but there was enough room for Kellen and the entire rescue party that had started out from Sentarshadeen (if they'd been there) to ride down the tunnel.

Suddenly the dragon stopped, stretching out his neck, his nostrils flaring.

"Oh, no—" he said in dismay. "We're trapped—"

For the first time, Kellen fell into battle-trance *immediately,* without having to invoke it; it fell over him as he cast off the *tarnkappa,* as if it were somehow taking the place of the cloak.

In a way, it was; the dual-sight allowed him to see in the dark as the cloak spell did. He saw the Shadowed creatures as they stalked forward out of the darkness just as clearly as if he were still wrapped in its folds. He did not, however, charge.

Instead, he drew his sword, and waited. Waited for his doubled-sight to show him that they saw him for what he was. The aura of threat that surrounded him was unmistakable—*that* he knew from his lessons in the House of Sword and Shield. He was armed, and he was waiting for their attack. Now it became their choice to fight or flee.

They saw him for what he was—and *they* charged. One of them threw the net it carried. As if it were floating like a puff of down, Kellen watched it drift toward him, and in that odd slowed-time, he cut it in half as it started to fly past his head, aimed at Ancaladar, evidently, and not him.

The moment that the steel of his sword touched it, the two halves of the net withered and dropped to the ground. Kellen continued the stroke with a sideways twist of his wrist, to take off the head of the unwary creature that was nearest him.

They were frail, these Shadowed Elves; he killed it, and the one behind it, then let the momentum of his blade carry him around in a spin to cleave another across the spine. He made a recovery move, blocked the sword of a fourth as he kicked a fifth in the stomach, cut under the blocked blade to eviscerate the fourth one and as the fifth staggered backward, followed, and gutted it as well. The sixth and seventh were no real challenge; he took them out as they stared at him, dumbfounded.

He whirled. Ancaladar was frozen in place, eyes wide. "Move!" he snapped.

Ancaladar managed to compress himself against the wall of the tunnel enough to let him squeeze by.

This time he *did* charge, catching the much larger party that thought it was sneaking up in the rear entirely by surprise. For all of the weapons that they carried, for all of their superior ability to see in the dark, they might just as well have had no defensive ability at all. They were absolutely no match for the special advantages of a Knight-Mage, not even at fourteen-to-one.

The battle-trance faded, and the world was utterly black once more. Kellen stood in the darkness, feeling a faint regret.

But nothing more. When he'd drawn his sword, they could have run. When he'd begun to kill the others, they could have run. They chose not to. If he had not fought, he and Ancaladar would have been killed or taken prisoner, and Idalia would die. Because he had refused to accept that, he had chosen to kill. That was the way of the Knight-Mage, the agent of the active principle of the Wild Magic.

He forgave them for attacking him, and he forgave himself for killing them, just as Jermayan had taught him.

Absently he wiped his sword blade dry on his cloak—there'd be time to give the blade a thorough cleaning later—and worked his way back up to Ancaladar's front.

"Any more of them?" Kellen asked, stooping to grope for the discarded *tarnkappa* and don it once more.

"No. You eliminated all of them . . . Knight-Mage." The dragon moved forward, stepping fastidiously over the corpses. They moved faster now. There didn't seem to be any need to try to conceal their presence any longer. Not only had the Shadowed Elves found them, but Kellen seemed to have killed most of the ones searching for them.

"They must want you really badly," Kellen said after a few moments.

"Has your world wholly forgotten my kind? I'm a *dragon*," Ancaladar said, with a note of bitterness in his voice. "And no doubt the Endarkened have a Mage or two in thrall, and an arsenal of spells to try to force a Bonding that they ache to try."

"Dragons Bond with Mages," Kellen said, half-remembered scraps of what Jermayan had told him about the Great War coming back to his mind.

"Almost correct. Each dragon is fated to Bond with one Mage—his Bondmate. After which that Mage becomes incredibly powerful—having an endless supply of spell-energy to draw on—and the dragon's life becomes incredibly short, for when his Bondmate dies, he dies as well."

"Oh." It didn't seem fair. All the advantage seemed to go to the Mage. All the dragon got out of the deal was dead. "What about Mageprices?"

"Bonded Mages don't pay them. Not with our power to draw on," Ancaladar said simply.

"Why would a dragon . . . ?"

"I don't know," Ancaladar said curtly, ending the discussion firmly. "We're nearly there, thank Sky and Fair Wind."

Up ahead, the tunnel opened out. Ancaladar stretched his neck out, extending it through the opening. Kellen followed along until he reached the edge of the tunnel.

He'd moved cautiously, and was glad he had. There was only a narrow ledge at the cave mouth, and it extended for only a few feet in either direction before vanishing entirely. The tunnel had opened out into another of the huge caverns Kellen was growing used to, but this one was different from any of the previous ones. Its floor was criss-crossed with other deep fissures—as though something very hot had cooled here—and littered with enormous boulders, as though there had been an explosion as well. He could hear a distinct sighing sound, as if something even bigger than Ancaladar was breathing, but it seemed to come from the cave itself.

He moved quickly to one side as Ancaladar flowed past him and down to the floor of the cave, then looked around in frustration. He couldn't climb down, it was much too far to jump, and as far as he knew, his Knight-Mage abilities didn't include the power of flight.

After a few seconds Ancaladar noticed his plight. The dragon turned back and plucked him from the ledge, depositing him on the cave floor.

"Not far now," Ancaladar said.

Was it Kellen's imagination, or was there a note of worry in the dragon's voice?

⟶

IDALIA was lying at the foot of a cliff at the far side of the cavern.

Kellen's heart twisted in his chest when he saw her. He knew the look of broken bones. He could see—and smell—the blood.

How long had she been lying here? Was she dead?

Then he saw the faint movement of her chest and knew that she was still alive.

He ran forward and knelt beside her. His first impulse was to waken her, but he knew that would be no kindness. She must be in agony.

He had to get her out of here. But even if Ancaladar would consent to carry her, he didn't dare move her while she was in this condition. Broken legs, broken arm and collarbone . . . undoubtedly a concussion . . . probably internal bleeding as well.

"I'll have to heal her before we can move her," Kellen said aloud.

Healing was not his strongest skill in the Wild Magic, and he'd never tried this major a healing, especially without someone around to share the Mageprice. He looked hopefully at Ancaladar.

But the dragon cringed away. "You go ahead," he said, taking a step backward. "I'll wait over here until you're done."

Kellen sighed. *I guess it's all up to me. I just hope I'm good enough.*

He had to be. For Idalia's sake.

These days, he always carried the components for the simplest of the Wild Magic spells with him, and healing was a very simple spell. Here where everything was stone, he didn't even need a brazier: he simply unwrapped his disk of charcoal and set it directly on the stone floor, and set it alight with a simple word. He pulled out the few herbs he'd need, and set them beside the burning charcoal.

His stomach twisted as he thought of the only other healing involving broken bones he'd ever witnessed. When Idalia had healed a unicorn colt's fractured leg, she'd worked all the pieces of the break into alignment first. He should do that here, to give the healing the best chance. But the colt had been dosed with a sleeping potion, and he had nothing to give his sister.

If you don't do it, she'll die. Do you want your squeamishness to kill her?

Kellen pulled off his armored gauntlets, then drew his dagger and cut a few strands of Idalia's hair, then a few of his own. He moistened the bundle with Idalia's blood, then pricked his finger and squeezed out a few drops of blood onto the dried leaves of willow, ash, and yew.

Then he tossed the bundle of herbs and hair onto the coals.

Heal Idalia—please! I swear I will pay the price! Kellen thought fervently. He knew he should be centered in a Wild-mage's dispassionate trance, but that was something he couldn't manage right now. He cared too much—and if that was something really wrong, then he supposed the Gods wouldn't have let him become a Knight-Mage in the first place.

The bundle should have smelled horrible while it was burning, but it didn't. It smelled like spring flowers and fresh-cut hay. Kellen saw the shimmer of the protective shields all around him, and hoped that protection would extend to keeping Idalia from feeling what he was doing.

First he straightened her legs. Feeling the bones move and shift under his hands made sweat run down his face in greasy droplets, but once he'd begun, he knew he couldn't stop.

Everything was glowing green.

Next, her arm. It seemed to him that it ought to be straightened, so he did that, as gently as he could. That led him to her collarbone—broken, as he suspected. There wasn't a lot he could do about it, but he prodded at it until he'd shifted the bones about into more-or-less the right places, and left it at that.

Everything was fire. Green fire.

He ran his hands over her head. They came away wet with blood, though Kellen knew that might not mean much. Even the smallest scalp wounds could bleed a great deal. Or it might be a concussion. Without being able to see her eyes, he didn't know.

Green . . . all green . . .

Her breathing was better now, which reminded him to check for broken ribs and broken pelvis. He ran his hands down over her ribs, pressing gently, but everything felt solid. He found her hip bones, and pressed gently, relieved to find that everything was solid there, too.

Abruptly Kellen sat back on his haunches and stared

down at his hands. They were trailing greenness as if he'd dipped them in a vat of liquid emeralds. Idalia, too, was green, as if she'd been soaked in the stuff.

When he'd healed Jermayan, the Healing Power had hit him like a hammer-blow, leaving him in no doubt of when the healing began and ended. This time it had snuck up on him; apparently he'd been healing Idalia while he thought he'd just been checking the extent of her injuries.

He wondered why the two healings had been so different. Perhaps because Idalia was such an expert Wildmage, and had been able to direct the healing in some fashion? Or was it for some other reason? Did the Wild Magic itself want her healed?

Slowly the green fire faded away, and Kellen waited to hear the price he would have to pay for this healing.

But to his surprise—and faint alarm—there was nothing. No inner voice setting his Mageprice. Only a certainty that somehow the price—even for this—had been paid in advance.

Kellen shook his head. He wasn't going to argue, and he wasn't going to complain.

The dome of protection vanished—Kellen was always surprised there wasn't an audible "pop" when it vanished— its work done. He felt a sudden rush of dizziness and exhaustion, as the price of the Casting caught up with him. He wasn't going to be good for much for a while—though he could fight if he absolutely had to—and Idalia would be utterly exhausted.

And they still had to get out of here.

He put his gauntlets back on, picked up the burning charcoal, and crushed it quickly into dust. Brushing the mess from his hands, he got to his feet. Idalia was still unconscious, but it was a natural sleep now, not a deathly coma. He'd like to wait here for her to wake—he didn't relish carrying her out, especially if they ran into more of those creatures on the way—but he didn't want to stay here one moment more than he had to.

He got to his feet, staggering a little with weakness. He

stood for a moment, breathing carefully until his head cleared.

Ancaladar approached carefully.

"Is it over?" the dragon asked cautiously.

"She's going to be all right," Kellen said. He wondered if the odd way the healing had gone had anything to do with the dragon's nearness, and decided not to ask. Ancaladar seemed to be a little touchy about being a living storage battery for Mages, and Kellen didn't want to suggest he'd tapped the dragon's power, even accidentally. "Now all we have to do is get out of here."

"Do you think . . . " the dragon seemed almost hesitant " . . . do you think I could come back with you? I'm tired of living in a cave and chasing deer. And they'll never stop looking for me now."

"You'll have to ask Andoreniel and Ashaniel if you can live in Sentarshadeen," Kellen said. "I can't promise that. But I don't see why you shouldn't come south with us and see; they've added some . . . unusual citizens to Sentarshadeen lately."

And if we're going to have to beware of Deathwings, it would be a good idea to have someone else around who flies.

"Fair enough," Ancaladar agreed.

The dragon headed off across the cavern, its enormous sable body moving over the boulders like a pool of midnight.

Kellen bent down, scooped up Idalia, and followed.

Halfway across the cavern, she began to rouse.

She reached up and felt his face—or rather, the hood of the *tarnkappa*—just as if she couldn't see. Kellen realized with a shock that she couldn't. *He* could see, but everything must be pitch-dark to her. He'd gotten so used to Ancaladar being able to see and hear him through the *tarnkappa* that he'd forgotten he was wearing it. But Idalia wouldn't be able to either hear or see him—not while he wore the *tarnkappa*—not that she could see anything down here, at any rate.

"Kellen?" she whispered. He nodded, knowing she could feel the movement.

She relaxed with a sigh, and Kellen knew she was figuring everything out—that he'd found her somehow and healed her with the Wild Magic.

"Put me down," she said a minute later. "I can walk—and you might need to fight."

She was right. It was only common sense, even though Kellen knew how tired she must be after such a major healing.

He set her carefully on her feet and led her the rest of the way to where Ancaladar was waiting for them. Their progress was a little slower, now that he had to lead Idalia, but Kellen was tired himself, and didn't want to risk a fall.

At the foot of the cliff that led to the tunnels, he stopped and pushed back the *tarnkappa*'s cowl so that he could speak to Idalia.

Instantly the darkness of the cave rushed in. It was like no darkness Kellen had ever experienced in his life: thick and absolute. There was no possibility of seeing anything, no matter how hard you strained your eyes.

For a moment he felt a bolt of panic, then he realized it didn't matter.

He didn't need to see.

He *knew.*

At the House of Sword and Shield, the Knights practiced blind-fighting, for it was always possible that you would be forced to defend or attack at night, in fog, or under other adverse conditions. You learned to have an *awareness* of where your targets were, to memorize the positions of your own people and keep them in mind. Kellen had learned then that he could not only remember where all the people on his own side were in a fight, but know where they were going to be. In practice sessions, he'd never hit any of his own side. Master Belesharon had said this was a manifestation of the Knight-Mage gift.

So was this, it seemed.

It wasn't that he could see in the dark. But he'd come this

way once, and apparently part of the Knight-Mage gift was to remember terrain *perfectly.* He wasn't going to need the *tarnkappa* to get out of here.

That was going to make things a little easier.

"There's an, um, dragon here," he whispered to Idalia. "He's going to lift both of us up to a tunnel a few yards up the cliff face."

"I remember the dragon," Idalia said dryly.

Before Kellen could raise the hood again, he felt Ancaladar's talons close around his middle, and heard Idalia give a startled squeak. He felt himself swept into the air and deposited, very gently, just inside the cave. He could see Ancaladar's eyes glowing like dim Elven lanterns, and could tell from their size that the dragon's head must be very close. He could even feel the dragon's warm breath. But he could see absolutely nothing.

"Hello," Idalia said to Ancaladar. "I guess I have you to thank for my rescue."

"It was my pleasure, Wildmage Idalia," Ancaladar said gravely.

"Oh," Kellen said, realizing he'd forgotten to introduce them. "Idalia, this is Ancaladar. Ancaladar, this is my sister Idalia." It felt very odd making polite introductions in the pitch-darkness when only one of the parties could see the other.

He swept the hood up for just a moment, to see where Idalia was, and led her a little farther into the cave. Then he took off the *tarnkappa.*

"Why don't you wear the *tarnkappa*?" he suggested. "I can get by without it. Oh, and Ancaladar can see you and hear you even while you're wearing it. I won't be able to hear you, though."

"Don't tell me you can see down here," Idalia said disbelievingly. Kellen sensed her reaching for the *tarnkappa,* and pushed it into her hands.

"No, but I don't need to. I can remember where we've been, and I'm pretty sure we're going back the same way."

"Yes," Ancaladar said softly. "It is not the fastest, but it will be sure."

Idalia put on the cloak. It was a very odd sensation for Kellen. One moment he could sense she was *there*. The next moment he couldn't.

There were a few moments of scraping and slithering while Ancaladar turned himself around in the cramped confines of the tunnel, and then they continued. They moved much faster now that Idalia could see, though she still leaned against Kellen from time to time for support. That was probably the strangest part of the whole adventure, because the occasional contacts seemed to come out of nowhere; Kellen had no sense of her presence until he felt her lean against him.

The absolute darkness wore on his nerves, though his internal map of the cave system was still as reliable as when he'd first discovered it. Now that he couldn't see, hearing and scent seemed to be magnified to compensate: he could hear a faint dripping of water; something that sounded like a distant river; the constant "breathing" sound of the cave; the faint sound of Ancaladar's passage over the stone and the louder sounds of his own movements. He could smell wet stone, blood and damp wool, leather and Elven steel and armor-oil, unicorn and horse, and a spicy indefinable scent that he eventually decided must be dragon.

And eventually, he could see light.

It was the faintest hint of light at first—nothing like enough to navigate by. But they were in the last long passage that led to the outside world, and Kellen could smell cold fresh air.

By now Idalia was staggering with exhaustion. Kellen wasn't feeling much better. All he wanted to do was throw himself down in the nearest snowdrift and sleep for a year or two.

"We're not going to be able to climb down that cliff," Kellen said in sudden realization.

"I know," Ancaladar said gently. "Humans are very fragile."

Whatever that meant. At the moment, Kellen was too tired to care.

By the time they reached the cave mouth his eyes were watering at the intensity of the light after so long in utter darkness, and he'd pulled up the hood of his travel cloak to try to shield himself a little. He was faintly surprised to note that from the position of the sun it was only early afternoon. It seemed as if he'd been down in the caves for sennights.

As soon as they'd neared the opening, Idalia had taken off the *tarnkappa* and bundled it across her shoulders like an over-large towel. She looked pale and exhausted, and there were deep shadows under her eyes. She was filthy with cave dust and dried blood, and her clothes were ragged and torn.

Ancaladar had hurried ahead once he saw the two of them could make it as far as the cave mouth under their own power. He was already outside, only his enormous head poking back into the cave, watching them anxiously as they staggered forward.

Finally they reached the cave mouth. Kellen shivered. He'd managed to forget how cold it was out here.

Once more the dragon reached out and lifted each of them out of the cave and—very gently—deposited them on the snow at the foot of the cliff. Then before either of them could say anything, it launched itself into the sky with a bound.

"Well, I—" Idalia began. Then her eyes rolled back in her head and her knees buckled. She fell forward into the snow.

Kellen lunged for her, feeling for her pulse, but both her breathing and her pulse were steady. She'd simply fainted from exhaustion—and no wonder, after walking who knew how far through the caves right after a major healing? At least he was in better shape than she was.

He looked around warily, but he saw no signs of enemies, and Ancaladar, soaring overhead, gave no sign that he saw anything amiss. Kellen picked up Idalia again—making sure his cloak was wrapped warmly around both of them—and began the long walk back toward the camp.

JERMAYAN and Shalkan met him halfway, and Kellen might have been in for a bad time if he hadn't had Idalia in his arms. Jermayan immediately took her up before him on Valdien, cradling her tenderly in his arms.

"Is she all right?" the Elven Knight asked, sounding closer to terrified than Kellen had ever heard him before. "Why does she not wake?"

It was a good thing they were operating under War Manners, which allowed Jermayan to ask direct questions. If he'd had to use the normal forms of Elven polite speech, Kellen thought he might have exploded.

"She's just had a major healing, and had to walk out of the caves on top of it," Kellen said soothingly, putting his arm over Shalkan's withers. "She'll sleep for at least a day, if she can." *And I wish I could.* "She's fine."

Jermayan held her close, looking unconvinced.

"You were fortunate to have found her," he said.

Just then, Ancaladar's shadow swept over them. Jermayan looked up.

Kellen had never seen Jermayan look quite so utterly and completely taken by surprise. It was rather gratifying. "What's that?" Jermayan sputtered, staring.

"It's a dragon," Kellen said, trying to hide a grin. "He's the one who showed me where Idalia was. His name is Ancaladar. He wants to come home with us."

He followed me home. Can I keep him?

Jermayan continued to stare in a stunned fashion as Ancaladar swept on over the end of the valley, wheeled, and headed back, soaring higher this time.

"Then . . . by all means . . . the dragon must be welcome . . . in our homes and at our hearths," he said at last.

"I don't know about that part," Kellen said doubtfully. "He isn't going to fit in *my* home, anyway, unless he can shrink."

THEY stopped to collect Idalia's horse, and then rode out of the valley following the route the rest of the party had taken the night before. Despite Kellen's tiredness and Idalia's need for rest, this was not a place any of them wanted to linger. Soon enough the Shadowed Elves would stop searching the caves and nerve themselves to face the punishing daylight. And Kellen didn't know how many more of them there might be.

Idalia rode in Jermayan's arms, wrapped in a blanket. As they went on, Kellen told Jermayan everything of what he'd seen in the caverns, particularly about the Shadowed Elves. The more people who knew about them, the better.

"Idalia mentioned an underground village, but I didn't see it. They were carrying weapons stolen from the caravan, so they're definitely the hooded figures I saw in my vision."

"Which means they are *Their* allies. Here—in Elven Lands. Living undetected," Jermayan said darkly. "Able to pass the land-wards at will. Andoreniel must hear of this without delay."

THEY rode through the rest of the day, but though they saw traces of the other party's passage, it had almost a full day's lead, and they had not caught up to it by the time Jermayan signaled a halt for the night.

"You are nearly falling from your saddle with exhaustion, Kellen, and Idalia could use better rest as well," the Elven Knight said, in tones that brooked no argument. "We will certainly catch up to them tomorrow—and travel all the faster for a night's rest."

Kellen reluctantly agreed. Even without Vestakia traveling with them to detect any hint of Demonic presence, Ancaladar's presence overhead ensured that they were nearly as safe as if they were within Sentarshadeen itself.

Although now that he knew that creatures such as the

Shadowed Elves could roam the Elven Lands at will, Kellen was no longer sure how safe that was.

Jermayan took most of the work of making camp upon himself, leaving Kellen to sit at Idalia's side beside the warmth of the brazier. She was awake now, but still very weak.

"Where's Ancaladar?" she asked.

"Flying around overhead, I guess," Kellen answered. "Unless he's asleep somewhere. I'm not sure where he'd sleep, though. He's much too big to perch in a tree, and there aren't any more caves around here." *At least I hope there aren't.* "Maybe he can sleep on the wing."

"I don't think dragons sleep at all, except when they're bored," Idalia said seriously. She shivered, but Kellen could tell it wasn't from cold. "Thanks for getting me out of there. I mean it." She sipped her tea.

"You'd do the same for me. And Ancaladar did all the real work. All I had to do was follow him." He thought about asking Idalia about the odd way the healing had gone, and decided to wait. It didn't seem to be an urgent problem that needed to be dealt with right now. "He wants to come and live in Sentarshadeen with us."

"Well, *that* should give the gossips something new to talk about," Idalia said. "Though if every time you leave, you bring back another odd stray, they might decide to confine you to the valley from now on." She yawned, her eyelids drooping, and Kellen plucked the teacup from her hand as her fingers relaxed.

Jermayan arrived, having settled the horses for the night, and stirred the pot of soup that was cooking over the fire. Kellen had already eaten several trail-bars, but was looking forward to hot soup.

"It will be ready soon," Jermayan pronounced. "Then you will both eat, and you will sleep."

"I think we can all sleep," Kellen said. "Idalia said that dragons don't sleep. Ancaladar can keep watch."

Jermayan glanced up at the sky. Ancaladar was invisible,

save as an enormous shadow that blotted out the stars as he passed between them and the ground.

"Two sets of eyes are better than one," the Elven Knight said simply.

There was no point in arguing with Jermayan, even if Kellen had possessed the energy right now. If there was one thing he had learned during the time he had spent in Sentarshadeen, it was that it was not an easy thing to change an Elf's mind, once he had made it up.

Well, if Jermayan wanted to keep watch, let him. No harm could come of it, after all.

They had to awaken Idalia so that she could eat. Jermayan cradled her in his arms while Kellen helped her hold the bowl. The sight of the two of them together made him faintly uncomfortable, but he put it down to exhaustion. She was asleep again almost before she'd finished, and Jermayan wrapped her tenderly in her blankets again, adding more fuel to the brazier.

"She must have been badly injured," he suggested, handing Kellen his own bowl of soup.

"She was," Kellen said briefly, bending his head over the bowl to inhale the steam. Jermayan seemed to be waiting for more. "She'd fallen off a cliff."

"Ah." Jermayan was silent for a moment. "I well remember my own weakness after you healed me."

"This . . . " Kellen hesitated for a moment, wondering how much to tell—and how much Jermayan would understand. Jermayan was no Wildmage: uncounted years ago the Elves had sacrificed their part in the Greater Magics for peace and length of years, so their legends told. There were no Elven Mages.

"This was a much more extensive healing," he finally said. "And it went differently. She's going to be fine," he added quickly, seeing the look of alarm in Jermayan's dark eyes, "but she's going to need a lot more rest and recovery time than you did." He thought of the days after he'd first come to live with Idalia in the Wildwoods, when she'd healed him of injuries sustained fighting the Outlaw Hunt. "Maybe as much as a moonturn."

"Then there are two reasons to return to Sentarshadeen as quickly as we may," Jermayan said consideringly. "Now I think it is best that you sleep as well."

WHEN he awoke the following morning, Kellen felt fully recovered—whatever gift had been bestowed upon him in the cavern to allow him to heal without Mageprice, it had granted him a quick recovery as well.

The morning had dawned damp and foggy; clouds had rolled in, shrouding the sun, and the trees were veiled in mist. The temperature had risen slightly, with a bite in the heavy air that promised snow before midday.

The horses were restless, sensing the coming snowfall, and even Idalia's placid bay mare, Cella, frisked and played up when it came time to saddle her.

Idalia was still too weak to ride, so once more Jermayan took her up before him on Valdien and tied Cella's lead-rein to his saddle.

They caught up to the rest of the party near midday. As Kellen had expected, it had begun to snow, and visibility was poor, but unicorn senses were keen.

"They know we're here," Shalkan reported, and a few moments later a unicorn-mounted knight came plunging back through the snowdrifts to greet them.

"Kellen—Shalkan—Jermayan—and Idalia as well!" Bendirean said. "Thank Leaf and Star! We had thought . . . "

"That misfortune had befallen us," Jermayan agreed. "And so it did, but as you see, we have all slipped free from the Shadow's grasp. We are fortunate to have reached you before you turned off in the direction of the Fortress of the Crowned Horns."

"We do not go there," Bendirean said reluctantly, as if to

impart the news pained him. He and Zanaleth turned and began walking along beside Jermayan and the others, at a distance that was comfortable for Zanaleth. "Vestakia says it is too dangerous. We return directly to Sentarshadeen."

Too dangerous? That doesn't sound good, Kellen thought.

"That is our destination as well, with all possible speed," Jermayan agreed, as calmly as if he were discussing a new fashion, or the best way to prepare roast partridge. "We bring news that Andoreniel must have at once—but we also bring a welcome ally." He pointed skyward.

Bendirean looked up.

As if he could hear them—and for all Kellen knew, he could—Ancaladar chose that moment to make a low pass over them. For a few moments he was plainly visible, even through the veils of snow, then he tilted the end of one vast wing and rose through the clouds again.

"That was a dragon," Bendirean said, with what Kellen thought was commendable calm under the circumstances.

Zanaleth and Shalkan exchanged eloquent—though silent—looks.

"Yes, Bendirean, that was a dragon," Jermayan said, his voice faintly unsteady. "His name is Ancaladar, and he wishes to be our ally."

⏤

THE reunion with the larger party was one marked by great relief on both sides. Sandalon was overjoyed to see Kellen again, bursting into unexpected tears and clinging to him tightly. When Lairamo saw that Idalia was alive—though far from well—Kellen thought she might actually lose her iron composure. As it was, the haggard lines of fear and despair in her face eased markedly.

Kellen was glad to see that all the children were well—at least in body. The scars of their captivity at the hands of the Shadowed Elves would be long in healing, and Kellen hoped that the Elven Healers would be able to do something to ease them. To his surprise, he found himself thinking with favor about Armethalieh, something he would have been willing to swear would never happen. But the High Mages were skilled in manipulating the mind: wouldn't it be a good thing if none of the children remembered any of the horrible things that had happened at all?

Or was this a case of good intentions leading to bad results? Armethalieh as it was now was certainly no paradise, but Morusil, Iletel, and even Idalia had said that the Mages had begun with the best of intentions. And it was wanting to do good that had allowed the Mages bonded to dragons to be corrupted by the Endarkened.

Fortunately this problem's solution wasn't up to him.

The stop was necessarily brief. While Vestakia did not sense pursuers, she had the sense that there were more of the Shadowed Elves in the area—and if they came in force, or with the same allies who had proved so disastrous to the first party, there might be little Kellen's people could do to stop them, even though they now had Ancaladar's help. With Shalkan's permission, Kellen took Sandalon up before him on his saddle, and they rode on.

The snow continued to worsen throughout the day, and they finally had to stop a few hours later to make camp. Kellen still felt restless, even though Vestakia didn't sense any trouble nearby, and decided to ride up the trail a ways to scout ahead for the next day's travel.

He unlimbered his bow and kept it ready to hand, shielded by his cloak. His archery wasn't as strong as his sword-work, but he might get lucky and surprise a rabbit or two. Elven trail-food was both nourishing and palatable, but after more than a sennight of eating nothing else, some fresh meat would be welcome.

KELLEN was a bit surprised at the relief he felt to ride away from the rest of the party. The winter silence seemed to envelop him like a soothing cloak, and the only sound was the hiss of falling snow.

"I, uh, didn't ask you if you wanted to come along," Kellen said after a while.

"You could hardly go without me," Shalkan said. "Besides, I thought you'd like to be alone for a while."

Kellen was grateful for his friend's understanding. Since the moment he'd realized that the convoy heading for the Fortress of the Crowned Horns had been attacked, he'd been drawn as tight as a bowstring with tension—first to reach the spot, then to find the missing children, then to rescue Idalia, then to get away safely. And while he knew they hadn't quite accomplished that yet, they were close. He could relax, at least a little.

"It's a real mess, isn't it?" he said.

"Having colonies of Shadowed Elves living within the Elven lands, ready to strike at the Nine Cities without warning? I suppose it depends on your definition of 'mess,'" Shalkan observed.

"I guess we're going to have to—Wait. What's that?"

There was a sound up ahead. But when he listened for it, it disappeared into the wind and the hiss of falling snow.

"I don't hear anything," Shalkan said, flicking his delicate ears back and forth.

That wasn't right. Shalkan's hearing was much more acute than Kellen's.

"Something's coming. I *think* something's coming. I thought I heard it."

"You probably sensed it. Knight-Mages know what they need to know. Shall we go see?"

"Yes," Kellen said. Shalkan broke into a quick trot. Kellen hoped that whatever it was, it wasn't more trouble than he could handle.

But when they reached the source of the disturbance Kellen had sensed, he discovered it wasn't trouble at all.

"Kenderk! Tyban! Dervasin!" he greeted the Elves he knew best by name. "I See you. And Calmeren—I am glad to see you so well recovered."

"I would not let them come without me," the unicorn said simply, inclining her head.

When he'd left Sentarshadeen, it had been with only those he could gather in less than a day, but Andoreniel and Ashaniel had not been sitting idle in his absence. From what Kellen could see here, they had gathered all the rest of the Knights they could call up in haste and sent them after Kellen as soon as possible—and not only warriors, but light supply wagons as well, to carry the extra supplies needed to engage in winter travel.

"I See you, Kellen Knight-Mage," Dervasin answered. "One hopes, of course, that the news you have to tell will make good hearing."

"The children are safe," Kellen said, since that was the extent of the good news. "We've made camp a way up the trail. I'll ride back with you. There's a lot to tell." *And not much of it good news.*

As he led Dervasin's party back to the others, Kellen provided an abbreviated version of recent events, including the details he now knew of the massacre of the party sent to conduct them to the Elven fortress.

"The fortress itself is safe, but Vestakia doesn't think it's safe to try to approach it. And we need to get Idalia and the children back to Sentarshadeen as soon as possible."

"As you say," Dervasin agreed.

Even with the snow and the gathering darkness, they were within sight of the camp by now. Kellen and Shalkan rode on ahead to let the others know that the relief party had arrived.

He wasn't quite sure Dervasin believed him about the dragon.

Yet.

THE arrival of supply wagons meant they could make a proper camp, with better shelter for Idalia, Lairamo, and the children. The relief party included several Healers as well, who quickly went off to consult with Evanor, to see if there was more they could do for the children and Idalia before they reached the city.

And more people meant they were less likely to be attacked . . . though there had been a substantial guard of Sentarshadeen's best warriors on the original convoy, and it hadn't saved them.

"Why so gloomy?" Shalkan asked a few hours later. "You've done what you set out to do. If no one attacked Dervasin's force on his way to us, we shouldn't have much trouble getting back to Sentarshadeen. So . . . we've won."

Kellen looked at his friend. He was fairly sure the unicorn was just being provoking—though he suspected he was right that they wouldn't be attacked on the way back to the city. From what Vestakia had said, the enemy forces were only interested in keeping them away from the Crowned Horns.

"No," he said slowly. "We haven't won. This is just the beginning."

ONE did not prosper in the World Without Sun without knowing the pattern of events almost before they were formed. And Prince Zyperis yearned to prosper. Though he had not known his mother's plans before she had at last unveiled them to him, once he knew the direction in which her interests lay, it was a simple enough matter to set his own spies—both magical and mundane—to follow the undertaking.

And so Zyperis knew almost as soon as it happened that Sentarshadeen rode out to rescue what Queen Savilla had taken. He waited, baffled, for her to order the captives removed from the hands of the Goblin Elves, but the cycles of rest and Rising passed, and she did nothing.

Almost—almost—he seized them himself, and carried them away to a place of greater safety, but he knew that his dearest Mama would see that as a direct challenge to her power, and Zyperis was not ready to attempt that. Nor did he ask her openly about her plans, for to do so would be to reveal his own sources of information.

And so he waited, frustrated and confused, as the accursed Elves, the Wildmages, and—worst of all—his wayward daughter Vestakia forged deep into the Mystral Range, discovering the lair of the Goblin Elves and carrying away the prize.

And adding unspeakable insult to unthinkable injury, carrying away the dragon as well.

Zyperis had known a dragon laired and hunted somewhere in the Mystrals. The Endarkened knew the spells to force a Bond between a human Mage and the greatest of the Otherfolk, and could he only have traced the creature to its lair, Zyperis could have sent one of his cringing Mage-men to it and claimed the prize for the Endarkened.

But now—thanks to Queen Savilla's maddening inaction—they had lost both Elves *and* dragon, and it would be long cycles of searching before he could locate another of the rare beasts.

Prince Zyperis was not happy.

⌐

THE loss of the dragon was an unexpected setback, casting a faint shadow of misfortune over her victory, but the savor of Prince Zyperis's frustrations at not being able to act upon his secret information nearly made up for that disappointment. And the creature had not Bonded with either of the Wildmages—so Savilla's spies reported—so there was yet a chance of reclaiming it to the service of *He Who Is*. And that would be so much easier now that they knew precisely where it was.

Her son really ought to learn to take the long view of things.

Queen Savilla was not unhappy with the progression of

events. And soon official word of her "defeat" would reach the Court, and she could savor new pleasures . . .

THE emissary of the Goblin Elves reached the Dark Court a handful of Risings later. Once he had left the Elven lands, Savilla had sent an escort—both to speed him on his journey, and to ensure he was not pursued.

She felt a mild curiosity at the prospect of personally viewing an example of this great and secret triumph over the arrogant and condescending Elves. Its creation had been the work of her father, Uralesse, who had mingled the blood of mind-blasted Elven captives taken in the Great War with that of Goblins and Lesser Endarkened to create a race that would deceive the land-wards of the Elves by virtue of its Elven heritage. For centuries, as the Children of the Light reckoned time, the Goblin Elves had been left to go their own way, living in the dark places deep beneath the Elven lands—but never let to forget to whom they owed their ultimate allegiance.

THE emissary's name was Hnn. Among his own people, he was a hunt-leader, cruel and fearless, but now he had been brought before his gods, and he crouched and cowered, drooling in fear.

Savilla had chosen to receive him in her formal Audience Chamber. She was seated upon the Shadow Throne. Carved of ebony and inlaid with black pearls, it made a striking backdrop for her scarlet skin.

The walls of the Audience Chamber were black as well— a frieze in darkened silver depicting all the ancient races which the Endarkened had destroyed. The ceiling of the chamber was paneled in the skin of a black dragon, its scales still luminous after all these centuries, and the floor was a single polished block of black topaz, so smooth and flawless that the ceiling and walls reflected in it as if in a mirror.

The chamber lent itself to the staging of very effective set-pieces. And was easy to clean up afterward.

"Sweet, isn't he?" Savilla murmured to Prince Zyperis. She had allowed him to attend—though this was by no means a public audience—and had even allotted him the signal honor of standing beside her throne.

"Barbarian," Zyperis commented. But he sounded intrigued.

Savilla waved a gilded hand, indicating that Hnn should approach. The Goblin Elf crawled forward on hands and knees, kissing her foot before flinging himself facedown at her feet.

"He's going to be difficult to talk to in that position," Zyperis drawled, gazing down at the trembling creature.

Savilla laughed. "*Talk* to him! My dear boy, they're incapable of producing civilized speech, and I have no intention of spending half an eternity barking like a coldwarg. No, a simple mind-touch will tell us all he knows. And then . . . kitchens? Or bedroom?"

Zyperis affected to consider the matter for a moment, and smiled. "Why not both?"

"Ah, Zyperis, you always know what will please me best," Savilla cooed.

She studied the creature at her feet for a moment more—rather attractive, really, all the more because one could see the remains of his Elven heritage spoiled and twisted within him—then gestured to the Lesser Endarkened that had accompanied him. They came forward, their hooves clicking on the topaz floor, and lifted him to eye level with the Queen. His pale bulging eyes widened further with terror and awe.

She reached out one hand to Zyperis, so that he could share in the spell. With the other she gripped Hnn's chin.

His fear cascaded over her like sweet perfume, kindling the spell. Delicately, she sipped at the images that lay on the surface of his mind, taking in the message he had come to bring. With him she shared the thrill of the stalk, the slaughter of the Elves, the capture of the strange hot foul-smelling captives. The joy at serving the Winged Ones.

And the terror, the fury, the sense of shame and failure, when the god-offering vanished from his grasp.

All that rushed into her mind and Prince Zyperis's in an instant. If the two Endarkened had not already been holding Hnn upright, he would have crumpled to the floor like a doll.

When she was sure she had all the information he had to give, Savilla released him. Hnn whimpered faintly. Urine ran down his leg and spattered on the floor, its musky scent filling the chamber.

"Now take him away and bathe him—thoroughly," Savilla said. "When you are done, bring him to my private chambers. We shall see what other entertainment our young envoy can provide."

SAVILLA was pleased to see that Zyperis contained himself until the two of them were alone, though his barbed tail lashed fretfully with the strength of his emotions. To tease him, she got to her feet and walked away from the throne—carefully avoiding the puddle—and walked about the room, admiring the designs upon the walls as if she'd never seen them before. So many races, quenched by the cunning of the Endarkened. And soon the Elves would join them.

"Mama—why?" Zyperis burst out, when he could contain himself no longer. "You had them within your grasp—all those tender morsels, and the Elven King's brat first among them! You could have brought them here before the cursed Wildmages and the others got anywhere near them! And you ordered the Goblin Elves not to pursue the party and take them back—that wretched barbarian didn't understand it, and neither do I! We've failed!"

"Have we?" Savilla turned to face him. "Why did I send the Goblin Elves after the children in the first place?"

"To take the King's son. And you did, Mama. It was beautifully done." But there was uncertainty in Zyperis's voice, as if he was not certain that was the whole truth. Savilla glowed with pride—it had been a subtle plot, and it was not his fault that he did not grasp it at once. That he realized he did not see all of her plan was to his credit, and indicated what a formidable adversary he would be in the years to come.

"If that was what I meant to do, do you not think that the puling brat would be weeping in my dungeons even now?" Savilla said gently.

Zyperis frowned, hesitating. "I . . . yes, dearest Mama. But if that was not what you wanted, why go after the caravan at all? Now the Elves know about their cousins. They will not rest until they have hunted them down, every one."

"Yes . . . " Savilla purred, and watched Zyperis's face light with understanding and delight.

"Now come, my son," she said, going to him and putting a hand on his arm. "There is much we can do to amuse ourselves until our guest is brought to us. And with such tender care, he will be a savory morsel at the banquet later."

Eleven

The Road Through the Border Lands

Cilarnen wasn't quite sure why the Elf was helping him. For a long time—bells—he was simply too numb to care. The creature gave him its pack mule to ride, doused its peculiar brazier and repacked its gear, and within two chimes, they were on their way.

Several times the Elf tried making conversation with him, even going so far as to offer its name—Hyandur—but Cilar-

nen only gave one- or two-word replies, and eventually the
Elf stopped talking.

Cilarnen couldn't think of what to say, anyway. He'd been
Banished. He was leaving the only home he'd ever known.
His Gift had been destroyed. He was nothing at all.

Eventually it occurred to him he ought to say something.
He needed to know what the Elf knew, if nothing else.

"One of my friends was Banished too. Did you—"

"I came upon the remains of a body in the woods today. It
wore a Felon's Cloak, and around it were the footprints of
dogs—heavy marks, as if made by creatures of stone. Perhaps it was he. If so, I am sorry for your loss."

The Elf's words were barely more than noise to Cilarnen.
He knew that Undermage Anigrel had said that Tiedor was
to be Banished. He knew that the Outlaw Hunt was com-
prised of enchanted stone mastiffs, like the Stone Golems
that—in other shapes—served so many functions in the
City. But somehow, in his shocked and benumbed state, he
could not bring any sense out of Hyandur's words.

"I don't understand," Cilarnen said at last.

"The body had been savaged by the Outlaw Hunt," Hyandur said patiently. "The Stone Hounds kill all who are declared Outlaw by the High Council, if they are still within
the City's lands at dawn."

But no matter how hard Cilarnen thought about Hyandur's
words, they still didn't make any sense. Why would the Outlaw Hunt kill anyone? They were just supposed to escort the
Outlaw to the borders. Of course they were.

The Elf had to be lying. That's what Elves did.

"Show me where he is," Cilarnen demanded.

"If we return to that place, we will not reach the edge of
the valley by dawn. If we do not leave Armethaliehan lands
by the time your Hunt is released, we will both meet the
same fate as your friend," Hyandur said calmly.

Cilarnen wanted to pull away, to ride off in search of the
body. Elves were dangerous—everyone said so—and he was

only now beginning to awaken to the fact that he might be in more danger from his companion than from the cold and the wilderness. But the mule's lead-rein was tied fast to the horse's saddle, and there was nothing Cilarnen could do but ride on, blindly, into the dark.

He was being kidnapped.

He vowed to escape at the earliest opportunity.

AS the sky began to lighten, Hyandur urged the tired animals to a faster pace. They were moving now through a gently rising landscape wholly unfamiliar to Cilarnen—a narrow path bordered by bare earth on both sides, as if someone had re-created the flower beds of the City gardens on a gigantic scale. Each enormous tract of earth was edged by a row of trees, and they seemed to go on forever.

Cilarnen hoped for the sight of a village where he could get help, but he did not see so much as the smoke from a distant hearth-fire.

Behind them, the sun began to rise. Cilarnen imagined it striking the gilded roof of the Council House with fire, heard in memory the sweet high carillon of Dawn Bells, its soft notes ringing out over the City. He swallowed hard with homesickness and loss.

"They will be coming soon," Hyandur said grimly. "We must hurry now."

He leaned forward, speaking softly to his mare. Her ears flickered back and forth, as if she understood what he was saying to her. He untied one of the knots in the lead-rope affixed to his saddle, lengthening it by several feet.

And the mare went from a trot, to a canter, to a floating run.

The mule lagged behind for a moment, pulling the lead-rein bowstring tight, and for a moment Cilarnen hoped it would snap. No mule was as fast as a horse anyway.

But this mule was apparently an exception, for after a moment, the rein went slack again as the mule followed after the mare at a pounding, jarring pace. Reflexively, Cilarnen crouched low over the mule's neck, urging it on. If he had been a lesser rider, he would have fallen off in the first few moments of their mad flight—and deep within, a tiny part of him was suddenly convinced of the seriousness of their peril. Surely no one, even an Elf, would misuse a horse this way without great need.

They passed the last of the open land and were back among the winter-bare trees, where patches of ice still covered the ground. Cilarnen expected them to slow down over such treacherous footing, but they didn't, and his heart hammered in fear—not for himself, but for the splendid chestnut Hyandur rode. If she slipped, if she fell, lameness would be the most fortunate outcome she could hope for. A broken neck—a broken leg—

But she danced over the ice as if she had wings, with the mule thundering after. The sun was higher now, flickering through the branches, the light making Cilarnen's head pound with feverish pain. His hands and face were numb with cold—it was as if he couldn't remember ever having been warm.

In the distance, the trees thinned out again. The road rose in a gentle curve, and he could see a gateway of sorts—or at least a place where someone had placed a large post at either side of the road. What could it possibly mark? There was nothing around it, and the land looked very much the same on one side as on the other.

But it must mean something, because Hyandur was already slowing the mare as they approached it. The mule was only too glad to slacken its pace without any urging on Cilarnen's part, and both animals passed between the posts at a dead slow walk.

It was snowing on the other side.

Or rather, it had snowed, recently and heavily. And the air was sharp with the promise of more, far colder than the air on the near side of the posts.

"This is the boundary of the City lands," Cilarnen said in

sudden realization. Or at least, the boundary of the Home
Farms.

"Yes." Hyandur dismounted from the mare and began to
walk back and forth with her through the fresh snow, speaking gently to her.

Cilarnen dismounted from the mule, wincing and staggering with stiffness. He rubbed its nose apologetically. He
wasn't sure what to do with mules. But he supposed it
couldn't hurt to treat it like a horse, and so he coiled up the
lead-rein that Hyandur had released and began to lead it
back and forth, as he had seen the grooms do with horses in
his father's stables.

As he did, he looked back toward the boundary. The snow
made it easy to see. The snow just . . . stopped, as though it
had run into an invisible wall.

As it had, of course. A wall of Magecraft. Just as Undermage Anigrel had said, the High Council must have extended the boundaries of the City to cover the entire valley
once more.

He wasn't sure whether to laugh or cry. The High Council
had reversed its decision. The Home Farms were part of the
City Lands once more, just as he and the others had wanted.

He'd ruined his life, caused his father's death, his family's
disgrace, for nothing.

"You may stop now," Hyandur told him, breaking into
Cilarnen's chaotic thoughts. "Unsaddle the mule, and build a
fire in the brazier. We will rest here before going on."

Cilarnen stared at him, too shocked to react. The Elf was
giving him orders?

Hyandur regarded him for a long moment.

"If you cannot do that, then go to the well and draw water
for the animals. They are rested enough to be ready to drink.
The well lies over there." He pointed in the direction of a
snowy cylinder of rock.

Cilarnen hesitated, but the mule nudged at his shoulder,
then lowered its head to mouth at the snow, obviously want-

ing water. There was no reason for the animals to suffer just because they belonged to an Elf. Reluctantly, Cilarnen trudged off in that direction, tucking his hands into his armpits to warm them.

He had never seen a well in his life, but it was a simple mechanical design, with a crank and gears to raise and lower a bucket on a rope, and after a few tries, he managed to get the cover off, find the bucket, and fill the trough at the well's foot with water.

If he'd had his Magegift and Wand, he could simply have Called the water up out of the well. As it was, it was at least a chime before he managed to fill the watering-trough, and he was sweating and damp—and very irritated with the Elf—at the end of it. If this was servants' work, then the servants in House Volpiril had not had as soft a life as he'd imagined.

But as he turned back to collect the horse and the mule, he forgot all his lesser problems.

Racing toward him, along the last patch of open ground between the woods and the marker-posts, was a pack of Stone Hounds.

They looked just like the pair outside the Arch-Mage's house, yet these were horribly animate, their fanged jaws opening and closing with soundless barking. There were almost a dozen of them, perfect in every detail from the spiked collars around their necks to the curved nails upon their feet. Every aspect of their manner spoke of murderous threat.

There was no Mage with them.

He ran back toward Hyandur and the animals—thinking he might be able to save the mare, at least—but before he could reach them, the Outlaw Hunt reached the invisible border between the lands claimed by the City and the world beyond.

They stopped as if they had run into a wall.

But even then they did not retreat.

Like any hunting pack frustrated and kept from taking its

prey, they milled back and forth on the far side of the invisible wall, their unblinking gaze fixed on Cilarnen. Some crouched on their haunches, barking silently. Some dug at the frozen ground, as if it were possible to dig beneath the magick and reach their intended prey. A few of the Hounds kept trying to cross the boundary, only to be flung back each time they tried, as if by some invisible hand.

The leader of the pack, a mastiff carved of white granite, simply stood at the far side of the posts and glared fixedly at Cilarnen. If it were possible for unliving stone to radiate murderous rage, the creature did.

Watching the pack go mad with failure, a slow cold wisdom settled over Cilarnen. The Elf had not lied. Anigrel had not lied. Tiedor was dead—any of his friends who might be Banished after him would die.

But Banishment was never meant to be a death sentence! It was only meant to cast people out of the City, not to kill them!

He did not know why this terrible ancient custom had been revived, but now he knew this: the Outlaw Hunt was not meant to conduct Outlaws to the borders of City Lands, but to kill them.

And if he had not had the great good fortune to run into Hyandur last night—if the Elf had not aided him for mysterious reasons of its own—he too would be dead now, savaged by stone fangs.

"You may take the animals to drink, now. Take care that they do not drink too much at first," Hyandur said, coming up to Cilarnen where he stood, still frozen in shock, watching the stone Hounds flail at what was to them an impassable border.

"Yes. I'm sorry," Cilarnen said, though he could not at that moment have said what he was apologizing for.

"They will not break through," Hyandur said. "It is, however, unsettling to watch."

Cilarnen shook his head, unable to stop thinking of himself surrounded by the Outlaw Hunt, pulled down beneath those unyielding stone bodies. He took the animals' lead-ropes—Hyandur had unsaddled them while he'd been fighting with the well—and turned away.

—

CHILD of the City and Mageborn he might be, but Cilarnen knew something of caring for horses. He was careful to let neither animal drink as much as it wished to, and when they were done, he brought them back to where Hyandur had laid out a ground cloth and the brazier. The Elf was brewing tea, indifferent to the Stone Hounds that waited beyond the Border.

They had stopped attempting to batter their way through the boundary, and now simply stood in a silent row, gazing hungrily toward Cilarnen. Eleven unmoving granite forms— but Cilarnen had no doubt now that if he took one step back across the Border, they would rouse terrifyingly into life.

And the Council's decree—its true, its *secret* decree— would be carried out.

Death for Cilarnen Volpiril.

But Mages do not kill . . .

"Come, stranger. We will drink tea," Hyandur said. "Then we will move on."

Cilarnen wrapped the stiff felt of the Felon's Cloak around himself. "I . . . my name is Cilarnen. Thank you for saving my life."

Hyandur bowed his head slightly. "The Outlaw Hunt is a foul thing. I would willingly leave no creature to its mercies. Perhaps someday we will talk of what caused you to leave the City."

Cilarnen just shook his head. He didn't want to talk about it, or even think about it. The farther away the events got, the less sense they made to him. All he knew was that people were dead, and it was somehow his fault.

He didn't want to ask where the Elf was taking him, either. He wasn't sure whether it was because he didn't care, or was afraid of what he might hear.

THE days after that passed in a numb haze for Cilarnen. They followed what Hyandur said was the caravan road the Mountain Traders used, though Cilarnen couldn't imagine how the Elf could see where the road was in the snow, much less follow it. He simply assumed it was some vile magic possessed by the Lesser Races.

He was always cold, though the Elf had gifted him with a heavier cloak and a pair of fur-lined gauntlets from his supplies. Cilarnen would have happily burned the Felon's Cloak, or at the very least abandoned it, but Hyandur had pointed out that his clothing was not suitable to the weather, and the Cloak was of sturdy fabric. He had taken the Cloak and crafted a pair of heavy leggings to lace over Cilarnen's trousers. The heavy felt kept Cilarnen dry, and if the leggings were ugly, he no longer cared what he looked like. There was no one around who mattered to see.

His head hurt all the time—a constant stabbing ache that the glare of sun on snow only worsened. He kept the hood of the new fur cloak pulled down as far over his face as possible, trying to shut out the light, but it didn't help.

Just when Cilarnen began to think he would be riding through wilderness for the rest of his life, they came to signs of civilization, at least of a very primitive sort.

Someone had built a wall out here in the middle of nowhere. It was like a crude tiny imitation of the City, though the wall was made of wood, not stone. As they approached the gates, they swung open, and a horseman rode out to meet them.

No.

Not a horseman.

Cilarnen swallowed hard, recognizing the abominable mingling of man and beast as another of the Lesser Races, one mentioned only in passing in his studies. A Centaur.

It wore human clothes upon his human half, with a short

cloak that came to its waist. Its horse half was shaggy with a heavy winter coat.

But Hyandur greeted it as if it were a sentient being, and even Roiry and Pearl did not shy away from the unnatural creature.

"Ho, Hyandur—so the humans did not put you into a cage after all!" the Centaur said, switching its tail back and forth.

"No, Grander. They would not see me at all, nor would they hear my words. Yet my journey was not accomplished without bearing some fruit, as you see."

"A human colt—City-born, I'll wager. Looks half-dead and half-frozen. This is no weather for gallivanting," Grander said disapprovingly.

"Nevertheless," Hyandur said calmly. "I had no choice, nor did Cilarnen."

"Well, Stonehearth will see you both warm and fed this night at least," Grander said. "Come, both of you—I'll see you housed in my own home, with the best of everything!"

"That makes good hearing," Hyandur said. "We thank you for your hospitality."

Hyandur dismounted, and regarded Cilarnen steadily until he had no choice but to do the same. The prospect of a hot dinner made his stomach churn. He wondered what Centaurs ate. Hay? Babies?

When they passed through the gate, he saw that there was an entire village crammed within its walls—almost like one of the poorest quarters of Armethalieh, but with everything much smaller. He expected the streets to be narrower, too, but they were wide, and swept free of snow.

Everyone Cilarnen saw on the streets was a Centaur, all of them dressed much as Grander was, in tunics and short cloaks, and wearing hoods or soft knitted caps. It did not make them look more human. It made them look as if someone were dressing up an animal for a play, but Cilarnen had no desire at all to see a naked Centaur.

Their horse parts were stocky and heavy-boned, like no

horse he had ever seen. Some of the creatures had elaborately braided tails, with ribbons or jewelry braided into the hair. Cilarnen tried not to look.

They reached what must be Grander's house. A younger Centaur appeared, and led Roiry and Pearl away.

"Hot dinner for them, too, and a warm stable," Grander said cheerfully. "Marlen can bring your packs to the house once he has them unsaddled. There will be time for a bath before dinner, I think—and we should be able to find you house-robes."

Hyandur smiled at that, as if at a private joke the two of them shared.

Grander's house was built all on one level. There was very little furniture inside, though what there was—a few tables—was beautifully, though simply made.

"You know the way. I'll send Marlen to you with the hot water as soon as it's ready. Sarlin will bring you mulled ale."

"I thank you for your courtesy to the weary traveler," Hyandur said. "Come, Cilarnen."

⁓

THE chamber at the back of the house was small by the standards Cilarnen was used to. It held a stove in one corner, a clothespress for storing clothes, a table, and a washstand with basin and ewer.

There was no bed at all. Cilarnen stared around in confusion.

"Few who are not Centaurs come to Stonehearth," Hyandur said, as if that were an explanation. He removed his cloak and gloves and set them in the clothespress, then turned to the stove.

As Cilarnen stood in the middle of the room, hesitating, there was a tap at the door. Before he could make up his mind what to do, it opened, and another Centaur walked in.

There was no doubt at all that this one was female. All she wore was a thin woolen blouse, heavily and colorfully embroidered. She was as opulently female as the figurehead on a Selken Trader's vessel, and her long, cream-blonde hair exactly matched the color of her horse-body. There were bright ribbons braided into her tail, their colors matching the embroidery on her shirt.

In one hand she carried a large, brightly-colored earthen-ware pitcher, its contents steaming, and in the other, two wooden mugs. Flung across her back was a pile of cloth.

"Ah, Hyandur, you'll never get that balky thing to light," she said cheerfully. "Let me—and drink up while the ale's hot. Grander would never forgive me if I let you wait until it went cold."

"Then we must not allow you to fall into disgrace, Sarlin," Hyandur answered. Cilarnen realized with a distant sense of surprise that Hyandur actually *liked* these creatures. He considered them to be his *friends*.

Well, you could hardly expect better of an Elf, he supposed doubtfully.

Sarlin walked past Cilarnen—who was still staring—and set the pitcher and mugs down on the table. Hyandur straightened up from his crouch before the stove and relieved her of the bundles of cloth, tossing one to Cilarnen. It fell in a heap at his feet.

Sarlin knelt—with more grace than Cilarnen would have expected—before the stove, and began to rummage purposefully about its interior. Hyandur moved to the table, and poured two mugs full of the steaming ale. He brought one to Cilarnen.

"Drink. And do not stare at her so. She's Grander's daughter."

"Oh, I don't mind a bit of staring," Sarlin said cheerfully over her shoulder. "But I'll kick him into next Harvest if he tries anything. I've heard about those City sorcerers and their ways. Tried to drive us off our own lands, they did! Ah, that's got it." She got to her feet, closing the door of the stove and brushing her hands clean of ash.

"I'm not a sorcerer," Cilarnen said, very quietly. He wasn't quite sure what that was, but it sounded bad.

"He's been Outlawed," Hyandur said. "I believe they take away their magic when they do that."

"Oh!" Sarlin turned to face Cilarnen, her broad inhuman features filled with sympathy. "Did they do that to you? How horrible!"

If there had been any place to run to, Cilarnen would have gone there. If he'd still had his Magegift and his wand, he would have happily reduced both Hyandur and Sarlin to a pile of ash. The one thing he was certain of was that he wasn't going to accept sympathy from a talking horse—or the next best thing to one, anyway.

He pulled off his gauntlets quickly, took the mug, and drank. He'd never tasted ale in his life, and it was filled with unfamiliar spices, but anything was better than having to answer her. He gulped it down, holding his breath to avoid tasting the foul bitter stuff, and felt its heat fill his belly. He hoped it poisoned him.

"He doesn't talk much. Maybe he's simpleminded," Sarlin suggested.

"Perhaps he'll talk later," Hyandur said.

She tossed her head. "Well! Father will certainly want to hear all about what they're planning to do next in the City, so I hope he knows." With another flirt of her tail, she walked out again.

Cilarnen rubbed his eyes with his free hand. He felt very much as if he ought to sit down, but there weren't any chairs. And the stove seemed to suddenly be putting out a great deal of heat. He undid his cloak and let it fall to the floor as well, then walked carefully over to the nearest wall and leaned against it.

"You will find things very different here than your life in Armethalieh," Hyandur said. He seemed to be trying to tell Cilarnen something, but Cilarnen wasn't sure what it was.

Cilarnen slid carefully down the wall and sat on the floor. He set his mug down on the floor beside him and pressed both hands against his face as hard as he could. Maybe the

ale *had* poisoned him, but his constant headache seemed to
be going away, just a little.

"There aren't any chairs," he said. It seemed particularly
important that Hyandur understand that fact.

"You are not accustomed to strong drink," the Elf observed dispassionately.

"Mageborn do not drink," Cilarnen told him grandly. It was
what they told the Commons, after all. The Commons believed that the Mageborn existed on nothing but air, pure well
water, and Communion with the Light, so the saying went.
But his power had been stripped from him, and he'd been cast
out from the City. Could he even call himself Mageborn any
longer?

Hyandur seemed to sigh, and went to place Cilarnen's discarded cloak in the clothespress.

A few moments later Marlen arrived, bringing Hyandur's
packs. He was not alone. Two more Centaurs accompanied
him—one carrying a large copper tub, and the other with his
arms filled with towels and with two large kegs of steaming
water slung across his back. They deposited their burdens in
front of the stove and left again.

"If there's anything else you need, just shout," Marlen
said. He glanced at Cilarnen, and frowned. "A Healer, or . . .
anything."

"You are most kind, as always," Hyandur said.

When Marlen left, Hyandur drew the latch and began
filling the tub. By then Cilarnen felt less dizzy. In fact, he
felt better than he had since the City gates had closed behind him.

He got to his feet and walked over to the pitcher, pouring
himself a careful half-mug of the ale. He knew about getting drunk—though his infrequent—and unauthorized—
experiments had been with the wine from his father's
cellars, and not with ale, which in Armethalieh was strictly
something in which the Commons indulged. While he had
no intention of getting drunk in the middle of a bunch of
talking animals, he liked being free of pain.

"You dislike the taste, yet you drink more of it," Hyandur remarked.

"It makes my head stop hurting," Cilarnen said. He didn't know why he felt the need to explain himself to Hyandur, but the creature had saved his life, so he supposed he owed the Elf common courtesy.

"And your head has hurt for a long time."

"Since I left the City. Or before that. I can't remember." Cilarnen raised the mug and drank. The ale still tasted vile, but he supposed he'd better get used to it.

"I have no skill in healing, but the Healer here is excellent. Perhaps she can craft a potion to ease your pain. Now we will bathe, and eat. Perhaps that will help as well."

As he spoke, Hyandur was removing his clothing, setting each piece neatly aside, and Cilarnen finally realized that Hyandur not only intended to bathe, but to bathe *right in front of him.*

He looked around desperately, but there was still nowhere to go. If he left the room, he'd be outside with a bunch of Centaurs, and that was unthinkable. So he did the only thing he could think of. He refilled his mug to the very top, draining the jug, and retreated to the far corner of the room.

By the time he'd finished that mug as well, everything had taken on a strange unreality. It seemed perfectly reasonable to take off his own clothes at Hyandur's insistence and climb into the cramped tub. It felt good to be clean again after uncounted days of sleeping and waking in the same clothes, and if the soap was harsh and foul-smelling in comparison to what he was used to, it did its job.

When he climbed out again and toweled himself dry in front of the stove, he put on the house-robe that Sarlin had brought. It was fur-lined, and fell past his knees. He still had to wear his own boots with it, but that didn't seem so bad. He was clean.

And maybe talking animals weren't so bad after all. Cilarnen liked horses.

HYANDUR guided him carefully down to dinner afterward. The dining table was as immense as anything that might be found in a Great House, and so high that Cilarnen thought it was going to be rather difficult to eat at, until he noticed two stools, obviously placed for his and Hyandur's use.

The food was what Cilarnen supposed coarse peasant food must be like—roasts and meat-pies and hot bread and dishes of preserved vegetables, all served without ceremony—and no one exhibited anything approaching proper table manners. The table-talk among the dozen or so Centaurs gathered there was rowdy and entirely impolite—if Grander was the patriarch of this peculiar family, then he certainly didn't seem to care whether people showed him proper respect or not.

It only proved, Cilarnen supposed, that the Other Races simply didn't have the same advantages as the inhabitants of the Golden City, though they did all seem to be enjoying themselves. He felt something that wasn't exactly homesickness—as this was entirely outside his experience—but he still felt as if he'd lost something that he didn't have any words for and was only now discovering it. The sensation frightened him.

But the food was hot and plentiful, and Grander kept encouraging him to eat more, and for the first time since that dreadful night in the cellar when the Stone Golems had come for him and his friends, Cilarnen discovered that he actually had an appetite.

After what Sarlin had said back in the room, he'd expected to be interrogated about the City and its plans, but to his relief, nobody asked him anything. And tomorrow he and Hyandur would be gone from this disturbing place.

After the meal was eaten, Hyandur suggested he go off to bed, and Cilarnen was glad enough to get away from the Centaurs to accept the Elf's suggestion readily, even though it still bothered him when the Elf gave him orders. When he returned to the room, he found that the bath-things had been

cleared away, and two large piles of furs and blankets had
been carefully laid out on the floor. Not proper beds, but after having slept for so long on the frozen ground, a soft pallet out of the wind and the snow seemed like paradise.
Cilarnen chose the one nearest the window, rolled himself
up in a couple of blankets, and was instantly asleep.

He awoke to the sunlight streaming through the slats of the
shuttered windows and sat up groggily. He looked around,
expecting to find Hyandur still asleep on the other furs.

But Hyandur was gone—as were his packs and everything
he had brought with him.

Cilarnen's own City clothes were there—clean and neatly
folded. He dressed quickly and ran from the room.

The first person he encountered was Sarlin. She was
working on a piece of embroidery at a large standing frame.

"Good morrow, Cilarnen," she greeted him cheerfully,
just as if nothing were wrong.

"I— He— The Elf— Hyandur— Where is he?" Cilarnen
gasped out.

Sarlin looked faintly puzzled. "Why, he left at first light.
Grander urged him to stay, of course, but he said he had
news to carry that would not wait." She regarded him for a
moment. "Surely you did not expect to go with him?"

Cilarnen stared at her in shock, realizing that, somewhere
deep inside, he'd expected exactly that. "He left me here,"
he said flatly.

"Well, you couldn't expect him to take you into the Elven
Lands, now, could you?" Sarlin said, as if it were the most
reasonable thing in the world. "But he made sure that you
would have a place in Grander's house. He says you are
good with horses. You can work in the stables. He said you
won't know much, but don't worry, we can teach you. Come
spring, you can help with the plowing—and at Spring Fair,
if you want to go to another village, why, no one will stop
you. What could be fairer? Marlen is even making you a
chair. Hyandur said you like chairs." She smiled encourag-
ingly.

Cilarnen took a deep breath as his world crumbled around him once more. *I can work in the stables. In the spring, I can help with the plowing.* He felt like screaming.

But he was a Volpiril. Even here, even now. His father had taught him that it was important not to make enemies without cause, and to be courteous to one's inferiors, because they could not help being inferior.

Of course, Lord Volpiril had not meant those teachings to apply to Lesser Races. But Sarlin could not help being a Centaur.

"Thank you," he said, though those were the hardest words he'd ever had to say. His headache was back full force, making it hard to see. He rubbed at his eyes, wishing everything weren't so bright.

"Come into the kitchen. I'll get you a bowl of porridge— I'm sure there's some left over from breakfast. Then I'll take you to the Healer—Hyandur said we should do that, too. Then you can go to the stables, and Marlen can get you started on your work."

Cilarnen nodded, barely hearing her words. It hardly mattered what these creatures did to him.

Hyandur had left him here alone. And now he truly knew what that word meant.

AS far as Vestakia could sense, they were no longer even being followed, and that made no sense to Kellen. Why would Shadow Mountain go to so much trouble to kidnap Sandalon and the other children, and then not even try to recapture them? It made no sense at all—and that made Kellen feel as if he was missing something important.

The storm blew over after a day or two, and the weather cleared again, and after that, everyone could see Ancaladar flying overhead.

The dragon was an awe-inspiring sight. Kellen never grew tired of watching him as he dipped and swirled through the open sky. He wondered what it would be like to ride upon Ancaladar's back, to see the world from that great height.

He also wondered how much a dragon *ate*. Something that size certainly wouldn't be satisfied with a goat or two.

Cows, probably. Lots of cows.

—

ONCE they were within a few hours of the city, Kellen decided it was safe enough to send messengers ahead to let the city know they were coming, and that the children were safe.

And that they'd brought a dragon with them. He hoped Andoreniel and Ashaniel would be willing to have him come and live in Sentarshadeen. They'd welcomed Vestakia, after all.

The caravan was met at the edge of the unicorn meadow by Andoreniel, Ashaniel, and many others, including the parents of the rescued children. The unicorn riders— including Kellen and also Vestakia—waited a little distance away from the main group, watching the joyful reunions of parents and children.

He wanted to share their joy—he truly did—but it was as if there were a veil between him and the glad celebration taking place in front of him. He knew that the presence of the Shadowed Elves was not yet general knowledge, but by now *everyone* in Sentarshadeen knew that the caravan taking the children to the Fortress of the Crowned Horns had been attacked. Why didn't they see that the war had already begun—a war of a different kind than any they had ever fought before?

"You're just tired," Shalkan told him.

"I don't have time to be tired," Kellen answered with a sigh. He dismounted and stood in the snow beside his friend. "We have to make plans—to get ready. And don't ask me for what, because I don't know."

"That does make it harder to plan," Shalkan agreed, leaning against him.

"Maybe that's the whole point," Kellen said glumly.

⟵

IN twos and threes, the others departed, but Kellen remained. Idalia was transferred to a small sleigh, and taken off with Vestakia and the two Healers, but Jermayan did not go with her. Instead, he rode over to where Kellen and Shalkan waited, alone now in the snow.

"I have spoken to Andoreniel and Ashaniel," Jermayan said without preamble. "They have said that Ancaladar is welcome in Sentarshadeen." He glanced up at the sky, but at the moment the dragon wasn't visible. Even when they'd reached Sentarshadeen, Ancaladar hadn't landed. Kellen got the idea he wouldn't come down until he was invited.

"Good," Kellen said. "It would be nice to know how we can tell him."

"He's coming," Shalkan said, looking eastward.

Both Kellen and Jermayan looked in the direction Shalkan had indicated. A tiny black dot was visible on the horizon. It swiftly grew larger, taking on the by now familiar dragon shape.

For the first time, Kellen was actually able to watch Ancaladar land. For something so large, the dragon was surprisingly graceful. When he was directly above them, he simply spread his great wings as wide as they would go and floated to the ground.

Valdien backed up nervously a few steps, but Jermayan patted his neck soothingly, speaking to him in a low voice, and the stallion quieted. Jermayan dismounted, leading the Elven destrier a little farther away from the dragon.

Ancaladar settled neatly to the snow and folded his wings across his back.

"So," he said.

"So," Jermayan answered, gazing at the dragon.

And Kellen had the odd sense that *something* was happening.

⌒

IT was the Elf.

Ancaladar stared enraptured into dark eyes and felt the pull of long-dormant instincts rousing. Here was his match. Here was the one who would be the conduit for his magic; his heart's twin, his Bondmate, to whom his life and his heart would be linked.

Fly away! Fly away now! a small voice inside him screamed. There was still time to refuse the Bond. It could be done. If he left now—

If he never saw Jermayan again—

But he had lived so long already—seen his friends and comrades die in the Great War. And these children said that Shadow Mountain was rising against the Lightfolk again. He'd seen proof of that. He did not think he could bear to hide and cower and save his life while watching others die yet again. He had been a coward and a failure once, and on the journey here he'd had a great deal of time to think about his choices and where they had led him.

And Jermayan was young as the Elvenkind reckoned years. They would have centuries together . . .

⌒

NO! Jermayan wrenched his gaze painfully away from the dragon's golden eyes. It was— It was—

It was impossible.

He knew what he was feeling. The Elves had long lives, and longer memories. The heart-tie that told them where true love lay was similar enough in kind, so the historians told them, to that Bond between a dragon and his Mage for

Jermayan to know what was happening. He was not in love with Ancaladar.

But they could Bond.

An Elf and a dragon.

Impossible.

Elves had no part in the Greater Magic. There had not been an Elven Mage since the time of Great Queen Vielissiar Farcarinon. Dragons Bonded with Mages—*human* Mages—because only through a Mage could a dragon express its innate magic.

⌐

"GO *away!*" Jermayan shouted desperately, staggering backward.

"Jermayan . . . " Ancaladar said.

"I am *useless* to you!" Jermayan said. "How is it that you do not understand that I am an Elven Knight, you who are ancient and wise beyond the dreams of Elves? It would all be for nothing!"

"I am useless without you," Ancaladar said, very softly. "You can learn. I know you can. In the First War, we fought for you, Jermayan. Your magic—Elven magic—woke us out of the bones of the earth. Do you remember?"

"No!" Jermayan said, sounding desperate.

Strange, so strange, that it would be *he* who was doing the urging now, and not the Elf-Knight. He, who had been a coward—

But he knew now that had been a choice, rather than what he truly was. As this was a choice. But this choice led away from failure, and toward bravery. He would not run anymore.

"War is coming," Ancaladar said. "A thousand years ago, while I cowered and hid, my brothers fought and died. I heard them weep as they went with their Bonded to serve the Demons. I felt the others die in the Light as their Bonded died. I cannot watch that again. This time I must fight. But I cannot fight alone."

⟶

KELLEN stood beside Shalkan, watching Ancaladar and Jermayan in amazement. "Do you know what's going on?" he whispered to the unicorn.

"Ancaladar and Jermayan can Bond," Shalkan answered in equally low tones. "If Jermayan accepts, he'll become the first Elven Mage since—oh, before the dawn of human civilization."

"Oh," Kellen said. "But he could refuse?"

"There's always a choice," Shalkan said. "You had one, when you decided to become a Knight-Mage."

⟶

JERMAYAN hesitated, clutching the hilt of his sword so tightly his gauntlet creaked. With all his heart, he yearned to look up, to meet Ancaladar's eyes, to let the Bond form.

But to become a Mage, a wielder of the Great Magics . . .

The golden eyes darkened, and Jermayan felt the sadness, the deep, inexpressible sadness. *He* had been the one feeling that sorrow not so long ago, when Idalia had refused the gift of his heart. Now it was, apparently, his turn to inflict that torture on another.

"I will go," Ancaladar said softly. "You will not see me again." The packed snow beneath his body groaned as he shifted his weight, preparing to take off again.

"No."

No. He could not do that to another living creature. Especially not this one, and not now.

Jermayan raised his head, and met the dragon's golden gaze. It was warmth and spring sunlight, it was the wind in the trees at high summer and the deep song of Life that underlay all things.

And he knew that even as he looked into Ancaladar's soul, Ancaladar was looking into his. Jermayan took a step forward, and then another. Ancaladar stretched out his long neck, and Jermayan laid his hand, very gently, against the side of Ancaladar's face.

He is mine, and I am his, and we shall be one, and together for the rest of our life.

THE following day, Kellen made his report to the Elven Council.

It was a frustrating experience, since he realized very quickly that nobody wished to hear his assessment of the situation, or what it might mean for the future. They only wished to know where he'd gone, what he'd done, and what he'd seen.

He wished Idalia were here, to help him figure out what to say, but she was still with the Healers, and they weren't letting anyone in to see her yet. He would have liked Jermayan to be here, too—but Jermayan was with Ancaladar, and would be meeting with the Council later, to explain—as well as the matter *could* be explained—what his becoming an Elven Mage meant to Sentarshadeen.

Kellen had never felt more like an errand boy in his life, and tried not to show his frustration. He knew the Elves were capable of quick and decisive action when they felt circumstances warranted it. He knew he had friends and allies on the Council. The Elves were not his enemies.

But the Elves did not hurry. Idalia had told him that, over and over. And Kellen was very much afraid that—this time—a lack of hurry was going to cost them in ways he couldn't yet put a name to.

THE next day, he was finally allowed to see Idalia.

The Healing House was within the House of Leaf and

Star, though to enter it, one came and went by a different entrance than the one Kellen was used to using when he visited Sandalon or his parents.

It was the most peaceful place he had ever imagined. If something could be the utter opposite of the Black Cairn, this was it. Just walking into the entry hall made all of his everyday worries seem as if they were simple problems that could be easily dealt with.

An Elf in the simple leaf-green robes of a Healer appeared almost instantly and brought him to Idalia's room. He saw no one else—though he knew that all of the children were here.

He was not surprised to see that Jermayan was already here, sitting beside Idalia's bedside.

She was sitting up, propped among a welter of colorful pillows. A table with a half-finished *xaqiue* game stood at the bedside, and there was a pot with teacups nearby on another low table. Idalia's cheeks were flushed with color, and she no longer looked exhausted to the point of death.

"Oh, good, you're here," Idalia said as soon as she saw him. "Now you can tell them I'm fine and I'm ready to leave."

Kellen glanced at Jermayan, but the Elf's face remained studiously blank.

"I'm not arguing with Elves," Kellen said, sitting down in a chair at the opposite side of her bed from Jermayan. "If you're feeling well enough to leave, *you* can argue with them."

Idalia snorted rudely. "Have *you* ever tried arguing with the Healers?"

Kellen laughed. "Not with the Healers—but I spent yesterday morning arguing with the Council—at least I think that's what I was doing—and I didn't get very far."

"You did, however, make something of an impression," Jermayan said, pouring tea and handing a cup to Kellen across the bed. Thanks to the Elven "small magics," the tea was still hot, and Kellen sipped it gratefully.

"Well, I'd love to know what it was. You'd have thought I was discussing the weather, instead of the fact that Shadow

Mountain's managed to stick a whole race of *things* smack
in the middle of the Elven Lands, where they can pretty
much do what they like."

"They're aware of that," Jermayan said broodingly. "And
they understand it is a grave threat, especially since the . . .
Shadowed Elves . . . can grant safe passage into the heart of
our realm to creatures who are truly of the Shadow, as we
have learned to our cost. Though the land-wards detect such
as they once they walk upon the surface of the land, our borders are not secure. We must return to the enclave Vestakia
discovered, and destroy it."

"You can't assume it's the only one, either," Kellen said.
It was the first truth of war that Master Belesharon had
taught him: never underestimate an enemy's strength and
resources.

"No," Jermayan agreed. "With Vestakia's help, we must
search out and destroy them all."

*Time. That will take time. Time to find each enclave of the
Shadowed Elves, time to fight the battles, time to search the
whole of the Elven Lands . . . and we only have Vestakia to
help us do it.*

And what will the Demons be doing while we do that?

"And what then?" Kellen asked. "When it's all done?"

Both Idalia and Jermayan were looking at him as if they
didn't understand, but to Kellen, it was as if a story were unfurling itself in his mind, almost as if he were remembering
one of Master Belesharon's old Teaching Tales. But this
wasn't something old. This was something new, something
yet to happen.

"When all the Shadowed Elves are gone," Kellen repeated
patiently. "What then?" He only realized then that he'd
asked a question—bad manners here—and rephrased it:
"Tell me what will happen next—and what the true Enemy
will be doing while we destroy the Shadowed Elves."

Idalia smiled faintly. "Kellen, it will probably take a very
long time to be sure we've gotten all of them. Maybe years."

"But we don't have years," Kellen said. He gestured at the

xaqiue board. "The Council thinks we do. Shadow Mountain puts up a barrier to starve the Elven Lands of water. We knock it down. We expect them to attack, then—though maybe after a very long time. But they don't. They show us something *we* have to attack: the Shadowed Elves. I'm not saying we don't: they're a threat, and if we don't destroy them, they *will* be used against us. But can't you see it? We didn't find out about them by accident. They were *shown* to us. It's like a *xaqiue* game. We'll commit our forces, we'll go after them . . . we'll probably destroy them. And then there will be something else."

"Their main attack," Jermayan said. "But we will have already gathered our army together. We will defeat them once again, just as we did before, though I do not deny that the cost will be high."

"No," Kellen said. He wasn't sure where the sense of *certainty* came from, but he'd never been surer of anything in his life. "Don't you *get* it, Jermayan? They're *never* going to attack—not this time. That's what you expect, because that's what they did the last time. That's what Andoreniel and Ashaniel are going to wait for—a big massing of Enemy troops; a formal declaration of war. And it won't happen."

For a moment he almost thought he'd convinced Jermayan. More than anyone else in Sentarshadeen, Jermayan knew him as a Knight-Mage, and knew what he was capable of—this instinctive understanding of War and how it worked. The more he trained with Master Belesharon—the more actual fighting he saw—the more Kellen realized just how his particular Wild Magic gifts worked.

But then Jermayan shook his head.

"Kellen . . . I do not say that you are wrong. But no matter what *They* plan, we must eliminate the Shadowed Elves first. Even now, Andoreniel sends word—not only to the Nine Cities, but to our allies as well, invoking ancient treaties. As soon as the children are safe—once I have persuaded Ancaladar to take them to the Crowned Horns—we go to muster at Ondoladeshiron. To fight in winter is hard, but he thought it best not to wait for spring."

Well, at least he'd convinced the Council of that much, Kellen thought. But it wasn't enough. He knew that, even though he didn't know—yet—what *was* enough.

"I'm going with you," Idalia said, a dangerous note in her voice.

"Such an army cannot be gathered overnight," Jermayan said reassuringly. "I am certain that the Healers will release you by the time we are ready to depart. And I will be grateful for the counsel of a . . . fellow Mage."

Idalia reached out and clasped his hand. "I know that Bonding with Ancaladar wasn't exactly what you expected," she said gently.

"*Nothing* about my life has been as I expected it would be," Jermayan said fervently. "Yet I would change nothing," he said, gazing deeply into her eyes.

"I think I'll see you both later," Kellen said, getting quickly to his feet. He set his empty cup down on the nearest flat surface, and backed hastily out of the room.

He doubted either of them noticed.

⟵

THE first person he ran into on his way out was Vestakia, and to his surprise she was also wearing a green Healer's robe.

"Apparently there are things I can do besides herd goats," she said cheerfully, noticing his startled expression. "How's Idalia?"

"She and Jermayan are fine," Kellen said, surprised at how disgruntled he sounded.

"And Ancaladar?" Vestakia asked, apparently not noticing Kellen's mood at all.

"Fine, I suppose. I haven't seen him at all, since, well . . . you know."

"Oh, he's found a nice place to live up in the meadows back beyond the House of Sword and Shield. Very private, so he isn't bothered too much by people who just want to stare at him. And much happier, he says, not having to spend all his time hunting his dinner. He says he much prefers the nice fat sheep and cows Jermayan is providing for him. Are you terribly busy right now, by any chance?"

"I ought to be at the House of Sword and Shield myself, catching up on all the lessons I've missed," Kellen said cautiously, "but . . . no."

"Then come and see Sandalon," Vestakia said, as briskly as as any nurse. "All the children would like to see you, come to that—and to hear about Ancaladar."

The children were gathered together in a bright light-filled room filled with toys and books. Sitting quietly in one corner was an Elven Healer, her hair the silvery-blue of great age.

Even Alkandoran was there. The Elven boy greeted Kellen with a wary smile. He looked hollow-eyed and unhappy, and Kellen felt a deep pang of sympathy. Alkandoran was still a child by Elven standards, but old enough to think of himself as an adult. He'd known better than any of the other children the true extent of the horrors they'd faced, but from what Lairamo had said, without his calm steadiness during their captivity, things might have gone much worse.

Kellen smiled back, and reached out and touched him lightly on the shoulder. "You did well," he said quietly. "You did all there was to do, and you did it well."

The boy's troubled expression eased just a little.

"Kellen!" Sandalon launched himself at Kellen. "Did you see the dragon? Is Jermayan—I mean, one *hears* that—"

"One *hears* that a dragon—his name is Ancaladar—has come to live in Sentarshadeen, and has Bonded to Jermayan, and so now Jermayan is going to become an Elven Mage, just like Great Queen Vielissiar Farcarinon."

"Perhaps Father will not mind if he is not King any longer," Sandalon said with a small frown.

"What . . . ? Oh. No, Sandalon. Andoreniel will still be King. Jermayan will just be a Mage. I don't think Jermayan would like to be King." *I don't think Jermayan wants to be a Mage, either, but he doesn't have much choice there.*

"Oh." Sandalon's frown cleared. "That's all right then."

"Perhaps you have come to tell us stories," Vendalton said hopefully, sidling closer. "About Jermayan and the dragon."

"Of course he has," Merisashendiel said firmly. "Nobody tells us anything here." She dragged over a low stool for Kellen to sit on, and the other children all picked up cushions and arranged them so that they were all sitting in a circle at Kellen's feet. They all regarded him expectantly.

For a moment he had no idea what to say, but then all the teaching stories he had heard so many times at the House of Sword and Shield came back to him.

"I will begin by describing dragons and their natures," he said, feeling for one odd moment as if he were back at the Mage College of Armethalieh—as a teacher this time, instead of as a student. "And then I will tell you how I met Ancaladar."

He spent most of the afternoon telling the children tales, letting them guide him in what they wanted to hear. He was surprised to find that what they wanted to hear about most was the story of their rescue—who had come for them, and how they had been tracked, who had actually found them, and what it had been like down in the caverns. Since the Healer in the room did nothing to interfere, though Kellen watched her closely, he answered all their questions as well as he could—though always keeping in mind the ages of his audience.

"But the evil creatures are far away, and can never find this place," Tredianala said.

"No," Kellen said firmly. "And soon you are going to the fortress—in a safe way, a way that nothing bad can possibly happen to you." He had no doubt of Jermayan's ability to eventually persuade Ancaladar to carry the children to the Fortress of the Crowned Horns—if "stubborn as an Elf" wasn't a proverb, it ought to be.

"But not by caravan," Merisashendiel said. She looked up at him with pleading in her gaze, and a hint of a shiver.

"*How* you will go," Kellen said firmly, "is a surprise—and a nice one, so I'm not going to spoil it."

Eventually Vestakia came in, announcing it was time for the children to take their medicine and their naps. Kellen, feeling quite as tired as if he'd spent the last several hours in practice bouts at the House of Sword and Shield, got to his feet and headed for the front door.

The aged Elven Healer followed him out.

"That was well done of you, Knight-Mage," she said simply.

"Huh? Me?" Kellen said, surprised, turning to look at her. She smiled faintly.

"There is nothing children fear so much as the unknown. But now there is no longer anything mysterious to them about their ordeal. Now all their terrors can become nothing more than a strange adventure—a frightening one, perhaps, but the fear will fade with time. Fare you well, Kellen Knight-Mage."

"Um . . . thanks."

He'd helped.

It felt very odd. Almost as if he'd done a healing, but . . . not quite. He'd gone through so much of his life trying not to be noticed—and trying not to notice everything around him. Finding the three Books had forced him to change. It had hurt at first. It had driven him out of the City. But here, it didn't hurt at all.

In fact, it felt good.

"IT would make things so much easier," Jermayan said, reasonably. Reason, however, did not seem to make as much impression on a dragon as he might have hoped.

"I am not a horse."

The land beyond the House of Sword and Shield was a series of pocket canyons, similar to those that made up the city of Sentarshadeen itself, though these had been allowed to remain in their natural state. The horses had adjusted to the intruder in their pasturage easily enough. Ancaladar had agreed not to bother them—his tastes, he assured Jermayan, ran to fat cattle and tasty sheep; even pigs and goats in sufficient quantity. Fortunately, Jermayan was wealthy enough to provide for Ancaladar's needs—though the dragon did not *need* to eat every day, he enjoyed doing so when the opportunity was provided, so each morning Jermayan led (or herded) Ancaladar's breakfast up to his new home.

Ancaladar had found a canyon that suited him—a relatively small one—and —with Jermayan's help—roofed it over, using those trees from the forest that had not survived the Great Drought. It was a crude shelter, but effective, and the dragon said it was comfortable enough. Come spring—assuming the time and labor were available—a more permanent and pleasing roof could be added to the canyon, and perhaps even a doorway of sorts constructed.

"A new caravan would take a sennight—perhaps two, in this weather—to reach the Fortress of the Crowned Horns. It would be vulnerable to another attack. Idalia is still recovering from her injuries, and tracking the creatures last time took a great toll on Vestakia. She is still not fully recovered. And each time she ventures forth from Sentarshadeen, she is at risk. She is a great prize for *Them,*" Jermayan said.

"I am still not a horse," Ancaladar said, stretching his head out so that Jermayan could rub the sensitive places just behind the eye sockets on the massive head. Jermayan had already learned that Ancaladar liked that.

"The children would be frightened," Jermayan said, after several minutes of silence. "To go again the way they did before, spending days upon the road, wondering each day if they are to be attacked again, to see their friends and companions slain before their eyes by monsters out of nightmare. I am afraid that such a journey would only undo what little healing has been accomplished." Jermayan thought he knew Ancaladar's weak point—that he had been slowly deprived of nestmates and companions until he found himself alone. "Those poor children—to know that their friends and their own kin were slain, and they were helpless to prevent it! And then, to wake in the darkness, and discover that they were all alone—"

"You can be truly annoying sometimes," Ancaladar grumbled. He thought for a while, while Jermayan walked forward a few steps and transferred his attentions to the soft skin just behind the armored plates at the hinge of Ancaladar's jaw. "If I did not know better, I would say this was an attempt to distract me from your lessons in Magery."

"I would say that I dislike them nearly as much as you dislike my plan," Jermayan said with a sigh.

What he learned from Ancaladar didn't seem to be very much like the Wild Magic as Kellen and Idalia knew it. He knew about the obligations and Mageprices involved there, but in Bonding with a dragon, all prices were paid by the Bond. The dragon surrendered its immortality, and all prices were paid in full, forever.

Nor was it anything like the High Magick practiced in Armethalieh. The Elves knew something of that: There had been hints gathered over the centuries that the Elves had traded with the Golden City, and Jermayan had pieced together a little more from the few disparaging comments he'd heard Kellen make. Elaborate incantations, complicated equipment . . . no.

To use Ancaladar's magic, all Jermayan needed was his Will. Each spell had a specific shape and color and *taste*— there was no better way to describe it. He had to hold the proper one in his mind and let Ancaladar's power pour through him, like sunlight through a crystal.

Spells for fire, for ice, for darkness, for invisibility, for flight. Thousands upon thousands of them, like trays of jewels.

And all he had to do, Jermayan thought wearily, was remember each unnameable colorshape perfectly, and always select the right one. At least Ancaladar was only putting a few of them into his mind at a time, though the dragon insisted he was only helping Jermayan remember them. According to Ancaladar, if Jermayan hadn't known them already, they never could have Bonded.

It was something Jermayan preferred not to think about. Elves were not Mages. Humans were Mages. Demons— Leaf and Star wither and blast them—were Mages.

Elves were not. Elves had given up their magic long ago,

in the childhood of the world. They had done so in order to save the world, and the Light—but that was something that was not spoken of outside of the Sanctuary of the Star. Humans and other races were not to know of this . . . he was not certain that even a dragon should be told.

Then again, he was not certain that a dragon didn't already know.

"Then if you will practice, I will take your children to the fortress," Ancaladar said, sounding both resigned and amused. "But you know I cannot land there. It was built when your kind had . . . reason to fear dragons."

"Andoreniel will send a message. We will land at the foot of the causeway. I think the children will be safe there for as long as it takes to get them inside."

"With what you have learned, certainly," Andoreniel said. "And now . . . practice. Make a flower."

Jermayan stared at the snow doubtfully.

"The canes are there, beneath the snow. They slumber. Wake one," Ancaladar said.

"It will freeze and die," Jermayan said, shaking his head.

"Then change them," Ancaladar said implacably. "Make flowers for the cold."

As clearly as if a voice had spoken inside his head, Jermayan could see what to do. He *reached*, and out of the snow beneath his feet, tender green rose-canes began to shoot up out of the snow, growing with unnatural speed.

But that wasn't enough. Roses were flowers for summer. They would die in the cold. He reached into them again and began to change them, even as they reached out toward the ice-covered walls of the canyon and began to twine and climb.

The pale green faded to the dark green of the mature plant, then faded further, into black. But not the black of death. The black of a different kind of life. The green leaves turned pale silver. They still had the shape of rose leaves, but now were much larger and thicker, sized to take in all the pale winter sunlight they could, and protect their fragile blossoms from the snow and ice.

The roses that had bloomed large and deep red a moment before fell from the twining vines in a shower of silken petals, replaced by tiny perfect white blossoms the size of Jermayan's thumbnail. They covered the now-dense vines like tiny stars.

Jermayan staggered back, leaning into Ancaladar as the spell ran its course. The jewel shapes faded from his mind, and the rapid growth of the ice roses slowed.

"See?" the dragon said. "Roses in winter. When the weather warms they will die back, but in the cold season they will bloom again. You have shaped a new thing. Proper magic for a dragon and his Bondmate."

You made me do that, Jermayan felt like saying. But he didn't. Only the power had come from Ancaladar. *He* had made the roses.

They were beautiful. They were harmless. There was nothing threatening about them.

He didn't know why they disturbed him so.

"You'll have to wear some sort of harness when you carry the children," he said aloud. "We don't want them to fall off."

Ancaladar blew out a long gusty breath.

"Now call fire," he said, not answering directly. "It's important, and useful, and you need more practice. A lot more practice."

Twelve

To the Crowned Horns of the Moon

It took a fortnight to make a proper set of harness for Ancaladar. The dragon grumbled quite a bit about it, but seemed, in the end, actually pleased with the results.

Then again, it was Elven workmanship, which was never

less than spectacular. He did not look like a "pack mule" as he claimed; as a matter of fact, he looked as if he had been fitted for a splendid costume of black leather and shining, sapphire-enameled metal. And there was no doubt in anyone's mind that the dragon was inordinately pleased with his appearance.

Idalia left the House of Healing after only a few days more, but she went to Jermayan's house to live, not back to the home she'd shared with Kellen. It was as if Jermayan's Bond with Ancaladar had eased some unshareable burden she'd been carrying—or perhaps it was only that having come so close to death, she now realized that there were things in life that should not be delayed.

Her departure left Kellen alone in the house they'd shared, but not for long. Within a day of Idalia's departure, Kellen discovered he had mysteriously acquired an assistant, one Vertai, whose business it seemed to be to keep Kellen's wardrobe in order, the larder stocked, simple meals available, and everything generally as tidy—or even more so—than when Kellen had shared the place with Idalia. Where this fellow had come from, Kellen had no idea; he was certainly more efficient and a lot more pleasant than any of the Tavadon servants had ever been.

In part, this might have been because Kellen rarely saw Vertai. Once he'd granted the man permission to come and go as he pleased—after consulting Jermayan, who seemed to think it was a good idea—Vertai seemed to do all his work while Kellen was at the House of Sword and Shield. It was like having a completely invisible servant, and one who managed to anticipate everything Kellen could have thought of.

Kellen had thrown himself back into his interrupted training with a vengeance. He knew that all around him important things were happening—Jermayan was learning magic, Idalia was creating weapons for the upcoming campaign against the Shadowed Elves, Andoreniel was calling up his allies and gathering the Elven army for the assault on the first of the enclaves of the Shadowed Elves—but nobody was telling him about them directly, or even asking him what he thought about them. He'd just been shunted aside, as if his opinion wasn't worth anything.

Was it arrogant of him to think otherwise? Should he *really* have a place on the Elven Council, setting policy for the Nine Cities? He knew he didn't want that. Trying to think like the Elves—trying to *talk* like the Elves—would drive him crazy within a sennight. Maybe less.

But still . . .

It doesn't matter, Kellen told himself fiercely, standing alone in the Great Hall of the House of Sword and Shield, practicing what Master Belesharon called the "simple forms" until his muscles ached and his tunic and leggings were plastered to his body with sweat. *They won't listen to you, whether you're right or not. JERMAYAN wouldn't listen to you. And the Shadowed Elves DO have to be destroyed. It's just that . . . we can't be concentrating on nothing except that. Shadow Mountain is being a lot smarter now. This is a diversion. It's an important diversion, but it's only a diversion.*

I have to find a way to make them listen.

And I have to figure out what Shadow Mountain's REAL plan is.

Without thinking, he broke form and spun around, his sword raised to block. Master Belesharon was standing behind him, his teaching staff raised to deliver an admonitory blow to an inattentive student.

"You seemed lost in thought, young Kellen," Master Belesharon said mildly.

"I was," Kellen said, smiling wolfishly. But not so lost in thought that his Master could catch him out as if he were a novice.

Master Belesharon smiled in turn. "Come. Bathe. Take tea."

When they were both immersed in the deep tub of the bathhouse—Kellen no longer even noticed having to walk through the snow to get to and from it—and a younger student had poured them both cups of dark fragrant tea, Master Belesharon broached his point with the unusual directness that Kellen had come to believe was a privilege of age among the Elvenkind.

"Soon you will hear, young Kellen, that Hyandur the trader has returned to Sentarshadeen. As you know, it was thought appropriate that he approach the City of a Thousand Bells to bring them warning that the Shadow walks the hills once more."

Kellen considered all the appropriate things he could say, considering what he knew about Armethalieh, and what the High Council thought about Elves. "I am pleased to hear that he has returned safely," he said at last.

"Doubtless this is because he was never permitted to enter the city, nor to deliver his message," Master Belesharon said, his voice neutral. "The city of your birth remains unwarned, and has promised death to any of our kind that approaches its walls again."

"That . . . " *Makes perfect sense. Because they're idiots.* "I thank you for telling me this, Master," Kellen said. Even though the water of the bathhouse tub was as hot as he could stand—hot enough to soothe away all the aches and bruises of a day's hard training—he felt his muscles tense beneath the scented water. Any mention of Armethalieh was like poking at a sore tooth.

"Hyandur said further that the City of a Thousand Bells begins to expand its borders once more. They had reclaimed the Delfier Valley as he left. Perhaps they will attempt to re-claim more land. He believes there had been unrest in the city before he came, and it seemed to be of a serious nature. Two were Banished that he knows of. Perhaps more. He warned those villages he passed on his way here of the city's plans. Word will spread."

"Wonderful," Kellen said with a sigh. He wondered what had changed on the Council. The last time Idalia had scryed and gotten a view of the Armethaliehan Council chambers, Lord Volpiril had pulled the City boundaries all the way back to the City walls. "At least it will take them time to re-claim all their old lands. Time and energy. And they hate all the Other Races—I'm sorry, Master—so at least we can be sure there's no way they'll ally themselves with *Them*. And I don't think one of *Them* could get into Armethalieh, anyway, even if it made itself look like a human. Armethalieh's . . . not a very nice place, but it's still the City of Mages. There are Wards everywhere. No one who isn't a citizen can pass them."

"So if they will not aid us, at least they will not give aid to the Enemy," Master Belesharon said. "Unfortunate, but not the worst that could happen."

"I suppose not," Kellen said. But something in his own words made him feel uneasy. He ducked his head under the surface of the water, dousing himself thoroughly, and came up, sweeping his hair back out of his eyes. "I suppose I'd better go and make sure Idalia knows. Maybe she'll be able to guess more of their plans."

THE ice storms were long past, and though the winter snows were heavy, the streets were kept clear enough so that walking—at least in cleated snow boots—wasn't difficult. Getting off the streets, now—that meant wading through snow that was up to the knees at least, and sometimes waist-deep, but Kellen didn't have to do that nearly as often as Jermayan did. Ancaladar was rather diffident about coming down into Sentarshadeen, where his appearance still rattled some of the inhabitants.

By now, Kellen had been to Jermayan's house at the forest edge many times. He admired it, while having no desire to possess anything like it. He'd grown up in one of the most intimidating mansions in the largest city in the world, and even though Jermayan's cottage could probably have fit comfortably in the suite of rooms Kellen had possessed in House Tavadon, it was still more room than Kellen wanted for himself.

Kellen crossed the arching footbridge—carefully, as the

slatted wood was icy and slick—and approached the house. It was still too early for lantern-lighting time, though the lanterns stood ready and waiting, and he noted that the seashells that had hung outside the door the last time he'd been here had been replaced with a set in the shape of golden flames. He wondered why. It might be a reflection of the seasons: the lanterns outside his own house had also been changed while he was gone, and were now pale blue.

He knocked at the door.

After a moment Idalia opened it.

"Home and hearth," she said cheerfully, the shortened form of the standard Elven greeting. "Come in, Kellen—you look half-frozen. Though if you've come to see Jermayan, he's with Ancalader. You know, I think he has finally met his match in stubbornness!"

Kellen grinned faintly at the thought; knowing Jermayan as he did, he doubted it.

"No," Kellen said, stepping inside, and immediately sitting down to remove his outdoor boots and heavy cloak. "I came to see you."

"Well, here I am. I'll get you some mulled cider. I'm sure Vertai isn't feeding you enough."

"He's doing fine. I'm doing fine." He tried to think of a good way to lead into what he wanted to say, gave up, and just launched into it. "Hyandur got back from Armethalieh today," he said, following Idalia into the kitchen.

"Oh, yes. I'd heard that. Rescued a Banished Mageborn boy and dumped him in the first Centaur village he came to." She looked over her shoulder at him, briefly, then went on with her work. "Well, I can't say I'll weep any tears for him, whoever he is. I'm sure it'll do him good to live among, ah, 'Lesser Races.' "

Kellen smiled at the small joke. Trust Idalia to have the gossip as fast as anyone. "Why was he Banished?" Kellen asked. "Did you hear that?"

"I don't think Hyandur knew. Maybe the boy didn't know either. *You* know what the Council's like, Kellen, especially now." Her voice took on a flippant tone. "He probably didn't return his books to the library on time." She took a jug of cider from the stove where it was warming and poured a mug full, pushing it toward him.

"They're extending the boundaries of the City lands again, too," Kellen said, drinking. "Back to the old places. Good news for the Home Farms, anyway. There's something to be said for getting their old weather protections back."

"Mmm," Idalia said. "That probably means a shift in power in the Council. I'll try scrying tomorrow and see if I get anything, but you know scrying isn't very reliable: I've been hoping to use it to help Vestakia find the enclaves of the Shadowed Elves, but I'm not sure I'll have much luck there, either."

"Maybe Jermayan should try," Kellen suggested, with a half-smile.

"Oh, *don't* say that to him!" Idalia begged. "He's like a bear with a sore tooth on that particular subject. And I thought *you* were a difficult student!"

"I wasn't!" Kellen protested, stung.

"You were, brother mine," Idalia assured him. "Of course, I was trying to teach you all the wrong things in all the wrong ways—neither of our faults—but still."

"Still," Kellen admitted, giving in.

"So. Was that what you came to tell me?" Idalia prompted.

"I suppose," Kellen admitted. "And to see if you knew anything more. I wish Hyandur had brought the boy with him. We could have found out what he knew."

"And how much did you know about what was really going on in the City on the day you were Banished?" Idalia asked, smiling gently to take the sting from her words. "Besides—our presence to the contrary—the Elves don't permit just *anyone* into their realm. He wasn't a Wildmage, Kellen, if that's what you're thinking. Hyandur would have known that, and Wildmages have always had safe passage through the Elven lands. And the Centaurs won't be unkind to him. They'll just knock some sense into him."

"I wish I could be there to see *that*," Kellen said with a faint grin, holding out his mug for a refill. "I wonder which of the spoiled brats he was? I probably knew him—or of him. I can't think of anyone that I'd feel sorry to see having to work for his keep in a Centaur village. Actually, it's the Centaurs I feel sorry for."

"Anyway, we've tried to warn the City. And it can't be done," Idalia said briskly. "And Hyandur carried the message about *Them* to every place he passed. It's winter, so the news wouldn't normally have traveled fast—but now that Andoreniel is calling up his levies, everyone's going to know. And soon." She looked off over his shoulder for a moment. "Maybe—if they haven't closed the City to *all* outsiders—we can get the Selken Traders to carry them the news once the harbors are open again in the spring. If we can spare a messenger."

He had wondered about that; and that made him think of something else. "Everyone keeps talking about 'levies,'" Kellen said. "But just what are they?"

"Well, we leave for Ondoladeshiron in a sennight. You'll see some of them there, though most of those who can gather that quickly are Elves. But . . . Centaurs, of course. The unicorns—not just the ones that live among Elves, but the Great Herds. The Wildmages will come—"

"Other Wildmages?" Kellen broke in, surprised.

"Of course," Idalia said. "Did you think we were the only ones? And—let me see—the Mountain Folk will come early, since they have no crops to tend. The Lost Lands folk will come next, for they must put their herds in order before they can come—but they will come as fast as they can, for as Vestakia has told us, they have been bearing the brunt of the Demon raids. The Wildlanders will come last, for they must get a crop in the ground before they can send troops. We will not see them before late spring. And such Otherfolk as can aid us—they will be with us as well."

"So many," Kellen marveled.

"I do not know, since I haven't seen them yet, but I suspect that all the humans the Elves will be able to call to their banners could be tucked safely behind the walls of Armethalieh—if it were empty, of course—with plenty of room left over."

Not so very many, then, after all. Kellen didn't know how many Centaurs there were, and though the Elves were formidable fighters, it had only—only!—been a thousand years since the Great War, and he knew from things Master Belesharon had said that the Elven population had suffered heavily during the Great War and not yet reached its former numbers.

None of the races had. Several of them had been wiped out entirely; the water-sylphs, the bearwards, the minotaurs, the firesprites. The dragons were nearly extinct—Ancaladar thought there might be others, somewhere, who, like him, had hidden and refused to Bond. How many, though, he could not even guess; they had avoided even each other. Only a Bonded dragon was fertile, Kellen had discovered, and unless they could somehow coax a female dragon—if there were any left—out of hiding and into a Bond, the dragons might as well be extinct.

Humankind was reduced to a few thousands scattered over the land in far-flung villages—and the inhabitants of the Golden City, home to tens of thousands, cowering behind their walls and their tyrannical laws. The great Centaur tribes were a shadow of what they once had been. The Allies had spent everything they had to defeat the Shadow in the Great War—had turned thousands of leagues of fertile fields and forest to stony waste where nothing grew, even now—and counted themselves lucky, because they had defeated the Shadow.

Only the Shadow hadn't been defeated.

"It has to be enough," Kellen said bleakly.

"It will be," Idalia said firmly. "After all, *we* have a dragon."

As if that were a summons, they heard the outer door open and close.

"Ah," Idalia said. "The Elven Mage has returned."

Kellen felt a strange tickle of unfamiliar magic—dragon magic made his nose itch—and knew that Jermayan must have been working with Ancaladar again, practicing sorcery. He set down his half-full mug and went with Idalia to greet his friend.

"Ah, Kellen," Jermayan said, seeing that Idalia was not alone. "It is good to find you here."

Jermayan looked both cold and exhausted. Perhaps things would be easier in the spring, but now, in the cold of winter, it was hard on him.

"You look frozen," Kellen said, with sympathy.

"I am assured that—with time—I can construct a suitable hall for our work, once I have mastered the appropriate skills," Jermayan said wryly, noting their concern. "However, by the time I have mastered them, the need for such a hall will have passed." He sighed, and sat down on one of the long padded benches that lined the sitting room. "Meanwhile, I call fire to burn upon the ice." He gazed down at his hands broodingly.

"Fire's supposed to be easy," Kellen said tentatively. It was the first spell a Student Apprentice of the High Magick learned back in Armethalieh, the first spell in the Books of the Wild Magic. Light a candle, call flame to tinder . . .

But Jermayan was talking about kindling a fire on the *ice* . . . How was that possible?

Idalia returned from the kitchen and set a cup of tea in his hand. "You do what you have to, Jermayan," she said.

"And having worked as hard as any apprentice in the House of Sword and Shield," Jermayan said, smiling faintly, "I have reconciled Ancaladar to necessity. Tomorrow we fly to the Fortress of the Crowned Horns. I would be honored if you would accompany us, Kellen."

Who, me? Kellen thought wonderingly.

"The children will be reassured by your presence, so Vestakia assures me," Jermayan explained. "And I thought perhaps you would find profit in seeing our greatest fortress."

Elves—even Jermayan—rarely did anything directly. Kellen knew that though this was partly meant to reassure him as to the extent of Elven military strength, it was also meant as a subtle rebuke for his criticism of Elven strategy earlier.

Still, he wasn't going to turn down the chance to ride a dragon. And he *did* want to see the Crowned Horns.

Because they say it can't be taken by direct assault. And I'm sure they're right. And I'm just as sure that whatever Shadow Mountain is planning, it isn't a direct assault . . .

"I thank you for this great honor," Kellen said in his best courtly style. "And I just know that Ancaladar will be thrilled at the thought of having another passenger."

"Dress warmly," Jermayan warned him. "Ancaladar says that the skies are colder than snow."

—

THE following day, Ancaladar came to the unicorn meadow to take the children to the Fortress of the Crowned Horns. The day was raw and overcast, but the clouds were high, and no storm beckoned.

As Kellen had seen in his vision of the Great War, when dragon fought dragon in the skies above an Endarkened battlefield, there was a saddle at the base of Ancaladar's neck, where Jermayan would ride. Kellen would ride behind him there. But for the others, different arrangements had needed to be made. Straps affixed a series of baskets to Ancaladar's massive sides: eight of them, for the five children, Lairamo, and two companions. Sand was added to some of the baskets, so that each one weighed exactly the same, because balance—so Ancaladar had explained—was the most important thing.

The children were all muffled warmly in furs, and then strapped firmly into their baskets, so that even if Ancaladar chose to fly upside-down (which he assured both Kellen and Jermayan he had no intention of doing) there was no possibility of the children falling out. It took ladders to get them into the baskets, but at the other end, Jermayan would simply have to walk down Ancaladar's back to free them.

If all went well.

And a trip that would take sennights on the ground would be compressed into less than a day.

Though for the children's—and their parents'—sake, Kellen behaved as though this were the most ordinary thing in the world, he couldn't help feeling a sinking sense of apprehension as he climbed up Ancaladar's side and took his place behind Jermayan. There was a belt there, fastened to Ancaladar's harness, and he saw that Jermayan already wore a similar belt buckled tightly around him. Well, if it was good enough for Jermayan . . . He strapped himself down, and looked over Ancaladar's shoulder toward the ground. It was like sitting on the roof of a three-story house . . . only houses didn't take flight and soar into the sky.

He knew he'd done far more dangerous things in his life— and more painful ones, too. But not only did this seem to be unnervingly unnatural, it roused the memories of buried ghosts, ghosts hundreds of generations in the past . . . but also of one particular ghost, who had also borne the name "Kellen," and who had fought for the Dark, Bonded to a dragon.

Before he could follow those bleak thoughts any further, Ancaladar reared up on his hind legs. Kellen heard the children squeal in pleased excitement.

"Hold on," Ancaladar said quietly.

He spread his great wings with a snap like sails filling with wind. He sprang into the air, slashed down—*hard*— with his wings once, then again.

It reminded Kellen—almost—of riding Shalkan when the unicorn was running all-out: that bounding gait that involved moments of weightlessness and jarring landings. Only here there were no landings, only moments of weightless falling before the dragon's great wings bit into the air again. Kellen closed his eyes tightly.

By the time he could bring himself to open them again, Ancaladar was moving smoothly, and the ground was hundreds of feet below. He looked back over his shoulder, and could barely see the green of the ever-blooming Flower Forest. The individual buildings of Sentarshadeen—well hidden even from the ground—were invisible.

"Comfortable?" Jermayan asked. Kellen realized after a moment that the question was directed to Ancaladar. "Nothing binding you anywhere, I hope?"

"Not bad. But don't make a habit of this," the dragon replied. He tilted a wingtip slightly, and they began a long curving upward spiral, taking them even higher into the sky.

Soon they were in the clouds themselves. Wet mist covered Kellen's face, and he could barely see anything at all. Then they were above the clouds, flying in the sunlight.

It was just as cold as Ancaladar had promised. The mist-droplets turned to ice crystals on Kellen's face—his only exposed skin—and the sheer dry cold took his breath away. The clouds below them—*below* them!—looked as solid as a snowfield, shining whitely in the sun, and the sunlight itself was bright and harsh. There was no sound save the whistling of the wind over Ancaladar's body, and the occasional squeals and outcries of delight from the children. Kellen was glad they were so firmly strapped in to their carrying-baskets: it would be far too tempting for the more audacious of them to try to climb out and take a closer look at this wonderland of sun and clouds.

His fear of flying was forgotten. He didn't even notice the cold. He wished this wonderful experience could last forever. Now—*now* he envied Jermayan, if this was the sort of thing that the Elven Knight was going to get to experience all the time.

As they continued north and west he could see the peaks of the higher mountains poking up through the clouds. The only thing that would make it better would be if he could see the ground below. He was Mageborn and had lived with magic all of his life, but *this* was the most magical moment of his life.

Too soon Ancaladar began to descend, flying into snow

and buffeting winds as they entered the realm of mountain storms. The ride now was much rougher, as the dragon glided from side to side, riding on the winds and tacking from side to side instead of fighting them directly. Now Kellen could see trees below, and had some way to judge their speed, and it was faster than anything he could have ever imagined. No wonder the Elves had wanted to send the children this way.

"Almost there," Jermayan said.

"I am *tired* of snow," Ancaladar complained, swerving again in response to a particularly prankish gust of wind. "What it does to the wind and thermals is simply disgusting."

"It's winter," Jermayan said soothingly. "And a particularly bad one. By next year, the weather patterns should be back to normal."

"We'll hope Andoreniel's message got through, then, with your weather and all. I have *no* desire to be shot at," Ancaladar grumbled, but Kellen could tell his complaining was merely a kind of bantering between the dragon and Jermayan. The Bond between Jermayan and Ancaladar was something he could not even imagine—far closer than his relationship with Shalkan—and words seemed almost unnecessary to it.

Even through the snow, Kellen could see the fortress up ahead. At first, it seemed merely an unusual outcropping, then he recognized the forms of Elven building—and then they seemed to be rushing at it at such a speed that there was no chance they could avoid hitting it.

Then the dragon tilted a wing, and suddenly the fortress was passing under them, in a dizzying, exhilarating panorama.

Ancaladar circled it once, and then landed at the foot of the causeway. A party of defenders was already waiting there for the children. Kellen unbuckled the belt and pushed himself free of the saddle, surprised at how stiff he felt, and immediately slipped off Ancaladar's back to fall sprawling in the deep densely-packed snow, for Ancaladar's scales were covered in ice.

Jermayan, naturally, fared much better—no matter how much and how hard Kellen trained, Jermayan was an Elf, with all the Elves' natural grace. Jermayan walked neatly down Ancaladar's back, cutting the straps that buckled the children into the baskets—for unbuckling the straps would take time, and everyone knew that here they were vulnerable if the Enemy wished to strike.

But Kellen had a hunch *They* wouldn't. At least, not today.

All the Elven children of the Nine Cities were here now— for as he'd heard recently, word of the attack on Sandalon's caravan had not reached the other Elven cities in time, and the last of the children had been dispatched to the fortress on the original schedule.

And reached their destination safely.

More than ever now, Kellen was sure that the whole point of the attack had been to show them the Shadowed Elves, and nothing else.

Kellen clambered up out of the snow in time to help with the last couple of baskets, and then set to work on the other needful task: cutting away the basket harness from Ancaladar's body. It had done its work, and was no longer necessary. Now only the saddle on the dragon's neck would remain, and the riding harness that held it there.

By the time he looked up from that, the children and those who had waited to greet them were gone. Only one warrior remained.

"I See you, Shentorris," Jermayan said.

"I See you, Jermayan," Shentorris said, bowing slightly in acknowledgment.

"I See you, Shentorris," Kellen said in his turn.

"I See you, Kellen Knight-Mage. I would be honored to make you welcome at the Fortress of the Crowned Horns."

"I," Ancaladar announced, "am going in search of clear air and sunlight. Call me when you need me."

The dragon took a few bounding leaps through the snow and was airborne. Jermayan and Kellen followed Shentorris up the causeway into the fortress.

⌐

EASILY *defensible,* Kellen noted on his way up. The removal of a few key blocks of stone would take down a substantial part of the causeway, isolating the fortress completely—assuming this was the only way in. Ancaladar had said that dragons couldn't land on the top of it—but Kellen suspected that the Deathwings that had destroyed the caravan that had originally been supposed to bring Sandalon here could, and they already knew that the Deathwings could carry a person. So . . . how many of them were there, and who controlled them?

And were there caves beneath the fortress that the Shadowed Elves controlled—or could reach?

He sighed inwardly. There were things he had to say to Shentorris—or whoever was in charge of defense here—that would not make good hearing, as the Elves would say. He hoped that Jermayan would take the lead in that, but if Jermayan wouldn't, he'd have to.

They reached the top of the causeway. There were massive bronze gates—crusted with winter's ice. In fact, the ice was so thick upon them that it was obvious they had not been opened in months. Shentorris led them around the edge—a pathway even narrower than the causeway, with a sheer drop to the rocks below—to a smaller door, also bronze. The walls looked as if they were made of a single piece of stone; there was nothing here that would burn or decay. The smaller door was barely large enough to admit one person at a time. It was closed. Shentorris knocked, and after a pause, it was opened. Kellen entered first, then Jermayan, then last of all Shentorris.

Kellen was used to Elven architecture being spacious, airy, and open, bringing the outdoors in so artfully that sometimes it was hard to tell where Nature ended and Elven craft began. This was beautiful, too, as all the work of the Elves was, but it was beauty of an entirely different sort. It was as if he'd suddenly stepped back through time, to meet a wholly different race of Elves—a race of warriors, not artisans.

The corridors were narrow, the ceilings low. Kellen had the sudden sense that this fortress was also a labyrinth, designed to confuse any invaders who got this far. Defenders would hide and attack, knowing the territory well, while their enemies circled about in confusion.

And the children who lived here now would find it a perfect playground, never realizing, as they played, that they were learning the skills that would keep them alive in the ultimate extremity.

Leaf and Star, Gods of the Wild Magic, let that day never come, Kellen thought fervently. If the Enemy broached this citadel, then all hope was truly gone.

There were no windows, of course, though the walls were painted with scenes of cities and forests that had not existed in a thousand years, and depictions of animals that Kellen had no name for. A sort of four-legged eagle, and something that looked more like a two-horned unicorn than it looked like anything else. A horse with wings—now surely *that* was wholly imaginary? A kind of a Centaur with a cat body instead of a horse body, and wings as well.

Kellen stopped trying to decide what was real—or might have been real—once—and simply followed the others. He wasn't lost—no Knight-Mage, as he'd discovered down in the caverns, could actually get lost—but unless he spent enough time here to learn the entire layout of the fortress, the only route he'd be able to take back to the door was the one he was following now.

"And here we come to what has—in times past—been the dining hall," Shentorris said, opening a door.

Kellen quickly understood the reason for Shentorris's odd phrasing, for it was obvious that the room was no longer a dining hall, and had not been used as one for quite some time.

It was now filled with children. All the children of the Nine Cities—except, Kellen supposed, for the very youngest, like Kalania, who were off in a nursery somewhere, and some of the oldest, like Alkandoran, who were probably continuing their knightly training.

But all the rest were here.

It was the largest room in the fortress. The floor had been marked with the elaborate patterns of children's games, the walls were lined with large tubs in which green plants grew, scenting the air with the perfume of growing things. High above, hanging from the rafters, were ancient war banners, an incongruous martial note in these surroundings.

There were fewer than fifty children here, yet Kellen knew that these were all the children of all the Elven Lands. But Elves lived for centuries, and children were rare among them.

Kellen watched as they ran and played together. Most of them had already been here for sennights. Long enough to get used to the idea of seeing so many others near their own ages. He wondered what kind of a difference it would make to them later.

The newest arrivals weren't here yet. Still getting settled in—and warmed up, Kellen thought, with a longing glance toward the enormous fireplace that filled one end of the great hall.

Shentorris caught the direction of his gaze. "But come. We will take tea. You shall meet Tyrvin, who is the Master of the Crowned Horns. He will be eager to hear the news of the outside world."

Shentorris conducted his two guests to a smaller room. Like every chamber Kellen had seen so far here in the fortress, it was windowless, but it had the look of a place that someone had tried very hard to make resemble home. Cushioned benches lined the walls, and there were low tables carved and inlaid in colored woods set here and there about the room. A tiled stove in the corner radiated a pleasant heat.

But the walls were hung with weapons. Not weapons for show, but weapons that could be grabbed at a moment's notice, and borne in defense of the precious treasure these walls contained.

A kettle in the shape of a fat-bellied faun stood heating on the stove, and from the cabinet beside the stove Shentorris took down a pot and a tea canister. While he was hesitating among the teacups—for Elves took the selection of the proper teacup nearly as seriously as they did the selection of the proper tea—Master Tyrvin entered the room.

He was not nearly as old as Master Belesharon, but Kellen could instantly see why he had been chosen as the guardian of the Fortress of the Crowned Horns. The same aura of absolute mastery of his craft enveloped him like an invisible cloak. He was, very simply, the best Andoreniel had to send.

Kellen faced him and bowed, the deep bow of respect, Student to Master.

Tyrvin looked surprised. "They told me you were a Knight-Mage," he said.

"I am still learning my craft," Kellen said honestly. "You have mastered yours."

"You should, at least, have learned not to flatter Elves in your time among us," Tyrvin said brusquely, moving to take a seat with his back to the door.

"I am not particularly good at flattery," Kellen answered simply, "but I have learned that Elves honor truth, and that respect is due to those who have earned it."

Jermayan and Shentorris both laughed. "The point goes to Kellen, Tyr," Jermayan said cheerfully. "And flattery is not the only thing he is bad at, I assure you. He cannot speak of the weather save to tell you whether it is wet or dry, and if his man did not dress him, dogs would run howling from the streets whenever he appeared. Nor can he brew tea that I would use for anything but killing parasites in my garden. He does not dance. But the children love him, Master Belesharon thinks well of him, and he fights like a firesprite whose nest has been burned. And he is Shalkan's rider."

"Well indeed." Tyrvin sounded surprised and somewhat mollified at this odd catalogue of Kellen's abilities—or disabilities. As for Kellen, he thought it was a peculiar sort of endorsement—especially coming from his oldest friend among the Elves.

But it was obvious that these three Elves were old friends, and an old friend among Elves was a very old friend indeed. So he tried not to take any of Jermayan's comments to heart, since certainly they were true—and probably pretty important from an Elven point of view. But why should his being Shalkan's rider be important to anyone but him and Shalkan?

Besides, he liked the tea he brewed just fine. He'd just remember not to offer any of it to Jermayan anymore. Or to politely suggest that Jermayan might like to brew his own.

"I suppose then, that if I wish to hear what has been going on in Sentarshadeen these last moonturns, it would be well to cast aside all vestige of dignity and manners," Tyrvin said, but there was a twinkle in his eye when he said it.

"Indeed," Jermayan said, taking a seat on one of the benches. "Though I am told that his speeches to Andoreniel's Council are memorable things."

Kellen sighed inwardly, sitting down as well and shrugging out of his heavy furs. He was being teased. He recognized that now, and resigned himself to it. It was better—much!—than being disliked. And he found that he very much wanted Master Tyrvin to like him.

"I only told them what they needed to hear. They didn't like it much," Kellen said, assuming a counterfeit air of innocence.

That startled another bark of laughter from Master Tyrvin. "The Council never wishes to hear what it needs to hear. And now Jermayan—perhaps, if he annoys me, I shall tell you what a difficult pupil he once was to me—has brought you to me so that you can tell me what *I* need to hear. And you think I shall like it as little as the Council did."

Kellen inclined his head, acknowledging that what Master Tyrvin said was the truth. He took a deep breath. He might as well give them the blunt truth they expected from humans, and he didn't really know any way that would render it palatable.

"I know that your fortress is not impregnable. I know it can be attacked. I know how, and by who. I don't know when, or if," Kellen said. "But I know how *I* would do it, had I the resources of the Enemy."

That got the full attention of all three Elves.

"Tell me, Knight-Mage," Tyrvin commanded, all business now.

"I don't think it will be soon. Perhaps not at all. But let me go back to the beginning, and tell you everything, and then you will know all that I know."

Carefully, Kellen began at the very beginning: the attack on the caravan that was to have brought Sentarshadeen's children to the Crowned Horns; with the frost-giants, ice-trolls, and coldwarg—and their allies, the giant Deathwings.

"They can carry a full-grown Elf safely, and they follow orders. I don't know who ultimately controls them, but I know they're creatures of Darkness that can, nevertheless, fly by day. I know Ancaladar said he can't land on top of the fortress, but I don't know what the top of the fortress looks like, so I can't say what *could* land there."

"You shall see it. Go on," Tyrvin said.

Kellen told the whole story, from the moment Calmeren had arrived at Sentarshadeen to the moment the rescue party had returned to it. He omitted no detail, whether he suspected Tyrvin knew it already or not. Whatever Tyrvin knew, he did not know the events as Kellen had experienced them.

"The Shadowed Elves weren't just using the cavern as a temporary camp, either. They had a whole city there, and Ancaladar said they'd been living there for a very long time. Since they . . . seem . . . to have Elven blood, the land-wards don't react to them."

There was a long silence. Jermayan knew all this, of course, but it was new to Shentorris and Tyrvin, and neither Elf was happy to hear it.

"How far do these caves go?" Tyrvin asked at last, with blunt War Manners.

"No one knows—yet. Not even Ancaladar. Andoreniel intends to wipe out the Shadowed Elves. He's calling up the levies in Ondoladeshiron." While Kellen had been telling the long tale of the rescue of the children, tea had been brewed and poured, and now he took a long sip of spicy Black Winter Tea to soothe his raw throat.

"The Fortress of the Crowned Horns is built atop a mountain of solid granite," Shentorris said, speaking at last.

"For the moment," Jermayan said. He needed to say nothing more.

"We will hear them if they dig. I will post listeners on the lowest level, where the spring that nourishes the fortress is—every hour of every day," Tyrvin said. "They will assist Ronethil in her work. But you say you do not think *They* mean to attack us, Kellen Wildmage?"

"I think *Their* plan was to lure us into a war with the Shadowed Elves—to make us commit all our resources into a battle to destroy them, as we shall. If we attack them in their caverns, we're at a disadvantage. If they attack us here, in our place of greatest strength, they're the ones at a disadvantage. I don't think they're after the children; I don't think that the children were ever their real target." He tried to choose his words with utmost care. "This is why: They didn't attack us to get them back once we'd rescued them, and until we met up with the second rescue party from Sentarshadeen, we were quite vulnerable. Nor did they attack any of the caravans that followed Sandalon's. The whole point seems to me to have been to allow us to discover the existence of the Shadowed Elves in a way that would make us determined to wipe them out." He knew he sounded puzzled, and he was, because he could not imagine what could possibly come next.

"An odd way of running a war," Tyrvin said. "Still, unless they can find a way of coming at us here in force, I am confident that if they *do* attack, we can hold them off—though your news is hardly calculated to help me to rest easy at night. But come. I will show you the rest of our defenses."

THE tour took the next several hours. Tyrvin showed Kellen over what seemed as if it were every inch of the fortress—though he saw no more of the children.

There were rooms filled with weapons: arrows and bows, the most fragile and easily-expended items of their defense; spears, swords, shields. Enough to arm and rearm every defender of the fortress a dozen times over.

There were other rooms filled with food: grain, both fresh and parched, dried fruit, dried meat, herbs and teas, spices. Enough to feed an army for years.

Everyone Kellen met—and there were female knights as well as male among the defenders—was in good spirits. No one here doubted the importance of their task, nor was inclined to grow soft and inattentive simply because one day passed seamlessly into another with no sign of overt threat. The Elves were a patient people.

Tyrvin even took him down to the deepest levels of the fortress, where the spring was. If Kellen had not been so intent upon learning all the citadel's secrets, it would have been an honor he would gladly have done without, for the way was long, down a winding stair that seemed to go on forever. He had the sense that the lanterns the Elves carried to light the way were mostly a courtesy to him.

"This is the lowest level of the fortress," Shentorris said, when they stood in the center of a great room hollowed from the living rock. In the center of the floor stood a deep round pool.

The others had stopped upon the stairs, letting Kellen go first, and now he knew why.

A unicorn stood beside the pool. Her coat was the grey of winter storm, and her horn was the clear shining brightness of winter's ice. As he approached, she bowed her head and touched her horn to the pool, and for a moment, the water shone blue.

"Yes," she said, "it is a spring, called from the depths of the Earth by magic in ancient times. But nothing of the Dark may try these waters and live—not while *I*, Ronethil, am here, or those who guard this place with me."

Without conscious thought, Kellen shifted to spell-sight. He looked down into the pool, saw where it flowed up through a crack in the stone so narrow that nothing of any size could pass through it. Nor could it be poisoned or bespelled, while Ronethil stood guard. Beneath that was rock. Nothing but solid rock.

He reached out, to the roots of the whole fortress, in the way a man might check his horse for soundness before he mounted. But he felt nothing. All was untouched. Nothing had come—yet—to try the citadel's defenses, at least from this direction.

"Safe," Kellen said with relief, as his spell-sight faded. Only then did he notice that a sort of conduit led from the spring, along the wall up the stairs. Well, he guessed it beat having to walk down all the stairs he was about to walk up again every time you needed water for tea.

"Your Magegifts have told you this," Tyrvin said. It was not a question.

"No one can truly say what future fruit the blossom of the moment may bear," Kellen said. It was one of Morusil's favorite sayings. Idalia said it was the Elven way of saying "Don't press your luck."

"He learns quickly," Jermayan said, a note of pride in his voice.

"Quicker than you learned to counter that low attack to your left side, when you were in my training," Tyrvin said.

"Ah, Master, I thought those bruises would never heal," Jermayan agreed ruefully. "Alas, that I have been unable to give Kellen ones to match them."

Tyrvin glanced at Kellen, and for a moment there was cold speculation in the Elf's dark eyes. Then he smiled. "Alas, that we do not have time this day for sport. I will show you the top of the tower, and then I think it will be time for you to depart to your duties. Remember us, on the field of battle."

"Remember us, among the children," Jermayan answered, and Kellen had the sense that he'd just witnessed one of those side-slips into an almost sacred formality that he guessed you'd have to live as long as an Elf to understand.

Him, he was just Kellen, a human Knight-Mage who (according to Jermayan) couldn't brew tea and fought like a firesprite—whatever that was. He wondered if asking Jermayan would get him any answers he could understand.

They stopped back at the room where they'd shared tea to collect their heavy fur cloaks and gloves. Kellen was sweating by the time they'd climbed yet another several sets of stairs to a room so small the four of them could barely squeeze into it. In order to make room for them, the two guards who had occupied it needed to retreat down the stairs to the landing below.

"This door," Tyrvin said, "opens onto the top of the tower of the Fortress of the Crowned Horns. There are always two sentries posted there, and as you have seen, two inside. In this weather, their watch is short. But the door is barred from this side, and can be barred from the other at desperate need. Should the sentries on watch here lose track of the time, or sleep, or fail of attentiveness, those without will die, for should they cry out, or hammer at the door, it cannot be heard from within."

Trust. That was the hidden message in Tyrvin's words. Each Elf—and unicorn—here at the fortress trusted every other to hold their lives as dearly as their own.

That was the Crowned Horns' true defense. Not sword and stone—the Demons could break through that if they came in strength. But *Their* greatest weapons were tricks of bribery and persuasion, of tainted promises. Kellen was sure now that any attempt to gain a foothold here by those means would fail.

Tyrvin unbolted the door. It thrust inward fiercely, pushed on an icy blast of wind.

"Hold to the guide-ropes!" he shouted over the howl of the wind, and stepped out onto the tower roof.

The "guide-ropes" were thick cables of twisted metal. Kellen grabbed for one instinctively. Without it, he would be pushed along the roof as if he weighed no more than an autumn leaf.

The rooftop was far too small for a dragon to land upon. Walls half the height of an Elf's body surrounded it, and at each corner was a strange five-pronged blossom standing twice that height—one prong sticking straight up, two curving outward, two curving in. From a distance, they probably gave the top of the fortress the look of a crown. All were sharp.

The surface of the tower floor was not smooth and open, either. Tall spikes were placed at intervals. The cable Kellen clung to was strung between them, making a virtue of necessity. Here, at the highest exposed point in the Icefang Mountains, the icy wind was punishing. It battered at Kellen like a living thing, making his flesh ache even beneath the heavy furs and his insulating Elven armor.

He saw the two sentries, groping carefully along the ropes, their gaze turned outward, toward the surrounding mountains and the sky. Tyrvin moved past him, going to each of them in turn and sending them inside.

Kellen groped his way to the parapet, or as near as he could get without letting go of the guide-rope. If he let go, the wind would take him over the side, unless he was quick enough to fling himself flat. This was a dangerous place.

But he was close enough to see the arrow-slits in the walls. They were clotted with ice now, but through them, a kneeling Elven archer could rain down destruction on an enemy. Or even stand to fire, for the range of Elven bows was long.

He caught Tyrvin's eye and nodded. He'd seen what he needed to see. Though if he wasn't in danger of freezing solid, he would have been happy to linger. The mountains were spread out below them in a breathtaking vista—in spring, in sunlight, this must be a beautiful place.

The Master of the Fortress of the Crowned Horns led them carefully inside, and waited until the next four sentries—two outside, two inside—had taken their places. Then he brought them all back to what Kellen now realized must be his private rooms.

"The posts that you saw are not only for show. There are charms of· unicorn hair attached to the top, renewed every spring. So none of *Them* will dare to try us," Tyrvin said with grim satisfaction.

Kellen thought carefully before he spoke. "I am not sure the Deathwings could land there, but they would not need to. They could come low enough to drop whoever they carried in their claws—or to carry someone away. They are small enough, and nimble enough, for that. And when spring comes—what are the winds like then? Are they constant, or do they soften or stop altogether? The Deathwings can fly by day, but they will be better still at night—and in a fog, or in the clouds, would any see them until it was too late?"

Tyrvin sighed. "Yet we must keep watch."

"Find another way," Kellen said bluntly. "Every time you open a door—any door—in this fortress, you expose a weakness. Close and bar it. Confronted with this fortress, if I were contemplating an attack, I would never even consider a frontal assault. I would try treachery, I would try stealth, and I would try by ones and twos, not by thousands. One or two can open the door to thousands, if they come at the wrong time and place. You cannot assume the Enemy to be less cunning than I am. Count your people. Count them constantly—"

At least here he could be single-minded. There was only one duty before these Elves. This was their posting and it was all they needed to concentrate on. Whether or not the attack on the children had been part of a ruse was of no moment to them. So Kellen, too, could be single-minded in his advice.

"And pray to Leaf and Star that someday we may open our gates again," Tyrvin said, agreeing. "It is good counsel, Kellen Wildmage. It is a great pity you were not born one of us, yet had it been so, you would not be what you are, and we have need of that."

"SOMETIMES you terrify me," Jermayan said conversationally, as they stood at the foot of the causeway, waiting for Ancaladar to arrive. Jermayan said it would only be a matter of a few moments.

"I only said what had to be said," Kellen said. He knew he sounded a little sullen, but he couldn't help it. Even Tyrvin seemed to be waiting for the Endarkened to show up as a massed army with banners—not sneak in at the changing of the guard and start slaughtering people. Which Kellen thought was far more likely, if they meant to attack the fortress at all.

"Someday you will say it to the wrong person," Jermayan said. "Leaf and Star! To speak so to Master Tyrvin!"

"He wants to keep those children alive. And so do—"

But Ancaladar had suddenly made his appearance, falling through the clouds like a black thunderbolt, fanning his wings wide at the last minute and making a graceful landing in a spray of snow. The dragon's great weight made him sink deeply into the snow, so that the saddle was only a few feet above Kellen's head.

"I trust that your visit went as you would have it go," the dragon said.

"It went as it went," Jermayan answered dismissively.

Ancaladar didn't linger a moment longer once Kellen and Jermayan had secured themselves in their seats, but bounded quickly into the air.

He had probably been trying to take things easy back at Sentarshadeen for the sake of his young passengers, and the air there had certainly been quieter. Kellen was glad he'd had that experience to prepare him for this one, because this take-off was nowhere near as gentle as the one that had preceded it. The mountain winds flipped and spun Ancaladar through the air as if he were one of Sandalon's toy boats upon Great Twovanesata, with Ancaladar taking expert advantage of every opportunity they granted him to gain height.

At last they broke through into the sunlight and comparative stillness of the upper air, and Ancaladar was able to spread his wings wide and level out.

"Everyone still there, I trust?" the dragon asked.

"It was . . . fun," Kellen answered. It actually had been, in a weird way. He'd been sure—fairly sure, anyway—that he wasn't going to fall off, and if he had, he had no doubt at all that Ancaladar would catch him before he could hit the ground. But all the same, he was just as glad it hadn't gone on *too* long.

"You have the oddest notions of fun," Jermayan said.

"Nevertheless, I do not think we will repeat it," Ancaladar said, a note of amusement in his soft deep voice. "The air over Sentarshadeen is calm and clear—I can feel it from here."

"So can I," Jermayan said, an odd note in his voice.

THE rest of the journey was almost a mirror of the first, though this time the sun was westering, treating Kellen to a spectacular show as it tinted the clouds with a thousand shades of gold. He missed the clouds when they left them behind, and was surprised to see that though here they were still in sunlight, the land below was already touched with twilight shadows.

Ancaladar landed in the unicorn meadow near the House of Leaf and Star, but only long enough for Kellen to dismount. With Jermayan still in the saddle, he launched himself into the sky again, heading for his home canyon.

Kellen stamped and stretched, working the stiffness out of his cramped muscles. It had been a beautiful flight, but still a cold one.

"And did you enjoy your day?" Shalkan asked, materializing out of nowhere. The unicorn was hard to see—Kellen realized it was almost dark; well after lantern-lighting time.

"It was instructive," Kellen said. "And cold. But the children are safe at the fortress now."

"And likely to remain so?" Shalkan asked.

Kellen regarded his friend broodingly. "Unless *They* try something I can't imagine . . . yes." *Or until they starve to death waiting for us to defeat Shadow Mountain.* Resupplying the fortress would be an easy matter come spring—but each time its doors were opened, all who were within were exposed to danger from an attack by treachery and stealth.

"But you're still not happy," Shalkan said, falling into step beside Kellen as the young Knight-Mage began the long walk toward home. "And after you got to ride Ancaladar, and meet Master Tyrvin. Such gratitude."

Kellen made a rude noise. " '*I am duly grateful for all the mercies and benefits visited upon me,*' " he said, quoting one of the sentences of the Litany of the Light that he'd had to recite each Light's Day back in Armethalieh. "I just think I'm forgetting something."

"Well, you'll have plenty of time to try to remember it on the ride to Ondoladeshiron," Shalkan said cheerfully.

THE journey to Ondoladeshiron took a sennight and a half, for not only did they move through deep winter, but they were restricted to the pace of the supply wagons that they escorted. These wagons held immense quantities of food and weapons, as well as much of the store of Wild Magic-infused articles that Idalia had crafted.

For the first time, Kellen traveled with an Elven army in formal battle array. Although he was certainly battle-seasoned, he had not yet won his spurs in the House of Sword and Shield, and even though he was a Knight-Mage, he was also Shalkan's rider, so for purposes of Elven battle protocol he rode under the orders of Petariel, Captain of the Unicorn Knights, as a junior knight.

Kellen found it instructive; he kept his eyes and ears open, and began to learn a great deal about the bonds of camaraderie that other Unicorn Knights had with their mounts.

The Unicorn Knights, of necessity, rode apart from the main army. By Elven standards they were all quite young, though they would have been grandmothers and grandfathers among humans. All of them were still mourning the loss of their comrades, both Elven and unicorn, in the Shadowed Elf ambush, for the community of Unicorn Knights was a small, close-knit one. Not every Elven fighter was even remotely interested in bonding with a unicorn.

Oddly, it was a community that Kellen had never really been a part of, until now. He wasn't a "real" Unicorn Knight—his bond with Shalkan was part of a Mageprice lasting a year and a day. That wasn't the same thing as choosing a unicorn for a companion—or being chosen by one. And what happened when the Elf fell in love with another Elf? He—or she—would never see their unicorn friend again. Not up close, anyway.

"You're thinking like a human, again," Shalkan observed, when Kellen confided some of these thoughts to him.

"I *am* a human, in case you haven't figured that out yet," Kellen said. It felt good to discuss—for a change—something that had nothing in particular to do with Shadow Mountain.

Shalkan snorted eloquently. "As if I could forget. Humans think the whole world revolves around them—but we have lives of our own, too, you know. The partnership of knight and unicorn is a fine thing, but in most cases both of the beings involved realize at the start that it's only going to be an episode—a relatively short one—in what will be long lives for them both. A year and a day probably seems like a long time to you—well, for most of these knights, *their* partnership won't seem to last much longer."

Uh-huh. That sounded awfully cold-blooded to Kellen. Maybe an Elf—who was going to live several centuries—could manage it. Or . . .

"How long do unicorns live, anyway?" Kellen asked.

"Longer than you're likely to if you keep asking foolish questions," Shalkan answered quellingly.

Ah. Evidently there were some things even Kellen wasn't supposed to know.

—

KELLEN didn't spend all his time with the Unicorn Knights. Fortunately, a Knight-Mage could go where he pleased, and Kellen took full advantage of that freedom.

Jermayan was flying with Ancaladar, doing most of the long-range scouting for the little army, but naturally he had brought Valdien with him. Under Deyishene's tutelage, Kellen's equestrian skills had improved to the point where— with Jermayan's permission, and after a proper introduction to Valdien to assure the destrier that it was, indeed, all right—he could take Valdien out of the horse-lines and ride the great storm-colored destrier among the main body of the troops.

He saw things there that greatly disturbed him.

He knew already that Elves were creatures of great respect for tradition. He saw now that the tradition extended to the organization of their army. The equivalent sons and daughters of these same Elven households had probably ridden in exactly these positions a thousand years ago, the last time the Elves had gone to war.

Which meant, Kellen thought with a frown, that when the Elven armies gathered to face Shadow Mountain, the Demon horde would know exactly who and where everyone was. Idalia had told him that the Demons weren't merely long-lived, like the Elves, but truly immortal. So it wasn't impossible that there were actual Demon generals out there that had faced the Allied and Elven armies *last* time.

He might not know everything about the Art of War yet, but he did know that it wasn't a good idea for the enemy to know what the entire disposition of your troops was going to be in advance. And if the Elves were as much creatures of Tradition as they appeared—which Kellen had no reason to doubt—Shadow Mountain already knew every possible battle formation they would use.

Not good.

Individually, the Elves were unstoppable fighters—and individually they were perfectly capable of improvisation if they put their minds to it. And they were smart enough to realize within seconds of an encounter that they were no longer playing by the same rules as they once had been. For some of them, that was fast enough to save them. But the larger the group, the more unwieldy and Tradition-bound it became.

The easier to defeat.

He'd identified another problem, Kellen realized with an inward sigh. It was just too bad he couldn't come up with a solution to it as easily. The Elven Commanders weren't going to throw out several thousand years of the "proper" way of doing things just on his say-so. And their tactics had worked the last time.

That's the root of the problem. It worked twice before. They know it did. So why shouldn't it work again?

The only bright spot in things—no more than a faint glimmer, really, to be honest—was that Kellen doubted whoever was running the Demon side of *this* war had any interest at all in engaging in a series of formal battles. As for the battle against the Shadowed Elves, it wouldn't be a traditional form of warfare at all, so it would rely on the Elves' strengths, not their weaknesses.

It was almost as if they were certain to win . . . and their victory didn't matter to Shadow Mountain's ultimate strategy. But if they ignored the Shadowed Elves, knowing them for the trap that they were, Shadow Mountain would mercilessly exploit that weakness in the Elven Lands' defenses.

We're trapped either way, Kellen thought, in grudging admiration for the unknown Demon general. *We have no choice but to do exactly what they want us to do. For now.*

Thirteen

Ondoladeshiron at Last

Sentarshadeen was a hidden city, a city of forests and canyons. Ondoladeshiron stood in the middle of a vast plain at the foot of a mountain range—Kellen recalled that Idalia had turned from a Silver Eagle back into human form here; if his memory was right, Ondoladeshiron was also where she'd met Jermayan.

The buildings of the Elven city echoed the rise and fall of the surface of the plain, and evoked the towering strength of the mountains behind them as well. Like the Elves themselves, Ondoladeshiron had the ability to hide in plain sight: though it should be easy enough to see a large city in the middle of a plain, especially in winter, Ondoladeshiron eluded the eye, deceiving one into thinking it no more than a natural tumble of stones. The buildings looked nothing like buildings of any kind; it was impossible to see anything that didn't look as if it had been formed entirely by the chaotic action of weather, wind, water, and time. Yet Kellen knew that whatever the Elves were doing to hide their city, they were doing it entirely without magic, merely the skill honed by centuries—millennia!—of observing the natural world.

One thing that assisted Ondoladeshiron to hide itself was the presence of the Elven army camped at the city's outskirts on the Gathering Plain. The encampment was as colorful as the city was circumspect, drawing the eye toward itself. At this distance, all Kellen could see was rows of pavilions in colors like the flowers in a spring meadow, and the horse herd beside it. Kellen wondered just how many of them there were: he, Idalia, and Vestakia had ridden here among nearly two hundred knights, all Andoreniel could spare from the patrols around Sentarshadeen.

Of course, like every Elven city, Ondoladeshiron also had its Flower Forest. In this season, it was the only spot of natural color in the snow-covered landscape. Though the trees at the outer edges of the forest were covered in snow, all were in leaf, and some were in flower.

"Courage, brother," Idalia murmured as they neared the encampment.

"What?" Kellen asked. He was riding Valdien today, and the destrier was (for the most part) behaving himself. Unfortunately, Jermayan's mount knew that Kellen's horsemanship wasn't the equal of his master's, and Valdien had all Jermayan's dry sense of humor. He liked to pull tricks on Kellen at odd moments, and then pretend he'd done nothing at all. It took all of Kellen's attentiveness to remain in the saddle sometimes, though it was doing wonders for his riding skills. It occurred to him that the destrier was giving him the equine equivalent of Belesharon's lessons in swordsmanship.

Idalia gave him a strange look. "You're the first Knight-Mage born in a thousand years. Don't you think a few people are going to want to meet you? Including other Wildmages?"

"Oh." *Oh.* "But nothing I should worry about, right?" Kellen asked with a crooked smile.

"Right," Idalia answered, smiling back.

⁓

ONCE again, being Shalkan's rider worked in Kellen's favor. Though the rest of the knights were grouped by the city of their residence, the Unicorn Knights' pavilions were all bunched together at the very edge of the camp, so that their mounts could come to them easily. By the time Kellen had turned over Valdien to the Sentarshadeen horse-master and found out where he was supposed to be, Petariel already had the wagons with their gear separated out from the rest, and he and the other Sentarshadeen Unicorn Knights were unloading them, while others that Kellen didn't recognize—even if all Elves looked fairly similar, even to Kellen, the armor of an Elven Knight was highly distinctive—were marking out the places where the pavilions were to be erected.

Kellen quickly got to work. No student of Belesharon's was afraid of a little hard work, and besides, he was looking forward to getting his bedroll unpacked and finding who was brewing the tea. Menerchel usually took charge of that— Kellen had tactfully assured the others at the outset that he would happily light any fires they liked, and do extra work putting up the pavilions, but that everyone would be a great deal happier if he did *not* do any of the cooking.

The other thing at the back of his mind was that surely, if he was hidden away in the midst of the Unicorn Knights, none of the other Wildmages would be able to find him.

It wasn't that Kellen was *afraid* to meet another Wildmage. Wildmages were, one and all, a force for Good. And he'd long since gotten over the time when he'd worried about being a not-good-enough Wildmage. That had ended at the moment when he'd discovered he was a Knight-Mage, a different sort of Wildmage entirely.

So, then, why?

Both his Wildmage training and Master Belesharon had taught him that such hidden reluctance was a warning, to be confronted and understood at once, if at all possible. Now that the pavilions were all in place—and firmly staked down against the wind—Kellen went and collected his equipment and Shalkan's armor. He dropped it in his tent, then procured a large mug of Winter Spice Tea from Menerchel, then returned to his tent to unpack his gear and think the matter over.

He wasn't afraid of the other Wildmages. He wasn't ashamed of what he was. And as for not wanting to be the center of attention . . . well, he was getting plenty of attention right here, since all of the other Unicorn Knights were just as fascinated by a Knight-Mage as any strange Wildmage might be, and if Elves were legendary for their stubbornness, they were equally known for their curiosity.

So that wasn't it.

"Cozy," Shalkan said, walking into the tent.

Since the pavilion was—naturally—in Kellen's "color," the light shining through it turned Shalkan's white fur a radiant pale green, which was a rather startling effect, Kellen thought.

"I guess it's going to be home for a while," Kellen said. "So I'm just as glad it's comfortable."

"Idalia's looking for you—or so I hear. There are some people she wants you to meet," Shalkan said, tilting his head to regard Kellen from beneath his long lashes.

"And I don't want to meet them. And I don't know why," Kellen sighed. "I'm trying to figure that out."

"Child of the City," Shalkan said, his voice unusually serious, "you are not responsible for the errors of your ancestors. Not even the most immediate ones."

"Of course not; I know th— Is *that* it?" Kellen said, catching himself in midsentence.

"Maybe," Shalkan said inscrutably.

Kellen thought about it. Idalia had been gone from Armethalieh more than half her life, but *he* hadn't. It was true that he'd been Banished, and Armethalieh had severed all its ties with him, but maybe, deep in his heart, he was still what Shalkan had called him: Child of the City.

And Armethalieh had not done well by the Wild Magic. It had set the High Magick in its place. It had cast out its Wildmages, denied their existence, killed them wherever it found them.

Now he could identify the peculiar reluctance to meet another Wildmage.

It was guilt.

"But they won't blame me," Kellen said aloud, exasperated with himself.

No, they won't—so stop blaming yourself. You had nothing to do with decisions made in the City centuries before you were born.

Kellen sighed, feeling the knot of tension and reluctance dissolve. "I'm always borrowing trouble, aren't I?"

"I don't see why you feel the need to," Shalkan said, "when the world is always willing to give so much of it away for free. Now, don't you have somewhere to be?"

"Yes," Kellen said. "And . . . thanks."

⟶

HE found Petariel and let him know where he was going, then headed off to find Idalia.

Sentarshadeen's encampment was at the far side of the Gathering Plain, so Kellen had to walk through most of the camp to reach it.

The tents of Ondoladeshiron were nearest the city itself, and Kellen recognized banners from Windalorianan, Deskethomaynel, and Thultafoniseen as he passed, for part of his training in the House of Sword and Shield had been in the heraldry of the Nine Cities. That meant Lerkalpoldara, Valwendigorean, Realthataladon, and Ysterialpoerin were yet to arrive, but they were the most far-flung of the Nine Cities, and it might be another fortnight before they arrived. Andoreniel's army should be on its way to the cavern before that, Kellen hoped.

He reached the Sentarshadeen pavilions, and saw familiar faces—but not the familiar faces he was looking for. In response to his puzzled expression, Dervasin took pity on him and observed that the Wildmage Idalia was to be found with Evanor, Vestakia, and the others among the tents of the Healers, and pointed him in the right direction.

Once more Kellen set off, discovering that he'd passed that collection of tents on his way across the field. Since the Healers weren't knights, their tents were a reflection of their personal style rather than knightly colors. Some were . . . very bright indeed, their surfaces as brilliantly and randomly colored as a field of wildflowers. Others were as plain and deceptively simple as an Elvenware bowl, or—in the way of Elves—carefully painted to look like something they were not. The pavilion Idalia shared with Vestakia, for example, was artfully crafted to look as if it had been stitched together from carefully-tanned deer hides, right down to the tiny stitches and the small imperfections in the leather. Only when you touched it did you realize that it was the same thick and durable silk canvas as all the others.

He wondered whose idea *that* had been.

He hoped Vestakia hadn't had any problems. They'd all grown so used to her appearance in Sentarshadeen that it only now occurred to Kellen that the rest of the Nine Cities might see nothing more than her outward appearance.

He dismissed the thought with a shrug. She had many friends and protectors now.

He found Idalia's tent without difficulty, and stopped outside to ring the bells braided into a length of cord suspended beside the entrance. Without a door to knock on, the ever-punctilious Elves had found another way for someone to announce his presence.

"Come in, Kellen," Idalia called immediately. She must have been expecting him. Or else by now, she could just *tell* when it was him.

Kellen pushed through the flap—resisting the urge to duck—and looked around.

Idalia's pavilion was larger than his—which only made sense as she might have to do healings here. Just now it contained a number of large chests, a standing brazier for warmth, and a low table with several stools that could be folded out of the way for night.

She and Vestakia were both here, and as Kellen's eyes adjusted to the lower light level after the wintry glare outside, he saw there was a third person present as well.

The man got to his feet as Kellen entered. He was human, tall and slender, his skin burned dark with wind and sun, making his age difficult to judge, though Kellen could tell he was certainly beyond middle years. He bore an odd elusive resemblance to Vestakia, and Kellen could feel the same sense of peace and intense focus—for lack of a better term—radiating from him that Idalia possessed.

"I greet you, Wildmage," Kellen said, bowing.

"And I you, Knight-Mage Kellen," the Wildmage said, holding out his hand.

Quickly Kellen pulled off his gauntlet and took the man's hand. He'd spent so long among the Elves that he'd almost forgotten there were other ways of doing things!

"This is Wildmage Atroist," Idalia said. "He's from the Lost Lands."

"He knew my mother!" Vestakia said excitedly.

"Yes. Virgivet was a dear comrade of mine. I had always wondered what happened to cause her to leave Wind's Bridge—but now that I know the whole of her story, I see that she had no choice in what she did. And she gave the world a splendid daughter—one to be proud of."

Vestakia smiled at the praise, her eyes glistening with happy tears.

The four of them sat down around Idalia's table once again. Kellen removed his helm, his cloak—it was quite warm in Idalia's pavilion—and his other gauntlet, setting them in a careful bundle at his feet. Idalia set a cup before him and filled it with hot spiced cider, refilling her own cup and the cups of the other two as well.

After an exchange of pleasantries—brief by Elven standards—Atroist got down to business.

"These are hard times for us in the Lost Lands. When the Firstling King's warning reached us, he told us nothing new. The Dark Folk have always walked openly in the hard western hills. But if they now turn their attentions to the east, we fear their hand will fall harder upon us than ever. And if that should happen, I do not think the Herdsfolk will survive."

Atroist glanced toward Vestakia, his expression grave.

"Ours is a hard land, with hard ways, as Virgivet knew. But the Dark Folk and their treacheries are a constant threat. They steal unprotected babies from the cradle, lure lone travelers to their doom, attack our flocks in the guise of monsters. Perhaps that is why the Wild Magic runs so strong in the West—we have great need of it there. Without our spells to discover and mark them, wanderers would be lured into the Haunted Places, and not all our Healing Arts could restore sanity to such a one afterward. When a kinsman is Overshadowed, a Wildmage can lift the spell before harm is done to the Light Within, if one is summoned in time. And when the Dark Folk raid in force—though once that was a rare thing— our magic often gives us warning enough to get the people and the flocks to safety, so that there is little loss of life."

Kellen looked at Idalia. Her face was gravely expressionless. When he'd ridden through the Lost Lands with Jermayan, the Elven Knight had told him that the place was dangerous, but listening to Atroist, Kellen figured they'd both been incredibly lucky. Vestakia had told him she had to spend a lot of time hiding from Demons, but Kellen had thought they were just coming after her personally. Apparently, the Lost Lands were practically a Demon playground.

And nobody had known.

"I see grim looks upon your faces," Atroist said with a gentle smile, "but this is the only life I, or any of my people, have ever known, so to us it seems very ordinary. The Good Goddess does not send to us a task beyond our strength, and each year enough Wildmages are born to protect the people and to replace those who go home to Her. So we had been content."

" 'Had been,' " Kellen quoted back to him. "But something's changed?"

Atroist sighed deeply, his weather-seamed face going grave. "In the last few turns of the seasons, the Dark Folk have grown bolder and more savage. Their raids increase in frequency and number." He bowed his head for a moment. "It is our custom to go in force to a village when we know the Dark Folk intend to strike at it, and so I was at Goatford that day with seven of my fellow Wildmages, though my home had been in Wind's Bridge since Virgivet left.

"It was the springtide, as it usually is when the attacks come, for then the flocks are spread upon the hills in search of the new grass, and the ewes and nannies are heavy with young. The flocks are the life of the Herdsfolk, and without them the people will starve; it was as important to get the flocks to safety as to shelter the people. We did not manage it in time.

"There was a great battle. We won—in the sense that the Dark Folk did not take any of our people alive. That is always a great cause for rejoicing among our people."

"Oh, yes," Vestakia said feelingly, putting her hand over his. Atroist took her hand, clasping it tightly as if for comfort. "Believe me—I understand. It would be much better for you to kill them yourself than to let them fall into *Their* hands. Your people would thank you for it, if they could."

"So the Good Goddess and Her Consort teach us," Atroist said somberly. "But you are one of us, so you know. And afterward, there were the wounded to heal, and the scattered flocks to retrieve. By the time my duties at Goatford were done and I could return to Wind's Bridge, three days had passed, but I was easy in my heart, for I had left my people well-protected with spells and charms."

He paused to take a deep drink from his cup.

"But when I arrived, Wind's Bridge was not there."

For a moment, Atroist's face crumpled with grief, but then he composed himself. "The village was *gone*. Not one stone stood upon another. The land itself was scoured as if by fire. No tree, no blade of grass, not even the village well remained. The very earth reeked of Taint and blood.

"For days I wandered the hills insensible. I saw no other living thing—not even a remnant of the herds. I realized that every living thing that had belonged to Wind's Bridge was dead—or alive in the hands of the Dark Folk. And more. I realized that they had somehow concealed the attack upon Wind's Bridge from the Wild Magic, allowing us to send our strength to Goatford and leave Wind's Bridge unprotected. For a full turn of the seasons I walked the hills, stopping no more than a few nights in any village as I railed against the Good Goddess, demanding to know how She could let this happen to the innocents under my care.

"At last She took pity on me and opened my heart to the knowledge I had been too wounded to bear: that if I, if a dozen Wildmages had been at Wind's Bridge that day, it would have made no difference. We would only have died along with our people, for such power as was brought to bear against Wind's Bridge that day was too great for the Wild Magic to stand against alone."

There was a moment of painful silence after Atroist finished speaking.

"It's my fault," Vestakia said at last. "They destroyed Wind's Bridge because of me."

"No!" Kellen and Idalia said in chorus.

"And if it is?" Atroist said. "What will you do?"

Vestakia blinked, staring at Atroist as if he'd slapped her. Then she took a deep breath. "I . . . no! It *isn't* my fault! I'm *not* responsible for what *They* do! How can I be? I can't control *Their* actions! Yes, *They* probably picked Wind's Bridge to destroy because Mama came from there, but it was *Their* choice, not mine."

"Good girl," Atroist said with a smile. "I had to learn that lesson as well, and it's a hard one. Just because you have a connection to a thing, you are not necessarily responsible for its actions.

"But to finish my grim tale quickly, this was nearly five turns of the seasons past. Since then, we have found that the Dark Folk raid more often, and will sometimes attack two or more villages on the same day, or within a day of each other. And so I come not only to bring my aid, but to speak for my people. They, more than any, do not wish to see the Shadow triumph. But if our Wildmages and warriors leave the people and the flocks, who will defend them against the Dark Folk? How can we fight, knowing that all we love will be gone when we return?"

Idalia cast a despairing glance at Kellen.

This was a heavy blow, but neither of them could blame Atroist. If things were as bad in the Lost Lands as he said, then asking the Herdsfolk to give up all their defenses was asking them to commit suicide. But most of the Wildmages left were in the Lost Lands and the High Reaches, and they were going to need them all.

"Would they come here?" Kellen asked. "Men, women, children—and goats?"

"Kellen!" Idalia burst out. "You can't offer the whole Lost Lands sanctuary in the Elven Lands! You don't have the power!"

"No," Kellen agreed. "But I think Andoreniel will agree to offer them safe passage *through* the Elven Lands, if we ask him to. There's a lot of unoccupied land between the Elven Border and the Wildwood, and more between the Wildwood and Armethalieh. The, uh, Dark Folk aren't raiding this far east. Not yet anyway. The noncombatants would be safe—if cold."

"Cold!" Vestakia scoffed. "*This* isn't cold."

"They would come," Atroist said with certainty. "To be safe from the Dark Folk—never more to fear the sobbing outside their shutters in the night, nor the sound of wings overhead in the darkness—not to live in terror that any stranger may be one of *Them* in disguise—Oh, yes, Kellen Knight-Mage, they will come. And gladly."

⟶

ALL that was needed to put Kellen's plan into operation was to get the request to Andoreniel and receive his permission in return.

Fortunately, he had a fast messenger available, assuming he could talk Jermayan and Ancaladar into it.

The arrival of the dragon at Ondoladeshiron had not caused panic, since Andoreniel had sent messages ahead of time, but Ancaladar's presence was an occasion of more curiosity than Kellen and Vestakia combined. When Kellen left Idalia's tent, he realized that Jermayan wasn't going to be that hard to find.

Jermayan and Ancaladar, making a virtue of the inevitable, had decided to put on a sort of aerial display for the encampment. Ancaladar was circling the Gathering Plain, flying low and slow enough for everyone to get a good look at him. Kellen could see the sunlight glint off the dragon's black scales, and see the blue flash of Jermayan's armor.

"Idalia—Vestakia—come look! Jermayan's brought Ancaladar down low enough for everyone to watch!" Kellen called, and the others crowded out of Idalia's tent to watch.

After a few minutes of circling, dragon and rider soared high into the sky—and there, to Kellen's astonished delight, Ancaladar performed a series of acrobatics that reminded Kellen of nothing so much as a selkie after a particularly choice fish.

It came to Kellen that what he was watching, however entertaining it looked now, had a grim and entirely serious purpose. These were the battle moves for sky fighting, the forms that Ancaladar would have to use against flying enemies. Jermayan would have to not only remain in the saddle, but be able to cast spells while Ancaladar was performing these maneuvers.

"I hope Jermayan didn't eat too much breakfast," Vestakia said, sounding faintly worried as she stared into the sky.

Idalia laughed. "Oh, he wouldn't make that mistake twice! This is hardly the first time they've done this. It's really quite enjoyable."

"I don't think I'd care for it," Vestakia said firmly.

Kellen glanced at Idalia curiously. She'd ridden Ancaladar? While he and Jermayan were doing something like *that*?

No, he didn't want to know. There were some things a man was better off not knowing about his sister. About women in general, probably. *Geas* or no *geas*.

"I'm going to go out in the open and see if I can get them to land so I can talk to Jermayan," Kellen said. "Wish me luck."

HE suspected that Ancaladar had seen and recognized him, because the dragon landed before Kellen had gotten very far away from the edge of the encampment.

Here there was nothing at all to break the force of the wind, and it cut like a knife of pure ice. Kellen was getting pretty tired of winter already, and Idalia said that there was more to come. Moonturns of it, in fact. No wonder it wasn't allowed to really penetrate Armethalieh's defenses against weather!

He bowed to Jermayan as Jermayan vaulted—with the ease of long practice—down from Ancaladar's back.

"It would be interesting to know when you learned to fly like that," Kellen said. "The display was most instructive. And I don't think you'll get Vestakia anywhere near Ancaladar, after that."

"I would promise to be good," the dragon said, sounding faintly hurt.

"I have been practicing," Jermayan said, obviously pleased. "And it may someday be needful that she ride with us. She is the only one who can tell where the Shadowed Elves lair. If she can do it from the air . . . "

Then she could cover the ground very fast— faster than on horseback. And a lot more safely.

"You're the one who's going to have to convince her, not me," Kellen said, grinning. "Or maybe you can talk Idalia into helping you. *She* seems to like flying."

"Never will she forget that she once had wings of her own," Jermayan said. "It is a hard loss to bear. I admit I had not thought our display might alarm Vestakia, but Ancaladar thought it best to present himself to everyone at once, so all might know him for what he is immediately. And it is a fine day for flying. The skies are clear, and the winds are relatively calm and steady."

"And the sky is blue, and the ground is white, and it's winter, and sooner or later it's going to snow again," Kellen agreed. "And as you know perfectly well, I didn't come out here to talk about the weather, but to tell you how I spent my morning."

Quickly and concisely, Kellen told Jermayan and Ancaladar about Wildmage Atroist, and the increasing frequency of the Demon raids in the Lost Lands.

"We knew they never stopped raiding there, but lately it's been getting worse. Atroist says that if they send us any help, they risk stripping themselves of all protection. But we need all the help they can give us."

"You have a plan," Jermayan said, studying Kellen's face. "Leaf and Star deliver us."

Kellen shrugged. It had seemed like a simple plan when he'd come up with it back in Idalia's tent, and frankly, he couldn't see any other way of getting the Lost Lands Wildmages on their side. He took a deep breath.

"Atroist says that he can get them *all* to come—all the Herdsfolk, with their flocks and herds. If Andoreniel will grant them safe passage through the Elven Lands, they can settle on the other side—in human lands—where *They* don't come. Then their Wildmages and fighters will be willing to leave them, knowing they'll be safe."

Jermayan took a deep breath, his whole body rigid with something beyond astonishment.

Ancaladar began to laugh.

Jermayan whirled and glared at his friend—Kellen could tell that much from his body language—but Ancaladar simply wouldn't—or couldn't—stop laughing. He shook his enormous head from side to side, scraping his chin in the snow, eyes tightly closed in mirth.

At last Jermayan's shoulders relaxed. He walked over to the twitching dragon and kicked it—gently—in the ankle.

"Very well, my friend. I stand rebuked," he said to Ancaladar. "Who am I, an Elven Mage, to bridle at the thought of humans within our lands when there are Shadowed Elves beneath them? If it will gain us help in an evil hour, it is foolish to cling to outmoded thoughts and old ways."

He turned back to Kellen.

"You did not simply come to tell me this, of course," he said.

"I need someone to go back to Sentarshadeen and ask Andoreniel for the safe conduct," Kellen said. "You and Ancaladar would be fastest, and I think Andoreniel will listen to you. So I thought I'd come and see if you were willing to go."

Ancaladar gave a last faint wail of mirth and raised his head from the snow. "Oh, yes. I am willing to go. I want to hear what he says."

"I see it is settled, then," Jermayan said. He sighed. "Kellen . . . I agree that we need their Wildmages. And no one could expect them to abandon their own people to *Them*. And it is equally true that the most direct route from the Lost Lands into human realms lies through Elven Lands. But I do wish you had found another way."

With that Jermayan turned back to Ancaladar, stepped up into the saddle, and took off into the sky.

Kellen shook his head. There was something else he was missing here. Probably another ancient Elven tradition that he hadn't had time to learn.

But Jermayan was right. They couldn't cling to those now. They had to change.

Or die.

—

JERMAYAN did not return that day, nor was he back by the following morning, when the full army was mustered together on the Gathering Plain, and Kellen saw General Redhelwar, and Rochinuviel, Viceroy of Ondoladeshiron, for the first time. Petariel had told him over morning tea that Redhelwar would be wanting to see both him and Idalia in his tent afterward, as the only ones who had actually seen the enemy up close, in order to plan the actual tactics of the campaign. But this was a purely ceremonial occasion.

Kellen had to admit that the army was an impressive sight. But the Elven destriers—and probably even the unicorns—

would be of no use in the caves, and against a Demon attack in force, even this much of an army wouldn't survive more than minutes. It would take more than physical might to defeat the Demons. And Kellen was coming to think—after what Atroist had told him—that it would take more than magic, too.

Some combination of both that he hadn't figured out yet, he supposed. Or maybe it was just as simple—and as difficult—as keeping the Demons from getting their hands on whatever objective it was that they thought would guarantee them victory.

Whatever *that* might be.

⌐

REDHELWAR was a grave and imposing figure in scarlet armor, mounted on a destrier whose coat was nearly the same color. Kellen saw him only from a distance, of course, since he stood with the Unicorn Knights. Kellen tried not to think about the fact that Redhelwar's experience with real war was as theoretical as his own: the Elves had been at peace since the end of the Great War, and certainly for all of Redhelwar's lifetime. But despite their heritage of peace, Kellen was coming to realize that the Elves were a warrior race, and he already knew they were master strategists. If they could only be weaned from so much love of Tradition!

But if Redhelwar did not approach the Unicorn Knights closely, to Kellen's great surprise, Rochinuviel did.

The Viceroy of Ondoladeshiron did not wear armor, having instead chosen to don the elaborate jeweled robes of state that Kellen had seen worn in the Council chambers in the House of Leaf and Star. The Viceroy rode a palfrey of dazzling whiteness—not as white as a unicorn, of course, but nearly. When he spoke—a short speech welcoming them to Ondoladeshiron in Andoreniel's and Ashaniel's names— Kellen realized that though he'd been automatically thinking of the Viceroy as "he," Rochinuviel was actually "she," not "he." It had been harder than usual to tell, between courtly jewels, winter furs, and the fact that Rochinuviel was not young and—so Kellen was beginning to find—Elves tended to become more androgynous with age.

The Vicereign finished her speech of welcome. Petariel's mount, a white unicorn named Gesade (white seemed to be the most common color among unicorns), thanked her for her kindness to them. Rochinuviel rode away.

It was all very sedate, and very little like what Kellen had imagined it would be, from the hints he'd gathered around the edges of Master Belesharon's tales at the House of Sword and Shield. Not that he expected everyone to be *enjoying* themselves, no, but this was the Mustering of the Army. He'd expected things to be noisier.

"I've heard you're in trouble," Shalkan said when Rochinuviel was out of earshot.

"I am?" Kellen said, startled. His partner had picked a fine time to mention it.

"You are," Petariel said, without turning from his position ahead of Kellen. "One hopes you will return from your audience with Redhelwar alive, as your presence is entertaining. One hears, however, that the absence of Jermayan and Ancaladar is because they have gone to Sentarshadeen to negotiate a safe passage through the Elven Lands for the Herdsfolk—all of the Herdsfolk, and their beasts—at your urging."

"That's true," Kellen said. He saw no reason to deny it.

"One observes," Petariel said, and there was a note of amusement in his voice now, "that no word of this reached your Captain—or the General of the Armies—before the event. Now *I* forgive a Knight-Mage all," he went on, holding up a hand, "knowing as I do that you are not truly one of us, Kellen, nor precisely under my command. But one wishes to observe that Redhelwar is from Windalorianan, and has not lately been a part of the great events in Sentarshadeen. He will not yet have had the opportunity to become used to the ways of Knight-Mages."

Great. In trouble again because I haven't gone through proper channels.

"Can we watch?" Gesade asked archly.

"No, rude one, we may *not* watch," Petariel told his mount firmly. "Kellen will explain his reasoning, and his feeling that speed was of vital necessity in making this information known to Andoreniel. He and Jermayan both acted properly, as Wildmages. It is merely that we are not yet reaccustomed to the ways of Wildmages."

"I told you that you were in trouble," Shalkan said.

"Maybe," Kellen said. He supposed he was in trouble if Redhelwar wanted to make it trouble, and not if not. And Petariel, in the indirect fashion of Elves, had given him all the clues he needed to smooth matters over, assuming he needed them.

BUT when he reached Redhelwar's tent almost an hour later, after the parade was dismissed and he'd unharnessed Shalkan and located where he was supposed to go, he found that Idalia was there before him, and seemed to have taken care of any feather-smoothing that needed doing.

"I See you, Kellen Knight-Mage."

"I See you, Redhelwar, Army's General." Titles were rarely used among the Elves, and in the most formal usage, they were placed last. Shalkan had coached him.

"Be welcome at my hearth. Now come, and tell me everything you know of the enemy we face."

Kellen stepped into the tent. It was the same shade of red as Redhelwar's armor and surcoat—which would have been unsettling without the bright golden light of the lanterns hung throughout—and large enough to hold a great many people. At the center of the tent was a large table, and pinned to it was a detailed map of the Elven Lands and much of the territory beyond. There was the Eastern Ocean. There was Armethalieh, the Wildwoods, the High Reaches . . .

Kellen looked down at it in delight. He'd learned to read maps at the House of Sword and Shield, but this was the largest and most complete map he'd yet seen. This was the *world*.

Or at least, if not the world, then a great deal more of it than he had ever seen before.

There was a small red dot in one place on the map.

"This is the location of the one enclave of the Shadowed Elves that we know of," Redhelwar said. "I have asked Idalia to draw as complete a map of the caverns as she can recall, and I will ask the same of you, so that we know all we can of the terrain before we attack. But she tells me you have actually faced the creatures in battle."

"Yes," Kellen said. He concentrated, thinking back. "I got the impression that they were physically not as hardy as we are; but if they have Goblin blood, their fangs or claws might carry poison . . . "

For the next two hours, Redhelwar questioned Kellen and Idalia closely about their experiences in the caves. Then the noonday meal arrived, and with it Vestakia, escorted by members of Redhelwar's personal staff.

Kellen still had trouble reading the expressions of Elves when they didn't want them read. But he thought these two looked . . . confused.

"Ah," Redhelwar said, getting to his feet—the three of them had been sitting around the map table—and going over to Vestakia. "Here is the savior of the children of Sentar-shadeen, the woman who helped Kellen Wildmage destroy the Barrier that had plunged the Elven Lands into drought. Be welcome, Vestakia, at my hearth." He took her arm and ushered her into the tent.

Kellen glanced at Idalia. Idalia smirked. It was pretty obvious that that little show hadn't been for Vestakia's benefit, but for her escort's, and it would be all over the camp within minutes, to good effect. If Vestakia had been having any trouble up until now, it had just been thoroughly and effectively quashed. Out here, you couldn't get patronage with more clout than that of the Commander of the Army.

Vestakia's escort left, and the service staff set out lunch—bread, soup, and roast fowl—on a second table.

"Thank you," Vestakia said, looking up at him shyly. "I hope my presence hasn't caused any—trouble."

"I will not have trouble in my army," Redhelwar said firmly. "And you are our greatest asset in this war. Besides," he added with a faint smile, "no one could doubt one for whom the unicorns have vouched. I was once a Unicorn Knight myself. They would not thank me for doubting them now, and their tongues are as sharp as their horns when they are annoyed. Now come. Eat. I have many questions for you."

Redhelwar said questions, and he meant exactly that, for this was an army in the field. After the meal was cleared away, he questioned Vestakia until he knew as well as she did the extent and range of her abilities and how they worked.

"It is a pity there is only one of you," he said when he was satisfied, "for we could surely use more. Idalia does not think her magics will be of use in detecting the lairs of the Shadowed Elves."

"I can try, of course," Idalia said. "I'll ask Atroist to try, too. His powers may have more of an affinity for this sort of work, since the Lostlanders defend against Dark Magic all the time."

"It will take four days to prepare the army to march. See what you can do in that time," Redhelwar said. "Meanwhile, take my thanks for all the help you have given me; it is invaluable, for foreknowledge of the enemy is as important as any weapon."

It was a dismissal, and they took it as such.

OUTSIDE, Kellen began walking Idalia and Vestakia back to their pavilion.

"Shalkan told me I might be in trouble," he said to Idalia, "but I didn't see any sign of it. I guess I've got you to thank for that?"

"You certainly do," Idalia said roundly. "If Redhelwar weren't reasonable—and you weren't a Knight-Mage—you would have been in real deep trouble." She shook her head with chagrin. "It's as much my fault as yours. I was so concerned about the safety of the Herdingfolk that I didn't even think of that at the time."

"Military chain of command. You and I were both thinking like civilians. Petariel says that Wildmages are outside it, technically, which means Jermayan won't be in for any trouble either"—he sighed—"but he and I both have to fight as part of the army, so we've got to figure out a way to fit in, and I guess that starts with not stepping on any more toes than necessary. Which means I should have told Redhelwar what I was going to do."

"If not exactly asked him for permission," Idalia agreed. "Just so you know, while he's not thrilled with the Herding-folk coming through Elven Lands, he agrees that if that's the only way to gain the help of the Lost Lands Wildmages, it's the best of our available choices."

BUT when Jermayan and Ancaladar finally returned, a little before dusk, it was apparent that not everyone shared Redhelwar's pragmatic outlook on matters.

"The Council . . . debates," Jermayan said wearily.

The four friends were seated around the table in Idalia's pavilion, sharing tea and the contents of a hamper of delicacies that Jermayan had brought from Sentarshadeen. Idalia had already set aside some of the sweet cakes for Kellen to share with Shalkan later.

Kellen took a deep breath. Jermayan raised a minatory hand.

"This time they will not be hurried. You have pushed them a great deal in recent sennights, and preparing for war has taxed their sensibilities to the utmost. This newest matter is the gust of wind that lays bare the tree, and if there is to be any hope of matters going as you would wish it, they must go slowly."

"But Andoreniel—" Kellen said.

"Sees the wisdom in your plan," Jermayan said soothingly. "As does Ashaniel. As does Morusil, and even Belesharon, and believe me, his word carries great weight. These and others speak as your advocates. But the matter must be thoroughly discussed to be sure that all aspects of the situation are seen."

Which means that there will probably be Demons walking the streets of Armethalieh before they come to a decision! Kellen thought uncharitably.

"I am sure that Atroist is anxious for word," Idalia suggested.

"I do not expect it will take more than a moonturn for the Council to provide Andoreniel with the fruits of its deliberations in full, and to provide its own solutions for the problems that it raises. Morusil has made the argument that in leaving the Lostlanders available for *Them* to prey upon, we are allowing the Enemy a source of strength and provision which it would be well to deny to *Them*. I believe that line of reasoning will influence the Council in the end. Meanwhile, we have battles of our own to fight."

⟶

FOUR days later, the Elven army marched on the cavern of the Shadowed Elves.

Idalia had done her best to try to detect other encampments of the creatures using the Wild Magic, but had had no more luck than on previous occasions, and Vestakia's power did not work at any great distance.

Atroist had made the attempt as well, both using the scrying bowl, and using an instrument new to Kellen and Idalia, something he called a hanging-crystal. When not in use, he wore it on a cord about his neck: it looked to Kellen like a clear, teardrop-shaped keystone, the narrow end wrapped with silver wire to make a loop for the cord to pass through.

But apparently it could be used to find things.

Atroist demonstrated in Idalia's pavilion. It found, in succession, a set of her hair combs, Kellen's dagger, and a pair of Vestakia's gloves, all hidden in various places about the tent as a test. When the crystal was working, it would point directly toward the object, even if it had to hover horizontally at the end of its cord to do so.

Then they turned to the map. Without difficulty, and with perfect accuracy, the hanging crystal located Ondoladeshiron, Sentarshadeen, Armethalieh, and the Wildwood.

But it was completely unable to locate any of the Shadowed Elf enclaves, even the one they already knew about.

"Well," Idalia said with a sigh, "we tried. I guess it's up to you, Vestakia."

Vestakia nodded grimly. None of them were happy about this, but none of them were surprised, either.

Just once, Kellen thought, as he made his way back to his tent, *just once it would be so nice to be pleasantly surprised about something in this war.*

⟶

THE Elven Knights of five cities marched in force, though not all of them would make the descent into the caverns. Once the caverns themselves had been cleansed, Kellen knew, Redhelwar intended to reclaim the bodies of their fallen comrades and fellow Elves lost in the attack upon the caravan from Sentarshadeen.

The Unicorn Knights rode nearly a mile ahead of the main army, functioning as its scouts and trailblazers, following a trail Kellen had last ridden less than two moonturns before.

At the end of six days of traveling, the Unicorn Knights reached the battlefield. They'd seen no sign of coldwarg, ice-trolls, or frost-giants, and Ancaladar had reported that the skies were clear of Deathwings. From here it was only two days to the Shadowed Elf caverns, at the speed the army traveled.

To the unaided eye, everything was pure and pristine, the bodies buried beneath several feet of new snow, but no one thought of it that way. This was a haunted place, drenched in blood and sorrow, and would remain so forever in the memories of the Elves.

Ancaladar and Jermayan circled low over the field, the wind from the dragon's wings stirring the loose surface-snow into dancing veils. A second circle, and Ancaladar headed westward again.

"It looks as if they'll find us a place to lay our heads tonight," Gesade said, stretching out her long elegant neck and shaking it. "Useful things, dragons."

"I have never said dragons weren't useful," Petariel said to his mount. "And if you could fly, Gesade, there's a faint possibility you might someday be of some use as well."

The unicorn snorted and did not reply.

⌒

THE campsite Jermayan and Ancaladar had found was, Kellen judged—perhaps three hours' ride from the caverns, in a sheltered valley surrounded by towering pines. It was a large enough open space to hold their entire force, and far enough away from the cavern that their arrival should not alert the Shadowed Elves.

Once the army and the supply train arrived, and the camp was in place, Redhelwar called his commanders—and Vestakia and the Wildmages—to the command tent to make his final dispositions for the attack, and to make certain that all the commanders had the opportunity to review the maps that Kellen and Idalia had prepared.

Vestakia would be going into the caverns with them. Kellen was worried about that. While Tandarion had made her a fine suit of Elven armor to protect her—with gold-washed vermilion enameling the precise shade of her skin—

she did not have either fighting skills or Wildmagery to protect her further.

But she *was* the only one who could sense the presence of
the Shadowed Elves.

Being able to see in the caverns was the major problem.
Idalia and Atroist had bespelled all the *tarnkappa* so that
they granted darksight, but they had only a couple of dozen
of them; such things were major Workings, and even with so
many willing to share the Mageprice, there had been a limited amount of time to make them. And the problem with
tarnkappa was that they concealed you from friend as well
as foe.

Lanterns and torches were a possibility. But they could be
easily extinguished by the enemy.

"Magelight," Idalia said. "It's a simple spell, and not very
costly. And nobody will have to worry about carrying
lanterns, either."

"Magelight?" Atroist asked, looking puzzled.

"This," Jermayan said. He cupped his hands, holding them
a little apart. The space between them grew misty, then began to glow, and in seconds he was holding a small blue ball
of light. He spread his hands, and it floated up over his head.

"Ah," Atroist said. "In the Lost Lands, we call that Coldfire. Yes, Idalia, an elegant solution."

"It would be well to know that enough can be made in
time," Redhelwar said.

"It can be done," Jermayan said. "I will do it, so that there
is no cost. There will be prices enough to pay for all by the
time we are done."

ANCALADAR had told them that the Shadowed Elves
moved by night, so Redhelwar made plans for a midmorning
attack, hoping to take them by surprise. Ancaladar said there
were only two ways into the caverns—the way he and Kellen
had taken to rescue Idalia, and the way she had taken to

bring out the children. Based on the descriptions of both, Redhelwar elected to send the army in through the latter. Jermayan and Ancaladar would go around by the "back way," meeting up with the main force as quickly as they could.

Redhelwar elected to divide his force into four groups: one, the main force that would enter the caverns and mount the attack. Two, a small force that would wait just outside the cavern mouth to secure it. Three, a mobile force situated halfway between the caverns and the camp to secure the line of retreat, and which could be called up quickly at need. And four, a sufficient force left behind to guard the camp in case the Enemy was only waiting for them to leave to attack it.

Considering the information they had available—which was very little—Kellen could find no fault with Redhelwar's dispositions. He thought it would be more tactful to keep quiet about that fact, though.

THEY left the camp an hour after sunrise, heading for the caverns. Each of them had a ball of Coldfire hovering over his or her head like a peculiar nimbus, the radiance only a faint shimmer in the winter sunlight. It would remain until Jermayan—or another Wildmage—dispersed it again.

Kellen was grateful that Shalkan didn't ask him if he was nervous. He hardly knew whether he was or not. His mind was filled with everything that could go wrong and a dull frustration that he hadn't thought of suggesting that someone—him—do a thorough scouting expedition of the caverns before they went in with their entire force.

But pulling back now would do more harm than good; what information they might gain would be offset by the damage to the morale of the army. And deep down, Kellen wasn't entirely certain that Redhelwar would have taken his suggestion.

That was the real problem. The Elves honored him. They respected him. But Kellen didn't set policy for the Nine

Cities. He didn't plan strategy for the army. And he didn't have a real voice in the tactics it would use.

Yet.

Yet?

The sudden thought—no, *realization*—startled him so much that he tensed all over. Shalkan craned his head around to gaze curiously at him, but Kellen shook his head wordlessly, and Shalkan went back to gazing at the path ahead.

Yes, *yet*. There would come a time—there *needed* to come a time—when the army did what *Kellen* said, not what Redhelwar said. But—he remembered the lesson of the Crowned Horns—you couldn't command that sort of trust. You needed to earn it.

He needed to earn it.

And fast.

Then Andoreniel would give him the army. Redhelwar would step aside without anger. The army would follow him.

If he was good enough. If he could prove he could lead an army, and keep it alive, and win. If he could *prove* that being a Knight-Mage made him understand strategy as instinctively as he understood fighting one-on-one.

One single moment of blind panic touched him. *I don't know how to do that!*

But he did. *Gan* had taught him. *Xaqiue* had taught him. Master Belesharon's story songs had taught him. Win a battle. Command a troop—and win. Command a larger detachment—and win.

Win, always. Plan—and show them his plans were better than theirs. And make the Elves see him as a Knight-Mage first, and a young human second. Better yet, get to the point where they looked at him and saw only the Knight-Mage, and the young human not at all.

And the first thing he needed to do to accomplish all that was to get through today.

"Here we are," Shalkan said.

The Unicorn Knights who had been chosen for the assault had ridden a little ahead of the main body of fighters. Now they dismounted to allow their mounts to get clear of the main army.

The cavern mouth was empty, and there were no footprints on the snow that lay before it. Kellen shifted to battlesight for a moment, but saw no sign of a trap.

That didn't make a lot of sense. The Shadowed Elves *must* know their lair

had been discovered. Any sensible creature would have posted guards, or blocked the entrance somehow.

But they hadn't.

"Is everything well?" Petariel asked.

"Much too well," Kellen answered grimly. "It's as if they can't imagine we could possibly ever come back."

"Maybe they left," Petariel suggested. "Vestakia will tell us soon enough."

Adaerion was at the head of the force that arrived a few moments later. Redhelwar was waiting with the mobile force—the General of the army was too valuable to lose. Vestakia rode beside him, and Kellen could tell with just one look at her posture—uncomfortably hunched over—that the Shadowed Elves had not left.

"They're still there," he said.

"Ah," Petariel said, following the direction of Kellen's gaze. "Well, I should hate to have ridden all this way for nothing."

⟿

THEY formed up in the way they had planned at the War Council the night before. Kellen and an Elf called Celegaer, Adaerion's lieutenant, would go first, with Vestakia and Idalia directly behind them. Vestakia would give warning the moment she sensed the presence of the Shadowed Elves.

"Leaf and Star be with you all," Adaerion said gravely.

Kellen nodded, forcing himself to wait until Celegaer took the first step toward the cavern before following. He kept himself from looking toward Vestakia and Idalia—or any of his comrades from the House of Sword and Shield.

Barring a miracle, this was the last time some of them would see the light of day. This was a war. Fighters died in war.

Get used to it.

Kellen walked into the dark.

The Magelight seemed to glow brighter the further they went along the passage, until it was the only illumination. The Elves moved silently, but he could hear the faint rustle of Idalia's clothing, and every sound that Vestakia's armor made.

Suddenly Vestakia gave a gagging whimper. "They're here—ahead—" she choked out.

"The passage widens just ahead," Kellen said quickly to Celegaer. "Hurry—we can't let them trap us here!"

Without waiting to hear Celegaer's reply, he ran forward.

At the end of the passageway, wider corridors opened out to the left and right, just as Idalia had described. They were crowded with the Shadowed Elves—too many to easily count—and this time the creatures were armed, not to capture a dragon, but to fight.

The Shadowed Elves wore bits and pieces of looted armor lashed to their bodies with strips of leather. But ragged and mismatched as their armor was, their weaponry was in gleaming earnest. Swords and shields—spears—

And bows.

Kellen dropped into battle-mind. Without thought, he raised his shield, and the first of the small deadly arrows fired out of the dark glanced off it.

The Shadowed Elves swarmed—there was no other word to describe their movement—forward. They obviously didn't like the light, but they weren't blinded by it as some of the Elves had hoped. Kellen cut down the creatures before him and pressed forward, he and Celegaer trying to clear the way for the Elves that were moving up behind them.

But he quickly realized that their tactics weren't working.

Individually the Shadowed Elves were comparatively frail. But they were attacking in enormous numbers, taking advantage of the cramped tunnels—and what was worse, they *weren't limited to the floor of the caverns.*

They climbed along the walls and ceiling, dropping into the middle of their foes to bear the Elves down by sheer weight of numbers. By ones and twos it was nothing to kill them, but they weren't attacking by ones and twos.

Kellen fought on, moving deeper into the right-hand cavern at the spearhead of a group of Knights. Up ahead, the Shadowed Elf archers were firing with deadly accuracy. He could see the arrows glowing dull green in his battle-sight, and knew from that that the arrows were poisoned. He would have shouted a warning, but it would have gone unheard. The cavern was filled with the screams of the injured; the clash of weapons; and the hoarse howls and barking of the Shadowed Elves. Kellen shut out the noise and concentrated on his task.

Cut, step, turn, and cut again. Block, attack, dodge. Celegaer was on his left, another Knight was at his back. One of the Shadowed Elves dropped down on him from above. Kellen grunted, bending forward with the impact, turning the move into a forward throw to dislodge the creature.

He felt the wind of an arrow pass his cheek. There was a muffled grunt behind him. Kellen heard—and felt—the Elven Knight fall to the floor of the cavern and die.

He killed the creature on the ground and moved forward.

At last the Elves' superior battle skills and heavier, more effective armor turned the tide. The battlefield opened up, and it soon became a matter of keeping the Shadowed Elves from escaping, and then it came to executing the enemy wounded and checking the dead.

And that was when Kellen found himself just standing there, sword hanging from his limp grip, staring at an empty tunnel.

"Kellen." Celegaer laid a gentle hand upon his shoulder. "Go back and rest for a moment. Then ask Idalia if Vestakia is well enough to come forward."

Kellen blinked, feeling almost as if he were rousing from a deep sleep. He nodded, and turned away.

He had to move carefully through the piles of corpses, and

the stone was slick with blood. It soaked the bodies lying in it, staining them all, Elf and Shadowed Elf alike, the same terrible scarlet color. The blue globes of Coldfire—so many, in such a confined space—made the scene shadowless and stark.

Grief and shame hovered over the battlefield like carrion birds. Kellen had expected the grief—there were too many Elven dead, and he knew that soon he would be mourning the loss of friends—but shame? He did not understand. They'd fought well. They'd won. There was no cause for shame.

Was there?

At the end of the corridor he found Petariel. The Captain of the Unicorn Knights had been wounded: a spear had taken him just behind the knee, at one of the weak points of the Elven armor. He leaned against the wall, a makeshift bandage over his wound, his helmet beneath his arm.

And to Kellen's astonishment, he was weeping.

"Oh, Kellen, our poor cousins. Leaf and Star, that we should be driven to *this*—!" Petariel said.

Kellen had no idea what he meant, but there would be time later to figure it out. "Come on," he said, getting an arm under Petariel's shoulders. "Let's get you out of here. Gesade and Shalkan both would have my head if I let anything happen to you."

Petariel laughed raggedly, but it ended on a strangled sob. "The worst has already happened," he said softly.

Kellen half-carried Petariel back up the passageway. He felt a deep pang of relief to see Idalia and Vestakia both there, unhurt—and quickly focused all of his attention on Petariel, lest his worry for Vestakia's safety turn into something he must not feel right now.

"Ah, another one," Idalia said lightly. "The stretcher-bearers will be back in just a moment."

"I can walk," Petariel said grimly.

"No you can't," Idalia said firmly. "Not if you want to be riding again soon."

Kellen helped Petariel to lie down among the other wounded. There were several Healers working in the narrow space, and a constant stream of the walking wounded were moving out toward the open air.

Everything was moving so slowly! But that was why the Shadowed Elves didn't bother with guards, Kellen now realized. They were sure no one could attack them in force.

Once he was sure his emotions were under control, he risked a glance at Vestakia.

Vomit stained the front of her surcoat, and she knelt beside Idalia, obviously dazed and exhausted by the presence of so much Taint. Kellen sighed reluctantly.

"Celegaer needs Vestakia," he said to Idalia.

"Now?" Idalia asked.

"I'm ready," Vestakia said valiantly, raising her head. There were deep shadows beneath her eyes, and she looked haggard.

"Not yet. Soon. He told me to rest," Kellen added, trying to make a joke of it.

"As if you would," Idalia said, handing him a waterskin. "Are you hurt?"

Kellen shook his head, and drank. The water was warm, but it was unicorn-pure. He felt better afterward.

"I think they threw most of what they had at us. Some of them got away, though. We'll have to find them," Kellen said.

"That will be my job," Vestakia said bravely.

"Come on, then," Kellen said gruffly, sounding far more brusque than he wanted to. But he couldn't help it. He felt as if he had no energy to spare for anything.

Idalia and Vestakia followed him back into the cavern.

Celegaer and several of the others were waiting for them just past the end of the bodies. All of them had the faintly stunned air of grief about them that Kellen had noticed before.

"Vestakia," Celegaer said, seeing her. "Are you well?"

"Well enough to do what you ask of me," Vestakia answered steadily.

"Then find our foe," Celegaer said.

Without hesitation, Vestakia pointed—not along the corridor, but at the corridor wall.

"The corridor curves," Idalia said. "That's the direction of the cavern village. There will be females and young there," she warned.

"We can leave none alive," Celegaer said wearily.

"I know," Idalia said gently.

"Celegaer," Kellen said. "If I can suggest . . . now we know where the village is, and Vestakia is too valuable to risk. Send her outside to wait with Adaerion until we think we have cleared the cavern, then bring her in to check to see if we have missed anyone."

"No!" Vestakia protested.

"Yes," Celegaer said. "An excellent suggestion, Kellen. Padredor, escort Mistress Vestakia back to Adaerion, and order the rest of the knights to come forward. Idalia Wildmage, will you also withdraw?"

"No," Idalia said, taking a moment to consider. "I think I can be useful here."

Fourteen

Blood and Sorrow

Soon they were moving forward again. Only about half their original force remained. There were not many dead, considering the savagery of the battle, but there were many wounded, and though some of the wounds were minor, Celegaer had not wanted to take wounded Elves into battle.

We're too spread out, and there's no way to avoid it in these tunnels. All the advantage is theirs, Kellen thought. *We're going to have to figure out how to fight this kind of battle—fast—in order to win it.*

At last the tunnel widened out into the great cavern that Idalia had described, with the narrow pathway leading around the rim, and the stairs going down to the village below. The cavern was so vast that the Coldfire coronas of the assembled army did nothing more than light their immediate surroundings. All they could see of what was below was the faint glow of the central firepit.

With a flick of her hand, Idalia sent her ball of Coldfire out to hover over the cavern. The light was faint, but enough to show that the crude stone village below was silent and still.

"Ambush," Kellen said with utter certainty.

"You can sense them?" Celegaer asked with surprise.

"No," Kellen said. "But I know they're waiting for us all the same. Or waiting for us to go away."

"Either course would gain them a victory, of a sort," Celegaer answered. "So we go down. But not unwarily. Archers—to the rim."

Once the archers were in place, the Elven Knights began descending the stair. It would have been the perfect place for an ambush, but the Shadowed Elves did not take advantage of it. When the first group of Elves was at the bottom of the staircase, their combined Coldfire illuminated the cavern, giving Kellen a good look at it for the first time.

It was as large as Merryvale—the entire village could have been dropped down neatly inside it, walls and all. There were scattered small huts, and along the cavern wall, Kellen could see holes—they reminded him uncomfortably of very large rat-holes—in the rock.

The Elves stood, silent, motionless.

What are they waiting for? Kellen wondered. He wasn't looking forward to this any more than they were, but it wouldn't get any easier—or any better—if they waited.

And where were Jermayan and Ancaladar?

He looked toward Celegaer.

Celegaer met his gaze, and there was despair in the black eyes. After a moment, Celegaer spoke.

"Search every structure, every hole. Find them all, down to the smallest infant. Kill them all. No survivors. No prisoners." The Elven commander's voice was harsh.

He turned away, striding toward the nearest hut.

The Elves fanned out, spreading across the cavern floor.

For a moment there was silence.

Then Celegaer screamed, and the cavern exploded in a harsh babble of barks and whines.

Kellen ran in the direction of the scream. He was too late. Celegaer was dead, his face and the front of his armor eaten away by a liquid thrown at him by a Shadowed Elf female who had just come out of the stone hut. The archers on the rim had filled her body with arrows, but they had been too late to save their commander.

Celegaer's troops were staring down at him in shock and horror.

"Search the hut!" Kellen ordered. "Keep your shields forward—we know they use poison as a weapon—now we know they use acid, too."

He moved on quickly, heading for the next hut. The doorway was low; he had to duck to get inside.

It was one room, windowless, and it stank. It contained a pile of furs and three small children.

I can't do this, Kellen thought in sick horror. He knew they weren't children—they were Shadowed Elves—but they were young things. Very young. They hissed at him, cringing back from the light.

Then suddenly all three of them shrieked and sprang at him. There was no fear in their bulging pale eyes, only the berserker madness of cornered rats. They swarmed up his body, scrabbling for every purchase, clawing and biting at everything they could reach.

Reflexively, Kellen knocked them away, but they kept coming back. He could see their glistening, needlelike teeth, smell their rank, poison-tainted breath. No matter how many times he flung them away from him, they sprang up and lunged for him again.

Then one of them pulled Kellen's dagger free of its sheath.

It was an Elven dagger, made of deadly Elvensteel and designed to pierce any opening or weakness in the Elven armor's defenses. Seeing the length of gleaming steel in the young thing's hands made all of his battle-honed instincts rouse at once. They weren't children anymore—they were the enemy.

With a gasping cry, he struck the Shadowed Elf child as hard as he could, then grabbed the other two and flung them against the walls of the hut, stunning them.

Then he took his sword and killed them all.

Bile rose in his throat as he retrieved his dagger, and Kellen breathed deeply, trying to center himself again. But the self-forgiveness he sought would not come. He had killed *children*. How could he accept that?

I will have to find a way. Or not. And whether I can or not, finding out if I can will have to wait. Because my comrades are dying now.

Gritting his teeth, Kellen left the hut.

All around him, the battle was going badly. There weren't as many of the enemy this time, but the Elves were taking terrible losses. They simply couldn't bring themselves to attack and kill what they saw—despite everything—as women and children.

And it was costing them dearly.

Suddenly the cavern was ablaze with light—as bright as the noonday sun at midsummer. Kellen looked up, and saw that the entire roof of the cavern was glowing with bright blue Coldfire.

Jermayan and Ancaladar had arrived.

"Pull back. I'm going to burn the huts." Jermayan's voice spoke quietly, as if in his ear, and Kellen could tell by the startled expressions on the faces of the Elves that everyone else had heard it too. They began to retreat.

But it was easier asked than done, especially when they had to protect their wounded and recover their dead, and it was several minutes of hard and bloody fighting before that could be accomplished.

The Shadowed Elves fought viciously, as much like animals—or insects—as like thinking beings. They did not

seem to care if they sacrificed any of their own—down to
the smallest infant—if it brought them a greater chance of
killing one of the Elves. In cold disbelief, Kellen saw the
Shadowed Elf archers using their own young as shields, saw
children younger than the ones he'd killed springing upon
Elven warriors, armed with jars of acid like the one that had
killed Celegaer. He dragged one of the Elves out of the way
just in time, striking his young attacker dead. The spilled
liquid fumed and bubbled over the corpse, smoking and
stinking.

The Elves were barely clear of the huts, fighting their way
toward the staircase, when suddenly every stone structure
within the cavern save for the staircase burst into flame.

That isn't possible, thought Kellen in awe. Any Wildmage or
High Mage could summon Fire—but only to burn what would
burn naturally. But this . . . ? The stone itself was burning as if
it were seasoned wood drenched in lamp oil. In seconds, a
roaring wall of heat separated the combatants from their prey.

Shadowed Elves—bodies aflame—ran from some of the
huts, only to be cut down by the archers, in mercy.

The Shadowed Elves who had not been in the huts were
trapped by the walls of flame. Their response to the sudden
wave of magic was one of utter terror. The archers who had
been holding living shields threw them down and tried to
flee, but there was nowhere to go, save into the Elven army.

It was no longer a battle, but a massacre. Some of the
Shadowed Elves ran toward the flames. Kellen saw females
grab struggling children and throw them into burning huts,
the structures already collapsing into ash. The archers shot
all they could before the flames took them.

It was over quickly. The huts were gone, the stone burned
away to ash. A wall of icy air filled the cavern, wiping away
the furnace heat. The stone floor creaked and groaned,
forced to cool as quickly as it had been heated.

Ancaladar launched himself from the rim of the cavern,
landing in the now-empty space.

Kellen glanced around quickly, feeling a deep pang of relief to see that Idalia was still on her feet, though her garments were tattered and blood-soaked and her face was grim.

All of the Elves looked stunned. They'd won the battle, but at a terrible cost, both physical and spiritual.

Which is what Shadow Mountain wants, Kellen realized with a flash of insight. *THAT'S what this war is about. It's just another kind of drought. The last one starved the land. This one starves the spirit.*

Realizing that, he felt his own soul-sickness ease. He'd hated what he'd done here today with all his being. But it had been necessary. The Shadowed Elves were Demonic in nature. They were creatures of the Endarkened, created as a trap for the creatures of the Light. To show them mercy would be to doom the Light.

I pity them, because I think they have no choice to be other than what they are. And I forgive them, because they have no choice. But I have a choice to fight for what I think is right, and I also forgive myself for making it.

But the Elves—oh, it was different for them. Not only had they been killing women and children, they had been killing kin. Blood of their blood. Tainted, but still their own.

I have to figure out how to take that guilt away from them . . .

Kellen took a few steps toward Jermayan and Ancaladar.

"It took you long enough," Kellen said. He could sense the tension of the Elves—normal Wildmagery was one thing, but what they'd just seen went far beyond that.

"We were hunting Shadowed Elves," Ancaladar said in his deep soft voice. "And a way here that I could pass through was hard to find."

Jermayan was looking past Kellen, searching the armored figures for familiar forms. He came over to Kellen.

"Celegaer?" he asked in a low voice.

"Dead," Kellen said. "Vestakia is waiting outside with Adaerion and the reserves. We didn't want to risk her."

"Better she not see . . . this," Jermayan said grimly.

"Kellen," Idalia said, coming up. Her voice echoed in the

empty space. "I hate to say this, but . . . Celegaer is dead, Padredor is badly wounded, and so is Tinbendon. They can't find Perchalas. And you're a Knight-Mage."

Kellen looked from Jermayan to Idalia, not understanding.

"You are the ranking officer able to command," Jermayan said quietly. "What do we do?"

He'd wanted the job. He just hadn't expected to get it *now.*

"Can you widen the steps to the surface? We need to transport the dead and wounded," he said.

"He doesn't ask much, does he?" Ancaladar commented.

"Yes," Jermayan said, answering Kellen.

Jermayan stretched out his hand. And the steps . . . blurred.

For a moment Kellen thought there must be something wrong with his vision. But when it steadied again, he could see that the steps were wider than before, as broad and easy as any grand staircase in a High Mage's house.

Kellen stared at Jermayan and Ancaladar, his emotions in turmoil. Awe, yes, and not a little fear. Not of his friends, but . . . this was power out of legend, out of wondertales.

"It comes at a price," Jermayan said quietly.

"Yes," Kellen said. If no other price than the price of being set apart from everything normal and familiar by living in a world you could reshape with a thought.

"Cover our retreat," he said to Jermayan and Ancaladar. "Then get out yourselves. I think we got them all, but we won't know until Vestakia tells us."

He turned and went back to the others.

"Gather up the dead. Prepare the wounded for transport. We're leaving."

Kellen had learned by watching that a good commander gave an order and left the details to his subordinates. He did nothing to interfere with the arrangements for departure. He was busy enough helping to bandage the wounded. Neither he nor Idalia dared to risk any healings—though everyone there would have been willing to share the price, they had been fighting all day, and it would have been cruel to ask it, nor did either Wildmage dare to risk deeper exhaustion and incurring Magedebt themselves.

But Jermayan was not so bound. He moved among the injured, Healing the worst of the injuries until Kellen saw him stagger with weariness as he rose from beside a supine body.

A dragon's power might be inexhaustible. But a Mage was not.

"Stop it," Kellen said quietly, going over and putting a hand under Jermayan's arm. "We need you to be able to fight if you have to. That's more important."

"More important than their lives?" Jermayan demanded in an anguished whisper.

"They'll be with the Healers soon," Kellen said. "And if you cannot fight when we need you, we may all die."

He did not know where the words were coming from. They were harsh and brutal, but they seemed to be the right thing to say, for Jermayan nodded slowly and walked back to where Ancaladar waited.

The Elves began moving up the newly-broadened staircase, carrying those too injured to walk—and the dead—in makeshift slings formed of cloaks and surcoats.

They carried the Shadowed Elf dead with them as well, all that they had been able to recover. Kellen was surprised at that, but had said nothing. He would never, he realized, truly understand the Elves, even if he lived among them for the rest of his life.

Kellen was the last up the stairs. At the top he stopped and looked back. The cavern was utterly empty save for Jermayan and Ancaladar, and a fine coating of grey ash upon the floor.

⌐

IT was twilight by the time Kellen stepped into the open air again. The corridors through which he had passed had been utterly empty. The Elves and the Shadowed Elves were gone, and only spilled blood remained.

The army had moved more slowly as the corridor narrowed, and the slower Kellen moved, the more it seemed he could feel exhaustion dragging at his limbs. When they reached the narrow corridor to the outside, he simply stopped, leaning against the wall and resting until Idalia came back for him.

"We thought you might have gotten lost," she said, handing him a wooden cup.

Kellen shook his head wordlessly. The cup held hot cider. He drained it in a few quick gulps.

"Vestakia?" he asked.

"She doesn't sense any Taint from where she is, which is good. Redhelwar wants her to go down to be sure, but that can wait until tomorrow, if you agree."

If I agree? When had Redhelwar started consulting *him?*

"She doesn't sense anything? How close is she?" Kellen asked.

"Right outside," Idalia said. "She said she could feel it when . . . " Idalia stopped.

"When we'd killed all of them down in the cavern," Kellen said gently. "Maybe she should go up to the other entrance now and check there, just to be sure. But I don't think any of them ran."

"Come on, then. You'll need to make your report."

—

THE reserve force had been brought up, and transport wagons were being used to carry away the wounded. The dead, to whom time no longer mattered, lay in neat rows in the snow, waiting to be carried away in their turn. Kellen looked away—there would be time enough later to find out who had died today.

Globes of Coldfire, interspersed with more conventional lanterns, flickered over the landscape, lending the twilight an ethereal, insubstantial quality, as if he were in a waking dream—or a nightmare.

Idalia led him toward Redhelwar. The general was seated

on his bay destrier, Vestakia at his side on a cream palfrey.
Her eyes widened in horror at the sight of him.

"I will not ask you for a detailed report now, Kellen
Knight-Mage," Redhelwar said, "but I will need a prelimi-
nary one."

"We entered the cavern village," Kellen said. "It was occupied by females and young, as well as by the survivors of the
first attack—mostly archers, I think. They hid until we entered the village and started going into the huts. They attacked
us with acid and poison weapons. Jermayan and Ancaladar arrived and set fire to the village, and we . . . did what we'd set
out to do. Celegaer is dead, two of his lieutenants were badly
injured, and the third is missing. So we left."

Redhelwar nodded. "Do you believe that more of the
creatures may be in hiding elsewhere in the caverns?" he
asked.

"No," Kellen said, shaking his head. "You didn't see how
they came after us. I'm sorry, but . . . I don't think any of
them wanted to get away from the fight, except at the very
end, and then they couldn't. But I'd like Vestakia to go up to
the other entrance—the one that Ancaladar uses—and see
what she can sense there, just to be sure."

"Yes. Best to be as sure as we can without going back inside tonight. Arambor, find horses for the Wildmages, and
gather a party."

While the horses were being brought, Kellen took the opportunity to clean the worst of the blood from his sword. It
felt good to be able to sheathe it again. He wished Shalkan
could be with him, but that simply wasn't possible.

The horses were led forward—Idalia had her own palfrey,
but the mare brought for Kellen—a dapple grey with a white
mane and tail—was a stranger to him. He took a moment to
stroke her neck reassuringly before swinging into the saddle,
blessing all those hours of lessons with Deyishene.

"Her name is Mindaerel," Redhelwar said. "She has lost a
friend this day." He paused, and added heavily, "As have we
all. Celegaer was her rider."

Kellen nodded. He'd seen the closeness of the bond between Jermayan and Valdien, more like that between dog
and master than between horse and rider. What would happen to all the Elven warhorses bereft of their closest companions by the battle today?

He urged Mindaerel forward. To his relief, she obeyed
without hesitation. If she was in some form of equine
mourning, she didn't show it. Unbidden, the thought came to
him. *She is a warrior too . . .*

He dropped into battle-mind easily, scanning the terrain
ahead for any sign of ambush, and saw nothing. When they
were still half a mile from the cave opening, he saw Ancaladar push himself out through it, springing upward into the
sky. Kellen waved, hailing the pair, and Ancaladar dipped a
wing in reply.

The small party reached the cliff face. High above, there
was a dragon-sized opening in the sheer, ice-covered expanse of rock.

"Anything?" Kellen asked.

Vestakia concentrated. She looked as if she were listening
very hard, although listening was not precisely what she was
doing.

"Nothing," Vestakia said after a long pause. She burst into
tears, and Idalia moved to comfort her.

IT was nearly midnight by the time Kellen was able to settle
into his tent at last. He wasn't alone; Shalkan had joined
him, as much for emotional support as because it was freezing outside. Kellen was happy to have him there for both reasons; the unicorn's body helped raise the temperature in the
tent appreciably.

Kellen had discussed the day's events with his friend already, settling them in his mind so that he could work
through them when there was leisure to (if there ever was),
but a few things still puzzled him.

"Shalkan, what did the Elves *do* with all those bodies—the Shadowed Elf ones, I mean? They went to so much trouble to get them—they brought all of them out of the caverns and back here; I saw them. But later, they'd disappeared."

The unicorn snorted gently, and snuggled closer to Kellen. "They did with them just what they did with their own dead. They took them into the forest and suspended them in the trees. You can go and see tomorrow if you like."

Kellen twitched. "No, thanks. But why?"

"You have to think like an Elf. If they buried them, it would shut the spirit away from the wind and the sun. If they burned them . . . well, that would be rather hard on the trees that were felled to make the pyres. And if they floated them down rivers, it would take their dead far away from home and hearth.

"As for why they're treating the Shadowed Elves the same way they're treating their own dead . . . well, you saw how they acted today."

"Yes. It was"—Kellen groped for words—"strange. I didn't understand it. Surely they realize that the Shadowed Elves aren't really Elves!"

Shalkan made a "hrumphing" noise. "What if Idalia did something really horrible?"

"But she wouldn't!" Kellen protested automatically.

"But imagine if she did. How would you feel?"

Kellen thought about it. First he had to imagine Idalia being somebody else entirely—but feeling just the same way about her. Then he imagined her doing something *awful*.

"I guess I'd feel . . . but I still don't . . . " he faltered.

"To you, the Shadowed Elves are creatures of the Dark. To the Elves, they are Elves—debased, Tainted, and twisted, but Elves nonetheless. Nothing you or I or anyone else can say or do will change that feeling. And so they feel responsible."

"Which is just what *They* want," Kellen said, feeling sick.

"I know," Shalkan answered.

THE following day, Kellen and a party of Elves entered the caverns once more, Vestakia in the lead. This time Redhelwar accompanied them—it was necessary, the Elven general said, to see firsthand the terrain over which he would be sending armies to fight in the future.

Once more Jermayan and Ancaladar entered the caverns from the other direction. The two groups met at the site of the village cavern.

The Coldfired ceiling still burned brightly over the cavern where the village had been. Eventually it would go out by itself if Jermayan did not extinguish it, but Coldfire—or Magelight—was such a simple spell that such castings were often left to run out by themselves. Redhelwar looked down into the cavern in silence.

Vestakia shook her head. "Nothing," she said, sounding relieved.

By the end of the day they had explored a great deal of the cave system. They found several more areas that the Shadowed Elves had used for various purposes—storerooms, larders, middens—but no further sign of the creatures themselves. And, thankfully, no prisoners. Kellen didn't think that anything could be held prisoner here for long and still be sane. At last everyone agreed that this cavern system was empty of Shadowed Elves.

"And now," Redhelwar said, "we must find their next lair."

⌒

"A message has come from Andoreniel in Sentarshadeen," Grander said. "Marlen, Sarlin, Erlock, Jarel, you must go to the other households today, and tell them there will be a Council at the Meeting House tonight."

"A message?" Cilarnen asked. "How could a message come now?" Not only had it been snowing for some time—and Centaurs, as he already knew, did not think winter a suitable time for traveling—but a messenger would have come first to Grander's house, and Grander would have in-

sisted on feeding him, and Cilarnen saw no stranger faces
gathered around the table for the noonday meal.

"What bird flies in winter?" Sarlin answered gaily, and
the others laughed.

If Elves never asked questions—and Cilarnen realized,
thinking back, that Hyandur had never asked him a single
question on the entire journey to Stonehearth—the beastfolk
seemed to more than make up for it, and worse, think a question was as good as an answer.

It was only one of their many annoying qualities.

Cilarnen knew he'd been very lucky to be taken in at
Stonehearth. Winter without weather-spells to tame it was a
terrifying thing. Without Grander's kindness—yes, kindness, and charity, too—he would be dead by now.

But while he could manage to be polite, he could not manage to feel gratitude.

What made it worse was that he knew that the beastfolk
were treating him far better than the Armethaliehans would
have treated one of them if the situation were reversed. He
was honest enough to admit that, even if he refused to say it
aloud. Grander had even helped him barter his few personal
possessions—his signet ring, his gold-and-sapphire chain,
his pencase and penknife, and the handful of silver and copper coins in his pockets—to buy himself suitable garments in
the days after his arrival, so that he would not start his time
in Stonehearth too deeply in debt to Grander's house. He'd
had to pay a harness-maker—who had used his City boots as
a template—to make him suitable footwear, but Sarlin had
made his new clothes without charging him for her labor.

⟶

"AND enough gold left over to buy cloth for summer
clothes," she'd said proudly, when she presented his new
outfit to him a sennight after his arrival. "Unless you'll be
wanting to buy something else?"

"Keep it," Cilarnen had said ungraciously, staring at the

bizarre garments. "What is there here that anyone could want to buy?"

She'd looked hurt, and his conscience had pricked him.

"I'm sure you know what I need better than I do," he'd said. He'd struggled to find something to praise, grateful in that moment that no one he'd ever known would see him wearing them. "The workmanship is very fine."

"Ah," Sarlin had said, perking up. "Spun and wove it myself, from our own sheep. You won't find better. And I only charged you what I'd charge family—not what I could get for it at Spring Fair, either!"

"That's . . . very kind," he'd said, as it seemed to be expected.

"Do you need help with them? You not being used to our wild ways, and all? Or—Is your head paining you again?"

"No. I—I will manage. Excuse me."

With the bundle of cloth in his arms, Cilarnen had fled to his room and quickly closed the door.

His new quarters were much smaller than the chamber he had shared with Hyandur. There were hooks on the walls to hold his few garments, and a pallet on the floor for sleeping. There was a chair—a welcome-gift from Marlen—and a small chest, which held a washbasin and a chamberstick. There was no stove, as the room backed on the great hearth's chimney, and so was usually warm enough.

Cilarnen had flung the armful of clothing down on his pallet and pulled out one of the drawers of the chest. Inside was a small glass phial, half-full of a brown liquid so dark it was almost black. He'd regarded it longingly for a moment, then put it back in the drawer and closed it again.

The first day, when Sarlin had taken him to the Centaur Healer, only the hope that the concoction would poison him on the spot had induced Cilarnen to try her remedy. The syrup she compounded was bitter, dark, and thick as honey.

But it had stopped the headaches. Completely.

"A spoonful—no more—night and morning—will stop the pain. Do not take more, young human, for it has dream-honey

in it, and it will make you thick-witted and scatterbrained."

He'd ignored her prohibition. Once. He'd never been tempted to repeat the experiment, no matter how much he craved oblivion, for whatever "dream-honey" might be, the dreams it brought with it when he took too much weren't nice ones.

He'd sighed and looked at the clothes. There was no point in putting it off. He might as well look as if he belonged here.

⟶

THAT had been a moonturn ago. One morning he had awakened at dawn in a full-blown panic, and only after several minutes of thought had he realized that this must be his day to go to the Temple of the Light and change out his City Talisman. Only he didn't have his Talisman, and they weren't likely to let him back into the City, now, were they?

After that, things got easier. His days settled into a routine of chores—once Marlen saw that Cilarnen was steady and trustworthy, he left more and more of the work of the stables to him. A stables built to accommodate the needs of Centaurs was an odd-looking thing, and of course the horses were draft horses, not riding horses—what would Centaurs need with riding horses?—but the animals were of good quality, and Cilarnen got on with them well enough.

"But what does King Andoreniel *say,* Father?" Sarlin demanded, bringing Cilarnen back to the present.

"You will find out soon enough," Grander said firmly.

⟶

ON Sarlin's way out the door, Cilarnen stopped her. Grander had been very mysterious about this message, and Cilarnen no longer had any taste for mystery. "Is Andoreniel your King?" he asked.

Sarlin stared at him for a moment, her broad face blank

with surprise. "Oh," she said at last. "But how could you know? You are from the human city, after all. No. Andoreniel is the King of the Elves."

And before Cilarnen could think of another question to ask, she was gone on her errand.

HE was not permitted to attend the Council, of course. He found out soon enough what it was about, as Centaurs weren't a terribly secretive lot—the Elven King was calling for the Centaurs to honor an ancient treaty, and send troops to his aid—but what no one would ever quite explain was *why*. They all said things like "Andoreniel wouldn't ask without good reason," or "we must honor our treaty," or "he would come if *we* asked," until Cilarnen wasn't sure whether the Centaurs knew why they were going or not.

Or whether they just didn't trust him enough to tell him.

What he *did* know was that it was some kind of emergency that couldn't wait until spring and better weather for traveling, and that one of the units would be mustering here at Stonehearth before traveling on. The whole village threw itself into preparations—packs must be sewn, storm cloaks reoiled, armor looked to, ice-boots fitted, provisions sorted out.

And Marlen seemed determined to spend every moment he wasn't training to go with them, cramming every possible detail of what to do for the horses in any conceivable emergency into Cilarnen's head.

Because Cilarnen wasn't going.

It wasn't that he *wanted* to go. It was just that he hated being dismissed as if he were useless. And . . . not that a bunch of talking animals were his *friends* of course, but he'd gotten *used* to Marlen and Grander. And to all of the others who were leaving. After they were gone, things would be different. And all of the changes Cilarnen had experienced recently had not been good ones.

There was almost enough work to keep him from thinking

of things like that, though, until the day when Stonehearth's gates were thrown open to the visitors.

A messenger—a Centaur this time—had arrived the day before to bring word of their arrival, and so by the time the troop cantered up, the great feast was nearly ready. Every house had been cooking and baking since the night before, and the entire village smelled like a cookshop. This afternoon there would be a great feast in the village square—he'd heard the hammering all morning as the trestle tables were knocked together—and tonight every home would hold visitors, for Stonehearth would be hosting fifty guests.

And tomorrow they would all be gone.

Maybe I'll just stay here until it's all over, Cilarnen thought, leaning his head against the flank of a grey mare. She'd been out in the paddock all morning, and her thick winter coat was clotted with ice. It needed careful brushing—but he had been at Stonehearth nearly two moon-turns now, and in that time he had become an excellent ostler.

He still wondered why the Centaurs didn't just hitch *themselves* to the plows. Maybe they did. Maybe they used the horses for something else. He'd undoubtedly get the chance to find out, if this Light-blasted snow ever melted.

He hadn't thought it was possible to be so cold. And even if his Gift hadn't been excised, there wouldn't be much he could do about the weather. He'd been an Entered Apprentice. You had to be a Master Undermage to do something about the weather.

He finished with the mare and looked about for something else to do, shaking his head at the Centaurs' foolishness. An outdoor banquet, in winter, without Mages to work the weather.

They'd all freeze.

"Cilarnen!" Sarlin came trotting into the stable, her cheeks flushed pink with the cold. "Come and see! The troop has arrived—and it's nearly noon! You'll want to have a wash before the banquet. And I made you a new tunic. A gift."

He was unreasonably touched. He knew that Sarlin saved

much of the money she earned from the sale of her cloth and finished clothing—she owned, Cilarnen had been surprised to discover, her own flock of sheep—to go toward her bride-money, which she would use to help set up her own house-hold when she married.

"Well, I'd better not wear it then," he said gruffly, to hide his feelings. "It will only be ruined by the snow that will undoubt-edly fall today. Whoever heard of eating outdoors in winter?"

But Sarlin only laughed merrily. "Oh, don't be foolish, City-man! They have brought a Wildmage with them, and he has done magic so that the weather will be fine!"

"A . . . Wildmage?" She might have said, "A Demon of the Dark" and Cilarnen would not have been less stunned. Except he didn't believe in Demons, and he *did* believe in Wildmages. He'd heard rumors that Farmer Kellen's disap-pearance had had something to do with Wildmagery. He hadn't believed them at the time, but . . . what if they were true? And what if Kellen had escaped the City, just as he had?

If Kellen was here, he was definitely the last person Cilar-nen wanted to see. And he certainly didn't want to see a Wildmage, whether it was Kellen or not.

But Sarlin had him by the arm, and was tugging him deter-minedly toward the house, so it was follow gracefully or be stepped on by great lumping Centaur hooves. And they had to pass through the village square on the way to Grander's house.

Despite himself, he looked for the Wildmage. And saw him, too. He was easy to spot—the only human in the great jostling press of Centaurs. To Cilarnen's relief, it wasn't Kellen, but a muscular fellow with a great black beard, wear-ing a large broad-brimmed hat and a fur cloak, looking more barbaric than the talking beasts surrounding him.

"Do you want to meet him?" Sarlin asked eagerly, slowing down. "His name is Wirance. He comes from High Reaches, in the mountains. We trade with the High Reaches at Mid-summer Fair—they're all humans there. Do you think you'd like to live in the High Hills? I hear it snows all the time there—"

"Come on!" Cilarnen demanded, and this time it was he who dragged Sarlin away.

～

THE new tunic was very fine. Cilarnen regarded it with a dull anger that he had not felt since he had first come to Stonehearth. It was of the softest, thickest lambswool, tightly woven and dyed a deep russet red, a cloth that would have fetched a premium price even in Armethalieh.

Sarlin had said that the Centaurs traded with the Mountain Folk. Armethalieh traded with the Mountain Folk as well. He wondered how many times before in his life he'd worn cloth woven by Centaurs and not known it.

The front and sleeves were covered with delicate, painstaking embroidery: Sarlin's finest work. This, he knew, would never have been permitted in the City—the colors were too exotic, the pattern of fruits and flowers and birds like nothing he'd ever seen before.

It was beautiful.

He hated . . .

He didn't know *what* he hated, but right now Cilarnen desperately wanted to hate something. There just didn't seem to be any suitable candidates. He thought he could manage to hate the Elves, if he worked at it for a while, since Hyandur was an Elf, and it was Hyandur's fault he was here. And now King Andoreniel—another Elf—was taking away most of the male Centaurs from the village, and it was Andoreniel's fault a Wildmage was here as well.

But Hyandur had saved Cilarnen's life, risking not only his, but Roiry's and Pearl's lives as well. And you couldn't expect Elves to know that the Wild Magic was, well, *wrong.*

Or is it just wrong in the City? a small voice inside him asked. Cilarnen shook his head. Wasn't wrong in one place wrong everywhere?

He wished there was someone he could ask.

He stripped down and washed quickly, then put on his new tunic. Sarlin would want to know how he liked it.

It is the most beautiful thing I've ever owned.

Why did the truth seem like a betrayal of something to which he no longer felt any loyalty?

⟳

TO Cilarnen's great relief, he was placed far away from Wirance at the banquet, among younger sons and apprentices, where he suffered—in silence—much good-hearted teasing about his new tunic. His head was starting to ache— as it hadn't in longer than he could remember—and he took great advantage of the pitchers of mulled ale that were kept constantly filled. He still hated the taste, but he'd come to like its effect.

He had no idea whether Stonehearth was large for a Centaur village or not. It was tiny by the standards of Armethalieh, and maybe even by the standards of the Delfier Valley farming villages, and so the Square was completely filled with the banquet tables. The village gates had even been left open to make more room—which was just as well, or else the apprentices would have been crammed against the walls. As it was, Cilarnen was in a certain amount of danger of being kicked and jostled by his fellows, but Centaurs were much smaller than the draft horses he tended daily, and he could hardly remember when he'd stopped worrying about it.

He was intent upon his food—and wondering if he could slip away to the stables without anyone noticing—when a stranger appeared at the gates.

Even for one of the talking beasts, his appearance was outlandish.

He wore armor, but not the simple steel that the other Centaurs wore. Over a heavy woolen tunic, he wore a shirt that seemed to be made of disks of metal sewn together. It dangled down almost to his knees in front, and spread across his withers behind. He wore a sword as well, hung parallel along his body, in the way that Cilarnen had seen other Centaurs carry swords. About his hips he wore a wide belt to which was affixed a number of small pouches, as well as a host of other ornaments that flashed and jingled. Around his neck, over the armor, was a necklace containing more such ornaments, and still more were braided into his waist-length hair. His hair was black, with a broad white streak in it, and despite the weather, he wore no cloak against the cold, though Cilarnen could see one—along with a small pack—lashed upon his back. Three of his feet were white, and one was black. He carried a long staff in one hand, although Cilarnen couldn't imagine why a Centaur would need one.

Seeing that Cilarnen was staring in the direction of the snow-covered fields, one of the other apprentices looked up.

"It is Kardus Wildmage!" he said. "Kardus Wildmage has come to join us!"

There was a great bustle as two of the apprentices—Tolin and Barcis—trotted forward to greet Kardus. Cilarnen hunched down in his seat, hoping they would escort the new arrival to the High Table where the esteemed guests were being feted. If he was a Wildmage—impossible as that seemed—undoubtedly they would want to honor him.

But to Cilarnen's dismay, Kardus seemed to wish to sit with the apprentices. And worse, next to the only human among them.

Him.

In Armethalieh, Mages were treated with dignity and proper respect. Apparently no one here had ever heard of that notion. Before Kardus had even removed his winter gauntlets and had a place laid for him—or gotten a mug of ale—the apprentices were pelting him with questions like the rowdy colts and fillies that they were. Where had he come from? Who had he seen? What was the news? Was he going to the Elven Lands with Captain Kindrius and Master Grander?

"How can you be a Wildmage? I thought Centaurs couldn't do magic," Cilarnen said, goaded out of his silence.

"And so I cannot, young human," Kardus said good-naturedly. "But I study the Three Books, and the Great Herdsman has given me the ability to know things unseen, and so I go where I am needed and do what I am given to set my hand to. And just as with my greater brethren, with each Knowing comes a Task."

"And do you have an, er, Knowing and a Task now?" Cilarnen asked. The others all stared at him, as if shocked by his presumption. But it was what they all wanted to know, wasn't it?

"Perhaps it would be best not to pluck that fruit before it ripens," Kardus answered calmly, reaching for the platter of roast meat in front of him. "And now. The news from Merryvale. The village flourishes, and Jenna has accepted Alfrin, so you may look for a great festival at Midsummer Fair. A new dozen of skeps have been put up, and Miele has split her swarm, so there will be more honey soon for you greedy ones, if you have sugar to trade—"

AS he spoke of the news from Merryvale—where he had meant to winter—Kardus saw the City-human slip away from the feast, thinking himself unobserved. He spoke on, though his mind was far from the gossip of the villages.

Since his Books had come to him as a young colt, he had followed the pattern of Tasks and Knowings set out for him by the Wild Magic. Though his race did not have the power to cast spells, the Great Herdsman taught that each had its place in the Great Cycle. And so his Knowings came to him, and he went where he was needed, doing what he could to set things into harmony with the Great Cycle. He had wide knowledge of the world, gained through years of travel, and if he did not have spellcraft to aid him, his knowledge of herbcraft—and the charms and potions given him by other Wildmages—were his to use.

And—just as his greater brethren did—he paid the price of each Knowing with a Task.

He had received his Knowing in Merryvale: to come to Stonehearth and be here to aid the human boy that he would find here. Perhaps the Knowing would unfold itself further once he had spent more time here. That the boy was unhappy it did not take a Wildmage to ken, but how a human boy had come to be so far from his own folk—and what Kardus's part in taking the Herdsman's Path might be—that he could not yet see.

But one did not herd ducks by chasing them, that much Kardus *did* know.

IT was no use. He was surrounded by them—Centaurs, Wildmages, and now something that managed to be an unholy combination of *both.* Excusing himself from the table as politely as he could—he no longer really had any appetite—Cilarnen left the feast.

Everyone in Stonehearth—down to the foals born that spring—was in the square, so Cilarnen had the rest of the village to himself. All he really wanted was the chance to be by himself for a while, but it seemed he was to be denied even that, because he hadn't wandered for very long before he saw someone else.

It was another human, a silver-haired man, dressed all in white. His garments were fine, and if they were not familiar in style to Cilarnen's eye, they were certainly more well cut and stylish than anything he'd seen on either the Centaurs or the human Wildmage. He must have come in with the Centaurs and found he had as little taste for the rustic feast as Cilarnen did.

The stranger smiled mockingly, seeing Cilarnen. "So, Arch-Mage's son Kellen, what a surprise to see you here. Have you tired of the Children of Leaf and Star and think to make your way back to the Golden City? You have nothing to return to now. Your father claims another as his son. He has given him the seat on the High Council that was to have been yours. And daily our foothold in the City grows stronger . . . "

Cilarnen stared at the man in shock. *The stranger thought he was Farmer Kellen.* As if he looked *anything* like the Mad Farmboy!

His shock—and denial—must have showed plainly on his face, for suddenly the stranger's face contorted in a snarl of furious realization.

And kept on twisting—

It—abruptly Cilarnen could no longer think of the stranger as "he"—began to grow, its white clothes vanishing like smoke. Its skin turned as red as if blood had blossomed from every pore, and great curving horns sprouted from its forehead at the same time enormous bat-wings shot out from its back. It growled and lunged at him, as fast as a cat might pounce upon a mouse.

If Cilarnen had not been Mageborn, he might have died in that instant. But if he did not have his Gift, he was at least used to seeing the impossible. He did not stand staring in disbelieving amazement. He turned and ran.

He felt a stabbing pain behind his eyes—worse than any pain that had ever preceded it. It made him reel blindly into a wall—the second thing that saved him—but before he could catch his breath, the pain was gone, taking even the memory of pain with it.

Fool! That thing isn't done with you yet!

He sensed the next attack seconds before it arrived, and in panic he acted without thinking, summoning up Mageshield to protect him.

And it was there.

Cilarnen and the Demon both stared at the dull violet

shimmer that hung in the air between them in equal amazement. Then the monster smiled, showing Cilarnen a mouth full of long sharp white fangs.

"Oh, Mage-man, I do so enjoy a challenge. Prepare your best spells. I'll be back for you."

Spreading its hideous scarlet wings, it leaped into the air and vanished.

Cilarnen slumped against the wall, panting as though he'd run at least a league. His Gift was back! He could feel it. And—maybe—the monster was gone. He could tell Grander—ask him what to do, what it had been . . .

No. He *knew* what it had been.

But that was impossible.

Demons did not exist.

His nurse had used to frighten him with tales of Demons. The walls of Armethalieh kept them out, but children—very bad children—called them in. And then they took bad children away into the Dark . . . and ate them. Demons had claws, and fangs, and long sharp teeth, and the horns and tails of beasts, and great bat-wings to fly over the walls with, and they were red with the blood of all the bad children they'd eaten.

Cilarnen slumped against the wall in despair. He hadn't thought about Demons in years. They weren't mentioned in the Cosmology of the Light, though it mentioned the Lesser Races. They hadn't been mentioned in his magickal studies, though those studies had covered the Elementals, the Lesser Races, the Embodiments of Magick, and the Illusory Creatures.

Demons are a nursery tale, he told himself desperately. *A Myth of Error.*

Then he heard the first screams. And over them, the Demon's shrieks of laughter.

⌒

"I wonder why he's come?" Grander mused, looking down the table to where Kardus sat at the center of a group of rowdy apprentices. It was a great honor to host two Wildmages—and one of them the only Centaur Wildmage anyone had ever heard of, besides!—but he did wonder.

"Perhaps because all of you are going," Wirance suggested. "I shall be sure to see what I can do for him before we leave tomorrow."

"I admit he's a useful fellow. Good to have on your side in a fight, too. Or when you don't want to fight. I remember a time when—" Kindrius began.

With an unearthly shriek, the Demon landed in the center of the table. The table collapsed beneath its weight, sending cups and platters flying everywhere.

For a moment, there was absolute silence. Some of the Centaurs at the farther tables began slowly to edge away, trying not to be noticed, but the ones closest to the Demon were frozen in terror.

"Mages *everywhere*," it purred, staring at Wirance with hot yellow eyes. "Oh, this is going to be *fun*."

Then it reached out, grabbing the nearest Centaur and yanking her toward it. It bit through her throat in one quick motion. She reeled back, choking and flailing as blood fountained from her ruined throat.

Someone screamed, and suddenly everyone was screaming and shouting. The Demon sprang away, licking its chops, to land on the back of another Centaur, wrenching the Centaur's head nearly off its shoulders before bounding away again.

"To arms!" Kindrius bellowed to his men.

"Get to your homes!" Grander shouted, equally loudly.

What had been a happy celebration moments before was now a panicked herd of Centaurs that the Demon attacked at will. Though they had worn their armor, the Centaur warriors had not brought their weapons or shields to the feast. Some ran to fetch their arms; other armed themselves with what they could grab from the table and attacked the Demon.

It was useless. The Demon turned on its attackers, its claws shearing through steel armor and leather padding as though it were the lightest linen. It seemed to delight in

wounding and crippling rather than killing, and soon the
screams of the injured were added to those of the merely
terrified.

And when it seemed that matters could get no worse, the
Demon added magic to its attacks.

It rose into the air and hovered, wings spread wide. It
pointed, and everywhere it pointed, something exploded or
burst into flame. Soon most of the houses around the square
were in flaming ruins. It pointed at the well, and the housing
dissolved in a spray of lethal stone shards. A great jet of water fountained into the sky, then water began flowing slowly
over the stones of the village square.

They could not reach it with swords—not that swords had
been able to cut its scarlet hide—but the Centaur warriors
were armed now with spear and bow, and the archers began
to fire from what cover they could find.

None of the missiles found their mark. The Demon batted
them all aside, laughing madly as if this were all great fun.
Even Kardus's arrows, which carried charms upon them, did
not find their mark.

⟶

WE *will all die here,* thought Wirance in despair. He
crouched inside the doorway of one of the few houses that
had so far escaped the Demon's attention and watched with
increasing fury as it slaughtered the Centaurs as easily as a
wolf might destroy a nest of field mice.

None of his spells were strong enough to defeat the
Demon—he thought he might be able to hold it for a moment or two, if he could Cast successfully, but the Demon
had marked him for its most dangerous enemy and broke
each of his Castings before it was fully formed.

*There must be something! By the First Frost, I must think
of something!*

⟶

CILARNEN could hear the sounds of the carnage even three streets away. The taste of his terror was sour in his throat. He had never been this frightened in his life. Not in the cell. Not looking at the Outlaw Hunt.

He could get away. He had his Gift back. That would be useful somewhere else. He could get away. Not out the Main Gate—that would be blocked—but there was another gate. Maybe the Demon wouldn't look for him. Maybe it would think it had already killed him. Maybe the Centaurs would kill *it*.

Cilarnen got to his feet and started walking slowly toward the Little Gate.

And stopped.

No.

These were his friends. They didn't care who Cilarnen *Volpiril* was—they didn't know a thing about House Volpiril, or the High Mages, or Armethalieh. They didn't want anything from him. They were just his friends. They had helped him even though they didn't have to.

Maybe he couldn't help them now. He didn't know much about Demons—he hadn't believed in Demons until a few minutes ago—and even if he *did* have his Gift, most of his spells were useless without the equipment to do a proper Working. He didn't even have a wand, for Light's sake!

But there was one spell he didn't need a Wand for, and he bet even Demons feared it.

He hoped they did.

He turned toward the Square and began to run.

⌐

HE reached the edge of the square and stopped. He'd never seen—never imagined—a sight like the one which greeted him. Bodies were everywhere. The cobblestones were slick with fresh blood. The houses that bordered the square were in ruins, burning. The well had been smashed, and water was sluicing over the stones, making the footing treacherous.

Cilarnen could see that the Wildmage kept trying to cast some kind of spell—he could actually *see* the energy—but the Demon kept breaking the spell before it could form. It could not strike the Wildmage, but others weren't so lucky. Cilarnen saw flesh crisped to ash—and worse. Even while he gaped at the fight in shock and horror, he saw the Demon's magic strike a young Centaur's hindquarters, and watched the flesh turn black and fall away from the bone like hot fat.

It should have made him sick. But somehow seeing what the Demon could do didn't make him more afraid. It made him hard and still inside; more determined—and more *angry*—than he had ever felt before. He stepped away from the wall he'd been hiding against and out into the Square.

Cilarnen raised his hand, summoning the power of the High Magick.

And the Demon burst into flame.

Burn! Cilarnen commanded, putting all his will into the demand, all his anger, all his fear. When he felt himself falter, he merely had to allow himself to see the dead and the dying scattered about the Square, and his fury welled up in him again. Never mind that a Mage was supposed to conduct all spellcasting in sublime detachment from everything and everyone; this rage gave him power he didn't even know he had.

He did not stop—a candle could not will itself to extinguish, but the Demon could—but willed Fire again and again—

—until, suddenly, unfamiliar weakness drove him to his knees.

And the Demon, its body charred and blackened, dropped from the sky.

⇌

WIRANCE felt the tingle of unfamiliar magic, and suddenly the Demon burst into flames.

For a moment he thought it was a trick, a trap, but then the Demon roared with pain, flailing wildly in the air as it sought to extinguish the flames that raced over its body.

Wirance glanced toward the edge of the square, following the line of magic stretched across the sky, and saw a slender human youth pointing his hand at the Demon, his whole body rigid with concentration and fury.

I don't know what you're doing, boy, but keep it up!

Kardus hurried to Wirance's side, forcing his way through the press of warriors. In his hands he held a thin length of shining white cord.

"I think—" the Centaur Wildmage began.

"Pray," Wirance said grimly, and readied his spell.

The Demon had stopped fighting now, and hung in the sky, a burning ember, its wings skeletal, its body ash and bones. But the moment the strange burning spell was lifted, it would begin to heal, and in moments it would be whole—and more savage than before.

Wirance waited for the instant the light of the burning spell flickered out, then struck with his own. This time it held: the Demon's body fell to the ground, surrounded by a white glow of Restraint.

"Quickly!" Wirance shouted, his voice harsh. "I cannot hold this spell for long!"

Kardus lunged forward, the rope of unicorn hair in his hands. He fell to his knees, looping it about the Demon's neck, and jerked it tight. The seared Demonflesh crackled as the unicorn hair burned through it, shearing through the neck and windpipe, and with a crack the head rolled free.

A moment later, the whole body dissolved into ash, and began to swirl away in the water.

Silence.

A terrible, heavy silence.

"Is it dead?" someone asked hoarsely.

"Yes," Kardus said, lunging awkwardly to his feet. "The Demon is dead."

Then the moaning, the weeping, the agonized cries for help began.

Wirance looked around. The village square resembled nothing so much as a slaughtering pen. In the cold, steam rose from the shattered bodies of the living and the cooling bodies of the dead, and the air was filled with smoke. He looked at Kardus. "We both have much work to do here. But we had best go find the boy first."

"His name is Cilarnen," Kardus said. "He is my Task."

Fifteen

At the Siege of Stonehearth

Cilarnen had not gone far. He was too weak to stand, but he had crawled back around the corner of the building and was curled up against it, trying to shut out the sobbing and groans of the wounded. His eyes streamed tears. But he was not weeping. No, not he. Surely.

"Cilarnen," Wirance said, squatting down beside him, "are you hurt?"

"It thought I was Kellen, you see," Cilarnen explained—reasonably, he thought. "And then it realized I wasn't. So it killed everybody. It tried to kill me first, but I still had my Gift. Lord Anigrel was supposed to take it, but he didn't. That was wrong of him, wasn't it? They're supposed to take your Gift when they Banish you."

"We don't know what you're talking about," Kardus said gently. "We know who Kellen Wildmage is. Kellen came from Armethalieh. Did you come from Armethalieh too?"

"Yes," Cilarnen said, sitting back and looking up at the two Wildmages. "I'm a Mage of Armethalieh. I was, anyway. An Entered Apprentice."

"And you used your Armethaliehan magic on the Demon?" Wirance asked.

"I used Fire," Cilarnen said, his voice thick with exhaustion, and with what was certainly not weeping. It was hard to form words. But now—now his vision was clearing at last, and—he was tired. So tired. He couldn't even think, he was so tired. All he wanted to do was sleep. "Even an Apprentice can do that."

"I know nothing of Armethaliehan magic. How do you pay for your spells?" Wirance asked.

Cilarnen stared at him in utterly exhausted irritation. There must be a thousand things that needed doing right now. Why was this man sitting here with him asking how the High Magick worked?

"Pay? You don't 'pay' for spells in the High Magick." Something occurred to him in the back of his mind, something about the Talismans, but the thought flew away and escaped him.

"All magic has a price, young Apprentice, and woe to your teachers that they did not teach you this. You have paid dearly for the spell you cast today, and now you must rest," Wirance said.

He put an arm under Cilarnen's shoulders, and lifted him to his feet. Cilarnen staggered, the world reeling greyly around him. Despite himself, he clutched at Wirance for support.

"It is as I said," Wirance said implacably.

Suddenly arguing with Wirance didn't seem worthwhile any longer.

"I will take him to a place where he may rest, then return to aid you," Kardus said, putting his arm around Cilarnen. Cilarnen leaned against the Centaur gratefully.

To his relief, they did not return to the square, but went back along the same back street he'd gone down not so long before. Kardus seemed to know Stonehearth as well as Cilarnen did.

When they reached the place where Cilarnen had encountered the Demon, he flinched, as if it somehow might still be here.

"It was here," Cilarnen said shakily. "It looked human."

"They can appear in any guise they choose," Kardus said.

Suddenly the Demon's words came back to him, as if he were hearing them at that very moment. Not the part about Kellen. That was Kellen's problem—and if Kellen really *was* a Wildmage, he wouldn't care if Lycaelon had supplanted him or not. But the rest:

And daily our foothold in the City grows stronger . . .

Were there Demons in the City?

"Wait—wait!" Cilarnen gasped. "It told me—it said—when it thought I was Kellen—that the Demons have a foothold in the City—in Armethalieh. I've got to tell . . . "

Who? Who could he tell? He couldn't return to the City. He probably couldn't even cross the Border and live.

"I've got to tell someone," Cilarnen said desperately.

"Indeed you must," Kardus agreed. "You must tell Kellen Wildmage, for he makes war against the Demons, and if there are Demons in Armethalieh, he will make war against them as well. It is my Task to bring you to him, but we will speak further of that when you are rested."

❦

KARDUS took him to the stables, not to Grander's house, but Cilarnen was so exhausted he didn't think to question it. He took a horse blanket and curled up in an unused stall, and was asleep before Kardus had left the stables.

When he woke again it was dark, and the stillness in the air told him it was snowing. There was no light in the stable, but he knew his way around it by touch after so long, and groped his way to the lantern and tinderbox.

He was reaching for the flint and steel when he realized he would never need them again. He concentrated, and the lantern bloomed into light.

He felt dizzy for a moment, and shrugged it off, closing the lantern door and watching the small flame steady to brightness. His momentary weakness didn't matter. What mattered was why he should be able to do this at all—or should have been able to cast the Mageshield that had saved his life when the Demon had first attacked him. His Gift should be gone, burned from his brain.

But it hadn't been. It had merely been . . . sleeping. And

this made no sense at all. He was grateful, no, more than grateful, he was elated—but it made no sense at all.

No Mage would have let him leave the City with his Gift intact, even if they expected him to be dead within bells. And it could not be an accident.

It must have been deliberate.

Undermage Anigrel had done this deliberately. But why? Had he hoped that the young Apprentice, if he left the Gift intact, could somehow use the High Magick to get himself beyond the reach of the Hunt? But that couldn't be right, because his magick *hadn't* worked when he'd first tried it.

Cilarnen shook his head. Whatever Undermage Anigrel's motives, he had more pressing concerns now. He picked up the lantern and left the stable.

It was snowing, and the snow had swept the smell of smoke from the air. It should have been peaceful; it wasn't. It was early evening, but the streets were oddly dark and quiet. Without cloak or hood, Cilarnen shivered in the cold night air. He felt unnerved and unsettled, and the silence filled him with an edgy energy.

He'd meant to go directly to Grander's house—as he shook off the last veils of sleep, he became more worried about what had happened to his friends—but as he walked up the street, he neared the tavern next to the smithy and finally started to hear voices. He hurried toward them.

As he approached, a strange Centaur male hailed him.

"You! Grander's boy! Come and help!"

Cilarnen came at a run.

The Centaur who had hailed him was one of the warriors who had arrived earlier that day. He was still bloody from the fight, and one arm was splinted and in a sling, but he looked vigorous enough. Looking past him, Cilarnen could see that both the forge and tavern had been converted to a makeshift hospital, and were filled with Centaur wounded.

"Someone said you were a Mage. Have you Healing skills?" the Centaur demanded.

Cilarnen shook his head, his spirits falling. "None," he said. "Wirance—or Kardus—"

"Both occupied with worse cases than these. They will come when they can." The Centaur looked weary. "I had hoped . . ."

"If there is anything I can do, I will do it," Cilarnen said quickly. "I work in the stables. I know you are not horses, but—"

"An able body and a willing pair of hands counts for much, if you are not afraid of blood," the Centaur said.

"After today, I do not think I will ever be afraid of it again," Cilarnen said bleakly.

FOR the next several hours, Cilarnen worked at the direction of others, stitching wounds, changing poultices over burns, and helping to draw limbs straight so they could be splinted.

Because those who had been lucky enough to escape injury were needed elsewhere—to search through the rubble of smashed buildings for trapped survivors, to build firebreaks, and to lend their strength (whatever that meant: Cilarnen wasn't sure) to Wirance's Wildmage spells—the injured had been left to tend to each other. Cilarnen learned, in scraps of conversations during the work, that the snow was Wirance's doing, so that the fires the Demon had set could be contained and extinguished, since the well had been destroyed. Half the homes of Stonehearth had been either damaged or destroyed outright in its attack, though this part of the village, the farthest from the square, was untouched.

It seemed to Cilarnen that there was no end to the wounded and burned . . .

And then, suddenly, there was. He found himself with bandages in his hands, and no one to put them on. "Here," said Comild, taking them from him gently and putting them with the rest of the scavenged supplies. "Go and wash yourself—there's water over there." He pointed with his

chin, and Cilarnen saw a bucket, and at the same time, realized that his hands were sticky with blood and unguents.

Holding down a surge of nausea, he hastened to cleanse
himself as well as he could.

"It will not be too difficult to rebuild the well, though it
may be best to call for a unicorn to purify it," Comild said.

"I suppose," Cilarnen said vaguely, not understanding
what a unicorn could have to do with a well. He looked up at
the Centaur. "What are you going to do now? You're not going home, are you?"

Comild shook his head. "Kindrius is dead, but it remains
to be seen if any of the other sub-Captains still live. If they
do, we will choose a new leader from among our number. If
I am the only survivor, the honor is mine. And we go on,
wounded or not. We will recover, and our allies need us."

"You're going to be a Captain?" Cilarnen asked.

"Not the way I would choose it," Comild said broodingly.
"I hope your friends are well. Best go and see. There's little
more you can do for my men."

Tired once more—but in a different way now—Cilarnen
stepped out into the street again. It was dawn now. He'd
worked through the night. This time the cold air felt good.

He looked down at his tunic. He'd rolled up the sleeves
when he'd set to work, but the front was as bloody and soiled
as if he'd been working in a butcher's shop. He blinked back
tears. Sarlin's rich gift, ruined.

He was glad—suddenly desperately glad—that he'd been
able to find the words to thank her for it when she'd given it
to him. He hadn't meant them properly at the time. He
hadn't understood why he'd said it. He hadn't understood
himself.

He hadn't understood a lot of things.

He'd find her now. He'd explain. He'd thank her
properly—tell them all how much they meant to him.

He began to run.

THE street that Grander's house was on was one of the lucky ones; its houses were untouched, though the roofs of the houses on the opposite side showed some fire-gaps through the snow. The street was awake; every house was filled with refugees. Centaurs in full armor patrolled the streets, and Cilarnen realized with a sudden flare of alarm that where there was one Demon, there might be more. The village could be attacked again.

He heard his name called a couple of times, but did not stop. He had to get home.

He pushed open the door of Grander's house. The common room was filled with Centaurs. All were villagers familiar to him, but he saw no one that belonged to the household.

"Blessed Herdsman—it's Cilarnen!" Corela gasped. The kindly middle-aged Centauress started forward, her face a mask of shock. "We thought you must be dead—now, don't move. Where are you hurt?"

"I'm not hurt," Cilarnen said. "It's not my blood. I'm all right. Are you— Is—Where is—?" He looked around, still hoping to see familiar faces, and saw none.

"Come into the kitchen," Corela said, coming forward and putting an arm around his shoulders.

There was soup, tea, and hot ale in the kitchen. Corela dismissed the Centaurs working there with a glance, and closed the door behind them with one well-placed nudge of her hind hoof.

"There is bad news," she said. "It is best given quickly."

Cilarnen nodded, unable to ask.

"Grander and Marlen are gone to the Herd. They are truly dead. I've seen their bodies. Not pretty, but quick. Jarel has lost an eye, but he will live, they think, with scars to brag on. Erlock's leg will heal, but it is likely he will be lame. Minor injuries only to the others of this house—so minor that they were all able to share price with Wirance, and so they are sleeping now. Sarlin, too."

"They can't be dead," Cilarnen said blankly. *I never told them how kind they were to me. I never thanked them.*

"They have gone to the Herd," Corela repeated gently. "And they will be reborn as good spring grass to feed our flocks. Now wash and eat. There are many tasks that need doing."

"The horses," Cilarnen said, with a pang of guilty realization. It didn't matter what else had happened in the world. The horses still needed to be looked after—fed and watered and turned out for exercise. "I have to go to the stables. I'll be back as soon as I can."

"Wash first," Corela told him firmly. "And eat."

IT was good advice, so Cilarnen took it. He didn't think that the horses would appreciate it if he came to them reeking of blood.

Once he'd finished his morning stable chores, it occurred to him that nobody probably had time for *any* of Stonehearth's livestock that morning.

Well, he did. He didn't need to sleep yet. He wasn't sure he could. There was something inside him, something that made his chest and throat feel tight whenever he thought of Grander, something that wanted to burst out. It was worse than when he'd been caught and told he was going to be Banished.

Much worse.

He didn't want to be alone with it.

The sheep and goat-pens were outside the walls, guarded by shaggy herding-dogs in their kennels. The great beasts came rushing forward when Cilarnen appeared, barking savagely when they caught his scent, then sniffing and nudging at him hopefully.

No one has been here to feed them either, Cilarnen realized. The sheep and goats could eat hay, but that wouldn't do for the dogs. He'd have to go find something to feed them after he unpenned the animals.

The barking had roused the pens' inhabitants, and a great bleating and baa-ing issued from within. Cilarnen opened each door in turn, jumping out of the way quickly to avoid being trampled by the outrush of hairy and woolly bodies.

The herd dogs, abandoning immediate hope of food, rounded up their charges and began herding them down to the river for their long-delayed morning drink. While they were gone, Cilarnen went to the storage barn, unbolted the door, and began dragging shocks of fodder out, dumping them in the snow. Centaurs might be able to carry them, but he wasn't nearly as strong as a Centaur.

He had no idea how many were enough, or what to do with them, but at least the animals wouldn't starve.

"That's enough."

Cilarnen looked up, to find Kardus standing in the snow behind him. The Centaur Wildmage had a large canvas bag slung over one shoulder, and a knife in one hand.

"Bolt the door, or the goats will get in among the fodder and gorge until they burst." As he spoke, he began cutting the braided lengths of straw that bound the fodder-shocks together. "Then help me spread this over the snow, or the strong will keep the weak away from the food."

By the time the dogs brought the herds back, Kardus and Cilarnen had covered the snow with hay, and both sheep and goats settled to browsing contentedly. Kardus reached into his bag and pulled out several large brown loaves. He tossed one to each of the waiting dogs, who were standing by expectantly. As they gulped them down, Cilarnen saw that the loaves were meat and bread mixed together, obviously what the dogs were used to receiving.

"I told Toria I would see to the flocks today," Kardus said. "But I see you got here first."

"I'd done the stables," Cilarnen said. "I didn't think anyone would have thought about the other animals yet."

"They have thought," Kardus said. "But there are many dead and injured, and not enough hands to do the work."

My friends are dead, Cilarnen thought bleakly, feeling his throat tighten and eyes sting again. And everyone in Stonehearth had lost friends. It was a small village. Everyone knew everyone else.

"Kardus—why did the . . . Demon . . . come here? Do you know? Tell me!"

But the Centaur Wildmage only shook his head wordlessly.

—

"CAN anyone tell me," Savilla asked with spurious mildness, "just *why* there was an open attack on that grubby Centaur village?"

Her highest-ranking nobles were gathered before her in the formal Audience Chamber, where she had summoned them as soon as the word of Yethlenga's attack upon Stonehearth had reached the World Without Sun. She did not know why he had attacked—and she could not ask him before she killed him, for the Lightborn had managed, not merely to defeat him, but to destroy him.

To destroy one of the eternal, beautiful children of *He Who Is*.

For that they would pay in the last full measure of pain and despair, but Savilla would not hurry either her pleasures or her vengeance.

Her own spies ranged freely and far, wherever magic and ancient land-wards did not constrain them. She had agents—both Endarkened and otherwise—in the Wild Lands—but Yethlenga had not been one of them. Her creatures knew better than to risk her displeasure by showing themselves openly, no matter what the personal cost.

"I will know what I will know," Savilla said dangerously.

She sat upon the Shadow Throne, dressed in scarlet as red as her skin and white as pure as shattered, aged bleached bone. There was utter silence. No one dared to speak, even though their Queen had asked a question.

"Highness." Prince Zyperis broke the silence at last, crawling forward and bending low before her, wings tightly furled in submission. "Yethlenga's action goes so strangely against your wise counsel that perhaps it was only . . . childish foolishness."

"And so you would excuse it?" Savilla hissed. She reached out with one foot and placed it on his shoulder, digging in with her talons until the blood flowed.

Zyperis raised his head to meet her gaze, though the movement opened deeper gouges in his back. "Never. Only beg that you question those who will give you proper answers, my Queen," he said softly. "Ask those who have been his companions and servants. If they knew his plans, and did not tell you, that is treason, and must be properly punished."

Savilla straightened, and pushed Zyperis away from her with a kick that sent him sprawling, bending his wings painfully beneath him. She waved him to his feet with a languid gesture.

"Rise, all of you. Chamberlain, bring Yethlenga's household here to me. Now."

Soon an odd assortment of beings were ushered into the Audience Chamber—several Lesser Endarkened, the squat misshapen cousins of their greater brethren; a collection of humans, and a blind Centaur. All knelt immediately.

"Your master, Yethlenga, is dead," Savilla said without preamble. "Your lives and fortunes depend on what you can tell me now. I will reward truth, and punish lies."

"Great Queen, we will tell you everything," one of the Lesser Endarkened said. "And so will the vermin."

The slaves knew very little, but the questioning of the servants produced the names of two of Yethlenga's companions: Anilpon and Iroth.

And when the slaves were sent to the Pits to await new masters, and Anilpon and Iroth were sent for, they could not be found.

"Where are they?" she demanded of her chamberlain.

"We are searching for them, Queen Savilla," Vixiren, underbutler to her household, said.

The tension in the Audience Chamber eased, just a fraction, now that Savilla's wrath had found a new target.

"It is nearly as good as a confession," Zyperis suggested.

Savilla glanced sharply at her son. He had been brave today, speaking out and risking her wrath. But had it merely been an attempt to divert attention from himself? Had Yethlenga been one of Zyperis's spies? Was this a conspiracy, and Anilpon and Iroth its other members?

Perhaps.

And perhaps not.

She did not think Zyperis was ready to challenge her just yet. And the attack upon Stonehearth had been—as he'd pointed out—strange. There was nothing to gain from killing a few Centaurs and terrorizing an isolated collection of mud huts. Zyperis would never make such a foolish mistake.

But was it so foolish?

Something at Stonehearth had been capable of killing one of the Endarkened.

And now she might never know what it had been.

⌒

"YOU *have* to know," Cilarnen pleaded.

"I do not lie to you when I tell you I do not," Kardus said. "I have traveled far—even into the Lost Lands, where the Dark Folk—as they call them there—raid among the folk as foxes among hares. But never have they come this far south since the end of the Great War. It is true that Andoreniel calls us to fight in honor of the ancient Treaties, but the Elves have seen only *Their* work, and *Their* creatures in the Elven Lands, not *They Themselves*."

"But one was here. And it said that *They* have agents in Armethalieh," Cilarnen repeated stubbornly, holding on to what he knew. So much of what Kardus was telling him simply didn't make sense to him, and he was really afraid to ask for an explanation.

What was the Great War? When had it been? Did it have anything to do with Armethalieh? Did that mean the Elves and Demons had fought before? What did that have to do with humans?

"Perhaps that is why the humans there would not heed the

Elves, when they tried to warn them," Kardus said. "I do not know. Perhaps Kellen Wildmage will know. We will ask him when we see him."

Would Kellen even care what happened to Armethalieh? Somehow Cilarnen doubted it.

Still, he had to try.

He turned and followed Kardus back toward the gate.

———

AT the end of three more days, the small party left Stone-hearth, heading for the Elven lands.

They left a badly damaged village behind them—and far too many dead—but in the days before they left, Wirance sent messages to the nearest villages, and help—in the form of food, supplies, and hands to help with the rebuilding—would soon arrive.

If it had been at all possible, Comild, Wirance, and the others would have waited until the others arrived. Nearly a third of the surviving Centaur soldiers were too badly injured to travel with them. But Kardus thought that Cilarnen's news must be brought before the Elves without delay, and Cilarnen reluctantly agreed, little though he wanted to meet the Elves.

And everyone agreed it was too dangerous for the two of them to travel alone.

Sarlin had given him a horse to ride. It was one of the draft horses—there was nothing else available in the Centaur village—but it was better than walking. She'd insisted he take it.

———

"YOU'VE already done so much for me," Cilarnen had said when she offered him the horse. She was the Lady of Stone-hearth now, and the responsibility weighed heavily on her young shoulders, but there was no one else to take it up. She had put aside her grief to take charge of the preparations for their leaving, gathering together supplies from the remains of the village's stores, finding clothing and armor for those whose possessions had been destroyed, making sure Cilarnen had proper clothing for the journey. Wirance had his own mount, of course—a sure-footed mule, the preferred form of transportation in the High Hills, especially in winter—but Cilarnen needed something other than his own two feet, or they'd not arrive at their goal until spring.

"You took me in, you and—and Grander, and Marlen—" His throat closed, and he swallowed hard. "I never told them . . . I never told you . . . "

Sarlin hugged him hard. "Oh, hush now, City-man! We knew. Hyandur told us how they'd hurt you there—how they'd killed all your friends, and worked their evil spells on you, and chased you off with their horrible stone dogs, and still you wouldn't say a thing against them because they were kin. That would put anybody off! And you worked hard for us, and never complained, and then . . . you saved our lives. You did. Wirance told us. The Herdsman gave you your magic back, and you saved us. The least we can do is give you a proper four legs to get on with."

"Oh, Sarlin!" Cilarnen said, caught halfway between laughter and tears. "I promise I'll come back—and I'll take good care of Tinsin, I will. I wish—"

"I wish Papa had been here to see this day," Sarlin said softly. "He always knew you'd amount to something, City-man. But go on with you. You've plenty to do to get ready. And don't worry about us. You won't know, being City-folk the way you are, but farming folk are tough. We'll get through this. We'll get a crop in the ground come spring—and come you back by Harvest, you'll see us doing well."

"I believe that, Sarlin. And we'll make sure you can," Cilarnen vowed.

He wasn't sure who "we" was—though it felt right to say it. Not the High Mages. They didn't care what happened to the folk of the Wild Lands—and they twice didn't care if those folk didn't happen to be human. And he wasn't sure—yet—whether the Elves cared either. But even if it was only he and Kardus—for Cilarnen knew by now that the Centaur Wildmage cared about all his people—Cilarnen would do his very best to see that Sarlin and her people were left to live their lives in peace.

"Be sure you do," Sarlin said, and kissed him lightly on the cheek. "Now go your ways."

⌐

THEY departed laden with small gifts: a packet of pastries, a skin of last year's mead, a well-wrapped honeycomb.

One thing that Cilarnen did not take with him was his phial of headache syrup. It had been nearly empty the day of the banquet, and Stonehearth's Healer had been one of those killed in the Demon's attack.

Even if she had not been, Cilarnen had the strong suspicion that his headaches had been linked to whatever had been blocking his Gift, for since it had returned, the one time he'd automatically taken a dose of the cordial, it had made him as sick as if he'd taken an overdose of it, and he'd given the rest of it to Sarlin for the use of the wounded.

Perhaps the headaches were gone for good.

⌐

THE entire village—or so it seemed—turned out the morning they left to see them off. Cilarnen was kissed and hugged and back-slapped by nearly everyone in the village—all of whom seemed to know some version of his role in the destruction of the Demon—until Cilarnen was grateful to clamber up on Tinsin's back and put himself beyond their reach. He wasn't sure how to gracefully ask them to stop thanking him when he felt deep down inside that they should be yelling at him for not helping sooner.

The big grey mare was not the ideal mount. She was a

draft horse, not used to having a rider. Cilarnen had practiced with her a few times in the past two days, and she'd
come to accept the idea of having someone on her back, but
not to like it. A set of tack had quickly been cobbled
together—really just a riding pad and stirrups—but though
he'd be in no danger of falling off, Cilarnen could already
tell he was going to be sore at the end of the day's ride.

It would still be better than walking.

Comild gave the signal, and the troop trotted out through
the gates of Stonehearth.

THEY stopped several hours later to eat and rest, at least
partly for the benefit of the two humans, who were grateful
for the chance to dismount and stretch their own legs for a
change. Not that Cilarnen's legs *hadn't* been stretched
already—quite too much, as a matter of fact, straddling the
draft horse's wide barrel.

As he'd been riding, Cilarnen had been thinking about the
future for a change. All the long sennights he'd been in
Stonehearth, he now realized, he'd thought no further than
his tasks for the day.

But the Demon's attack had changed everything. It wasn't
just that he had his Gift back—though that was part of it—or
finding out that the City he still loved, despite all it had done
to him, was in terrible danger. It was that somehow the world
had become much larger than he'd ever imagined it could
be, and he needed to find where he belonged in it, and what
he could offer it.

There were his Magegifts, of course, and as much training
as he possessed. More than his tutors had suspected, of
course, but how much use was it here, outside the City?

His Gift was fairly useless without the appropriate appa-
ratus. Much of that he could make, with the proper resources, but it was unlikely he'd have access to them
anytime soon. High Magick was so very complicated . . .

But there was one item he might be able to make right here, and it was absolutely essential, the first of all tools.

At their rest stop, he waited until everyone was finished eating, and then sought out Kardus. He found Kardus less intimidating than Wirance—he and the Centaur Wildmage seemed to be bound together, somehow, though Cilarnen still didn't understand Kardus's talk of Knowings and Tasks, any more than he'd understood when Wirance told him that magick had to be paid for. Commons paid for magick, not Mages.

"Kardus," he said, walking over to the Centaur. "Is there an ash tree around here anywhere?"

The Centaur Wildmage regarded him curiously. They were stopped in a forest of young trees, their branches winter-bare.

Cilarnen shrugged when Kardus said nothing. "I wouldn't know one tree from another. Is any of these an ash tree? Or a willow?"

"Willow trees grow best near water," Kardus said with a gentle smile. "But there is an ash here. I will take you."

He led Cilarnen away from the others, stopping before a slender tree with smooth grey bark, which looked pretty much like every other tree in the woods to Cilarnen. "And now?" the Centaur asked.

"I need a straight length of wood about as long as my arm and as thick as my thumb," Cilarnen said, gazing up at the tree. There seemed to be some suitable branches, but they were fairly high up. "Living wood."

And I have now merited Banishment all over again, speaking of the secrets of the Art with a non-Mage. Oh, well. They'll have to catch me before they can Banish me, Cilarnen thought with bleak humor.

Kardus reached out and put his palm against the trunk of the tree. "Dryad, if you sleep here, know that we do not ask this lightly. We will take only what we need, and use it well. I promise you this." He turned to Cilarnen. "Climb and cut. Take only what you need."

One of the gifts that the folk of Stonehearth had pressed upon Cilarnen at his leavetaking was a good heavy knife, more than capable of cutting through a tree branch if he was careful. But getting up the tree looked like more of a problem. At last, Cilarnen managed to reach the branch he was after by standing on Kardus's shoulders and clinging to the slender trunk of the ash for dear life.

That left him only one free hand. It would have been easier to just saw away a big cluster of branches near the trunk, and then take what he needed after it had fallen to the ground. He started to do that, but then he remembered Kardus's words.

He'd spoken to the *tree*. As if there might be something *alive* inside.

As if dryads were real.

Demons were real. Maybe dryads were more than Illusory Creatures.

Cilarnen hesitated, then adjusted the placement of his knife, reaching far out along the branch and feeling the strain in his shoulder as he stretched. At last the length of wood he wanted eased free.

And Cilarnen, caught off balance, fell sprawling into the snow.

He landed flat on his back, winded but unhurt—the snow was thick, and he hadn't fallen all that far.

He staggered to his feet, brushing snow from his clothes. He'd dropped both the branch and the knife, of course, but the knife had made a deep hole in the snow crust where it had fallen, and the branch was sticking up out of the snow like an arrow. He picked them up.

"Now you must thank the tree, for giving so graciously of herself," Kardus said.

"Is there really a dryad in there?" Cilarnen asked cautiously, turning toward the tree.

"I do not know. I do not have the magic to see her if she is there," Kardus said, a little wistfully. "And this would be her season to sleep, in any event. But it is always proper to give thanks for the bounty of forest and field—and to the Other-folk, even if you cannot see them."

Cilarnen nodded. "Thank you, dryad," he said to the tree. "I really need this." He felt strange talking to a tree—but then, he'd felt equally strange talking to Centaurs not so very long ago.

"Good," Kardus said approvingly.

Cilarnen looked down at the length of wood in his hands. It looked nothing like the polished, elegant tool he had used back in the City. "I need to trim this," he muttered under his breath.

He found an outcropping of rock and used it to steady the branch while he trimmed the ends flat. He carefully cut away all the tiny twiglets sticking out from it, measured it against his arm, and trimmed again.

Not elegant. But a wand of living ashwood. If it wasn't polished smooth with virgin beeswax and bound in fine silver, those things shouldn't matter.

"Eleph. Vath. Kushon. Deeril. Ashan."

The sigils every first-year student committed to memory. The building blocks of the High Magick. Cilarnen traced them in the winter air, whispering their names under his breath.

They hung before him, perfect shapes of colored fire.

Cilarnen let out his pent-up breath in a sigh of relief.

⟷

THE difficulty with finding the next lair of the Shadow Elves was that it might, literally, be anywhere. Or nowhere. This might have been the only enclave of the creatures—or the Elven Lands might be riddled with them. No one knew—and they dared make no assumptions.

And Vestakia was the only one who could find them.

If the Elves knew that, then Shadow Mountain must know it as well. Her life was in constant danger, for without Ves-takia, their only alternative was to seek out every cave in the

Elven Lands—and even the Elves weren't quite sure where they all were—and search them all blindly. And such a task could take an Elven lifetime to complete.

And that was time they did not have.

Not knowing where the next enclave of the Shadowed Elves might be, Redhelwar made the decision to regroup at Ondoladeshiron. The rest of the Elven Knights would have arrived by now, and the wounded could be better cared for there.

The army moved more slowly on its retreat, handicapped both by its burden of wounded and by the bitter winter weather. The only mercy was that none of the horses or unicorns had been hurt in the battle—Kellen didn't think he could have borne that.

Idalia, Jermayan, and Atroist worked tirelessly among the injured—the sword cuts were bad enough, but these were things that the Elven Healers were used to dealing with, and they were masters of the healing arts. But the wounds caused by acid and poison were resistant to everything the Healers could do, and there the skills of the Wildmages made all the difference.

Here Kellen faced a great dilemma. It was not that he was unwilling to help his friends and companions in every way he could, though no Knight-Mage would ever be as good a Healer as a true Wildmage—but the Wild Magic exacted a price for every spell, in the form of a task the Wildmage must complete in payment. What if one of those tasks somehow ran counter to doing what needed to be done here?

"Don't worry about it," Idalia told him, when he brought the question to her. "I don't *know* of course, but I'm pretty sure the Gods of the Wild Magic want Shadow Mountain out of the way as much as we do. They aren't likely to set you a Mageprice that will interfere with that. And you need the practice. Someday you might be the only Healer around, and what then?"

So at the end of each day, Kellen joined the others in the Healers' tents, doing what he could. Some of the prices he incurred were small and relatively easy to discharge, like going to comfort one of the unicorns whose rider had been slain. Some of them he could not discharge for years to come, if ever—like the order to visit the homeland of the Selken Traders.

And some were simply odd, like being told to forgive one whom he thought of as an enemy.

That was puzzling. Kellen didn't have any personal enemies. Armethalieh had banished him, but even he had to admit there was nothing personal about it. He was trying to exterminate the Shadowed Elves, but again, it was because they were Tainted, not because he hated them personally. He didn't get along with every single Elf in the army, or in Sentarshadeen, but as far as he knew, he didn't have any enemies in either place.

Still, if a personal enemy showed up, Kellen supposed he'd keep his Mageprice in mind and do his best to forgive whoever it was. Of course, that didn't mean he wouldn't kill that person, but he'd forgive them as well.

Between the long days of riding, and working half the night as a Healer, he was nearly always tired, and the icy conditions didn't help. It was hard to get to sleep at night, shivering in his blankets, and harder to wake up sooner than he wanted. He learned to get by on less sleep than he would ever have imagined possible, to both eat and sleep in Shalkan's saddle, and—somehow—stay alert for danger through it all.

WHEN they reached the Gathering Plain, Kellen saw that the encampment had grown, even without the presence of most of the knights from Ondoladeshiron, Sentarshadeen, Windalorianan, Deskethomaynel, and Thultafoniseen. He recognized the banners of Lerkalpoldara, Valwendigorean, Realthataladon, and Ysterialpoerin: the four northernmost of the Nine Cities had arrived.

And there were other tents—non-Elven tents—besides.

"Mountain Traders," Petariel said cheerfully. Though his leg was still stiff, the combination of Healer skill and Wild-magery had him back in the saddle once more. "I'm glad they're here. We can use more Wildmages. Oh, not that you're not very efficient, Kellen," he added teasingly.

"I think you said at the time that you'd rather be healed by a snow-bear than let me anywhere near you," Kellen re-minded him with a grin. "And if Gesade hadn't threatened to stand on you and hold you down, I might have gone and found a snow-bear."

"I should have let you," the unicorn said consideringly. "It would have been fun to watch. And we could have skinned it afterward, and the stubbornest Elf in the Flower Forest would have had a lovely new cloak."

"Only if I could have left the bear in it to share it with him," Kellen said.

Petariel's injury—a spear through the knee—had looked bad enough at first, but it was only a day or two later that the Healers had realized how serious the Shadowed Elf poison could be. Nothing they'd been able to do had stopped the spread of the infection that ate the flesh from within. Not even the touch of Gesade's horn had been able to purify it. Only a Healing Spell had been able to lift the Taint from the wound so that the Healer's drugs could take effect. By the time Kellen had been called to Petariel's side, the Unicorn Knight had been delirious with pain and poison . . . and a very bad patient.

KELLEN unharnessed Shalkan before seeing to anything else, but by the time the wagons carrying the rest of their gear got to the Unicorn Knights' encampment, a messenger had arrived as well. It was Dionan, a junior member of the General's staff.

"I See you, Kellen Knight-Mage," Dionan said, bowing.

"I See you, Dionan," Kellen said. He returned the bow as best he could with his arms full of Shalkan's armor.

"You're wanted in Redhelwar's pavilion in two hours," Dionan said. "He's gathering all the commanders, and everyone with special experience in fighting the Shadowed Ones."

That would be me, Kellen thought with an inward pang. "Thank you. I'll be there."

Two hours would barely give him enough time to change into the cleanest clothes he had—and maybe, if he was lucky—get some tea. His stomach growled. Food, unfortunately, was going to have to wait.

He set Shalkan's armor in a convenient location and went looking for his packs.

—

IDALIA left her palfrey with the horse-lines—someone else would untack Cella and turn her out with the herd, then clean her tack and bring it to Idalia's tent. There was little deference to rank among the Elves—at least not in the same way there was among humans—but the work of the Healers was hard and often dangerous, and that brought them a few privileges.

With Cella seen to, Idalia went off toward the Mountain Traders' camp to see if she could find some old friends and catch up on the gossip.

The wind here on the Gathering Plain was sharp and piercing—Idalia, having spent a winter in Ondoladeshiron several years earlier, had dressed for the weather, but even in fur-lined garments, with a heavy fur cloak over everything, she shivered in the wind. The Mountainfolk probably thought this was no more than a brisk spring day, though—it snowed early in the High Reaches, and spring thaw came late. Because of this, the Mountainfolk did very little farming, hunting and trading for most of their needs. They worshiped the Greater Powers in the form of the Huntsman and the Forest Wife, and were careful to do nothing to offend Them, lest They should withdraw the game and the fruits of the forest.

The tents of the Mountainfolk were designed to withstand the heaviest of snows, being low domes constructed of waxed canvas with thin rods sewn into the fabric to stiffen it. Once unfolded and staked into place, no amount of snow could collapse them, nor wind overset them. In fact—Idalia could see as she approached their encampment—all of the dun-colored tents had been edged around with high-packed snow for added warmth and stability, so that only the very tops protruded from the mounds of glistening white.

"Hail, stranger." A man anonymous in winter furs greeted her as she approached. "Are you lost?"

"Looking for old friends," Idalia answered, pushing back the hood of her cloak so he could see her face.

"By the First Frost—Idalia! Come to give me my mule back, have you?"

To Idalia's surprise and delight it was Kearn, one of her closest friends among the Mountain Traders.

"No more than you're here to give me my *tarnkappa* back, Kearn," she responded with a grin. "I'm fond of that mule, and I traded for her fair and square. Besides, she's back in Sentarshadeen, and I'm not going all the way there just to fetch her to you."

"Well met nevertheless," Kearn said. "I'm glad you made it away from the Wildwood safely. There's many that didn't, so I hear."

"What have you heard?" Idalia asked, more sharply than she'd intended. If not for the discovery of the presence of the Shadowed Elves, she'd intended to head south into the Wild Lands this winter, to try to discover more about the aftereffects of Armethalieh's ill-advised expansion of its Borders.

"Come along, and I'll tell you, then. It's not so very cold out here, but the wind on the flat makes my bones ache. Resel, come and keep watch. The Elves are good folk, to be sure," he said in an aside to Idalia, "but I think we understand them as little as they understand us, and a man can grow old waiting for them to come to the point when they want something. So it's best to have someone waiting at the entrance of the camp for when they show up, so we can try to find out what they want and give it to them as quickly as possible."

He led Idalia deeper into the camp, back to his tent. Idalia negotiated the low entryway with ease. The space inside was roomy enough, though of course it wasn't possible to stand upright, and dimly, though adequately, lit by a candle in a glass lantern. The sides of the lantern were thick, double-paned, and filled with water to magnify the flame—and for added safety, should the lantern break.

Idalia sat cross-legged in a corner while Kearn lit a small spirit-stove and quickly boiled tea.

It was nothing any Elf would have been willing to drink: black as *kaffeyah*, twice-boiled, and served with a generous dollop of frozen goat's butter for seasoning. But the extra calories were welcome in the cold mountain environment that was the Traderfolk's natural home, and the bitter salty taste was oddly refreshing. Idalia wrapped her hands around the wooden mug to warm them.

Kearn squatted down on his heels, holding his own cup, and gazed down at the pot as if seeking inspiration for his tale. At last, when Idalia was almost afraid she'd have to prompt him, he began.

"Last autumn, when you gave me the warning of what the City planned, I went home as swiftly as my girls would go, passing the word of Armethalieh's encroachment everywhere I stopped. We expected that we would see Lowlander folk coming into our mountains from the Wild Lands—aye, and Otherfolk too. I cannot say that we were happy at the thought, but neither would any of us choose to turn them away, and leave them to the mercies of the City-folk. So we did what we could to prepare, and hoped that the winter would be kind.

"At first they came in numbers. No one knew how far the City's thievery would go, so there was much confusion. We made all welcome who came—Centaurs whose homes lay closest to the old border, it was at first, and Lowlander humans who had no taste for City rule. Fauns came too—I did not see them myself, but they spoke to those who serve the Wife, and they said that all the Lowland Otherfolk were coming to us, creatures of air and earth, of river and lake and tree."

Kearn stopped, staring broodingly into his cup.

"But something went wrong," Idalia prompted at last.

"Oh, aye," Kearn said. "It did that. Many that we expected—that the Centaurs expected, that the humans expected, that the fauns told the Children of the Wife to expect . . . they never came.

"We did look for them, Idalia. We went down the trails— even into the new so-called City lands, for we have free passage as far as Nerendale, you know, for the trade caravans, and the City magistrates would not trouble us overmuch if they encountered us upon the road. We found a few Wildlanders still heading for the Reaches, and heard that some had decided to stay where they were and fight, though in the end the City pulled its borders back before it had even knocked upon the gates of half the villages in the Wild Lands. But the rest . . . ? I know no more than that. When word reached us that the City had tucked its tail between its legs and run craven, the farmers that had come to us returned home for the most part, since the children of the plow do not find our mountains hospitable. The rest are with us here, come to fight since they cannot farm. As for the Shining Ones, who can say? I think they would wish to return to their own lands if they could, and perhaps they have."

Idalia nodded. Kearn's story made little more sense to her than it did to Kearn, but what was certain was that it wasn't good news. There was no way to tell now how many folk— human, Centaurs, and Otherfolk—had simply vanished, but she could make a pretty good guess at *how* they had vanished.

Demons.

Demons needed blood and pain and death to fuel their magic, and while the raids they conducted on Atroist's people could have provided enough victims to do something like build the Black Cairn, they would have needed to replenish their store of power afterward. Armethalieh's attempt to annex the Wild Lands had provided the Demons with a perfect opportunity to conduct secret raids among the refugees, harvesting hundreds—perhaps—of victims, all unnoticed. In all of the confusion and chaos, who would have thought to look for Demon raids?

"You've thought of something," Kearn observed.

"Nothing encouraging," Idalia said, taking a swallow of her bitter black tea. "And it's not even a theory, really. Just a supposition."

Just then Resel poked his head into the tent's opening. "The Elves," he announced in long-suffering tones, "are looking for the sister of the Knight-Mage. I promised I'd look, else they'd have set the place on its horns. Do we have such an item as a sister anywhere about the camp, Kearn?"

"That," Idalia announced, setting down her mug, "would be me. I'd better go find out what they want. I thank you for your news, Kearn—though I'm not sure thanks is really the right word."

"It so rarely is these days. So much of the news is bad," Kearn agreed somberly. "Fare you well, then, Idalia."

He escorted her to the edge of the Mountainfolk camp, and Idalia, tucking her cloak tightly around her against the eternal winter wind, went off to find out who wanted to see her.

⟶

SHE caught up with Dionan fairly quickly. He had Vestakia with him, and they were searching among the Healers' tents, obviously looking for her.

"Idalia!" Vestakia cried, sounding breathless with relief. "We've been looking everywhere for you!"

"So I discover," Idalia said dryly. "Here I am. I See you, Dionan."

"I See you, Idalia Wildmage," Dionan answered, bowing respectfully. "Redhelwar asks, if you would find it convenient, if perhaps it would please you to join him in his tent."

No wonder the Elves drive the Mountainfolk crazy, Idalia thought wryly. From her long experience with the Elves, she had no difficulty understanding that she had been bidden to come to the Elven General at once—whether it "pleased" her or not. But few humans without equivalent experience of the Elves would find Dionan's words as easy to decode.

"Of course," Idalia said. "It would please me greatly," she added for good measure.

Dionan led her—and Vestakia as well—through the milling and confusion of the camp. Redhelwar's scarlet pavilion was an oasis of serenity in the midst of all the apparent disorder—though nothing in an Elven camp was ever really disorganized.

When they reached the tent, Dionan bowed them in ahead of him. Idalia entered first, and found that the pavilion was filled with people.

Kellen was there, and Jermayan, as well as a number of the high-ranking Elven war leaders. More surprising—for this seemed to be a strategy meeting—Rochinuviel, the Vicereign of Ondoladeshiron, was there, and Atroist as well.

Naturally, tea must be served and drunk before the business of the meeting could be discussed, though things went swiftly by Elven standards. When the delicate Elvenware cups had been collected and set aside, Redhelwar spoke.

"We have been blooded by the foe, and he will be a difficult enemy to master," Redhelwar said. "Yet by the grace of Leaf and Star, and with Vestakia's aid and that of our Wild-mages, we shall find the dark places in which he bides and scour his presence from the land, so that *They* have no foothold here, and the poor tortured spirits of our cousins can find rest at last."

There was a profound moment of silence, and Idalia remembered what Kellen had told her: even while they devoted every fiber of their being to killing the Shadowed Elves, *their* Elves never stopped thinking of them as Elves, and hating the necessity that drove them to slaughter what they considered to be their own kind.

"Yet this is a fight that cannot be won with sword and spear alone," Redhelwar said, continuing. "We must once more take up our alliance with those who wield the Wild Magic, as it was in the time of the Great War. To that end, Rochinuviel brings word from Andoreniel."

Rochinuviel bowed, stepping forward. The Vicereign was gowned as elaborately as she had been on the day that she had greeted the Unicorn Knights on the Gathering Plain. Diamonds and moonstones glowed and glittered in her long black hair, and she wore a cloak of thick white fur over a gown of white velvet banded in ermine and satin as bright as ice. But despite the fact that she was dressed for Court in a pavilion full of men and women wearing armor and coarser furs, she did not look out of place. She was simply Rochinuviel, as inviolate as the snowcapped peaks.

"Your words honor me, Redhelwar. The words of Andoreniel will bring change to the Elven Lands. It is, as I am sure you expect, a hard counsel, but wise, and in time of danger, new ideas must not be set aside merely because they are new. Andoreniel's words are these: the Lostlanders must come south, every man, woman, and child of them, every goat and sheep, every household chattel. No living thing which they value is to be left behind. They will be granted safe passage through the Elven Lands, escorted by our own people, all the way to the lands of Men. Then shall their Wildmages fight among us against the Shadowed Elves, and those of their young men who are willing as well. All of the Lostlanders who take up arms in honor of the ancient treaties shall be our valued allies, and all the rest shall be safe in the Lands of Men, and all who aid them there shall have the gratitude of the Elves. So says Andoreniel, Lord of the Nine Cities."

Atroist let out a deep sigh of relief, bowing his head.

"I shall tell them this at once, Lady. You are more than generous."

"It is not I who am generous," Rochinuviel said, rebuking

him gently, "but Andoreniel, who speaks through me. I have given his words, and now I will go, and leave you to see to the matters of war. You will tell Andoreniel when he may expect your people to arrive."

She drew her white cloak more firmly around her and walked from the tent. Her escort—another Elf, dressed almost identically, but in shades of palest grey—followed silently.

"To know this thing will make good hearing," Redhelwar observed, in the silence that followed.

"I can speak to Drothi today," Atroist said. "With help it will be easier, but—"

"Of course we'll help," Idalia said firmly, glancing at Jermayan and Kellen. "Just tell us what you need."

"Ah." Atroist smiled. "Then when Drothi tells me how soon the folk can be ready to move, I can tell you, Lord."

"Useful," Redhelwar observed, to no one in particular. "Now. We will discuss the Battle of the Cavern, and what we may learn from it in order to be able to fight more efficiently in future battles."

FOR the next several hours there was a brisk discussion—both among those who had been at the battle at the cavern in the Mystral Mountains and those who had just arrived on the Gathering Plain—about the sort of fight the Shadowed Elves had put up, and whether they could expect the same sort of battle the next time. Kellen found himself having to tell the story of what he had done and what he had faced over and over again. There were things he wished Vestakia didn't have to hear, but there was no help for it. It was no consolation to hear the others who had also been in the caves echo his story from their own perspectives. The memories were still hard and painful ones.

What was clear to Kellen was that they dared not risk another such battle as the one they had just fought. Though their losses had been comparatively small, they'd been far too high when one remembered that this was only the start of the campaign against the Shadowed Elves—and that they had the Endarkened still to fight.

"Perhaps that was the only enclave of the creatures," an Elven Knight named Belepheriel suggested, when the battle had been gone over from every possible aspect.

"It is true that we do not yet know the location of other enclaves—or, indeed, if they exist at all," Redhelwar agreed reluctantly. "Therefore, we must wait until Vestakia has discovered another nest of the creatures to see what we must do. But it is best to be prepared, for I do not think that *They* would lead us so easily to the only infestation of our enemy. *They* are not in the habit of bestowing such rich gifts upon *Their* foes."

And with that grim assessment, everyone present had to agree.

REDHELWAR dismissed his commanders soon thereafter: the meeting had been for the purpose of providing everyone there with information; soon, he told them, he would want to hear strategies for dealing with the special problems of invading the Shadowed Elves' underground lairs.

The four Wildmages and Vestakia left together, intent upon their more immediate concerns.

"What is it that we have to do to help you send your message to Drothi?" Idalia asked.

"There must be a Speaking Circle," Atroist answered. "We use them to pass messages over long distances in the Lost Lands. Drothi will be awaiting a Sending from me, though she knows not when one may come. It is a thing best done with"—he glanced around at the bustle of the camp—"perhaps some privacy."

"Well, if Jermayan's going to help, it needs to be someplace where Ancaladar can be close by anyway," Idalia said in practical tones. "There's an old orchard out behind the Flower Forest—you remember the place, Jermayan. We can meet there."

"Sounds cold," Kellen muttered. It was hard to remember at the moment the last time he'd been really warm.

"It won't be when I'm done with it," Jermayan said with a smile. "Perhaps you will tell me, Atroist, what you require for this Speaking Circle."

"A place to build a fire—a small one—where we can gather around," Atroist said simply. "I have brought all else I need with me."

"Then let us meet there at dusk. Ancaladar and I can go now to prepare the place, and Idalia can bring the two of you, if that is amenable to all of you."

"I thank you for your aid, Wildmage," Atroist said, bowing.

Jermayan nodded and walked away, leaving the others behind.

"I'd better go check back with Petariel to see what else needs to be done at the Unicorn Camp," Kellen said. He glanced at the sky. The day was overcast, but it was still possible to mark the position of the sun through the clouds. "We have a few hours yet."

"And Vestakia and I will have a few things to do among the Healers," Idalia agreed. "Meet us at the Healers' tents an hour before sunset. It's a bit of a walk to the orchard."

Sixteen

Ghosts upon the Wind

Just at dusk they arrived at the old orchard. The trees were bare and black with winter, but Kellen barely noticed them.

Jermayan had indeed been busy.

A pavilion of ice stood at the spot where they would need to do their work. It was all of a piece, as seamless as Mage-crafted stone and as transparent as glass. The light of lanterns gleamed from within, making the whole structure glow softly in the fading twilight.

A human Mage would probably have made a simple square building and let it go at that, but Jermayan was an Elven Mage. He had created a replica of Redhelwar's pavilion—the available interior space, of course, would be much smaller, because the ice walls needed to be thicker for the pavilion to stand—but the exterior was exact in every detail, down to the fringe and tassels along the upper edges of the walls, the folds in the "fabric" of the tent, the stakes and peg-ropes, even the pennons hanging from the centerpole and from each of the four corners. Even the door-flaps that stood pinned back from the entrance—they would not close, of course, being made of ice, but they were so detailed that they looked as if they could.

"Oh, my," Idalia said, mirth bubbling in her voice.

"Do you like it?" Ancaladar asked, appearing out of the Flower Forest to their right and moving quickly through the winter orchard toward them. He cocked his head, inspecting the ice-pavilion. "The boy shows promise."

"It's . . . not something you see every day," Kellen said weakly.

Here, as in the Shadowed Elf village, being confronted with the sheer *scope* of the magical power his friend could command gave him a moment's pang. It was not that he coveted it for himself—Gods of the Wild Magic forbid it!—or that he did not trust Jermayan utterly. It was just that there seemed something almost unnatural about it.

It was true that to a non-Mage, there would seem to be very little difference between what he and Idalia could do, and what Jermayan could do. But Kellen saw a very great difference. What he did, at least, was just—almost—an intensification of what an ordinary man might do, or what the natural world did on its own. He could make the healing process go faster, but he could not call back the dead. He could see things invisible to others, but that was because his Gift gave him the power to understand tiny clues that they could not see, and showed him the results in visions. He could call fire, but he could not burn things that a natural flame would not burn. He could not reshape stone with a thought.

But he had seen Jermayan burn stone as if it were oil-soaked kindling, and shape granite as if it were clay on the potter's wheel. And now this—calling ice out of thin air to make a place for them to work in.

Was the only difference between what Kellen could do and what Jermayan could do that Jermayan had Ancaladar's power to draw upon? Was it that Jermayan was an Elven Mage and Kellen was human?

"Is this what your Wildmages do in the south?" Atroist asked, sounding stunned.

"I'd have to say that Jermayan isn't exactly a typical Wildmage," Idalia said comfortingly.

"Come," Jermayan said, stepping out of the ice-tent's entrance. "Be welcome."

The three of them crunched through the heavy snow and in through the entrance of the "tent."

It was warm inside, even though the structure was made of ice. The walls were smooth and featureless, save for brackets of bronze in the shapes of wyverns that were set into the walls. The lanterns illuminating the space hung from their jaws. The floor of the tent was hard-packed snow, providing cold—if certain—footing. Jermayan's pack was tucked into a corner, and the inevitable brazier was already brewing water for tea.

"It looks very much as if you've done this before," Idalia commented, looking around as she shed her pack. Kellen and Atroist quickly followed suit.

"As Ancaladar does not wish to be treated as a pack animal—yes, I had to find a way of making shelter on my journeys, since I could not carry it," Jermayan agreed.

"Pack animals walk," Ancaladar said simply, poking his nose into the doorway of the tent. "I fly."

"That you do," Idalia agreed, squatting down in front of the dragon and reaching out to rub his nose, gradually working her way up to gently scratch the brow-ridges above his eyes. The huge black dragon closed his eyes with pleasure.

Atroist was busily working through the three packs—all of which contained his supplies—and laying them out in the center of the tent. He made a circle of what Kellen recognized as keystones, though very large ones—so *that* was why the pack he'd carried had been so heavy!—two rings of them, with a third set balanced upon the first two, and, at the center of the ring, a carefully woven pyre of sticks and small logs, all black and tarry with resin.

"So long as the fire burns, I can Speak with Drothi," Atroist said. "This is the wood of the ghostwood tree. I will call the fire away when we are finished, in case I need to speak again—I have not seen ghostwood here in the south."

"You have not been to the Flower Forest," Jermayan said. "We call these trees *namanarii*. We use the sap in medicine; it sends healing dreams. I did not know that they grew any longer in the lands of Men. If you need more of it for your spells, send to Andoreniel for permission to take what you need, and you may have it from any of the Flower Forests in the Elven Lands."

As he had been speaking, Jermayan had been brewing tea.

He paused now to pour it out and to hand the filled cups to each of them.

This was a set of cups Kellen had never seen before. They were tiny, holding no more than a sip or two—the sort of cups the Elves used for "polite" occasions. They were Elvenware, delicate as moonlight, and of a color Kellen had never seen before: black.

But their surface shone with a red fire, like flames, and somehow it seemed as if he could see a black dragon dancing through those flames. Kellen thought he'd gotten used to the beauty the Elves could create, but this was truly the most exquisite piece he had ever handled.

"They are for drinking out of, not looking at," Jermayan reminded him gently.

Kellen grinned, and sipped the tea.

It was bitingly hot. He tasted woodsmoke and fruit—the tea was some kind he'd never had before, and a stronger flavor than most of the Elven blends. It was odd, but he liked it.

"Oh, Jermayan, I didn't think you had any of this left," Idalia said, her eyes going wide as she tasted it.

"Very little," Jermayan admitted. "But it is a good tea for this time and place."

"Take pity on a poor round-ear who can't be trusted to boil water," Kellen pleaded.

"The tea is called Auspicious Venture," Idalia said. "It's made with the fruit of the *vilya,* among other things. It's very rare, because the *vilya* is always in flower, but it fruits only once a century. So you see."

"Maybe," Kellen said cautiously. He sipped the tea slowly, trying to make it last, but trying to finish it before it cooled. The flavor seemed to change with every sip. He guessed he'd better not get to like it *too* much, if it was as rare as Idalia said.

Jermayan finished first, and to Kellen's horror, dropped his exquisite teacup to the snow and ground it to shards underfoot.

"Things of beauty are not meant to be guarded at the expense of more important things," he said. "We cling to them at our peril. Only when we release them are they truly ours—and are we truly free."

Idalia finished her tea, dropped her cup, and did as Jermayan had done.

Kellen looked down at the empty cup in his hands. Destroy such a beautiful thing? When would he ever see something like it again?

"We cling to them at our peril . . . "

He dropped the cup to the snow and crushed it beneath his boot. The sound it made as he broke it seemed to resonate through his entire body.

Atroist broke his cup in turn, grinding the fragments into the snow.

"Come," he said, seating himself close to the ring of keystones.

The other three seated themselves around the ring of stones as well.

"Who will share the cost of this Working with me?" Atroist asked formally.

"I," said Jermayan.

"And I," Ancaladar said from the doorway.

"I will," Idalia said.

"Me, too," Kellen finished.

"Then let it begin," Atroist said, stretching his hand out toward the wood. "Walk with me."

The wood burst into flame, and Kellen felt the familiar sense of Presence as the shield that marked the beginning of a spell of the Wild Magic appeared.

But nothing else was the same.

Suddenly he was not in the ice-pavilion at all.

He got to his feet—moving without his own volition—and as he moved, he saw he was in a small cottage. The light was dim—the illumination coming mostly from a fire that smoldered on the hearth—but his body moved with certainty, as if it knew this place.

"Drothi."

It was Atroist who spoke, not Kellen, and when he did,

Kellen realized that he was not truly present at all, merely hearing and seeing all that Atroist did. The illusion of *presence* was so real that it was strange not to be able to move at his own will, and only now did Kellen realize that although he could see the fire that smoldered on the hearth, he could smell nothing at all, not even the smoke of the burning ghostwood.

The woman sitting at the hearth looked up. She was dressed much as Vestakia had been when Kellen had first seen her, in a long tunic of coarse homespun with wide calf-length trousers, and heavy boots of rough leather. Over that she wore a large shawl, woven in a complicated pattern of crossed stripes that would probably have been very colorful if there had been more light to see by. She was not a young woman; her face was seamed with the lines of age, and her eyes looked almost white in the firelight. As she gazed in his direction in an unfocused fashion, Kellen realized she could not see Atroist at all.

"What news do you bring, kinsman?" Drothi asked. Aged she might have been, but her voice was young and vibrant with power.

"The Firstlings beg our aid, as we knew, yet they would not deny us help as well," Atroist said. "I have told them how it is with us, and of our struggles with the Dark Folk, and so they bid us travel to find sanctuary in the lands where the Dark Folk do not come. The Firstling King offers us safe passage through his lands for flock and herd, and for every man, woman, and child of the Folk. The Wildmages here speak of a land beyond the Firstling borders where we may settle; an empty land that we may take for our own. And the Firstling King gives his word that all who aid our people beyond the Firstling borders shall dwell in his grace, and here his word is no light thing, even in the lands of Men."

"Welladay," Drothi said coolly, "so the walls of the Great Border fall at last, even for kern and chicken. It will not take so very much to persuade the people to come, I think—aye, and swiftly."

"What is the news?" Atroist asked, and now Kellen heard a note of fear in the Wildmage's voice.

"The raids, as you expected, have continued," Drothi said simply. As she spoke, she picked up a spindle from the basket beside her and began pulling carded wool into thread with deft sure motions. "And to make matters worse, the winter has been harder than any we have seen in a long-hand of years. Had Torchen not warned us it would be so when the rains began, there would be starvation now. But that is no matter, since it has not happened. There are things that are worse.

"The Great Wolves have come again. When the snows began to fall, the folk heard them singing at Icebridge and at Songhythe, which lie nearest to the Stone Wastes, as you know. The folk there had left their cattle to winter in the near fields, and one day they woke to find them slaughtered, every bull and cow, with nothing left behind but blood and polished bones. They knew the marauders for Great Wolves by the tracks, and did the only thing they could: they turned their flocks out as a sacrifice and fled south. This is what the survivors say. There were not many, for the Great Wolves harried them as they went, pulling them down in ones and twos, running them like the deer until the weakest dropped from exhaustion and the strongest must leave them behind or die as well. It was a cruel jest the Dark Folk played upon us that day, to leave any alive when they could have taken all so easily."

Atroist sucked in a trembling breath, but Drothi went on with her spinning implacably. This was old news to her, Kellen realized.

"Yet the Great Wolves can be killed. We have fought their kind before, but now creatures have come into the land that have not been seen since before the Settling, if then. We have seen creatures in the sky like giant bats—they do not come near, but they bring fear to all who see them. In the Haunted Places there are tracks upon the ground as if of giant serpents—you remember the songs I taught you as a child, Atroist, of the icedrake whose body is colder than the coldest ice, and whose breath is poison? I think it must have come again among us, though I was certain it was only a legend from the Oldest Days.

"Other folk speak of black things that look like bears but are as tall as two men, beasts with glowing red eyes and the power of human speech. Of things like horses, but with cloven hooves, the teeth of wolves, and the tails of serpents.

"No man dares leave his village to hunt, no woman to draw water from the river. The Lost Lands have become an abode not only of the Dark Folk, but of monsters, and our people suffer terribly.

"I shall pass the word at once that we are to leave. We will come as swiftly as we may. Pray to the Good Goddess that we survive the journey."

"I shall," Atroist said. "And I will come to you myself and render what aid I can."

"Let it be so," Drothi said. "Now leave me. I have much work to do before I sleep."

THERE was a moment of disorientation, and suddenly Kellen was back in the ice-pavilion, blinking in confusion at his fellow Wildmages over the now-cold fire. He breathed in deeply and coughed, suddenly aware of the lingering spicy scent of woodsmoke.

"This does not sound good," Idalia said mildly.

"Coldwarg, and icedrake, and shadewalkers, and serpent-marae, to judge by Drothi's description," Jermayan said grimly. "And the Deathwings that we know to be the creatures of the Shadowed Elves as well. The Deathwings we had never seen before, and all but the coldwarg we had thought to be gone—destroyed in the Great War."

"I guess they're back," Kellen said. He yawned—he couldn't help it; now that the spell had run its course, the energy he'd lent to its working left him feeling drained.

"I must go," Atroist said, getting to his feet and beginning to pack the keystones and the half-burned ghostwood into the packs again. "I will leave at first light. I cannot leave my people to face such a journey alone, when I might be able to protect them on their way."

"Of course you can't," Idalia agreed. "Return as soon as you can, and make your journey safely."

"May the Good Goddess will it so," Atroist said.

"What about this?" Kellen said to Jermayan, indicating the ice-pavilion.

"Oh," Jermayan said, a faint overelaborate note of casualness in his voice, "I thought I'd just leave it. It won't melt, you know."

"Not until spring," Ancaladar agreed, from his position in the doorway.

"And I might have a use for it later," Jermayan continued, far too innocently.

"Whatever," Kellen muttered. He wondered if there was any chance of getting a bowl of hot soup back at the Unicorn Knights' camp, or whether he'd have to make do with cold trail-rations. At least there'd be tea. In an Elven camp, there was always tea.

"Don't tease him, Jermayan," Idalia said sharply.

"What?" Kellen said blankly.

"I do apologize, Kellen," Jermayan said, sounding truly contrite.

Kellen was puzzled. Something had just happened, and he had no idea what it was, but Idalia was mad, and Jermayan was upset.

"Look," he said with a sigh. "I'm tired, I'm hungry, and I'm cold. All I want is to help Atroist get his stuff back to his tent so I can go get some dinner, okay?"

Idalia smiled, and reached out to ruffle his hair. "I do love you, Kellen," she said with a smile.

"Sure," Kellen said. Sometimes sisters were just as baffling as Elves.

Since a good portion of the ghostwood had been burned

in the Speaking Spell, the remains and the keystones fitted neatly into two backpacks. Kellen took one, and Atroist took the other, and they headed back in the direction of the Gathering Plain. It was only after they'd passed the edge of the Flower Forest that Kellen realized that Idalia and Jermayan had stayed behind. He shrugged. Probably quoting poetry at each other. He hoped Jermayan had brought more teacups.

"The Firstlings are . . . not as I imagined they would be," Atroist said after a while.

"The Elves? I guess they take some getting used to," Kellen agreed. "I didn't even know they existed—not really—before I left the City, so I wasn't really sure what to expect. Good thing too." Not that he'd had a lot of choice about coming to Sentarshadeen. But he'd have worried—and it would have turned out to be for no good reason.

"The Golden City of Mages—your City—is a place we only know of in legends," Atroist said. "Someday, perhaps, we will speak of it further."

"Um, well, Armethalieh probably isn't very much like your legends either," Kellen said tactfully. He supposed the Lostlanders thought of Armethalieh as a sort of paradise, the way the wondertales wrote about the Mage College.

"In our legends, it is a place that shines with painful brightness to mask the darkness of its Mages' hearts; a place where there is no night or day, no winter or summer; a place where the citizens have no souls, for they have been stolen to fuel the magic of the Mages. Music fills the air eternally to mask the cries of despair rising from the captive populace," Atroist said simply. "I apologize if my words offend you. They are only legends."

Oh.

"They're close enough to the truth," Kellen said sadly. "Except that nobody's in despair. Everybody's perfectly happy with the life they have—or most of them are, anyway. They're"—he thought long and hard for a good analogy— "sheep, and the Mages are the shepherds, except that these shepherds not only keep them shorn of every scrap of wool they grow, but would probably throw them to the wolves if wolves showed up. But they don't know that, and so they're completely content."

"You weren't," Atroist pointed out.

"No," Kellen agreed. "Idalia wasn't either. But most people are. The High Mages make sure of it." He supposed he ought to hate Armethalieh and the High Council for what it had done to him. Certainly they'd acted out of pettiness and spite, and tried to kill him, but since he'd been Banished, he was happier than he'd ever been before in his life.

And to his surprise, he was worried about them. They were blind, self-centered, bigoted idiots, true, but *nobody* deserved to be the Demons' victims.

Kellen and Atroist had reached the edge of the camp by now, and a few minutes more brought them to Atroist's tent. The two men stepped inside, and Kellen set down his pack with a sigh of relief.

"I'd better be going. Shalkan will want to know what happened," Kellen said. "I hope your friends get here safely."

"As do I," Atroist said. "Fare you well, Kellen Knight-Mage."

"You, too, Atroist Wildmage," Kellen said.

WHEN he returned to the Unicorn Camp, Kellen was grateful to find not only tea, but soup and fresh bread waiting.

"The advantages of being chosen for night patrol," Petariel told him cheerfully, handing him a steaming bowl. "Not you, Wildmage. I order you to report to your bedroll at once. You look exhausted."

"I'll make sure he gets there," Shalkan said, walking around the corner of one of the tents and staring pointedly at the jar of crystallized honey until Petariel laughed and offered him a disk of it.

"Huh," Kellen said inelegantly, squatting near the large brazier and filling himself with bread and soup with brisk efficiency. "Thanks." And that was all he said for long enough to fill himself up to the brim with hot food and drink. After half a loaf of bread, three bowls of soup, and two mugs of tea with a great deal of honey, he felt a lot better—well enough, in fact, to realize how tired he was. He stumbled off to his tent, one arm over Shalkan's shoulder, glad he was awake enough to remember where it was.

"So," Shalkan said, once they were inside.

"Atroist spoke to Drothi. The Lost Lands are being used as a breeding ground for monsters," Kellen said, struggling out of his armor. When he heard his own words he stopped, blinking in surprise. But it was true, wasn't it? The Demons had to put them *somewhere* while they were rebuilding their numbers. "I have to tell Redhelwar."

"The news will keep. And you'll present it so much more elegantly if you're awake when you do it," Shalkan said cuttingly. "Now finish taking off your armor and go to bed."

KELLEN awoke when the sun was high, feeling as if he ought to have had restless dreams, but unable to remember any of them. Shalkan was already gone, on business of his own. Kellen dressed—not armor, but camp clothes—and made his way from the tent. He'd check with the Watch Commander for orders, then go to the tents that served as the common dispensary for food in the settled camp to see about breakfast, then bathe if his schedule allowed it. A fixed camp allowed for a number of luxuries—though he wouldn't have thought of them as luxuries a few months ago. Hot food he didn't have to cook himself, hot water for bathing, and more fur blankets on his bed than he could carry in a pack or on a packhorse that he shared with three others.

Riasen was the captain of the Morning Watch—since Petariel had been on patrol last night.

"Nothing for you to do while we're in camp, Kellen," Riasen said cheerfully. "Except stop wearing yourself to the bone working as a Knight and a Healer both. If that's what being a Wildmage is like, I thank Leaf and Star I was born Elven."

"I did all right," Kellen said, stung. He hadn't thought he'd looked *that* tired.

"We were all taking bets on when you'd fall over," Riasen said frankly. "But you saved Petariel's leg, and so . . . if there's ever anything you need: ask."

"I hope I won't have to," Kellen said. "But I will, if . . . "

"And Leaf and Star defend us from the day," Riasen agreed. "Now, I have heard that Rochinuviel has sent bullocks from her own herds, and cheese from her own cellars. You won't want to miss that."

"Probably not," Kellen agreed. And if he was going to go give bad news to Redhelwar, he wanted to do it on a full stomach.

THE dining tents were enormous; the largest single structures in the camp, designed to seat and feed hundreds at a time, and to serve as a place where a large percentage of the troops could be gathered in one place in foul weather—or as a hospital, in case of true disaster.

The tables and benches were delicate yet strong, designed to be folded and stowed for easy transport, in the event that the entire army should need to move somewhere. Despite having been constructed for function and efficiency, the space maintained the ethereal beauty common to all the work of the Elves, and Kellen was reminded, suddenly, of the teacup he had broken last night.

Were the Elves themselves like that teacup? Must the Elves themselves pass away for Shadow Mountain to be destroyed this time? Was the attempt to save the Elves the attempt to preserve Beauty that would doom them all?

Did Jermayan know?

If the Elven Knight-turned-Mage *did* know, then one

thing was sure: he wouldn't tell Kellen. Maybe knowing for sure would be the one thing that would tip the balance toward disaster. Maybe working without knowing for sure was the only chance they had.

Kellen shook his head. It sounded like something out of *The Book of Stars.*

Even at this hour—late for breakfast—the tent was half-filled with Elves. Kellen walked the length of the tent, toward the far end where it opened into the cooking area.

The army that had traveled into the mountains had contained only fighters and Healers, but an army, Kellen was discovering, needed much more than that to function properly. Not only fighters, but everything from blacksmiths to wagon drivers to armorers to launderers to cooks—an army was essentially a small mobile city.

The kitchen staff, seeing him, took instant action without a word from Kellen, presenting him with a heavily laden tray burdened with roast meat, cheese, fruit buns, and even—amazingly—a few apples. They were a little withered from winter storage, but fresh fruit at this season was nothing short of a miracle.

Kellen took his food to the nearest table and worked his way slowly through it, trying to at least pretend he had table manners. He wrapped one of the fruit buns in his napkin and tucked it into his tunic, knowing Shalkan would relish the treat later. Sometimes he wondered how the unicorn had indulged his sweet tooth before he'd had Kellen to cadge treats from.

Breakfast over—and feeling comfortably stuffed—Kellen went off to look for Dionan. He knew better than to think he could just barge in on Redhelwar, Knight-Mage or no.

⟶

DIONAN'S tent was near Redhelwar's. Kellen waited outside while Dionan dealt with another matter—from the armor, Kellen recognized Belepheriel, the Elf of the previous evening who had suggested that there might not be any more Shadowed Elves. When Belepheriel had left, Kellen walked up to the tent and courteously shook the bells attached to the tent flap.

"I See you, Kellen Knight-Mage. Enter and be welcome," Dionan said.

"I See you, Dionan," Kellen answered in return. He entered the tent.

Dionan's tent was set up as an office, with a table and chairs. A smaller table held a teapot and cups—it would have been startling if it did not. Kellen took a deep mental breath and resigned himself to attempting the Elven dance of politeness once again.

"One observes," he began, "that the Working last night went well, and that because of that, the Wildmage Atroist journeys back to the Wildlands."

"So very direct," Dionan sighed. "I will pour tea."

"Thank you," Kellen said meekly. He'd thought he was doing pretty good. He hadn't come to talk about Atroist, after all.

"I have recently tasted a most exceptional tea," he said, trying again.

"It would please me greatly to know the name of this tea," Dionan said, setting a tall pottery cup before Kellen. Kellen lifted it and sipped, tasting the familiar flavor of Winter Spice Tea.

"The name told to me was Auspicious Venture," Kellen said. "I am told it is a very rare tea. I am pleased to have had the opportunity to have tasted it."

"A rare tea indeed," Dionan said. "One may go half a lifetime without tasting it."

"It had a strong flavor," Kellen said. "And it seemed to me that the flavor changed constantly. I am sure I did not appreciate it sufficiently. I am gratified by the variety of teas available for me to taste."

"Indeed," Dionan said. "You will find the teas of springtime to be strong and complex, when they come into season.

I look forward to aiding you in your education, should it be possible. Many humans are not interested."

"I discover that I do not brew tea well," Kellen said. "I do not see that this should be a drawback to appreciating its taste."

"The two go together," Dionan said, a note of faint reproach in his voice. "Still, if you will begin by appreciating the taste, you will come to understand the making, for they are both part of the same thing."

The odd thing was, Kellen believed him. Tea and the making of tea *had* to go together, like—like swordplay and the proper stance. If you had one, you'd have the other.

"You enlighten me," he said, bowing where he sat.

Dionan smiled. "Come to me to understand the spring teas, and I will teach you the making with the summer teas, for they are the most subtle, and in the summer teas, the making is all. Any fool may brew a winter tea." He made an elegant motion—not a shrug, but an indication the subject was about to change. "But perhaps you did not come to speak of tea."

"Perhaps I did not know that I needed to come to speak of tea," Kellen said, "but wisdom is not summoned, only discovered." Another of Master Belesharon's favorite sayings. "What was in my mind when I awoke this morning that Redhelwar would wish to know what I had done and learned since I left him."

"Perhaps it is so," Dionan agreed. "If you come to his pavilion at the second hour after noon, you may speak to him of the Wildmage Atroist and other matters touching on the current campaign. I shall see to it that you have the opportunity to sample Ice Mountain Wind as well. You should find it interesting."

"I look forward to that opportunity," Kellen said, rising to his feet and bowing. *And I hope we're both alive in the spring, so you can teach me more about tea.*

KELLEN spent the time waiting for the next move in this "game" of war on the hundred homely tasks that had been neglected while he'd been in the field—laundry, a proper bath, a thorough cleaning of his sword and armor—and Shalkan's armor—now that he had light and time to do them. He discovered that his helmet-crest needed refletching—the feathers had gotten thoroughly battered and blood-soaked—and dropped it off with the armorer on his way to Redhelwar's tent.

Part of him chafed at this constant focus on inessentials—what did it matter whether he had feathers on his helmet or not, or what they looked like?—while another part of him was resigned to it. He could not change the way the Elves did things overnight. In fact, he probably could not change much—permanently—in his lifetime. When—if—they all got through this and beat the Demons back, the Elves would probably go right back to their old ways the next day. And until they found the next enclave of the Shadowed Elves, there was nothing more vital to be doing.

As he crossed the camp, he could see mounted parties out on the plain, drilling on horseback with the long Elven lance. It was beautiful to watch . . . but it would be next to useless fighting underground.

He reached Redhelwar's pavilion and waited. After a moment, Dionan summoned him inside.

"Dionan observes that you have recently had the good fortune to taste Auspicious Venture," Redhelwar said, once Kellen was seated. "Perhaps you would favor me with your opinion of it. It would be gratifying to perceive this tea through a human's senses."

Kellen's heart sank. This was high formality indeed, something he was terrible at. And despite his growing interest in Elven teas, they were very different from the teas brewed in Armethalieh, and he'd never really been much of a connoisseur. Tea had always been something you drank when you were thirsty, and that was about it. And of all time to start comparing the finer points of leaves—

Still, if that was what Redhelwar wanted to talk about, he guessed he'd better do his best. He needed to understand the Elves if he wanted to be able to persuade them that he was right about Shadow Mountain. But oh, it was very hard to be patient at a moment like this!

But he put on a serious expression. "You honor me with your interest. I know very little about tea, and my tastes are uneducated as yet, but I shall explain as best I can. I am told that it is flavored with the fruit of the *vilya*. To me it tasted of fruit and smoke, and the taste seemed constantly to change. I found it a strong-flavored tea, and to me that was very agreeable. It was unlike any tea I have ever had, and yet it seemed to remind me of something, in a way I cannot define."

"It is a good description, for one unversed in tea," Redhelwar said. "One observes that it is odd for a knight to escape Master Belesharon's tutelage without learning the ways of tea."

"I have much more to learn in the House of Sword and Shield," Kellen said simply. "And many of the . . . more subtle arts had been set aside to concentrate upon those which Master Belesharon considered more needful to my position and his limited time."

If that wasn't enough of a hint—

Apparently it wasn't. "We shall do what we may to continue your education here," Redhelwar said. "Now come. Try this tea."

Cups were set before Kellen and Redhelwar, and Dionan seated himself with his own cup. Kellen raised his cup, inhaling the fragrant steam.

It was hot, yet somehow it managed to smell of the cold purity of ice. The paradox was so odd, that it actually distracted him from his ever-present anxieties. Kellen sipped cautiously.

It wasn't a tea for drinking carelessly, like Winter Spice. This was a tea that had to be paid attention to, almost like listening to music. It was herbal, like most of the Elven teas, and there were flavors of grass and metal in it—it sounded unpleasant, but it wasn't, not really. And over all, the sense of winter combined with the heat of the tea seemed to offer a promise that no matter how cold the day or how deep the snow, spring would always come.

"It is a riddle," Kellen said, setting down his cup after several sips. "It's hot—but there's ice in it, somehow. Snow—and green things."

Dionan exchanged a pleased look with Redhelwar. "I did suggest that perhaps the brewing would not be wasted on him, Master."

"I admit I had my doubts, but you have convinced me," Redhelwar said. "Yes. Winter Mountain Ice is one of Teamaster Thenandelet's most subtle creations, the recipe for its creation passed down in my family for many generations. When you have finished, we will pour something that requires less attention, and speak of necessary things."

Kellen finished his cup slowly, still trying to figure out how something so hot could make him think of cold. He didn't quite manage to solve the riddle before the cup was empty.

Dionan removed the cups, and replaced them with larger ones. Kellen caught the familiar comforting scent of Winter Spice Tea. Good. At least it wouldn't distract him from what he had to say.

"Dionan mentioned that you wished to speak of matters touching upon the Wild Magic, and of the Wildmage Atroist," Redhelwar said, when the new tea had been tasted.

"As you know already, he left this morning for the Lost Lands," Kellen said. "Last night, he spoke with Drothi, another Wildmage there. She said she will bring everyone south as quickly as possible, and that because of the great trouble in the Lost Lands, it will not be difficult to convince them to come."

"Go on," Redhelwar said.

"Drothi told Atroist—it was as if I were actually in her presence, and could see her and hear everything she said—that *Their* raids on the Lostlanders have continued through the winter, and in addition, monsters have begun appearing in the Lost Lands. I did not recognize all of them from her descriptions, but Jermayan did. He said that there are cold-

warg, icedrake, shadewalkers, and serpentmarae in the Lost
Lands, and the Lostlanders have seen the Deathwings that
attacked the caravan near the Crowned Horns as well. The
coldwarg have destroyed two villages in the Lost Lands, but
she was not clear about where the others were, only that they
are close enough to the villages to be a constant, and urgent,
threat."

*And please, please, someone make the Elves understand
that* urgent *means* urgent!

Redhelwar sat and thought for several minutes after
Kellen had finished speaking.

"This is fell news, but good to have," he said at last. "I
shall send troops west to support the rangers Andoreniel has
sent to conduct the Wildlanders to the eastern border. If
these creatures follow the Wildlanders toward the Elven
Lands, it may be that our ancient land-wards will not stop
them all, nor do I wish to witness a slaughter just outside our
protection. But perhaps you will favor me now with your
views on why these creatures should have so suddenly appeared in the Wild Lands, where they were not before."

This is a test. Kellen knew it, with a sudden cold shock of intuition. A test, as—in its way—Kellen's opinion of the tea had
been. Redhelwar was testing him. But for what? After the Battle of the Cavern, Redhelwar already knew how well he fought.

He chose his next words with great care.

"Drothi hasn't given us much information to go on, but it
seems clear to me, from what she said last night and from
what Atroist has said before, that *They* have long considered
the Wild Lands their special private hunting preserve. I think
that now *They're* using it as a place to breed up and collect
these creatures in great numbers. Jermayan said most of
them hadn't been seen since the Great War, and that he'd
thought most of them were extinct. Drothi said the Wildlanders only knew them from ancient story-songs.

"It seems to me, from the tactics we've seen *Them* using so
far, that *They* are not anxious to meet us on a battlefield. *They*
did that in the Great War, and *They* lost. If *They* intend to try

it again at all, I think *They* want to make sure we're very weak before *They* do. So They're using tactics of attrition. First *They* struck at your water supply, and that failed, but if *They* can strike at crops and flocks—and game, in the case of the Mountainfolk of the High Reaches—*They* don't need to meet us on the battlefield. *They* can starve us to death."

There was a long pause after Kellen had finished. Both Redhelwar's and Dionan's faces were expressionless, in the way that Elven faces often were. At last Redhelwar spoke.

"And all of these are creatures of cold. If they are stopped by the land-ward barriers, they will simply follow the mountains until they come to a place where they may pass, and enter into human lands," the Elven general said grimly. "The coldwarg and the icedrake must stay in the realms of cold unless they are spell-guarded, but the serpentmarae and the shadewalker may roam where they will."

"Unless those who have created them are keeping them back to use later," Kellen said. "We won't know until it happens."

"As with all things in war," Redhelwar agreed. "A reasonable analysis, given the scant information that we have ... and I admit, I have found *Their* continued reluctance to take the field against us somewhat puzzling. Nevertheless, there is another matter that it is in my mind to speak to you of today.

"As a Knight-Mage, you fight for the Elves, and your valor is unquestioned, but you are not truly *of* my command. I would change that, were you willing. It is in my mind that you might be one of my *alakomentaiia*. You would lead a troop under my orders, and work as one with the other *alakomentaiia*.

"Of course, you would need to take a destrier as your mount, and for this I am truly sorry. If Shalkan consents, it is also in my mind that Mindaerel is without a rider, and grieves at her loss. You might take her, did you find favor in one another's eyes."

Kellen sipped his tea without answering, glad that the rules of Elven formality allowed him time to gather his thoughts before he answered. The *alakomentaiia* were subcommanders. The Elves didn't use a lot of ranks; there were generals, commanders, and sub-commanders, and everything else was just "understood" by people who had known each other and worked and trained together for centuries. As far as he could figure out, he'd have equivalent rank to Petariel, but below Adaerion.

And the root word *komen*—which was Old Elven—didn't really mean "commander" or anything like it. It meant—as close as you could come to it in non-Elvish—"brotherhood." Try to translate the whole thing, and what you got—besides a headache—was "the servant of the brotherhood." What Redhelwar was proposing was as much an adoption as it was a military promotion.

But . . . give up Shalkan? Kellen wasn't stupid or dense enough to think this was nothing more than a polite suggestion on Redhelwar's part that he could lightly decline. He wouldn't be with the Unicorn Knights anymore, and he wouldn't have the protections against the Demons that riding Shalkan undoubtedly gave him. But it would give him a visible and acknowledged place—not only in the army, but in the War Councils as well.

"Nothing would please me more than to accept your generous offer," Kellen said, thinking hard. "And I believe it would be for the good of all. But as you know, Shalkan and I are bound together by an unfulfilled Mageprice. It would not be wise or appropriate for me to answer without consulting him."

"A proper answer. Do so," Redhelwar said, rising to his feet to indicate that the interview was finished. "Then make matters known to Dionan. And Leaf and Star guide and counsel you."

Kellen rose to his feet and bowed.

ELSEWHERE in the vast camp—it was as large as the larger Elven cities, by now—Jermayan sought out Vestakia on an errand that would, he knew, require all his arts of tact and persuasion.

If they were to find the rest of the enclaves of the Shadowed Elves quickly—or determine with reasonable certainty that there weren't any, something Jermayan doubted was likely— the only efficient method was for Vestakia to search for them from dragonback. It would certainly be the safest method as well, for in that way he and Ancaladar would be able to protect her from nearly anything that might seek to harm her.

All he had to do was manage to obtain Vestakia's agreement to the plan—and he knew the child was terrified of flying.

There were only a limited number of places she might be; having tried the more obvious places to no avail, Jermayan tracked her down at last in the Flower Forest. Vestakia would have been shy of crowds even without the added handicap of her Demonic appearance; having spent the first seventeen years of her life with little more company than a herd of goats, she sought solitude whenever she could.

Before the First War, the Flower Forests had covered all the world, and before the Great War they had still been thick upon all of the Elven Lands and much of that terrain that was now bleak and sterile wasteland. Now all that remained of the great Elven forests and their vast diversity of species existed only in the lesser woodlands that adorned the Elven cities. It was said that one day, when the Endarkened were utterly defeated, the Flower Forests would begin to spread once more, but Jermayan wondered if perhaps that day was not meant to come.

It was winter, but at every season the Flower Forest was lush. Jermayan followed the faint tracks in scattered snow and blown leaves deeper into the forest until he found Vestakia moving carefully through the wood. Her gathering basket was already half-filled—Idalia or one of the other Healers must have sent her here for supplies and some much-needed solitude.

She stooped to gather a handful of winter mushrooms from the base of a tree, then rose to her feet, turning to face him.

"Jermayan," she said. She sighed, and her shoulders slumped. "I know why you have come," she said forlornly.

"I suppose you must," Jermayan said. "Yet I would not even ask, were the need not so grave. And I shall do no more than that."

"But the others—they would think I was such a dreadful coward, if—if I did not do it!" Vestakia burst out. "And it's true, of course—if I were just to *fly* over the Elven Lands, and see if I could sense the Shadowed Elves, everything would be much faster. It might be the only way! But it is so very high—and I could fall, and—"

She was speaking very fast, and her voice had gone thin and high with fear. Jermayan stepped over to her, took the basket from her arm and set it on the ground, and gripped her shoulders gently.

"Vestakia. It *is* very high. But you will not fall. Neither Ancaladar nor I will permit it. Nor is it the only way. Ancaladar and I believe it to be the safest, but that matters not if it will not work. You must be calm and easy in your mind to be able to sense the Shadowed Elves, and I do not believe that will be so if you are in fear of falling from my Bonded's back."

Vestakia managed a weak giggle. "No. I guess not. But . . . " She hesitated for a long moment. "Maybe we should just go look at him?"

"Indeed," Jermayan agreed, picking up her basket. "We shall go and look at Ancaladar."

THE dragon was waiting beside the ice-pavilion that Jermayan had created two nights before, his great body dwarfing the structure completely. For a few moments Vestakia's attention was distracted by the glittering structure of ice, but she knew why she was here, and her attention quickly returned to Ancaladar.

She'd seen him before, of course, but that was before she'd actually considered getting on his back.

"He's very tall," she said faintly.

"I am not so tall when I am airborne," Ancaladar assured her gravely. "And once I am in the sky, my flight is as steady and level as you might wish, my lady, though I cannot control the winds. Jermayan will be sure to pick only the calmest days for flying, though, I am sure."

"That I should," Jermayan said. "And Ancaladar can sense the weather and how it will run from a great distance, you know. There is very little possibility that we might fly into a storm unexpectedly. And there are all manner of ways in which we can secure you to his back."

"Would we have to fly . . . very high?" Vestakia asked in a very small voice.

"The higher the flight, the more serene the winds," Ancaladar replied. "But we would fly at your direction, Lady Vestakia. No one else's."

"I don't know from how far away . . . " Vestakia whispered, almost to herself. She looked pleadingly at Jermayan.

He shook his head.

"I cannot tell you that you must do this thing. And I cannot tell you that you may not. Perhaps you would be comforted to take tea in the pavilion and consider matters further. It will also give you the opportunity to inspect Ancaladar's saddle."

"Hmph," the dragon snorted. "It is *your* saddle, Jermayan. *I* have no need of a saddle."

"But your Bonded is a weak and feeble thing," Jermayan responded with a fond smile, "who requires many such aids. And it is a work of art, very fair to look upon."

"Thank you," Vestakia said. "I would very much like a cup of tea."

TO her surprise, it was quite warm inside the tent of ice. There were carpets upon the floor—just like in the pavilion she shared with Idalia—and lanterns hung from the walls, for despite the fact that the day was bright and the ice was very clear, its thickness made the interior of the ice-pavilion a bit dim.

One corner of the room was taken up with what must be Ancaladar's saddle, and just as Jermayan had promised, it was a work of art—though Vestakia hadn't yet seen anything made by the Elves that wasn't, and privately she thought they wasted a good bit of time on making things beautiful that only had to be serviceable. She inspected it more closely while Jermayan brewed tea.

She knew by now that every Elven Knight chose—or had chosen for them—a particular color of their own. Jermayan's was dark blue, so she was not surprised to see that the saddle and everything about it was in that color. The leather was stamped with a pattern of tiny stars, some subtly burnished with gold and silver leaf, some merely indentations in the leather. It was heavily lined with thick fleece, both where the rider sat and where it would rest upon Ancaladar's neck. Several sets of wide padded straps went around the dragon's neck, and there were footbraces for a rider—very much like the horse stirrups she was already familiar with—set into two sets of the straps.

The saddle itself was similar to a destrier's saddle, except that it was higher in the back and in the front, and a second seat behind—which explained the second set of stirrups. This must be how Kellen had ridden to the Fortress of the Crowned Horns. And when there was no passenger, Jermayan could carry things there.

Continuing to inspect the saddle, she encountered a set of very wide straps, one set for each seat. She picked one set up, wonderingly. They were too short to be part of the girth-straps, but she couldn't quite figure out what they were for.

"That is so I do not fall off," Jermayan said, not turning from his tea preparations. He'd heard the faint clinking, of course; Elven hearing was sharp. "It would be foolish not to take every precaution—though I am certain Ancaladar could catch me if I *did* fall."

"I could," Ancaladar said, poking the end of his nose through the opening of the pavilion. "I would always catch you, Jermayan. And you, Lady Vestakia. But the straps are strong. And more could always be added, as many more as you thought might make you feel secure."

"And the tea is ready," Jermayan said, gesturing to Vestakia to come and sit beside him.

"What will—I mean, do you know—" She stopped, frustrated by her inability to phrase her remark as anything other than a question. Kellen made it sound so easy!

Jermayan smiled, and handed her a cup of tea.

"For the next sennight—at the least—Redhelwar will consult with his commanders—of whom I am not one, thank Leaf and Star—to decide what tactics will serve us best when we next engage our foe. Perhaps new weapons will be needed, and those must be made, and we must train in their use, as well as in the best way of confronting the enemy. All these things will take time. And we do not know what those who oppose us may do. Should they do anything at all, our plans will change."

Vestakia sipped her tea. *And it is all up to me. I must tell them where to go—where the enemy is. Or . . . not.*

She knew she was the only one who could find the Shadowed Elves. The Wildmages had all tried—even Jermayan, whose power worked so differently from that of the other Wildmages—and none of them could sense where the enclaves of the Shadowed Elves lay. Only Vestakia had the power to sense Demon-taint and find the Shadowed Elves.

I must try. She had led Kellen to the Black Cairn, though that had been the most terrifying thing she had ever done in her life. She had gone down into the cavern of the Shadowed Elves, and that had been worse. And there had been true danger both times; the threat of immediate death from an enemy who was trying to kill her.

But neither venture had made her sick with fear the way the thought of climbing onto Ancaladar's back and soaring into the sky did.

Once, when she was a child, before Mama had died, she had gone with her, accompanied by Aunt Patanene, to the Icewild River to fish. The river had been in full spring flood, and she had been far too young to be of much help, so while Mama and Aunt Nene worked the nets, she had wandered away and walked out onto the slippery river stones.

And fallen in.

Her heavy cloak had soaked through at once, pulling her toward the bottom, as the swift river current swept her along below the surface. Fortunately she had been upstream of the nets, so Mama and Aunt Nene had been able to rescue her before she drowned, but ever afterward she had remembered the cold of the river and the airless choking darkness.

The thought of going up in the sky brought the memories back sharply. Flying made her think of drowning, and her heart beat faster with fear.

If she did not agree to fly upon Ancaladar's back, she knew, Jermayan would not rebuke her. But if she did not agree to fly, they would have to search for the caverns on foot. It would take moonturns instead of sennights.

"Do what you can do. You can do no more than that."

Suddenly it seemed as if Mama was beside her, speaking in her ear. Mama had always said that—and after she had died, Aunt Nene had said it for her.

It was as if Mama had given her the right words to say now.

"If I am ... too afraid, up in the sky," Vestakia said slowly, "then I will not be able to do what you need. But maybe ... we don't need to do it all at once? If we could just practice a little? To see if I could get *used* to flying?" Her voice trembled, and she stared hard down into her teacup, hoping that Jermayan could not see how terribly afraid she was to say even that much.

"Yes, of course," said Jermayan calmly, as if this were the simplest thing in the world. "Today you will watch me put the harness upon Ancaladar, and sit upon his back. He and I will help you get in to and out of the saddle as many times as it may take to make you feel comfortable with doing so.

Then, tomorrow, as the weather will hold fine, we will take a short flight, if you like."

━━

FINDING a white unicorn in a snowfield might be a difficult task, but not when you had a sticky fruit-bun left over from breakfast tucked into your tunic.

"Is that for me?" Shalkan asked, coming up silently behind Kellen.

"Of course it is," Kellen said, unwrapping the treat and holding it out for his friend.

"Um," Shalkan said, finishing the bun in three bites. "Next time get one of the marzipan-stuffed ones. I think they're serving them at dinner tonight."

"Uh-huh." Kellen had no idea what Shalkan's sources of information were, but they were always accurate, especially when it came to sweets. "I need to talk to you."

"You're even less happy than usual—and that's saying a lot," Shalkan observed, falling into step beside Kellen.

"Redhelwar offered to make me an *alakomentai*," Kellen said bluntly. There was no reason to mince words, not with Shalkan. Thank heavens. At least there were a few beings in this army he didn't have to do verbal dances with for hours before he could get to the point!

"And you accepted? Or . . . not?" the unicorn asked.

"I'd have to ride a horse! Unless—?" Kellen said hopefully.

"No. There are limits," Shalkan said firmly. "Which horse?"

"He offered me Mindaerel."

"She's a good choice," Shalkan said. "Gentle and well trained. She'll give you a lot less trouble than Valdien does. And you know how to ride. Not very well, but you probably won't fall off."

"But—"

Shalkan stopped and nuzzled him gently. "We're not forever, Kellen. Or even for as long as a pair like Petariel and

Gesade, you know. I will always be your friend, but—I will give you full honesty, here—a year and a day bonded to you will be quite enough for both of us. And we both know that if you want those stiff-necked Elves to listen to you, they've got to see what you're made of. Redhelwar is offering you a good place to start. Just don't think he's offering you an easy one."

"I don't," Kellen said. He'd expected Shalkan to object—he realized now that part of him had been *hoping* that Shalkan would object. But Shalkan thought it was a good ideas as well. And that, Kellen knew, meant he was going to do it.

He'd ordered Jermayan around, on the way to the Black Cairn. He'd led the rescue party on the first expedition to the caverns. He knew he *could* do it . . . in the abstract. But this was all real and immediate and a little daunting. And much more formal than anything he'd ever done before. He wasn't good at being formal: discussing tea and talking about the weather, the way the Elves seemed to expect their military leaders to do even when there was a war on. Give him something to hit with a sword, sure, he was fine, better than fine, but the rest of it . . .

He'd have to learn. That was all there was to it.

"All right. Then—since you think I should—I will," Kellen said, taking a deep breath.

"And don't think you're going to be leaving me behind if you happen to get sent off on any interesting missions, either, because that isn't going to happen," Shalkan said firmly. "You'd only get into trouble if I let you go off by yourself."

"Right," Kellen said, feeling a bit better. So he wouldn't be riding Shalkan, but the unicorn wasn't going to let him go off into danger alone. "No interesting missions."

Shalkan snorted eloquently, switching his tail. "Just be sure to tell the armorers, so they can change Mindaerel's colors. Oh, you'll be quite the dazzling sight. I can't wait."

"Do you want a faceful of snow?" Kellen demanded.

"Do you think you can manage it?" Shalkan drawled

archly. Before Kellen could react, the unicorn bounded forward and kicked back, sending a thick shower of snow into Kellen's face.

Kellen fell backward, coughing and sputtering—and quickly assembling several snowballs to hurl, with deadly accuracy, at his friend.

"Hah!" he cried gleefully as his missiles found their mark.

For the moment, troubles were forgotten.

"IF they're going to fight the way the first ones did, there's no point in risking Vestakia in the first assault wave," Kellen said.

"We do not know that they will. Nevertheless, point taken," Adaerion responded. "We should risk Vestakia as little as possible. We dare not lose her."

There were days that Kellen almost felt as if he were back in the House of Sword and Shield. Mornings were spent in battlefield drill with his new command, afternoons at what seemed a never-ending series of convoluted strategy meetings that made Andoreniel's Council look straightforward. Every time he tried to drop a hint that the Enemy wasn't acting the way *They* had in the last war, the session turned into an excruciating analysis of what had and had not happened, not what the Elves were going to have to do in order to deal with it. It was enough to drive him mad.

At least they might have something real to fight soon. Jermayan had actually persuaded Vestakia to fly with him, and they spent their days covering an expanding ring of territory centered on Ondoladeshiron. The area that they'd "cleared" was marked on a large map suspended in a frame in Redhelwar's tent, and each day a new segment was marked off—a tiny segment, in comparison to the vastness of the Elves Lands, but far better than nothing.

And much faster than if they'd had to do it on foot.

After almost a sennight of meetings, Kellen knew both the

komentaiia and the *alakomentaiia* rather well, though Redhelwar still remained an enigma to him. Of the senior commanders, Padredor, who had gone down into the caverns and faced the Shadowed Elves sword to sword, tended to favor Kellen's suggestions, and thankfully *did* understand that something had to be done to ready the fighters for an entirely new sort of warfare. Adaerion was conservative, but hated to lose troops or assets for any reason, and favored cautious plans that forced the enemy to commit its resources without forcing him to commit his own. Arambor preferred to draw the enemy out with a display of supposed weakness—Kellen suspected his tactics might work fine in theory, but in practice an enemy might take a pretended weakness and turn it into a real one.

And Belepheriel still preferred to believe that there might not be any more Shadowed Elves at all—and if there were, they could certainly be dealt with by the tactics that had served his ancestors in battle for the last several thousand years. His resistance was quiet, but firm.

Of his new fellows-in-rank—all of whom were old enough to be his grandfather, at the very least—several had been newly raised in rank following the Battle of the Caverns, and tended to be quieter than the others. Petariel—Captain of the Unicorn Knights—and Rulorwen—Master of the Engineers—tended to be the most outspoken of the rest.

"Vestakia is not the only one who needs protection," Keirasti said. "Our shields serve us well against sword and mace, but not against a bucket of acid." She winced faintly; Kellen knew Keirasti had lost many of her command in the battle at the underground village, and also knew that her long sleeves hid acid-scars and still-healing burns from that encounter.

"I will hear suggestions for a defense," Redhelwar said formally.

No one spoke.

Why didn't they say anything? Kellen wondered. They all knew what the answer was—everyone in this room had been trained by Master Belesharon, and he would certainly have told them, just as he'd told Kellen. *"If you cannot be where the blow is not, you must arrange matters so that the blow strikes something other than yourself."*

Maybe it was some kind of weird Elven etiquette having to do with doing things the way that things had always been done. Maybe they just didn't *want* to acknowledge the truth. But Kellen remembered what Rochinuviel had said: *"In time of danger, new ideas must not be set aside merely because they are new."*

"A larger shield," Kellen said, when it became obvious nobody else was going to say anything. "They're no use on horseback, but you're fighting on foot in the caverns. Something large enough to hide behind."

"Hide! The Children of Leaf and Star do not *hide*," Belepheriel objected.

"If acid would improve your complexion, it would not improve mine," Arambor said tartly. "Yet the crafting of such shields would be the work of moonturns."

"If Kellen can show me what he is thinking of, I believe my armorers can have at least a few ready within a sennight," Artenel said. "We have seen that good Elvensteel is no defense against the vile liquids that such a shield as this must repel. If they need not be metal, then the work should go quickly."

"Let such shields be made," Redhelwar said. "Bring the first one to me here as soon as it is completed."

The discussion moved onward. Kellen let out a breath he hadn't known he'd been holding. Keirasti shot him a grateful look.

Petariel edged over.

"You're just lucky there probably won't be a Flower War this spring," he whispered. "I'd hate to face Belepheriel in the field, and *you'd* probably lose your lance, your garlands, and your colors besides, Knight-Mage or no."

Kellen nodded politely. He had absolutely no idea what Petariel was talking about.

Seventeen

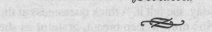

On the Wings of Dragons

𝕴t's beautiful!" Vestakia shouted over the rush of the wind. Jermayan nodded, and Ancaladar laughed aloud, his deep voice booming through the sky.

Today was the sixth day they'd flown, and every day she grew to love it more. She couldn't imagine now why she'd feared it so. Even riding behind Jermayan, there was a freedom and a solitude here, and she hadn't realized how much she'd longed for it. She'd been alone for so much of her life that she'd not only grown used to it, that solitude had become a part of her fundamental nature. Living in the densely-populated city of Sentarshadeen—and then in the even-more-crowded war camp—she'd yearned for something like this far more than she'd realized.

In the beginning she'd been constantly afraid that she'd fall off. Her first flights were only minutes long, and had left her shaking and sweat-drenched, but stubbornly determined to master her fear. And suddenly the moment had come when she was *not* afraid; when she could look around her and see the wonder of the world below as only birds—and dragons—saw it.

And then their true work had begun.

Each morning Vestakia dressed in her warmest furs—by now she had special clothing just for flying—and rode her palfrey to the orchard where Jermayan and Ancaladar waited. They flew throughout the day, landing once or twice to eat and brew tea, for it was cold up in the high sky.

As they flew, Vestakia concentrated on the ground below, willing herself to be aware of any hint of Demon-taint. But as one day followed the next and she felt nothing, Vestakia began to wonder if—though none of them thought it possible—her Gift really wouldn't work from the air.

Then, suddenly, today, she felt it. A thick queasiness at the pit of her stomach. She drew a deep breath, grateful as she had never been before to feel the onset of the misery that signaled that Demon-taint was near. And she was even more grateful to realize by the way she felt that it was not just that she was high above that attenuated the sensation. She tapped Jermayan's shoulder and pointed. North.

He nodded, and Ancaladar veered off in that direction.

Because they were moving so fast, the nausea swiftly worsened, and soon Vestakia was gasping and shuddering, clutching with mittened hands at the raised cantle before her.

"Down there—" she gasped, knowing that either Jermayan or Ancaladar would be able to mark the spot close enough for the army to find it. "Ah!" The yelp was torn from her as they passed directly over the site.

She expected the pain to begin to fade immediately as they flew away from the spot, but to her dismay, it didn't. "Keep going!" she choked out.

Ancaladar had begun to swerve back toward Ondoladeshiron. There was a slight bobble as he returned to his original course, and Vestakia whimpered as the pain began to increase again.

"There . . ." she whispered. It was the last thing she remembered.

Some time later she realized she was no longer in the sky. She was sitting on a blanket, leaning back against Ancaladar's side. No matter how cold it was, the dragon's body was always warm, like summer-warmed rocks. It was as if he radiated sunlight.

She took a deep breath. Her chest hurt.

The light brightened as Ancaladar folded his wing back.

"She's awake," Ancaladar said softly.

"I know I'm awake," Vestakia said, feeling slightly cross. "And at least we know it works."

"We do indeed," Jermayan said, folding her hands around a cup of hot sweet tea and helping her raise it to her lips. "And while I am grateful for the news, it is perhaps somewhat distressing to learn that we have not one, but two enclaves within a short day's ride of one another to deal with . . . and both of them very close to Ysterialpoerin, most ancient of the Elven cities."

"That isn't good, is it?" Vestakia said, after a pause.

"No," Ancaladar assured her. "There really isn't any way to make news like that sound good. But we're very glad to have it, all the same."

⌒

SINCE Idalia worked with strong and sometimes toxic chemicals in her salves and potions, Kellen had brought her into the discussion with Artenel. The Elven armorer already knew the shape of the shield Kellen wanted—long and square, but curved for strength.

But what to make it out of was another question.

"Metal's right out," Idalia had said frankly. "Acid will eat right through it. Glass is best to stop acid."

"If it's thick enough to stop a sword blade—and it will have to stop one or two—it's too heavy to lift," Kellen protested. "And it's fragile besides."

"Nay, that is a myth," Artenel protested. "Indeed, glass does become fragile with time. But new glass is supple, and when thick, is very strong. Yet a mace will crack it if it is not reinforced, nor have I the resources here to make shields of glass."

"What about wood?" Kellen asked. "The acid will eat through it, but not fast, if it's thick."

"And wax," Idalia said. "It's not as good as glass, but it's lighter and a lot more flexible. If you layer wood with sheets of wax—or even just cover a wooden shield with wax—it should be even more resistant to acid. They don't have to last forever; just for one battle. It'll burn like a torch, though."

"But I will cover it in the finest leather," Artenel said, brightening. "And the leather may be water-soaked before battle, then wax laid atop the leather as well. I think we may have discovered the very thing that will serve to confound the foe. It would even serve to hold a *thin* pane of glass, should some be found in time."

Just then Ancaladar returned to camp. The dragon swept low over the camp once, signaling that there was news, before disappearing into the distance.

"He's found them," Kellen said, staring after the dragon.

"It would be more accurate," Idalia said tartly, "to say that *Vestakia's* found them. I'm going to go see if she's all right. *You* stay here."

⟶

THE news had spread throughout the camp by the time Kellen returned to his tent: Shadowed Elves had been found near Ysterialpoerin. Messengers had already been dispatched to Andoreniel and to the Viceroy of Ysterialpoerin to give warning, and the army was making ready to deploy in all its strength, since not one, but two enclaves had been found.

Shalkan said Vestakia was fine, though very tired. Kellen very carefully kept from going to see for himself.

Not seeing Vestakia left him plenty of time to worry about other things, though. All he knew about Ysterialpoerin was that it was the oldest and northernmost of the Nine Cities—which meant it would be even colder there than here, if possible.

He'd barely begun going over a list of things to do—and orders to give—when the bells at his doorway jingled. "Be welcome," Kellen said, turning.

It was Kharren, who was to Adaerion as Dionan was to Redhelwar, though she also commanded a force of her own. Adaerion was Kellen's direct superior in the military hierarchy, which it had relieved Kellen to learn when he'd eventually discovered it. Better Adaerion, steady and fair, than someone he could never hope to impress—like Belepheriel.

Kharren stepped inside and stood in the doorway of his tent, regarding him politely.

"I See you, Kharren," Kellen said, remembering his manners.

Kharren bowed slightly. "I See you, Kellen Knight-Mage. Adaerion wonders if it would be convenient for you to attend him."

Kellen bowed in return. "It is always a pleasure to receive Adaerion's wisdom."

⌒

AFTER the formalities in Adaerion's tent had been observed, and tea had been poured, Kharren departed, leaving Kellen alone with Adaerion.

"One observes that you distinguish yourself well," Adaerion said, sipping his tea, "and that your discourse is always refreshing."

Kellen tried not to frown. What was *that* supposed to mean? Adacrion's expression was impenetrable. Kcllen wasn't sure whether he'd just been insulted or not.

"I thank you for your notice of me," he finally said.

Adaerion smiled. "Impatience is a poor General, yet decisiveness wins many an engagement. This evening Redhelwar dines with his senior commanders, to discuss how best to approach the coming problem. Were you there, perhaps you would contribute some remarks to the conversation."

But I won't be there, because Belepheriel, at the very least, would pitch a fit, Kellen supplied mentally. Even if it would be logical for a Knight-Mage to be present this evening, Senior Commander or not.

Suddenly he realized what this little tea party was *really* about. Adaerion was giving him the chance to tell him what he wanted them to know, so that Adaerion could present Kellen's ideas.

Kellen hesitated, trying to figure out how to phrase his remarks in the indirect fashion that Elven protocol demanded.

"Oh, come, Kellen," Adaerion said gently, and for the first time, allowed a commiserating smile to curve his lips. "Do you think I have never spoken with a human before? I shall not shatter, I promise you. Nor think less of you for being what you are, for if you are human, then you are also a Knight-Mage, and Shalkan's rider. You are impatient, and this is a good thing, for some among us have far more patience than is needful. Speak as you would to one of your own kind. No one else is here to hear."

Kellen relaxed. "Thank you," he said with real warmth. "I think—now that we have found them—it's important to know the layout of the inside of the Shadowed Elf caves before we enter in force. We still don't want to risk Vestakia for that, though we might need her to find the entrances. But we still have Idalia's *tarnkappa,* and they worked before to conceal our presence from the Shadowed Elves. What I think is that before the attack, scouts wearing *tarnkappa* should be sent into the caverns to map them. If they're lucky, they might even discover a route to the villages inside. Then we'll have some idea of what we're facing."

"So you would scout ahead," Adaerion said, nodding. He paused, as if to gather his resources. "Who would you choose?"

Kellen looked surprised, more at the content of the question than that Adaerion had asked it; he was becoming used to the Elves dropping into War Manners now and then when it was the only convenient way to speed a conversation along. "The best scouts. And—anyone with experience in caves, or rock-climbing. Some of the cave paths are pretty narrow, and the *tarnkappa* won't protect someone from being discovered if they're bumped into. So they might have to climb to get out of the way."

"How many would you send?"

Kellen shrugged, forgetting for the moment that this was a human gesture Adaerion might not understand. "It won't matter too much—once they're wearing the *tarnkappa,* they won't be able to see or hear each other. Two or three, perhaps, so that at least one returns. No more."

"Would you go yourself?" Adaerion asked.

The question seemed somehow *different* from those that had come before it, but Kellen answered it just as honestly. "I would go if I was asked to. I do not think that I would be the best one to send. If I used the Wild Magic, it might make them aware I was there—and during an important scouting mission is not the time to find out. In some ways, I am the best suited to the task, and in some the worst. I do know that while I would volunteer, I am not the person best suited to make the decision."

"These are good answers. Very . . . simple." Adaerion seemed to be relieved to be finished with his questions, and Kellen was reminded once more that Elves found questions not only rude, but sometimes very difficult to ask as well—perhaps even more difficult than he found their mode of speech.

"I find some things simple, other things hard," Kellen said. "I think perhaps everyone does."

" '*Beware he who finds all things simple, for that one will make all things difficult,*' " Adaerion quoted. "Yes. Perhaps you are right to think so. Now. There is much to do before we set out upon the war-road again. I think you will find this journey very different than the first."

"Different," Kellen was to find, was the greatest understatement he'd heard yet from any of the Elves.

THE High Mage Anigrel Tavadon—Lycaelon had said his elevation in rank was only a matter of time, and so it had been: a very *short* time—was a very busy—and very contented—man. His days were full, and his master—and more important, his Mistress—were both more than pleased with him.

As the head of both the Magewardens and the Commons Wardens, he now knew everything that took place in Armethalieh, from the sullen grumblings in the lowest dockside tavern to the rash speculations of the Entered Apprentices who drank at the Golden Bells. Finding Commons who would inform upon their fellows—from nobles in need of ready money to pay gambling debts, to merchants hoping their warehouse fees could be eased, to laborers who would tell what they knew for a bottle of brandy and a bag of coppers—had been child's play, and Anigrel's spells ensured that all of his informants were entirely trustworthy.

Finding Mageborn who would act "for the good of the City" had also been easier than he'd expected. Fear had done his recruiting for him—some had come to him anxious to prove that they were not involved in his imaginary conspiracy. Others were equally anxious to align themselves—after the Banishings and resignations—with the new power in the City.

All were useful.

For Anigrel not only collected information, he dispensed it. Rumors were the weapons in his arsenal, and he deployed them with the skill of a master strategist.

Now the Mageborn remembered—no one was quite sure who first spoke of it—that the Lady Alance, Lord Lycaelon's wife, had been Mountainborn. And that the two children— yes, two—that she'd borne to the Arch-Mage had both been Banished for practicing the Wild Magic. Everyone knew that the Mountainfolk were overrun with Wildmages— undoubtedly Alance had insinuated herself into the City in an early attempt to destroy it through Wildmagery, and had passed the heretical taint down to her children. Praise the Light the Arch-Mage had been spared.

But it only proved how deep the plots against the City ran.

And that even humans would ally themselves with the treacherous Otherfolk—and worse. The inhabitants of the Golden City could trust no one but themselves.

And did not the Elves consort with Wildmages as well?

Had not, in fact, the recently arrested sons of the deposed Council members been attempting to learn Wild Magic, possibly with Elven help?

Elves had been seen in the Delfier Valley near the time of the arrests. Undoubtedly coming to the aid of their confederates. Praise the Light they had been stopped.

Soon this tissue of lies and half-truths was common "knowledge" among the Mageborn. They accepted it without question. Why should they not? It fed their pride—and their deepest fears.

Among the Commons, the rumors were simpler.

The Wildmages had caused all the recent trouble in the City, because Wildmages hated cities, and destroyed them wherever they could.

They meant to destroy Armethalieh.

They could hide undetected among ordinary folk, but would always reveal themselves because they did not follow the precepts of the Light, and so did not believe in the wisdom and goodness of the High Mages.

Everyone knew that to become a Wildmage, a blood sacrifice was needed. Since Wildmages were corrupted young, they usually murdered their parents. The Archmage had discovered the horrible truth about his son when Kellen Tavadon had gone mad and tried to kill him. Only the glory and wisdom of the Light had protected the Arch-Mage, and allowed him to survive to destroy the monster in human form that his son had become.

Slowly, the City became a place of fear. In the Low City, brawls and riots increased as the fearful Commons turned on one another. The riots were, of course, the work of the Wildmages.

To protect against them, spells and protective Talismans were needed—and now the costs of such things were higher than ever before.

Each sennight Anigrel came to the Council, bringing reports of the rumors he had gathered—rumors he himself had started, now distorted out of all recognition. And the Council acted upon his reports.

The Watch was increased in numbers, patrolling the streets constantly. New and tighter curfews were introduced for the commons—now everyone in the City must be able to present a Talisman glyphed with their residence and their occupation upon demand. The City was divided into districts, and a permit was required from the newly appointed District Magistrates—all of whom reported to Anigrel—to travel outside of one's home district. And in their fear, the Commons and Mageborn alike not only tolerated these changes, but welcomed them and clamored for more, all in the name of "safety" and "protection."

Anigrel found it all immensely gratifying. The City was growing more and more terrified and disaffected, and blamed one cause: the Wildmages.

The Commons had never heard of the Endarkened—the Mageborn had made certain of that. And the true history of the City—of the banishing of the Wildmages, of the creation of a magick wholly under human control—was a secret shared by only the highest ranks of the Mageborn.

Soon Anigrel would be ready to proceed with the next step of his plan. All he must do now was tighten his grip upon the Mageborn even further—persuade them that their enemy was not the Endarkened, had never been the Endarkened.

That it was—had always been—the Wildmages.

And that only the Endarkened could save them.

ONCE more the moon waned to darkness. Once more Anigrel retreated to his private rooms within the Mage Courts, bearing with him a small black bag, such as Mages used to transport the smaller Tools of their Art. By now he had rooms in a dozen quarters in the City, where he was known by a score of names, but for his Communion with his Dark Lady, only this place would do.

Here, Anigrel met with some of his Magewardens, and kept an ever-growing collection of documents and information on his brethren.

There was High Mage Corellius, with his low taste for beer—and his Tradesman father. Over the years, Corellius had developed a number of interesting appetites that would prove quite embarrassing to him were they exposed to public scrutiny. Possibly even fatal, in the current climate of opinion.

And Mage Nadar Arbathil, whose son Perulan had needed to be dealt with so thoroughly. In his youth Perulan had engaged in quite a correspondence with folk across the sea. Who was to say that Lord Arbathil had not assisted him in doing so? Such a man might easily deal with Wildmages as well.

There were more—many more. Some in positions of power, some the sons of powerful men. All . . . malleable.

And two who were not.

With Anigrel's appointment, the Mage Council's number remained at eleven. There were two seats vacant, and so far Lycaelon had blocked every attempt to fill them.

Anigrel intended to winnow the Council further.

Vilmos would be easy to remove. The man was half-senile and tottering toward reunion with the Eternal Light. A little gentle pressure from Lycaelon would gain his resignation—for health reasons, of course.

And if Vilmos would not see reason, it would be a simple matter some night, when he and Anigrel stood together in the Circle, to see that some Great Working went just wrong enough to cripple the old dodderer, or perhaps even kill him. Vilmos had been excused from the Circle lately on account of his age, but it would be easy enough to goad him into returning.

Perhaps that would even be for the best. There had been too many resignations from the Council recently. A death in service would be more fitting—and uplifting to the Commons.

Arance and Perizel were another matter. Both men were

in their prime—both stood in the way of Anigrel's plans—
and neither was susceptible to pressure—on themselves, or
their sons.

A man who had begun his rise to power by murdering his
own father—as Anigrel had—certainly did not blink at a little more blood on his hands. But the High Mages were well
guarded—and difficult to kill.

But at the moment, a more pleasant task awaited him.

From its small casket, Anigrel removed the iron bowl, and
set it on the desk that now occupied the center of what had
once been his sitting room. Now that there were visitors to
his rooms, the casket shimmered with Spells of Warding, and
would open only to his touch. But that in itself attracted
no attention—the High Mage Anigrel Tavadon was known
to have many secrets, all of which he kept for the good of
the City.

From the pencase at his belt he took the knife he would
use, and set it beside the bowl.

Now he opened the bag and lifted out a large grey cat.

No doubt it had been some Mageborn miss's pampered
pet, but Anigrel had seen it walking along the top of a garden
wall, and the opportunity had been too good to pass up. It
had been the work of an instant to enchant the creature into
Sleep and tuck it into his bag. No one had seen him.

Now, before the animal could rouse fully into wakefulness
again, he lifted the cat over the iron bowl and slit its throat
with a quick deft motion. Blood spurted into the bowl with a
ringing sound, filling it to the brim—cats held so much more
blood than the pigeons he had been forced to employ for so
many years.

And a child . . . a child would be even better. But he must
be careful. His dominion over the City was not yet complete.

A mist of power formed over the steaming surface of the
blood. Anigrel leaned forward, dropping the lifeless body of
the cat carelessly and opening his mind to his Dark Lady, as
he had each Dark Moon for almost his entire life.

"What do you have to tell me, my slave, my love?"

Her darkness filled his mind and his soul, completing him in a way that nothing else ever had and ever could. From the moment he had first seen her reflection in a mirror in his father's house when he had been a child of eight, he had been hers utterly. She had been his first and best teacher. He would do anything to be with her always.

Quickly he told her everything.

"And soon they will be yours entirely, Mistress," Anigrel said humbly.

"Yet something troubles you, my pet. I sense it."

"Two inconvenient Mages. They must be removed."

He felt the rich glow of his Dark Lady's amusement.

"Umbrastone is what you need, my jewel, my slave. It will poison a Mage-man and send him to his bed. Mixed with another poison, it will render that poison undetectable by magic."

Anigrel felt a thrill of delight. Two members of the High Council poisoned in their beds! With only a little care, he could make it look as if their own families were responsible . . .

"Now that I have done something for you, you must do something for me. It is so hard for me to come to you, sweet Anigrel. You must change the Wards that bind the City. You have the power now . . . "

"Yesss . . . " Only let him remove three more members of the Council, and it would be a simple enough matter to suggest that the Mage Council was now stretched too thin for its members to stand in the Circle for every Great Working. To suggest that maintaining the City-Wards be turned over to a specific *trusted* body of Mages who performed no other task.

Anigrel would select them. Anigrel would lead them.

And Anigrel would corrupt them thoroughly.

"It can be done. I will need a little time. But it can be done. I swear it shall be done."

He felt his Dark Lady's delight flood through him, filling his body with black heat. Anigrel's body shuddered in ecstasy, the intolerable pleasure building until he collapsed to the floor, insensible.

—

IT was just as well, Savilla reflected, once the connection was broken, to occasionally reward one's slaves. It made the eventual betrayal so much sweeter.

And she looked forward with longing to the day when she could bring her sweet Anigrel here, to the World Without Sun, and teach him what it truly meant to love the Queen of the Endarkened.

It was nearly a quarter of a century—as the Lightworlders counted time—since she had made her first move in the war. She had acted in secret, for she knew the work would cost her dearly, and in her weakened state, any of her nobles might have challenged her.

She had withdrawn to a secret place, deep within the World Without Sun, and there she had worked tirelessly, destroying hundreds of captives gathered in secret—and all of her own folk who knew of her plan.

And then she had struck at Armethalieh.

Even with all her gathered power, she had barely been able to slip through the wards the City wrapped about itself. But her effort had borne fruit.

She had touched a child's mind.

Receptive, eager, willing to learn all she had to teach . . . Chired Anigrel—now Anigrel Tavadon—had provided the crack in the City's defenses that would soon bring them utter dominion over their loathed enemy. He had become hers utterly, growing in Darkness and strength through the years, moving ever closer to the City's heart of power.

It was not a true breech of the City's wards. As yet, it was only a way for her to communicate unnoticed with her most devoted slave, willing to work toward any task she set.

And now . . .

Victory was near.

She could *taste* it.

Just as she would taste the blood and flesh of her sweet slave, when he was no longer useful to her.

THE Centaur party continued to travel toward the Elven Lands. After the first few days, Cilarnen's aches and pains subsided, though riding a draft mare was just as uncomfortable as he'd thought it would be.

In every spare moment, he practiced with his new wand. The need to practice burned in him; he had his Gift back, and being able to use it again felt better than anything he could have imagined. It was as if he'd had a hand cut off, learned to live imperfectly without it, and then suddenly had it regrow before his eyes. He was only an Entered Apprentice, but he had been studying so hard to try to impress his father that he already knew many of the more complex spells that kept the City running—spells to purify water, spells to bind and unbind, spells to banish vermin, spells to calm animals and send a non-Mage to sleep, dozens more.

But though he built the glyphs that summoned his spells until his eyes ached and his body trembled with weariness, he was careful to leave them incomplete. There was no need for them here, after all, and he really wasn't sure what would happen if he completed them. For some of the spells, he lacked some of the needed components. For others . . . well, the more powerful the spell, the more necessary he had been taught that it was to work it within a warded Circle. All his teachers had said that over and over from the first day he'd entered the gates of the Mage-College. Cilarnen wasn't really sure what would happen if he did them out here. Summoning Fire was one thing—and Mageshield could be done anywhere. But the others . . .

He didn't know. And there was no one to ask.

Seeing his difficulties with the High Magick, Wirance and Kardus had offered to try to teach him their heretical sor-

cery. Cilarnen had accepted with very little reluctance. He
was cast out by the Light already, so it didn't really matter to
him one way or the other, and Kardus was the closest thing
to a friend Cilarnen had among the Centaurs, though he felt
an odd aversion to Wirance . . . not a dislike, precisely, but
more as if Wirance simply wasn't someone he should be
around.

⌐

"THESE are the Books of the Wild Magic," Kardus said,
placing three worn volumes into Cilarnen's hands one night
as they gathered around the fire. "All the wisdom of the
Herdsman's path is written in their pages. Perhaps you will
learn what you seek herein."

Cilarnen accepted them gingerly. There was a certain il-
licit thrill in handling them.

Cilarnen opened the first of the three books. The leather was
stiff and slippery in his hands, the covers oddly hard to open.

"There's nothing here," he said in surprise.

"Say you so?" Kardus said, frowning. "Look deeper."

"At what?" Cilarnen demanded irritably. "There's nothing
to see. The pages are blank." He handed the three books
quickly back to Kardus, who looked down at the first book
thoughtfully, shaking his head in puzzlement.

"Try mine." Wirance, who had been standing a few feet
away, stepped closer, holding out a single slim volume.

Cilarnen took it reluctantly. It was one thing to tell himself he was willing to investigate other kinds of magic. It
was another to have his nose rubbed in the reality of it. Kardus could obviously read what was written on the pages of
his three Books perfectly well, but to Cilarnen, those same
pages were blank.

Unlike the Books of the Centaur Wildmage, Wirance's
Book seemed to burn in Cilarnen's hands, writhing under his
fingers as if it wished to escape. It gave him the same feeling
he had around Wirance, only magnified a hundredfold.

He gritted his teeth and pried the book open.

It was blank.

He let the covers snap shut with a sigh of relief. When he relaxed his grip, it was as if the book flew from his hands and back to Wirance's.

"Nothing," Cilarnen said. "It was blank, too."

"Well, we know that whatever you are, you're not a Wildmage—nor meant to be one, it seems," Wirance said thoughtfully.

"I am a Mage of Armethalieh," Cilarnen said. He'd never been so sure of anything in his life. Half-trained—maybe never better-trained than this—and lacking most of his tools, but still a Mage of the Golden City.

And he would save her if he could.

"A great pity we do not know more about what that means," Wirance said, slipping his Book back into his pack. "Perhaps the Elves will be able to help."

Cilarnen nodded politely, but privately he doubted it. Hyandur had been kind, but as much as he stretched his imagination, Cilarnen could not imagine the Elf tutoring him in magick.

⌒

"WE should be near the border of the Elven Lands soon," Comild said. He had to raise his voice to be heard over the wind wailing through the trees—as Wirance had predicted before they'd left Stonehearth, the fair weather had only held for so long, and for the last several days they had been traveling through increasingly heavy snow. More and more, Cilarnen found himself longing for the comforts of the City—it never snowed in winter there, and there was always hot water whenever you wanted it. Hot water, hot food, hot baths . . .

"Declare yourselves."

The voice came out of nowhere. A figure had appeared in their path where none had been before—hooded and cloaked in white furs that made him almost impossible to see through the snow. He held a short bow pointed at them, an arrow nocked and ready.

"Wirance, Wildmage of the High Hills, brings Comild of the Centaurkin and his warriors to answer Andoreniel's call," Wirance answered.

"Yet do I see one among you who is neither Centaur nor Wildmage," the Elf observed, his weapon unwavering.

Cilarnen had been riding at the front, with Kardus, Comild, and Wirance. Now he wished he'd stayed toward the back. Maybe they just wouldn't have noticed him then— though that was unlikely. On Tinsin's back, he towered over the rest of the troop.

"I am Kardus Wildmage. It is my Task to bring the human Cilarnen to Kellen Wildmage," Kardus said, stepping forward.

There was a long pause. Cilarnen blinked, unable to believe his eyes. Suddenly there was a second Elf standing beside the first. The two of them were identical in every way, except that the second Elf held a long staff instead of a bow.

"You will accompany me," the second Elf said.

He turned and walked off through the winter forest, without waiting to see if they followed.

As they rode through the trees, Cilarnen realized they must be in Elven Lands now. He looked back, but the first Elf had vanished again.

They rode now in silence broken only by the whistle of the wind and the crunch of the snow beneath their hooves. Where before the quiet had seemed companionable, now it was awkward, as if all of them felt that someone might be listening and judging all that they might have to say to one another. For the first time it occurred to Cilarnen that he could have been stopped and turned back at the border. What would have happened then—to him *and* to Kardus, since Kardus would have been unable to complete his Task? Would it have been like the magickal backlash to a spell of the High Magick gone wrong? Or would Kardus simply have camped on the border until his patience wore them away?

Their guide walked steadily onward, never looking back. At last, as the short winter day drew toward a close, they reached a clearing that had obviously been prepared for them.

Windbreaks had been strung between the trees in a half-circle around the clearing to block the brunt of the winter wind. The ground had been swept clear of snow and leaves very recently, and Cilarnen could see that it was as smooth and level as the floor of a house. The sense of this place being a sort of outdoor house was heightened by the fact that in the center of the clearing was a tall cylinder. Its exterior was covered with the most beautiful tilework Cilarnen had ever seen, and through the openings in the side, he could see the gleam of embers.

A stove? Who would put a stove out in the middle of a forest?

Elves, he supposed.

"All you need is here. Others will come for you. Remain until they do," the Elf said.

With that their guide vanished, as if he'd possessed no more substance than the snow itself.

"Elves," Comild said with a sigh of relief as their guide departed. "Elder brothers, and all, but still . . . " He trotted into the clearing, the other Centaurs following him.

Cilarnen hung back. It wasn't that this place made him uneasy—not even as much as Wirance did, and down deep inside, he trusted Wirance—but ever since they'd ridden across the Elven border, he'd had the peculiar sense of being inside a dream he couldn't wake up from, and this place just made it worse.

Kardus looked up at him inquiringly.

"Kardus . . . back at the border . . . if they hadn't let the two of us through, what would you have done?" Cilarnen asked.

"We would have waited until they did," Kardus replied simply. "It is my Task to bring you to Kellen Wildmage, and yours to go."

"But how long would we have waited?" Cilarnen asked, pressing for information.

"Until they did," Kardus said. "I have been in Elven lands before. The Elves are not like humans, nor like Centaurs. They are cautious, but they are not unjust, nor would they deny a Wildmage who needed to complete a Task. Sentarshadeen, the King's city, lies near the border. If we did not leave, they would send to Andoreniel, and he would tell them to let us pass."

So his guess had been right. Kardus had been perfectly prepared to wait the Elves out. Cilarnen felt—relieved. Kardus wasn't going to abandon him.

"Are we going to Sentarshadeen?" Cilarnen wondered what a whole city full of Elves would look like.

"I do not know. But come. It is cold here, and Elven stoves give good heat."

The Elves had left them more than a well-prepared campsite and a stove with a good fire. At the edge of the campsite were more provisions: casks of cider and mead, bread, cheese, and the carcass of a deer, skinned and dressed for roasting.

After weeks on the trail with nothing but dried food and trail-rations to sustain them, the Centaurs fell upon the fresh food with shouts of delight, and soon the savory scent of roasting meat filled the clearing, and the smoke of bubbling fat spiraled up toward the trees. As they waited for the chunks of meat to cook, they shared out the bread and cheese, and filled their tankards with cider and mead.

After trying the mead, Cilarnen stuck strictly to the cider—he'd had a thorough education in alcohol by now, and the mead in those barrels packed a kick like a Centaur's hoof. Maybe if things were different, he might welcome the release that came with surrendering to the light-headedness that a bit of intoxication would bring. But here, now—no. The last time he had relaxed, a Demon had come. When it happened again, he would not be unready.

Wrapped in his blankets, belly full, some of Cilarnen's sense of unreality faded, leaving him time to worry about what was to come.

What was he going to say to Kellen Outlaw when they found him? Cilarnen wasn't quite sure. The Demon's words were etched in his memory—he'd never forget those—but their meaning seemed constantly slippery. There was only one thing he could be really sure of.

He had his Gift.

And he shouldn't.

CILARNEN woke—as had become his habit long before they'd set out on this journey—just before dawn. In Stonehearth, Grander's house would already be awake and stirring; he would wash and dress, grab a quick breakfast of porridge and hot watered ale with the other apprentices, and go off to his morning chores at the stable. On the trail, his first duty in the morning was to see to the fire.

He'd learned to sleep with his boots inside his bedroll. He pulled them on without letting too much cold air in and got to his feet, his blankets wrapped tightly around him. There was a moment of shocking cold as he dropped the blankets and pulled his hooded cloak around himself, then Cilarnen was ready to face the day. The Centaurs were just beginning to stir.

Last night Kardus had showed him how the Elven stove worked. The Elves had left a good supply of the charcoal disks they used for fuel. Cilarnen opened one of the bottom gates of the stove. Good. There was still a good bed of embers left. He picked up several of the disks and set them on the embers, then went to see to Tinsin. There was a water trough nearby, but they'd emptied it last night. He supposed he could fill it with snow and melt the snow to give her and Wirance's mule a morning drink.

But when he reached the place where the animals were tied, there was an Elf there.

Automatically, Cilarnen glanced down at the snow. There were no footprints.

"This is not a riding animal," the Elf observed, regarding Cilarnen unblinkingly. He looked enough like Hyandur to be his twin. Did all Elves look alike?

"Centaurs don't have saddle horses. I had to ride something," Cilarnen said. "Are you—"

But the Elf had vanished again.

Cilarnen shrugged, and went to find a bucket and his wand.

The same spell that warmed his bathwater at home turned a trough full of heaped snow into a trough full of water without much trouble. He led Tinsin and the mule down to it for their morning drink.

He brought them back up and secured them again. Out of habit, the Centaurs made quick work of breakfast, and by the time it was done, Cilarnen could see a cart coming toward them through the trees.

It was on runners because of the snow, and was drawn by four of the most beautiful horses Cilarnen had ever seen. Draft horses, yes; there was no doubt they had been bred to pull heavy loads; but beyond that, they resembled his Tinsin as little as a swan resembles a duck.

Their heavy winter coats shimmered like the finest velvet, and all four of them were so closely matched in color that there was not a hair's worth of difference among them. They were a pale bronze color, and their manes and tails were the color of heavy cream. Their harness was only a few shades darker than their coats, and the cart they pulled of wood a few shades darker still; it was as if the whole was some fabulous carving in amber: a rich man's toy.

Riding beside it were two Elves on horseback.

Cilarnen had thought that Roiry was the most beautiful animal he'd ever seen, but the two stallions utterly eclipsed the Elven mare. Both were greys—one nearly white, the other a dark dapple grey—and they moved with an elegance and grace that made him think of dancing.

The cart pulled to a stop. One of the Elves dismounted and walked forward. He approached Comild.

"The others precede you by many days. The army

marches to Ysterialpoerin. It is a great distance. Here are supplies for the journey, and a guide. I make known to you Nemermet, who will accompany you."

Kardus stepped forward and bowed. "I See you, Nemermet. May Leaf and Star grant us all a safe journey, by the Herdsman's grace."

The Elf on the back of the pale stallion bowed slightly. "I See you, Kardus Wildmage. May the Herdsman watch over your people, by the grace of Leaf and Star. Take what you need from what is here. More will be provided along the way."

"Get to work," Comild ordered his men.

With a wrench, Cilarnen forced himself to stop staring at the Elves and the Elven horses. He quickly saddled Tinsin and packed his gear upon her back, then went to aid the others in emptying the cart under the watchful eyes of the Elves.

Soon the entire contents of the cart—food, blankets, even a couple of braziers and a store of charcoal—had been transferred to the Centaurs' packs. There was even grain for the horse and the mule. Cilarnen hoped that Nemermet was telling the truth about there being places to restock along the way, because there certainly didn't seem to be any grazing to be had—or any hunting either. It would be hard enough finding running water, though he could always melt snow.

"It is good that Luermai made known to us Nemermet's name," Kardus said to Cilarnen, as he helped him fill Tinsin's packs. One of the few advantages of riding a draft horse was that she could carry a great deal in addition to her rider.

"Luermai? You know him?" Cilarnen asked.

"We have met before," Kardus said. "But if he wished to be known to all, he would have given his name. To give us Nemermet's name is kindness enough, as the Elves reckon things."

Cilarnen puzzled that out for a moment. "But aren't *we* doing *them* a favor?" he said at last.

Kardus looked at him. "If the Dark Folk strike first in the

Elven Lands, is it a favor to the Elves to fight them there? Or is it better to wait until they come *back* to Stonehearth?"

Cilarnen blushed. "I guess you're right. But it just seems as if they ought to be more . . . welcoming."

"No one save Wildmages has crossed the Elven Borders in a thousand years. That there is need for anyone to do so now"—Kardus switched his tail—"upsets them."

When Kardus put it that way, it made more sense to Cilarnen. He supposed it was just like, well, Elves and Centaurs in Armethalieh.

Only not quite.

Because the Elves *were* letting them in, even though they apparently didn't like it all that much. And the High Council hadn't let Hyandur in at all.

When everything was ready, Nemermet turned his stallion's head and began to ride off through the trees. The Centaurs, Wirance, and Cilarnen followed.

———

ADAERION had been right about this journey being different from the last. For one thing, there was someplace Kellen was supposed to be every single minute of the day, from before dawn until well after dark. For another, this time he didn't ride among the Unicorn Knights, and he found he missed their free-and-easy companionship more than he'd expected to.

And he missed Shalkan most of all, for now that he was riding Mindaerel in the middle of the army, he only saw Shalkan for a few hours each day, when he could steal time from his other duties—and there were many of them.

Now that the army was on the move, watches and patrols were added to the drills and planning meetings—not that there was much time for drilling, since they were heading toward Ysterialpoerin as fast as the full army could travel.

The weather worsened the more they traveled north. Almost every day now brought snow, and in the deep night

Kellen could sometimes hear the howling of wolves. He didn't envy Jermayan and Ancaladar their post, flying above the army—and back and forth through the clouds—all day, keeping an eye on the territory ahead.

They were a sennight out of Ondoladeshiron when the first attack came.

That day began like any other. Up in the greyness of false dawn. Into his armor, pack his gear, and off to the cook-fire assigned to his group for a quick breakfast of tea and pastries—the cooking tents weren't unpacked at every stop—then to the horse-lines to collect and saddle Mindaerel and gather his troop and find their place in line. By then it was dawn, and the army had begun to move.

As they rode, Kellen realized that he felt unsettled—just as he had the day that Calmeren had come back to Sentarshadeen bearing news of the ambush at the Crowned Horns.

Leaving his troop in Ciltesse's charge, he rode back through the line until he found Adaerion. Collecting his commander's attention, the two of them rode a little aside from the line and stopped.

"Something's going to happen," he said bluntly, though keeping his voice pitched as low as possible. "I don't know what. But soon. I felt like this the day we learned that the children had been taken."

Adaerion glanced back toward the line, to where Vestakia was riding beside Idalia. She seemed completely untroubled. Whatever Kellen sensed, it owed nothing to Demon-taint.

Not all of the creatures that served the Demons bore Demon-taint.

"Ride up and warn Petariel to be on the alert. Then pull your force out of the line and ride to flank." Adaerion rode back toward the line, but Kellen could hear his next words clearly. "Kharren, allow Keirasti, Shunendar, Duarmel, Churashil, and Thenalakti to know that it would please me greatly if they would ride to flank this morning and be alert for any inconvenience."

Kellen urged Mindaerel up toward the head of the army.

The mare seemed grateful for the opportunity to stretch her legs, and soon overtook the unicorn riders, who were, as was the custom, riding far ahead.

"A vision! A vision of spring!" Petariel cried, sighting him. Gesade wheeled around and came trotting back toward Mindaerel, seeming to run across the top of the snow rather than through it.

Kellen reined Mindaerel to a stop and waited for Petariel and Gesade to reach him. "You're to be especially alert today." He hesitated. "I have a feeling."

"What kind of a feeling?" Shalkan asked, trotting up. Now that he was no longer Kellen's mount, Shalkan continued to stay with the Unicorn Knights most of the time—to keep an eye on things, he'd told Kellen.

"Like . . . the day Calmeren came. That something bad is going to happen," Kellen said. "But Vestakia doesn't feel anything."

"Not *Them* then," Gesade said, switching her tail. "Anything else?"

"I'm not even sure about that," Kellen said. He wouldn't have confessed it to anyone else, but the Unicorn Knights, Petariel especially, were the closest thing to family he had here, outside of Idalia, Jermayan, and Vestakia. "But . . . "

"We're glad of the warning, all the same," Petariel said, nodding. "And even if nothing comes of it, don't hesitate to give it again. I'd rather a thousand warnings that came to nothing than to miss one we needed."

"Me, too," Kellen said fervently. He turned Mindaerel's head about and headed back toward the line to find Ciltesse.

THEY'D been riding in flank for nearly an hour when he heard Ancaladar's shriek of fury.

Kellen looked up, just as a flash, like lightning out of season, lit the sky. It silhouetted the dragon against the clouds, surrounded by a flock of winged wheeling shapes like an eagle harried by crows.

Deathwings!

"Ware!" Thenalakti suddenly shouted from across the column.

Horns blew, taking up the warning call. With the precision of a dance, the Elven army stopped and deployed for battle.

Suddenly Kellen could see all of it, spread out before him like the markings on a map. The Deathwings above, and the coldwarg packs heading for the army, preparing to strike the column at several places at once under cover of the growing storm. Thenalakti, Duarmel, and Shunendar were on the far side. He couldn't reach them. But he, Keirasti, and Churashil were here, and the flanking units became skirmishing units when the call to battle was given.

"Coldwarg," he said to Ciltesse. "They'll go for the unicorns first." He stood in his stirrups and drew his sword, making himself as visible as he could. "Skirmishers! To me!"

THIRTY mounted Knights pounded up the line. They were ninety by the time they reached the head of the line, and Kellen saw his first coldwarg in the flesh.

The creatures were nearly the size of a unicorn. Their remote ancestors might have been wolves, but wolf was only a small part of their nature now. They carried their heads low, their thick necks and heavy shoulder-hump of muscle giving killing power to the enormous jaws that could crush a limb—or a neck—with one bite. Their silvery fur was faintly dappled, giving them perfect winter camouflage, and their thick wide paws were perfectly adapted for running over snow. They were the ultimate predator, and the pack sweeping toward Petariel and the others outnumbered the Unicorn Knights three to one.

Kellen swore softly to himself, seeing the perfection of

the trap. The unicorns could not retreat to the safety of the army, and they could not outrun the pack.

People will die here.

It was Kellen's last private thought.

"Archers!" he shouted. "Keirasti! Churashil! Split them up!"

Suddenly the air was filled with arrows. He'd seen Jermayan drop an ice-tiger in seconds with the deadly Elven bow, but though every arrow found its mark in a coldwarg body, the arrows barely seemed to inconvenience the monsters.

They did, however, make the coldwarg aware that Kellen's force had arrived. Half the pack split off from attacking Petariel's knights and came for Kellen's, flowing over the snow toward them like a ripple of wind.

The skirmishers could expect no assistance from the main body of the army. Kellen could sense that it had problems of its own. Ancaladar and Jermayan weren't able to stop all the Deathwings. Some of them were getting through. And not all the coldwarg were going after the unicorns.

Chursashil and Keirasti had split off. Keirasti drove past him, heading for the coldwarg that had nearly reached Petariel's force.

Kellen and Churashil drove into the other pack side by side. The Elvensteel-shod hooves of their destriers plowed the shattered bodies of the coldwarg that hadn't moved fast enough to escape into red ruin beneath them.

But it wasn't enough.

The horses grunted as they wheeled, presenting tight walls of hooves and armor to the pack. It was the traditional defense against coldwarg, but defense would not serve the Elves this day. The moment the Knights had taken their position and braced for attack, the coldwarg facing them turned away and took off to resume the assault upon the unicorns once more.

Follow, and they were vulnerable. Yet there was no choice. Kellen spurred Mindaerel to the attack once more.

As soon as they left the safety of close formation, the coldwarg turned back and attacked.

It became a deadly dance over the snow. Through his battle-sight, Kellen was aware that Thenalakti, Duarmel, and Shunendar had joined him, but the other commanders were as handicapped as he was by the coldwarg's tactics. The beasts would not stand and fight the skirmishers, and when the cavalry gave chase, they were easy prey. All around him he could hear the shouts of Elves and the screams of horses.

Despite their best efforts, the Elves were too spread out. Every time they tried to regroup, the coldwarg went after the unicorns again. The Unicorn Knights were clustered together, but the rest of the skirmishers, Kellen included, were scattered by now in a wide ring around them. He could see it as clearly as if he sat upon Ancaladar's back. And the coldwarg were taking every advantage of that, scattering them further.

He had to make them come to him.

"Shalkan!" *Oh, please don't let Shalkan be dead; I don't think I could stand it—*

"Kellen." The unicorn appeared out of nowhere. He was red with blood; he looked as if he'd been bathing in it. But he was alive. Why hadn't Kellen made him wear his armor? He'd make him wear it every day from now on; he swore it.

"I'm going to form square around the unicorns. Make them stand when I do."

"They won't—" Shalkan began.

"Make them."

Shalkan sprang away. A coldwarg leaped out of concealment in the snow and bounded after Shalkan. Without a thought Kellen sent Mindaerel after it, sword poised to strike. A single downward blow severed the creature's spine.

For a moment he had a breathing space. He looked around, unable to see anyone he recognized. Where was Keirasti? Where was Thenalakti?

"Square!" he shouted at the top of his lungs, unable to tell if anyone could hear him. "Square around the unicorns! Skirmishers!"

On the fields of Ondoladeshiron he'd seen the Elven Knights practicing their maneuvers and thought of those maneuvers as only a pretty dance, useless in the war they were about to fight.

Today Kellen learned differently.

All about him on the battlefield, a ripple seemed to move through the Elven Knights as the order was passed. They moved as the fingers of one hand, fighting through their separate retreats to execute the order Kellen had given. He urged Mindaerel down into the fray, closing up with the Knights to either side.

Slowly, bloodily, the square formed. The Knights fought for every inch of ground. The pack seemed to sense what was happening, and tried to drive through the gaps in the forming lines, but at last the monsters were fighting on the Elves' terms. They met a wall of steel and sword and hoof, and at last the impenetrable square closed around the Unicorn Knights.

"Is everyone—" Kellen began.

"Oh, Leaf and Star." Beside him, Duarmel's voice was flat with despair.

Kellen looked. His heart sank.

Across the battlefield, he saw Keirasti riding toward them, her mare running flat-out. Petariel was behind her in the saddle. Limping along beside the mare on three legs, her top speed now only that of the mare's, was Gesade.

There was no hope. Gesade must have been wounded, Keirasti had stopped to cover her retreat. And now the three of them were going to die in sight of sanctuary, because if Kellen broke the square to send out a rescue party, the coldwarg would take more of them, not just his friends.

The coldwarg circling the square saw them in the same instant.

"Archers, fire," Kellen said, his voice rough. "Everyone, hold steady."

He had no spells that would stop a coldwarg pack. Jermayan did, he was sure, but Jermayan wasn't here.

But he was a Knight-Mage.

"Duarmel, take command. Hold them." He gathered up Mindaerel's reins.

"Take me. I'm faster." Shalkan was suddenly at his side.

Kellen didn't question how Shalkan knew what he was going to do, or what it cost the unicorn to stand so calmly among the knights. He flung himself from Mindaerel's back to Shalkan's, and with a bound, they were away.

Shalkan flew over the snow like a blast of wind. Kellen barely noticed that he had no trouble keeping his balance on Shalkan's bare back. The Elven arrows flew all around them, but despite the wind and the snow, Kellen knew that none of the shafts would strike Shalkan.

The coldwarg were not hurrying as they loped toward their prey. The death of their victims was certain, and they would savor the fear before the kill. Though some fell to arrows, the others did not slacken. It would only take one or two to accomplish the kill.

Kellen saw Petariel push himself from Keirasti's saddle and fall to the snow beside Gesade. He saw the Unicorn Knight rise gracefully to his feet and draw his sword.

Closer now.

There weren't many of the pack left alive; seven, perhaps eight. Of those that had begun the attack, many had fled, many had died. Kellen and Shalkan were within reach of the stragglers now. He could attack them, but that wasn't the point. The point was to defend Petariel, Gesade, and Keirasti.

Keirasti had turned back when she felt Petariel's weight leave her saddle. He could hear her shouting. Gesade was shouting too. Kellen didn't bother to listen to the words. He was focused on what he must do.

The coldwarg could have attacked him and Shalkan as they passed, but they didn't. Kellen hadn't thought they would. The creatures would find it far more entertaining to let them reach the others and kill them all together.

He was counting on it.

"Help me," he said to Shalkan, almost conversationally.

"Yes," the unicorn answered simply.

They reached the other three. Shalkan was running flat-out, bounding over the snow. Kellen thrust himself off backward, landed standing in the snow, whirled, and drew his sword.

The coldwarg, sensing at last that something was not right with their prey, abandoned their lazy lope and began to run. They closed the distance between them and Kellen in seconds.

The world became nothing more than a series of targets. Kellen had no time to think, only to *be*. Afterward—long afterward—he would realize it ought to have reminded him of fighting the Outlaw Hunt, but it didn't, and it never would, because the Kellen who faced the coldwarg in the Elven snow was a very different man than the frightened boy who had faced the pack of stone dogs sent by Armethalieh. That boy had been unsure of himself, uncertain of what to do.

Kellen knew exactly what to do.

He cut through the neck of the first beast that leaped at him. The second didn't die, but it ran, badly wounded. He stopped counting after that. Each blow merged into the next. It was as if they moved to meet his blade. He knew where they were; knew where they would be. It was snowing harder now, masking the world in an impenetrable veil of whiteness, and it didn't matter. Kellen saw the world in patterns of blue and green and red: his attacks, their attacks; defense, retreat.

He did not plan to retreat. He would not be where their blows landed; they *would* be where his blade could find them. It did not matter if he killed, or merely wounded, all that mattered was that *he* became the center of their attention, the foe that could not be ignored, that he dominated their thoughts until there was room for no other prey in their minds.

Except, of course, that he was not the prey.

They were. They just hadn't realized it yet.

Here was the dancing circle, as it had been drawn for him by all his teachers—Jermayan, Master Belesharon, those who had taught them, back to the beginning of the World. Within it was what he had sworn to protect. Attack came from every side; he crossed the circle again and again, his sword spraying blood across the snow like dark stars.

At last there were no more targets.

The patterns faded around him and vanished into whiteness. And his sword suddenly felt too heavy to lift.

Warily Kellen gazed around. With his own eyes, he could see nothing but blowing snow, but the battle-sight told him the coldwarg were gone.

Or dead.

He looked around. Where were the others? There was no one in sight.

They *had* to be here.

"Shalkan?" he said hoarsely. "Keirasti? Petariel? Gesade?" Now that it was over, he could feel the ache in his muscles, the weariness of long exertion in the cold.

Before he could panic, a mound of snow a few feet away thrashed. Shalkan got to his feet and shook vigorously, then Petariel and Keirasti climbed out of the hollow where they had been shielding Shalkan. The two of them gently lifted Gesade to her feet, then at last Keirasti allowed her mare to rise from where she had been lying. The animal shook herself exuberantly, and snorted as if in disapproval of the entire matter.

"I believe I now know what a carpet feels like," Petariel observed, his voice absolutely emotionless.

"You—I—Wait. I *stepped* on you?" Kellen said, confused.

"Several times," Shalkan said. "I thought it best if we stayed out of your way."

"I put Orata down to use as a shield, and Gesade next to her. Shalkan told us all to curl up as tight as we could," Keirasti said.

He'd said he'd help, Kellen remembered with a sudden flash of gratitude. If he'd had to concentrate on protecting the others—if they'd been visible targets for the coldwarg . . . well, things might not have worked out so neatly.

"I'm sorry," Kellen said contritely, his voice thick with the exhaustion that poured over him like winter honey. "I didn't mean to step on you."

Petariel stared at him as if he'd gone mad. Kellen could read the expression very clearly, even through Petariel's helmet. "You saved our lives. You saved *Gesade's* life. And now you're apologizing for it. It's true what they say. Wildmages are all mad."

"Let's go," Kellen said. He shook his head to clear the snow that was falling into his face through his helmet slits, and found enough energy to lift his sword and sheathe it. "Those things won't be back today, but I'm tired, cold, and we need to get back and report. If you can walk that far, Gesade?"

"I can run, if I have to," the unicorn said proudly, lifting her head.

"Let me go on ahead," Keirasti said. "I'll let them know that Leaf and Star have favored us this day." She vaulted into Orata's saddle and cantered off in the direction of the army.

Kellen looked up at the sky. He could see nothing. Now that he had the luxury of worrying, he hoped the rest of his friends were all right.

He knew as clearly as if the coldwarg had the power of human speech what their intent had been. Attack the army, kill as many of the Unicorn Knights as they could. They could not hope to destroy the entire army, but every warrior they could kill was a small victory for those they served. And if the Deathwings had managed to kill Ancaladar . . . or capture Vestakia . . .

"You killed a coldwarg pack," Petariel said in tones of awe, breaking into his thoughts. "I wish I'd been able to watch."

"There weren't a lot of them," Kellen said, realizing the moment he spoke that the words sounded like the worst sort of false modesty. He tried again. "Petariel, I'm a Knight-Mage. That kind of fighting is just one of the things I'm good at, because of the Wild Magic. Like Idalia can heal. It's not like—like something I trained all my life to have. I mean, it's just something I am, not something I had to earn. It doesn't mean . . . " He wasn't sure what he meant to say, so he stopped.

"But you came for us. You and Shalkan," Petariel said.

That reminded Kellen of something. He rounded on his friend, fury giving him a burst of energy he wouldn't have believed he had left only a moment before.

"And what did you mean by *that?* Coming out here with me like that? You didn't have a scrap of armor on! You could have been *killed!*"

"I wanted to see the fun," Shalkan said innocently. "Besides, I knew you'd protect me." Shalkan stretched out his neck, batted his lashes, and managed to assume an infuriatingly sappy expression of hero-worship, despite the fact that he was still covered in drying coldwarg blood.

"I really ought to beat you senseless," Kellen said fervently.

Gesade snorted. "Oh, *don't* make me laugh!" she begged. "It *hurts.*"

The four of them began to walk slowly back toward the others through the thickening snow.

Eighteen

The Price of Power

Cleaning up after the battle took all of that day and the next. Vestakia was unhurt, and Idalia said that according to Jermayan, the greatest injury he had sustained in the battle was having to listen to Ancaladar complain about how the Deathwings tasted.

"There would be more dead had you not given warning," Jermayan said later that night.

Kellen had helped Idalia heal Gesade—a coldwarg had bitten through her foreleg, crushing the bone—and then visited with his wounded in the hospital, and then made his second—and more complete—report of the day to Adaerion. He should, by rights, be so completely exhausted he couldn't stand, but he found that he was too keyed-up to sleep. He'd gone to the horse-lines to check on Mindaerel, and found Jermayan there with Valdien. Jermayan, sensing

Kellen's mood better than Kellen did, had brought him back to Jermayan's tent.

"But there *are* dead. It isn't enough," Kellen muttered, staring down into a mug of mulled cider.

"You would save all the world, if you could," Jermayan said.

"Yes," Kellen said simply.

It was that, but it was more than that. Today the responsibility for saving the lives of others had been real—not an abstract, not a distant thing. The lives he had to save were right there in front of him, and people lived or died by how fast he could think, and how many right decisions he could make in a very short time. It had been his first taste of the responsibility he had chosen, the responsibility that would only become greater the longer he pursued this path. The weight of that responsibility felt like iron chains.

And every day would not always end in victory, as this had. Someday he might have to stand and watch friends die because that was the only way to attain a greater victory. He knew that, and wasn't sure that he could bear it.

"Kellen." There was a note of urgency in Jermayan's voice that startled him. He looked up.

Jermayan was studying him as if he were a problem to be solved. "In the Great War . . . the Wildmages who fell to the Dark . . . they had fought first for the Light. They saw friends, brothers, sisters, loved ones, all die. Perhaps they wanted to save the world as well."

"I . . . *oh.*" Kellen blinked as Jermayan's words sank in. "But I can't stop caring that they die."

"No," Jermayan agreed. "But don't let your caring heart do the Enemy's work for him. Now go to bed."

AFTER that first assault, flank patrols became the order of the day during the march. Every unit of the army took a turn at riding them.

Though the coldwarg and the Deathwings never again attacked the army in the same numbers they had the first time, Jermayan reported that both creatures trailed the army at a distance constantly. Everyone knew this before very long, and everyone was on edge, waiting, wondering what was going to happen next. Though Jermayan and Ancaladar could easily have flown back and destroyed the packs, to do so would have meant leaving the marching column vulnerable to aerial attack—and Redhelwar was certain that this was precisely what their enemy was hoping for.

Kellen agreed, and had said as much. Since the coldwarg attack, his position in the army had undergone a subtle change. He had proven himself—shown that he could think quickly and well in battle, and act efficiently to save lives and form strategies that would kill the enemy. The senior commanders gave greater weight to his advice.

As for the sub-commanders, and the field knights, Kellen was welcomed at every fire and in every pavilion. He spent as much time with them as he could, knowing, deep in his heart, that the day would come when he would have to command them. He wondered if Redhelwar suspected it as well.

The progress he was making toward his goal should have made him happy—it was what he needed, it was what he was working for—but all Kellen could see was the pressure of needing to be both right and lucky the next time he went into battle as well. Each time the stakes were higher, and to gain his ultimate goal, he could not afford a single misstep.

But at least they listened. The creatures—Deathwings and coldwarg both—were obviously acting under orders, and Kellen wasn't the only one to suspect that Vestakia was their ultimate target. The Elves knew that the Deathwings could snatch a rider from the saddle—they'd seen it done one day, when one of the white-furred monsters had slipped past Ancaladar and Jermayan's defenses, though the archers had forced the creature to drop its prize unharmed—so now Vestakia rode in one of the wagons. It was stuffy and far less comfortable than riding on horseback, but at least she was safe from being snatched out of the saddle.

But others would not be, and so Ancaladar flew over the army, and let the coldwarg follow it.

⟷

THE land around Ysterialpoerin was heavily forested. Dense pine woods made it utterly impossible to keep to anything resembling a formal line of march, and slowed the army's progress as alternate routes had to be found, time and again, for the supply wagons. Once they entered the forest, the Deathwings had stopped shadowing them, but the coldwarg did not. The trees provided far too much cover for the coldwarg; everyone knew they were there, but Jermayan and Ancaladar could not always see them. The Elves hunted them when they could, but no matter how many they killed, it never seemed to discourage the rest.

Kellen waited. He knew something was going to happen, and it would be when they let their defenses down.

And it did. When the army was two days away from Ysterialpoerin, the coldwarg attacked again, this time by night when half the camp was asleep.

Kellen was roused out of unquiet dreams by shouts and horns, and was halfway into his armor before he was even awake. Grabbing his sword, he ran toward the horse-lines. They were heavily guarded—next to the unicorns, the horses were the most attractive target for the coldwarg, since without their mounts and draft animals, the army would be crippled.

The battle this time was brief. They lost a few of the horses, and less than a dozen Knights, but once Ancaladar was able to find a place to land and take Jermayan onto his back, the victory was not in doubt.

⟷

THE third attack came days later, this time at dawn, just when they were all encumbered with packing and harnessing up.

One moment, Kellen was tightening the saddle girth—the next, only a glimpse of something moving at the edge of his vision warned him.

Then the coldwarg were on them.

They came on as if driven, and this time there was something desperate in the way they flung themselves at the Elves. There was no thought and no science in this attack; they attacked as the Shadowed Elves had, with hysterical ferocity, as if they were not only trying to overwhelm the Elves with mere numbers, but as if the unseen hand directing them had decided to sacrifice them entirely.

Kellen made a target out of himself. And in a moment, he was surrounded by the coldwarg, which was exactly how he wanted it.

And he began his deadly dance.

Perhaps it had seemed clever to the enemy, to attack now—but it was the worst of all times for them to try, when the warriors were fresh, well rested, bodies still warmed and not stiff and cold with long riding.

The red and blue shadows of battle-sight dodged around him, circling, driving in, dashing out—

Be where they aren't—

Making feints, snapping enormous jaws—

Be where they aren't expecting—

It was what Jermayan would call "a challenge."

Be the target they can't ignore.

With a new challenge involved—the Elves had come to understand that his battle-sight allowed him to see every danger, including friendly fire, and were taking advantage of that. So while he made an irresistible attraction of himself, they surrounded him and sent arrow after arrow into the ring of coldwarg around him. Now his own dodging had to include the arrows that missed their targets.

And even a Knight-Mage grew tired—

Kellen drove his sword through the body of a coldwarg. He was beginning to tire, and as a consequence, the strike was clumsy—he'd missed vital organs—and the monster dragged itself along his blade, jaws snapping as it strained to reach his throat.

He flung himself onto his back, pulling his dagger, and jammed it with all his force into the beast's eye. He felt the tip of the blade grate against the inside of the back of its skull as the blow drove home.

As it thrashed, he got his feet into the coldwarg's chest, and shoved with all his might, flinging the dying creature away from him. He rolled to his feet, and looked around for fresh targets, but his battle-sight was strangely clouded. A blue haze filled it, though to his normal vision, the scene was clear.

And with normal sight, he could see the coldwarg walking—slowly, stiffly—away from their prey. Their heads and tails were down, and their hackles stood up stiffly.

Something is happening.

"Let them go," Kellen said quietly to the Elves around him.

The coldwarg staggered away from the horses, into the trees, moving in an eerie silence. Kellen could see their sides heaving; the beasts were panting as if they were running. When they were a bowshot's distance away from the horse-lines, they stopped.

And burst into flames.

They burned as the stone houses in the Shadowed Elf caverns had burned, with a hot and furious flame that touched nothing around them. The fires burned so quickly that none of the beasts had time to utter so much as a yelp, and in seconds nothing remained but pools of snowmelt where the coldwarg had stood.

The Enemy had discarded its weapon.

THE day they reached Ysterialpoerin, Redhelwar and Adaerion rode down into the city, with Kellen's troop along as escort, as the army continued onward toward the place where it would settle itself semipermanently.

Ysterialpoerin was the closest in form—Jermayan had told Kellen—to how the Elves had lived in the days before the Great War.

As they rode, Kellen kept waiting to see a sign that they had reached the city, and finally realized that there wasn't going to be one. They were already *in* it. He looked around, as much as he could without changing position. It was nearly impossible to tell where the trees stopped and the buildings began, so artfully did they blend together. Kellen had to look very closely as he rode, but yes—there was a house, built somehow *between* two of the largest trees, several dozen feet over their heads. And there was another, on the ground this time, its stone surface nearly indistinguishable from the stone outcropping thrusting into the forest beside it. Only it wasn't stone, he realized a few moments later, but tile made to look like stone.

And some of the trees weren't trees at all, he realized with a shock—unless trees had doors in them, and windows.

He'd thought that Sentarshadeen was beautiful, and that its dwellings blended into the landscape, but riding into Ysterialpoerin was like riding into a dream while you were still awake. Even the snow seemed to have fallen here with the intent to fall beautifully.

At last—Kellen suspected they'd ridden all the way through the center of the city to reach their destination, but he hadn't seen a single Elf, and very few things he recognized as a house—they came to what would be, in human lands, the Viceroy's Palace.

The forest opened out into a clearing. At the far side of it stood a house, the first one Kellen had seen here that was easily recognizable. Like the House of Leaf and Star back in Sentarshadeen, it *was* a house, not a palace, though it was quite large. Unlike the House of Leaf and Star, it was made entirely of wood—ancient wood, weathered to grey by the passing of untold seasons. Like the House of Leaf and Star, it glittered with winter's ice, but everywhere that Kellen could see, the wood was carved; delicate intricate carvings of vine and flower, leaf and bud. It was as if the house itself might burst into flower at any moment and take root in the earth beneath.

Standing upon the portico of the House were two Elves wearing elaborate jeweled and feathered cloaks of white, pale grey, and ice-blue.

The riders stopped. Redhelwar dismounted and walked forward. He bowed deeply.

"I See you, Kindolhinadetil, Voice of Andoreniel in Ysterialpoerin. I See you, Neishandellazel, Lady of Ysterialpoerin."

"We See you, Redhelwar, General of Andoreniel's armies. Be welcome in the House of Bough and Wind, Branch of Leaf and Star, you and those who ride with you."

"We come on the wing to speak our word," Redhelwar said, not moving from where he stood.

"Yet be welcome, as the wind that shakes the bough is welcome," Kindolhinadetil said.

At this second invitation, Redhelwar moved forward. Adaerion dismounted, and gestured for Kellen to follow. The three Knights followed the Elven Viceroy and his Lady into The House of Bough and Wind.

Kellen resolved not to say a single word while he was here, no matter what. The Knights of Ysterialpoerin had seemed just like the rest of the Elves Kellen had met, but on reflection, he realized that must be because they'd left Ysterialpoerin and traveled extensively through the Elven Lands—and spent a number of years at the House of Sword and Shield besides. Kindolhinadetil and his Lady were another pot of tea entirely. He suspected they wouldn't have any particular patience with round-ear informality, Knight-Mage or no.

He knew the Elves were an ancient race—far older than humans—but walking into the House of Bough and Wind was the first time he truly *felt* that age. Walking through the doorway was like walking into a summer forest. It looked nothing at all like a human house. He smelled the green scent of new growth, heard the twittering of birds, and saw the flash of butterflies among the trees. The fantasy was perfect. Yet there was no magic in it, only Elven artifice and the love of illusion.

Passing between two trees, they found themselves in a "clearing." There were other Elves present—not dressed in winter's white, but in the soft bright colors of summer. They stood so very still that only Kellen's Knight-Mage senses made him certain they were there at all, and not merely some vividly lifelike artwork created to serve the same function as statuary.

Kindolhinadetil and Neishanellazel removed their long cloaks. Beneath them, they, too, were dressed in summer colors; Kindolhinadetil in shades of green and blue, Neishanellazel in copper and gold.

Servants—somehow Kellen had no doubt there were servants in Ysterialpoerin—came forward to take the Knights' heavy winter cloaks. As they did, Kindolhinadetil and his lady seated themselves on elaborately carved chairs and turned their whole attention to Redhelwar.

"It would please us to hear all that you may tell," Neishandellazel said, speaking for the first time.

Concisely—at least for Elves—Redhelwar explained about the Shadowed Elves; how Vestakia had discovered evidence of their lairs nearby, and how he and his army had come north to exterminate them.

There was a silence after Redhelwar had finished speaking. In a human conclave, it would have been filled with questions, but on consideration, Kellen supposed they were all pretty irrelevant. The Elves of Ysterialpoerin would know that Redhelwar would do the job as fast as possible, and the best way possible, and protect Ysterialpoerin as well as he could. So what else was there to ask?

"What Ysterialpoerin can do to aid you will be done, in Andoreniel's name," Kindolhinadetil said at last. "Send your injured to us that they may find peace and rest, and know that our forests stand ready to succor those who are heartsick for the forests of home. Know also that we will provide the Last Gift to all who require it."

"The gifts of the Voice of Andoreniel are great, and his counsel makes good hearing," Redhelwar said, bowing very low once more. "And now I must return to my army, so that all may be done as Andoreniel wishes."

"Let it be so," Kindolhinadetil agreed, rising to his feet.

⌐

IT took Kellen some time to figure out what the Viceroy had meant, but he had nothing *but* time as they rode to catch up with the army. The Last Gift must be burial—only the Elves didn't bury their dead, they hung them in trees. And Kindolhinadetil had been saying—must have been saying—that it would be appropriate to put the Shadowed Elves there, too. He couldn't fathom it—how they could still feel kinship with those creatures—but it wasn't up to him, after all. Perhaps it would make them feel a little less guilty.

As for the rest, Kellen hoped there wasn't going to be any need of it. But pragmatically thinking, with two enclaves to clean out, he knew there'd be losses. And the Herdingfolk Wildmages hadn't arrived yet, though the army had added several more Wildmages from the Mountainfolk.

When they caught up to the army, Dionan told Redhelwar that Jermayan and Ancaladar had scouted ahead and found a place suitable to make an extended camp. Padredor and Belepheriel had taken several units ahead to secure and prepare it for the arrival of the main force and the baggage wagons, while Jermayan and Vestakia made an overflight to determine the exact location of the caves.

"All is as I would have it," Redhelwar said with satisfaction.

⌐

BY a few hours before dusk, most of the camp was in place, though it would be another full day before all the larger pavilions were unshipped. An hour earlier, six Elven Scouts carrying *tarnkappa* had ridden out to the locations now marked on Redhelwar's map—just as Vestakia had sensed in her first overflight, the two enclaves were only a short distance apart. Ancaladar had been able to spot separate entrances, but that was no guarantee that the two sets of caves did not connect beneath the ground. Perhaps the scouts would be able to tell them whether they did or not when they returned.

For now, Vestakia was resting in the Healer's tent. The strain of coming so close to such a large concentration of Demon-taint and then doing such delicate work of detection had exhausted her, but fortunately the camp was located far enough away that she was not constantly affected by the nearness of the Shadowed Elves. And there was nothing Kellen could do to help her.

Once again Kellen forced himself to stay away from her bedside, trying to give Vestakia as little thought as he'd give a sword, or one of Artenel's new shields. Idalia or Jermayan would tell him if there were anything truly wrong. Meanwhile, he forced himself to focus on other things—the strange and somehow deeply-unsettling beauty of Ysterialpoerin; the fact that there was to be a strategy meeting after supper. The proximity to Ysterialpoerin and the fact that they could finally unship the ovens from the carts meant that the food would be better. Though Elven food was never really bad, Kellen was getting tired of an endless diet of tea, soup, stew, and porridge—though it did occur to him that he ought to be grateful to have the luxury of being tired of food of any sort. The Mountainfolk had been existing on much less, and the time might be coming when he would look back on soup, stew, and porridge with longing.

"You're restless tonight," Ciltesse said, coming up to him with a cup of tea.

Kellen took it gratefully, warming his gloved hands. He knew now why fighting in winter was something a sane man avoided at all cost. The weather was another enemy to fight; one that never got tired, and never retreated, and had the terrible weapons of cold and storm forever in its arsenal.

"I suppose I wish it were over with," Kellen answered. "Or at least, that we knew more than we do."

Ciltesse smiled faintly. "As do we all—the caverns cleansed and we home at our firesides. And better yet, that there were no need to have cleansed them at all. Yet all things come at a price."

Is the fighting now the price of the centuries of peace in Elven Lands in the past? Kellen wondered. Or was it the price to pay for centuries of peace in the future—if they won?

He didn't know. He only knew that he felt terribly uneasy. About what was to come? Or . . .

There was a scream from the Healers' Tents, and all Kellen's sense of unease coalesced into a sudden terrible sense of *warning.*

He flung away the cup, with no idea where it went, and gave poor Ciltesse a shove in the direction of the Unicorn Knights. "We're going to be attacked—go! Warn as many as you can!"

Kellen whirled and ran headlong through the camp, toward Redhelwar's tent, giving the alarm to all he passed. It had been Vestakia who had screamed—she could sense Demon-taint at a great distance. Kellen's own abilities relied more on hunches—the more he faced a particular enemy, the more accurately he could predict how that enemy would behave in battle. And sometimes the Wild Magic gave him advance warning of danger to come.

But not enough to do any real good, Kellen thought in bitter, frantic frustration.

He reached Redhelwar's tent and barged inside, not stopping for courtesies. Redhelwar was disarming himself, as Dionan stood by. In the distance, Kellen could hear a few of the Elven warhorns blowing, sounding the watch-and-ward.

"The Enemy is attacking!" Kellen blurted out. "Vestakia sensed it too!"

Suddenly the calls of some of the horns changed. An enemy had been sighted.

"Yes, so it seems," Redhelwar said with remarkable calmness, reaching again for the pieces of his discarded armor. "See to your command."

Kellen sketched a salute and pelted off again, as fast as his feet could take him.

⌒

THANKS to Vestakia and Kellen, the Elves had gotten some advance warning, but the camp was large, and there hadn't been time to spread warning throughout the entire camp before the first attackers appeared.

Coldwarg attacked the sentries, appearing out of the snow like ghosts.

This time they were accompanied by Shadowed Elves.

Showing no concern for their own survival, the Shadowed Elves ran directly toward the center of the camp, side by side with their four-footed allies.

Not all of them reached the camp. Those already beneath the trees Jermayan could not reach, but those still on open ground were easy prey for his magic.

But those who did get into the camp caused damage enough. They were armed with bows, not swords—the terrible poisoned arrows that the Elves had learned to fear in their last battle—and with worse than that; sacks of small fragile spheres filled with acid. They threw them with deadly accuracy, and as the spheres shattered, the thick syrupy liquid inside burned through anything it touched.

But because they were fragile, the spheres were vulnerable targets as well. The Elven archers quickly learned to aim, not at the Shadowed Elves, but at the sacks that they carried, shattering the contents with a volley of arrows and leaving the acid-soaked carrier screaming in agony upon the ground for a few brief minutes until a merciful sword stroke ended his life.

There was no order of battle, no organization. Kellen had not even managed to reach his troop again before he found himself facing a slavering coldwarg over the body of a dead

Knight. The monster's jaws dripped blood and saliva. It gazed at Kellen with glowing yellow eyes for a timeless moment, growled, and sprang.

Kellen stepped forward, into its leap, bringing up his sword like a boar-spear. The weight of the coldwarg knocked him flat, but the beast was dead before they both hit the ground, impaled through the chest. He rolled out from under it, wrenching his blade free as he did, and went looking for fresh targets.

He smelled smoke. Some of the tents were burning, and the reek sent a wave of panic through him.

Then discipline took hold of him. *Stop. Think.*

Kellen took a deep breath and stood where he was. There was nothing to gain by running around like a chicken trying to avoid the barnyard axe. He must use his gifts.

The Shadowed Elves weren't stupid. Alien to everything the Elves knew, but not stupid. Even with the coldwarg to help them, they were outnumbered here, and had thrown over their main advantages of absolute darkness and confined spaces to make this attack. The Elves would kill them all and they must know it. Yet they had attacked anyway.

Why?

They are creatures of the Shadow. The Shadow fights a war of the spirit. What is the greatest blow it could strike against the Elves this night?

Suddenly he *knew.*

This is a feint. The Shadowed Elves mean to distract us from discovering their true target until it is too late.

And he knew—with a sudden awful certainty—what it was.

He ran toward his tent.

There were Shadowed Elves and coldwarg along the way that he could have killed. He did not stop.

He found Isinwen near his tent. The rest of his troop was scattered, attacking the attackers, but he sensed them nearby.

"Ciltesse?" Kellen demanded.

Isinwen shook his head.

Kellen had ordered Ciltesse to spread the alarm. He might be anywhere. There was no time to wait for him.

"Gather the troop. Get to the horses. We ride at once. Stop for *nothing*."

"Alakomentai!" Isinwen said. He turned away, running toward the others to pass the word.

Kellen moved through the chaos of the camp, giving the same order over and over.

He blessed the Gods of the Wild Magic, blessed Leaf and Star, blessed all the trust he'd earned in the sennights passed—his men abandoned the camp and the battle and followed him. By the time he reached the horse-lines, Isinwen and the others who had gotten there first had retrieved their mounts and saddled them.

Kellen vaulted onto Mindaerel's back and set her off as fast as he dared, away from the camp and back into the forest. Through deep snow, at night, in the woods . . . there were a thousand ways for a horse, even an Elven destrier, to break a leg on uncertain footing.

But some of them must get through. And that meant they all needed to know why.

"This attack is a trap to occupy us," Kellen called back over his shoulder. "They strike at Ysterialpoerin! I think they mean to burn it."

Unconsciously, he shifted Mindaerel's path to the left, and realized he'd sensed an obstacle beneath the snow. "Behind me, and follow like my shadow!" he ordered, and shifted to battle-sight. By this time, he had learned to rely upon it as he did his muscles; it was less like shifting to a different way of seeing, and more like focusing on something you wanted to see clearly.

There. The path to take—the clear path, the *safe* path—burned a bright clear blue against the snow, often narrow, always twisting. He set Mindaerel upon it, urging the mare to her fastest speed. He felt the body beneath him gather, and her speed redouble.

An ordinary horse would not have run so for her rider. A

horse's night-sight was not good, and where a horse could not see, it would not go. But Mindaerel was an Elven destrier. She would answer her rider's commands until her heart broke. She ran through what to her must be utter darkness, trusting absolutely to Kellen's touch to guide her. Behind him, the Elven Knights in his command followed in a single file, all riding at breakneck speed in Mindaerel's hoofprints.

Back in Armethalieh, Kellen had never believed in the Light. Idalia had called it "bloodless," and it was—even more unconnected to the reality of daily life than the study of the High Magick. Jermayan and the other Elves swore by Leaf and Star—and Kellen had fallen into the same habit— but he wasn't at all sure what that *meant*.

As for the Gods of the Wild Magic . . . well, Kellen believed in the Wild Magic, because he worked with it daily. He had no doubt that it had a purpose outside itself. Maybe that was what the Gods of the Wild Magic were, but they didn't seem to be anything you could talk to directly.

Right now he wished they were. He'd ask anyone—the Gods of Leaf and Star, of the Wild Magic, the Great Herdsman of the Centaurs, the Huntsman of the Mountainfolk, Vestakia's Good Goddess—for help in reaching the Shadowed Elves before they did whatever they intended to do. He was certain now that they'd left for Ysterialpoerin before the second group had struck at the camp, and if Sentarshadeen was the head and the crown of the Elven cities, Ysterialpoerin was surely its heart. To attack it, to burn it as the whole might of Andoreniel's army stood by, oblivious . . .

Would be precisely the sort of thing Shadow Mountain would love best. It's why they never did it before. They were waiting for an audience. They want us to see how helpless we are, and despair. They want to break our hearts and our spirits.

He strained his senses as Mindaerel raced over the snow. He had gone now beyond hope, beyond prayer. He *willed* their victory, because they dared not fail.

He could sense Ysterialpoerin ahead. Its boundaries were

as clear to his Knight-Mage senses as if they were lines upon a map. He could see its Elven sentries, and knew that they saw nothing—not the Shadowed Elves, not the Elves racing toward them.

But *he* could sense the Shadowed Elves.

He urged Mindaerel onward. In the darkness, he dared not take his hands from the reins to unlimber his bow, for his hands were her eyes. He was by far the poorest shot in the entire camp—except perhaps for Vestakia—but a bow had more range than a sword, and even if he didn't hit any of the Shadowed Elves, he could at least get their attention.

Once they were in range.

At last his battle-sight told him that they were.

And the shining azure path—the path of safety for a running horse—widened out, ringing the city with a band of manicured protection. In that moment Kellen blessed the Elves' attention to perfection, for now the path was smooth enough that not one destrier would put a foot wrong between here and the city.

"Go!" Kellen said, motioning the others up as he reached for his bow.

He knew if he looked with his eyes he would see only darkness. He knew the Elves' night-sight was better than his, but he wasn't sure how much even they could see, here under the overshadowing trees.

Balancing on Mindaerel's back, he strung his bow and nocked an arrow. Without thought, he drew and fired.

Without waiting to see whether he'd hit the target he fired again; neither as fast nor as sure as the Elves, but by his arrows the enemy knew it had been discovered.

All around him now, the Elven bows were singing. Kellen flung his own aside and drew his sword.

The Shadowed Elves could have run—or tried to. But as always, the sight of true Elves seemed to wake some madness in them. They turned and the eight warriors among them began launching arrows of their own. Kellen could see the green fire of the poison upon their arrowheads.

Their bows did not have the range of the Elven war-bows, but the Elves were easily within range of their arrows now. Their only defense was to ride the Shadowed Elves down before they could launch too many of their deadly poisoned shafts, hoping none of the darts struck true, and everyone riding with Kellen knew it. The Shadowed Elves' only defense was to cut them down at a distance; they knew that, too.

They were twenty against eight, and the Shadowed Elves wore no armor. Speed and momentum won; when they closed the distance, it wasn't even a battle.

In seconds the Shadowed Elf males were no more than heaps of rags upon the snow, struck down by Elven arrows, trampled by the horses' hooves. Several of the Knights dismounted and ran forward, swords drawn, to make sure they were truly dead.

"Kellen!" Isinwen cried, pointing.

Kellen saw the four survivors—all females—running toward Ysterialpoerin. They ran in pairs, each pair carrying a large jug between them. Without hesitation, he urged Mindaerel after them.

Once he would have hesitated to attack them. It seemed like an eternity ago now. He took Mindaerel to the right as Isinwen swung left. His sword flashed out, and the nearest female's head went flying. He spun Mindaerel, facing the other, and struck again. Beside him, as if he were Kellen's reflection in a mirror, Isinwen did the same.

It was over. Kellen breathed a sigh of relief.

And then, slowly, Mindaerel sank to her knees in the snow. Kellen sprang from the saddle as the mare rolled to her side, her ribs heaving as she gasped for breath.

"Mindaerel!" he cried. She raised her head.

"Mindaerel. Lady—" Kellen choked, sinking to his knees beside her. Now that he looked, he could see the baleful green of poison, the Shadowed Elf arrows sunk into the muscle high upon her foreleg, just below the protection of her armor.

Yet during the fight, she had given no sign of her wounds.

She had run on, fleet as the clouds before the Moon, had done everything he asked of her—

"Mindaerel—" he whimpered. Hearing her name, Mindaerel lày her head down in the snow again, stretching her neck out toward him. Kellen reached out to touch her muzzle. But before he could complete the gesture, she gave a great sigh.

And stopped.

She was gone.

A moan escaped him as his throat closed.

"We hail the bravery of a great warrior," Isinwen said quietly, dismounting to stand behind Kellen. "May she run forever through the Fields of Vardirvoshan."

Kellen bowed his head, feeling his eyes fill with tears. He'd lost . . . a comrade, a friend . . . one who hadn't, perhaps, truly understood the battle or the need to fight it, but who had given up everything she had to it. Out of love. He stroked her muzzle, but it was a pointless gesture; the flesh was already cooling beneath his fingers, for Mindaerel was truly gone. Perhaps her spirit *was* running free through the Fields of Vardirvoshan where she had been foaled. He hoped so.

He took a deep breath, and got to his feet. The task was not yet complete. He knew what the Shadowed Elves intended, but not how they were going to do it.

"Let's see what was in those jugs."

When they broke the wax seal and pried off the lids, they found that both jugs were filled with oil and dozens of rings of a strange whitish material. Four of the male Shadowed Elf dead were carrying a second set of bows—larger and heavier than their usual ones—and quivers of iron arrows with oddly shaped tips. Kellen used one of these to hook one of the white-metal rings out of one of the pots of oil— cautiously, as he trusted nothing to do with the Shadowed Elves.

He held it up, puzzled, as the Elves gathered warily around. As the oil dripped from the ring, it began to smoke, then to burn, glowing brightly, and the shaft of the arrow began to glow red-hot.

Startled, Kellen dropped the arrow into the snow, but to his dismay, the snow did not quench the ring's fire. If anything, it burned more brightly, melting down through the snow and the ice beneath, and curls of smoke began to rise from the buried leaves. Kellen scrabbled through the snow until he found the arrow shaft—it was hot even through his gauntlets—and plunged the ring swiftly back into the oil. The ring sizzled and smoked, the oil simmering with its heat, and he shook the arrow gently, wincing at the heat, until the ring dropped off. He quickly tossed the arrow aside, and to his relief, it cooled in the snow like ordinary metal.

"The metal burns like one of Jermayan's fire-spells," Sihemand said, sounding troubled.

"There's no magic to it. Not that I can sense, anyway," Kellen said, puzzled. But it would have burned as well as a fire spell. Oh, yes. Those metal rings, launched into the trees and houses of Ysterialpoerin, would have burned the forest and anything else they touched, no matter how much water the Elves had thrown on the blaze.

"Declare yourselves," came a voice out of the darkness.

A little late, aren't you? Kellen thought uncharitably.

"Kellen Knight-Mage," he said, turning in the direction of the voice. He racked his brain. He *knew* there were proper forms for this sort of thing, but he didn't know them!

"*Alakomentai* to Adaerion, *komentai* to Redhelwar, Army's General, hand of Andoreniel, by the grace of Leaf and Star ruler over the Nine Cities," Isinwen supplied smoothly, not missing a beat. "We come in a good hour, for as you see by the blood on our swords, there are those who wish ill to Ysterialpoerin, heart of the land, and to Kindolhinadetil, Voice of Andoreniel, and Neishandellazel, his Lady." Isinwen's voice took on the force and melodious tone of one making a speech. "These who would harm the forest came in the night, bringing fire to the trees out of season, and in a way not willed by the great balance that governs all things. Yet we came before them, as the wind comes before the storm, and so the forest stands strong by the will of Leaf and Star, and all who would harm her lie dead by the will of Kellen Knight-Mage and the ways of the Wild Magic."

That should shut him up, Kellen thought, impressed.

Unfortunately, there was very little that could truly silence an Elf.

"I See you, Kellen Knight-Mage," the sentry said, bowing, a great deal less impressed than Kellen was.

"I See you, Ysterialpoerin's guardian," Kellen said, bowing in return. Damn it all, this was no time for Elven formality!

But it appeared that the sentry was bound and determined to hold to convention. Kellen felt like a wild thing lunging against a tether; he desperately wanted to get back to the camp and bring these strange new Shadowed Elf weapons with them. But despite his feeling of urgency, he knew that offending the Elves of Ysterialpoerin would only make trouble for him later. He had to hold on to their respect. He took a deep breath and restrained his impatience.

"Perhaps you will allow me to carry your word to Kindolhinadetil," said the sentry, "that he may know what aid and honor will best sustain you in the completion of your task."

Now what was he to say?

Once more Isinwen saved him. "Compared to Kindolhinadetil's burdens, Ysterialpoerin's guardian, our own are light indeed, and we would be greatly honored not to add to them by more than the word of what has transpired here this night. And we are but come upon the wing. Our duty to Redhelwar, Army's General, calls to us like hind to hart in spring, and our hearts leap to obey."

"Let it be so, then." The sentry bowed again, deeply, and seemed to vanish without moving, but by now Kellen was practically used to that.

"We need to take the strange weapons," Kellen said. "Handle the jugs carefully. They can't be allowed to spill. Leave everything else. I'll tell Adaerion what happened here."

And let someone else worry about it for a change.

Before they left, however, the Elves arranged the Shadowed Elf dead neatly in the snow. It was not only a mark of
respect, but would make handling the bodies easier later,
since they'd certainly freeze solid in the night. Kellen took
the opportunity to look around for other traps, but saw none,
and sensed no further danger to the city.

At least not tonight.

He walked back and collected his bow from where he'd
thrown it, slinging it over his shoulder, and as he did he saw
the faint trail of blood in the snow from Mindaerel's
wounds.

If he'd known Mindaerel had been hit, would he have
stopped, tried to heal her? Could he have saved her life if he
had? Even as he asked himself the questions, Kellen knew
the answer was "no." No, he wouldn't have stopped, couldn't
have stopped, not until the Shadowed Elves were all dead.

And by then it would have been too late.

"It would honor me did you choose to ride with me," Isinwen said, trotting up beside Kellen on Cheska.

"Thanks," Kellen said. He took Isinwen's hand, and
pulled himself into the saddle behind him.

They rode back toward the camp—more slowly now, following their own hoofprints in the snow. The horses were
tired, and Kellen sensed no need for haste. The fight back at
the camp was certainly over by now. And if they'd stayed to
fight it, Ysterialpoerin would already be burning.

He didn't want to be alone with his thoughts just now.
They kept returning to Mindaerel. He knew that a good general had to use the people and materials available to him to
win—use them *up* as often as not. He wondered if Redhelwar regretted every death of those under his command.

Suddenly Kellen found himself hoping so—fiercely. So
far he'd been lucky. His people had been wounded, some
gravely, but no one had died. But when they attacked this
new set of caverns, some surely would die. He would not
only send them to death, he would lead them to it, just as he
had led Mindaerel. And afterward he would mourn them,

just as he mourned her now, but he would know—he knew now—that it was something he did open-eyed, and would do again the next time there was need.

What was he becoming?

A leader. A commander. Someone who can face Shadow Mountain—stand against the Demons—and not flinch.

Nobody said it was going to be fun.

He wondered if this was how a sword felt while it was being forged.

But right now he needed something to take him outside his thoughts, if only for a little while.

"You're good at that," Kellen said to Isinwen as they rode. "Talking to the sentry. They're very . . . formal . . . here."

"Yes. I was born here," Isinwen said blandly. Kellen stiffened in surprise. If it had been Jermayan, Kellen would be sure he was being set up for one of the elaborate and obscure Elven jokes, but he didn't know Isinwen well enough to be sure.

Isinwen chuckled. "One does not forget the ways of Ysterialpoerin easily."

Kellen was only glad he was riding behind Isinwen, so the Elf could not see his expression, but apparently it wasn't hard for Isinwen to guess by the way Kellen twitched. He hoped desperately that he hadn't offended Isinwen, though he was pretty sure by now that Isinwen was amused—by something, at any rate.

"I *did* leave," the Elf added. Perhaps it was supposed to mean something to Kellen, but he wasn't sure what to say. After a moment, Isinwen spoke again.

"One hears that the human city is punctilious in its ways, and everything must be done just so," Isinwen said in his most neutral "discussing the weather" tones. "And some cannot bear it, and leave. Perhaps, then, you would understand that when I went to the House of Sword and Shield to train as a Knight, I knew I could never bear to return to Ysterialpoerin. In Sentarshadeen, in Ondoladeshiron, in the eastern cities, life is . . . different."

Different? That was something that stretched Kellen's imagination. He'd gotten used to thinking of all of the Elves as being as alike as they looked. So the Elves had the equivalent of Armethalieh? And this was it? That was something he'd never thought of. Except that their "Armethalieh" didn't have High Mages, of course—and they could leave any time they wanted to, and go somewhere they liked better. Or go *to* Ysterialpoerin, if that was what they wanted. It occurred to him that for every Elf like Isinwen, who couldn't stand the place, there probably was one who found that it was their heart's desire.

So . . . everybody who was in Ysterialpoerin *wanted* to be there.

What if Armethalieh could be like that? What if people could not only choose, but actually know what they were choosing?

"You give me much to consider," Kellen said.

"A proper Elven answer," Isinwen said, "yet brief, as they are on the Borders."

"And consider me as grateful as whatever you like that you were there to speak for me," Kellen said, "since I don't think it would serve Redhelwar's purposes if I insulted everyone in the city with what was taken for unpardonable rudeness. And . . . if it's anything like Armethalieh"—he hesitated, not wanting to insult anyone, even in absentia—"it would suit some very well, and perhaps not others."

"We will not be here long, by the grace of Leaf and Star," Isinwen said, "nor should you have need to go among the folk of Ysterialpoerin, called the great city of the forest's heart, as they would say, again. Yet should there be need, I will teach you some simple forms that should serve you. I memorized them all, in the days of my youth, for I am no poet, and that, Kellen, is among the greatest of the reasons why I left!"

By now they approached the camp, and as they passed the sentries, they met groups of Elves bringing bodies into the forest in wagons. In the distance, Kellen could see the lights of the camp.

Rulorwen was with the groups carrying off the dead, and Kellen hailed him.

"I See you, Rulorwen. It would please me to know what you may tell," Kellen said automatically. The awkward circumlocution seemed almost second-nature by now. Even if it was "brief, as they are on the Borders."

"I See you, Kellen. It is good to know that you live," Rulorwen answered, with the same intonation as if they had met in a garden. "The day was ours, by the grace of Leaf and Star. Vestakia and Idalia Wildmage are well: I have seen them. Adaerion lives, and will wish to know that you live also."

That was the equivalent of being told *report at once.* "I go in haste," Kellen said.

"Take Cheska," Isinwen said, swinging down from the saddle. "There's work here."

Kellen slid forward and gathered up the reins while Isinwen had a quiet word with his mount. He looked over his shoulder.

"Sihemand, Rhuifai, come with me. The rest of you, look to Rulorwen."

He rode down into the camp. Sihemand and Rhuifai—who were carrying the jugs of metalfire and the Shadowed Elf weapons—followed.

The camp was still disorderly in the aftermath of the battle, but there were no bodies to be seen. The fires had been put out, though the smell of burning and the rank stench of poison still hung in the air, making Cheska shake his head and snort. Soon, though, Kellen knew, it would be as if the attack had never occurred.

Kellen reached Adaerion's pavilion, but before he could dismount, Kharren stepped outside.

"He is with Redhelwar," she said without preamble. "Go there."

Kellen turned Cheska's head toward the great scarlet pavilion at the center of camp. When he got closer, he saw that it had not escaped the night's battle unscathed. The front was nearly charred away, and a network of ropes—obviously new and hastily added—held the structure upright.

Kellen dismounted, motioning for the others to do so as well, and stopped before the wide-open front of Redhelwar's tent, where Dionan stood guard. Adaerion, Redhelwar, and several others were inside.

"Bring the jars, and the weapons. Then go. Find Ciltesse, and tell him what has happened. Take his orders. If you cannot find him"—*If he is dead*—"return to Isinwen."

Sihemand and Rhuifai bowed, a brief acknowledgment.

"Be welcome," Dionan said gravely.

Kellen and the two Elves entered. His men set down the heavy stone jugs, the bows, and the quivers of iron arrows just inside where the doorway would have been, bowed again, and departed. They mounted their horses, and led Cheska away with them.

Kellen waited, and as he did so, the last of his energy seemed to drain away. Redhelwar was behind the others, speaking with someone he couldn't see. At last the general finished and came over to Kellen.

Kellen bowed very low, since he knew in his bones that this was the only thing in the way of proper Elven formality that he'd be able to manage tonight. Reaction was setting in. Only the knowledge that they had saved Ysterialpoerin from burning was keeping him going now.

"I See you, Redhelwar, Army's General," he said wearily.

"I See you, Kellen, *alakomentai,* Knight-Mage. One observes that you do not ride Mindaerel this night," Redhelwar said.

"She's dead," Kellen said. He took a deep breath, and held back another sudden burst of sorrow. "The Shadowed Elves killed her."

"May her spirit run free in the Fields of Vardirvoshan," Redhelwar said sympathetically. "I have had grave news this night, and I would have your counsel."

"With all respect, I do not think what I have to say can wait. And for my brevity I beg pardon," Kellen said. "The attack on the army was a feint. The Shadowed Elves went to burn Ysterialpoerin. They had new weapons. I think it would have worked."

"But it did not work," Redhelwar said, his manner suddenly intent.

"We killed them all and brought the weapons back with us," Kellen said. "The city is unharmed."

"Yet it would be good to know how the Knight-Mage knew to ride after these Shadowed Elves," Belepheriel said, coming forward. "Or how it is that he so often gives warning—and never soon enough to prevent losses. I would be interested to know what we will find in the caverns ahead if we continue to rely upon his warnings."

The note of contempt in Belepheriel's voice was impossible to mistake, and Kellen felt rage fill him, as if he faced an enemy on a battlefield. He had thought he had come to the end of his energy; he had been wrong. This new challenge filled him with a strength he had not known he still possessed. He swung toward Belepheriel, the fury in his face so plain that even Belepheriel stepped back. Redhelwar placed a hand on his shoulder, but Kellen stepped out from under it, taking a step toward the Elven commander.

"I am a Knight-Mage, Belepheriel," he said, very softly. "My Magery is the Art of War. Tonight the Wild Magic showed me that the attack upon the army was a cloak for an attack upon Ysterialpoerin, and so I stopped it. Would you see the Heart of the Forest burned to ash for your foolish pride in the Ancient Ways? Or shall I withhold the warnings I can give so that you may rejoice in a slaughter unrestrained by the Wild Magic? You are free to ask me for that, Belepheriel. *Or will you call me a liar and face me across the Circle?*"

There was utter silence in the pavilion.

"You cannot . . . " Belepheriel began, aghast. "It is unseemly! We are in the field!"

"I will permit it," Redhelwar said. "This once."

Abruptly his fury left Kellen, though the cold anger still

burned deep. Belepheriel had been a dead weight in their councils ever since Kellen had been admitted to them—and undoubtedly long before—and they could no longer afford that.

And now he remembered what the Circle was—though a moment before the words had come without thought.

When two Knights could not resolve a difference—great or small—any other way, they fought within a Circle. The one to push the other out—or kill him, though that was so rare as to be the stuff of legend—was the winner, and the matter was considered settled for all time.

Duels were strictly banned for armies in the field. Yet the commander of all the armies was suspending that ban. *He* knew Belepheriel for the dead weight that he was.

And now Belepheriel must know that he had been measured, and found wanting.

"I would hear your word to Kellen, Belepheriel. You waste my time," Redhelwar said implacably.

"Honor to the Knight-Mage," Belepheriel said at last, his voice utterly without color. "By the grace of Leaf and Star, good fortune to him and long life, and to his endeavors on behalf of the army as well, which come in a good hour. If there are no further matters that require my attention here, I would see to my command, Redhelwar."

"Go," the Elven General said. It was the most abrupt dismissal that Kellen had ever heard from Elven lips—and as such, very nearly an insult.

Belepheriel walked stiffly from the tent.

"Dionan, bring tea," Redhelwar commanded. "Kellen, show me these weapons."

Still feeling a little dazed—he thought he might have just cast a spell, but this was certainly the first time he'd done it without knowing about it in advance, or without any of the tools of the Wild Magic!—Kellen walked over to the jugs, knelt, and lifted the lid of one of them. Picking up one of the arrows, he explained what he'd seen and done with the strange weapon as well as he could.

While he was talking, Dionan appeared at his shoulder

and offered him tea—not just a cup, but a large wooden tankard. Kellen took it gratefully and drained it in a few gulps, even though it was steamingly hot. It was very sweet, and he tasted allheal in the brew. He handed it back with a nod of thanks, still talking.

"—the white rings burn when they are no longer in the oil. I think they'll even burn through the iron eventually. Nothing makes them stop burning—not water, anyway, and I think they'd keep burning no matter how much earth you shoveled over them. I don't know what they are, but they're not magic."

"Perhaps Artenel will know. We shall give these to him and tell him to be careful," Redhelwar said.

Dionan brought another tankard of tea. Kellen sipped this one more slowly, getting to his feet. The combination of allheal and honey was bringing him back to himself.

"I accept that the Wild Magic told you of the second attack," Redhelwar said. "But it would make good hearing to know more, if there were more to tell."

Kellen frowned, thinking hard. Redhelwar certainly had a right to know, but it was hard to put into words.

"It seemed to me," he began hesitantly, "that there was no reason for their attack upon the camp. They were giving up their only advantage—their caves—to attack us in the open. So there had to be a reason that seemed good to them. It came to me—there's really no other way to explain it, I'm sorry— that the attack must *only* be to focus our attention upon the camp, and there had to be a reason why they wished us to do that. The only possible reason could be that they had a second target, and there is only one other target nearby worth taking."

"Ysterialpoerin," said Redhelwar gravely.

Kellen nodded. "Those that the Shadowed Elves serve want to break our hearts. There's no better way than by destroying what we're sworn to protect while it's directly beneath our hand. So I rode after the Shadowed Elves that were heading toward Ysterialpoerin. I didn't know what they planned, and I wasn't sure it *was* Shadowed Elves. I just knew there'd be a strike at Ysterialpoerin, because . . . because there *had* to be. I *knew* it." He held his hands out, palm upward, and shrugged. "The rest you know."

"Magic," Adaerion said, a note of despairing humor in his voice. "We must become accustomed to it, Redhelwar."

"Yes," Redhelwar said. He studied Kellen for a long moment. "Now come and give counsel in time of peril, Knight-Mage, as it was in the days of my great-grandfather."

Redhelwar led him over to the table. The others stood aside, and now Kellen could see there was someone sitting there. He was bloody and battered, though he had obviously already been in the hands of the Healers—one arm was lashed tightly to his body with a sling and a network of bandages, and his head was bandaged as well.

With an effort, Kellen dredged his name up out of memory. Gairith.

One of the scouts they'd sent out earlier tonight.

"The others are all dead," Gairith said wearily, meeting Kellen's gaze. "The enemy came upon us as we rode toward the caves. We were not wearing the *tarnkappa* then. We fled, hoping to give warning, but they cut us down. My lady, Emerna . . . died."

"May her spirit run free in the Fields of Vardirvoshan," Kellen said softly, finding the proper words. "My own also died this night at their hands."

"Yet she saved my life in her death," Gairith said proudly, "for I lay beneath her, and they did not stop to see if I lived or died. I claimed the *tarnkappa* of the others, lest they should fall into evil hands, then donned my own and ran back to the camp as fast as I could. Yet I was too late . . . too late to warn . . . " His head drooped with exhaustion and pain.

Kellen glanced at Redhelwar. The Elven General made a small gesture, as if to say he left the matter in Kellen's hands.

"I would question you, if you can bear it," Kellen said gently.

"Let it be so," Gairith said wearily, raising his head.

"Where were you, when you were attacked?"

"At the stream that runs below the caverns, a mile from the opening of the nearer. It is the last cover of any kind before the caverns, and there is not much, as Ancaladar has said. There we would go our ways, Kolindearil, Alanoresen, and Morwentheas to ride north, I and my comrades to leave our mounts and go ahead. But we did not get the chance."

"Was it wholly dark by that time?" Kellen asked, trying to judge the timing of the attack.

"The sun was behind the mountains, and the light had left the sky, but we could see well enough. We saw them. They saw us. And then the coldwarg came at us from upwind, where the horses could not smell them."

"One last question—and I know you may not have an answer for me," Kellen said after a moment of thought. "Did you see females among them, or pairs of Shadowed Elves carrying large jugs, very heavy?"

"I saw no jugs as you describe," Gairith said, his voice a whisper of exhaustion. "For the rest, I do not know. They had bows, and swords, and . . . clubs. That I saw."

"Thank you," Kellen said. "You have helped me greatly. I honor you."

"Dionan, take Gairith back to the Healers," Redhelwar said.

Dionan came forward, lifted Gairith from the chair, and half-carried him from the tent.

"It would please me to know he will be all right," Kellen said, when the two Elves were gone.

"He lost a brother tonight—one of the other scouts. As was one of Belepheriel's sons," Redhelwar said in expressionless tones.

Kellen winced inwardly. It did much to explain Belepheriel's behavior.

But it didn't excuse it.

They had no time for excuses.

He was laboring under an unpaid price of the Wild Magic: to forgive an enemy. He wondered if—just now—he'd failed to pay it, and searched his heart.

But no. Belepheriel was not an enemy, no matter how harshly they had treated one another. He was only an obstacle. Kellen was truly sorry that Belepheriel's grief had caused him to force the issue that lay between them, and not to leave it for some other time. He would make amends for that, if it were possible. Jermayan would know.

"Your counsel, Knight-Mage," Redhelwar said, interrupting his thoughts.

"You see what I have seen, Redhelwar," Kellen said. "The scouts did not see the second party, the one that went to burn Ysterialpoerin. It may have left earlier, perhaps to lie in wait until the attack on the camp began. Perhaps not. We know they can move through the day if they must."

Be right. No matter what, you always have to be right. Especially now.

"The plan to destroy Ysterialpoerin is good in their eyes," he went on. "The plan to map the caverns before invading is good in ours. They know we're here. They know what we mean to do, I think."

He took a deep breath, closing his eyes, trying to call up the intuitive understanding of the enemy that he needed.

"Sit," Redhelwar said. "I ask too much of you."

Kellen sank into the chair that Gairith had so recently vacated, feeling as if his bones were suddenly made of Artenel's most fragile glass. "You ask what must be asked," he replied, knowing, if he knew nothing else, that this was the right thing to say. "And I must give what must be given." There was an answer here, somewhere, just beyond his reach.

"If we cannot send scouts in to map the caverns," Adaerion said reluctantly, into the silence, "we must go in with Vestakia to lead us. And that means we can only attack one enclave at a time. And we do not know how many entrances or exits they may have."

"Ancaladar saw only two," Padredor said. "His eyes are sharp."

"So we will guard the one, so that nothing may pass it, and attack the other. Kellen is right: the Enemy would love nothing better than to destroy Ysterialpoerin in the face of our gathered strength, so we must guard it as well. We shall send a third of the army to do that—and all the unicorns, for their senses may discover what ours do not. A third again to the farther cavern, and the Mountainfolk with them, as they are expert in matters of snow and ice, so that no matter what seeks to escape the cavern or through the mountains, nothing shall—and if there are other exits elsewhere in the mountains, there will be sufficient forces to dispatch against what may issue from them. Ancaladar will tell us what he sees, for I think there is no way this time for us to gain his strength beneath the ground."

"No!" Kellen burst out, feeling a jolt of *warning* course through him.

Everyone stopped and looked at him.

"Will you speak, Knight-Mage?" Redhelwar said courteously. But this time Kellen sensed impatience and reluctance as well. This time, Redhelwar did not wish to hear him.

Redhelwar meant to split the army into thirds, and send Vestakia into the nearer cavern with the attack force. It wasn't the splitting of the army that disturbed Kellen, because they couldn't get the full force of the army into the caverns anyway. Having to do without Jermayan and Ancaladar was a blow, but the dragon would be useful outside, and it wasn't impossible that they'd manage to find him a back door once they were inside.

Intuition had struck with the force of a blow. It still wasn't clear to Kellen what they should do, but suddenly what they must *not* do was completely clear to him.

If Redhelwar sent his forces down into that cavern without scouting ahead, there would be a disaster.

"Redhelwar, hear me. You asked my counsel, and now I give it. Wait. Guard the city, guard the entrance to the other cavern, yes. But send Idalia and me into the nearer cavern before you send the army in. She can map it. I can protect her. If we can find the village at the cavern's heart, we won't need Vestakia when we invade. She can come in afterward to check that the cavern is clear, and we will protect our most valuable asset."

"What speaks to me, Knight-Mage," Redhelwar asked, his voice cool and expressionless. "Your head . . . or your heart?"

"Neither," Kellen answered, honestly confused. He was sure that by now he'd offended everyone here, and he only hoped that truth could make up for that. "The Wild Magic speaks, Redhelwar, and only the Wild Magic. Send me alone if you wish—I am not as good at maps as Idalia, but—"

Adaerion leaned over to speak into Redhelwar's ear, saying something too low for Kellen to hear.

"You say this now, Knight-Mage, yet you did not say it when I asked for your counsel," Redhelwar said, his voice still neutral.

Kellen struggled to put what was only a *feeling* into words, knowing that he must convince Redhelwar, Adaerion—everyone here. How had the Knight-Mage of the past ever managed it?

"I was listening, Army's General," he said. "To . . . what comes." He looked past Redhelwar, and his eye fell on a *xaqiųe* board, set up and ready for play. Ready for play—but as yet, no moves had been made on the board.

He got to his feet and walked over to the board.

"Redhelwar," he said, "tell me how this game will play out."

The Elven general looked at the board. "No one can say, Kellen. None of the pieces has yet been moved, nor do I know who the players are."

"Yet if I were to move a piece, you could begin to say," Kellen said.

"Yes," Redhelwar said. "And were you to be my opponent, I could also say who would win."

"At *xaqiųe,* this is indeed true." Kellen agreed. "I am a poor player. But the game is a fine teacher. Tell me you wish to guard Ysterialpoerin, to seal the far cavern with troops . . . I see no opening for *Their* victory. Tell me you mean to send your troops down into unmapped, unscouted caverns . . . and the Wild Magic shows me an opening *They* can exploit."

"But no more," Redhelwar said.

"Not yet," Kellen said, wishing to shout at them, *But it shows me that. And you* have *to listen!*But he did not dare; did not dare offend them, not when they had only just begun to take him seriously.

"Discussion," Redhelwar said to his commanders.

"While we wait for Kellen and Idalia to return—or not—from the caverns, the Shadowed Elves could launch a second attack at Ysterialpoerin. The first force evaded our scouts and our sentries. Perhaps a second one would as well. Then Ysterialpoerin would burn because we had not attacked the Shadowed Elves immediately," Ninolion said.

"If the caverns can be mapped, so that we can attack without risking Vestakia in the forefront of an attack, it is the more prudent course," Adaerion said.

"But perhaps it is a feint within a feint; perhaps they wish us to commit our strength to the cavern and leave Vestakia at the camp. Then while we are engaged in the caverns, they will attack the camp and take her there," Arambor suggested.

"Having somehow moved sufficient strength to do so out of either of the caverns directly beneath our regard," Adaerion noted dryly.

Redhelwar raised a hand, stopping what promised to become a long, drawn-out byplay.

"Whether Vestakia goes or not," Padredor said slowly, "whether the Shadowed Elves attack us or not, it would be good to know how the caverns lie before we are in them. It seems to me that they worked very hard to turn us from reaching them—and now that we are here, it seems that they wish to distract us from entering them. To discover the reason for that would be a thing worth knowing, I believe."

Around the pavilion it went, with each of the commanders giving his opinion—let Kellen go, attack at once, find another plan entirely.

"Dionan, you have not shared your thoughts," Redhelwar said, when everyone else had spoken.

"We cannot attack the caverns tomorrow, not if all the

armies of Great Queen Vielissiar Farcarinon, their dragons, and their flying horses, were here to aid us," Dionan said simply. "We must place three armies into position—one of them around Ysterialpoerin—and establish them against the weather, which grows no more clement. The day after tomorrow, if Leaf and Star favor us, is the earliest we can descend against the Shadowed Elves. Therefore, my counsel is this: let Kellen move his piece in the game. When he returns, and can tell us more of the enemy's mind and disposition, we shall be ready as well."

There was a silence after everyone had spoken. Kellen could almost *feel* Redhelwar weighing the possibilities—the opinions of his commanders, the condition of his army, the situation at Ysterialpoerin . . .

And more.

Sending Kellen to scout the caverns would change the balance of power in the Elven army. Kellen couldn't quite grasp it—not in a way he could put into words—but he could *feel* it, the way he'd learned to feel changes in the weather.

And Redhelwar knew it, and was deciding whether *that* was worth the risk, as well as all the rest.

At last he spoke, turning to look directly into Kellen's eyes.

"I have heard the counsel of my *komentaiia*, Kellen Knight-Mage, now here is my word to you," Redhelwar said. "I will not risk your life and that of Idalia Wildmage for so little gain. But neither will I risk Vestakia's, when experience has shown us that our Tainted cousins will attack in force the moment we advance into their lairs. She will remain here, safe, while they expend their strength against us. Now go to your rest. There is much to do on the morrow to prepare for our assault."

Kellen stood for a moment, stunned, as Redhelwar's words sank in. He'd *told* Redhelwar that a simple assault on the cavern without advance scouting would be a complete disaster.

And Redhelwar hadn't listened.

At last he managed to bow. "I thank the General for his wisdom. I go," Kellen said.

He made his way through the camp by instinct alone, still feeling as if he'd been struck. *Redhelwar hadn't listened.*

This was his fault. When Belepheriel had provoked him, he should have ignored it. But no. His Knight-Mage instincts told him he had been right to do what he had done; to remind them all of what he was. Belepheriel's would have been the loudest voice in favor of a direct assault; he was certain of that.

But Belepheriel hadn't been there. And the plan was going forward anyway.

I saved Ysterialpoerin for them tonight. They know that. And this is how they reward me? Kellen thought bitterly.

But that wasn't the right way to think either. He'd saved Ysterialpoerin, yes. But not in order to be *paid* for it, as if— as if he were a High Mage of Armethalieh!

Kellen took a deep breath, willing anger and hurt pride away. What mattered was the problem at hand, and he needed time to consider how best to deal with it. There would be answers in his Books, of that he was certain.

His steps had taken him back to his home tents. It was still early enough that several of his people were gathered around the communal brazier. With a pang of relief, he saw that Ciltesse was there, and Isinwen had returned from the forest. They got to their feet as he approached.

"I share your sorrow at Mindaerel's death," Ciltesse said, bowing. "Many destriers in the horse-lines go without riders now. By your leave and Adaerion's, I shall select another to share your life."

"That . . . makes good hearing," Kellen said slowly, forcing himself to concentrate on more homely and immediate problems. "You will know what I need better than I do myself, Ciltesse. Mindaerel . . . I don't. . . . "

"We will handle matters at first light, *alakomentai*," Isinwen said. "There is a way such things are done in Ysterialpoerin." He smiled slightly, at the small jest they both shared.

For a moment Kellen had a wild vision of the Elves hoisting Mindaerel into a tree, and shook his head sharply, banishing the freakish fancy. However they handled things in Ysterialpoerin, he was sure it wasn't that. He nodded.

"That makes good hearing. She died a warrior. And I would know now, Ciltesse, if it pleases you to say, how fare those who did not ride with me tonight." Blunt words, and a flat-out demand by Elven terms, but he hoped Ciltesse would forgive him.

"All live, by the grace of Leaf and Star," Ciltesse said, looking pleased. "And there were only the most minor of injuries, and none from the Blight-cursed arrows of the Shadowed Elves. All have been seen by the Healers, and are at their rest."

"And so I will go to mine, and encourage you to go to yours. Tomorrow Redhelwar disposes the army for the attack upon the nearer cavern, and there will be much to do."

Nineteen

The Wisdom of Betrayal

Kellen entered his tent, buttoned the flap closed, and called fire into the brazier and the lantern. He opened the small pack he kept always with him—it was the same pack he'd been given in Armethalieh on the day of his Banishing—and drew out his three Books. Perhaps they would grant him wisdom.

He still wasn't quite sure why Redhelwar had refused to allow the second scouting expedition—surely he knew that *Kellen's* life wasn't at risk, and he could have agreed to let Kellen go without Idalia if he were really worried about *her* safety. Perhaps it was because it just "wasn't the way things have always been done," or perhaps Redhelwar saw the consequences of the cusp-point that Kellen had only sensed, and feared them.

He didn't know. And it didn't matter now.

He ran his hands over the worn leather covers. Which one would serve him best tonight? Without hesitation, he opened *The Book of Stars* at random and began to read.

"A Wildmage's honor is not what honor may seem in the eyes of the world. The honor of a Wildmage lies in always paying the price of the Wild Magic, no matter what that price may be, and no matter what path the price may unfold. The world's honor takes many paths and many forms, but to the Wildmage, there is only one path and one form, and so it must ever be."

Kellen closed *The Book of Stars* and stared unseeingly into the lantern's flame. He couldn't remember seeing that passage there before, but in a way he'd suspected its existence ever since he'd begun to be a Knight-Mage.

He knew Redhelwar's plan of attack. Redhelwar wasn't going to change it. If Redhelwar followed it, there would be disaster.

Kellen knew it. The Wild Magic had told him so.

Do what Redhelwar had ordered him to do? Or do what was right?

They won't be ready to attack for at least a day and a half. Dionan said so. A full day at least to make ready, and Redhelwar will want to go at midday, when he judges the Shadowed Elves to be weakest, so he might even hold off another full day rather than attack late in the day.

Time enough for me to reach the nearer cavern and see what's there—and get back again. Even if I have to go on foot.

The realization of what he was contemplating shook Kellen. He was a member of the Elven army now—an *alakomentai*. If he disobeyed orders—if he just *left*—it would be a serious thing. He had no idea how serious—he suspected he'd lose his command at the very least. He would have betrayed everyone who'd trusted him—Adaerion, Ciltesse, Isinwen . . . he could sit here until dawn naming names and not be done with the list. And everything he'd done toward convincing everyone that they should listen to him as a Knight-Mage and not just tolerate him as Idalia's younger brother who happened to be good with a sword would be gone.

It isn't worth it, Kellen thought wildly. *I can't throw all that away!* If he lost his position in the army, if the Elves went on doing things as they always had—fighting the last war and expecting their enemy to do the same—they'd lose. Shadow Mountain would win. Wouldn't the greater good—the long-term good—be just to sit here and let Redhelwar do as he pleased, no matter what consequences Kellen foresaw?

But suddenly Belepheriel's words came back to him.

"Yet it would be good to know how the Knight-Mage knew to ride after these Shadowed Elves. Or how it is that he so often gives warning—and never soon enough to prevent losses."

This time Kellen had a warning that had come in plenty of time to prevent *all* losses. How could he even *think* of disregarding it for what—when you came right down to it—would be personal gain?

"A Wildmage's honor is not what honor may seem in the eyes of the world . . . "

Always pay the price. Because to refuse to pay it, as he'd learned when Jermayan had begun to teach him about the Great War, would ultimately lead a Wildmage into the service of the Demons.

He'd been given a gift by the Wild Magic: a warning that would save hundreds—thousands—of lives. The price of that gift was personal disgrace.

He would pay it.

Kellen bowed his head over *The Book of Stars,* trembling as he thought of how close he'd just come to doing something horrible. Better his friends should be alive to hate him than that they should be dead still thinking well of him. *He* would know he'd done the right thing, no matter what they thought.

For the first time tonight he felt light and free. He saw his path clearly. Get to the caverns. See what the Wild Magic wanted him to see. Get back and tell someone—Shalkan,

Ancaladar, and Jermayan, if no one else would listen to him. Then let Redhelwar do with him as he chose.

All that remained was "how"—a simple enough problem for a Knight-Mage trained by Master Belesharon.

Kellen packed his Books away, quenched his lantern, and lay down, feigning sleep.

IN the darkest part of the night, when the camp was as quiet as it ever got, Kellen slipped out of his tent.

Within the camp itself, he simply had to not be seen, for it would be best for all when Redhelwar asked after him if no one could say they had seen him go. That was a comparatively easy matter, with his battle-sight to guide him. But eventually he reached the point where he needed to pass the sentry-ring and leave the camp entirely.

If he'd had a *tarnkappa*, evading the mounted sentries riding post would have been as simple as covering his tracks in the snow, but he hadn't dared risk lingering in camp long enough to steal one. Without one, it took him over an hour to work his way past the rings of guards, and it was the most agonizing hour of Kellen's life.

He used his battle-sight to spot the sentries, and their movements to mask the sounds of his own. He carried a blanket with him, and dragged it behind him to blur his tracks in the powdery snow. It was snowing again, and the wind was a constant wail through the trees, and that helped to mask the sound of his movements as well. The greatest danger of discovery would come when he had to strike off away from camp. They might well see him then.

But the outer ring of sentries rode to a fixed pattern, and by now Kellen had timed it out exactly. When they were on the opposite sides of the camp, he would run. When they were in a position to see him, he would throw himself down in the snow and wait until they'd passed. After half a league of that, he should be out of sight.

They were in position. Kellen grabbed up his blanket and began to run. At the end of ten minutes, he flung himself facedown in the snow to wait.

"I do hope you weren't planning to go anywhere without me," a familiar voice said from above his head.

"Yes," Gesade added. "Where *were* you going?"

Kellen choked on a mouthful of snow, barely managing not to yelp. Knight-Mage Gifts were one thing, but unicorns were *sneaky.*

He thought about ignoring them. He thought about telling them to go away. He might as well have wished for a *tarnkappa*—or wings.

He rolled over on his back, looking up at the two unicorns. Both of them were gazing down at him with identical expressions of polite interest, their bodies white blurs against the snow.

"I'm deserting," Kellen said, after a long pause.

Shalkan cleared his throat in the manner of a unicorn that was trying *very* hard not to laugh and wanted to make sure everyone knew it.

"In that case," he said mildly, "I'm going to need my armor and my saddle."

"Come and have tea," Gesade said. "You look half-frozen. Humans don't like snow-baths. Come to that, Elves don't like snow-baths either. Petariel will get Shalkan's things."

I wonder if you can strangle a unicorn? Make that two *unicorns.*

"Look," Kellen said, gritting his teeth. "I'm telling the truth. I really am deserting. Redhelwar told me not to leave the camp, and I'm leaving. So no one can know. Do you understand?" The snow had now had ample time to melt, and he'd have to wait at least another ten minutes—probably more—before he could move again, even if he could talk the unicorns into leaving. His cloak felt damp, and his armor . . . well, his armor felt like cold metal. Which it was.

"All right," Gesade answered reassuringly, as if to a small child. "We won't tell anyone. Come and have tea. Because if you don't, you're going to find out how loud I can scream," she added, her voice taking on a warning edge.

"Oh, do get up, Kellen," Shalkan said, sounding bored. "You can't desert if you've got the coughing sickness. Everyone will hear you for leagues. And I understand that Idalia's remedy for that tastes *really* awful."

"One . . . " Gesade said, laying her ears back and switching her tail meaningfully.

Kellen scrambled to his feet.

⇌

"THIS is *important*," Kellen said to Shalkan, as the two of them followed Gesade back to the camp of the Unicorn Knights.

"It's all right," Shalkan said, rubbing his head against Kellen's arm.

For a moment Kellen almost felt an urge to hit Shalkan, then draped an arm over the unicorn's neck instead. "People are going to die," he said, and heard his voice tremble.

"No," Shalkan said firmly. "I told you not to try to go off somewhere interesting without me, didn't I? You should have remembered."

⇌

THE camp of the Unicorn Knights was silent and dark—no need of Elven sentries here, with the unicorns to keep watch. Gesade walked into Petariel's pavilion—opening the flap neatly with her horn—and a few moments later, Petariel came out.

The Captain of the Unicorn Knights had obviously been roused from sleep. His long hair was loosely braided, and he was still pulling a heavy fur cloak around him. But his expression was alert as he saw Kellen.

"Leaf and Star—you're soaking wet. Gesade, Riasen and Menerchel, if you please." He went to the banked brazier and began adding charcoal, then went back into his pavilion, coming out with another cloak.

"Here. Take this. Not your color, but at least it's dry."

Kellen dropped his wet cloak to the ground and took the dry one gratefully. Gesade had roused Menerchel and Riasen now, and Kellen wondered with a sinking heart just how much worse things could possibly get.

"Kellen's deserting," Gesade said brightly. "So we need Shalkan's saddle and armor."

"Tea first," Petariel said. "Kellen, you're as blue as ice."

"I have to get out of here," Kellen said desperately.

"You need to tell us what else you need," Riasen said as Menerchel began to prepare tea.

"I'm deserting," Kellen said, wondering if they'd all gone deaf.

"Yes," Petariel said. "We all heard you. Tell us how to help."

Kellen stared at them. He'd been expecting . . . he didn't know *what* he'd been expecting. But not this. For a moment, he felt as if the earth had opened under him—except that he also felt as if the moment it had, he'd discovered how to fly.

"I think he should sit down," Shalkan said. "Over here, next to the brazier. I'll tell you what *I* know while his wits unthaw. Sit down, Kellen."

Kellen sat. If he'd learned nothing else in the past several moonturns, he'd learned that arguing with Shalkan was worse than useless.

Quickly Shalkan summarized the evening's events, including most of what had gone on in Redhelwar's pavilion. "So now Redhelwar has changed his battle plans, and I imagine Kellen hasn't been able to talk him out of them, don't you?"

"Huh," Gesade said, stamping her forehoof. "They must be really bad plans."

"No," Kellen said, stung to Redhelwar's defense. "They aren't. Not really. It's just . . . he doesn't . . . "

"Better tell," Shalkan said.

Kellen sighed, giving up.

"He isn't going to risk trying to scout the caverns again. Without maps, we can't attack them both at once, and he's concerned about leaving Ysterialpoerin undefended. He's going to divide the army into thirds and guard Ysterialpoerin and the further cavern. There's nothing wrong with either of those ideas," Kellen said, knowing it sounded bad, but he was *tired* of mincing words! "But he means to send the third force into the nearer cavern using the troops to draw the Shadowed Elves to attack."

"And that's bad?" Gesade asked.

"It must be," Shalkan said. "Because Kellen's deserting. To scout the nearer cavern before Redhelwar can get the army into position, I suppose. All by yourself?"

"I'd wanted to take Idalia," Kellen said unwarily. "But I can't ask her now."

"*We'll* ask her," Riasen said. "That way the army will have decent maps, at least. She has a fine hand at mapmaking."

"And you'll have someone along to keep you out of trouble," Shalkan said with satisfaction. "Though I'd hate to be the one to wake her up."

"Fortunes of war," Riasen said. "We'll draw lots for it."

"I— Hey— Wait—" Kellen said desperately. How had things gotten so completely out of his control?

"Tea," Menerchel said, passing Kellen a cup.

Kellen took it. "You can't do this," he said, trying to make them understand. "It's one thing for *me* to disobey orders. I'll be in trouble—I don't know how much, but probably a lot—but if you help me, you'll all be in trouble, too. I can't let you—"

"Kellen," Shalkan said, interrupting him, "tell them what will happen if Redhelwar proceeds as he plans, and no one scouts the nearer cavern before he sends the army in."

Kellen focused on what he'd felt in Redhelwar's tent, trying to bring it into words. There was nothing but dread—a terrible sense of death and loss. "I—" he began.

"No," Riasen interrupted somberly. "Your face tells us too

much. Once I said you might call upon the Unicorn Knights at need. Now the day has come." He glanced at the others. Petariel and Menerchel both nodded. "Drink your tea before it cools."

Kellen drank the tea.

This was mutiny. A whole troop of the Elven army—the Unicorn Knights, the elite scouts—were disobeying Redhelwar's orders to follow his. Or at least to help him, because try as he might, he didn't seem to be able to order them *not* to help him.

"I give up," he muttered.

"Good," Shalkan said, nuzzling his ear. "I'd almost thought you were going to be as stubborn as an Elf."

On the other side of the brazier, the three Elves were playing an elaborate—and quick—guessing game: Wind, Water, Tree. Kellen had never been able to master it—the Elves learned it as children, and played it all their lives, and though Kellen had mastered the simple gestures easily enough, he'd never understood it well enough to play. Petariel lost the round, and shook his head with a sigh.

"I will go to waken Idalia and tell her what she must know. But you, Menerchel, will bring Shalkan's armor here."

Menerchel bowed elaborately, a courtly reverence filled with mockery. He straightened, fading into the darkness beyond the edge of the lantern light.

"There will be time for a meal before you go, if we are quick," Riasen said. He went into his tent.

"I don't understand Elves," Kellen said to Shalkan.

"The beginning of wisdom," Shalkan said.

Kellen opened the jar of honey-disks and fed several to Shalkan. "Won't they get into trouble? Someone's sure to look for me in the morning."

"And displease us?" Shalkan asked haughtily, switching his tail. "But you're asking the wrong question. The question is, will they say they've helped you? And will Redhelwar ask them?"

Kellen thought about that for a few moments as he finished his tea.

"I *really* don't understand Elves," he finally said.

Riasen came out of the tent with a large bundle of cloth and a flask. He spread out the bundle near the brazier. It held half a chicken, a meat-pie, and some tarts.

"The cordial will be warm, but the rest must be cold," Riasen said. "It's the best we can do."

"You honor me," Kellen said, pulling off his gauntlets and reaching for the chicken.

By the time he'd finished eating, Menerchel was back with Shalkan's armor, and the cordial was warmed. Like most of the decoctions of Elven brewing, it contained very little alcohol. This one tasted strongly of sweet cherries, and banished the last of Kellen's chill. When he'd drunk it, he got to his feet and began armoring and saddling Shalkan, first rubbing him dry with his discarded cloak. It wasn't much of a chore—the downy unicorn fur seemed to shed snow as if it were bespelled; and maybe it was.

"You'd better dry that if you're going to wear it," Shalkan pointed out, so Kellen stood over the brazier, holding his cloak to the heat. Soon Petariel would return—without Idalia, he was sure—and they could be on their way.

But not long after that, Petariel returned—*with* Idalia.

She was leading Cella, saddled and ready for a journey. The palfrey even had full saddlebags and a bedroll lashed to her saddle.

"Well?" Idalia said, swinging into the saddle. "Are you ready?" Quite as if they were going off for a snow-picnic.

Kellen nodded, taking off Petariel's cloak and exchanging it for his own now-dry one. He swung into Shalkan's saddle.

"Don't worry about the pickets," Gesade said. She'd backed away when Idalia entered the camp, but her voice was quite audible. "We'll take care of them."

"Thank you," Kellen said meekly.

"Fare well and safe journey," Petariel said. "And return to us in a good hour."

"I'll make sure of it," Idalia said.

Shalkan took off at a brisk trot, and Cella followed.

⌒

FOR a long time they rode in silence, wary of their voices carrying back to the camp. The trees were few and far apart, not thick enough to blunt the force of the wind, and it was so cold that the snow was more like powdered ice. Finally the wind shifted, and then dropped altogether. Kellen could tell that the clouds would probably start to break up soon. That meant it would get colder. There were two kinds of weather in winter, he'd learned—bad and worse.

"You didn't have to come," he said, now that the wind had slacked enough to make conversation easy. They were riding side by side—though far enough apart to be comfortable for Shalkan.

"You're welcome," Idalia said. "*You* may be deserting your command, but *I* am a Wildmage, and if I want to go wandering off into the Shadowed Elf caverns on a whim, that's my business."

"Oh." Well, at least there was one person who wasn't risking Redhelwar's displeasure tonight.

"Kellen, what did you See?" Idalia asked.

"Nothing. I don't know." He shook his head, wishing desperately that he had something more concrete to tell her. "I really . . . I couldn't tell Redhelwar either. But we—*I* have to go look."

She gave him a long look, her face hidden in the shadows of her hood. "Petariel said you told Redhelwar you wanted me along."

"You're better at maps than I am," he told her honestly. "But he said he couldn't risk us."

She coughed politely. "That's not all that got said in Redhelwar's tent tonight, from what I hear." Her voice softened. "I'm sorry about Mindaerel, by the way."

"Belepheriel's son was one of the scouts who died out

here tonight. And then, later, in Redhelwar's pavilion, I called him a fool," Kellen said, half answering.

Kellen could feel Idalia's gaze even though he wasn't looking at her. "They said he challenged you to a Circle, and you refused, but I'm sure that's wrong. Redhelwar wouldn't permit it."

"Redhelwar *would* permit it," Kellen said wearily. "And *I* challenged *him*. He called me . . . well, he said the warnings I gave were conveniently useless."

"Let's go back," Idalia said after a pause, and now her voice had an edge to it that could cut the wind. "I'll challenge him myself."

"No," Kellen said, feeling tired of it all. "It's all right. Well, it isn't. I'll have to make it right later. But he apologized."

"Storytelling is obviously not a Knight-Magely gift," Shalkan said. "*I* heard that after he apologized to Kellen, and wished him all honor and long life, Belepheriel left Redhelwar's pavilion, and so did not take part in further discussion of the planning and strategy."

"Did he?" said Idalia in an odd voice. "What did you say to him after he'd apologized, Kellen?"

Kellen thought back. "He didn't give me a chance to say anything. I challenged him, nobody said anything, Redhelwar demanded his answer, he gave it and asked to be excused, Redhelwar said 'go,' and everybody started acting as if he'd never been there."

"Elves," Idalia sighed. "Well, what else?"

Once more Kellen summarized what he'd told Petariel and the others about Redhelwar's change of plan.

"And it's all . . . reasonable, I suppose," he concluded. "We didn't know before tonight that they'd try something like attacking Ysterialpoerin. So it makes sense to defend it. And blockading the farther cavern and taking the two enclaves one at a time . . . the Mountainfolk will be put to good use guarding the farther cavern. But attacking the nearer cavern without scouting ahead, even without Vestakıa there . . . " Kellen shook his head.

"A Finding Spell might locate the village. We haven't tried that yet," Idalia suggested. "Let's see if we can find it on our own, first. I brought the *tarnkappa*, but I have lanterns, too. You can decide which we'll use."

"Thanks," he replied, touched beyond words that she was delegating the decision to him.

"Knight-Mage's privilege," Idalia told him. "And I brought food, tea, and a brazier—all items that I'm sure you forgot. Nothing I like better than spending a night in a cozy snowdrift, followed by a day sneaking around a cave filled with murderous monsters." She made her voice sound light, though Kellen was very certain she felt nothing humorous in the situation. "And it's actually a relief to get away from the camp for a while. All those people! When this is over with, I'm going to find myself a nice high mountaintop and sit on it—alone!—for about ten years, I think."

"You and Vestakia," Kellen said, grinning to himself. Idalia's matter-of-fact confidence in his judgment and abilities lightened his spirits. They *could* do this. And they would.

They were over halfway to the nearer cavern now, and Kellen was automatically sensing rather than seeing to find his way through the dark. He looked up, suddenly startled, as six pale ghosts rode past.

Oh.

The Elven scouts, who'd ridden this way earlier in the day. Kellen watched them, fascinated.

But why was he seeing them? He'd "read" the site of a past battle before, but he'd done it deliberately.

Ah, but sometimes the Wild Magic showed him things of its own accord, when there was need. Was this one of those times?

"Idalia—" he said softly, "I'm seeing our scouts."

She knew exactly what he meant. "Tell me. Show me."

He kept looking.

And saw, moving through the scattered trees, the Shadowed Elves as they moved toward the camp. And beyond them, off in the distance, a second, smaller party.

"Ah," he said. "There." He pointed off to the right. "That's where the party going toward Ysterialpoerin went. I was right. They circled wide around the army, but they were on the move at the same time as the party the scouts ran into. I think they might have come from the upper cavern. No wonder the scouts didn't see them."

"That's another reason you wanted me to come along, isn't it?" Idalia said, quietly. "In case there were still more of them."

"If there was a third force in hiding, waiting to attack the army just when things started to quiet down, someone would have to ride back and warn them," Kellen agreed. "And that would have been you. But I don't see one. And Vestakia and Ancaladar can warn them of most things now as well as I can."

No matter how untrue it was, Belepheriel's accusation still rankled. Couldn't Belepheriel *see* that Kellen wanted desperately to be able to give better warning than he did— that every time someone died because of something he didn't see, he felt as if it were his fault?

"I somehow think the Elven army in full arrày, with a dragon, an Elven Mage, and a woman who can sense Demon-taint to help them, can muddle along without us for a few hours," Idalia said. "Plus—oh, yes—a full score of High Reaches Wildmages to lend their poor powers to the fight."

"No," Shalkan drawled, "Kellen's right. They absolutely can't get along without him. We'd better turn back now."

"Thanks a lot, both of you," Kellen grumbled, without rancor. He took a deep breath, feeling more of the tension ease. They were both right. He *couldn't* do everything himself. And trying to was a sort of trap. No one was indispensable. Even if they lost Vestakia, they'd find another way—somehow—to discover which of the caverns held Shadowed Elves.

Even if he died in the caverns, somewhere there was another Knight-Mage. He was sure of it. And now the Wildmages knew to look for the signs of Knight-Magery in those called to the Wild Magic. They would find him—or her, Kellen realized with a pang of realization—and send them to Master Belesharon for training. And the fight would go on. The Wild Magic itself would see to it that he was replaced, just as the Wild Magic had seen to it that he had come into his power.

They'd nearly reached the stream, but he didn't want to spend the few remaining hours of the night among the Elven dead, and he doubted Idalia did either.

"Let's—" he began.

"We'd better check for survivors," Idalia interrupted. "Gairith said they were all dead, I know, and he stopped to take their *tarnkappa*—but he was wounded himself, and if they were only badly hurt, he might have missed vital signs."

So they rode on.

They found the bodies of the horses—six of them. Kellen dismounted, drawing his sword and motioning to Idalia to stay in the saddle. Something was not right here.

No bodies.

The Elves had not come to carry away their dead—not this soon. And the coldwarg had not eaten them, for they would not have stopped with the Elven bodies, and save for attack-bites, the horses had not been touched.

He paced around, moving back and forth across the area. He found Emerna, her throat and belly torn open. There was still a hollow in the snow beneath her where Gairith had lain. He scratched at the fresh snow with the tip of his sword, uncovering Gairith's frozen blood.

At last he opened himself, reluctantly, to See the battle.

He watched the shadows of the Elven scouts ride silently down through the falling snow in two files. Saw them stop, and see the Shadowed Elves advance. He turned and watched the Shadowed Elves come toward them over the snow, the forward ranks of the horde breaking into a run.

Saw the Elves rein in and turn to run, only to be met by the fury of the waiting coldwarg. Three of the horses went down in that first instant, and by then it was too late. The Shadowed Elves overwhelmed the scouts, leaping onto the horses' backs, clawing at the riders' armor. It was like watching something eaten alive by maggots, if that were possible. Kellen watched as one of the Shadowed Elves stabbed one of the scouts to death with his own dagger, slamming the narrow deadly blade home over and over again. Saw others, their armor stripped from them, bludgeoned to death with clubs.

It was over in a handful of minutes.

The Shadowed Elves moved on, like the horde of plague rats they so much resembled. A few moments passed, and he saw Gairith work his way painfully from beneath Emerna's body. One arm hung useless at his side, and his face was covered with blood. The Elven scout staggered, regained his balance, and after checking the others, moved off into the forest, following the Shadowed Elves.

⟜

KELLEN waited, but nothing changed. The bodies were still there. He blinked, shook his head. *Let me See what happened to them!* he demanded silently.

He had the sense that time passed—hours. And then, moving over the snow, came a band of now-familiar cloaked figures. Shadowed Elves. Not warriors, but a hunting party; one had a brace of hares hanging from his belt, another carried the body of some animal Kellen couldn't identify.

When they saw the Elven dead, they grew excited, gesturing to one another. Then they quickly gathered up the bodies—and all the weapons and pieces of armor—stowing them in the curious slings that Lairamo had described from her captivity in their hands.

And they were gone.

Kellen blinked, banishing the vision. He shuddered. There was no doubt what the Shadowed Elves meant to do with the bodies.

"They're all dead," he said. "And Shadowed Elves came and took away the bodies.""

"Why?" Idalia said, dumbfounded.

"To eat," Kellen said. There was no doubt in his mind.

"Kellen . . . are you sure . . . ?"

"I saw them die," Kellen said gently. "None of them were alive by the time the Shadowed Elves came. They died . . . very quickly."

"Good," Idalia said resolutely. "And we can tell Redhelwar and the others what happened to their bodies. They'll want to know. Now let's find a safe place to camp and wait for dawn."

———

THEY found shelter behind a granite outcropping a few hundred yards uphill from the stream, spread a blanket on the snow, and huddled in their cloaks while Idalia unpacked the tea-things from Cella's saddlebags, lit the brazier, and prepared to brew tea. The quiet night, and the simple, every-day preparations helped to still Idalia's mind, and keep her from thinking too much about what might lie ahead of them.

Now and then, over the years since she'd left Armethalieh, Idalia had wondered about what had happened to the brother she'd left behind. She hadn't thought about him very often, for thinking about the life she'd left behind held pain, and her scrying-visions had never shown him to her. She'd always imagined him safe and happy—Lycaelon had wanted a son as much as he'd been indifferent to a daughter—probably growing up to be the next Arch-Mage of Armethalieh, if Lycaelon had his way, and never wondering what lay beyond the walls of the City. Never in her wildest dreams had she ever imagined she would see him again, much less that their lives would intertwine so intimately.

When Shalkan had staggered into her clearing in the Wild Lands a half year ago, she'd realized the Wild Magic had possessed other plans for Kellen all along—even before she'd found the three Books in his pack. She'd been happy to be able to train him—and more frustrated than she'd ever let him suspect when the Wild Magic didn't come as easily to him as it had to her.

But all had been explained once Jermayan discovered that Kellen wasn't a Wildmage, but a Knight-Mage. Since Kellen had come into his true power, he'd grown up frighteningly fast. She didn't think the Elves could see it—everything that humans did was fast, to them—but she could. He was nothing like the boy who'd been pitched out of the gates of the City so short a time ago. That boy would have never, ever have been able to face down an Elven general.

She knew much more of the story of what had happened in Redhelwar's pavilion than she'd let on when she'd been questioning Kellen. She'd been the Healer to treat Gairith after he left there, and Gairith had been a silent witness to the entire confrontation between Belepheriel and Kellen. And as a scout, no matter what his condition, his memory was sharp, and near-perfect as to details.

She did not doubt that the Wild Magic had been involved in what had happened. She had told Kellen many times that healing was such a simple matter for her because so often all she needed to do was "step aside" and let the Wild Magic do as it wished. Apparently there was something similar that operated to assist a Knight-Mage, and Kellen had done it—or been possessed by it—when he'd shamed Belepheriel. And now that they were heading for the caverns in such haste, it was obvious to Idalia that the Wild Magic wasn't done with Kellen yet.

But it was equally true that Kellen didn't understand what he'd done, nor did Redhelwar wish him to understand it. Though it had not, in fact, come to a Circle, Belepheriel had lost his Challenge, and all that was once Belepheriel's was now Kellen's, by Elven custom.

Including his rank.

It was an ancient custom, and there were many good reasons to ignore it in this instance. Belepheriel was one of the most senior commanders. Kellen was a very junior sub-commander.

But Kellen was also a Knight-Mage, honored and well liked, and there had been far too many witnesses to what had happened for the truth to remain hidden for very long.

The Elves liked ritual, custom, order, and tradition—as she knew to her cost. They had long since given up their share in the Greater Magics, but had always welcomed the Wildmages among them, since the Wild Magic was a magic of, when all was said and done, "setting things right." It worked in small quiet ways, and the Elves liked that, and found it . . . suitable.

But Kellen's form of Wild Magic . . . didn't operate in small ways, nor in quiet ways. He was a Knight-Mage. As he'd told Belepheriel, his Magery was the Art of War, and that was hardly small and quiet at the best of times. At times like these, when the need was so great, he was a weapon that the Wild Magic would use in ways that were not what the Elves were used to.

And he won't stop pushing. He can't. Even if it were in his nature—which it isn't—I don't think the Wild Magic will let him. Not until Shadow Mountain is destroyed.

"Ah . . . I think the water's boiling," Kellen said. "Unless you want *me* to make the tea?"

"Gods forbid," Idalia said with an absent smile. "I've been told your tea is poisonous."

"So they say," Kellen said, holding out the pot.

Is that why Redhelwar forbid him to go to the caverns? Because he knew Kellen well enough to know he'd go anyway? And that would give Redhelwar some sort of pretext to leave Belepheriel in command? All he had to do was explain it, and Kellen would have done whatever was needed. Or Redhelwar could have forbidden the Challenge in the first place. But to dismiss a Knight-Mage's warning . . .

Idalia poured the water into the pot, swirling it between her hands to mix the water and the leaves. She could not read Redhelwar's mind, or know what had been in his thoughts. Perhaps it *had* truly been as simple as him not wishing to risk Kellen's life. Perhaps tomorrow—if Kellen had stayed—he would have been invested as a commander, supplanting Belepheriel. Perhaps Redhelwar would have had second thoughts.

They'd never know now. The Wild Magic wanted Kellen to act, and act he would, and they would deal with what came of it.

Idalia poured the tea, and they drank it quickly before it cooled—or froze solid.

"Dawn's coming," Shalkan said.

Idalia looked at the sky. The clouds were starting to break up, and the stars she could see were faint.

"We might as well go," Kellen said, rising to his feet. "Let's wear the *tarnkappa,* but take lanterns, too. Either the *tarnkappa* will shield us or they won't. And there doesn't seem to be anything out here." He furrowed his brows. "And you know, now that I think about it, that's just . . . strange. They know we're here. But there aren't even sentries at the cave entrance."

"You can ask them about that when we see them," Idalia said, trying to sound as if this was the sort of thing she and he did every day.

She replaced the tea-things in Cella's packs, emptied the brazier into the snow, cooled it, and packed it as well, then took out the two *tarnkappa* she'd brought. She handed one to Kellen, along with a piece of blue chalk.

"We won't be able to see or hear each other while we have these on. But I'll be able to see the marks you make on the cave walls, and follow those," she said. "And I'll leave my own—in yellow—so if we get separated for some reason, you can use them to find me."

"Try not to do that," Kellen urged. "I really don't want to have to try to explain how and why I lost you to Jermayan."

"Come to that, I don't want to have to explain the reverse," Idalia said. "Well, go ahead. I can follow your footprints in the snow as far as the entrance."

"Enjoy yourselves," Shalkan said, with a shake of his head. "We'll be right here."

KELLEN put on his helmet, then shook out the *tarnkappa* and flung it around himself. As soon as the hood dropped over his helm, the darkness became eerily bright. Making sure he could reach his sword and dagger easily, Kellen started off.

The *tarnkappa* muted the sound his footsteps made in the snow, but it could not erase his tracks. He walked in a weaving pattern toward the cavern's entrance—a straight line would draw the eye of any watcher, as there were few straight lines in Nature. He reached the entrance and peered inside, but there was nothing to be discerned by either the *tarnkappa*'s darksight or his own Knight-Mage-enhanced senses.

He stepped inside, chalked a small blue arrow just inside the entrance, and went on, moving slowly and carefully.

The entrance passage was low and narrow—the Shadowed Elves might have been able to walk upright in it, but Kellen found himself crouching reflexively.

Up ahead he could see the corridor broaden. He was about to quicken his pace when a thread of green fire at his feet stopped him. He froze, looking down.

A few inches above the floor, stretching across the whole width of the corridor, was a shining strand of greyish material. It glistened to his battle-sight with baleful intent.

He flung off his cloak and spread his arms wide, feeling something bump into one of them. "Stop," he whispered hoarsely. The cavern was pitch-black to his vision now, all but the thread of green fire.

"What?" Idalia whispered after a moment, having removed her own *tarnkappa*.

"There's a trip-wire here. Low to the ground. Do you see it?"

There was a long pause, while Idalia put on her *tarnkappa* and then took it off again so she could talk. "Yes."

"I need to see what it does. I hope I won't trigger it. Step back."

Kellen pulled his cloak back down. Once more the cavern

was bright. He knelt down in front of the trip-wire and studied it carefully, willing himself to See it deeply, to Know it.

Suddenly, in his mind, he could See the trip-wire breaking, and as it did, the section of floor on which he and Idalia were standing pivoted and fell away, leaving a deep pit where the floor had been. How deep, he wasn't sure; but the fall would kill all who were standing in this length of corridor when the wire was broken.

Kellen got to his feet and backed away. He pulled off the cloak again.

"If we'd broken that wire, the floor would have fallen away, and we'd both have been killed," he whispered into the darkness.

There was a moment of silence.

"Kellen, if we're attacked by a horde of poison-flinging Shadowed Elves, you *can* protect me, right?" Idalia said, a strangled note in her voice.

"Yes," Kellen said with certainty.

"Then let's use lanterns. Because I really don't want to miss you warning me about the next trap because I can't hear you. And they're easier to put out quickly than Coldfire."

They lit their lanterns and went on, stepping carefully over the trip-wire after marking its position with chalk-marks on the floor to either side of it.

The corridor opened out into a small chamber. Long thin poles were stuck into the rock at intervals, jutting out into the room. The only way through them was a narrow corridor down the middle.

Disturbing one of those would bring a jar of acid pouring down.

"Don't touch any of those unless you want a faceful of something bad," Kellen said grimly.

They went on.

Each of those traps—the pit-trap and the acid-trap, would have caused losses. But they could have built a bridge across the pit—or even jumped it—and once the acid jars were empty, that trap would be harmless, too.

Neither was bad enough to make the army turn back. And from there on, they'd be alert for more traps.

But if the Shadowed Elves were attacking at the same time, they wouldn't have the chance to spot them. They'd be forced into them.

The next trap was a patch of corridor that looked like stone to the unaided eye, but when Kellen threw a coin into it, it sank beneath the surface instantly. He chalked a mark at the near edge, Saw where the far side was, and jumped it. Idalia did the same, chalking a mark to indicate the far boundary.

"It must have taken them a long time to make all of these traps," Idalia said consideringly, looking back at the pool of artfully-disguised quicksand. "Moonturns, maybe."

"There weren't any of these in the first cavern. Did they build these just for us? And if they did, how did they know we were coming?" Kellen wondered aloud. He was glad of the breathing space. The need to be constantly alert—and the knowledge of the penalty if he wasn't—was draining.

"And where are they?" Idalia asked, putting into words what Kellen had been wondering since they'd begun to descend into the cavern.

"That's what I'd like to know," Kellen said grimly. "These traps—bad as they are—aren't enough to stop the army— only to make it pay dearly for every foot of tunnel it takes. Let's keep going. We need to find the village."

It seemed they could not go more than a few steps without encountering another trap. Some were as simple as poisoned spikes jutting out of the walls, or a rain of stones set to fall from the ceiling when a trip-wire was broken. Some were as complicated as the jet of air rushing between two low holes in the walls—they crawled beneath that one, and didn't stop to find out what would have happened if they'd interrupted the flow of air. Some trip-wires seemed to have no purpose at all that Kellen could see—that probably meant they triggered more distant traps, perhaps to seal the whole army into the cave system, so it could be dealt with at leisure.

And no matter how far they went, they saw no sign of the cavern's inhabitants.

Several side caverns had been hastily filled-in with rubble, as if the Shadowed Elves did not wish the invaders to get lost—or to find shelter.

"They're leading us right to them," Idalia said. "Or to the village, at least."

Kellen had no doubt of that. And the army, having gotten this far, having sustained horrific losses, would be thinking of nothing but closing with its enemy.

The corridor they were following made a sharp left turn, and suddenly they were there.

The last village had been at the bottom of an enormous cavern. This time, the corridor opened directly onto the village floor. Though their lanterns cast very little light, Kellen had a sense of vast open space stretching off in all directions—all directions but overhead, because the ceiling was still only a few inches above his head.

The lanterns did give them enough light to see the same cluster of stone huts as before, and in the distance, the banked embers of the communal firepit glowed redly.

But to Kellen's battle-sight, the whole of the low ceiling glowed with the evil green of a Shadowed Elf trap.

He swallowed hard, realizing what he was seeing. Here—somewhere—was the trigger that would bring the whole ceiling down, crushing everyone beneath it as a man might crush an insect between his two palms.

"Idalia—" he said, turning.

And stopped.

Idalia wasn't there.

⌐

OH, *good, now we can go home,* was Idalia's first exhausted thought when they reached the edge of the Shadowed Elf village and she saw the cluster of stone huts. Following Kellen into this chamber of horrors had been nerve-wracking; at times only the thought of the lives they would save had given her the energy to push herself on. She knew she hadn't seen all the traps that Kellen had; it had been bad enough seeing the ones he'd pointed out. For a while tonight she'd begun to think that the time had come to pay her Mageprice, the one she had offered up to save Sentarshadeen.

But dying down here would serve no greater good, and she had the faint suspicion—no more than that—that when the time came to pay her Price, the Gods would see to it that her death counted for something.

At least so she hoped. Accidents—if anything in war could be called an accident—were still possible. But when she died, she hoped it would be in the light and air, and not buried beneath tons of rock . . .

Someone was calling her.

Idalia heard it clearly. A voice, off to her right, a voice that claimed every bit of her attention, and made her weariness vanish as if it had never been. Without thought, she set her lantern aside and moved toward it. She didn't need light to see where she was going.

KELLEN looked down. Idalia's lantern rested on an outcropping of rock at his shoulder.

"Idalia!" he shouted.

The echoes almost masked the scrabble of claws against stone.

Kellen whirled back, tossing the lantern he held at the first of the creatures emerging from the rock and the darkness. It broke against the creature's skin, engulfing it in flame.

He recognized them from Jermayan's description. Goblins.

They were less than half the size of the Shadowed Elves, but bore a horrible resemblance to them. Their frog-wide mouths gaped as they sprang toward Kellen, exposing multiple rows of glistening, needle-sharp teeth, and their skins were bruise-dark. They squinted their bulging pale eyes against the light of the remaining lantern as they bounded toward him, running on hands and feet both. They seemed to rise up out of the stone itself, as if it were like water to them.

And they could spit poison. A unicorn could heal it, but Shalkan wasn't here.

And this was not the time to think of any of that.

Kellen let all thoughts and questions drop from his mind, slipping into battle-trance now without even realizing he had done so. The goblins ceased to be goblins, and became targets for his sword.

In the back of his mind, where some part of him made cold calculations and plans, was the knowledge that he dared not move very far from where he stood, for to enter the village might be to bring the entire roof down. No matter how his attackers came at him he spun and pivoted, backing and turning only in his own footsteps—he knew that was safe—and hacked away at the goblins.

For every one he killed, three more took its place. There seemed to be an unending supply of the creatures, but for all their vaguely manlike shape, they didn't seem to be even as intelligent as the coldwarg, and they kept interrupting their attack to devour their own dead and fight with each other.

But no matter how many were diverted, there were always more than enough to take their place.

In his brief breathing spells, Kellen grudged every moment he had to spend on them, but he dared not leave any of them alive. They were creatures of the Dark, and if he broke off the attack, they might have been given orders to trigger the collapse of the cavern roof.

He dared not stand too close to the cavern walls, either. As far as he was able to tell in the midst of fighting them back, they could move through rock, hiding themselves within stone as easily as Elves could hide within a forest. Time and again Kellen felt hands reach up out of the stone on which he stood to clutch at his ankles, trying to pull him down so that the goblin horde could devour him. He could feel their teeth grate against his armor, searching for any way through its defense, even as he cut and kicked at them.

There were spells he could use to make the fight end sooner. Fire was easy to summon, and he'd already seen how well they burned. But he didn't dare. Every moment of the fight, a part of his mind was focused on the cavern roof, so precariously balanced. He did not know what would bring it down—perhaps even a Wildmage's spell—but he knew that if it collapsed, neither he nor Idalia—wherever she was—would survive.

And so he fought on, grimly, killing the goblins by ones and twos. He had no choice.

And then, at last, he cut the last three down—and no more came. Kellen lowered his sword. The goblin bodies were already starting to dissolve, and the acrid stench of their decay made Kellen's eyes water. He stepped hastily away from them, along the edge of the cavern, toward cleaner air, and came out of his battle-trance.

And the first thing that leaped into his mind was Idalia.

Where was Idalia?

Suddenly he became aware of an odd desire to go deeper into the caverns. He was sure he'd find . . .

What?

Kellen stopped, realizing he'd taken several steps into the darkness without noticing.

And that something deep inside him had jerked him to a halt with a thrill of alarm.

He probed his own feelings, the way he would probe a wound. The yearning sensation was still there, but suddenly Kellen felt no desire at all to yield to it. It was like the revulsion he'd experienced at the Black Cairn turned inside-out, but he had no doubt its source was just as Tainted.

It's what would lure the army deep into the caves, Kellen realized in horror. If it worked on Elves—and he had no reason to think it didn't—the Knights would have followed it to their doom.

As Idalia had followed it.

But why wasn't he affected? Certainly he felt the call, and could follow it, but he could resist it, too.

He remembered what Jermayan had said, when the Elven Knight had first discovered what Kellen was.

"A Knight-Mage's gifts turn inward, refining himself, so he cannot be turned away from his path once he has chosen it. A Knight-Mage can withstand forces that would destroy a Wildmage, for his power lies in endurance and the alliance of his knightly skills with his Wildmagery."

In other words, he was stubborn. Well, everyone had always said so. Kellen bared his teeth wolfishly. Whatever was calling was going to find out it had called up more than it could handle.

He looked at the lantern, still burning undisturbed on the outcropping of rock. Should he take it?

No. Idalia had gone into the dark without it, and he would follow her the same way.

He fumbled in his belt for the *tarnkappa* and pulled it on. At once the cavern was sharply lit. He could see the vast sweep of it—far more than the lantern light had shown him—an enormous area, stretching at least a mile.

And all of it carefully arranged to collapse, as soon as the proper trigger was tripped.

He turned in the direction of the Call.

⌐

THE way was long, but her steps were made smooth. Idalia hurried forward impatiently, anxious to reach her destination.

Which was . . . what?

She stopped, frowning. Where was she going? Where was Kellen? And why was it so dark?

She fumbled at her belt for her *tarnkappa,* but before she could complete the gesture, the call reached out to her again, washing over her in a warm wave. Her hands dropped to her sides and she continued walking.

⤳

THOUGH there were no traps that Kellen Saw past the village cavern, once he reached the edge of the village there were several tunnels. For a moment he wasn't sure which of them Idalia had taken, but then the Call lured him toward the centermost one.

It was smooth as glass and perfectly round, as if made by the passage of some rock-eating worm. At the far end, it opened out into what Kellen had come to think of as a more "traditional" underground cave—a high vaulted cavern filled with tall spikes and pillars of rock. Here he could hear the breath of the mountain, and realized that sound had been absent from the labyrinth of tunnels he and Idalia had just passed through.

He had the sense that this part of the cave system was one that the Shadowed Elves rarely used. But there was *something* here—these caverns were filled with life. He could sense it—and what he sensed was mixed. Some was Tainted, but some was not. He moved forward slowly, sword ready.

And then he saw Idalia.

She was walking forward, as easily as if she could see, directly toward a monster such as Kellen had never seen before.

It squatted on its haunches, its arms clasped across its stomach, crouched upon a hummock of stone. Its body was squat and wide, and it did not seem to be very large, perhaps the size of a Shadowed Elf, but much wider. Its skin seemed to be a dull black. It was covered, not with fur or feathers or scales, but with little fleshy polyps of skin that gave it a nauseatingly shaggy appearance. If it had any eyes at all, they were so tiny as to be lost in the nest of facial polyps, and it seemed to have neither nose nor ears. Its mouth was slightly open, forked tongue lolling over curved fangs as it radiated the Call that had lured Idalia to it. And by the time Kellen saw her, she was nearly within arm's reach of it.

Fast as he was, Kellen couldn't reach Idalia in time.

He drew his dagger. He could put it through her leg, even at this distance. The wound would stop her without killing her.

But then, he realized with a sudden feeling of horror, the creature would know someone was here. And it could spring up and rip her throat out before Kellen could reach it. He could stab the creature, but he didn't know if that would kill it—or what stabbing it would do to Idalia's mind.

With a strangled cry of desperation Kellen began to run. He had to try to reach her. No matter what, he had to try!

And oblivious to it all, Idalia continued to walk forward, caught in a spell she could not break—

Suddenly half-a-dozen furry white, softly-glowing spiders dropped from above, directly onto the black squatting creature. It closed its mouth with a startled snap, and the *calling* Kellen had been following stopped abruptly.

The spiders were the size of young lambs, and swarmed nimbly and quickly over the creature's body as it writhed and batted uselessly at them. Silently it battled the swarming arachnids, frantically attempting to catch them, but they flowed away over the cavern floor as quickly as they'd arrived.

It was no more than a momentary distraction, but it gave Kellen the time he needed. Idalia had stopped moving forward, and began groping for her *tarnkappa*, shaking her head as if she'd been roused from sleep. As Kellen passed her, he shoved her hard, knocking her sprawling, his mind already full of what he must do.

He reached the creature and struck unhesitatingly, taking its head from its shoulders in one clean blow. It was not like cutting into a man or a coldwarg—or even a goblin. Beneath the skin, the creature's flesh seemed almost jellylike, and Kellen's blow did not meet the resistance of bone. He leaped back, and just in time. Its flesh began to melt away as soon as its head rolled free of its body, dissolving like wax plunged into a furnace, filling the cavern with the sick-sweet scent of decay and something worse.

Kellen looked down at his sword, wondering if it would ever be clean again, and saw to his horror that the metal was black and flaking where it had entered the monster's body. With a sinking feeling, he set the tip of the blade against the stone floor and pressed gently. The sword bent, then snapped like rotting wood.

Kellen winced. Not the worst thing that could happen, but high on the list. He wasn't helpless with only a dagger and half a sword, but he wasn't happy about the situation.

He turned back to where he'd left Idalia. Time for them to get out of here.

Her body was covered in spiders.

Their bodies weren't just glowing whitely now, they were pulsing in pale colors: green, purple, yellow, pink. And Idalia wasn't moving.

⌒

SUDDENLY it was dark—the blinding darkness of the caves—and Idalia knew something was terribly wrong. The last thing she remembered clearly was the cavern, the deserted Shadowed Elf village, and then . . . it was almost as if she'd been asleep.

She groped for her *tarnkappa*, but before she could pull it free, a savage blow from out of nowhere knocked her sprawling. She hit the stone floor of the cave hard, and in the utter silence could hear nothing but the faint sound of the cave's "breath" and the pounding of her own heart in her ears.

Then she felt fingers plucking at her clothes.

No.

Not fingers.

Legs.

: Do not fear us. We are friends.:

A voice spoke in her head. More than a voice. Pictures— images—memories. She pulled off a glove and reached out hesitantly. She touched stiff silky bristles.

: Good. Easier.:

Who are you? Idalia thought back.

She could see them—and herself—a strange disjointed picture, relayed by multiple eyes. Spiders. But like no spiders ever seen in the outside world. And with that picture came something she had not expected. Peace—warmth. Welcome, the welcome of one ally recognizing another, one creature of the Light (though these spiders spent their lives in the darkness of the caves) acknowledging one of like spirit. Strange as it seemed, and as repugnant as most humans found spiders to be, these *were* friends. She relaxed, and opened her mind a little further.

: We are Crystal,: came the reply. *:This is our home, and it has been ravaged by the Black Minds. Those you call Shadowed Elves come, and take our webs, our eggs, our children.:*

She felt their anger at the pillaging. The Shadowed Elves ate the Crystal Spiders, and used the silk from their webs and cocoons for their own purposes. Idalia felt a flash of alarm, purely her own this time. If the Shadowed Elves were here in the caverns, and triggered any of their traps—

: They are not here now. For—long—they have made the traps. And brought the others to lure you in. Then they left.:

"Idalia?" A voice, with an edge of panic to it. "Idalia, can you hear me?"

Kellen. Alarmed. Sounding not-quite-certain the Crystal Spiders were a threat, but ready to believe they were.

"It's all right. I'm all right, truly, there's nothing to worry about. They're friends, allies, a People of the Light. They're talking to me," Idalia said, trying to concentrate on the spiders and Kellen at the same time. "That's why they're sitting on me, I think it's the only way they can speak to my mind." She turned her thoughts back to these new allies. *Go on. Tell me more. None of the Shadowed Elves are here?*

: Gone. All gone to their other place. It is not far. We are there too, and we know. Other Black Minds, like the one who Called you, are there as well. Beware, for the Black Minds do not need eyes to see. That which is invisible is visible to them.:

The Crystal Spider sent a blurred picture into Idalia's

mind, and she shuddered. A *duergar.* They were cousins to the ice-trolls but could not bear even as much light as their cousins. They lived in the deepest caves, and lured prey to them with their mental powers.

And they were utterly blind, so a *tarnkappa* would not conceal its wearer from them.

"What are they saying?" Kellen demanded, still sounding unconvinced. Well, she couldn't blame him—here she was, covered in spiders, after being lured down here by a *duergar*!

"They live here. It really *is* all right, Kellen," she replied, making her voice sound reassuring. "They're friendly, honestly—didn't you see how they distracted the *duergar* so it lost control of me for a moment?" She had seen that in their minds as well. "They don't like the Shadowed Elves, and they see us as their allies. They told me that the Shadowed Elves set up the traps in these caves—and called in some other Black Minds, they say, then left."

"Yeah," Kellen said with a sigh. "I've already met some of the other 'Black Minds'—a pack of goblins. But what was that thing that was after you?"

"Duergar," Idalia said briefly. "They lure prey with their minds. *Tarnkappa* don't work against them, because they can't see."

"Oh." Kellen sounded slightly chastened. There was a pause. "We need to set off all those other traps. And I think if we do, this whole cave might collapse. The roof of the village cavern is set to come down, but I couldn't see the trip-wire for it, or any other way of triggering it."

Do you understand? Idalia thought to the spiders. *I don't want any of you to be hurt. But this place is too dangerous to leave as it is.*

: We understand,: the Crystal Spiders "said"—they seemed to speak as one, or perhaps all of them together made up one mind. *: Wait . . . :* There was a long pause, and Idalia sensed that the spiders were consulting among themselves and picking through her surface thoughts, trying to find a concept they would all understand. *:Wait a day before you make the caverns*

safe, and we will not be harmed. And when next you hunt the Shadowed Elves, we will give you what help we can.:

"I promise we will wait," Idalia said aloud. "And I thank you for your help."

There was a wave of movement, and the shining carpet of enormous spiders that had covered her scuttled away. Idalia sat up, watching as the balls of glowing pastel light disappeared into the darkness, actually seeing them for the first time.

"Why—they're beautiful," she said aloud, in surprise. "Poor things—never harming anything but insects, suddenly finding themselves hunted by Shadowed Elves—"

"I guess we're not the only ones the Shadowed Elves are hurting," Kellen said quietly.

"They're hurting everything that lives," Idalia said grimly. "That's what they were designed to do. Hurt things."

"Why?" Kellen asked plaintively, and suddenly he sounded very young and fragile. "Why would they want to do that? It doesn't sound like any kind of life. What possible kind of existence is that for anything?"

"Kellen," Idalia said, her voice suddenly sharp with fear. "You said you were attacked by goblins. Did any of them bite you?"

"Of course not," Kellen said indignantly, but there was a dreamy undertone to his voice that Idalia didn't like. "Some of them chewed on my armor a lot, though. I couldn't help that."

"No, of course you couldn't. Come here and let me see."

She cupped her hands and concentrated. A faint mist began to coalesce between her palms, growing denser and brighter until it burned chill and blue. She gestured, and the ball of Coldfire rose to hover above her head.

In its light she could see Kellen standing a few feet away. His *tarnkappa* was hanging from one hand, his sword—*half* his sword—was hanging from the other. She got to her feet, retrieving her discarded glove in the process, and walked over to him.

She leaned over and sniffed. His armor reeked of goblin venom, but it seemed to be in one piece. If any of them had spit in his face, he wouldn't be standing here debating the nature of Evil, Knight-Mage or no. He'd be goblin dinner.

But if any of it had gotten through the joins in the armor and soaked into the padding, and through the padding. . . .

"I think I might have been poisoned after all, Idalia," Kellen said somberly, and with a slight slurring in his voice. "I don't feel—quite right."

"I think so, too," Idalia said. "But not badly. You'll just be a little . . . drunk. And Shalkan can fix that once we're out of here." She hoped. A unicorn could cleanse a poisoned wound, but how could Shalkan reach the poison that had soaked into Kellen's skin?

Kellen laughed bitterly. "Can you get out of here without me?" He began removing his armor. "Without triggering any of the traps we passed on the way in? Can *I* keep from triggering them?" He set the last of his armor aside. The damp blotches of poison were visible now on the legs and thighs of his leather underpadding. Kellen began to remove it as well. "Because if not, you've got to heal me now, or we've got to figure out something else that will work. And if we can't, we've failed. And the army is going to die."

Where the goblin poison had reached his skin through the underpadding, there were raised red welts. Kellen rubbed at them absently, shivering in the cold of the cave. He was wearing nothing but a hip-wrap now, but at least it was untouched by goblin poison.

He was right, Idalia realized.

She had no idea where she was in the caves now. She was sure Kellen could lead her back to the village cavern, even in this condition, but even though they'd marked them carefully on the way in, Idalia wasn't completely certain of her ability to navigate past all the traps on the way out without a Knight-Mage's battle-sight to point them out. And Kellen might not be able to do it at all if the poison fogged his mind any more deeply.

And if she did leave him and make the try, and succeeded, then she'd have to come back in and try to get him out later, when he was in even worse shape from the slow working of the poison he'd absorbed—because Shalkan couldn't get in here at all. Though he might possibly manage to throw off the effects of the poison by himself eventually, it was a gamble she didn't want to take, and they couldn't afford to wait.

And leaving him here, alone, sick, without sword or armor—well, she doubted she'd have a brother to come back to, considering what else the Crystal Spiders said was prowling around down here.

But if she did heal him, there was no one here to take any of the physical price, even if her Mageprices seemed to have all been paid in advance. The effort would leave her exhausted. And navigating the labyrinth of traps took a huge amount of physical stamina. She wouldn't be able to do it after doing a healing. And Kellen wouldn't be able to do it carrying her.

But there was one thing she could try.

Idalia began to rummage through her possibles bag.

"Here are the choices as I know them," she said. "If I leave you and go for help and to warn Redhelwar, I *might* be able to get out by myself, but I don't guarantee it. Meanwhile you get sicker, and I—or someone—still have to come back in and get you out. Or I can heal you here, after which you'll probably have to carry me out, and I don't think that will work either."

Kellen laughed giddily, caught himself, and shook his head.

"Or you can drink this," she said, having found the phial she'd been looking for. "It's not a healing. It's not really a medicine. It's a cheat. It convinces your body it's well—for a little while—no matter how badly you've been hurt—or poisoned. But when it wears off, what it's done to you has to be paid for with a true healing, or a lot of rest, or both."

"Why would you make a bad thing like that?" Kellen asked, sounding less than half his age. He rubbed at his head, as if it hurt, dropping the *tarnkappa* to the cavern floor.

"Sometimes a man needs to be able to walk off a battlefield with two broken legs," Idalia said. "This will let him do it. But he pays for it afterward."

Her brother suddenly shook himself, all over, like a dog

shaking himself dry. "Gods of Leaf and Star!" Kellen swore, sounding like himself for just a moment, "if you told me it would kill me in a day, I'd still take it. Give it to me, before I get too stupid to know how to drink."

Idalia placed the thumb-sized glass phial in his hand, blessing the impulse that had caused her to bring it with her when she'd packed for the journey.

Kellen broke the seal and quickly tossed it back, shuddering and gagging at the taste.

Twenty

The Order of Battle

Why did all of Idalia's herbal medicines seem to be made of the bitterest herbs she could find? The taste made his eyes water and his teeth ache, and Kellen swallowed hard, resisting the impulse to retch.

But the disconnected floating feeling that he'd been fighting off ever since he'd killed the *duergar* was gone. He was himself again. He took several deep breaths.

"I feel better," he said.

"You won't in half a day," Idalia warned.

In half a day the Elven army would have been warned about this trap. At the moment, that was all that mattered.

Kellen inspected the pile of discarded armor and garments. The sheen of goblin poison glowed sickly green to his battle-sight in far too many places. He picked up his heavy fur cloak, inspecting it carefully—it was clean—and put it on, then looked at his armor regretfully.

"There's no way to carry it safely, and half of it's covered with goblin spit. I'll miss it." He picked up his dagger and his broken sword. "Come on."

"First let's do something about your feet," Idalia said, taking out her dagger and beginning to cut her *tarnkappa* into strips. "It won't be much, but it's better than having you try to walk out of here barefoot."

⟾

THE return trip seemed to go far more swiftly than the trip in. Idalia's Potion of False Healing filled him with energy, so that Kellen had to be careful to adjust his pace to hers. He felt as if he could run all the way.

But making their way back through the traps was still a painstaking process, one that required the most exacting concentration. Kellen breathed a sigh of relief when he and Idalia stepped over the last of the trip wires.

Idalia hugged him tightly.

"I never, never, *never* want to go down there again," she said fervently.

"Neither do I," Kellen said. Now that it was over, he could acknowledge the fear—and more, the disgust—he'd felt every moment he'd been down in the Shadowed Elf caverns. There was something horribly *unclean* about those traps. Compared to them, the goblins and even the *duergar* had been wholesome.

"I'll cut up the blanket I left with Cella to make you a pair of leggings," Idalia said, "but I'm afraid you're going to have a cold ride back."

"At least it should be day when we get out," Kellen said. "I just hope it isn't snowing too hard."

They reached the entrance of the cave.

It was dusk. They'd been underground a full day. But sunset wasn't the only thing that greeted them.

Spread out across the valley, starting a bowshot's-length from the cavern and running all the way to the stream and beyond, was a third of the Elven army.

They sat on their destriers like statues, as if they had been waiting there for centuries, and were prepared to wait for centuries more. A light snow was falling, and from the way it had collected on their cloaks and armor, they had indeed been waiting here for some time. The only movement was the flutter of the war banners on the wind, and the occasional shake of a destrier's head.

Facing the army was Shalkan, standing firm right in the mouth of the cavern. His horn glowed deep scarlet, and every inch of fur not covered by his armor was fluffed straight out.

"It looks like they got here early," Idalia said noncommittally.

Kellen looked out over the assembled host. With a sinking heart, he saw not only Adaerion's banner, but Belepheriel's and Redhelwar's as well.

Ninolion had been wrong. The general *had* been able to make his dispositions in less than a day. Or else, finding Kellen gone, he'd put everything else aside to bring a force to the nearer cavern.

And now Shalkan was holding them off.

⟳

"GOOD to see you," Shalkan said, not moving, as Kellen and Idalia walked slowly up to stand with him.

"I was right," Kellen said. "The whole cavern's been turned into one enormous death trap."

"You might want to let Redhelwar know," Shalkan replied, as outwardly calm as if Kellen had just remarked on the depth of the snow. "Ah, here he comes now."

The general rode into the first rank of the assembled Knights, but came no closer. Considering the way Shalkan looked, he probably didn't dare.

"You'd better go out to him," Shalkan said. "I believe he was unaware until now of how protective a unicorn can be."

Wincing inwardly at the thought, Kellen stepped out of the cavern mouth into the snow, wrapping his cloak around him as tightly as he could. The snow was knee-deep, and soaked through the rags of the *tarnkappa* wrapped around his feet instantly. As he had been taught at the House of Sword and Shield, he shut the pain and the cold away in a small part of his mind, and concentrated on the task ahead.

He reached Redhelwar's stirrup and bowed, as formal a bow as he could manage under the circumstances.

"I See you, Redhelwar, Army's General," he said.

But Redhelwar did not greet him in return. Instead, he bent his head only enough to look stonily down at Kellen through the slits in his helmet.

"What do you have to say to me, Kellen Knight-Mage?"

Kellen suspected that this was not War Manners, but the attitude of a commander who is about to issue a great deal more than a simple reprimand. Either way, it did not matter.

He took a deep breath. No matter what was done to him after this, at least he would have prevented a disaster with his disobedience. "I say that the cavern is a death trap, Redhelwar. There are no Shadowed Elves here. It is filled with a series of traps, cleverly concealed, to destroy the army if it enters. And if the army actually reached the village cavern, the entire roof would collapse upon them." The commander's eyes widened, but Kellen wasn't done yet. "Further, the Shadowed Elves brought allies to ensure that the army would advance into the caverns at any cost: within the caverns are both goblins and *duergar*. I have seen and slain both, but more remain." He closed his eyes for a moment, and picked his words with the utmost precision. "Whoever entered that cavern mouth would never come out again; neither living, *nor* dead. This was not only meant as a trap, it was meant to destroy one-third of our army."

Elves were ageless and beautiful. Even the tales told of them in Armethalieh said so. And though Kellen had seen that they *did* age, the marks of age came slowly and at the end of a very long life, and even in age they were still beautiful.

But in that moment Redhelwar's Elven beauty drained

away like water poured into drought-parched earth. For a moment, Kellen saw the Elven general not only surprised, but terrified.

He lowered his eyes quickly, not wishing to see more.

"If I had done what I wished to do, followed the plans I had made . . . " Redhelwar said. His voice sounded hollow, as if he bore a burden of unendurable pain.

"I would ask a boon, Army's General," Kellen said, keeping his teeth from chattering with an effort. The wind seemed to find every gap in his cloak, and the snow burned against his skin. He couldn't feel his feet at all.

"Name your boon, Kellen Knight-Mage," Redhelwar said. His voice was stronger now, and Kellen dared to look up again. Redhelwar's face was still haggard, but it no longer looked quite so . . . naked.

"We escaped the cavern alive through the help of allies. The caverns are far too dangerous to leave with their traps intact, but we have promised our allies time to escape before we destroy the traps. They ask for a day."

"All shall be as you wish," Redhelwar said hollowly.

He raised his hand and gestured. Dionan rode forward.

"Sound the retreat," Redhelwar said, his voice steady now, but without expression. "We return to camp."

Dionan raised his horn to his lips and blew a complicated series of notes. Instantly the army was in motion, its elements turning in place and beginning to move away from the cavern.

"Bring Ninolion to me, and fetch Idalia's mount. My compliments to Belepheriel, and let him know it would please me greatly if he and his people would continue to watch over this cavern for untoward events. Under no circumstances are they to enter it."

"And could someone find something for Kellen to wear?" Idalia demanded irritably, forging through the snow to stand at Kellen's side. "He hasn't got a thing on under that cloak."

"The, uh, Goblins poisoned my armor. I had to take it off," Kellen explained, blushing furiously. He thought he'd actually rather freeze than have Idalia explain things.

"See to it," Redhelwar ordered, still in that terrible, flat voice. Dionan rode off.

"Shalkan will assist you," Redhelwar said to Kellen. "Go to him. Dionan will see what may be done. And . . . my thanks to you. You have saved me from a great error."

Kellen bowed. He couldn't think of anything to say. Idalia grabbed him by the arm and dragged him back toward Shalkan.

Shalkan's horn was back to its normal pearly-white color now. "Get on," he said, seeing Kellen.

It took Kellen several tries to mount—by now he couldn't feel either his hands *or* his feet—but once he was on Shalkan's back, he felt better. Even through the armor, the unicorn was radiating heat like a furnace, and soon Kellen's teeth stopped wanting to chatter, and he stopped shivering.

Was everything going to be all right now? Or as all right as things got these days? At least Redhelwar had believed him.

It hadn't occurred to him until just now that the Elven general might not have. What could he possibly have done then?

"Where am I going to get another set of armor?" he said aloud, turning his mind with relief to things that didn't matter quite so much. "And another sword?" He was beginning to feel a bit of that muzziness return; he wasn't quite sure where the broken one had gotten to—or his dagger. He thought he'd left them both back inside the cavern just after the last trip-wire.

The majority of the Elven army had withdrawn to beyond the river now. Only Redhelwar and his adjutants remained, and Belepheriel and his command.

"Both of those things are Artenel's problem, and I'm sure he'll rise to the challenge," Idalia said. "How are you planning to trigger the traps in the cave?"

"That's Jermayan's problem," Kellen said, with a certain amount of relief. "I'm sure he and Ancaladar will rise to the challenge. Tomorrow."

"I take it Redhelwar didn't have a problem with that?" Idalia said.

"I think he'd have given me the whole damned army if I'd asked for it just now," Kellen said.

"Ah," Idalia said. "There's Cella."

Ninolion had led the palfrey up to Redhelwar's side. Idalia went out to the mare and led her back to Kellen and Shalkan. She was carrying something else in her other hand, but by now it was too dark—and, once again, snowing too hard—for Kellen to see it clearly.

"Here," she said. "Put these on."

Kellen reluctantly untucked his hands from his cloak to take what Idalia was holding out to him. It was a pair of the long heavy sheepskin boots that were worn over armor as a further protection against the cold. They were an Elven pair, of course, so even without armor, Kellen could barely cram his feet into them.

Idalia rooted around in her packs and came up with several blocks of journey-food. She gave one to Shalkan, handed one to Kellen, and unwrapped the third for herself. Kellen wolfed it down as quickly as he could, then wrapped himself tightly in his cloak again.

"Let's go," she said, mounting Cella. "I want to get you back to camp and into the hands of the Healers before you fall over."

"You go ahead," Kellen said. "Shalkan and I will follow as closely as we can. I promise."

Idalia nodded, and trotted after the retreating army.

Kellen glanced once more at Redhelwar and the others. Without Shalkan, he might have been tempted to join them—or at least think it was his duty—but with Shalkan, it was impossible. Shalkan made an exception for Idalia—at need—but for a whole troop of Elves?

Impossible.

Fortunately. No doubt now; he was beginning to feel unpleasantly drunk.

"Let's go home."

"YOU'LL have to make your own way from here," Shalkan said, trotting into the circle of pavilions that made up the camp of the Unicorn Knights. "I'd suggest stealing some clothes, but nothing will fit."

"Where is everyone?" Kellen asked, looking around. None of the lanterns in front of the pavilions were lit, and even the communal brazier was cold and dark.

"Probably off at Ysterialpoerin," Shalkan said. "Where I'm going, to get this armor off and get a good meal, as well as to catch up on the gossip, so don't worry about me. Now, go—straight to the Healers, if you please. I can smell that potion Idalia gave you, that and the goblin poison both. You need to get them both taken care of. *Now.*"

"I'm going," Kellen said meekly.

He'd forgotten what a long cold walk it could be from the Unicorn Camp back to the main camp—of course, he'd never done it wearing nothing more than a cloak and a pair of too-tight boots before. At least there was a string of lanterns to mark his way, though the snow—the everlasting snow—had drifted so high that they seemed to rest directly on its surface, and some of them had melted small craters in it, so their light gleamed against walls of ice.

And he had the awful feeling that Idalia's potion was wearing off very quickly now, because he didn't seem to be able to keep the cloak closed. It seemed to take too much effort, somehow, and he had the strongest desire just to lie down right here in the snow and sleep.

"Halt and declare yourself." A sentry's voice came out of the darkness.

Stopping was the best idea Kellen had heard in hours. He opened his mouth to explain who he was.

And that was the last thing he remembered.

⟿

"—BE all right now. The poison is gone, and I've healed him of the potion's effects. All he needs now is rest and food."

A stranger's voice, one that Kellen didn't recognize.

"Thank you, Arozen. I'll see to it that he gets both."

Idalia.

"You should rest as well, Idalia," Arozen said.

"Hey," Kellen said weakly. He pried his eyes open, though that seemed to take a great effort.

Idalia was glaring down at him as if he were a personal enemy. A man stood next to her, dressed in High Reaches furs: Arozen, presumably.

Vestakia was there, too, and Ciltesse, Isinwen . . . all his command. He struggled to sit up.

"Don't—you—dare—move," Idalia said, strong-arming him flat with one expertly-placed blow.

"I'm not moving," Kellen said hastily, now entirely bewildered. Why was Idalia so angry with him?

"It was . . . a difficult healing," Arozen said, explaining. "The potion Idalia gave you is, in its way, a kind of poison as well, and you were already poisoned. And you were also paying Mageprice, so . . . you were closer to death than you realized. And it is cold out there in the night."

"Well, I'm not dead now," Kellen said. "Honest." *Paying Mageprice?* He couldn't think of any spells he'd cast.

Unless . . . back in Redhelwar's pavilion . . . what he'd done to Belepheriel *had* been a spell after all? If the price had been to go off to the Shadowed Elf cavern in the middle of the night, taking complete disgrace on himself, then he guessed he'd paid the price in full.

"Idalia—Vestakia—Ciltesse—I'm fine," he said. "Tired, but—fine." He knew Arozen wouldn't have let Idalia share the Mageprice of his healing, as tired as she'd been, but he suspected that the reason the others were here was because they had.

Including Vestakia.

"That makes good hearing, *alakomentai*," Ciltesse said.

"Now go and rest," Kellen demanded. "All of you. Please. Idalia, if you don't think I'll be smart enough on my own to stay here, you can find . . . you can find . . . "

He didn't manage to finish his sentence before he was asleep.

HUNGER and the smell of food woke him. Daylight was shining through the walls of the Healer's tent, and Isinwen was there with a large covered tray that smelled *wonderful*.

Kellen scrambled into a sitting position and reached for it. Isinwen set it carefully on Kellen's knees and removed the cover.

"I See you, Isinwen," Kellen said. "Tell me what I need to know, of your courtesy." The tray was piled high with enough food to feed three people, and Kellen was so ravenous he was sure he could eat all of it. Thinking back, he wasn't sure when the last time was he'd had a full meal. One day? Two? He thought it might have been the journey-meal on the march the day they'd reached Ysterialpoerin, but he wasn't quite sure. He reached for the tall mug of tea first.

"You have slept only through the night, which should please you. The farther cavern is quiet, as is the nearer. You will need to see Artenel today for a first fitting for your new armor, and to choose a new sword. Ciltesse has selected three destriers for you to choose from, but thinks you will pick Anganil. There have been wagers placed, of course."

Kellen found himself grinning around a mouthful of bread and cheese. He'd discovered that Elves would place bets on the most unlikely of things, and at the most unlikely of times. Even in the middle of war. Probably in the middle of battle.

"Redhelwar wishes to see you when you are fully recovered. And . . . Belepheriel begs the favor of an audience as well."

Kellen nearly choked on a mouthful of roast chicken. *Belepheriel* wanted to see him?

He took a deep breath, and prepared to eat crow along with his chicken. "Isinwen, I fear I have offended Belepheriel greatly by my rash and ill-considered words. It would please me if you, who are wise in the ways of the Elves, can help me to understand what seems strange to me."

Isinwen smiled. "Your manners improve. Kellen, the whole camp knows what happened in Redhelwar's pavilion that night, though certainly no one would say so. Belepheriel's words are just as I have said them to you. He spoke so to Ciltesse in my hearing. He comes as a petitioner. It is for you to say 'yes' or 'no.' "

"That's not a lot of help," Kellen muttered, swallowing chicken and reaching for a meat-pastry.

"You would wish to know his reasons for asking," Isinwen said. "I do not know them. I do know that he will not offer you insult, should you come as a guest to his pavilion. If you would seem gracious, accept. If you wish a . . . distance . . . to grow between you, say nothing. If you wish to truly sever all connection, then refuse to see him: But that course could lead to . . . awkwardness."

"Awkwardness," Kellen suspected, was a mild understatement of what would actually happen. And whatever his—or Belepheriel's—feelings, the army could not afford a feud.

"I'll see him," Kellen said quickly. "I did not know that his son was one of the scouts who died. I wish I had."

"We searched for their bodies and did not find them," Isinwen said sadly.

"You won't," Kellen said. Abruptly he lost all appetite. He pushed the tray away. "The Wild Magic showed me their deaths. They died quickly and well. But then—after Gairith had left them—the Shadowed Elves came and took their bodies." Kellen hesitated for a long time. "It was a hunting party, searching for food."

Isinwen made a quick gesture over his heart, and bowed his head for a moment. "Tell Belepheriel so. It is better to know, no matter how black the news."

"I will tell him. I wish . . . it seems there are very many people I must see this day." His mood of good humor was quite gone now. He would have liked to enjoy it just a little longer.

Isinwen nodded. "Were I to have the choices set before you, I would go first to Belepheriel, then to Dionan to discover Redhelwar's pleasure. The rest of what you must do can be set about those things. And now, clothing was prepared for you while you slept. I have had it brought."

When Isinwen said that clothing had been "prepared," he meant precisely that. The garments he presented for Kellen's inspection were nothing Kellen remembered ever seeing before, though it was all in his colors.

The skintight pants that the Elves favored had been made in his size, woven of soft heavy wool, with a twining pattern of leaf and vine worked into the weave. Thigh-high boots of smooth leather, lined in sheepskin, with a tapered heel so that Kellen could ride in them at need were also a perfect fit. A sleeveless quilted undertunic was a superior replacement for the one he had lost. He wasn't sure what it was made of, but its surface was as soft as down. A heavy, long-sleeved tunic—also wool—that came nearly to his boot tops, again, a perfect fit, better than the old one, for he suspected he had been putting on some muscle in the chest. A pattern matching the subtle weave in his leggings was worked into it in silver thread. Gauntlets of the same leather as the boots, their cuffs lined with vair, which would be welcome against the cold. A baldric and belt—but no scabbard—its entire surface stamped with a twining pattern of vines in Elvensilver, was again superior to what he had left behind. The buckle was of green enamel, and through its glassy surface, Kellen saw, not more leaves, but stars.

"And last of all, lest you freeze again, your cloak," Isinwen said.

On the outside it was the thickest, softest green velvet Kellen had ever seen. The lining was white fur, faintly dappled. The fur looked oddly familiar.

"Coldwarg fur," Isinwen said proudly. "It will not freeze, no matter the temperature, even if it gets wet. Petariel said that if anyone deserved a cloak made from those wretched hellbeasts, you did."

Kellen took the cloak and swirled it around his shoulders. It felt oddly heavy in his hands, but once he had it on—like his armor—he didn't notice the weight.

Where had all this stuff *come* from? He didn't think even Tengitir could have produced this quantity of clothing overnight. And then there were the boots. Boots took *time* to make. . . .

He wasn't going to ask. He thought, all things considered, he was probably better off not knowing. At least he wouldn't have to face Belepheriel looking like a street urchin. Assuming the Elves, who valued children beyond all treasure, had any such thing.

"You'll have to show me where Belepheriel's pavilion is," Kellen said to Isinwen. He didn't feel at all ready, but then, he doubted that he ever would.

⟿

BELEPHERIEL'S knightly color was a pale blue-violet, and so was the pavilion that Isinwen conducted him to before bowing and leaving Kellen to face the unknown alone.

I don't want to do this. For all of Isinwen's assurance that Belepheriel had "petitioned" to see him, and would not insult Kellen while he was Belepheriel's guest, Kellen was doubtful about what was to come, and his ability to deal with it appropriately. He'd been right to do what he'd done, and once he would have thought that was all that mattered, but he'd grown up a lot since those days. Now he knew that being right wasn't enough—at least not among the Elves. You had to be right in the right way.

Or so it seemed.

And the Elves had a lot of ways of insulting people. Well, he would just have to be man enough to take it.

He stepped up to the doorway, took the rope of bells in his hand, and shook it gently. At least the first part of what he needed to do was accomplished. Everyone in camp had seen that he had come when Belepheriel had asked.

"Enter and be welcome."

Kellen stepped through the flap of the pavilion.

The pale violet light shining through the silk gave everything an unearthly pallor. Belepheriel stood to face him. The Elven commander was alone.

"I See you, Kellen Knight-Mage."

"I See you, Belepheriel *komentai*."

The Elven commander's tent was similar to Adaerion's and Dionan's, containing several tables, chairs, a brazier, lanterns, and a number of large chests. All the furniture could be folded away for night, but Belepheriel's pavilion was large enough that this wasn't really necessary, though Kellen saw no sign of a bed.

"It would please me greatly if you would take tea with me," Belepheriel said.

"I would be honored," Kellen replied instantly. Well, at least he wasn't going to be slapped across the face with a gauntlet.

At Belepheriel's gesture, Kellen seated himself at the table. He'd never wished so hard in his life that he'd managed to get all the way through Master Belesharon's training before all this happened. He was sure this exact situation would have been covered somewhere. The only thing he did know was that he mustn't rush matters. There was certain to be a good half hour of talk about the tea and the weather before they even began to discuss whatever Belepheriel wanted to discuss.

Belepheriel did not disappoint him. They began with the weather—the winter was far more severe this year than in previous years. Ancaladar promised them a break in the weather, but not for at least a sennight. A winter this severe ensured a wet spring, which would certainly mean deep mud and hard travel. The rice crops would undoubtedly flourish, though the wheat would probably not do as well as in previous years, and it might well be a waste of time to plant rye at all.

By then the tea was ready. Kellen sipped it cautiously, and looked at Belepheriel in surprise.

It was Armethaliehan Black—his own favorite.

"You do me great honor, Belepheriel," he said, setting down his cup.

"One should not stop learning," Belepheriel said. "My master and yours said that, in the House of Sword and Shield. I fear I set aside that lesson."

"We are all finding out things we did not wish to know," Kellen replied, slowly, and only after a moment of thought.

"Yet we must learn them!" Belepheriel responded, with emphasis, as if it were he who must convince Kellen of this. "If I had not set my face against the Wild Magic . . . "

"All would have gone just as it did," Kellen said quickly. "Your voice was not the only voice in Redhelwar's tent. *His* was the decision, for he is the leader of us all."

There was silence for a while.

"I do not know how to say this," Kellen began hesitantly. "You know I am . . . uncivilized." Before he'd come to live among the Elves, he'd certainly never thought of himself that way, and he still didn't—not really. But considering the news he'd come to bring, he thought it best to give Belepheriel all the warning he could.

"You are not Elven, nor can you ever be," Belepheriel said simply. "You do as much as a young human may to honor our ways. And you are more than that. You are a Knight-Mage, sent to us by Leaf and Star. Speak, if you would."

"There is something I would tell you. It is a thing of ill hearing, and it will bring you grief." Kellen sighed heavily. "There is no good, no *civilized* way to impart it."

"I am warned," Belepheriel said. "Wait." He refilled both their cups.

"I did not know, that night in Redhelwar's tent, that Imerteniel was one of the scouts. First, I am sorry for your loss. But there is more of this matter that I must speak on. After I had left the camp, when I rode out over the battlefield, I saw the bodies of the horses, but the bodies of the scouts were gone." He licked lips gone dry, and clutched his cup so that his hands ached. "The Wild Magic lets me see how a battle has happened, and so I saw what had taken place. Imerteniel and the others died very quickly, fighting to the last. Afterward"——Kellen took a deep breath, told his muscles to relax, and went on——"a Shadowed Elf hunting party came to the spot where the bodies lay and took them away. They were looking for—food."

Belepheriel got to his feet and turned away. "I thank you for bringing this news to me," he said quietly.

Kellen sat silently. He didn't think even Master Belesharon could have told him the proper thing to say to someone when you'd just told them their son's body had been eaten by Shadowed Elves.

Belepheriel spoke without turning. "Once I mocked the warnings you brought to us. I wish you to understand: our land has been at peace since the city in which you were born was no more than grass and sand. My grandfather would go to the place where it now stands to swim and fish. The seafolk found those waters a pleasant place as well. In those days, my family had a summer-season home on one of what you now call the Out Isles. The flowers there were very beautiful, and in the orchards there grew a kind of salt-plum that I do not think grows anywhere now since the great storms that came to scour the coast. The sea-folk prize fruit and flowers greatly. They would come to the shore and trade shells and pearls for fruit and flowers. We always traded fairly with them." There was a sad smile on his lips that did not reach his eyes.

"Now that house is gone. My father and my grandfather are gone. My sons . . . Imerteniel was the last. I have no wife, and no daughters. I shall have no more children." The ghost of a smile was gone. "There is no one left to carry on my line, no one left who will remember that pleasant summer home, or the scent of the wind in the sea-grass, or how the storm-light fell upon the sands."

Kellen looked up at him mutely, unable to think of any way to respond.

"I thought the threat that we faced to be a small and simple thing, easily dealt with." Belepheriel shook his head slowly. "Even when I saw proof that it was not, I refused to see. I wished things to be as they had always been. But the world does not go according to our desire, but after the patterning of Leaf and Star. And it is the Wildmages who help it to do so."

Kellen was far out of his depth, and he knew it.

"It is not the Wildmages, Belepheriel," he said, "but the Wild Magic that works through us. We are nothing but the hands, or the sword that those hands wield. I pay my Mageprices. I try to do what it asks of me. That's all. Sometimes it moves through me in ways I do not understand, having me do things I do not yet know the meaning of. That night—in Redhelwar's pavilion—"

Belepheriel turned and looked at him, studying Kellen's face intently. "The Wild Magic spoke through you. I see. And you do not fully understand what you did."

"I insulted you," Kellen said. "I know that now, though I did not then. I challenged you to a Circle. I understand what a Circle is now as well."

"Then you also understand that you won," Belepheriel said.

No! But . . . Belepheriel seemed to think he had.

What if he had? Frantically, Kellen cast his mind back over everything he'd learned about the Challenge Circle at the House of Sword and Shield, but all that he could remember was that it settled all arguments. He shook his head.

"I do not understand what winning means," he said carefully. "But it would please me greatly if the whole matter could be forgotten as if it had never been. We have an enemy that will take all our strength to defeat. We do not have to make enemies of one another, nor weaken ourselves by . . . misunderstandings." He'd seen enough of the squabbles between Mageborn families back in Armethalieh. The last thing he wanted was to start something similar here.

Belepheriel continued to study him. Kellen kept his face still, but he knew that the Elven commander could read it as easily as Kellen could read a book of wondertales. He only hoped he wasn't making matters worse, but he couldn't think of anything else to do. Redhelwar needed *all* his commanders, able and ready to fight.

"Your words go against all custom. Yet we must all learn new things, if we are to survive in these dark times," Belepheriel said. "Let it be so, then. I would give you a gift, if you would accept it. And let it be known, if any should wonder, that the gift would have been given no matter what words you said here to me today."

"I will remember," Kellen said. "And I will let it be known. I am honored to receive a gift from your hands." He *really* had to find Jermayan and find out what he'd just done, but whatever it was, it seemed to have smoothed things over with Belepheriel, and that was all that mattered right now.

Belepheriel went over to one of the chests, and drew forth two silk-wrapped bundles, one small, one very long. He placed them upon the table.

"You have earned these," he said, opening the smaller bundle. "And I have the right to give them."

Spurs.

There were three degrees of Elven Knighthood. The first was the sword—Kellen had gotten that by default, since he'd taken a sword with him on the quest for the Black Cairn, before anyone had realized he was a Knight-Mage. The second was the shield. Jermayan had given him that—a shield looted from the body of one of the bandits he and Kellen had slain along the way, but it had still counted as a formal shield of Knighthood.

The third was the spurs.

Kellen had spurs, of course—they were necessary to give commands to an Elven destrier. But they weren't the formal ritual badge of completed Knighthood.

These were.

They were made of Elvensilver, the instep-plate covered with a mosaic of tiny gems in a dozen colors. They glittered as brightly as sunlight on ice, but Kellen could not make out the pattern, if there was one. Maybe human eyes couldn't.

"I have not completed my training in the House of Sword and Shield," Kellen said quietly.

"Only Leaf and Star may say whether any of us will see its walls again," Belepheriel said. "And I say that whatever graces Master Belesharon has yet to teach you, you are now a Knight in all the fullness of the rank, and so you shall be honored. Stand."

He took the spurs in his hands. Kellen got to his feet.

Belepheriel knelt before him and buckled the spurs into place over Kellen's boots. When he had finished, he rose to his feet.

"And now, the other." He went to the table and laid back the wrappings.

It was a sword. Kellen had already guessed that from the shape.

The scabbard was black, smooth, and utterly plain. Some sort of leather. But looking closer, Kellen could see that it seemed to shimmer, casting back not only the color of the pavilion's silk, but shimmering with other colors as well, like . . . like Ancaladar's scales.

The sword itself was as ornate as the scabbard was plain. The quillons were designed to resemble rolling waves; the metal looked blue, but it was difficult to judge colors here in Belepheriel's pavilion. For a moment Kellen thought that the hilt was encrusted with pearls, but then he realized that it was mother-of-pearl made to look like pearls.

But it was the pommel-weight that drew the eye.

The Elves rarely used faceted stones, preferring the play of light and color to be found in the smooth cabochon cut. But the pommel-weight of this sword was a faceted transparent sphere the size of a large apricot. It glittered brightly, casting rainbows across the walls of the pavilion.

"Her name is The Light at the Heart of the Mountain," Belepheriel said. "She has always been victorious. It is said that she fought at Vel-al-Amion, but as to that, no one can say in truth. She is a thousand-year sword, forged when we knew to craft weapons of war, forged to teach the Enemy the taste of defeat and dissolution."

Kellen regarded the sword uncertainly. He knew perfectly well that Belepheriel was doing him an incredible honor, and that many of the other Elven Knights had swords just as elaborate, but he couldn't imagine riding into battle carrying a piece of . . . jewelry. The grip looked slippery, just to begin with.

"Try her," Belepheriel said.

He had no choice. Kellen stepped forward, and took the scabbard in his hand, lifting the sword from the table. He gripped the hilt.

It wasn't slippery at all.

He pulled. Light at the Heart of the Mountain slipped free of the scabbard with a hiss.

He felt himself automatically settle into guard position, as if the sword were alive. His last weapon had been a good one—nothing that came from the Elven forges was flawed—but this was better than that. A *great* weapon. Ancient. Perfect. She answered to him exactly as if he and she were one being; he knew precisely where every atom of her was, even with his eyes closed.

After a long moment, he realized he was just staring at the play of light along the surface of the blade, and reluctantly sheathed it again.

How can you bear to part with this? he thought.

Gently, Belepheriel took the scabbard from Kellen's hands, and hooked it to his belt. "Use her well," he said. "And know that you will always be honored in my house and at my hearth."

"And you. In mine," Kellen said. "I, uh, don't actually know if I *have* a house or a hearth, Belepheriel . . . ."

"But I shall take the desire for the deed, Kellen Knight-Mage," Belepheriel said, bowing. "And now, I believe you will need to surprise Redhelwar."

IT didn't take long for Kellen to discover what Belepheriel had meant.

He presented himself at Dionan's pavilion as soon as he left Belepheriel. As usual, Redhelwar's adjutant was busy, even with two-thirds of the army elsewhere—if an Elven army didn't run on paperwork, then endless meetings and consultations seemed to take their place. If Kellen didn't receive any looks of open curiosity, he was at least thoroughly inspected by everyone he passed, and by everyone who found a reason to pass by Dionan's tent while he waited. He had no doubt that the information about the spurs and the sword would be all over the camp by the time he was finished here.

At last he was able to enter.

"As we await Adaerion," Dionan said, pouring tea, "it would please me to hear anything you wished to tell."

This was briskness indeed from the Elves! Well, he could certainly match it. "You will have seen that I bear gifts given by Belepheriel's hand," Kellen said. "He wished it known that the gifts would have been given no matter what I said to him today."

Dionan looked . . . puzzled. "We will drink tea," he said, after a long pause.

Adaerion arrived a few moments later.

"Belepheriel has given Kellen gifts," Dionan said, without preamble, as brusquely as any human. "He has given him The Light at the Heart of the Mountain. He has given him the spurs of Knighthood."

"Leaf and Star!" Adaerion said. He inspected Kellen closely. "It would please me to hear how Belepheriel fares, if you would care to oblige me in the telling."

Elves. I will never understand Elves, Kellen thought. *Do they think I've killed him?*

"He looked well when I saw him, and when I left him," Kellen began cautiously. Well, if they were going to be as straightforward as any human, then he would take the rare opportunity to do likewise! "Isinwen told me when I awoke that Belepheriel wished to see me. I went to see him. I apologized for being rude to him. I told him how Imerteniel had died, and what happened to his body. It and those of the other scouts were taken by Shadowed Elves. About the Challenge . . . he told me I had won it. I don't understand that, because we didn't fight. I asked him to just forget it had ever happened, because we don't need to fight among ourselves. He gave me the sword, and the spurs, and said he wished it known that he would have given them to me no matter what happened between us. I apologize if my brevity offends," Kellen added, for good measure.

There was a very long pause. Adaerion and Dionan looked at each other, then back at him. Both of the Elves were watching him as if he might faint, or explode . . . or turn into a dragon right before their eyes.

"Kellen," Adaerion said, speaking slowly and carefully, "do you understand that by winning the Challenge, you had the right to take Belepheriel's place in rank? And that you gave it up to him by your words to him?"

Oh. *Oh.* No wonder everyone had been acting so oddly. And no wonder Adaerion had felt it necessary to speak so bluntly now. Kellen knew enough by now about how Elven gossip ran to know that everyone in camp must have a pretty clear idea of what had happened between him and Belepheriel in Redhelwar's pavilion that night. And it looked like running off the way he had hadn't changed his position particularly—at least, it seemed his so-called rights under the "Challenge" would still have been honored. Everyone must have been expecting him to take over Belepheriel's command the moment he was on his feet again.

Kellen shook his head.

"Adaerion, Dionan . . . you both know that I want Redhelwar to . . . listen to my counsel, when I have something to say that is given to me by the Wild Magic. To say that I don't want what Belepheriel has would be a lie. But I wish to earn it—*not* to take it away from someone else. Not by—" He was about to say "playing children's games" and stopped. "Not this way," he finally said. "Earning it would be right. Having it because we have lost a commander, and I was needed would be right. Taking it would be wrong."

"You would renounce being a commander of hundreds because it did not suit you?" Adaerion asked.

"No! No, nothing like that. I renounce being a commander of hundreds because I do not yet have those skills," Kellen said frankly. It was true; he could command a smaller force in the field easily now, and certainly he could advise Redhelwar about what he thought the army should do, but as for being able himself to think of and give the orders on such a scale—those skills he still lacked.

"I must learn all that you, and Dionan, and Redhelwar—yes, and Belepheriel—can teach me about the use of an army. And quickly." He let out a breath he had been holding in without realizing it. "And I honor Belepheriel. It would be wrong for all of us for me to claim what I cannot properly govern. It would be as if I had been foolish enough to claim the Light at the Heart of the Mountain when I did not even know the use of a dagger."

And I have to figure out what Shadow Mountain is really after. All of this with the Shadowed Elves, bloody and dangerous as it is, is just delaying tactics. There has to be something Shadow Mountain wants—and doesn't have yet. When it has it, the real *war will start. And if we can't fight it properly, we'll lose.*

He already knew that. The Elves might be able to bring more fighters into the field, but to do so would be to utterly strip their cities of protection. Shadow Mountain was waiting for that, he was sure. The Demons themselves might not be able to enter the Elven Lands, but many of their creatures could. Even when the Elves destroyed the last of the Shadowed Elves, they wouldn't be safe from the other creatures of the Endarkened.

The Centaurs, the Mountainfolk, the Herdingfolk Wildmages, the Wildlander farmers—all of them would add to the army's numbers, perhaps even double its size, but that wasn't enough to gain them victory. Not without an enemy who would stand and fight. And against the Demons . . .

It would still be suicide.

"Then your decision is made," Dionan said.

Kellen nodded. He wasn't sure if he'd made a terrible mistake and insulted everybody, or done exactly the right thing. It felt right to him, that was all he knew.

"Then perhaps you will wish to see what Artenel can do to replace what you have lost," Dionan said. "At the third hour past noon, it would please Redhelwar to drink tea, and hear your thoughts on tomorrow's attack upon the farther cavern."

"Yes," Kellen said, getting to his feet. "Of course. It would please me greatly to drink tea with Redhelwar."

He exited Dionan's tent with a feeling of intense relief.

FORTUNATELY, it was nearly impossible to get lost in an Elven war camp once you'd learned the disposition of the tents. Kellen found the tents of the armorers without difficulty.

The first thing that caught his eye were several of the new shields, racked outside the cooper's tent for transport to the farther cavern. He picked one up and hefted it experimentally.

Heavy, yes, but not as heavy as he'd expected. It was half as long as he was tall, and would provide good protection in the caverns. Leather over wax over wood, just as he, Idalia, and Artenel had decided. Water-soaked, it would be heavier, but he'd still be able to lift it, he judged, and the Elves were much stronger than he was.

"Kellen! This is no time for idleness. We have much to do," Artenel said, walking out of the main armorer's tent and regarding him sternly.

Meekly, Kellen followed the Master Armorer into the tent.

"One wishes, of course, that you had not had the misfortune to lose every piece of your armor all at once," Artenel said, sounding mournful. "But it is not without precedent. And fortunately, knowing that you would be . . . difficult to fit, I began my preparations sennights ago."

He gestured at the long table at the center of the tent, and drew back a protective cloth with a flourish. All the components of a full set of Elven battle armor in Kellen's size lay there, waiting.

The armor Kellen had just lost had been covered with a subtle pattern like wood-grain. The armorers said the patterns added strength to the metal, and the pattern chosen to ornament the metal of the armor was apparently another matter of great importance to Elves. Jermayan's had a pattern of tiny stars over its entire surface, and, knowing the Elves as well as he now did, Kellen had no doubt that it was an accurate representation of the night sky at some season. Master Belesharon had called Kellen's armor plain and dull, because it had been made in such haste that there had been no time to add the coat of glistening enamel that was the final touch on normal Elven battle armor. Kellen had liked that just fine.

But apparently Artenel had had a lot of free time to spend on making a new set of armor, just on the chance that Kellen might need it, because the armor he unveiled for Kellen's inspection was as green as Shalkan's eyes. Each piece glittered like glass.

And instead of wood-grain, the metal beneath the enamel was covered with a tiny intricate pattern of twining vines similar to the pattern worked into his clothes. Here and there, Kellen could see an occasional star glisten palely among the leaves.

Leaves and stars. Leaf and Star? He felt a sudden cold chill. *Who do these people think I am?*

The Elves swore by Leaf and Star, just as the Herdingfolk did by the Good Goddess, and the Centaurs by the Herdsman. When Kellen thought about it at all—which was rarely—he thought they were all probably different ways of seeing the same thing he and Idalia—and every other Wildmage—touched when they invoked the Wild Magic: the Power that set Mageprices and kept the world in balance.

Certainly one of the first things that Idalia had taught him about the Wild Magic was that paying whatever Mageprices the Wild Magic set was a way of keeping the world running properly, even if he didn't understand at the time how the prices he paid—some of them quite small and personal—could really help. How had rescuing a servant girl's kitten back in Armethalieh, for example, helped the wider world?

But knowing that you were a tool of Greater Powers, and accepting that fact, Kellen realized, was far different than knowing that everyone else knew it too.

He'd been able to handle the thought of being scorned, outcast, relieved of his command, a lot better than he was handling this, Kellen realized. Because he was *used* to being the goat, the misfit, the butt of a thousand jokes. He'd been that all his life. When he'd become a Knight-Mage, well, the Elves were tactful, and he'd gone almost immediately into training in the House of Sword and Shield, where Master Belesharon had treated him like the humblest apprentice, so while life had been much more pleasant, his status hadn't seemed appreciably different from what it had been before.

Now things were changing, and rapidly.

You wanted to command the Elven army, and you didn't think things would change along the way? What would Shalkan say if he knew you thought that?

"It is very beautiful," Kellen said gravely. "I am honored."

"It is unworthy work, filled with flaws," Artenel said dismissively. "Done in haste under the worst possible conditions. Had I dared to present such a piece to my Masters as evidence of my craft, I would still be feeding the forge fires in the guild-house. But it is sound and strong, and will turn a blow, I promise you that. And in a few moonturns, better will come from Sentarshadeen."

Better than this? Despite Artenal's protests, Kellen could see no flaw in the armor—and if Artenel said it would protect him, he could be certain that it would.

But though the pieces were complete, the armor was far from finished, for now it had to be assembled on the body of the man for whom it had been prepared, and a thousand modifications made.

⏥

"NEARLY done," Artenel pronounced with satisfaction a few hours later, "though you will undoubtedly wish to make the last adjustments yourself."

"As you say," Kellen said, hastily scrambling from the undertunic and leggings he'd worn for the armor-fitting back into his clothes. "But at just this moment, I am called elsewhere."

⏥

KELLEN ran all the way to Redhelwar's pavilion, and suspected that he was late anyway, but if that was the case, the Elven general gave no sign of it.

To his surprise, Redhelwar was alone. Kellen had somehow expected this to be a less private occasion. He wondered if he was going to get the scolding he still felt he might deserve—or at least that protocol ought to demand. He *had* disobeyed orders—no matter how strong the need, and no matter how right he'd been to do so, there was still that.

But as always, they began with a—mercifully brief—

discussion of the tea and the weather. Soon, however, Red-helwar changed the subject.

"You come before me as if your spirit lies heavy, Kellen. Yet already today I have had Adaerion's good counsel, and Dionan's and Belepheriel's as well. And I have been privileged to hear all that Idalia Wildmage could tell me of the nearer cavern." Redhelwar leaned forward a little. "So. I would know what lies unsaid between us, that you look upon me as one who expects ill tidings."

Well, if that wasn't an opening to come straight out with what was bothering him, he had never heard one. "When you made me *alakomentai,* you gave me a place in your army," Kellen said, thinking his words through slowly. "Army officers follow orders. You gave me an order. And I didn't follow it."

"Yet you are also a Knight-Mage, a voice of the Wild Magic. And if I would command the Wild Magic, then perhaps I shall step outside and command the wind and the weather to answer my will as well," the General said dismissively. "It would be as efficient a use of my time. You risked both life and honor to save the army. Let that be an end to this matter."

It was an order, and Kellen took it as such. Seeing Kellen's assent and relief in his expression, Redhelwar smiled, every so faintly, and turned to more practical matters.

"The first of the Centaurs will arrive at Ysterialpoerin within a sennight, so Jermayan tells us. Not so many as we will see come spring, but a goodly number for the season— and the weather, which remains difficult. Unfortunately, the Wildmages tell us that to bring truly calm weather here would take all their power, and worsen the weather elsewhere, so they do not advise it. Perhaps it is just as well that our battles this season take place below the earth. A number of High Reaches Wildmages travel with the Centaurs, of course. It will be good to add their numbers to those already with us."

But it still wouldn't change the weather. Kellen remembered that Idalia had never wanted to meddle with the weather without a very good reason, and right now the weather patterns were still trying to settle back to normal after the long unnatural drought. That was one of the reasons this winter was as bad as it was—and a good reason why it was a good idea to leave the weather strictly alone, no matter how bad it got. But . . .

"If the Shadowed Elves are changing the way they attack . . . " Kellen began.

"That thought has been much in my mind," Redhelwar said somberly. "Idalia has spoken to me of the traps she saw in the first cavern, but says that you saw more. Yet from what she described, such traps as were there would be the work of moonturns to create."

"Yes," Kellen agreed. "They knew we would be coming. And they knew it—perhaps—before we were led to their first lair. All that we do here to fight them is planned for us by others. But we have no choice."

"No," Redhelwar said quietly. "And tomorrow we discover what further entertainment they have planned for us."

"Goblins and *duergar*," Kellen said instantly. "The Crystal Spiders said there were more of them in the farther cavern. And all the Shadowed Elves will be there—the ones from both caverns. So we'll be facing more of them than we expected." He felt a surge of gratitude to the Crystal Spiders, odd creatures though they were. If they hadn't come to Idalia's rescue, if they hadn't made the effort of talking to her—

"Yet if we face more of our foe than we expect, the reverse is also true, for we have evaded their trap, by the grace of Leaf and Star and the intercession of the Wild Magic." The commander tapped the table with one finger, betraying his own tension in a manner that Elves seldom indulged in. "Light will keep *duergar* at bay, and we shall have that in good measure—but it will not stop one from luring prey within reach of another foe," Redhelwar added, consideringly. "Wildmage Athan has suggested that he might work a spell of Calling to cause the Shadowed Elves to come out to us. They are easier to kill outside their caves, and we would be beyond reach of their allies."

"A good plan, if it works," Kellen agreed. "Idalia said that the *tarnkappa* don't work against *duergar,* but they might work against goblins. They move through stone, though."

Redhelwar dismissed goblins with a shrug. "We have hunted goblins many times in the past. They are foolish and easily lured, when they are hungry enough. With the Shadowed Elves dead and unable to control them, they will be simple enough to kill. The *duergar* will present a more difficult problem. Only a Knight-Mage, it seems, can withstand their call."

"There might be a spell that would help. I'll ask Jermayan and Ancaladar. And the Crystal Spiders don't like the *duergar* any better than we do. They'll give us all the help they can," he added.

"Then we are well begun by honoring our promises to them. And now, perhaps, once you have settled a matter of no small interest to the army, we shall ride out to the nearer cavern and see that promise completed," Redhelwar said, rising to his feet.

⌒

KELLEN was never precisely certain exactly how the Elven destriers were organized. He did know that taking care of several thousand horses—even several thousand horses who knew their names and invariably came when called—was a large job for someone. Several hundred someones, probably, even though the Knights did much of their own horse-work.

The animals that were going to be immediately needed waited in the horse-lines, standing quietly in orderly ranks. Those that would not be needed as quickly seemed to wander at will, though Kellen was sure that was only an illusion.

He saw Idalia's Cella and Redhelwar's blood-red bay

waiting patiently; Dionan's stone-grey mare and the thirty mounts of his own troop standing by as well, all under saddle and ready to ride out.

Ciltesse had been loitering nearby—there was really no other word, Kellen thought ruefully, to describe his second-in-command's behavior.

"I See you, Ciltesse," Redhelwar said, greeting him. "It would be pleasant to discover the nature of Kellen's new mount."

"That is yet to be known," Ciltesse said gravely. "I See you, Kellen Knight-Mage," he said formally.

"I See you, Ciltesse. It would please me greatly to be presented with the fruits of your wisdom," Kellen said, bowing.

Ciltesse led him to the end of the line of horses. Three destriers, without saddle or bridle, stood waiting.

"Here are those which I judge could best meet your needs, gathered from those which are available," Ciltesse said. "It is for you to choose, of course."

"Nor will you tell me their names, for the whole camp is betting on which one I will choose," Kellen said, smiling. He wondered if his choice would match Ciltesse's.

He turned and regarded the horses.

Two were stallions, one was a mare. They all regarded him with wary curiosity, ears flicking back and forth.

As he had when he had chosen Deyishene, he cleared his mind and regarded them through spell-sight.

The young stallion he rejected immediately. The black was a beautiful animal, young and filled with fire and spirit, but Kellen neither needed nor wanted that much eagerness in a mount.

He considered the mare next, and shook his head. She was a dark dapple grey, and had the grace and quiet spirit he wanted and needed, but she had loved her rider too deeply to be quite ready for a new master yet. He paused to stroke her neck gently. Would he have to reject them all? Maybe Jermayan would loan him Valdien for the day. Or he could take the mare—but not as a permanent battle-mount.

He turned his attention to the last of the three. The buck-skin stallion was by far the oldest of the animals Ciltesse had collected, and though his coat was well-kept and without flaw, Kellen's battle-sight showed him the ghosts of old wounds, well-healed. To his surprise, Kellen could feel that he was being judged as much as he was judging. He could tell that if the destrier found his rider lacking, it had an arsenal of tricks that would put anything Valdien had ever imagined to shame. But he could also tell that the stallion was calm, steady, and smart. It would stand unafraid in the face of a pack of coldwarg—if it trusted its rider to know his business.

Now you, old warrior, I think might be what I need. Your experience just might make up for my lack of it. And I hope I'm your match in courage. Shall we show them all? Kellen wondered, looking up into the stallion's eyes. *I won't be the best rider you've ever had. But I'll let you teach me everything you know.*

Animal speech was one of the gifts of the Wild Magic, but like so many of the powers of a true Wildmage, it was one that Kellen lacked. Yet the stallion seemed to understand *something* when Kellen looked into his eyes, because he lowered his head and butted Kellen—hard—in the chest.

"This one," Kellen said, staggering back a step. *Did I choose you? Or did you just choose me?*

"It is as I said," Isinwen said to Ciltesse, sounding smug. "He would choose Firareth over Anganil."

Twenty-one

Blood on the Moon

Anganil, Kellen discovered, was the name of the young stallion. The mare's name was Grayn. Firareth had apparently rejected several potential riders already—though always with great courtesy, Isinwen assured Kellen.

"I thank you for bringing me to his attention," Kellen said. He wasn't sure quite yet whether he meant it or not. He offered Firareth a piece of dried apple—Ciltesse had brought them—and the stallion accepted the treat with grave politeness.

"A commander must do more than look to his mount," Isinwen said. "Ciltesse was born in Windalorianan, among the Fields of Vardirvoshan, where, it is said, one learns to ride before one learns to walk. It is indeed true that Anganil is the finest of the available destriers, young and in his prime, while in a very few years Firareth will return to Vardirvoshan to live out his days, if Leaf and Star are with him. But he is wise, and can keep a rider safe even when such a one may be . . . occupied by other matters."

And what seemed like "a very few years" to the Elves might seem like a considerably longer time to a human, Kellen reflected. And—listening to what Isinwen did *not* say—he got the impression that Ciltesse's opinion of Kellen's horsemanship might be just a bit better than Kellen's actual skills.

"I am pleased with my choice. Leaf and Star grant that my choice is pleased with me." *And that I can keep him alive.*

It was a prayer that Kellen seemed to be making more and more often these days. He didn't think he could bear the heartbreak of losing another destrier so soon.

⌐

SOON they were riding out toward the nearer cavern. Kellen took the opportunity to get to know his new mount, and suspected that Firareth was taking his measure as well. Fortunately, between them Deyishene and Mindaerel had managed to teach him enough horsemanship for him to reassure his new mount that he *did* know what he was doing, and after a while he felt Firareth relax a bit.

Idalia had contented herself with saying that she was glad to see he was looking so well. Apparently nobody was going to scold him today.

On the other hand, he hadn't seen Shalkan yet, though he suspected the unicorn was following them at a comfortable—for Shalkan—distance.

When they reached the cavern, Jermayan and Ancaladar were already waiting.

"Better go tell him what you'd like," Idalia suggested.

Kellen rode forward to where the enormous black dragon crouched in the snow. He was pleased to see that Firareth approached Ancaladar calmly.

"Farneyirel would be pleased to know that Firareth has found a master who will honor him as he deserves," Jermayan said. "He has waited long to return to the field."

"I think we'll do well together," Kellen said. "Idalia said I should instruct you on how to trigger the traps."

Ancaladar snorted gustily. Firareth flicked an ear, but was otherwise unimpressed. "Say, rather, you should tell us what you have seen of them. Jermayan will do the rest," the dragon said.

"I am so instructed," Kellen said ironically, bowing where he sat. "Most of the ones I saw involved a trip-wire. I saw a lot of trip-wires that didn't seem to activate any traps I could see. In some places, there was quicksand disguised as stone—that needed no trip-wire at all. In other places, there were rods sticking out of the cave walls, and if you brushed against them, jets of—something—would spurt out of the rock, or jars of acid or poison would be broken or tilted on you. In one place, there was a jet of air flowing continuously across the passage: I don't know what would have happened if that had been interrupted. And the entire roof of the cavern village is set to collapse—it's a huge place; I don't know how they managed it. The trigger for that must be somewhere in the village, I think, but I didn't go into the village to look for it."

"A prudent child," Ancaladar commented. "So, Jermayan, let us snap the wires and smash the sticks, and see what comes of that." The dragon looked up, studying the snow-covered slope of the mountain. "And I would suggest that everyone stand well back, just to be safe."

Kellen rode back to the others.

"Ancaladar suggests we move back," he told them. "And on the whole, I think we ought to be even more cautious than he suggests."

They retreated to the edge of the little stream. By the time they turned back, Ancaladar had moved back as well, far enough from the cavern mouth so that he'd have plenty of room to launch himself into the air quickly.

Jermayan gestured. A spark of blue fire flew from his hand and vanished into the cavern mouth.

For a very long time, nothing seemed to happen at all. Then the ground beneath the horses' feet began to tremble and shake, a long low shuddering rumble that went on and on. The Elven destriers shied madly, backing into a streambed that suddenly held ice but no water, as their riders fought to steady them. Kellen could see a plume of—smoke?—dust?—steam? issuing from the cavern's mouth, as he did his best to reassure Firareth. The destrier might be tranquil and mild-mannered, but this was something wholly unexpected. But the shaking subsided fairly quickly, and the animals steadied, though they were still restless and unhappy.

The traps—there must have been a lot more of them than I saw, Kellen realized. And whatever spell Jermayan had used, it had set off every single one. The cavern mouth . . . well, it wasn't *there* anymore. The ice that had covered the rock face had fallen away in large sheets, and there were deep raw cracks in the exposed granite of the cliff face as the mountain seemed to have . . . settled.

I hope for their sake all the Crystal Spiders got out all right.

"Look!" Ciltesse said, pointing.

High above where the opening of the cavern had been, the snow on the mountain began to shift. It meant nothing to Kellen, who had never seen either snow or mountains before this winter. But others knew better.

"Snow-spill!" Isinwen shouted. "Ride!"

The horses needed little encouragement to run. Kellen looked back and saw Ancaladar bound into the air. The snow was halfway down the mountain face by now, spreading like a fan.

A large fan.

He could hear it now. A roaring, like a waterfall, but faint and far-off—for the moment.

How much snow was on that mountain?

Was it all coming down?

If the entire army had not come this way the day before, breaking a deep trail in the snow that even another night's snowfall had been unable to fill, they would not have been able to try to outrun it.

But "try" was all they were able to do.

The roaring now was as loud as the fury of a battle, and the wave of snow pushed wind before it. Kellen felt the rush of air at his back and braced himself even though he knew that it was the most futile of gestures—

Then he felt the spell as it was being cast, and saw two waves of snow as high as Ancaladar's shoulder pass them by on either side, racing along beside them as fast as a running horse. A few hundred yards further on, the force of the snow-spill was spent, but without Jermayan's spell it would certainly have been enough to bury them all.

The troop reined in—Kellen had been bringing up the rear—and stopped. Kellen looked back.

There was a deep sheltering "V" in the snow along their track. Beyond that, and to either side, the snow lay white and smooth—and deep. There was no sign of the cavern mouth—or even of the cliff face.

Ancaladar landed a few yards ahead. The dragon kicked up a great plume of snow with his landing, then settled deeply into the snow. Jermayan dismounted, and walked through the snow to Redhelwar. Kellen urged Firareth forward.

Jermayan bowed.

"It seems the cave was more extensively mined than anyone properly understood," Redhelwar said.

"Ancaladar expected a . . . small snow-spill," Jermayan admitted. "He has seen them before, when the snows have been heavy. And we thought—when I sent the wind to scour the caverns—that when the roof of the village cavern collapsed there would be some disturbance, but . . . "

Jermayan looked a bit shaken, and more than a little drained. Kellen was reminded, once again, that if Ancaladar's storehouse of power was infinite, Jermayan's energy was not. He wondered just how much energy it had taken to turn aside that wall of snow.

"But we are all still alive thanks to you, and the caverns are gone, and so are the traps, which is what matters," Kellen said. "And I do not think, from the way Idalia is looking at us, that either you or I will have to worry about tomorrow's battle if you do not go and rest now."

"So I have said," Ancaladar said, speaking up now. "But I am a mere dragon, so of course my Bonded would not listen to me. No. We must land, and he must assure himself twice-over that what he could see with his own eyes was indeed so, and stand here in the snow when a warm fire and a hot meal is what he truly needs."

It was amazing, really, how much Ancaladar could sound like Shalkan when he tried, though Kellen had the impression Ancaladar was reserving the worst of his lecture for when he and Jermayan were alone.

"Then let him go to them at once," Redhelwar said, speaking directly to Ancaladar.

Jermayan bowed once again, and walked back through the snow to Ancaladar.

"Men," Idalia said in disgust, coming up beside Kellen.

"Wildmages," Kellen corrected absently. "Or maybe Elven Knights. Keirasti isn't any more sensible, and she's a girl."

"'Girl'—she's old enough to be your grandmother," Idalia said with a snort.

"Great-grandmother, probably," Kellen said agreeably. "And I suppose the Healers all take care of themselves very sensibly? Or do they work themselves until they drop, going without food and sleep when there are wounded to care for?"

Idalia laughed, looking surprised. "You're getting far too good at arguing, little brother. And the worst of it is, you're right—as you know perfectly well, since you've worked in the Healers' tents."

They ducked their heads, covering their faces as Ancaladar took off, raising a shower of snow. When the black dragon was well airborne, Dionan gave the signal, and they began to ride back toward the camp.

"You're sure you're all right?" Idalia asked.

"Fit to fight tomorrow," Kellen told her, allowing himself just the briefest moment of preening, thinking about his new glory of armor and weaponry. "I'll be a stunning sight, too. You just wait and see."

THAT night, Kellen attended the meeting of the senior commanders to plan the placement of the troops. No one had remarked about his presence at all, either for or against it. Kellen kept his mouth shut and his ears open. If he wanted to learn how to handle an army—not just set policy for it, or to react to an emergency facing it—here was the place to begin.

Kellen had expected they would attack the farther cavern sometime during the next day, but Athan Wildmage had said that his Calling Spell needed to be timed to the moon's appearance in the sky above the cavern mouth. The Shadowed Elves were more likely to come out at night, too, and for once they *wanted* them to come out.

So the army would have one last day of grace to finish its preparations for attack. One more day to rest, to heal, to mend armor and weapons and make new ones, to plan. The trouble was, without knowing what, exactly, they were going to face, it was difficult to plan.

Redhelwar's decision was to divide the army into very small, very mobile, sections. It was more likely the Shadowed Elves would attack if they thought the odds looked to be in their favor. The third of the army that was to have been used to attack the nearer cavern would be kept well back and hidden until the enemy was thoroughly committed, and those who were already there had been ordered to spend the day appearing to scatter their forces, on the pretext of building a more permanent set of camps and organizing several hunting parties.

Their strategy was founded on the hope that the Shadowed Elves were just as uncoordinated and barbaric as they had been at the first cavern. There was every possibility for the plan to turn to a disaster if the Shadowed Elves showed any organization and generalship at all. And everyone gathered in Redhelwar's tent that night knew that every battle they'd had with the enemy thus far might be all part of one long feint: the Shadowed Elves might not actually be the feral half-animal rabble that they seemed. If that was the case, the Elven losses would be heavy tomorrow.

But there was no way to know. Kellen's Knight-Mage gifts couldn't truly show the future. At best they seemed to give him a wider view of the present—he'd "seen" the attack on Ysterialpoerin because it was already in motion, and the nearer caverns had already been mined when he'd given his warning that they were too dangerous to invade. And he already knew his battle-sight could be blocked by Demonic magic.

When it came to the outcome of tomorrow's battle, he knew as little as Redhelwar did. The sole advantage they had was that they had *not* lost a third of the army to the trapped caverns. Kellen only hoped the enemy did not know that, but there was no way to be sure.

⟶

THE following morning, he went out to say good-bye to Shalkan before taking his troop out into position. The morning meal had been lavish—the cooks had truly outdone themselves, since it was the last proper meal the fighters would probably see for a whole day at least—and Kellen was certain he was not the only one who did his best to try not to think of it as a farewell feast.

When he buckled on his new armor for the first time—it had been waiting in his tent when he returned from the meeting the previous night—he had to admit that despite his reservations about what he could not help thinking of as its gaudiness, Artenel had done a magnificent job. As long as he didn't *look* at it, it felt just like his old armor, nearly as comfortable as an ordinary suit of clothing. At that, the showy armor actually made him relax a little—it was very difficult to picture himself going out in something that looked like a fancy-dress costume to actually fight. Never mind what his head knew, his insides took one look and didn't believe. His sword, of course . . . well, he'd never mistake Light at the Heart of the Mountain for his old sword, but that was not a disadvantage. The sword moved like an extension of his hand—no, his *thought*. And if he had to kill any more *duergar*, well, he'd use a spear.

Tucking some delicacies saved from breakfast into his new surcoat, he went up to the Unicorn Knights' camp. Even if he didn't have much of an appetite this morning, that never seemed to hinder Shalkan.

Though the Unicorns were posted at Ysterialpoerin now, there was a great deal of traffic back and forth between the city and their camp. Once Kellen and the others were in position, Redhelwar intended to move the units that had been guarding the cavern back to the main camp for a few hours as well. If the Shadowed Elves *were* watching, the more confusion about who was where, the better.

"I See you, Kellen Knight-Mage," a familiar voice greeted him from the edge of the Unicorn Knights' encampment.

"I See you, Riasen," Kellen said. "I've come looking for Shalkan. I ride out to the farther cavern in a few hours, and I hoped to see him."

"And I back to the city." Riasen shook his head ruefully. "I should have brought an edifying scroll or two—you cannot imagine how very dull it is there! But that's all to the good, when one is hoping *not* to be attacked, of course." He glanced out toward where the unicorns were drifting toward the camp. "One imagines Shalkan will be along in a few moments, if only to admire the fact that you have something near to proper armor at last."

"Urm. Yes," Kellen replied, blinking owlishly at him.

Riasen chuckled, and motioned to him to follow toward the center of the Unicorn Knights' encampment. "Only think what Artenel could have done with enough time and the proper equipment—but still, no one will think badly of you. It is wartime armor, after all, and you will soon have better. And no one, indeed, could find any fault at all with your spurs and sword. Quite fitting, since you come from the sea-city." He picked up a cup from a table inside the door of his own pavilion, and filled it from a pot steeping on the brazier there before offering it to Kellen. "Tea?"

"I suppose it must be fitting, since the one who gifted me with them is long in years and wisdom," Kellen said, accepting the inevitable cup of tea with real gratitude. He'd never thought of Armethalieh as a "sea-city" before. He could see the wave pattern in his sword's quillons, but he still couldn't make out the pattern on his spurs, even in the strongest sunlight. The stones glowed brilliantly, and he could tell there *was* supposed to be a pattern, but that was all.

And Riasen, perfectly casually, seemed to find as much fault with his armor as Artenel had.

"Utterly stunning," Shalkan drawled, mincing into the center of the circle of pavilions. He struck a pose, and somehow managed to remind Kellen of some of his most dandified classmates back in Armethalieh, the ones who spent every moment they weren't studying the High Magick arguing about clothes. "I can see I shall have to have a new saddle and armor—immediately."

"Barely worth putting on, I assure you," Kellen said, doing his best to match Shalkan's tone. "Still, Artenel does wonders with the poor resources at his command."

Shalkan snorted rudely. "As if you could tell the difference."

"Well, I can't," Kellen admitted, dropping the pose. "He says it's sound where it counts, and that's all I really care about."

Shalkan shook himself all over in silent laughter. "If you *did* live a thousand years, I still don't think they could manage to make an Elf out of you."

"Probably not," Kellen agreed.

He finished his tea—it was cold before he was done with it, but the arid winter weather left him constantly thirsty—bowed courteously to Riasen, and followed Shalkan off beyond the circle of pavilions.

"I see you've won your spurs—and gained a fine sword," Shalkan said when they were private. Or as private as things got in a war-camp, anyway.

"Belepheriel wanted me to have them," Kellen told him, still a bit bemused by it all—and still worried that he might have done something wrong by Elven standards. "I hope I did the right thing by accepting them."

"If he hadn't wanted you to have them, he wouldn't have given them to you," Shalkan said inarguably. "The way the

Elves see things, you honored him by taking them. And if I do say so, you managed your way out of the whole mess fairly gracefully, all things considered."

"I'm still . . . well, no. I *do* know how I got into that mess. And I think I know 'why,' too." He started to rub his eyebrow with his gauntleted hand, then realized what he was doing, and shrugged instead. "The Wild Magic needed to change Belepheriel's mind about the way he was seeing things before he made some bad decisions. But it wasn't very comfortable."

"Magic often isn't," Shalkan said shrewdly. "At least today you'll be dealing with simple straightforward actions with no worry about Elven manners: riding places and killing things."

"That isn't exactly straightforward either," Kellen muttered. Oh, the battles themselves were. But they were brief, compared to the time spent preparing for them and recovering from them. That was *filled* with complications.

"I brought you some honey-cakes. And I have a question."

"Honey-cakes first," Shalkan said firmly. Even though the cold had made them rock-hard, the unicorn enjoyed them thoroughly. "And the question?" he asked, when he'd finished the last crumb.

"Is there supposed to be a pattern on my spurs?" Kellen asked.

From the look on Shalkan's face, this wasn't the question he'd been expecting. "Lift your foot," the unicorn finally said.

A reasonable request; both Kellen's boots were buried in snow up to the calves. Kellen lifted his foot and brushed the instep-plate and rowel of the spur clear of snow. Shalkan inspected both closely.

"It's seashells in ocean foam," he finally reported, in the kindly tones of someone describing a sunset to a blind man.

"Oh." Kellen put his foot down again. "He told me his grandfather used to go to Armethalieh, that they had a home on one of the Out Islands."

"If you can call 'going to Armethalieh' visiting a place before it exists, then . . . yes," Shalkan agreed blandly. "The Elves once ruled the seas as well as the forests. But that was a long time ago, even as Elves think of time."

Kellen took a deep breath, and regretted it immediately as the cold air seared his throat and lungs. "Are you going to be—" he began.

Shalkan interrupted him. "I'm fine. I will be fine. Now stop worrying about me. As Riasen says, those of us at Ysterialpoerin should probably have brought *xaqiue* and *gan* to keep from getting bored. You're the ones who will be facing moments of unusual interest tonight."

"That's one way to think of it," Kellen said.

But when he had trudged back to his own pavilion again, Kellen somehow felt a little better, though he could not have said why.

⇒

IN fact, he and his thirty spent much of the afternoon being as cold and bored as any of Ysterialpocrin's nearer defenders. Despite knowing Redhelwar's plan, Kellen felt very much like a *xaqiue* piece himself—over and over, it seemed they'd no more than settle into one position than the order would come to shift to another. At least the constant shifts in position kept the horses from freezing solid—if the Shadowed Elves *did* come out as Athan hoped, there'd be a good deal of mounted combat tonight, and none of them could afford to be stiff.

The farther cavern was in a more elevated area than the nearer one. The only entrance the scouting parties had been able to locate was at the end of a twisting path halfway up the mountainside. Kellen knew that there were troops actually *on* the mountain—the men of the High Reaches, and most of the Knights of Ysterialpoerin, who were most familiar with the local terrain. Kellen certainly didn't envy them their posts. If it was cold down here—and it was—he could only imagine how much colder it must be farther up the mountain.

One thing a day spent emulating a *xaqiue*-piece did was give everyone a good idea of the ground they'd be fighting over later. Jermayan had set Coldfire spells over all of them that would trigger with a single word of command, but until that moment, Redhelwar had given orders that there was to be no light at all.

⌐

THEY moved through the dark to their final position. It was almost half a league away from the mouth of the cavern, but Kellen knew why his command was here and not in the front lines. Redhelwar was taking every possible precaution against a repeat of the feint against the camp and the attack upon Ysterialpoerin.

He could feel the army around him, waiting. Above the clouds, Jermayan and Ancaladar circled. A light snow was falling; the Wildmages had been willing at dire need to shift the heaviest of the weather a league or so westward, but warned that the lull would only be a day at most, followed by a brutal storm.

Kellen knew, without actually seeing it, the moment that the moon rose above the mountain and Athan began his spell.

Imagination and spell-sight showed him what his own eyes could not: Athan kneeling at his small brazier, his Great Grey Owl perched upon his shoulder; Athan casting the dried herbs upon the coals and calling upon the Wild Magic. Kellen knew from what Idalia had told him beforehand that Athan had asked for no aid to his spell: whatever price the Gods of the Wild Magic asked, Athan would bear the whole cost of the spell and the Casting alone.

Now the price had been asked and agreed to, and Athan's Calling began, though only the Wildmages gathered here could sense it. Still there was nothing but silence and darkness and the faint moaning of the wind.

Kellen felt, rather than heard, a flicker of movement, and looked up. Athan's owl glided by in utter silence overhead, a keystone clutched in its talons. The keystone was brilliant with power to Kellen's spell-sight.

It must be the focus of the Calling spell. Wherever it is, that's where the Shadowed Elves will try to get to.

Athan still had not moved. The Wildmage stood alone, armored and ready, just below where the path leading up to the cavern opening began.

With a sinking sense of dread, Kellen suspected he knew what the price of Athan's spell had been: not suicide—for the Gods of the Wild Magic did not ask for things like that—but to *offer* his life by being the first to meet the Shadowed Elves' attack. He was a Wildmage, and, standing in the open, he would be an irresistible target for any Tainted creature. For those who fought the Calling spell, his mere presence could serve to draw them out.

He might well survive. There was a chance. And there was no rule that said Athan could not defend himself. But the Mageprice Athan had accepted—had *probably* accepted, Kellen reminded himself, for he did not know for sure—carried with it a terrible peril.

Still there was silence and an eerie tranquility. Despite the fact that two-thirds of the Elven army shared these woods with him, Kellen could hear nothing, nor did he see anything beyond the men and mounts of his own troop. The moon was the faintest shine in the clouds overhead, casting no light on the snow below.

He felt his stomach knotting again, and his hands were clenched inside his gauntlets. *Let Athan's spell have worked. Let it have worked. If it hasn't, we'll have to go in, and if we fight on their ground, they'll have all the advantages.*

Suddenly the false peace of the night shattered. He heard distant shouts—the ring of steel on steel—and a moment later, the entire forest was full-moon bright, as balls of Cold-fire appeared over the heads of every Elven Knight.

But he felt Athan die in that same moment, a shining beacon that existed only in his mind, extinguished between one breath and the next.

"There's more than one exit from the cavern. Be ready." Jermayan's voice spoke as if in his ear.

"They're out," Kellen said to his troop, grimly. "There are multiple exits from the cavern. Let's go."

He could "see" the battlefield nearly as well as Jermayan and Ancaladar could. As Redhelwar had hoped, the sight of their Elven enemy drove the Shadowed Elves to attack recklessly. They swarmed from their cavern like hornets from a nest—and not just from the exit the Elves and Vestakia had first identified. They were burrowing up out of holes concealed by ice high on the mountain as well, attacking the defenders there.

But Redhelwar did not want to contain them or push them back. He wanted as many of them to come out as would come. So the Elves offered little resistance to the attack of their foes, falling back before them.

In Redhelwar's tent, it had seemed a simple plan, with little that could complicate it.

Kellen's first hint that things were about to go badly was the arrival of the Deathwings. They'd never flown at night before but suddenly an enormous flock of them appeared.

Half of them went after Ancaladar. The other half swept in low over the army, through the areas of heaviest fighting, but in a few moments it became clear that to attack the Elves was not their purpose.

Again and again they swooped down, snatching up the Shadowed Elves by ones and twos and bearing them over the Elven lines and away. Ancaladar could do nothing to stop them; he and Jermayan had their own battle to fight. Any archer not actively engaged in combat shot at the ghostly targets—aiming for the Shadowed Elves, rather than the Deathwings, as the Shadowed Elves were easier to kill—but it didn't seem to help. If they managed to kill or wound one of the Shadowed Elves, the Deathwing simply dropped its burden and went back for another. And the Deathwings themselves were nearly impossible to kill with simple arrows.

They have a cache of armor and weapons hidden some-where else for just this emergency. Kellen knew that with a sudden sinking feeling, without knowing either how he knew it or—worse—knowing how to find it. He only hoped that whatever else the cache contained, it did not contain any of the white rings of metalfire.

Follow them?

No.

It was tempting, but if he pulled his unit out of the outer ring to follow them, he would break the wall of Redhelwar's defense. And he'd received no clear warning from the Wild Magic that there was a crucial need. It would be the height of folly to go charging off without a direction—leaving a hole in the lines that the others were counting on to be filled.

And without Jermayan in the sky to tell Redhelwar how the battle was progressing on the ground, Kellen was needed here more than ever. He felt Jermayan and Ancaladar being driven further and further away, leaving Redhelwar essentially blind so far as the battle was concerned.

Suddenly he knew what he had to do.

"Ciltesse, take command here. Don't let them break through, whatever you do." He touched his spurs lightly to Firareth's sides, and rode to find Redhelwar.

He'd gone less than a quarter mile when he encountered Shadowed Elves that had broken through the ring. Their tactics against mounted Knights were savage but effective: they struck first against the destrier, if they could, shattering its legs with heavy clubs, and then springing on the downed Knight, using poison, or acid, or thin-bladed knives to destroy the armor's defenses and kill the Elf within. Every Knight they killed gained them new Elvensteel weapons as well as eliminating an enemy.

The Shadowed Elves swarmed toward Kellen and Firareth. Kellen had an instant's warning as he felt the stallion gather himself. He took in a sharp breath, and a shiver of energy ran through him; not quite fear, but a close relative—

And then Firareth plunged into the midst of the Shadowed

Elves, spinning and striking with hooves and heels and teeth. Kellen struck as well, reaching with his sword what the destrier could not.

Once—it seemed a long time ago now—Jermayan and Valdien had showed him what an Elven destrier was capable of on the field of battle. Kellen had been sure then that he'd never master the intricate cues that would tell his mount what to do, and in fact, he didn't know them yet. But Firareth obviously knew exactly what the situation called for, and after Master Belesharon's training—and Shalkan's—Kellen could stay in the saddle no matter what his mount chose to do.

And Elven-made equestrian armor was just as flexible as anything the Elves made for themselves. So he let battle-sight and Firareth tell *him* what to do.

It was a dance, a dance in which two moved as one. A deadly dance of hoof and steel, and one that the Shadowed Elves were not prepared for. Firareth might have had some form of battle-sight himself, the way he anticipated what the enemy was going to do next, and met the threat before it could even evolve.

It was over before the Shadowed Elves realized that they were outclassed and outmaneuvered; not one of them escaped.

"Good fellow," Kellen said a few moments later, patting the side of his mount's neck—armor against armor, but it would have to do. Firareth turned to look at him—with, Kellen imagined, an air of equal approval. Then he snorted, and looked about, head high. The stallion was excited, obviously looking for more targets.

The Shadowed Elves were trying to break through the line, drawn by the Calling Spell and by the nearness of their enemy. With the arrival of the Deathwings, there was no more question of luring them out—it had become a matter of killing them before they escaped, and everywhere Kellen looked, the fighting was heavy. The skirmishers weren't armed with the Elven lance, but the line units were, and for all its unwieldiness, it proved their most effective weapon against the Deathwings.

Kellen saw one Elven Knight stand in his stirrups, heft his lance, and fling it skyward like a javelin. It transfixed the body of one of the Deathwings and brought it crashing to the ground. The others with him rode quickly forward, their mounts trampling the creature until they were sure it was dead.

The fighting was frenzied now, but Kellen did his best to detour around it. His goal was to reach Redhelwar.

He found the Elven general on an outcropping of rock overlooking the cavern mouth. Redhelwar was surrounded by his personal guard, and by mounted messengers, whose purpose it was to take orders to the various units engaged in battle.

"Sir!" he called, to catch the commander's attention.

He caught it, all right. The Elven commander turned in his saddle to stare. "Why are you here?" Redhelwar demanded.

"Jermayan can't see the battlefield for you," Kellen said, as his battle-sense and Wildmagery told him just how far they actually were. At the moment Jermayan and Ancaladar were far to the west of Ysterialpoerin. Kellen could locate them as easily as his own right hand. "The Deathwings have driven Ancaladar off. But *I* can tell you what is happening. The Shadowed Elves are breaking through our lines. And they have weapons and—*something*—cached somewhere between here and Ysterialpoerin. I don't know where."

"If you can see the battlefield, then tell me what you see," Redhelwar ordered sharply.

Automatically, Kellen closed his eyes, responding to the command as if he'd been bespelled himself. For a moment the world seemed to spin, then everything steadied, dream-like and impossibly tiny, a pattern in his mind, in colors that only Elves could see. As if it were nothing to do with him, as if it did not matter, he heard himself reciting the places where the line was weak, where units had been decoyed out of position—or slain entirely.

THEY had assumed the numbers of the Shadowed Elves would be similar to what they had encountered in the first cavern—doubled, of course, since they were facing the warriors of two caverns here, but of the same order.

They'd been wrong.

There were far more of them here. The Shadowed Elves thrived on darkness and cold. And they'd been preparing for this battle for a very long time. If Redhelwar had fallen into their trap, and lost a third of his force in the nearer cavern, tonight wouldn't be a battle at all. It would be a slaughter.

Redhelwar was giving orders to his messengers now, and they sped off like arrows from an Elven bow, but Kellen didn't listen. The important thing was to see the picture and report it. Would a time ever come when he could see *and* fight?

"They're behind the line," Kellen heard himself say. "They've really broken through now; they've driven a gap in the lines."

"Where?"

"East and north." Not just the few dozen that the Death-wings had managed to carry over their line, but a number that could pose a serious threat to Ysterialpoerin. "A hundred, perhaps more." He could see how they'd done it—the long perilous climb over the glacier, the bitter clash with the High Reaches warriors, then down the side of the mountain and into the night.

"Go. Find them. There's little more you can do here," Redhelwar said.

Kellen opened his eyes, drawing in a deep breath of icy night air, and for a moment the battle spun crazily around him before everything settled again. The world seen only through his human senses seemed oddly flat and simple.

But now urgency tightened his gut, and he had orders to follow. With a quick salute, he turned Firareth about and rode back to his men.

The fighting was heavier now, and several times Kellen was delayed, though he went as quickly as he could. By now the skirmishing units had been drawn into the fighting, called up to replace fallen comrades and to draw the ring of Elvensteel tighter around the enemy.

Kellen located Isinwen—he did not see Ciltesse—at the head of the troop. They had obviously just withdrawn from a clash with the enemy, and were looking about for fresh foes. Isinwen was not riding Cheska, but a strange destrier whose caparison and barding was drenched in blood.

"Ciltesse?" He did not want to know, yet he must ask.

"We were separated," Isinwen replied, voice cracking and hoarse from shouting. "I have not seen him since."

There was no time to worry about a single member of the troop. He would either be alive, or dead, and they had a job to do. "Disengage! We have orders! Come with me!"

Isinwen raised the warhorn to his lips and blew a short call. A few moments later a few more members of Kellen's troop came riding up, their swords black with blood even in the blue light of the Coldfire. Ciltesse was not among them.

"Follow!" Kellen called. "They've broken through the lines! We've orders to stop them!"

Kellen set a hard pace, and the others followed him in the direction of where the Shadowed Elves had broken through the lines in his battle-vision. Kellen wasn't sure what their plan was. Escape? To attack Ysterialpoerin? It didn't matter—whatever they planned, he had to stop it. If he could do no more than warn the defenders of Ysterialpoerin, that would be enough. If this was not completely familiar land, it was familiar enough now, with the Coldfire to help, that he dared take them at a hard canter. They pounded through the soft snow, a growing urgency in him, though no direction as yet.

By now he'd lost all track of time. Athan had not cast his spell until the moon had risen above the mountains, so the battle had begun several hours after sunset. At a guess, it must be after midnight now, but the clouds were denser than ever. The only illumination was the crowns of blue fire each of them carried with him, casting blurred and changing shadows over the snow and against the trees. Only the nearer trees and undergrowth had any definition at all; a few yards away, everything blurred into an insubstantial misty grey.

He carried the map of the terrain in his head—half memory of the maps in Redhelwar's pavilion, half memory of what his battle-sight had shown him. Their path and the path of the fleeing Shadowed Elves should intersect somewhere ahead.

The forest made pursuit more difficult. Kellen never thought there'd come a time when he'd be wishing for the open icy plains that led up to the nearer cavern, but he did now. He would have been able to see for leagues there, and they could have let the destriers run all-out.

At last Kellen could sense open space ahead. He raised his hand, slowing the horses to a walk.

With the Coldfire, they didn't have the advantage of surprise, but whatever was there, he wanted to *see* it before they rushed to engage. And the animals could use a breathing space, even if only for a few minutes.

They reached the edge of the trees.

Ahead of them stretched a long shallow valley. All was black, without even the shadows of trees to give it shape. In the distance, his battle-sight showed him piles of dirt-covered snow, where the Shadowed Elves had dug all the way down into the frozen ground. Two sets of ropes were attached to something beneath the surface of the snow, and the Shadowed Elves—the ones that the Deathwings had lifted over the lines earlier, he thought—were pulling with all their strength. Axes and shovels, and unused coils of rope, were scattered over the surface, discarded when they were no longer needed.

Not a weapons cache. Or if that, then more. A tools *cache. But why?*

What was buried here that was so important to them that they would dig down through ice and snow and frozen earth to get to it in the middle of a battle? And why now? Why not earlier?

There was something *beneath* the ground as well. Kellen couldn't quite make it out, and knew he didn't have the time to spend trying. The Shadowed Elves were trying to get to it, which meant it would be very bad for the Elves.

"I don't know what they're doing, but it doesn't matter. They want what's there. We must stop them from getting it," Kellen said to Isinwen—and, with his heart leaping into his throat, gave the signal to charge.

THEY rode down the valley toward the work party of Shadowed Elves. The second group of Shadowed Elves caught sight of them and began shouting in their strange barking language, running toward them.

"Isinwen, who has the fastest horse?" Kellen shouted, over the sound of their snow-muffled hoofbeats.

"Nironoshan's Cerlocke is fastest," Isinwen answered without hesitation.

"Nironoshan—ride to Ysterialpoerin—now—and tell them the Shadowed Elves have broken through our lines. They may expect company!" Kellen ordered at the top of his lungs. His party was outnumbered six to one—at least—and at those odds, it was a more than equal fight. And he dared not assume this was the only group of Shadowed Elves that had broken through Redhelwar's careful defenses.

"I go!" Nironoshan spurred Cerlocke off at an angle from the main charge, the pale destrier he rode quickly drawing ahead of the others.

Kellen expected the Shadowed Elves to go for weapons as his troop bore down on them, but they only increased their desperate hauling on the ropes. Soon he was close enough to see them by Coldfire instead of battle-sight.

And then to slaughter them.

It was almost too easy. The only difficult thing for him and his troop was reaching them to attack, as the piles of earth and snow on either side formed a natural bulwark that made them difficult to get to. But even while they were being cut down, the Shadowed Elves would not relinquish the ropes leading down into the pit, not even to defend themselves.

And a few seconds after the last of them fell dead, the second wave of Shadowed Elves reached the pit's edge.

Unlike the others, these were well armed: in the light of the Coldfire, Kellen could see the gleam of looted swords and daggers in their hands.

"On foot!" Kellen shouted, vaulting from Firareth's saddle and giving the destrier the command to leave the field. Mounted, the Elves were vulnerable to attacks against their horses—the Shadowed Elves had proven that to them time and again this night.

On foot, a chance against these greater numbers. Perhaps.

Once more, his world narrowed to a series of feints and targets, as Kellen's mind forced his aching cold-stiffened muscles to obey. Each foe he killed was one less for his war brothers to face, and no matter what they did here, Ysterialpoerin was warned.

In a distant part of his mind—the part that must assess things, even now—he knew the battle was going against them. Time and again he felt his comrades die, and fed his fury at their deaths into the fight. Though it cost him dearly in his exhaustion, he summoned Fire, and set a dozen of the enemy burning like torches.

But fire was easy to put out in the midst of a snowfield, and in the moment he was distracted by setting the spell, two Shadowed Elves got past his guard, swarming him like starving rats. It was his cloak that saved him as much as his armor—the coldwarg fur was heavy and thick; it tangled their blades, buying him the vital moment he needed to throw them off.

The ground began to shake.

Kellen hadn't thought there was anything that would make a Shadowed Elf break off an attack once one of the creatures had begun. But the two that were attacking him actually cowered back, and in their moment of inattention, Kellen killed them both.

Suddenly the pit behind him exploded upward and outward as if it were a stopped-up fountain, spewing ice, stone, and earth high into the air.

And something was rising with it.

Kellen's first confused impression was "snake"—and he hated snakes—but this was only as much like a snake as the Deathwings were like true bats.

It was the white of dirty snow. It had a head vaguely similar to Ancaladar's, but there all resemblance ended. The eyes were dead black and malignant, the body that of a serpent's—if a serpent were large enough to swallow bulls without choking. It radiated cold like a palpable force—the temperature dropped quickly enough to make Kellen's face hurt, and the pooling blood on the bodies of the Shadowed Elves he'd just killed froze solid with an audible crack.

"Ice-drake!" Sihemand shouted.

One of the creatures Shadow Mountain had bred in the Lost Lands. They radiated cold and exhaled poison.

"Get to the horses!" Kellen ordered. Suddenly it was difficult to talk.

He looked around. The rest of the Shadowed Elves were gone, faded into the darkness. They'd run the moment the ice-drake had burst free.

And the temperature was still dropping. He'd thought he'd been cold before. Now he knew he'd never known the meaning of the word. The ice-drake radiated a cold as intense and deadly as a forging-furnace's fire. He backed unsteadily away from the pit. His blood-drenched surcoat was frozen to his armor; it tore like paper when he moved.

The ice-drake towered over him, rising as high as the tallest trees in the forest of Ysterialpoerin before arching its neck and beginning to lower itself slowly toward the snow.

Kellen switched to battle-sight, but instead of the familiar overlay in glowing blue and red—showing him the creature's attack-pattern, and where he might attack in turn—he saw nothing but the same queer fog that had surrounded the coldwarg when they'd been Demon-bespelled.

"Kellen!" Isinwen shouted, rousing him from his daze. "Run!"

He tried, but by now he was so cold that even to move was agony. He managed a few steps and fell, and knew that he couldn't get up again.

"You will learn to do that which you think you cannot do." He could hear Master Belesharon's words in his head. He tasted snow and blood from cold-cracked lips through the facepiece of his armor. He couldn't run, but he could move. Clutching at his sword, he used it to lever himself to his feet again.

Cold. Even the ice-drake's presence was lethal. If he stayed here any longer, he would freeze to death.

The ice-drake appeared in front of him, its chin landing in the snow with a soft thump. It opened its jaws. They were large enough, Kellen realized with a distant sense of astonishment, that he could just walk down its throat. But that obviously wasn't what it had in mind.

And there was no way he could get out of its way.

Fire. I'll summon fire, he thought desperately.

But there was nothing here that would burn.

Suddenly the ice-drake burst into flames. Its jaws snapped shut and it reared up, looking affronted. A ragged cheer went up from the Elves.

Kellen stared, bewildered. Though every inch of its body was covered in flames—the snow all around it was melting—the fire seemed to have no effect on the monster itself at all.

And then Jermayan and Ancaladar struck from above with all their might.

The great black dragon stooped down out of the sky and seized the ice-drake just behind the head, as an eagle might seize a snake. With great pounding wingbeats, the dragon carried its far-from-helpless prey into the sky.

Kellen almost fell, the relief of rescue was so intense; instead he forced himself to his feet and began to stagger through the slush. Isinwen met him halfway, and dragged

him the rest of the way to the horses, boosting him into Firareth's saddle.

"Can you see it? Can you see Ancaladar? Kellen, tell us!"
he demanded.

Kellen shook his head to clear it, looking skyward.

THEY'D barely arrived in time.

Jermayan and Ancaladar had fought the Deathwings before, but never in such numbers, and this time their intent
was clear—if they could not harm Ancaladar they would kill
his Bonded, for the death of one meant the death of the other.

And they *could* harm Ancaladar, for the dragon, though
large, and fast, and possessed of a tough armored hide, was
still flesh and bone and blood.

Their fight carried them far from the mountains, far past
Ysterialpoerin. For every one of the white-furred horrors
slain by Ancaladar's teeth and claws—or Jermayan's sword
and spells—two more seemed to take its place. When the
creatures could find no other way to attack, they simply
threw their bodies at the dragon and his rider, attempting to
batter them from the sky by sheer force.

But at last the sky was clear.

"Where now?" Ancaladar asked. Jermayan could feel his
Bonded's weariness. It matched his own. But there was still
work to be done; the fight was by no means over, not for
them, and not for the army below and behind them.

"Back toward the battlefield. Fly below the clouds. I want
to be able to let Redhelwar know how the land lies between
Ysterialpoerin and the cavern."

"Of course," Ancaladar agreed, curving a wingtip in a
gentle arcing descent.

Ysterialpoerin was quiet, as was the camp. But then, running through the snow below, Ancaladar spotted a lone
horseman riding at top speed through the snow in the direction of the city.

"That's Nironoshan. One of Kellen's troop," the dragon said.

"Follow his tracks," Jermayan ordered tersely. Kellen had sent his fastest rider as a messenger to Ysterialpoerin—but why?

A few wingbeats later, he knew.

The ice-drake reared up out of the earth, spraying rock and ice about it with the force of its exit, and then lowered itself to the snow, seeking food. The creatures would eat carrion, or the frozen victims of their radiated cold, but they preferred to stun their prey with their breath and swallow their paralyzed quarry before it died.

Jermayan could see the remains of a battle on the snow below, and a handful of Elven Knights still alive.

And Kellen, directly in the ice-drake's path.

Jermayan summoned Fire, enfolding the creature in flames. But to his dismay, it was not consumed. The flames coated it like a cloak. They annoyed it. But they did not harm it.

The ice-drake reared back, lifting half its length from the snow and looking for its tormentor.

And Ancaladar stooped upon it, seizing it behind the head, and dragged it into the sky, his mighty wings straining. The ice-drake hissed and thrashed, spewing clouds of poison vapor that were blown harmlessly away by the winds of the upper air before they reached Jermayan.

As the white worm flailed, Jermayan tried spell after spell, before realizing that all of them were useless. No spell that he knew had the slightest effect on the creature. All he could do was use his spells to constantly heal the damage it was doing to both him and Ancaladar with its radiant cold, for as long as his strength held out. Beyond that, this was Ancaladar's fight alone.

The dragon raked the ice-drake's body with his formidable hind talons. The ice-drake used its body like a whip, attempting to wrap itself around the dragon's neck and break it, or strike his wings hard enough to break them.

And no matter what, Ancaladar dared not let go of his grip on the ice-drake's head.

⌐

"THEY'RE fighting," Kellen said, in response to Isinwen's question. His battle-sight showed him the combatants, locked in struggle above the clouds. "Ancaladar will win," he added, with a certainty he did not feel, "and then he and Jermayan can give you all the details." He shook his head to clear it; there was still work to do. "Come on. Half the Shadowed Elves ran off when that thing came out of the ground. We need to find out where."

The others were as tired and nearly as battered by the cold as he was, and of the twenty who had ridden away from the main battle with him, five would never ride again.

"The snow is fresh. Let me try," Reyezeyt said.

⌐

EXHAUSTION tugged at Jermayan, but he knew he dared not fail. A moment's inattention to his spells, and both he and his Bonded would freeze to death. It would not matter which died first, for the other's death would follow in a heartbeat.

Ancaladar roared with pain and fury as the ice-drake slammed its muscular coils once more into his ribs. This time he was quick enough, darting his head down and to the side. His jaws sank into the ice-drake's body with a sound like ice breaking on a frozen pond.

For just an instant, the creature went still in agony. Jermayan could taste the foulness of its blood in his own mouth as well as the acid pain of burning cold. But in that instant, Ancaladar claimed the victory.

He curled his hind talons upward, sinking them deep into the ice-drake's body in an unbreakable grip. It was impossible for him to fly in such a contorted position, but he had flown very high during their battle; now he folded his wings back and simply *fell*, pulling at the struggling body in his grasp with claws and teeth.

At last, the ice-drake . . . *tore*. Jermayan felt it die, felt the ancient and inimical energies fade, and felt Ancaladar's surge of triumph at the same moment. Ancaladar's jaws snapped shut—he quickly opened them again, spitting out fragments of flesh—and he straightened his body with a snap, letting the wind pull his wings open.

The ground had been very close.

Relief gave Jermayan new energy, and Ancaladar's magic was a boundless well for him to draw from. He healed the damage—the last of the damage, for with the ice-drake dead, there would be no more—and sent up a silent prayer of gratitude to Leaf and Star that they had won. He let his own joy and relief spill out to Ancaladar, and felt the dragon share his own.

Ancaladar circled low over the pit from which the ice-drake had emerged, and fastidiously dropped the pieces of the dead creature beside it. There was no blood—that had been spattered to the winds above—and the corpse was already softening in the quick dissolution of creatures of the Dark.

Ancaladar landed, and walked over to the pit, peering down into it curiously.

"I wonder where it leads?" he asked.

"Nowhere we want to go," Jermayan said grimly. "Nor do I think our enemies should have the use of it."

The Spell of Unmaking was one of the most complicated spells he knew—and one of the most dangerous, for it returned things to their original condition, and so must be used with great care. But Ancaladar had insisted that he practice it, over and over and over again, and now Jermayan had good reason to be grateful for his teacher's stern determination.

He cast it now, focusing upon the pit.

Stone and earth and ice shivered; snow leaped up into the air; all caught in the dance of magic. A moment later, the pit was gone, sealed once more.

"Now we return to the fight," Jermayan said.

"Yessss," Ancaladar agreed, and Jermayan smiled, just a little, to feel the dragon's strength return as they launched back into the sky.

⟵

THE tracks of the Shadowed Elves led quickly into the trees and scattered, and then vanished altogether. Try as he might, Kellen could summon no vision of What-Had-Been to tell him where they'd gone, nor could Reyezeyt find any trace of them—not even the piles of ash that Shadow Mountain tended to leave of servants it was displeased with.

But it shouldn't be displeased with these servants, should it? They and the others had done exactly what they'd meant to—unleashed another Shadow-born monster to ravage the Elven lands. If Jermayan and Ancaladar couldn't kill it . . .

After at least an hour spent searching for a trail that didn't exist, even Kellen was willing to give up.

"Come on," he said wearily. "We'd better report to Redhelwar. But I want to take a last look at the pit, first." He paused a moment to try and find Jermayan and the dragon with his battle-sense, but even that was weakening as exhaustion claimed him.

When they got there, Kellen received one of the few pleasant surprises of the night. The pit had been filled in—as if it had never been—and lying in the snow atop it were the two halves of the ice-drake.

Like the Deathwings, it seemed to be decomposing with supernatural swiftness, and the destriers, well-trained though they were, flatly refused to approach the stinking remains.

"At least we know who won," Kellen said. *I hope they're both all right.*

They turned their horses back toward the cavern, bearing their dead and leading the now-masterless destriers.

⟵

BY the time Kellen and the remains of his troop returned to the lines, the tide of battle had shifted firmly in the Elves' favor. Belepheriel met them as they were coming in. The Elven Commander rode at the head of a full hundred; for all their numbers, still only a fraction of the troops under his command.

"To see you gladdens my heart, Kellen Knight-Mage," he said, as serenely as if there was not still fighting going on all around them.

"And mine to see you, Belepheriel," Kellen said, "though the news I bring makes ill-hearing."

"Jermayan and Ancaladar have returned, and told us of the ice-drake's destruction," the commander replied. "The battle goes well for us—there are only scattered knots of resistance from the enemy now, and our line holds firm. Jermayan has sealed the main entrance with ice, so they may not retreat, and by dawn the field will be ours."

"And I have failed," Kellen said bitterly. "I lost the Shadowed Elves I was sent to find—they escaped, and I could find no trace of them. I sent Nironoshan to warn the city, but . . . "

"And if you had not, Jermayan and Ancaladar would not have known to seek out the ice-drake, and we would have lost far more this night than the location of a few Shadowed Elves," Belepheriel said reprovingly. "One warrior does not win the war, as Master Belesharon will surely have told you. Come. You have done your part, and now that I have found you, I have done mine. With the line secure, Redhelwar has ordered the Healers' wagons brought up. You and your men need healing, rest, warmth, and tea. I will make your report to Redhelwar."

Kellen wanted to argue the point, but he was too tired, and far too cold—and he certainly owed his command and their mounts a rest. So he followed Belepheriel to the Healers' encampment, a circle of wagons set up half a mile away from the lines.

He was unsurprised to find Idalia there as well. She came out of the Healers' Tent to view the new arrivals, took one look at him and ordered him into the Healers' Tent.

"But I'm not—" Kellen began.

"*Now.*"

Kellen sighed and obeyed. "Go warm up," he said to the others.

It was bright inside the Healers' Tent, and after so long outside, it seemed swelteringly hot. Frost formed on the exposed surface of Kellen's armor and melted immediately.

"Jermayan told me about the ice-drake. You know what they can do. Didn't it occur to you that it was going to kill you? Take off your armor," Idalia commanded.

He blinked at her in confusion. "Well, yes, but, I—now?"

"No, *after* the flesh has fallen from your bones with frost-burn," Idalia said acidly.

Kellen unhooked his cloak and dropped it to the floor of the tent, then pulled off his helmet. Idalia studied his face critically.

"Not too bad," she pronounced. "Come on—boots and gauntlets."

His hands and feet had been numb with cold before; the warmth of the tent made them ache now. Clumsily, he managed to get his gauntlets off, and barely remembered to keep his leather gloves on to remove his frost-cold sabatons and greaves—sitting down first on a wooden stool that Idalia impatiently indicated. At last his bare hands and feet were exposed.

The skin was white with cold, but whatever horrible affliction Idalia was looking for, she didn't find it. Nevertheless, she pulled a pot of salve from her apron pocket, knelt before him, and rubbed it into his feet briskly.

It hurt.

Kellen kept his mouth shut, though. She might think of something worse.

When she was done with his feet, she did his hands—and that hurt even more. Then she wiped her hands clean, took a pot of something else entirely, and daubed it liberally over his face. That, at least, was pleasant—the thick salve smelled of honey and lanolin.

"All right. You can armor up again. You were damned lucky," Idalia said grudgingly. "I *know* you were warned about frost-burn."

"Well, yes," Kellen admitted. Too long in the cold, and the flesh died on the bone, and then rotted if not seen to. The Healers had been very graphic about it. "But it's not as if we had time to stop and build a fire."

Idalia grunted, reluctantly and wordlessly conceding his point.

Kellen gratefully put his armor back on, and picked up his cloak. There were deep slashes in it from Shadowed Elf blades, but perhaps someone would be able to repair it later. He got to his feet.

"Idalia, I lost track of Ciltesse and several of my other people earlier," he said hesitantly. "Have you seen . . . ?"

Idalia shook her head, compassion in her expression now. "I haven't seen them. But I'm not the only Healer here. Someone else may have. Or they may not have been wounded at all. Check with the others."

Checking with the Healers might be a good idea, but as Kellen left the tent, two more Elves were brought in, one bleeding from a deep sword-cut, the other shaking from poison. Right now the Healers had enough to do.

He left the tent and passed behind the ring of wagons. The horse-lines were set up there, with lanterns illuminating large braziers heating the ever-present kettles of soup and tea. He quickly found the others.

There's bad news. He could tell that from Isinwen's posture alone, as the Elven Knight stood huddled against the brazier's heat, his helmet beneath his arm.

"Tell me quickly," Kellen said, coming up.

"Ciltesse is dead," Isinwen said. "I saw Jolia in the horse-lines, and I asked. Others—Valhile, Penerniel, Aldere—"

"Gone to Leaf and Star," Reyezeyt said softly.

Kellen took a deep breath. He'd seen Ayihletevizi fall earlier tonight in the fighting: Lirgrinteko, Rirnas, Airiren . . . and those the Shadowed Elves had killed at the pit as well.

He'd lost more than half his command tonight. Elves he'd ridden with, trained with, lived with. Trusted his life to.

And sworn to keep safe.

He bowed his head, feeling his throat swell with unshedd-able tears.

"*Alakomentai,*" Isinwen said gently, "it is not easy. But it happens, in war. You were not generous with our lives. You were our *mayn* against the enemy, first in every battle."

Mayn meant "shield" in the Old Tongue of the Elves. Kellen was not comforted. He took a deep breath.

"If our losses were so heavy . . . " he began.

"Ah. No. Do not fear *that,*" Reyezeyt said, sounding al-most relieved at what he thought was the cause of Kellen's distress. "The skirmishing units took the brunt of the en-emy's attack. We and the Mountainfolk took the heaviest losses, I hear. The army is still strong."

It was cold cheer, but it would have to do.

"Come," Kaldet urged. "Take tea. It is crude and simple stuff, but it will warm you."

Twenty-two

Smoke and Storm

At dawn the warhorns blew the victory. Hours before, carts of wounded had begun moving back toward the camp, well guarded by line units that could now be spared from what was by now little more than a series of execu-tions. Kellen and his people remained, having no orders oth-erwise, and slowly a few last stragglers from Kellen's troop found them: Rhuifai. Janshil. Krinyen.

Kellen knew that Isinwen was right. Loss was the price of war. No one blamed him for the deaths.

Except himself.

You've got to stop this, or you'll go mad, he told himself. *If Belepheriel can forgive you for Imerteniel's death, then you have to forgive yourself now, because the deaths of those who died tonight are no more your fault than Imerteniel's was. If you can't forgive yourself, you'll be useless in this fight. And the stakes are too high for that.*

They knew what they were doing, and they did it willingly and gladly. They were Elven Knights, trained for war. Don't dishonor their deaths by letting them make you less than what you are.

"We will always remember them," Kellen said, heavily.

He'd been silent a very long time. Isinwen looked up in surprise when he finally spoke.

"Yes," he said simply. "Their names will be entered in the Great Book in the House of Sword and Shield. The House will remember them, and so will our children. And Leaf and Star will remember also, as long as the forests bloom and the stars burn."

And it's our job to make sure that the forests bloom forever, Kellen thought grimly. *I'll make sure they do. I swear it.*

⌐

A few hours after dawn, Adaerion rode down with the order for Kellen and his troop to retreat back to camp.

"And make sure you eat and sleep when you get there. You're going into the cavern tomorrow," Adaerion said when they were mounted and ready to ride.

Wearily, Kellen turned Firareth's head toward camp.

⌐

KELLEN missed the next battle, which took place that very night. Redhelwar brought the Unicorn Knights up from Ysterialpoerin to the farther cavern, backed them with a hand-picked selection of volunteer cavalry that could work in close proximity to unicorns, and arranged for Jermayan and Ancaladar to slaughter a small herd of deer directly below the cavern mouth.

He didn't ask Jermayan to unseal the ice barriers over the cavern openings. There was no need.

The ever-voracious Goblins, lured out into the darkness by the scent of fresh meat, swarmed toward the mound of venison through the ice and rock. And once they began to feed, the Unicorn Knights attacked. One thrust of their mounts' horns would kill a Goblin, and though the creatures spat poison, the touch of a unicorn's horn could quickly heal the hurt.

Though the Elves slew them in great numbers, the lure of food—dead deer, the bodies of slain Goblins, and the prospect of living prey—kept the creatures coming. They must have been more than usually ravenous; perhaps the Shadowed Elves had kept them short of prey. Many of them stopped to eat instead of attacking, and Elven lancers, riding in and out of the fray, quickly added the new arrivals to the swiftly growing mound of dead at little risk to themselves. Goblins would rather eat than kill and would break off an attack in order to feed. Only in the absence of food were they truly dangerous to an enemy. So long as there was something to eat, they could be killed with relative impunity.

And at last, no more Goblins emerged into the upper air.

As Redhelwar had told Kellen, the Elves had hunted Goblins many times in the past.

THAT was the tale Kellen heard when he was roused at dawn of the next day. He might have slept even longer, save for the fact that someone was shaking the bells at the door of his tent—and had been for some time, by the sound of things.

He staggered over to the doorway, still wearing his armor's underpadding. Idalia was standing there, a roll of cloth under one arm and a covered mug in the other.

"Oh, good," she said. "You're still alive. You certainly slept like the dead." She dumped the bundle on the floor of his tent and held out the mug. "Armethaliehan Black. I figured you'd need something stronger than Winter Spice this morning."

"How long . . . ?" Kellen croaked, snatching for the mug and flipping back the lid. The fragrant smell of—very strong—tea filled the pavilion. He drank eagerly.

"Let's see," Idalia said, pretending to think about it. "It's dawn, so the battle at the cavern ended yesterday morning. Last night the Unicorn Knights—with a little help from qualifying cavalry—lured out and killed what's probably all of the Goblins from the caverns. Now Redhelwar wants to see you as soon as you've eaten. So you should probably get dressed and go see him." She dropped the tent flap and walked off while Kellen was still coming to terms with being awake.

Kellen finished his tea and put on his armor—apparently he'd cleaned both before passing out yesterday, though he didn't remember doing it—and put on a fresh surcoat. The bundle Idalia had dropped was his coldwarg-fur cloak, mended.

I have to remember to thank her for that—if she won't take my head off for it.

———

PETARIEL was in the dining tent, and Kellen got a more detailed version of the slaughter of the Goblins from him as he worked his way through a platterful of food.

"I wish I'd been there," he said, surprised to find it was true.

"Well, we can't let you have all the fun," Petariel said reprovingly. "It made a nice change from riding picket around the Heart of the Forest, I assure you. We return Nironoshan to you, incidentally—while we thank you for the warning, if you've lost any Shadowed Elves, I assure you, *we* haven't found them."

"They've probably run off to some other rat-hole," Kellen said darkly. "Just . . . in case they haven't . . ."

"We'll continue to look for them," Petariel assured him. "But I don't think I can promise to return them to you in the condition you last saw them."

Kellen shook his head, smiling painfully. He knew Petariel's lightly-mocking words were a mask for the grief that all the Elves shared at being forced to execute those they thought of as their own kind.

He understood it better than he would have once. Petariel had offered Kellen neither sympathy nor acknowledgment for the members of his troop he had lost in the battle, though he was sure Petariel knew about them, and for that, Kellen was profoundly grateful. If Petariel had, Kellen wasn't sure he'd have been able to stand it.

"I wouldn't dream of asking you to return them at all," he said, striving to match his friend's tone. "One does not ask for the return of a gift."

"Since you have given me such a rich gift, I shall have to ask Gesade what I may gift you with in suitable recompense," Petariel said. "But you must go now, else you will be late for the day's interesting events."

———

WHEN Kellen arrived in Redhelwar's pavilion, the senior commanders, Idalia, Vestakia—in her scarlet armor—and Jermayan were already there. Once he would have fretted about being late. Now Kellen simply assumed that if Redhelwar had wanted him earlier, he would have sent someone to fetch him.

"Kellen Knight-Mage," Redhelwar greeted him. "It is now time to finish what we have begun. Vestakia must lead us to the Shadowed Elf village."

Kellen thought about it for a moment. "Will it work?" he asked bluntly. "I know you can sense Taint, Vestakia, but the Shadowed Elves aren't the only Tainted things still in there—even without Goblins."

Vestakia nodded. "I know I can't tell one kind of Tainted

creature from another, but from what Jermayan says about the *duergar,* if we go in lit with Coldfire, they'll sense it and get as far away from us as possible—and the Shadowed Elves won't."

We hope, Kellen thought grimly.

"We've killed all—or nearly all—the Goblins, and most of the fighting males," Redhelwar said. "What you should face today should be only females and young, though in greater numbers than you have faced before."

Kellen nodded. "Then Vestakia will be able to lead us to the village. And once she's found it, she'll return to the surface immediately."

"I won't object," Vestakia said with a rueful smile.

⌒

JERMAYAN and Ancaladar were waiting for them at the cavern mouth. The day was dark, and even cold as it was, the air felt heavy instead of crisp. Kellen remembered what the other Wildmages had said about the weather. Because of that—and because clearing the caverns of all their Tainted inhabitants would probably not be the work of a single day, Redhelwar would be making a second, temporary, camp here, once the battlefield had been cleared. The Elves were still working to remove the bodies of the slain Shadowed Elves as the fighting force rode through, and everywhere Kellen looked the snow was churned and stained. He found himself looking forward to the snow to come.

Before they'd arrived, Jermayan had improved the path to the cavern mouth—now it was a long gentle slope instead of the steep twisting path the Shadowed Elves had carved. As those who would enter the cavern began to dismount, he banished the shield of ice that had barred the entrance.

"First ranks, take your shields," Adaerion ordered.

The supply wagon with Artenel's experimental shields stood ready and waiting. Kellen collected his and hefted it. Artenel had made some improvements, including a shoulder-piece that would allow the shield's weight to be more evenly-distributed. There weren't enough shields for everyone, but at least those in front would have greater protection than before from the Shadowed Elves' preferred weapons.

They ascended into the cavern. Kellen and Isinwen led, with Idalia and Vestakia directly behind him. As before, the passageway was straight at first, and narrow enough that only two Elven Knights could walk side-by-side. Kellen walked carefully, alert for trip-wires. Just because they didn't expect this lair to be catch-trapped didn't mean it might not be. And a quickly prepared trap could be just as lethal as one that had been moonturns in the making.

But he saw nothing at all—not trip-wire, goblin, nor Shadowed Elf—and soon they came to the first point in the cavern where a decision as to their direction must be made. By now, the only light came from the Coldfire that crowned them all.

Behind him, he heard Vestakia's breathing grow ragged, though she tried hard to control it.

"Which way?" Kellen asked.

"Left—far left," she corrected, as the tunnel branched in all directions here.

⌐

UNLIKE the last two Shadowed Elf caverns Kellen had been in, this one was a honeycomb of tunnels and chambers, and after the second turn, he sent someone back to mark their path, for without clear signs, they might never find their way out again. Still they saw no sign of the enemy, and Kellen began to believe that, once again, the rest of the Shadowed Elves meant to make a stand at the village.

Surely they know that's useless? Kellen thought. There was something disturbing about the idea that this part of the battle would repeat the previous one. Everything they'd seen so far told them that the Shadowed Elves had learned from the first battle. They would know that hiding wouldn't save them.

"There's something wrong here," he said to Isinwen.

"Tell me," Isinwen said instantly.

"Nothing clear." *Of course.* "It just doesn't feel as if things are quite as they should be here. I can't tell more than that."

Behind him, Vestakia choked out a laugh, then gagged and began to cough.

"Let me make this known to Redhelwar. Any information is better than none," Isinwen said.

"Yes." Kellen stopped while Isinwen moved back through the line to find a runner to carry the message. "Vestakia, are you all right?"

"Oh, I'm fine," Vestakia said, sounding breathless and a bit irritated. "I don't know what you mean about things being not quite right here. They certainly feel normal to me—all wrong!"

Isinwen returned, and they continued.

Vestakia grew weaker the deeper they went into the mountain, until Kellen wondered if she would actually be able to lead them the entire way to the village. Her breathing now was punctuated by strangled whimpers of pain, and Idalia was all-but-carrying her.

But she never faltered, giving them their directions in a clear—though shaking—whisper each time the path became confused. Her courage was as true as a sword blade. If there was a single Elf in the entire army who still doubted her—after today, that doubt would be gone.

"There," she said at last, in a voice so faint Kellen had to strain to hear it. "Look . . . ahead . . . to the left . . . "

"Wait here," Kellen said to Isinwen.

They stood at the entrance to a huge cavern. By now Kellen had lost all sense of time; without Vestakia's guidance, he would have been certain they'd been wandering in circles. He left the others and crossed the cavern, senses alert, looking for any exit to the left.

He nearly missed it. The opening was small and narrow, as Shadowed Elf passageways tended to be, but when he looked cautiously through it he could see—at the bottom of a short series of shallow terraces—the glowing firepit that marked a Shadowed Elf village. And though it was too dark to see clearly, in the cavern beyond, he sensed Life in abundance.

And the sense of wrongness he'd felt before came back again, stronger.

But still no clearer.

He saw no traps.

For a moment Kellen considered retreating. Adaerion was in charge of the assault, but he was certain Adaerion would listen to him if he said they should leave.

But no. There was something down there. Even if it didn't turn out to be Shadowed Elves, they needed to either kill it, rescue it, or talk to it. Their job was to find out which—just as soon as Vestakia was safe.

He returned quickly to the others.

"That's it. Get her out of here," he said to Idalia. "Go with her. Tell Redhelwar . . . something's not the way it's supposed to be. I can't figure out anything more."

"I'll tell Jermayan, too," Idalia said. "Maybe he can help."

⌐

THE cavern outside the entrance was large enough for them to gather a good portion of their assault force there as they waited for the others to get back to the surface. Kellen tried to bring his sense of foreboding into sharper focus, but could not. Something was not right. That was all he knew.

"Kellen, you must go first," Adaerion said. "If it is an ambush, you will be able to tell us at once. After you, all those with Artenel's shields. We shall surround the village if we can, and . . . do what we must."

Kellen and the others nodded. None of them liked the necessity that lay before them but it had to be done.

And what other terrible things will have to be done, before the power of Shadow Mountain is broken? Kellen wondered uneasily.

AT last it was time. Kellen hefted his shield and stepped through the doorway.

He quickly slipped to one side, keeping the rock at his back. His battle-sight showed no threat. There was utter silence in the cavern, save for the faint sound of water dripping steadily somewhere far away.

The Elves followed him quickly, each crowned with Cold-fire. The more that came through, the brighter the cavern became. They spread out along the terraces—five shallow broad steps, Kellen now saw, something the cave itself had created, smoothed and evened by the passing of countless generations of Shadowed Elf footsteps.

The cavern itself was a beautiful thing. The stone ceiling dripped with eternal icicles of stone, some of which, at the edges of the cavern, had grown long enough to touch the floor. The cavern had obviously once been filled with them, and—just as obviously—those in the center had been cut away and used to build the village huts, giving many of them an odd resemblance to the log house Kellen had shared with Idalia in the Wildwood.

This village was larger than the last one they'd seen, the structures more elaborate, indicating longer habitation. But all the life Kellen sensed here was concealed within those huts—though this cavern had many exits, Kellen could not perceive a single Shadowed Elf lurking in ambush.

Soon the attack force had moved into position. And still there was no sound, no movement, from the Shadowed Elves everyone knew were there.

Adaerion indicated the nearest hut, and pointed to Keirasti, communicating solely by gesture. She pointed to five of her command, and moved toward it.

Then everything began to happen at once.

They can't possibly all fit into these huts! Kellen realized belatedly. A dozen yelping children swarmed from the hut just as Keirasti and her troops reached it.

As if their screams had been a signal—or perhaps because they could not bear to lie concealed a moment longer—the door of every hut burst open, and barking, yelping Shadowed Elf young burst forth, running at the Elves. They were every size from those barely able to walk on their own to those half-grown, and they attacked the Elves in the manner of starving rats.

There was not one full-grown Shadowed Elf among them.

"Children," Kellen whispered in horror. "Nothing but children."

He ran into the first hut, the one Keirasti had approached. Lying on the floor, pushed into a corner, he saw half-a-dozen Shadowed Elf infants. A couple were still moving feebly. The others were already dead.

They starved to death. There was no one here to care for them, and they starved to death.

Because their mothers were elsewhere . . .

He ran back outside and grabbed the nearest Elf he could pull from the fighting. "Go—run—tell Redhelwar. *All the adult females are somewhere else. They aren't in the caverns.*"

He saw the Elven Knight turn away to carry his message, and raised his sword, covering the warrior's retreat.

THE Winged Gods had warned them centuries ago that this day would come, and so, against the Time of Testing, they had prepared, digging their long tunnels deep into the rock, preparing weapons, making all ready.

When the day came that the Hated Ones summoned the Brothers into the night to die, the Sisters were ready. They gave their last orders to their young. They went to the tunnels. And there they waited, knowing they must not dig their own way to the surface until they knew all was lost.

But all was not lost.

The last of the Brothers came for them, just as the Winged Gods had promised that they would. They brought them into the terrible cold bright world of the upper air, promising them blood and meat enough to atone for the death of every cub. With weapons in hand and death in their hearts, the Sisters and the Brothers hurried toward the place where the Hated Ones made their home.

⌐

THE Unicorn Knights were working a wide circle through the heart-forest, carefully searching for anything out of place, while the regular cavalry patrolled the city just outside its boundaries. Despite the fact that there had been no attack—nor was likely to be one—neither group was less than alert. Elves were a patient people.

"Centaurs coming," Gesade said, sniffing the wind. "A day or two, I think."

"It will be good to have the reinforcements," Petariel said. "And good of them to travel so far from their farms in winter. We must make them welcome."

Gesade sniffed again. "The wind's wrong, but . . . Something. Let's go look."

Unicorn and rider trotted off along their assigned path through the snowy forest.

⌐

VANDELT and Merchan had been partners rather longer than the usual pairing among the Unicorn Knights; a little over a century now. Vandelt had never found the Elf to whom his soul could bond, and Merchan simply said that Vandelt was incapable of managing without him. Vandelt might have been Captain of the Unicorns if he'd chosen— he'd certainly been a Unicorn Knight longer than anyone else currently serving among them—but he was far more interested in his garden, and he was quite willing to admit that he had no interest in command. Let Petariel have that honor, with Vandelt's great goodwill.

But he had seen his fragile and delicate garden at Deskethomaynel turn to dust in the Great Drought, and he was as willing as anyone to strike out at the servants of those who had killed his beloved plants. And he was by no means stupid, merely unambitious.

So when Merchan warned that someone was approaching from the direction they had been set to watch, Vandelt blew a warning immediately, even before he rode out to investigate further.

It did not save them.

The arrow took Merchan squarely in the chest. It did not penetrate his armor, but it clung, and it *burned*. Vandelt could smell the stench of burning fur, see the shimmer of heat, and see wisps of smoke as the padding beneath Merchan's collet began to kindle.

But of their attackers, he saw nothing.

"Run, Merchan!"

The unicorn turned, heading back toward their own lines. Vandelt raised his horn to blow a second, more urgent warning, but it was too late. Merchan had only gone a few yards before a net fell over them from above, tangling them in its meshes and sending Merchan crashing to the forest floor.

Before Vandelt could cut them free, the Shadowed Elves dropped from the trees, long knives flashing in the weak sunlight. Merchan and his rider died within seconds of each other.

The Shadowed Elves cut the ring of burning metal carefully from the unicorn's body, handling it with tongs, and spiked it to the nearest tree.

Then they moved on.

⌐

"KELLEN says that something's wrong."

Idalia passed Vestakia into the hands of the waiting Healers, who would take her back to the temporary camp a mile away as quickly as possible—distance was truly the best remedy for what ailed her; that, and a great deal of rest—and turned back to the Elven general.

"He will have given you all the information he had, of course," Redhelwar said imperturbably.

"Well, his precise words were 'tell Redhelwar something's not the way it's supposed to be,' if that helps. He couldn't tell me more than that. He *did* try."

"I know Kellen. He will have—" Redhelwar broke off, looking past her. He'd looked grim a moment before. Now he looked appalled.

Idalia followed the direction of his gaze. A single Elven Knight was running toward them from the cavern mouth, running as if more than his life depended upon it.

He slid to his knees at the feet of Redhelwar's bay destrier.

"A feint," he gasped. "The females are not there. Kellen said—the females are not in the caverns."

"But the children were," Idalia said with sudden bleak understanding. "They left them behind, so Vestakia would have something to follow."

Redhelwar barely moved. His voice did not waver.

"Dionan, tell Jermayan what Tildaril has said. Request him, if it is possible, to find where the females have gone."

Dionan rode away immediately to where Jermayan and Ancaladar waited on the cliff above the cavern entrance.

"Padredor, I leave this secondary camp in your keeping. Guard it—and Vestakia—well. When the others return from the caverns, tell them we proceed as planned," Redhelwar continued.

"Yes, Redhelwar," Padredor said. Whatever might be happening elsewhere, the caverns must still be scoured.

"Tildaril, Idalia, I thank you both for your warnings. When you see Kellen next, tell him he did all that anyone could ask of him. I must return to camp. If the females are gone, we must look to the location of the next attack."

He turned and rode away.

Yes, Kellen has done all that anyone could ask of him— not that he'll believe that, Idalia thought with a resigned sigh. She went to fetch Cella for the ride back to the nearer camp. Her tools were there, including her favorite scrying bowl. Perhaps she could see something useful.

⌐

VANDELT'S warning had not been in vain, for it was heard and relayed across the forest by a dozen horns even before he was struck down. But it had been a warning only: the Unicorn Knights were still not sure what they faced as they rode toward Vandelt's patrol area.

"I smell blood—and smoke," Gesade said, alarmed.

Suddenly she leaped forward. A net fell to the snow in the place where she'd been.

"Above!" Petariel cried.

Unicorn Knights fired into the trees as their mounts dodged madly, evading nets, spears, and deadly fragile bottles of acid. A few bodies fell, but not enough—and from their concealment in the trees, Shadowed Elf archers were returning fire, with the terrible poisoned arrows that the Elves had learned to fear.

In the rear of the vanguard, Menerchel blew the Call to Battle, loudly enough to wake the forest itself.

Leaf and Star, guard and guide us this day! Petariel thought. Their ambush having failed, the enemy revealed themselves plainly now: not the two-score refugees from the battle that Kellen had warned them of—hundreds of Shadowed Elves swarmed through the trees and over the forest floor. They attacked where the army was weakest: Ysterialpoerin.

And Gesade had been right. Now he smelled it too.

The forest was burning.

⌐

ALMOST before Dionan had finished speaking, Ancaladar took to the air. The oncoming storm made the air currents turbulent and hard to predict; higher altitude would have made flight easier, but to seek greater height was the one thing they could not do. He and Jermayan must find the vanished Shadowed Elf females that Kellen had warned them of, and to do that they must fly low enough to see the ground.

Ancaladar saw nothing moving below, save for Redhelwar and his troops making their way back toward the main camp. He swept past the camp, in a long curve—east, then north. The ground was harder to see here—there were fewer patches of open land, and more forest—but Ancaladar had hunted his own food for over a millennium. He was an expert tracker, and his eyes were sharp. He studied the ground closely, searching for signs of their prey.

"Ancaladar—look."

His Bonded's voice was tight with fear.

Ancaladar raised his eyes to the horizon.

In the distance, near the Elven city—smoke.

Fire.

⌒

THERE was no thought of containment, no possibility of a careful battle plan. Even being near these creatures was utterly painful to the unicorns—a disastrous miscalculation that their enemy was quick to capitalize upon.

The Unicorn Knights fought on foot at Petariel's command. They'd ordered their mounts to run, but the unicorns couldn't—or wouldn't—leave their partners.

The cavalry units fought on foot as well, for they had all learned quickly that a mounted warrior was at a disadvantage against this foe. Even Kindolhinadetil's Guard had come at the sound of the warhorns to lend its strength to the fight.

The Shadowed Elves died—but taking far too many of the Elves with them.

And the forest was burning.

NOW Jermayan saw tracks where no tracks should be—looking down through the trees, he could see places where the snow had been trampled by the passing of hundreds of feet.

And ahead, curls of smoke rising from Ysterialpoern's forest in a score of places. Smoldering still, but about to burst into true flame. And when they did . . .

The fire would take The Heart of the Forest with it.

Once before, Kellen had stopped the Shadowed Elves from bringing disks of ever-burning metal to the trees. This time they must have succeeded. He could call those pieces of metal forth from their hiding places, but it would take time—time to find them, time to bespell them—and meanwhile the forest would catch, and kindle . . .

And his comrades would die, while he spent himself on this, instead of coming to their aid.

"You know how to stop this," Ancaladar said quietly. "The snow is near. Bring it now."

Yes. Jermayan took a deep breath as Ancaladar made a wide sweep around the heart-forest. He forced himself to set aside his fury and uncertainty to become an untroubled vessel of magic. The snow would keep the fires from spreading, buy him time to come to the aid of the army.

He could feel the patterns of the weather through Ancaladar's senses. Now he reached out with his magic to the coming storm, bringing what would have been here by tomorrow's dawn *immediately.*

The sky darkened. Wind lashed the trees below, forced into the valley by storm clouds wrenched from their proper places. The air currents boiled like an icy broth, and Ancaladar battled to stay skyborne.

The blizzard came, as inexorable and deadly as a breaking wave. An updraft sucked dragon and rider suddenly high into the clouds; instantly Jermayan was blinded by wet icy mist; deafened by the crash of air colliding with air as solidly and loudly as boulders in a flood-tossed streambed. Jermayan felt his skin begin to prickle, and barely threw a shield around both of them in time. Lightning chained across the sky, striking against his shields again and again, as if the weather itself were angry about its mishandling.

It was needed, Jermayan thought, as he and Ancaladar were hurled across the clouds. *Forgive me.*

Ancaladar fought for altitude, his wings straining in their sockets, and after a desperate battle they were above the storm, soaring through calm winds and sunlight as sheets of ice crackled and fell from the dragon's great wings. Jermayan looked down at the roiling cauldron of black snow-heavy clouds that filled the Ysterialpoerin valley. It was snowing now, a blizzard that would not spend itself easily or quickly. And though snow would not quench the Shadowed Elves' burning metal, nothing else would burn. The damage to the forest would not spread.

"Not an elegant execution," Ancaladar said at last, sounding both amused and breathless. "But effective. Are you well, Bonded?"

"I shall be better when the enemy is vanquished," Jermayan said. "Though I wish it did not have to be. Are you ready to return?"

"I shall be quick," Ancaladar said. The great black dragon folded his wings and dove through the storm, falling to earth as swiftly as if he were a thunderbolt himself.

AT last the bitter work beneath the ground was done. Not without casualties—for even the Shadowed Elf young fought with desperate intensity—but it was done. All were dead, even the infants—and that, the Elves could tell themselves, was an act of mercy, for the youngest had obviously gone untended by their siblings.

They settled the bodies neatly, but left them behind to recover later, for Adaerion was uneasy about what might be happening above.

Kellen had led the host going in. This time he was last out, for the caverns were not yet safe, even if no Shadowed Elves or goblins remained here. There were still the *duergar* to hunt down; Adaerion could be certain Kellen could resist their lure, and could protect the others from giving in to it.

Figuring out how to hunt them down—so the caverns could be finally cleared—was a problem for another day.

And even when we clear this place out, who knows how many more lairs remain? Kellen thought wearily. *And this isn't even the war. This is just another of Shadow Mountain's strategies to weaken us BEFORE the war.*

He had never felt so close to despair.

⟶

BY the time he reached the surface, Kellen already knew—from talk passed back up the line—that the promised blizzard had come early—magically early. No one knew why, but everyone was agreed that the Wildmages would not have called it.

Fresher information came the closer Kellen got to the surface, but it was frustratingly incomplete. A battle at Ysterialpoerin. Their own orders remained the same: stay here and clear the caverns.

At last he reached the end-tunnel, and almost wished he hadn't.

Snow was blown along half its length. He could see nothing beyond the entrance but dim whiteness. Each pair of Knights who walked out through the entrance was visible for only a few seconds before vanishing into the dense all-concealing snow. Their heavy cloaks whipped around them as if they were made of thin silk.

Kellen hurried forward, all but shoving Isinwen ahead of him. They must have won at Ysterialpoerin. Redhelwar would surely have been able to get the reserves from the camp to the city in time to support them.

He was grateful that Jermayan had taken the time to re-shape the ramp out of the caves. The wind was fierce, and the snow that covered it had been packed down to ice by the feet of those before him. If it had been any steeper, it would have been a slide, not a pathway.

He looked for Adaerion, but it was Jermayan who came toward him out of the snow.

"Shalkan is asking for you. Come quickly."

"Shalkan?" *Shalkan was at Ysterialpoerin!*

"He is unhurt. But . . . hurry."

⌒

JERMAYAN had brought the storm. Kellen gathered that much from the Elven Knight's half-distracted explanation on the flight to Ysterialpoerin. That, and that the Elves had won the battle.

"I thought for the forest, and the city. It did not matter to the Shadowed Elves or to their masters if they all died, so long as they accomplished their task of destruction, and so I looked first to the trees. Snow would slow the burning, and its cause could be looked to later. So that is a great victory." Jermayan's voice was bitter, carried back to Kellen as they flew through the clear air and sunlight above the storm. "When poets unborn sing of this day in centuries to come, surely they will say that we won."

"Jermayan—" Kellen began. If he couldn't get some straight answers out of Jermayan soon, he was fairly sure he was going to start shouting.

"Not now," Ancaladar said.

The dragon tilted his wings, diving back into the storm, and speech became impossible in the maelstrom of their descent.

Kellen was working the saddle-straps before Ancaladar had quite settled. The dragon had landed in a clearing barely big enough to accommodate him—a neat piece of flying

with the winds as strong as they were. Kellen slid down the
dragon's ice-covered ribs into a drift of snow.

"Shalkan!" he shouted.

"That way." Ancaladar extended his neck in the direction
Kellen needed to go. "Hurry."

Kellen ran.

⌒

HE came upon it all at once, a scene so hideous that at first
his mind refused to admit what it saw, and then when he realized what he was seeing, Kellen staggered back against a
tree, bile rising in his throat.

Dead unicorns.

There were . . . too many to count. They had been laid in
the snow in rows, neatly, as the Elves set their own dead,
fresh-removed from the battlefield. Their bodies were rapidly being covered by the falling snow, covering the hideous
wounds, the shattered horns.

Dead, they looked so *small* . . .

"Kellen. Come."

Shalkan appeared in front of him, blocking his view of
the dead and rousing him from his horrified daze. The unicorn was glowing, just as he had on the night Kellen had
first seen him.

Kellen reached out his gauntlet blindly and closed it over
Shalkan's mane, letting the unicorn lead him away.

"Shadowed Elves did this," Kellen said a few moments
later. It wasn't a question.

"The females from the caverns attacked, led by the males
that escaped Athan's call. The females had all borne young.
It made things difficult. Now." Shalkan stopped and looked
at Kellen.

"Many of us are hurt. I am taking you to where the Healers are caring for us—but as you know, only a particular sort
of Healer can be of use to us."

"A virgin," Kellen said. "A *chaste* virgin."

"Fortunately there are a few of those around," Shalkan said, with a ghost of his usual dry humor. "So you will see blood and wounds in plenty, but nothing the Healers cannot handle. And the Knights may go to the Wildmages, of course—as soon as the rest of them manage to here. I don't say the blizzard wasn't necessary. But it causes problems."

The Knights can go to the Wildmages. But the unicorns can't. Because—

"I can't be—" Kellen began, embarrassed and outraged.

"You are," Shalkan said inexorably. "The only Wildmage who can touch us. You have seen a unicorn healed. If you can heal Gesade, she will live."

Gesade!

"Idalia—Jermayan—" Kellen said desperately.

"Cannot approach her. It would kill her," Shalkan said. "She is very badly hurt. You are her only hope."

I can't do this! "I need tools," Kellen said, shutting away his fear. "And someone to share the price."

"Both are waiting," Shalkan said. He hesitated for a moment. "There's something else you probably need to know. Petariel is dead."

Kellen took a deep breath. He'd shared his morning meal with Petariel. They'd joked together about Petariel going off to a dull day of guarding something nobody was going to attack. And now he would never speak to Petariel again. He knew, somewhere in the back of his mind, that eventually he would weep. Now, though, all he could feel was a terrible emptiness.

Though it was not as terrible as the emptiness that would move within Gesade.

Shalkan began to move forward once more, as quickly as the deep snow would allow.

"Does she know?" Kellen asked.

"We aren't sure," Shalkan said.

A few moments later they arrived at the clearing where the wounded unicorns were being tended. It had been hastily enclosed with awnings of heavy silk canvas hung between the trees and overhead, and the ground was covered with sleeping mats, cloaks, and even carpets. Several heavy braziers heated the air.

Kellen and Shalkan stepped inside. Here the air was moist, and filled with smells, some familiar to Kellen, some not. The cinnamon scent of unicorns. The oddly-sweet scent of Elven blood. The rank scent of Shadowed Elf blood, and—faintly—the acrid scent of the poison they used on their weapons. The cloying smell of burn ointment, and the flowery scent of Night's Daughter, the herb that Jermayan had used so liberally on Kellen's burns to numb the pain. He could never smell it without remembering that long torturous journey back from the Black Cairn, and ever since then, the scent recalled unpleasant memories.

He knew everyone here, but he didn't dare stop, didn't dare let himself *see* any of them. Not now. He had to think of only one thing right now.

Gesade.

She was at the far end of the tent, lying on her side. The overpowering reek of Night's Daughter nearly made him gag; she smelled as if they'd bathed her in it. Her fore and hind legs were tied together. Trigwenior and Ansansoniel knelt before her, holding them gently, and Menerchel sat on her shoulders. Even though she had been heavily dosed with a sleeping cordial—Kellen could smell it from where he stood—she was thrashing weakly, trying to get to her feet. The three of them spoke to her soothingly, trying to calm her, but she was beyond hearing.

Her entire head and most of her neck were completely swathed in salve-soaked cloths. There was an airhole at the end through which he could hear her whistling gasps for breath, her agonized whimperings, but they sounded . . . wrong.

Menerchel looked up as Kellen approached. His face was streaked with tears. He said nothing. There was nothing to say.

Kellen moved behind him, kneeling at Gesade's back, as

close to her as he could get. He pulled off his helmet and gloves. What he needed was already laid out.

"Hush, Gesade, hush," he said, speaking to her as if she were Deyishene, or Lily. "It's Kellen. I've come to help. Just lie quietly, if you can. I'll help you, I promise."

He didn't know if she heard.

He cut a few strands of his hair, and a few from the base of Gesade's mane, below the ointment-soaked cloths. Then he reached for the bandage at her neck. Already others— Elven Knights, unicorns, even one or two of the Healers— were gathering around to share the price, just as Shalkan had promised.

But Shalkan was nowhere in sight.

"No—don't," Menerchel begged, seeing what Kellen was doing.

"I need her blood for the spell," Kellen said gently. "And I need to know how she's hurt."

"Acid," Menerchel said starkly. "They threw acid in her face."

Kellen closed his eyes for an instant, fighting back the images Menerchel's words evoked. Acid was a favored weapon of the Shadowed Elves. He'd seen the wounds they caused. Armor was no defense—acid ate metal, slipped through every crack.

And the unicorns went into battle only lightly armored.

Kellen peeled back the edge of the bandage, exposing raw burned flesh slick with numbing ointment. Gritting his teeth, he wiped a small patch of skin clear. Blood beaded to the surface. He soaked the hairs—his and hers together—then quickly replaced the bandages.

He picked up the knife—a small Healer's knife, wickedly sharp—to cut himself, then realized he'd almost forgotten to ask the vital question. No Wildmage could ever assume that help would be offered. It must always be asked for.

"Who will share the price of this healing with me?"

"We will—all of us," Menerchel said.

Kellen looked up at those waiting, making sure that all

agreed. Then he cut his hand, mingling his blood with
Gesade's.

Quickly now, he summoned the brazier alight, and added
the proper leaves: willow, ash, yew. A thin coil of blue
smoke began to spiral upward.

Leaf and Star, let this work!

He motioned for Menerchel and the others to move
back—Gesade's struggles were weaker now—and gently
dropped the knot of bloody hairs onto the coals. Then he laid
his hands on Gesade's exposed neck and shoulder.

She quieted at last beneath his touch, and for a terrible instant Kellen thought she was dead, until he saw the slow
steady rise of her ribs. The peace that filled her gave him a
moment of calm as well; when he saw the shimmering dome
of protection form around them all, he felt a spark of hope.
The Gods of the Wild Magic had heard.

"Forgive. Forgive and forget."

The words filled his mind, and Kellen knew that this was
the price They set upon Gesade's healing—and that it was
twice now that the Wild Magic had commanded him to forgive. His previous Mageprice was still unpaid, but that
wouldn't matter. Idalia had told him that prices could run
unpaid for years; all that mattered was that you paid them
willingly when the time came. He did know that you knew
when the time had come to pay a Mageprice, although figuring out *how* to pay it was left up to the individual. But none
of that was important now. He would have accepted the price
if it had been far higher. *I will,* he promised.

The sense of *listening* departed. All that was left was the
work of healing.

It was the hardest yet, as if he tried to lift the weight of the
earth itself from beneath his feet. Again and again he struggled to become a conduit for the Healing Magic, feeling as if
he tried to touch something just out of reach.

And every moment he struggled, he felt Gesade growing
weaker.

"Don't try. Be."

Master Belesharon said that in the practice circle. Only when you could step aside from your thoughts of what you should be doing, and do the thing itself, was the thing accomplished.

He stopped *trying*.

He thought of Gesade, whole.

He remembered her looking down at him in the snow, the night he'd tried to escape from camp to scout the nearer cavern.

He remembered her—yes, and Petariel—running at the head of the Unicorn Knights on a day that was bright and clear. Powdery snow had sprayed up from beneath her hooves as she ran, and the sunlight had sparkled off their armor . . .

He realized he was lying curled around her body, his face pressed against her stomach, breathing in her warm scent. It was an awkward position, and Kellen straightened with a stifled groan. He didn't remember moving, or closing his eyes.

He blinked. He felt as if he'd been asleep, though he was sure he hadn't. The protective shield was gone, so whatever was going to happen, had happened. He felt hollow and light-headed, but that was normal after a healing, for Healer and Healed alike.

"You . . . glowed," Menerchel said.

That was encouraging, Kellen decided, but he was still reluctant to lift the bandages and see what lay beneath. At least Gesade was sleeping now, not writhing in heavily-drugged agony.

He lifted the lower edge of the bandage again.

White fur. Thickly soaked in ointment, but there was no trace of burn or scar. Eagerly now, Kellen lifted away the rest of the cloths—they had not truly bandaged her, only wrapped soft cloths loosely over the terrible burns. The flesh beneath was perfect. Whole.

Then he reached her head.

It took him a few seconds to understand why what he was seeing looked so wrong. Her horn was unblemished. Her soft muzzle was whole.

But her eyelid was sunken into its socket. Frantically, Kellen lifted her head. The other side matched exactly, the eyelid sunken over an empty socket.

She had no eyes.

SHALKAN found him several hundred yards from the unicorn's clearing. He was kneeling beside a tree, gagging up what felt like every meal he'd ever eaten in his life.

"Kellen—"

"Go away!" He couldn't bear to see anyone right now. Especially Shalkan. Not after what he'd done.

"Kellen—"

"I *hurt* her! I blinded her!"

How could a healing have gone so wrong? Was it because he'd come here straight from the caverns? What had he done to her? It was all his fault—

"I saw her before the Healers got to her." Shalkan's voice came to him, harsh and rasping, as if the unicorn had been weeping until his throat was raw. "You didn't. She was already blind. Shall I tell you what a bucket of acid in the face does to a person—or a unicorn? I could describe it in great detail, if you'd like." Shalkan's words were cruel, but they penetrated Kellen's own grief and horror.

"Stop it," Kellen said wearily. "I already know. I've seen it too." He sat back, scrubbing his face with snow. "But . . . I healed her. Or I could have. If I'd been good enough." And that was what was so horrible. He hadn't been good enough, not nearly good enough, and he had been her only hope.

"No." An Elven Healer Kellen didn't know came and knelt in the snow beside him. "I am no Wildmage, but I have aided them in their healings, and I have heard them speak among themselves. The power of the Wild Magic to heal is indeed great, but it cannot create that which is not there. That which will—or might—grow with time will grow at a Wildmage's touch. But that which is lost is lost forever." The

Healer took his shoulder in one hand and shook it. "Look at me, Kellen Knight-Mage. See the truth in me!"

Kellen studied the Healer's face. She regarded him with grave compassion and faint puzzlement, as if she had never seen anything like him before. Kellen knew without having to ask that she was from Ysterialpoerin.

She's right. The storm of rage and grief—and guilt—that had filled him a moment before was gone, leaving only aching numbness.

It isn't fair! he thought wearily. Would Gesade want to live without sight?

But that's her decision to make, isn't it? Today you've given her the power to make her own choices again.

"Now, if you'll accept the Lady Arquelle's word that you did all you could do, perhaps you'll be sensible, come inside, and rest," Shalkan said crossly, his voice still sounding hoarse. "Or perhaps you'd like to give the Healers even more to do?"

"No," Kellen said, getting stiffly to his feet. His bare hands were numb and aching with cold. "I'm coming."

He felt battered, both physically and emotionally, and he wasn't quite sure whether Shalkan was really angry with him, or simply knew that the last thing Kellen could take right now was his sympathy.

"No one rejoices to see the Star-begotten in pain," Arquelle said softly as Kellen walked back through the snow. "It has overset stronger hearts than yours, Kellen Knight-Mage."

And that, perhaps, was the truest thing he had heard in a day of terrible truths.

CILARNEN, Wirance, and the small party of Centaurs traveled west and north. As Luermai had promised, each time their supplies began to dwindle, Nemermet led them to a fresh cache—tea, salt, charcoal, grain, honey, spices, and the blocks of compressed rations that Nemermet simply called journey-food.

It never seemed to stop snowing.

He ought to be used to it by now, Cilarnen told himself. He'd never seen snow actually *falling* before this winter— the little snow allowed to alight within the City walls came at night, and certainly wasn't allowed to fall where it would inconvenience anyone—but this journey seemed determined to repair the lack of every day of those eighteen winters.

Snow, in addition to being cold, painful, inconvenient, and sometimes actively dangerous, Cilarnen decided, was boring. But there was nothing else to look at. There was Snow With Trees, and Snow Without Trees. There were cloudy days when it snowed, and (fewer) cloudy days when it didn't snow, and (very infrequently) clear days when you had a dazzling vista of . . . snow.

Kardus, who was the only one of them who had traveled in Elven Lands before, said that the snow was unusually heavy this year. Nemermet had no comment to make on this—but then, as Cilarnen had quickly discovered, their guide apparently had no desire to engage in conversation with them at all. His only interest seemed to be to hurry them along as quickly as possible, pushing them to the limits of their endurance every day.

After the first sennight, it became obvious that Tinsin was slowing the party's pace. The draft mare obeyed Cilarnen's orders willingly, but no amount of willingness could make her as fast as a mule or a Centaur—let alone as fast as Nemermet's ice-grey stallion. She was meant for plowing fields and pulling wagons, not gallivanting cross-country.

The next time they stopped at one of the trail huts for supplies, there was a mule waiting there.

The mule was obviously of Elven breeding; it looked very much like the one Hyandur had loaned him. It was a russet color, with a cream mane, belly, and tail-tuft, and quite elegant . . . for a mule.

"In the morning, you will take Oakleaf," Nemermet said as he unsaddled his mount, speaking directly to Cilarnen for the first time. "Leave Tinsin here."

"No," Cilarnen said, surprising himself. "I'm responsible for her. I won't abandon her. What will she eat?" A hundred dangers ran through his mind. "What if there are wolves? Or bears? Or—something?" he ended, lamely.

Nemermet regarded him expressionlessly. "She will be cared for." His task finished, he began to turn away.

"That isn't good enough," Cilarnen said. All his anger and frustration at days of following orders he didn't quite understand came boiling to the surface, but he did his best to keep his voice low and even. "Sarlin of Stonehearth gave Tinsin to me. I promised I'd bring her back safe. Everyone says we're not supposed to ask you questions. If you don't want me to ask you questions, then give me answers."

For a moment, he didn't think Nemermet would answer him. Then the Elf seemed to reach a decision.

"Tomorrow, when we are gone, a rider will come. He will take her to winter with our own stock, cared for as if she were our own. In the spring, we will see her to Stonehearth if you cannot."

Nemermet turned away, indicating the conversation was finished.

"I will say this for you, boy—you've got more courage than sense," Comild said, coming up to him.

Cilarnen leaned his head against Tinsin's shoulder. "I just don't like being pushed around." *Elves, or—or High Mages. I don't like being pushed around.*

Had he really hated life in Armethalieh that much?

No. He'd loved living there, and the thought that he could never go back hurt so much that he didn't dare think about it.

But . . .

Mageborn keeping secrets—saying things were "for the good of the City" when that was a lie—plotting against the City and moving other Mageborn around as if they had no more worth than pieces on a *shamat*-board . . . no, Cilarnen didn't like that at all.

If they will do that to their fellow Mageborn, they will do that to anyone. Citizens. The Delfier Valley farmers. The

Mountain Traders. The Selkens. The Wildlanders—like Sarlin and Comild and Kardus.

And he wasn't sure anyone could stop them. Not if what the Demon had told him at Stonehearth was true.

He sighed, and began the awkward business of removing Tinsin's saddle and bridle.

———

ONCE Cilarnen had been remounted, their journey went faster, and in another sennight they began to see faint signs that another—much larger—party was traveling in the same direction. Now Nemermet's insistent haste began to make sense: Luermai had said that "others preceded them," and Nemermet was obviously trying to catch up with the other party.

By now they were well into the mountains—Kardus said that beyond this lay high plains, but further than that into the Elven Lands he had not been. Though Cilarnen missed Tinsin—and despite Kardus's assurances, wasn't entirely certain he trusted Nemermet's word that she'd be cared for and returned to Stonehearth—he had to admit that Oakleaf was much easier and more comfortable to ride. And the Elven-bred mule was certainly better-suited to the terrain they had to cross.

In the middle of their third sennight of travel, they finally caught sight of the other Centaurs. They'd crossed the last of the mountain passes and were starting down into the valley.

"Look!" Comild said, pointing.

Cilarnen peered through the falling snow. Dimly, he could make out a blot of darkness in the distance, moving slowly over the plain below.

"There are your fellows," Nemermet said. "You will join them tomorrow, if we hurry now."

———

THEY lost sight of the Centaur army when they reached the plain—the rest of the levies would have crossed the Elven border together, Cilarnen realized; Comild's people had been delayed by the Demon attack upon Stonehearth—but they were only half a day behind them now, and the wide deep track the others had made with their passage made travel for Comild's party both easy and fast. They pressed on that day until well beyond their usual stopping time, until Wirance finally called a halt.

"It's as dark as the inside of a goat's stomach now," the Wildmage said bluntly, "and I'm not minded to spend tomorrow healing the fool that lames himself on the ice tonight. We'll stop here. You may be able to see in the dark, my Elven friend, but we can't and neither can these poor mules."

Reluctantly, the others agreed.

There were no sheltering trees on the High Plains, but by now all of them carried pieces of heavy canvas designed to be joined together by collapsible hollow tubes—a gift of the Elves, left for them at one of the trail huts many days ago. Each piece alone could serve as a windbreak. When they were all joined together, they formed a shelter large enough for humans and Centaurs both to take refuge together from the worst of the storms.

Assembling it was a tricky matter, however, and something they'd never done in the dark.

Cilarnen hadn't worked any High Magick since Nemermet had joined them—even so simple a thing as lighting a fire. He wasn't sure why; he didn't *think* Nemermet would try to throw him out of the Elven Lands just for being a High Mage. But there was no longer any point in wondering. They needed light. And Mage-light was a simple spell, one that every Student-Apprentice knew.

He concentrated. The ball of blue light grew between his hands. When it was as large as he wanted, he spread his hands. It hovered above them, a small full moon.

"You're full of tricks," Wirance said approvingly. He swung down from his mule's back and began to unpack his piece of the shelter. Cilarnen dismounted as well. The

sooner the shelter was assembled, the sooner they could begin to get warm. He thought longingly of tea—though the
hot water Nemermet called "tea" was a poor substitute for
the real thing.

"You did not name yourself a Wildmage when you stood
upon the Border." If Nemermet's voice held any expression
at all, Cilarnen would have said it sounded faintly accusing.
But of course it didn't. He wasn't entirely sure Elves *had*
emotions.

"I'm not a Wildmage," Cilarnen said, struggling to match
Nemermet's even tone. "I'm a Mage of Armethalieh."

"Armethalieh!" Now there *was* emotion in Nemermet's
voice.

Surprise . . . and contempt.

Kardus stepped forward, placing his body between Cilarnen and Nemermet.

"He was Banished, as was Kellen Wildmage," the Centaur
said, and there was warning in his tone. "He has lived for a
season among the Centaurs of Stonehearth, and fought
valiantly in their defense. And it is my Task to bring him to
Kellen Wildmage."

"Then do so," Nemermet said briefly, his tone gone flat,
and turned to help the others erect the shelter.

In the glow of the Mage-light, Cilarnen stared at Kardus
in shock.

Hyandur had known he was from Armethalieh, and had
helped him escape. The Centaurs had known where he came
from—and they'd pitied him for it, he now realized ruefully.

He hadn't expected *this* reaction.

"Armethalieh, too, had a treaty with the Elves," Kardus
said quietly. "But they have not honored it."

"To *help* the Elves?" Cilarnen wasn't quite certain he'd
heard the Centaur Wildmage correctly. "Like the Centaurs? To
send . . . troops?" Even after all that had happened to him in
the last few moonturns, Cilarnen found that an impossible
concept to quite imagine. High Mages—and citizens—*leave*
the City?

"Yes. But they would not even allow Andoreniel's envoy to warn them."

A dozen disparate pieces of information came together in his mind, all in a rush. "Hyandur. He was the one who came to warn the High Council, wasn't he? They didn't let him in." He paused, and added, wonderingly, "He saved my life."

When the City denied him—he still saved my life!

"And so you see that the Elves can be kind. Remember that."

There were times when Kardus sounded *just* like his old tutor Master Tocsel, Cilarnen thought ruefully, though certainly Master Tocsel would never have had a good word to say about the Elvenkind.

He turned to help assemble the shelter.

Twenty-three

Journey's End

Much later, crowded in among the Centaurs—cramped but warm—Cilarnen found himself lying awake. His mind was filled with questions, but of them all, only one was really important.

If Elves were like humans, or Centaurs, with individual likes and dislikes, well and good. But if Armethalieh actually *had* somehow had a treaty with the Elven King, and had broken it, how likely was it that the Elves would help Armethalieh now?

And if Kellen Tavadon was living among the Elves, which side would he take? Human—or Elven?

AS Nemermet had promised, they caught up to the main body of the Centaurs the next day.

A few hours after they broke camp that morning, another Elf—this one on a bay mare wearing beautifully fitted armor enameled in a rosy hue several shades lighter than her coat—came galloping back to them.

"I See you, Nemermet," the mare's rider said.

He was wearing armor as well, though it hardly looked to Cilarnen as if it would be of any use in a battle. It matched the mare's exactly, and like the mare's looked more like jewelry than armor.

"I See you, Linyesin," Nemermet said, bowing slightly. "Here are the stragglers from Stonehearth: Comild and his levy, and the Wildmage Wirance who accompanies them. I also present to you the Centaur Wildmage Kardus, whose Mageprice is to bring the Banished High Mage Cilarnen before Kellen Knight-Mage."

Linyesin lifted a horn from his saddle and blew a few notes. After a moment, Cilarnen heard an answering echo of that horn-call in the distance.

"Andoreniel thanks you for your care of them, and asks that you aid the others in helping the Herdingfolk across our eastern border safely," Linyesin said.

"I go with pleasure," Nemermet said. Without a word to the others, he turned his stallion around and headed back the way he'd come.

"Come," Linyesin said to them. "Your comrades await you. We are grateful for your strength, and are eager to hear your news."

"Not much to tell," Comild said gruffly, as they followed Linyesin toward the other Centaurs. "One of *Them* came down on us at Stonehearth. Our losses were heavy—ours and the villagers both. But the Wildmages killed it—them and Cilarnen."

There was a pause, but though Cilarnen was expecting a sudden barrage of questions from Linyesin, it didn't come.

"That is welcome and interesting information," the armored Elf said at last. "It nearly outweighs the discouraging news that one of *Them* has been seen east of the Elven Lands. That is puzzling news indeed. But perhaps you will have told Luermai or Nemermet more of your tale than you have told me."

"No," Wirance said simply. "As for why it came, we are not sure."

Cilarnen hesitated. He didn't want to deliver the whole of the message he had for Kellen to this stranger—only Kardus and Wirance knew that the Demon had spoken to him, or what it had said—especially considering how the Elves seemed to feel about Armethalieh. But it couldn't hurt to fill in a few of the details.

"It saw me," he put in, hoping he didn't sound as ineffectual as he felt. "I don't know why it was there, either, but at first it thought I was Kellen Tavadon. It looked like a human, and it spoke to me, telling me I couldn't go back to—to Armethalieh. When it realized I wasn't him, it attacked me. I fended it off, and it decided to destroy the village first before coming back to kill me."

He stopped, wondering if he'd said the wrong thing. Linyesin was staring at him intently.

"It would be good to know—and it would please me greatly," the Elf said, "if you would say further how you fended off the attack of one of *Them* and survived."

"It was Mageshield," Cilarnen said. Thinking back, he wasn't sure his shield had been all that effective. It was more as if the Demon, seeing he was a Mage, had simply decided to kill him last.

"It must have meant to take you captive when it discovered that you were a Mage," Linyesin said, echoing Cilarnen's thoughts. "Or to take a very long time over your death. Fortunate indeed that matters occurred otherwise."

Cilarnen shivered. From all he'd seen at Stonehearth, "fortunate" was an understatement.

By now they were within sight of the Centaurs. There were a couple of hundred of them, and with them were more

Mountainfolk and several more Elves, all in armor. Each suit of armor was a different color; they looked like a handful of spring flowers somehow transported to the midst of winter.

And there were supply carts, like the one Cilarnen had seen just inside the Elven border, but these were much larger, drawn by six draft mules instead of by a pair of horses. He wondered how they'd gotten them over the passes.

Comild gave a grunt of satisfaction at the sight of the carts. "Decent meals at last."

Linyesin laughed. Cilarnen would hardly have been less surprised if the Elf had dismounted from his mare and turned cartwheels in the snow. "Oh, yes, Comild, 'proper food.' Nemermet brought you to join us as fast as he could, and the food the scouts travel on can be less-than-satisfying, but we don't mean to starve you before we reach Ysterialpoerin."

⌒

HE would hardly have called it "luxury" a moonturn before, but fresh meat, pancakes, hot cider, and a warm place to sleep—even if it was a tent he shared with three of the Mountainfolk—made Cilarnen feel more confident than he had since he'd left Stonehearth. The Centaurs had been eager to exchange news as they marched, and apparently their new guides—Elven Knights—were freer with information than any of the Elves Comild's party had dealt with up till now. In the few hours Cilarnen had ridden with the army, he and Kardus had learned more about what was going on than they had in all their time riding with Nemermet.

All Nemermet had told them was that their eventual destination was a place called Ysterialpoerin. Now they knew that, weather permitting, they would reach it in two sennights. Three at the most—assuming nothing attacked them along the way.

And attack was possible at any moment, though so far they'd been lucky—another reason Nemermet had hurried them along so swiftly. The Elven Lands were already under assault. Not by the Demons directly—apparently they couldn't come here—but it seemed that they had found a way to slip their creatures past the land-wards. The Centaurs had been warned to be on the watch for a kind of wolf the size of a pony, bats as large as small ships, and (apparently worst of all) things called "Shadowed Elves," which had to be destroyed at all costs. Though nobody said anything directly, Cilarnen got the impression that the Demons meant to destroy the Elves and the Elven Lands first.

These Demons—nobody called them anything but *Them*—were nothing like the Armethaliehan nursery-tales he'd been terrified by as a child. He managed to figure that out, though nobody wanted to talk about them much. Cilarnen doubted that the Centaurs he'd talked to knew much more than they'd said; and he wasn't quite ready to try questioning any of the Elves.

He suspected that Kardus knew more, but the Centaur Wildmage would not answer any of his questions. "This is neither the time nor the place," was all Kardus would say. "Wait for better."

Remembering the sight of the Demon at Stonehearth, Cilarnen reluctantly decided to take his advice.

THEY were two days away from Ysterialpoerin when the blizzard struck.

The Wildmages traveling with the army had been warning of truly bad weather to come—in a day, perhaps two. Cilarnen knew that Linyesin was hoping that they would at least reach the edge of the forest before it began, so that they would have some shelter and protection from the storm. The Centaurs had rejoiced when the Wildmages told them that weather magic had been done by the Wildmages with the Elven army, pushing back the storm and giving them an extra day's grace.

But then the storm struck without warning, and far too early.

It was an hour or two past noon. Cilarnen was riding beside Kardus near the supply carts when suddenly he heard the horns begin to blow.

"What is it? Are we being attacked?" he demanded in alarm.

"No," Kardus said, puzzled. "It's the signal to make camp."

Suddenly the temperature dropped sharply, and the sky turned black.

Cilarnen looked up, alarmed.

The sky was . . . *boiling*.

There was no other way to describe it. He heard a rumble, and a sudden crash of thunder, and saw lightning flash across the sky.

A wall of wind—fierce enough to make Kardus stagger—came howling down out of the north. Oakleaf began to sidle and balk as thunder boomed again and heavy wet flakes of snow began to sheet down out of the now-black sky.

Belatedly, Cilarnen realized what the horns had meant. The promised blizzard had come *now*. And if they all didn't get under cover they were going to freeze.

He swung down off Oakleaf's back. The mule fussed and balked, but Cilarnen managed to lead him over to the wagon and tie him fast.

—

THEY formed the supply carts into a windbreak, and fought to get the shelters up, for without shelter they would freeze, and quickly. But it was useless. The wind was too strong.

It was the Mountainfolk who realized what must be done to save them. They emptied the supply carts, flinging the contents haphazardly into the snow as the Elves struggled to unhitch the mules so that they could be brought to shelter. So great was the force of the wind that the wagons' contents blew everywhere. Already snow was mounded against the windward side of the wagons, and no one could see more than a few feet in any direction.

Every coil of rope they found, the Mountainfolk passed to the Centaurs, who used it to link themselves together, so that none would be lost in the blinding snow.

Cilarnen found himself unceremoniously lifted—he didn't see by whom—and tossed into one of the now-empty carts. He landed hard, and immediately tried to scramble back out again.

"Stop that, boy. Do you want to freeze? I've never seen a storm come up this fast—not even a Called one," an unfamiliar voice said out of the darkness. It was one of the Mountainfolk. Others crowded in quickly, and then pulled the tarp closed over the end of the wagon.

"But, Kardus—" Cilarnen said. The wagon shuddered with the force of the wind.

"Your Centaur-friend is warm and safe in the middle of the herd," the stranger said. "Which is more than you or I would be out there just now; they're hardy folk. Have patience. The worst of this should blow itself out in a day or two and we can be on our way. And then, I admit, I'd like to have a word or two with whoever Called this blizzard."

"Called?" Cilarnen said blankly.

"Of course," the stranger said calmly. "You don't think this came naturally, do you? This weather was supposed to come tomorrow, or the day after—and not a storm this hard, either. A Wildmage called this up, and I'd like to know why."

As the wind howled around them, and Cilarnen buried his head under the shelter of his cold arms, he decided that he wanted to know why, too.

Very badly indeed . . .

"I need to get back," Kellen mumbled aloud. He was exhausted from the healing but he thought he might as well rest back at the cavern as here. Where he was supposed to be right now anyway.

"You're exhausted," Shalkan told him, not unkindly, as Kellen sat at the front of the unicorn's tent, wrapped in blankets and drinking a cup of soup someone had brought him. "You're not thinking clearly. If you insist on going tonight, wait for Ancaladar to get back. A horse won't be able to make it even as far as the main camp in this weather—and don't make eyes at me. Even if I were willing to take you—and I'm needed here—you'd freeze by the time I could get you there."

He knew Shalkan was right—the snow was coming down even heavier than before, if that was possible, and in full darkness, even a unicorn might get lost. And getting back to the cavern camp wasn't really an emergency.

"Why is it snowing?" Kellen finally thought to ask. "The weather wasn't supposed to turn so soon."

"The Shadowed Elves tried to burn the forest. Jermayan is pretty sure they used the ever-burning metal you stopped them from using before. He had to bring the storm to stop the fires from spreading. Kindolhinadetil's foresters are out looking for the pieces now. Perhaps they will be able to save the individual trees that were set afire. But whether they can or not, the forest itself is safe."

"I should go and help," Kellen said groggily, trying to get to his feet.

"You should stay where you are, and drink your soup," Shalkan said firmly, lowering his horn meaningfully. "I will wake you when Ancaladar returns."

Kellen had no intention of falling asleep—especially here. Not when there was so much to do. But Shalkan was right. He needed a little more strength, and he could get that from the soup. It wouldn't hurt anything or anyone just to sit there until he finished it.

SHALKAN woke him a few hours later. "Come on," he said, prodding Kellen with his horn; it was the prod of the horn, rather than Shalkan's voice, that stirred him out of an unrestful sleep.

Kellen was glad to be awakened. He was as groggy as if he hadn't slept at all. His dreams had been unsettled, filled with shadowy menace and battles. He'd woken with the same feeling he had all-too-frequently these days: that time was running out; that while they spent their energy on inessentials, Shadow Mountain was winning the larger war.

He got unsteadily to his feet and staggered after Shalkan into the thigh-high snow, pulling his heavy cloak tightly about him. The snow was still falling heavily and steadily; there was a narrow trench where others had walked, but even that was filling quickly, and the snow showed no sign at all of stopping. If the wind kept up like this, they'd have snow dunes up to a dragon's eye before long.

Ancaladar and Jermayan were waiting for Kellen in the same clearing as before. Balls of Coldfire hung in the trees, illuminating the blowing snow and very little else.

"The forest is secure," Jermayan said, raising his voice to be heard over the sound of the wind. "The foresters have found every ring of the Shadowed Elf metal."

"Good," Shalkan said, shaking to rid himself of the snow that clung to his fur. "And Kellen has done what he came here to do. So you may take him back to the caverns—as he insists."

The cold had woken him thoroughly at last, which was a mixed blessing. Kellen clambered up onto Ancaladar's back, slipping on the dragon's ice-covered side. He wondered if Ancaladar even *noticed* the cold. He wished he didn't.

Jermayan seated himself in the forward saddle with a great deal more grace, and pulled the riding straps tight. But they didn't take off at once. Instead, Ancaladar trotted quickly through the trees, to Kellen's initial puzzlement. At last he figured out the reason.

Of course. He can't just jump into the air. He may be able to land straight down, but in this wind, he needs more room than there is here to get into the sky. Kellen made sure his own riding straps were tight. Having experienced several of Ancaladar's takeoffs, he had no desire to fall off, especially in this weather and at night.

Soon they reached an area where there were fewer trees, and Ancaladar spread his wings, springing into the wind. The force of the storm spun him like a kite, and he used its power to pull him into the sky, rising in a tight swooping spiral. It seemed to snow harder the higher they went, until suddenly the snow was gone, and darkness was replaced by light: the brilliance of the moon and the stars. Beneath them, the clouds looked like the snow-covered landscape.

"We have paid a heavy price for victory this day," Jermayan said quietly, as Ancaladar leveled off.

Petariel. Gesade. So many of those Kellen had ridden with, fought beside, dead or terribly wounded in these last battles. And how long until Idalia, Vestakia, Jermayan and Ancaladar, were added to the list? Everyone he knew, everyone he loved . . .

"Yes," Kellen said, tightly. The last thing Jermayan needed was a display of emotion when he himself must be feeling worse than Kellen. He must have known his friends and fellow Knights for—a century, at least! These were Elves who should have been spending the next several centuries contemplating their gardens, practicing their arts, making beautiful things, and perfecting themselves. And now—now they were gone.

"We must take what comfort we can in having won," Jermayan said somberly. "For the consequences of defeat are too great to bear."

But are we winning, Jermayan? Kellen looked at his friend's back, heard the weariness and near-despair in his voice, and did not ask his question aloud.

THE following day, Kellen, Vestakia, and Keirasti met with Adaerion to discuss the best way of ridding the caverns of *duergar*. By now both their units had been brought up to full strength again, as Redhelwar reconfigured the hard-hit skirmishing units, and formed new ones.

The blizzard still hammered the land. The pavilions of the cavern camp were all half-buried in snow, and ropes had been strung between them to allow people to find their way between them. Without that, there was every chance of becoming lost, even in the few feet that separated one pavilion and the next.

"Kindolhinadetil has opened the archives at Ysterialpoerin to Redhelwar, so we now know something more than we did of the habits of *duergar*. They are not accustomed to luring many victims at one time, so if you approach them in force, at least some of you should be safe from their call, and able to attack them while the others are held in thrall," Adaerion said.

"But our light will drive them into hiding, as it did the last time we entered the caverns," Keirasti said.

"You will not have light," Adaerion said. "The Wildmages have worked upon this problem since we understood we would have to hunt *duergar*. They have crafted Darksight hoods—enough for both your troops. They will not render you invisible as *tarnkappa* would, for we now know that would be useless, but you will be able to see your prey and approach him in darkness. And Artenel's artificers have made you spears and nets, which will be of more use against these creatures than your swords."

"So we can hunt them," Keirasti said with grim satisfaction. "But it would be pleasant indeed to hear how we will find them."

"The Crystal Spiders will tell us," Kellen said. "They're as eager as we are to free their home of what they call Dark Ones. They said they would give us aid. If we go into the caverns—past the village cavern—I think they'll come out and speak with us."

"All that remains is getting there," Keirasti said. She glanced at the doorway of Adaerion's pavilion and winced faintly as the wind shook the fabric vigorously.

"We might as well move into the caverns until we've cleared them," Kellen said reluctantly, although the last thing he wanted to do was to move underground. "The big chamber near the entrance would do for a base camp. If we light up enough of the caverns—I can cast Coldfire on the walls, or Jermayan or one of the other Wildmages can—we'll be safe from the *duergar.* And we won't have to keep coming back and forth through the snow." The camp was a mile away from the cavern mouth—close enough in ordinary winter weather, but not something he wanted to ride through twice a day in a storm. And it would be warmer underground as well; so much of their energy was being wasted in keeping warm that everyone was exhausted.

"A reasonable suggestion," Adaerion said, with equal reluctance.

"Will the Crystal Spiders be able to tell you when the caverns are . . . empty?" Vestakia asked, speaking up for the first time.

"I'm not sure," Kellen admitted. "They're not very much like anything we've ever seen before, though they're not Tainted. So when they say the caverns are empty, that's when I'd like you to check and see what you feel."

"Nothing, I hope," Vestakia said. "But . . . you did say they could talk to each other, didn't you? That the one lot in the trapped caverns talked to the ones here?"

Kellen nodded, frowning faintly in puzzlement, wondering what she was thinking.

"Well," Vestakia said, "once the cavern is clear, maybe someone should find out just how far away they can talk to each other. Because the weather's getting so bad now—if these storms keep up—that Jermayan and Ancaladar and I won't be able to fly to search for the next Shadowed Elf cave, but if there are Crystal Spiders living in all the caves in the Elven Lands, and they know everything that goes on in their caves, and they all talk to each other, maybe *they* can tell you where the next cave you need to go to is."

Everyone stared at her. It was such a simple, practical, *obvious* solution that none of them had thought of it. And it would save them an enormous amount of time—and danger to Vestakia.

If it worked.

"That is an excellent notion, Lady Vestakia," Adaerion said with grave enthusiasm. "It is certainly something we must try, once the caverns are safe to enter."

Kellen felt a sense of relief. Not so much at the thought that Vestakia wouldn't be in constant danger—though that thought was never far from his mind—but at the thought that, if her plan worked, she would no longer be completely irreplaceable.

"Well," Kellen said, "once we've gotten rid of the *duergar* and you tell us the caves are clear, I'll introduce you to a bunch of giant glowing spiders and you can ask them yourself. How would you like that?"

Vestakia grinned at him. "Better than flying around for sennights freezing my . . . feet off, to tell the truth! And spiders certainly won't care a bit what I look like, so we won't have to persuade them that *I'm* not Tainted!"

KELLEN and Keirasti moved their troops into the caverns. When the blizzard blew itself out, they barely noticed—their days had settled into a wearying, hideous routine as they searched the caverns, hunting *duergars*. With the darksight hoods the Wildmages had made for them, they could approach their prey in darkness and still see and hear one another, and the Crystal Spiders kept their promise, letting them know where to hunt.

The creatures had approached them eagerly as soon as they had ventured past the now-empty Shadowed Elf village. Remembering what Idalia had done, as soon as he saw them approach, Kellen pulled off his gauntlet and held out his bare hand.

The enormous spiders had climbed over him eagerly, until he was covered in them. Though they looked as insubstantial as thistledown, the whole swarm of them was surprisingly heavy. One of them walked out on his arm, and settled its body in his palm.

:*You return.*: He heard the voice in his mind. It tickled faintly. :*Now we can help. You hunt the Black Minds. We know where they are.*:

Show me, Kellen thought.

Pictures appeared in his mind—parts of the cave system he hadn't seen yet. They were blurred, impossible to decipher.

The Crystal Spiders must have sensed his bewilderment, for the pictures ceased. :*We will take you—near. And then you will know.*:

Know? How? Kellen thought in bewilderment.

:*You will know,*: the voice in his head repeated.

The carpet of spiders ebbed from his body, and the Crystal Spiders began to scuttle away with surprising speed.

"We follow them," Kellen said to the others.

Soon enough he understood what the Crystal Spiders had meant. After they had followed the Spiders for a while—being careful to mark their trail at intervals in order to find their way back—two of their party simply dropped their weapons and began walking forward.

"Rhufai!" Reyezeyt said sharply. "Janshil!"

"Let them go," Kellen said quietly. "They'll lead us right to where we need to go."

The first kill was easy: though the *duergar* held ten of them spellbound at the end, it didn't seem to understand that it was still vulnerable. The others rushed forward, confusing it, and Kellen and Keirasti spitted the *duergar* on their long wooden spears. In death it dissolved instantly, filling the cavern with the same gagging sweet-sick stench Kellen remembered from his first *duergar* kill.

It was the last time their hunts were to be this easy. The

duergar seemed somehow to be able to silently communicate with one another. Once Kellen and the Elven Knights had killed the first one, the others seemed to understand there was a need to hide.

And if they could not hide, attack.

⌒

"WATCH him! Watch him!" Kellen shouted. His voice echoed eerily in the vastness of the cavern.

A dozen of the Elves stood like sleepwalkers. The *duergar* was backed into a small alcove just off a larger chamber deep within the mountain. It crouched and snarled, revealing a mouth filled with formidable teeth.

Then it sprang at the entranced Elves.

Keirasti barely blocked its rush toward the helpless ones, sweeping it back toward the alcove with the shaft of her heavy spear. Then she, too, dropped the spear, sinking to her knees in a daze. The weapon clattered to the ground as she fell beneath the *duergar's* spell. Some of the first victims were rousing now, as the creature turned its powers on other prey: Kellen, rushing forward to attack, found his way blocked by Seheimith and Nironoshan. He thrust them aside, but by then the *duergar* had released them and claimed others.

Seeing its way blocked only by those who were powerless to hinder it, the *duergar* bounded forward, away from Kellen and toward the freedom of the deep caves.

Kellen hefted his spear and threw.

It did not go in as deeply as he hoped, but it broke the monster's concentration. The Elves carrying the net rushed forward, flinging the net over the creature and trapping it. Seconds later, it was dead.

"Not as bad as it could have been," Kellen said, relieved.

"At least this time no one died," Keirasti said tightly. When one of the creatures had bitten Tildaril—one of her command—there had been no time for Kellen to even try to

Heal him. Tildaril had died in seconds, screaming in agony as armor and flesh had boiled away from the bite like smoke.

They left the net and spears where they were. They were useless now that they'd come into contact with *duergar* blood.

"Let's find the next one," Kellen said.

As he'd expected, the Crystal Spiders appeared almost immediately. Once the *duergar* had begun to hide, the Crystal Spiders had needed to lead Kellen and the Elven Knights closer each time.

Kellen knelt down and removed his gauntlets. As they had each time before, the Crystal Spiders swarmed over him, nestling into his outstretched hands. The long furlike bristles that covered their bodies tickled his hands, as if they were as much cats as spiders.

Each time they touched his mind, the contact became easier, though Kellen always had the impression that he baffled them as much as they confused him. If Vestakia went ahead with her plan, and tried to get complicated, detailed information from the Crystal Spiders, she wasn't going to have an easy time of it.

:Dead. Webs, eggs, babies. All safe now,: came the voice in his mind.

You need to show us where the next one is, Kellen thought back, forming the silent words carefully.

:All safe now. All safe.:

Kellen sighed mentally and tried again. The Crystal Spiders weren't stupid. They were just . . . alien. *Where is the next Black Mind that we need to kill?*

There was a pause. He felt a *riffling* through his mind, as he did whenever the creatures were trying especially hard to make him understand something.

:There are no more. Not here.:

"Not here," Kellen said aloud. If the Spiders made a distinction between "here" and "not here," maybe that meant they *were* able to sense the other caverns, and the "Black Minds" there.

There are no more Black Minds in these caverns? We have killed them all? he thought back.

:All dead. All. Webs, eggs, babies, all safe,: came the reply once more.

Good, Kellen thought back. *That's good. I want to bring a friend of mine to talk to you—about other Black Minds, in other caverns. Will you talk to her?*

He sensed confusion and uncertainty, then a long pause, as though the Spiders were conferring among themselves. Or perhaps they were simply thinking—in all the times he'd talked with them, Kellen had never decided whether they were one group-mind, or separate creatures.

:She will kill Black Minds?: the Spiders finally asked.

She helps us kill Black Minds, Kellen answered. *Yes.*

:Then we will speak with her,: the Spiders answered.

Thank you, Kellen thought at them, as the mass of Spiders flowed off his body and scurried away into the dark.

He got stiffly to his feet—it was cold in the deep caves, a constant damp chill that made his bones ache—and looked at the others.

"They say that one was the last," he said.

"Good. I am *tired* of sleeping in a cave," Keirasti said simply. "And I am tired of wearing a bag over my head. Now we can go back."

They gathered their remaining weapons and headed for the surface.

~

DESPITE the warmth of the bodies packed around him, Cilarnen was cold, though he knew he was lucky not to be freezing. He was thirsty, and as the bells passed—he still reckoned time by the standards of the City, even if no one around him did—he began to be hungry as well. How long were they going to be trapped here?

Tarik had told him—the man had eventually introduced himself—that the Elves they'd been riding to meet would probably come looking for them soon. Cilarnen hoped so. It would be a cruel jest on the part of the Light if the people coming to aid the Elves were slain, not by the enemy, but by a storm Called by one of their own people.

In addition to everything else, being packed in so closely with a bunch of Wildmages was uncomfortable in a way Cilarnen couldn't quite define, like being forced to listen to an annoying sound, or a ringing in your ears that went on and on and wouldn't stop. But there was nothing to be done about those things, and so he resigned himself to being miserable. And he hoped—if it came to the unthinkable worst—that at least Kardus would survive, and take his message to Kellen.

AS it happened, Tarik was quite right. Late the next day, Cilarnen was roused from an uncomfortable half-doze by shouts and the violent shaking of the wagon. The tarpaulin at the back was hauled away, and light, snow, and fresh arctic air streamed into the cramped confines of the wagon. .

"Ah," Tarik said with satisfaction. "Rescue."

The others clambered out of the wagon, and through the snow-tunnel at the foot. Cilarnen simply sprawled where he was, luxuriating in the absence of the Wildmages. It was as if someone had finally stopped banging on a sore tooth. At the moment he didn't care if he stayed here and froze.

"Cilarnen? Come." Kardus was leaning into the wagon, looking worried. "A rescue party has found us. They will take us to their camp. It will be a long cold journey, and we must travel through the night, but better that than to remain here."

For a moment Cilarnen thought of telling Kardus to go on without him, that he was fine where he was, but he realized that that was ridiculous. He'd freeze here, and his message would go undelivered. He had to go on, for Armethalieh's sake, if nothing else.

Everything hurt as he crawled across the floor of the wagon toward Kardus. The Centaur lifted him down and carried him through the snow as if he were a child, and Cilarnen was too weak to protest.

It was still snowing heavily, and the wagons were nearly buried. The Centaurs had dug down a large ring of firm ground for themselves and the mules and horses, but outside it the snow was Centaur-shoulder height.

The snow was still blowing down—not as heavily as when the blizzard had first struck, but it was impossible to see more than a few yards. He could barely make out the forms of their rescuers, blurred by the snow.

"Can you ride?" Kardus asked.

"Yes." He had no idea whether he could stay on Oakleaf's back or not, but Cilarnen knew he was going to try.

⟜

THEY left the wagons behind, and the heaviest of their gear. Linyesin said that they could come back for it when the weather cleared. Cilarnen wondered when that would be. Spring?

From the others, he learned that their rescuers were more of the so-called Elven Knights, and a few more men of the High Reaches. The Centaurs were already organizing themselves into marching order, moving slowly along the path the rescue party had broken through the snowdrifts.

Kardus handed him a wineskin. "Drink this—all of it. It will warm you and strengthen you for the journey."

Cilarnen took the wineskin gratefully. To his surprise, it actually contained wine—not the mead the Centaurs preferred—and it was *hot* wine besides. He gulped it down quickly, for once not caring about the taste, and without wondering how it had been heated. When he had finished, Kardus took the wineskin back.

"Stay with me. This will be no pleasant journey—but far better than remaining here in the open."

SEVERAL bells later, Cilarnen decided that Kardus had a great gift for understatement. The sun set, but they did not stop. All through the night they traveled, at a plodding pace little better than a walk. He had thought the journey thus far had been near-unendurable. It had been a mild spring jaunt compared to this.

Cilarnen hated to think of how long Oakleaf had gone without proper care. At least he understood why this was happening; the poor mule didn't.

At dawn they stopped, but only long enough to give the animals a little water and some broken cakes of journey-food. It was simple enough to melt a hole in the snow; the edges turned instantly to ice and formed a natural watering trough—as long as you could keep the water from freezing. Once Cilarnen saw what the Wildmages were doing, he did it as well, and allowed Oakleaf and the mules that were being led along behind him to drink. Though he could usually summon Fire without difficulty, this time the effort left him giddy and breathless, as though he'd run for a long time without stopping. He did his best to conceal his difficulty from Kardus, but he suspected the Centaur Wildmage noticed, all the same.

But the rest was all-too-brief, and soon they were on their way again.

They traveled faster with light to see by. Soon they were among the trees, where the snow was not as deep, and the wind did not cut so sharply. The only drawback to that was that at intervals the overburdened boughs would bend and dump a load of thick wet snow on whoever was unfortunate enough to be beneath them at the time.

He supposed it would be a breathtaking sight, assuming he could actually see it through the veils of snow. He'd read Perulan's pastoral tales—along with everyone else in the City—with their detailed descriptions of woodland groves and shady glens. But Perulan had been describing the tame forests of the Delfier Valley, not something this . . . wild. The trees were taller than the masts of the Selken ships, larger than the pillars that lined the Great Temple of the Light. And those were just the ones he could see.

But even the forest could not distract him from his cold and exhaustion for long. He had never been so tired, and all he really wanted was to lie down in the snow to sleep forever. But of course, even he knew that was the last thing he could possibly do.

⌐

THE sound of horns roused him, and Cilarnen realized he'd been asleep in the saddle—or near to it. He jerked upright, every frozen muscle protesting, and looked around wildly, certain they were being attacked. The light was the dark blue of twilight, and they had moved out of the shelter of the great trees.

"We're within sight of the camp," Kardus told him. "It's nearly over."

Cilarnen didn't remember the rest of the ride at all. All he knew was that eventually someone lifted him down from Oakleaf's saddle and carried him into a place filled with light and warmth. He roused enough to drink when a cup was held to his lips.

"Oakleaf—" he said.

And that was the last he knew for quite some time.

⌐

IT was day when Kellen and the others reached the surface again—and snowing only lightly, which was a pleasant change. The air was drier and colder here than down in the caverns, but fresh, and Kellen breathed deeply as he walked down the ramp.

Kharren and a half-dozen Knights were standing guard outside the cavern. Kellen greeted her with a careless wave.

"I See you, Kharren. The Crystal Spiders tell us the caverns are now free of *duergar*," he said.

"That makes good hearing, Kellen Knight-Mage," Kharren responded. "I will send Elatar for your horses. Adaerion has news for you, but he will wish to give it himself."

⌒

SOON Kellen was following Kharren into Adaerion's pavilion. He wondered what the news was, but if it had been anything truly urgent—and bad—Kharren would surely have delivered it herself.

"I See you, Kellen," Adaerion said, motioning for Kellen to sit.

"I See you, Adaerion," Kellen said, bowing respectfully before he sat.

Pircano poured tea for all three of them. Kellen sipped it gratefully; tea had never seemed to get hot down in the caverns.

"Perhaps you will indulge me by letting me know how your work fared below," Adaerion said.

Bad news first. "As you know, we lost Tildaril," Kellen said quietly. Now the good news. "But other than that, we were lucky, and sustained no real injuries. The Crystal Spiders tell us that we have killed all the *duergar*. Now Vestakia can go down and see if the caverns are indeed free of Taint. And the Spiders have agreed to talk with her as well, so that she can see whether they are truly able to communicate with others of their kind in other caves. It might take her a while to find out anything useful, though," he added.

"That work may have to wait," Adaerion said. "Four days ago, the Centaurs who came at Andoreniel's summons reached our camp. Traveling with them was a High Mage of Armethalieh."

Kellen stared at Adaerion in disbelief. *A High Mage? Here?*

"It would be interesting to know how it was that a High Mage was permitted to cross the border into the Elven Lands," he said, after a long pause.

"We did not know, then, that this is what he was. He came in company with a Wildmage, whose price it was to bring him to you."

"To me?" Kellen echoed blankly.

"He—and the Wildmage—were both quite certain of it," Adaerion said kindly. "There is more. Linyesin—who has heard some of the boy's story, but not, he thinks, all—says that he was living at Stonehearth, a Centaur village, when it was attacked by one of *Them*. Fortunately, there were Wildmages there as well, because some of the levy was mustering there, and they managed to kill the creature, with the High Mage's help. The boy says that *It* mistook him for you, and when *It* realized *Its* mistake, set out to destroy the village."

"This doesn't make any sense," Kellen said, puzzled. "High Mages don't leave the City. They just *don't*. And the only business any High Mage has with me is to finish what the Council started." He shook his head, baffled. *But . . . he killed a Demon? I'd certainly like to ask him how he managed that.*

"Nevertheless, Kardus has his price to pay," Adaerion said.

And only Kellen could help him pay it. But . . . a High Mage consorting with a Wildmage? Voluntarily?

"I will see him," Kellen said reluctantly. *Maybe he isn't a High Mage,* he thought hopefully. *Maybe he's lying.*

He'd thought he was done with Armethalieh forever, and the thought of having to confront it—or one of its emissaries at least—unsettled him in a way that no battle could.

"But I want to make sure the caverns are clear first," Kellen added, only partly from a desire to put off the confrontation with this ghost from his past for as long as possible. "If he's waited this long, certainly he can wait a while longer."

"Indeed," Adaerion said, his voice conveying nothing of his thoughts. "And while you complete that task, we shall begin dismantling this camp, for its purpose is finished."

KELLEN collected Isinwen, and told him to ready Idalia's and Vestakia's horses. His troop would accompany him back into the cavern to guard Vestakia, while a second troop waited outside to guard the entrance.

Then he went looking for Idalia and Vestakia.

He found them in Idalia's tent, playing *xaqiue*—or rather, Idalia was playing *xaqiue* against herself while Vestakia watched with interest, moving the green pieces at Idalia's direction.

"Ah," Idalia said, when Kellen poked his head into the pavilion. "You're back. And Adaerion's told you about our wandering Mageborn. Oh, come now, brother dear—what else could make you look like a faun dragged through a bramble bush backwards?"

"I want to know who he is and what he wants," Kellen said, between gritted teeth. The anger in his voice surprised him.

"Well, his name is Cilarnen, and he wants you," Idalia said matter-of-factly. "Leaf and Star know why. I don't suppose you know him?"

"Cilarnen . . . Volpiril?" Kellen asked, stunned. No two living Mageborn bore the same given name, by the custom of the City, and Kellen knew of only one Cilarnen.

"Well, no one knows his family name; he didn't give one," Idalia said.

"You *do* know him!" Vestakia said. "I thought you might! Why else would he be asking for you?"

"I was at school with him." Hazy memories surfaced, of a time so long ago that the events that occurred then might have happened to someone else. Cilarnen had always been everything Kellen wasn't—the golden young Mageborn who'd excelled in all his studies and been the Masters' petted darling. Except for one day, a few sennights before Kellen was Banished, when, for some reason, Master Hendassar had chosen to humiliate Cilarnen in front of the entire History of the City class. "He's no more a High Mage than—than I am!" Kellen said indignantly.

"But if he *is* Cilarnen Volpiril, his father's a member of

the High Council, which makes it even odder that he's here," Idalia said, her eyes narrowing.

"And traveling with a Wildmage, don't forget." Kellen laughed bitterly. "I'd certainly like to know how *that* came about, considering what the High Mages think of the Wild Magic! But the pampered little Mageborn can certainly wait until we're sure the caverns are clean. The Shadowed Elves have surprised us enough times already. I want to be sure our backtrail is safe this time."

And he wasn't at all averse to having Cilarnen cool his heels. It would do him good to discover he wasn't the most important creature in this universe.

KELLEN and Pihrandet rode back to the caverns with their troops. Though no one expected trouble—the caverns were supposed to be empty—both Idalia and Vestakia wore armor; Vestakia, her full suit of scarlet Elven armor, and Idalia, her heavy shirt of Elven chain.

Kellen found himself wishing that Shalkan were here to talk to. The news that Cilarnen had come to Ysterialpoerin—and was claiming to be a High Mage of Armethalieh—had unsettled him more than he'd thought possible. Why in the name of the Gods of the Wild Magic had he come?

Banished? Lord Volpiril would never let that happen.

But then why—?

Resolutely, Kellen forced all questions and speculations from his mind. He had to concentrate on the task ahead.

"Are you all right?" he asked Vestakia as they reached the cavern mouth.

"I don't feel anything," she said, her voice light with relief. She swung down off her palfrey—Pihrandet moved to assist her, but her riding skills had improved greatly since the start of the campaign and she dismounted without help—and began to walk toward the cavern mouth.

"Wait," Kellen said, dismounting from Firareth's back.

He paused to give the stallion a companionable pat, then drew his sword and moved forward. "Don't get yourself killed for overconfidence."

The others moved up, and, with Vestakia and Idalia in their midst, moved back into the caverns once more.

They had lanterns with them, of course, but for the first part of the journey, they didn't need them. Kellen had cast Coldfire on the rocks and walls of the cavern—it had been the surest way to keep the *duergar* from creeping up on them as they slept—and the walls glowed a faint pale blue. The spell would wear off eventually, but he saw no reason to dismiss it.

They went all the way down to the village cavern, and Vestakia felt nothing.

She looked at Kellen and shook her head. "No. If there were anything here—anything at all, I'd feel it. I'm sure of it."

Kellen hesitated, but Vestakia and the Crystal Spiders both agreed that the caverns were empty of Tainted creatures, and he had to admit that his hesitation stemmed from the fact that once they went back, he'd have to confront Cilarnen.

But that was his problem, and not a reason to keep everyone else standing around in the cold.

"Let's go back, then," he said with a sigh, then smiled. Smiled broadly, in fact. "Good work, Vestakia."

She ducked her head, but it seemed to him that she was so happy she was glowing.

⌒

THEY reached the main camp just before dusk. Kellen sent the others on ahead. There was a stop he wanted to make first. It wasn't just that he wanted to avoid the meeting with Cilarnen. It was that there were other obligations he felt he had to discharge that were just as pressing, and almost as uncomfortable to deal with.

In the sennight that he'd been underground, the Unicorn

Knights had returned to their old camp. Many familiar pavilions had been struck—the encampment was barely half the size it had once been—but Kellen wanted to pay his respects. He'd fled like a coward the night he'd healed Gesade. The least he could do was ask after her. Perhaps someone here would know.

He rode into the center of the encampment and dismounted.

Riasen's pavilion was now in the place where Petariel's had been. He came out at the sound of Kellen's arrival.

"Kellen! You come in a good hour," he said. "We had begun to think you loved the caves so well you intended to spend the rest of your life underground."

"It began to seem as if I was," Kellen replied, with a shake of his head. "But Vestakia says that the caverns are now free of Taint."

"And so I suppose we shall be moving on, once she finds the next one." Riasen shrugged. By now the other Unicorn Knights had appeared as well. Kellen saw many familiar faces—but as many more were missing, gone forever. Petariel. Vandelt. Melchia.

Too many to count. He swallowed hard.

But Riasen was still speaking.

"—and once you have dealt with this High Mage who has come all the way from Armethalieh to speak with you, of course. Kardus says he was Banished—if this goes on, there will be no one left there at all, and we might as well live there ourselves."

Kellen had forgotten how fast gossip traveled among the Elves. Riasen undoubtedly knew everything there was to know about Cilarnen. But before he had to reply to that, a welcome interruption spared him the need.

"I See you, Kellen," Menerchel said with pleasure, poking his head out of his own pavilion. "I do not doubt that you have come for a proper cup of tea."

"Tea would be welcome," Kellen said gladly. "We could not make it properly in the caverns—at least it never tasted right."

"It is a wonder you all did not die of thirst," Menerchel said, in tones of mock concern. "I would not myself care to engage in such hazardous duty. No proper tea! It is not to be thought of. I shall see to it at once." He disappeared back into his pavilion to bring out the tea-things.

"It would please me greatly to hear what you have heard of this Arme-thaliehan," Kellen said, "but I came first of all to see if you were . . . well. And to ask after Gesade."

"Why not ask me yourself?" a familiar voice came from behind him. "I'm only blind, you know. Not deaf."

Kellen turned around quickly. Gesade and Shalkan were standing behind him, shoulder to shoulder.

"He looks stricken," Shalkan said to her. "You know the look."

"Indeed I do," Gesade replied, sounding as if nothing much had ever happened to her. "Very much as if he's done something wrong and is waiting to be scolded for it. Well, Kellen? Have you done something wrong?"

She looked completely restored to health—except for the closed sunken lids and the hollow eye sockets.

Kellen couldn't speak.

Gesade walked carefully forward, with Shalkan at her side to guide her. She reached Kellen, and he automatically raised his hand to stroke her neck.

"Well, boy?" she said tartly. "Would you rather I was dead?"

"No!" Kellen said instantly—and honestly. "But—"

"—you'd rather I could see," Gesade finished for him. "Well, so would I, of course. We'd all rather a great many things that we don't get. But this is *not* the end of the world, or my life, so kindly don't carry on as if it is, if you please."

"But . . . what are you going to do now?" Kellen asked.

Gesade leaned into his hand, stepping back a pace so he could rub the particularly soft spot just behind her ear.

"I'm going to stay in the heart-forest until spring, then I'm going to go home to the Great Herd and run with them," Gesade said. "Someone will come to be my eyes for that.

And I'll live my life—which I could not have done without your help. And that is that, boy. It's charming of you to wallow in self-pity over me . . . when I know very well that you'd happily have strangled me more than once!"

"Yes, but—" Kellen sputtered.

"That was before I was a helpless cripple?" Gesade said sweetly.

Shalkan snickered.

"I pity the person who thinks you're a helpless cripple," Kellen said feelingly.

"Good," Gesade said, giving him an encouraging nudge. "Thank you for healing me. I am very pleased to be alive, and I intend to extract every moment of pleasure from life that I can. Now drink your tea, and then go find out what that other silly human child wants here—and then be sure to come back and tell us all about it."

"First," Kellen said, accepting a mug of tea from Menerchel gratefully, "tell me what *you* know."

"Not much," Shalkan said, flicking his ears back and forth. "Andoreniel sent Hyandur to Armethalieh to warn the City about *Them*, as you know. The City wouldn't let him in to give his warning—as you knew. As he was leaving, the gates opened and they threw Cilarnen out, wrapped in a Felon's Cloak. Hyandur had already seen the remains of another body, torn to pieces by a Scouring Hunt, so he knew what was coming. He took Cilarnen with him over the Border—fortunately, it wasn't very far, and they reached it before dawn.

"He went on to Stonehearth to warn them, and left Cilarnen there. And that would have been the end of the matter, except for the fact that some moonturns later, a Centaur Wildmage named Kardus received a Task—"

"A Centaur Wildmage?" Kellen asked. "But Centaurs can't do magic."

"Who's telling this story?" Shalkan demanded. "Kardus's Task—a Mageprice to anyone else—was to go to Stonehearth and help the human boy he found there. He arrived at the same time that a part of the Centaur levy was mustering there, preparing to head over the Border. Well, one of *Them* showed up, mistook Cilarnen for you—so Cilarnen says—and tried to destroy the village to cover up *Its* mistake. Kardus, Cilarnen, and Wirance—a High Reaches Wildmage—working together, managed to kill *It*, but the levy took heavy losses and so did the village. Cilarnen decided he had to come and talk to you, and since Kardus's Task was to help Cilarnen, along they came with what was left of the Centaur levy. Which is all anybody knows. Except that he's definitely *not* a Wildmage, and he *does* have magic."

Once again Kellen was impressed at how much Shalkan managed to find out—though the unicorn certainly couldn't be sneaking around the main camp picking up gossip. He couldn't imagine how Shalkan did it. Or did everyone come to *him* to tell him the news?

All it did was add to the mystery.

"Why me?" Kellen asked.

"*Do* come back and tell us," Shalkan said archly. "And now, I suspect everyone—including Redhelwar—would like an answer to that question."

Reminded of his other responsibilities, Kellen quickly finished his tea and bid farewell to the Unicorn Knights, mounted Firareth again, and rode down into the main camp.

Seeing Gesade again had made him feel better. He hadn't thought it would—he'd thought being reminded of his failure would make him feel terrible—but somehow it didn't. Her refusal to wallow in self-pity, even after her maiming, reminded him that no matter how terrible the loss, there was always something left with which to begin anew.

⌒

WHEN he reached the horse-lines there was a message waiting for him to report to Redhelwar "at his convenience." Kellen grinned to himself and turned Firareth over to one of the ostlers for untacking, brushing down, and turning out. He'd dawdled long enough.

He presented himself at Redhelwar's pavilion, relieved to see only familiar faces there: Redhelwar, Adaerion, and Idalia. He bowed.

Redhelwar regarded him with a lifted brow. "Idalia has told me of your sortie into the caverns, and what you found—or, rather, did not find—there, and Adaerion has acquainted me with your suggestion that the Lady Vestakia attempt to communicate with the Crystal Spiders. Perhaps there is something that you will wish to add to that which they have told."

"I am sure they have told you everything that I would have said," Kellen said. "All I have to tell that they do not know is that I have seen Gesade, and that she is well and in good spirits. I ask that you forgive my tardiness, but . . . I wished to know how she was," he added awkwardly.

It could have been viewed as manipulation of the most blatant sort to offer up *that* excuse for his lateness, but Redhelwar had once been a Unicorn Knight himself, and Kellen knew he would understand. Besides, it was no more than the truth.

Redhelwar's expression softened. "You did all you could for her, Kellen."

Kellen grinned. "And so she told me—very firmly. And since the unicorns know all the gossip, I think I know as much as anyone does about our . . . guest."

"Guest." The word tasted sour, tarnishing his good humor.

"And what we know of him certainly doesn't add up to a logical whole," Idalia said. "He's used magic—everyone agrees about that. But when a Mage is Banished, they Burn the Gift from his mind before they cast him out, so he'll have no chance at all against the Scouring Hunt. They must have done that to you, Kellen," she finished, her voice puzzled.

"No," Kellen said. "But then, I wasn't even a Student Apprentice. I was the worst student in the entire history of the Mage-College; I could barely light a fire—or so everyone assumed. I *did* know a couple of First Level spells—I wasn't supposed to—but as far as anyone knew, I hardly had the Gift at all. I think I've forgotten them now." He thought hard.

"I suppose Lycaelon was supposed to do it when he came to see me anyway, just in case—but I made him so furious I guess he just forgot."

Dredging up those old memories required an act of will, and Kellen was surprised at how much they hurt.

"Lycaelon was a great one for forgetting things," Idalia said caustically. "And when you were Banished, the Boundaries were so vast that there shouldn't have been any way for you to get across them before the Hunt caught up to you even if you'd *had* an intact Gift—in fact, even with Shalkan's help, you didn't manage it. If you hadn't been a Knight-Mage-to-be, you'd be dead."

"But Cilarnen was a *good* student," Kellen said resentfully. "He'd already been a Student Apprentice forever, and that was last spring. They'd certainly have Burned him."

"But they didn't," Idalia said. "He's cast Fire, Magelight, and Mageshield, from what the Centaurs say. The first two are also spells of the Wild Magic—don't look so surprised, Kellen; an awful lot of magic comes from the same root, and the High Magick *has* to have come from the Wild Magic originally—but *I* can't cast anything like Mageshield."

"Well, neither can I," Kellen said sulkily, well and truly irritated now. It was a simple spell, too, a First Level spell, one that a Student Apprentice had to master for his own safety before moving on to more elaborate and dangerous work. Most of the First Level spells didn't even require wand and sigil work, just visualizations and cantrips . . .

But he'd never managed to learn them.

He shook his head, disgusted with himself. It was sickening how quickly all that dead-numbing rote memorization came flooding back into his mind. As if he'd never left the City at all. As if he were still trapped within its walls, buried alive.

And he'd had a chance to think about this—an Armethaliehan Mage, arriving here at this time, this place—and he didn't like the conclusions he had come to.

IDALIA watched her brother with carefully-concealed dismay. It was as if the past half-year had suddenly been stripped away. This was the "old" Kellen; the boy she'd first met—unhappy, uncertain, angry.

If Kellen had a weak point, it was Armethalieh. He hated and loved it at the same time—she was positive even he wasn't sure which. The same way he—still—hated and loved Lycaelon, though—and she was *quite* positive of this—he'd convinced himself he didn't care about his father at all. And since Lycaelon was Arch-Mage of Armethalieh, Father and City were very nearly the same thing. Certainly Lycaelon had always thought so.

She knew nothing about Cilarnen Volpiril, except that his father was Lycaelon's rival on the High Council, but from what Kellen said about him, it was obvious that Kellen saw Cilarnen as everything he had never succeeded in being: excellent student, beloved son.

And now Cilarnen was here, reminding him of every failure, every fault.

And Kellen wasn't thinking clearly at all.

"Well, as a Knight-Mage, you have precious little use for Mageshield, now, do you?" Idalia said, trying to draw him back to the present and make him focus on what he *did* have.

Kellen looked at her, startled. "I . . . suppose not," he said, slowly.

"It would be good to know just *why* he was Banished from the City," Idalia continued ruthlessly.

"That is something he has told no one," Adaerion said. "And we do not know enough of the ways of the human city to know for what cause it casts out its folk."

Kellen looked at Idalia. She was relieved to see that he seemed to have come back to himself a bit.

"You and I were Banished for studying the Wild Magic," he said hesitantly. "But . . . they would have let me stay if I'd apologized and given it up."

"Well, we can rule out studying the Wild Magic," Idalia said. "Because we know he hasn't done that." She frowned. "There's hardly anything else the Mages Banish someone for. For any other crime, you either do penance, pay a fine, get your memories excised, or all three."

"Idalia," Kellen said after a moment's silence, an odd note in his voice, "what *is* studying the Wild Magic? If you're a High Mage? If someone has studied the Wild Magic, what actual crime—the name of the crime, I mean—are they committing against the City?"

Idalia thought hard. It had been almost half her lifetime since she'd discovered her three Books in the Records Room of the Council Hall, and from the moment they'd come into her hands, she'd known she was committing . . .

"Treason," she said. "To study the Wild Magic is to commit treason and heresy against the Light."

"Ah," said Redhelwar with satisfaction. "We progress."

"No," said Kellen. "We don't. We could talk until the sun came up and get nowhere," he added harshly. "What we need to do is ask Cilarnen questions, not each other. So I'll see him. I'll question him. And if I don't like his answers, I'll kill him."

"Kellen!" Idalia gasped, stunned.

"That's what I'm here for, isn't it?" Kellen said bleakly, and now Idalia could see the pain in his eyes—the pain of a man carrying a burden far too heavy for him to bear. "To kill things? We can discuss why he's here and how he got here for as long as we like. But in the end, it comes down to one thing: a Wildmage brought Cilarnen to me, because that's his Mageprice. I don't think there was anything in that price about me letting him live."

Idalia would have liked to deny the truth in that—but in all honesty, she couldn't.

"I don't know why an Armethaliehan Mage—whatever his rank, Banished for treason or not—is here. It doesn't seem really likely that they'd let him go with his Gift intact, or when they knew an Elf was lurking around outside the City ready to help him escape the Scouring Hunt. It sounds like a trap to me. I'll see," Kellen finished simply.

"And certainly there will be time enough for that on the morrow," Redhelwar said, as smoothly as if Kellen had not just proposed to murder a guest under Elven protection. "Tonight, I believe he still recovers from his ordeal in the blizzard—I know not where. For yourself, Kellen, I am certain a warm bath, a hot meal, and a good night's sleep will be welcome before you are called upon to try this stranger's motives. The tea that can be brewed in the caverns, so I am assured by Adaerion, is foul, and you will wish for better. Belepheriel has made you a gift of some of the Armethaliehan Black that you favor; I shall send Dionan to your pavilion to brew it for you after you have bathed, and see you to your rest."

For a moment Idalia thought Kellen would object, but he caught himself in time. He bowed, deeply.

"You do me too much honor, Redhelwar. It is cold in the caverns, and colder without. It will be good to spend the night in reflection, and I will welcome the tea."

He bowed again—to Redhelwar, to Adaerion, to Idalia, and left quietly.

There was silence in Redhelwar's pavilion for a time.

Someone please tell me that Kellen didn't just suggest killing Cilarnen, Idalia thought.

"If the Mageborn boy is indeed a threat . . . " Adaerion began.

"Then Kellen will deal appropriately with him in the morning," Redhelwar said. "I trust him to do as the Wild Magic wills."

But not, I notice, enough that you were willing to let him know where Cilarnen is now, Idalia thought.

Bowing, she took her own leave.

⌐

HE was sure Redhelwar was right. He thought he was sure.

Actually, he wasn't sure of anything other than that he was cold, hungry, and tired.

But a hot bath and fresh clothes—he'd spent the last sen-night living in his armor, and it was certainly time for a change—did much to make Kellen feel better, as did a hot fresh meal that hadn't started life as blocks of journey-food. After that he returned to his tent—where Dionan was wait-ing to brew the promised tea—and drank the entire pot, while giving his armor and sword a thorough cleaning.

It made him feel better—as long as he didn't think about Cilarnen.

The uppermost emotion in Kellen's mind—he was honest enough to admit—was outrage. How *dare* Cilarnen come here? This was *Kellen's* place, Kellen's life—he'd worked hard to make a place for himself here, and now Cilarnen was coming to—

Take it all away? Is that what you really think?

Kellen snorted, surprised, disgusted, and amused—all at the same time—by the direction of his own thoughts. Even if Cilarnen were a fully invested High Mage with an army at his back—which he wasn't—he couldn't do that. *But what if he ISN'T Cilarnen at all? What if he's a Demon who's fig-ured out some way to pass the bounds of the Elven Lands?*

And conceal himself from Vestakia? Unlikely, but possible.

What was slightly more possible was that he was some other kind of enemy. Something Vestakia couldn't sense, something that could pass the bounds of the Elven Lands, but an enemy nonetheless.

If he's an enemy, I'll deal with him.

But you have to deal with yourself first, a small inner voice said.

Kellen sighed, and set his sword and armor aside—both gleamed with oil and polish—and sat down cross-legged on his sleeping mat. He sat quietly, not emptying his mind but letting it fill with whatever it chose.

His losses came first. Ciltesse. Petariel. The dead friends he had not yet had time to mourn in the need to cleanse the cav-erns of *duergar*. The lost members of his thirty, replaced al-ready by near-strangers who had not yet had time to become friends. He was afraid to get to know them well, afraid to lose them too.

Elves were supposed to live for centuries. There were Elves in Sentarshadeen as old as *Armethalieh!* They were supposed to be living in peace in their beautiful cities, studying, crafting, making life itself into an art. They weren't supposed to die—drowning in their own blood, spilling their guts out on the snow, vomiting and convulsing as they died of Shadowed Elf poison . . .

Screaming as they were eaten by acid.

They weren't supposed to die.

But they do die, Kellen told himself. *They die so their children will live. They die so the Centaurs will live. They die so the trees will live.*

He remembered the barren wasteland he and Jermayan had ridden through on their way to the Black Cairn—the land that, so Jermayan had told him, had been a lush and fruitful forest before the last time Shadow Mountain had gone to war.

Yes, they fight because of that.

If there had to be war, that was a good reason to fight. Because to see the whole world turned into that—and worse—was unthinkable. Anything his friends had to do to stop it was worth it.

Even die.

But Gods of the Wild Magic, he would *miss* them—!

He let his grief wash over him, and through him, and when its first violence was past, he looked deeper.

Hatred. Anger. Fear. They came racing into his consciousness like coldwarg over the snow, all centered on the image of a young man he remembered only dimly.

Envy. Spite. Malice. He hoped that Cilarnen had suffered every step of his journey here, had loathed falling into the hands of the "Lesser Races," had been terrified of the Elves.

Grief. Despair. He hoped, when Cilarnen had heard the gate slam shut behind him—he'd realized his high-and-mighty father had betrayed and abandoned him—he'd realized that the High Mages cared for nothing but power, for nothing but themselves. That everything he'd done every day of his life to excel, to please, had come to nothing in the end.

Kellen realized he was crying silently, tears streaming down his face.

Is that it? he thought wonderingly, even as his heart ached with loss and despair. *But I don't care—*

Apparently he did.

"I don't," he whispered aloud, wiping at his eyes. He had *everything* here—friends, a life, work that mattered, a gift to cherish and train.

But the thought of Cilarnen coming here . . . frightened him.

Because Cilarnen was—or had been, at least—everything that Kellen had once desperately wanted to be. And it was as if . . .

As if I'm afraid that if when I see him again, everything will go back to being that way. I'll be Kellen-the-failure again, and he'll still be . . . perfect.

It was a ridiculous thing to fear. In Armethalieh, Cilarnen had belonged, and Kellen had been out-of-place. Here, Kellen fit in.

Only he didn't. Not really. He was a Knight-Mage. Knight-Mages didn't "fit in."

There.

That was the root of his anger and fear.

He didn't fit in here either. He was just as alone here as he had been in the City.

Kellen bit back a heartfelt sob.

Oh, it was a completely different situation, of course. In Armethalieh, conformity was the highest goal. Here, everyone valued him for being different. His Knight-Mage gifts were esteemed and honored.

But he was still different. Set apart. In a way that even Idalia wasn't.

And now, if Cilarnen came and fit in . . .

You'll be jealous. You'll still be jealous. Of him.

Kellen managed a shaky laugh and wiped his face dry once more.

But he thought he'd worked his way to the heart of the problem. It had been as painful as lancing an infected boil, but he felt better now. And he thought that tomorrow, when he faced Cilarnen, he could judge him fairly—for whatever he was.

I won't like it. I won't like HIM. But I can do it.

Thoroughly exhausted now, Kellen rolled into his bed-clothes and doused the lanterns with a gesture.

Twenty-four

Shadows of the Past

Cold air and a hint of movement woke him. Kellen rolled out of his bedclothes and grabbed his sword in one fluid movement. Someone was moving toward him. He reached out and grabbed the front of the intruder's tunic, flinging him to the bedroll he'd just vacated, the edge of his sword at the shadowy figure's throat.

"Hey!" the intruder yelped. He must have felt the cold of the steel at his throat then, because he went absolutely still.

With a gesture, Kellen lit the lanterns.

And stared down at someone who could only be Cilarnen Volpiril.

He'd seen that face, Kellen realized with a shock—and since his Banishing. It was the same face that had appeared in Idalia's scrying bowl the day he'd gone to Ashaniel to ask her to warn Armethalieh: russet hair, pale blue eyes, narrow aristocratic Mageborn features. He was freshly shaved, and his hair was still cut short in the manner of the City, but no proper Mageborn son would have a complexion so roughened by wind and weather.

"Cilarnen Volpiril," Kellen said in disgust, getting to his feet. "Close the flap," he said without turning around, "it's cold in here."

When he turned to pick up his sword sheath, he got a good look at his second "guest."

The Centaur had waist-length hair—black, with a broad white streak—and, uncommon for male Centaurs, was clean-shaven. His tail had a white streak in it as well, and he had three white feet. Charms were braided into both his hair and his tail, and around his neck, over his tunic, he wore a necklace from which were strung many more. Kellen's mind caught up with his body, and he knew then what this was all about.

"You must be Kardus," Kellen said, sheathing his sword. How a Centaur could still be a Wildmage without having magic was a question for another time. He reached for his tunic and pulled it on. "I'm Kellen. Is your Task fulfilled?"

"Yes," Kardus said. "My Task was to bring Cilarnen to you. But I have grown fond of him on our journey. I would stay to help him, if I may."

For a moment Kellen thought of ordering him out, then shrugged. "It'll be cramped, but sure. Tea?" He was glad, now, that Dionan had left the tea-things behind. It occurred to him that maybe he'd better apologize for nearly decapitating Cilarnen. "Ah, sorry about the welcome. We sleep lightly around here; it wouldn't be the first time that the Enemy has tried to infiltrate the camp."

He rummaged around until he found his camp boots and slipped them on, and began setting up the tea brazier.

"DON'T you want to know why I'm here?" Cilarnen demanded.

When he'd awoken in the Healer's tent several days ago—unutterably relieved to discover that Kardus had kept the Wildmage Healers away from him—he'd wanted to see Kellen immediately.

Only Kellen, it seemed, wasn't here.

Nobody was willing to tell him when—or even if— Kellen would be back, either, and so for nearly a sennight Cilarnen had waited in the Centaur camp, hoping for word.

Tonight he'd finally heard that Kellen had returned— from a Wildmage Healer who had been with Kellen at someplace called the further cavern—but still the invitation Cilarnen impatiently expected didn't come. Finally he'd taken matters into his own hands. He'd demanded that Kardus show him the way to Kellen's tent, or he'd go by himself, and a little to his surprise, the Centaur Wildmage had agreed without argument.

He hadn't expected the tent to be green silk.

He certainly hadn't expected to be attacked when he opened the flap and stepped inside.

"I said—" he repeated.

"Probably to annoy me," Kellen answered coolly, and went on with his tea preparations as if Cilarnen wasn't there.

Cilarnen regarded Kellen with a mixture of fear and despair. He *had* to listen to what Cilarnen had to say!

But this was *not* the same Kellen he and his cronies had taunted back at the Mage-College. Oh, they'd called him "Kellen Farmboy" even then because of his hulking size, but now . . .

He was muscled like a dock-laborer and surely even taller than he'd been then. There was nothing of the Mageborn about him. He looked nothing like Lycaelon Tavadon—he looked like one of the High Reaches folk—and his hair was long enough to braid.

And then there was that sword. As large and heavy as a Ritual Tool, but Kellen handled it as if it weighed no more than a practice rapier. And his speed—

Cilarnen had never seen anyone move that fast in his life—not even the Centaur warriors. He'd barely taken two steps into Kellen's tent before he'd been seized and flung to the floor, feeling something cold and sharp at his throat, and when Kellen had lit the lanterns—by magic, *Wild* Magic— he'd seen that Kellen was holding that monstrous blade to his throat, glaring down at him with a face like Death Itself.

And now he was making tea.

"My news is urgent," Cilarnen said. "It concerns the good of the City."

"It can wait until the tea is ready," Kellen said maddeningly. "Or, of course, it can wait until the morning. I *really* don't like being woken up in the middle of the night."

"You're still thinking only of yourself," Cilarnen said bitterly. "But then, you always did."

"Have you always been an idiot," Kellen asked pleasantly, "or did frost-burn addle your brains? You don't know anything about me, you've come halfway across the world to ask for my help, and now you're insulting me. What would your father say?"

"He's dead," Cilarnen said bleakly. "I killed him."

⇌

"WHAT?" *Oh, good going, Kellen, you've really put your foot in it this time.* What was it about Cilarnen that sent him back three seasons in his manners? As if the Elves hadn't taught him better by now. Leaf and Star—if he'd thought about it, the most annoying thing he could have done was to have been completely polite, and if he hadn't, then he wouldn't have put himself in the wrong. "Cilarnen, I—"

"You don't care." Cilarnen's voice was flat. "Why should you? Your father and mine were enemies."

"My father condemned me to death, actually," Kellen replied slowly. "He wanted me dead so badly he sent three packs of the Scouring Hunt after me. When he found out I was still alive, living outside City Lands, he expanded the Boundaries so he could try to hunt me down again. Whatever our fathers are—were—to each other, *we* are not enemies. Or at least, we shouldn't be."

As he said it, he felt a sense of Presence.

A price to pay.

Forgive an enemy.

Yes, Cilarnen *had* been his enemy. Perhaps not for what he had done—though Kellen had certainly suffered enough from his youthful tormenting—but simply for what he *was*—the symbol of what Kellen could have been, as much so as the Other Kellen he had confronted at the Black Cairn.

Cilarnen had been—and still was—his enemy.

Forgive an enemy.

Forgive—forget—it was time to pay the price of Gesade's healing.

Kellen swallowed hard. He'd thought then it was a small price, a light price.

I forgive you, Cilarnen. I think it will be the hardest price I have ever paid, but . . . I forgive you. I think you were as much a victim of the City as I was.

He got up to reach out to Cilarnen.

"No," Kardus said quietly. "The touch of a Wildmage is . . . uncomfortable to him."

Kellen settled back and concentrated on preparing tea, saying nothing. This was no simple price, over and done with in hours or days. He would be paying this price for moonturns to come. Perhaps for the rest of his life.

I can try, he thought desperately. *I can only try my best.*

"Was *that* why Lycaelon wanted to expand the City Bounds?" Cilarnen asked in horrified wonder.

Kellen took a deep breath, and forced himself to sound calm. He could *act* as if Cilarnen weren't his enemy. That was a beginning.

The sense of Presence—of listening—withdrew.

So he nodded, and made his expression serious, but open and pleasant. "Yes. We're fairly sure, anyway. When we found out, my sister and I escaped into the Elven Lands, because we knew that no matter what, the Council wouldn't dare push the Bounds past the Elven border."

"And then everything went wrong, and the Council drew

back the Bounds to the walls," Cilarnen said, taking up the story as if it were his to tell as well. Well, maybe it was—he knew what Kellen did not, what had gone on inside the City. "The farmers stopped sending food—they said with so much rain in the fall they would need all their food for themselves. There were no weather spells to protect them anymore, you see. I was an Entered Apprentice then. I *saw* all the storehouses." There was a hint of desperation in his voice. "They were half-empty, and every day it was worse. The price of grain kept rising. The Council agreed to buy grain from the Selkens, but of course nobody knew if they would send it. And it made us look so weak!"

The tca was ready. Kellen poured, and held out a cup to Cilarnen, dropping several honey-disks into it for good measure. In the cold, honey was energy. The boy—Kellen couldn't help thinking of Cilarnen as a boy, though he knew Cilarnen was a year older than he was—took it automatically.

Heavy rains. When the Black Cairn had burst, it had affected the weather everywhere. Normally that wouldn't have included the Delfier Valley, granary of Armethalieh, but when the Mages had restricted the Bounds, they had removed the weather-spells from the valley, exposing it to the full force of the freak storms. Anything still in the fields would have been beaten down and drowned; rotted. He hadn't known. Of course, if he had, it still wouldn't have changed anything, but—

"You couldn't let that go on," Kellen said quietly.

"We had to stop them!" Cilarnen said passionately. "The High Council wouldn't listen—my *father* wouldn't listen. It was his plan to reduce the Bounds to the walls, to shame Arch-Mage Lycaelon, and he would not reverse his position. The Arch-Mage would have listened. I know that now. I know it! But I thought he wouldn't because of who my father was, and I couldn't see the City starving before my eyes!"

Odd as it was to imagine, Kellen thought Lycaelon *would* have listened. Leaving the City without any way to feed itself was suicidal. But if the rest of the Council had backed Volpiril, and not Lycaelon . . .

"And I couldn't see the City starving before my eyes." At that moment, Kellen felt something he hadn't expected for Cilarnen: respect. As Mageborn, Cilarnen would have been one of the last to suffer; in fact, the hardships of the City would scarcely have touched his life at all. Yet he had taken on the responsibility his elders were too enwrapped in political wrangling to claim.

"What did you do?" he asked gently.

"We made umbrastone," Cilarnen said miserably. "Light deliver me, I don't even know why now! There were six of us, and Master Raellan: Jorade Isas, Geont Pentres, Kermis Lalkmair, Tiedor Rolfort, Margon Ogregance, and me. Margon's father was on the Merchant's and Provender's Council, so he knew exactly how bad things were. Kermis was the one who had the recipe for umbrastone. It eats magic—I think we thought that if we made enough of it, we could get into the High Council chambers and make them listen to us."

"Leaf and Star," Kellen said softly. Treason, they'd guessed back in Redhelwar's tent, and here it was: conspiracy to overthrow the High Council and meddling with forbidden magic. He'd read about umbrastone in the *Ars Perfidorum, the Book of Forbidden Acts.* It was one of the products of the *Art Khemitic,* and as such, as much anathema to the High Mages as the Wild Magic was.

"We were arrested before we even made the first batch," Cilarnen said, sounding baffled and grief-stricken. "I don't know how they found out. But we had all the ingredients, so that was good enough for the High Council. I don't know what happened to any of my friends—I think at least one of them was Banished before me, and died. Hyandur said there was someone in a Felon's Cloak, and the Hunt . . . I didn't believe him then. Or maybe . . . Undermage Anigrel said my father was dead, when he came to Burn away my Gift. He said the conspiracy was Lord Volpiril's idea."

"He lied," Kellen said instantly, though the mention of

Anigrel's name made him want to twitch. It wasn't only kindness that motivated his words, but common sense. Why would Lord Volpiril instigate a conspiracy whose sole purpose was to overthrow him and support Lycaelon's position? Anigrel must have been lying.

Cilarnen held up a hand. "That doesn't matter," he said, his voice rough with grief. "This does: Undermage Anigrel came to Burn away my Gift. I still have it."

Kellen started, but didn't interrupt.

"For a long time I didn't." Maybe Cilarnen interpreted Kellen's expression of startlement as skepticism, because he nodded vigorously. "Truly. Even *you* have to believe I'd know whether it was there or not. I spent two moonturns at Stonehearth, and I didn't have it—just the worst headaches you can imagine. Then—the day that *Thing* came—it came back."

"And it's all there?" Kellen wasn't sure quite what he was asking, or what good the information would do him. He *knew* how the High Mages fueled their spells—by power stolen from the citizens of Armethalieh through their City Talismans. Even if Cilarnen hadn't had his Gift Burned out of him, he had nothing now beyond his personal power to draw on to fuel his spells.

"Yes," Cilarnen said, smiling bitterly for a moment. "For what good it does me. I was nearly ready to test for Journeyman when I was Banished—but here, without tools, without spellbooks, what good am I? Unless, of course, you need someone to take care of horses. I can light fires and boil water. But just touching those cursed books you Wildmages are so proud of makes me feel sick. And there's something *missing* when I try to cast a spell. But I don't know what it is."

I do, Kellen thought. *And bless Leaf and Star that Anigrel was so willing to parade his superior knowledge before me that day. I can explain to you how the High Magick REALLY works, and why your spells don't.*

But whether that was something he *should* do would require more thought. And he wasn't sure that even if he *did* explain, it would help. Cilarnen would still need a power source—quite a lot of them, in fact—and they would have to donate their power freely and willingly.

"I'm glad that you told me all this," Kellen said, "and I really am sorry about your father—not because I liked him, or any of the High Mages, but because I think he was unjustly killed. And I *know* that you and your friends were unjustly punished. It should have been the *first* thought of every High Mage on the Council to take care of the City, not to spend their time in wrangling over who was to blame. But this isn't why you came, is it?"

"No," Cilarnen said. "I came because of what the De— *Thing* told me at Stonehearth." He closed his eyes, obviously concentrating, and when he spoke again, eyes still closed, Kellen sensed he was reciting something he had carefully committed to memory.

" 'So, Arch-Mage's son Kellen, what a surprise to see you here. Have you tired of the Children of Leaf and Star and think to make your way back to the Golden City? You have nothing to return to now. Your father claims another as his son. He has given him the seat on the High Council that was to have been yours. And daily our foothold in the City grows stronger . . . ' "

Kellen rocked back on his heels, the words striking him like separate blows.

The Demons were in Armethalieh.

Or . . . wait. He was fairly sure the Demons couldn't enter Armethalieh, any more than they could enter the Elven Lands. If he could trust a single word Lycaelon had said to him that night in his cell, the High Mages *did* remember the Demons, and were still terrified of them. So they'd have spells to keep them out of the City.

But . . . a foothold. That was bad enough.

It would have to be a foothold of a different sort than they had here in the Elven Lands with the Shadowed Elves. Something that could pass the City-wards and flourish unnoticed.

But what?

"Well?" Cilarnen demanded. "Aren't you going to do something?"

"Yes," Kellen said. "I'm going to have another cup of tea. And I'm going to think."

"Think!" Cilarnen cried. "What good is thinking going to do? You've got to stop them!"

"Really?" Kellen replied, his tone dry. "One would be interested, of course, to hear how this was to be accomplished at all, much less this instant. I can't go back to Armethalieh and neither can you. And even if we could fight our way in, do you think the High Council would listen to us? Would the Arch-Mage listen to *me*?" *And Lycaelon rules the Council now. He must, now that Volpiril's dead. I have to talk to Idalia about this. She kept watch on the High Council for years. She'll have a better idea of how the power would have shifted with Volpiril gone. And . . . Lycaelon has adopted someone, and given him Volpiril's Council seat. Who?*

"So you're going to leave them to die," Cilarnen said bitterly. "I knew you would." He started to get to his feet.

"Sit down," Kellen said firmly. "Drink your tea. And *think,* Cilarnen. By Leaf and Star, you were the best student at the Mage-College—you must have *some* brain in that pretty head of yours. I wouldn't give my worst enemy over to *Them*—I'm certainly not giving *Them* a whole city of innocent people to play with. *Their* sorcery is fueled by torture and death—and the more powerful the Gift in their victim, the more power *They* gain from destroying him. If they take Armethalieh . . . if they *can* take Armethalieh . . ."

Then They *win.* They'll be unstoppable.

"It's cold," Cilarnen muttered sulkily, sitting back down.

Kellen lifted the pot. Cilarnen held out his cup. Kellen refilled it. Cilarnen sipped. "Now it's bitter," he said, a faint whining note in his voice.

Kellen sighed inwardly. He wondered if he'd ever been anything like Cilarnen. Probably. He refilled his own cup. "I don't make very good tea. Ask anyone," he said mildly. He passed Cilarnen the jar of honey-disks and sipped his own tea. It tasted fine to him—strong, but that was just as well. He hadn't gotten much sleep.

"You say you're going to help. But you don't say what you're going to do. And the only reason you're going to help is because if those *Things* destroy Armethalieh, it'll be bad for the Elves, who are the only ones you really care about," Cilarnen retorted belligerently a few moments later.

If Kellen hadn't had something really important to worry about now, if he hadn't had the paying of his Mageprice fixed firmly in his mind, he might actually have gotten angry. As it was, he simply stared at Cilarnen in bemusement. Why in the name of anything you cared to call upon was the boy trying to pick a fight with him?

Because Cilarnen was afraid.

The intuition came to him suddenly. He glanced up at Kardus, and saw acknowledgment in the Centaur Wild-mage's dark-eyed gaze. Cilarnen was terrified.

For Armethalieh.

Kellen had been afraid when he'd been Banished, but only of the unknown. From the moment Armethalieh's gates closed behind him, he'd been looking forward, not back.

But Cilarnen . . .

Cilarnen *missed* Armethalieh. The way Idalia would miss Jermayan, he imagined vaguely, or he would miss Shalkan. Cilarnen felt about Armethalieh the way Jermayan and Ancaladar felt about each other.

But a city is wood and stone. It can't love you back.

He supposed that didn't matter. The Elves loved Ysterialpoerin, and had fought desperately to save it. *He* had fought desperately to save it.

Compassion warmed his next words.

"Yes, many of the Elves are my friends. But I'd help anyway, even if Armethalieh's destruction weren't a danger to them. If *They* destroy Armethalieh, *Their* victory will be bad for more than just the Elves. It will give *Them* the power to destroy every creature of the Light, every tree, every blade of grass, until there's nothing left in the world but *Them* and *Their* slaves. *They* tried twice before. The first time was before there were humans, and the Elves fought them alone. The last time was around the time Armethalieh was built. Everyone—Elves, humans, Centaurs, unicorns, dragons, and Otherfolk who don't exist anymore—all joined together to defeat *Them*. They thought they'd won forever.

"They were wrong."

Cilarnen just shook his head. Plainly it was more information than he could handle.

"Kellen will aid Armethalieh, Cilarnen, and so will the Elves, for all the races of the Light depend on one another, like a spider's web. Cut one strand, then another, and soon there is no web at all. Do you see?" Kardus said, as simply as if he were talking to a small child.

"But the Elves went to ask the City for help," Cilarnen said, shaking his head. "And we wouldn't give it. Why should they help now?"

Kardus glanced at Kellen questioningly.

"Well, the Elves weren't actually asking for help. Andoreniel already knew that the High Mages wouldn't fight for the Elves—or for anyone outside the City," Kellen said, trying to keep his explanation simple. "He was only trying to warn the City so they could protect themselves."

"But they wouldn't let Hyandur in!" Cilarnen said angrily. "They wouldn't let him warn them—and he still saved my life! Roiry and Pearl could have been *killed* outrunning the Scouring Hunt, but he still helped me."

Kellen wasn't sure, but from the context, "Roiry" and "Pearl" seemed to be Hyandur's riding animals. Odd that one of the Mageborn should care about anything like that; young Mages-in-training didn't have pets or favorite mounts any more than they had girlfriends. They were supposed to focus their entire being on the High Magick to the exclusion of everything else.

"If what the creature you met at Stonehearth told you is true," Kellen said, still thinking his way slowly through everything Cilarnen had told him, "Hyandur's being barred from the City may have saved not only your life, but his. He probably wouldn't have been left alive to deliver his message—depending on the nature of this 'foothold.'"

Cilarnen looked surprised, as if the thought had never occurred to him.

"So . . . it worked out for the best?" he said tentatively.

"It went as the Wild Magic wills," Kellen said automatically.

Cilarnen recoiled in disgust, wincing faintly.

Kellen sighed ruefully. Cilarnen was more difficult to talk to than the Elves of Ysterialpoerin! "You can't have *that* much objection to the Wild Magic. You came here with a Wildmage," he said, with just a touch of chiding in his voice.

It was an hour before dawn now; he wasn't going to get any more sleep tonight. He might as well get dressed and take Cilarnen to be fed. At a slightly more civilized hour he could present him to Redhelwar—hoping Cilarnen did not insult the Army's General too thoroughly—and they could begin to plan what to do.

"Kardus is different. He doesn't make my skin crawl," Cilarnen said with a shattering lack of tact. "And anyway— I'm already Banished. What difference can it make *who* I associate with? But Wild Magic . . . it doesn't make any sense."

Kellen looked at Kardus, puzzled.

"As you know, I have no magic. Yet when the Books came to me, I did my best to live by their teachings, and to follow the Great Herdsman's Path. There are times when I Know what others do not, and in payment for these Knowings, I am always set a Task. I Knew in Merryvale that I must go to Stonehearth, and help the human child I would find there. When I reached Stonehearth, my Knowing unfolded further, and I realized, after the attack, that my Task was to bring him to you, in order to give him the help he truly needed.

"Both Wirance and I found that his magic was of a kind neither of us knew. We tested him with the Wild Magic, and found that Wirance's Books caused him true distress where mine did not, though he could read neither Wirance's set nor mine. Yet their spells worked together well enough at Stonehearth."

"Huh," Kellen said. One more mystery. Well, given time and enough information, this one could probably be unraveled too.

He pulled off the tunic he'd grabbed at random and opened his clothes chest.

"What are you doing?" Cilarnen asked nervously.

"Getting dressed." For some reason Kellen was starting to feel like Cilarnen's *much* older brother. "It's almost dawn. Then the three of us—by your courtesy, Kardus Wildmage— are going to go and eat, because I didn't get much sleep and I'm hungry, and as the Mountainfolk say, 'Sleep is food, and food is sleep.' By then the day-watch of the camp should be on duty, so I'll go to Dionan or Ninolion and see when we can see Redhelwar—the General of the Elven Army, Cilarnen, and he's the most important person here, so try to be extremely polite. The Elves set a great store by politeness. Then, when we *do* see him, you can tell him what you've told me, and we'll figure out what to do about it."

As he spoke, he finished dressing, and buckled on sword, dagger, and spurs. It was a little cramped with Kardus in the tent, but he managed. Quickly running a comb through his hair, he braided it into a tight club at the base of his neck, tied it with a ribbon, swung his cloak around himself, and picked up his gloves.

Cilarnen was staring at him, jaw hanging.

"You look like an Elf," he blurted, scrambling to his feet.

Kellen bit his lip. Hard. "Cilarnen, have you actually *seen* any Elves? I look about as much like one of them as a draft horse looks like a unicorn. Come on." He doused the lanterns and worked his way around Kardus to the door of the pavilion.

⌐

CILARNEN followed the other two out of the now-dark green tent, gasping a little as the sharp bite of the cold air. It was still black as night, for all Kellen Tavadon's talk of it being nearly dawn, and snowing—of course. At least Tavadon had listened, though Cilarnen wasn't really sure how much he understood. He had kept talking about things that had happened a thousand years ago, not about what had happened back in the village. And about Elves.

Always Elves.

Cilarnen seethed with resentment. Like any properly-raised Mageborn, Cilarnen knew about Elves. They were deceitful, they were one of the Lesser Races—

Of course—he felt a wash of confusion—Centaurs were a Lesser Race, too. And Sarlin and Kardus were Centaurs.

But they were different. They didn't make him feel quite so . . . unfinished.

Elves bothered him. They were so haughty, so terribly aloof.

And the Chronicles of the Light *specifically* said that Elvenkind had been created by the Light as a rebuke to humankind. That Elves never told the truth.

But Hyandur had been coming to tell the truth about the Demons, hadn't he?

Cilarnen felt his head begin to hurt. This was not how things were supposed to be going.

⌐

THE dining tent was bright and warm. The night watch was there, lingering over their meals before retiring to their beds. With the caverns cleared, the army, by the grace of Leaf and Star, would be granted a breathing space to heal itself before it must fight again.

Kellen caught Cilarnen gazing around himself curiously, as if he'd never been here before.

"You've been staying with the Centaurs?" he asked. That would make sense, if he'd been in Kardus's care. The Centaurs had a separate section of the camp, with everything—including their eating place—arranged to accommodate their physical requirements.

Cilarnen nodded dumbly.

"We can move one of the benches for you, Kardus," Kellen said. "But I'm afraid the table will be low."

"It is of no matter," the Centaur said kindly. "The food here is excellent." He switched his tail in anticipation.

They went and collected trays of food. Kellen noticed there were few items on Cilarnen's tray, and added more.

"Will you stop doing that?" Cilarnen demanded irritably, after Kellen put on the third dish. "I'm not that hungry."

"It's cold out there. You need to eat," Kellen said, spying a platter of honey-cakes fresh from the oven and taking several. Warm, they were delicious. Cold, both Shalkan and Firareth liked them—and he knew he'd have to make time today to get up to the Unicorn Camp to tell them the news.

Bad as it was.

"I *don't* need to eat," Cilarnen said pettishly. "And if I did, you couldn't make me."

"I could tie you in a knot and feed you your own feet," Kellen said, making his tone pleasant just to keep the boy off balance. He had the feeling that the more he kept Cilarnen bewildered, the better chance there would be for new ideas to sink into that too-pretty skull. "At least drink if you won't eat."

"Not if it's more boiled grass," Cilarnen said peevishly. At least he kept his voice down—not that it mattered, as the Elves could hear him perfectly well.

Kellen added a tankard of hot cider to Cilarnen's tray.

"Boiled grass." He'll drink tea in Redhelwar's pavilion if I have to strangle him.

Kellen and Kardus worked their way steadily through hearty breakfasts—Kellen, as was his usual habit, wrapping several of the honey-cakes on his plate in a cloth and tucking them away for later—while Kellen took the opportunity to catch up on news from the Wild Lands, since Kardus had come from Merryvale.

Haneida was well—Kellen was grateful to hear that, as

the elderly beekeeper had refused to leave the village when the Scouring Hunt had come—

"And Master Eliron as well," Kardus said, smiling. "Still in his place, still swearing he is too old and too busy to serve as a Councilor. Most of the villagers returned to their places in the Wild Lands as soon as the new Bounds collapsed."

"And Merana? And Cormo?" Kellen asked eagerly.

Kardus bowed his head, suddenly grave. "Cormo is here. Merana . . . was lost upon the road, as many were."

Kellen swallowed around the sudden lump in his own throat. Lost, if Idalia had guessed right, to Demon raids. "I'm sorry." *I hope she died quickly.*

Out of the corner of his eye he could see that Cilarnen was only picking at his food. In fact, he didn't look well at all.

But he'd seemed fine back in Kellen's pavilion. And he hadn't eaten or drunk anything Kellen hadn't. As Kellen watched, he set down his eating knife and rubbed fretfully at his eyes.

He'd mentioned having headaches back in Stonehearth.

"Look, why don't we go over to the Healers' tents and find you something for your headache?" Kellen suggested. "You'll probably feel more like eating then. And you need a clear head when you talk to Redhelwar."

Cilarnen stared at him in a combination of misery and shock.

"You look awful," Kellen said, in explanation. "Didn't they give you something for your headaches in Stonehearth?"

"Yes," Cilarnen finally—reluctantly—said. "I don't know what. It was brown. It had dream-honey in it. I took it twice a day. But I haven't had any headaches since . . . " His voice trailed off.

Kellen managed to keep his face still, but it took all the practice he'd had living among the Elves. What little he knew about healing-cordials he'd learned listening to Idalia, but he knew that dream-honey was powerful stuff, not used lightly.

"Well, the Healers will be able to come up with something. And this is probably just because of a weather change."

"But what if I'm losing my Gift again?" Now Cilarnen had an edge of panic in his voice. Kellen thought he knew why, and for just a moment, he felt a little sympathy. Magic, after all, was all that Cilarnen had left of his old life. And the thought that he might lose even that must make him mad with fear.

"Cilarnen," Kellen said firmly, getting to his feet. "You know *much* more about the High Magick than I do. You know you can't just 'lose' a Gift. The High Mages either Burn it out of your mind, or they don't. So since they didn't, no matter what happens, or what you feel, you still have it."

Cilarnen stared up at him, the same dumb fear in his eyes as a cornered hare. Kellen shook his head. This should have been the moment when he felt superior, at long last, to the too-perfect boy who was everything Kellen Tavadon should have been and wasn't. But he didn't. Oddly, all he felt was ir- ritation. "Now come to the Healers' tent," he said gruffly, "—or be carried. It's all one to me."

BY the time they reached the Healers' tent, Cilarnen was staggering along between Kellen and Kardus mechanically and very nearly *was* carried there. They brought him inside the tent designated for minor injuries—a mere headache, no matter how bad, could not compare with the severity of the injuries the Healers usually treated. Cilarnen sank down on a waiting bench and leaned forward, his forehead nearly touching his knees.

Even a sennight after the battle at Ysterialpoerin, the Healers' tents were still filled with recuperating wounded, for the Wildmages could only cure so many, and the rest must be left to heal by more conventional means.

A Healer approached as soon as they entered.

"I See you, Kellen Knight-Mage."

"I See you, Healer Yatimumil," Kellen said, bowing to the Elven Healer. "Here is Cilarnen, a human High Mage. He suffers from headaches that Centaur Healers in Stonehearth were treating with a potion containing dream-honey. We thought the cause of those headaches was past, and this headache may not be of the same sort. It came on very suddenly."

Yatimumil bowed again, looking at Cilarnen critically. "Idalia is here. I will send for her. I think perhaps that a human should look into this."

A few moments later, Idalia and Vestakia entered the tent.

"So you found him," Idalia said neutrally.

"Say rather that he found me," Kellen said, grimacing.

Idalia moved toward Cilarnen.

"No," Kellen said quickly. "Don't. Kardus says that Wildmages make him uncomfortable." He shrugged. "I don't know why."

"Well, *I'm* not a Wildmage."

Vestakia moved forward and knelt in front of him. "Cilarnen, please look up. I need to see your eyes."

Cilarnen looked up.

Recoiled.

Tensed.

Oh, NO.

Kellen had long since stopped noticing what Vestakia looked like. She was just . . . Vestakia. His comrade in arms, sometimes his weapon in battle. And by now everyone in the Elven army thought of her the same way.

But when Cilarnen had looked up, he hadn't seen *Vestakia.* He'd seen a Demon.

He scrabbled for the knife on his belt, his face white with terror.

If he kills her—or so much as hurts her—the Elves will kill HIM.

If I don't kill him first!

Kellen dove between them, knocking Cilarnen and the bench over backward before anyone else had a chance to move. He measured himself full-length atop Cilarnen, one hand clasped over the wrist of the hand that held the knife—a Centaur-made blade, heavy and sharp—the other firmly clasped over Cilarnen's mouth, lest he say words that could not be unsaid.

"I'm sorry," he said into Cilarnen's ear. "I'm sorry. I should have warned you. I didn't think she'd be here. I didn't *think*. Her name's Vestakia. She's a friend. Her father was one of *Them*, but her mother was a great Wildmage, and she worked a powerful spell, so that Vestakia would be human, and good—inside, where it counts."

Cilarnen struggled violently, but he was no match for Kellen's strength. Kellen supposed he was hurting him— one way or another—but right now he had no choice.

"I promise you that she's never hurt anyone in her life"— it was stretching the truth a bit, but certainly Vestakia had never hurt anyone Good—"and she isn't one of *Them*. *Think*. Would Kardus be standing here quietly if she were?"

Finally Cilarnen lay still, and Kellen dared to take his hand from over his mouth.

"I— But— She— But— Women can't do magick," Cilarnen sputtered irrelevantly.

Behind them both, Idalia made a noise like an exasperated cat.

Kellen plucked the knife from Cilarnen's hand and tossed it into the middle of the room, then hauled him unceremoniously to his feet, stepping back warily.

"You'll find that women can do a great number of things. Probably even High Magick, if the High Mages weren't so unreasonable about it," Kellen told him, though not as sternly as he might have. "You have a good mind, Cilarnen Volpiril. See with your own eyes, hear with your own ears, and use what you find to draw logical conclusions."

He glanced around cautiously.

Vestakia was cowering back against Idalia, looking stricken. Kellen looked away quickly.

Kardus picked up the discarded knife and moved to stand beside Vestakia and Idalia.

"It is true," he said. "She is a daughter of the Light. I will prove it to you now."

From one of the pouches at his belt he removed a short coil of shining white rope. Kellen recognized what it was instantly. Unicorn hair, braided into a thin rope.

"Child, I beg you, of your courtesy. He has seen friends die at *Their* hands," Kardus said to Vestakia.

Tears welled up in Vestakia's eyes. She held out her arm, pushing the cuff of her tunic back to expose the skin.

Slowly and deliberately, Kardus wound the length of rope around her arm.

Kellen turned away. He could not watch. How many times did Vestakia have to prove herself? Instead, he watched Cilarnen.

Cilarnen was staring at Kardus and Vestakia intently. At last he moved forward slowly, stepping over the fallen bench.

Kellen forced himself to turn to keep Cilarnen in sight, but he still would not look at Vestakia.

"Citizen Vestakia," Cilarnen said, bowing before her. He stopped, obviously searching for words. "I beg that you will accept my . . . very humble . . . apologies. I have been . . . unjust. It must be a terrible thing to be seen as . . . as what you seem . . . instead of as what you are."

"Citizen." Not sure of her rank, Cilarnen had chosen to address her by the honorific that properly belonged to *any* inhabitant of the City, from High Mage to dock-laborer. From someone who still thought of himself as an Armethaliehan, it was an incredible honor. Kellen hoped Idalia would explain it to Vestakia later.

Vestakia held out her hand. Cilarnen took it without hesitation.

"We shall both blame Kellen for this, and not each other," she said decisively. "For he should certainly have warned you."

She shook her head, as over a careless child, and Kellen felt himself flushing. "Sometimes," she said, with a sidelong glance at Kellen, "he is not very practical. Now come and sit. We must still discover the cause of your headache."

"Oh, it doesn't hurt now," Cilarnen said hastily.

"Then it will not hurt you to be examined," Vestakia said implacably, leading him over to another bench. "I am a Healer, and you must allow me to do my duty." Kardus followed.

Kellen picked up the fallen bench. When he straightened, he found Idalia looking at him.

"Still want to kill him?" she asked.

Kellen shook his head in exasperation. "If you happen to see a Selken Trader though, I wouldn't mind stuffing him in a sack and selling him to them. Still, I suppose, if I'd gotten dropped in things as thoroughly as he has, I wouldn't have handled things much better." He took her arm and led her to the far side of the tent, and continued in a lower voice. "He told me his news. It's bad. *Very* bad." He shook his head at her unspoken query. "Not here."

"Where?" she said.

"Whenever Redhelwar can see us. But he wouldn't eat this morning, so I brought him here. That was *after* he sneaked into my tent last night and I nearly killed him."

"Poor Kellen," Idalia said with fulsome sympathy. "Bearded by the terrible High Mage in his bedroll."

"Entered Apprentice," Kellen corrected absently. "And ready to test for Journeyman, which means he knows the spells—if he could figure out a way to use them."

Vestakia came over to them then.

"He has no head injury, and it is not any kind of cold sickness I know, nor poison—and Kardus says that if a spell *had* been cast upon him, he would probably have been a great deal sicker than he was. Kellen, did you see what happened to him?"

Kellen thought about it. "Nothing happened. We were in my pavilion, drinking tea—Armethaliehan Black. I drank it, and so did Kardus. He was fine then. We went to eat. He was sick by the time we got there, I think."

Idalia shrugged. Vestakia looked baffled. "Well, he swears his head does not hurt now," she said.

"We can't just knock him over and have a passing Knight-Mage sit on him every time he develops a headache," Idalia retorted. "It wouldn't be convenient—and you might start to like it, Kellen." She tapped her lips with one finger, thinking. "I'll make up a cordial for him to take if his head starts hurting again. If it doesn't work, bring him back. Oh—and you might want to see about getting him something warmer to wear. What he's got is good enough for Stonehearth, or for camp, but if we have to go any further north, he's going to freeze, and he must be cold already."

Kellen sighed—he seemed to be doing a lot of that lately. But when had he been appointed Cilarnen's nurse? Still, proper Mageborn like Cilarnen were small and slender. They might even be able to fit him from the clothing the dead had left behind.

It was a gruesome thought, one he wouldn't have had a moonturn ago, but it came to him now with simple matter-of-fact practicality.

"I'll see to it," he said. In fact, he'd tell Isinwen to see to it. That way, Cilarnen's clothes would not only be warm, but suitable.

Idalia went to see to the making of the cordial, taking Vestakia with her. Kellen went over to Cilarnen.

He really did look better. Whether it was the sudden shock, or just because the headache had run its course, he seemed to be fully recovered.

"I'm sorry, I didn't mean to hurt her feelings," Cilarnen said quietly. "I didn't think . . . "

No, Kellen thought. *They didn't teach any of us to think in the City, did they? But you started thinking there—or trying to—and that's what started all your problems.*

Just the way it started mine.

"The fault was mine," he said. "I didn't think, either, and as a result, I gave you a terrible shock, and she was upset. Let it be forgotten."

"If I will not be needed here," Kardus said, "there are matters elsewhere that require my attention. Follow the Herdsman's Path, Cilarnen. Kellen will be your friend."

"I have kept you too long already," Cilarnen said, with automatic courtesy. "Go with the Light."

The Centaur trotted quickly from the tent, leaving Kellen and Cilarnen to share an awkward silence. A few moments later Idalia came back with a bottle of amber liquid and a horn spoon.

"Here you go," she said to Cilarnen. "It's not the same thing you were taking in Stonehearth, from what Yatimumil says, but if your head starts hurting again, take two spoonsful of it. If that doesn't work, come back here."

"Yes," Cilarnen said. "Thank you." He was regarding Idalia curiously, as if there were questions he longed to ask her, but didn't quite dare.

Kellen felt—strongly—that those questions had better go unasked just now. Cilarnen might have been able to repair his lapse with Vestakia, but Vestakia had an essentially forgiving nature. He wasn't quite sure how Idalia would react to any questions along the lines of how she—a mere female—had managed to learn magic.

"Come on," he said, giving Cilarnen a quick gentle shove toward the opening of the tent.

—

"NOW," he said, once they were outside. "We are going to see Redhelwar's adjutant, whoever is on duty. He may offer us tea. Drink it; believe me, it is an honor to be offered tea. Do *not* tell him it tastes like boiled grass. Do not even *think* that it tastes like boiled grass. Elves have *very* sharp hearing. And—"

"Don't ask them any questions?" Cilarnen suggested.

"Right," Kellen said, relieved that Cilarnen had figured out that much. "They may ask *you* questions. Don't be surprised. It's called War Manners, and this is an army in the field, so in an emergency, the forms of etiquette are relaxed. But generally questions are considered incredibly rude.

Like—" He groped for the proper comparison. "Like barging into someone else's house and making yourself at home, I guess."

"You lecture like Master Tocsel," Cilarnen grumbled, shivering. "How long did it take you to figure all this out?"

"I didn't figure any of it out," Kellen told him honestly. "Fortunately Idalia—my sister—had lived with the Elves before, and she told me so I wouldn't make, well, too many mistakes."

"Sister?" Cilarnen said, blankly. He might not have noticed the last time Kellen had mentioned having a sister, but he did now.

Just too late Kellen remembered that Cilarnen would have known perfectly well—along with everyone else in the City—that Kellen Tavadon was Arch-Mage Lycaelon's only child. For a brief moment, he wondered how Lycaelon had managed *that*. Cilarnen was Kellen's age, or near it; certainly he wouldn't have known about Idalia any more than Kellen knew about Cilarnen's family. But there was Volpiril—or Cilarnen's mother, who might actually have *known* Idalia . . . Kellen wondered for a moment how many other nasty little secrets the Mageborn families shared.

"She's my older sister. Lycaelon's firstborn. Banished for practicing the Wild Magic ten years before I was," Kellen said.

"You never mentioned her."

In all the intimate conversations we had at the Mage-College?

"Lycaelon made sure I didn't remember her," Kellen said briefly.

"I don't think that's right," Cilarnen said, a new, hard note in his voice. Then a few moments later, he spoke again. "Kellen?"

"Yes, Cilarnen?" Trying *very* hard not to sigh.

"If she was Banished ten years before you were, you would have been seven, and I would have been eight. Was it a full legal Banishing?" His voice was full of a sharp urgency. "Did she appear before the High Council? Did she wear the Cloak? Did they send the Hunt?"

"Yes, and yes, and yes, and yes, and why does it matter?" Kellen said, beginning to get irritated despite his best intentions.

Cilarnen swallowed audibly. "It matters because of a course at the Mage-College you never took: Jurisprudence of the City. They taught that there hadn't been any Banishings for over a century, that it was an ancient custom from the Dark Times, fallen into disuse now." And now there was yet another note in his voice—one that said the bottom had fallen out of his world. "They *lied*, Kellen!"

Kellen stopped and turned around. "Yes, Cilarnen, they lied," he said patiently. "About the Banishings, about Wild Magic being evil, about the so-called Lesser Races, about— too many things to go into right now. The entire City is built on lies. We're going to save it anyway."

I hope.

⟳

DIONAN was not there when Kellen and Redhelwar arrived, only Dionan's assistant, who was tidying the tent and setting out the tea service. After a moment, Kellen dredged up his name. Alenwe.

"I See you, Kellen Knight-Mage," Alenwe said, bowing courteously.

"I See you, Alenwe," Kellen said. "I make known to you Mage Cilarnen of Armethalieh."

"I See you, Mage Cilarnen," Alenwe said, bowing again.

"I See you, Alenwe," Cilarnen said, following Kellen's lead.

"Perhaps, if you are not called elsewhere, it would please you to enter and take tea, for I know you have been welcome in Dionan's tent many times before," Alenwe said.

"To be welcomed into Dionan's tent is always an honor, each time as much as the first," Kellen said.

There was no need for Alenwe to send anyone in search of Dionan; even if Dionan weren't planning to return immediately from whatever errand had called him away, the Elven gossip-chains that ran faster than a bolt of summer lightning would ensure that he knew Kellen was here.

And in fact, before the tea-water had boiled, Dionan came walking into the tent, as unhurriedly as if he'd been out for a morning stroll.

"I do thank you for your patience with me, Alenwe, and your hospitality to my guests. Let us find something new for Kellen to try, and to honor the visitor from Armethalieh. I think perhaps Golden Pearl would be suitable. It is an excellent warming tea."

As the tea was prepared, they discussed the weather, which, according to Dionan, would continue hard and cold, but without any more blizzards like the one they had just weathered, or so the Wildmages said.

At least Kellen and Dionan discussed the weather. Cilarnen remained resolutely silent, though Kellen could sense his growing frustration and bewilderment as if it were itself a gathering storm.

The tea was poured. Kellen sipped.

Most Elven teas were herbal. Some were heavily-spiced as well. This was one of the heavily-spiced ones. It tasted . . . not like fresh-baked bread, but like the *idea* of fresh-baked bread: warm with more than heat. It reminded him of honey, though it was unsweetened, yet it had a subtle biting undertaste he couldn't quite identify.

"Perhaps we shall allow our guest to give his opinion first," Dionan said. "Cilarnen High Mage, perhaps you would wish to favor us with your opinion of this brew, of your kindness."

Oh, please, don't let him say it tastes like boiled grass! Kellen thought in near-desperation.

Cilarnen considered the matter for a moment, taking a second sip of the tea. "It lacks the body of a cured-leaf tea, of course, though perhaps that is not a flaw, as it allows the subtle interplay of flavors to bloom more fully upon the tongue. I taste saffron and ginger—a *very* slight hint of chamomile—and, I think, *rendis*. The illusion of sweetness, along with the complex hot finish, makes this, as you say, an excellent warming tea. But I do not believe it would keep well, or repay oversteeping. Of course," he finished modestly, "I am no expert. My own tastes, as I have said, run to the cured-leaf teas."

Kellen stared at Cilarnen, nonplussed. Cilarnen shot him a triumphant look.

"An excellent description indeed," Dionan said, with approval. His gaze shifted to Kellen expectantly.

"I must thank Cilarnen for giving me the words to say what I am yet too untutored in the Way of Tea to yet express," Kellen said, firmly suppressing a flash of jealousy. "I could only have said that it made me think of homely things, like bread, without knowing why it did. And I would give much to know how a thing can seem sweet, and yet not be so."

"Ah, you would be instructed in *all* the arts of Tea," Dionan said, with the faintest of smiles. "If Leaf and Star permit, someday you will not only brew properly, but blend. What a joyous day that will be for us all. But I have indulged myself sufficiently. Perhaps you would wish to share with me your purpose in coming to drink tea before the day has fairly begun, for I know you came weary from your labors at the caverns yesterday."

"I had hoped, if it was not inconvenient, that it might be possible to make Cilarnen known to Redhelwar, were Redhelwar not occupied with more important matters. It would please me greatly if Idalia might also be present to hear what might be said then, and whoever Redhelwar thought prudent, that Cilarnen might be made known to all at once. Though he has journeyed for many sennights through the Elven Lands, he has seen little of Elven ways, and what he would speak of is a grave matter indeed."

"Indeed, and grave matters must be conducted with unseemly haste," Dionan agreed. "Present yourselves at Redhelwar's pavilion in three hours, and all shall be as you desire."

"I thank you for your courtesy and your quickness," Kellen answered. He stood and bowed.

⇌

"A bell and a half is unseemly haste?" Cilarnen demanded, once they were a few yards away.

"Unless someone is actually attacking—yes," Kellen said. "Elves live a thousand years, and they do not hurry." He shrugged. "Well, think about it. If you lived for a thousand years, what would a few bells seem like to you? And we have plenty to do between now and then. And for somebody who thinks Elven tea tastes like boiled grass, you certainly seem to be able to say a great deal about it."

"Awful, wasn't it?" Cilarnen said, grimacing. "Give me a good pot of Phastan Silvertip any day. Still, you don't spend hours in the Golden Bells without being able to talk about tea, no matter what it tastes like. And you said to be polite."

⇌

THEIR first stop was Isinwen's tent. Kellen's Second was still asleep, but Kellen showed no pity. He shook the bells until Isinwen unpegged the flap and stood in the doorway.

His long black hair was still loosely braided for sleep, and he had hastily thrown his cloak on over a tunic and leggings, but he regarded Kellen alertly.

"Alakomentai," he said.

"I make known to you Cilarnen of Armethalieh," Kellen said. "Idalia assures me he will surely freeze if we do not find him something warmer to wear. And we are to go before Redhelwar in three hours."

"So it would be as well if we could present him to advantage," Isinwen said, stepping out of his tent to regard Cilarnen critically. "Armor will be impossible. Not in three hours."

"He is no knight," Kellen said. "But he'll need something soon. Not today, though. Clothing, however, he is in great need of."

"Artenel will rejoice to hear it," Isinwen said blandly. "I go upon the wings of the wind, though Leaf and Star alone know what I shall find. I shall leave my poor scavengings in your pavilion."

"I thank you for your help and courtesy," Kellen said. "And I am sorry to have interrupted your rest."

"At that," Isinwen said, slanting a glance at Cilarnen, "I think I must have gotten more than you did. But we were all sure you could handle two intruders by yourself."

Thanks a lot. Once more, Kellen was reminded of the utter lack of privacy in the camp, but if Isinwen had heard anything of what Cilarnen had said to Kellen early this morning, he would be far too polite to say so. To Kellen, at least.

"As always, you instruct me," Kellen said, bowing with overelaborate courtesy. Isinwen retreated into his tent to dress, and Kellen took Cilarnen off again.

"If you haven't figured it out, everyone here heard you come to my pavilion last night," he told Cilarnen.

"They didn't stop me," Cilarnen said, doubt warring with accusation in his tone.

"They knew they didn't need to," Kellen said. Let Cilarnen figure out the rest. Right now, he was trying to decide what to *do* with Cilarnen for the next couple of hours. He wasn't sure that taking him up to the Unicorn Camp was a good idea. For one thing, he wasn't sure the unicorns would tolerate him—he didn't know that much about Cilarnen, after all, and celibate—as the young Mageborn were—didn't necessarily mean chaste. For another, it would only be appropriate to give Redhelwar the bad news first.

But he didn't really want to be alone with him either. Paying his price was one thing. Refraining from throttling Cilarnen for new annoyances was another.

"Have you seen much of the camp?" he finally said.

Cilarnen shook his head. "After I thawed out, I stayed

with the Centaurs. Comild—he became the leader of the levy that gathered at Stonehearth after Kindrius died—said it was best to stay out of the way of the Elder Brothers as much as possible."

"Good advice as far as it goes, only you aren't going to be able to do that anymore. You'll never *be* an Elf, but they'll make allowances for that. Your manners are good, when you bother to use them. So pay attention and learn how to fit in."

"The Elves don't seem very . . . useful," Cilarnen said tentatively. "All they seem to do is talk about tea and the weather . . . and half the time I can't figure out what they're saying! And their armor—your clothes—it's all so . . . pretty." From Cilarnen's tone, "pretty" was not a compliment.

"Elven ways are not human ways. Sometimes they don't make sense at first. Sometimes they never make sense to humans at all." Kellen tried to sum up everything he had learned in a few simple sentences. "They love beauty, so much that they try to make everything into an art. That means fighting and weapons too. Let me tell you, that pretty armor is strong, and tough, and flexible. It's saved my life more than once."

As they spoke, Kellen found that he was walking in the direction of the horse-lines. A good destination. There'd be time to give Firareth a little exercise—and to test Cilarnen's riding skills as well.

By the time they got there, though, he was weary with more than a night's lost sleep. Every answer he gave Cilarnen seemed to breed more questions. So he had armor? Was he a Knight? If he was a Knight, where had he learned to fight? How could magic teach someone to fight?

Though Kellen knew that half Cilarnen's questions were an honest attempt to gain the information that would allow him to fit in to his strange new world and the other half an attempt to distract himself from his worries, they still nibbled at Kellen's composure like a swarm of hungry mice at a bread loaf. Leaf and Star—he didn't know the answers to half of them—and the ones he could answer, he didn't know *how* to, not in any way Cilarnen could understand.

Any mention of the Wild Magic seemed to simply baffle Cilarnen, like attempting to explain color to a blind man. True, it had confused Kellen when he began to study it, but even then he'd realized that there was a *pattern* within it— somewhere.

Cilarnen seemed wholly unable to grasp that pattern—or even the *idea* that there *could* be a pattern.

He's not a Wildmage. He'll NEVER be a Wildmage.

They reached the horse-lines. And Cilarnen—blessedly— shut up, staring at the waiting ranks of destriers.

"I thought we'd go for a ride this morning. I'll have to go out and catch Firareth first, though. What were you riding when you came?"

Cilarnen seemed to wilt slightly. "A mule. A very *nice* mule of course—his name is Oakleaf, but—Kellen, the Elves keep their promises, don't they?"

"Did someone promise you something?" Kellen said carefully.

"When I came from Stonehearth, Lady Sarlin gave me a horse. Her name was Tinsin. She was a plowhorse—the Centaurs didn't have any riding horses, of course. She wasn't very fast. Nemermet—our guide—didn't like that. He took her away from me. He said she'd be well treated, just as if she were Elven stock, and returned to Stonehearth in the spring, but . . ."

"Then she will," Kellen said firmly. "The Elves honor their allies, and if you told Nemermet that Tinsin was your responsibility, he'd take that very seriously."

"Oh," Cilarnen said. He seemed to relax a little. "I wasn't sure."

"Be sure," Kellen said seriously. "Don't ever call an Elf a liar. Don't even think it." *Or you might find yourself in a Challenge Circle, and I'm not even sure you can lift a sword.* "Remember about them making everything into an art? Their honor is an art, too, and they spend a lifetime perfecting it."

They walked out into the herd. Kellen stopped to pat fa-

miliar friends, looking for Firareth. He should be with the
nearer herd, those who still had riders.

"They're all so beautiful," Cilarnen said longingly.

"Elven-bred, from the Fields of Vardirvoshan, and trained
for war," Kellen said. "We should be able to find you something faster than a mule—you'll need it, to keep up with the
army when it's on the move. How well do you ride?"

"Better than you do," Cilarnen said smugly.

That's the last straw. Kellen turned to the nearest horse
handler, who was moving through the herd. "I See you, Ana-
mitar. It would please me greatly to know if Anganil has yet
found a rider."

Twenty-five

Gifts and Promises

T he young black stallion was yet unpartnered. By the
time Kellen had brought in Firareth and saddled him,
Anganil had been brought to the horse-lines, and his gear
had been brought from storage. He wore no armor, and his
saddle-trappings were now all in white.

By the time Anganil was saddled, they'd collected something of an audience.

Kellen supposed it wasn't very nice of him to set Cilarnen
up for a quick flight into a snowbank—but Leaf and Star, the
boy needed to stop making so many assumptions!

"He's war-trained," Kellen warned, swinging into his saddle. "He's young, and he hasn't been ridden for a while. If he
likes you, and you can stay in the saddle, he's yours to ride
for as long as you're with the army."

He felt safe in making that much of a promise, especially
since Cilarnen's possession of Anganil wasn't likely to ex-

tend much beyond the next five minutes. After that, they could find him something he *could* handle.

He tried not to think of Ciltesse, who had chosen Anganil, hoping Kellen would ride him. Ciltesse would have enjoyed this moment very much.

Or been appalled by it.

But apparently Cilarnen did know something about horses. He took the time to make friends with the stallion, stroking his nose and speaking gently to him. Kellen offered him a piece of honey-cake, and Cilarnen fed Anganil the sticky-sweet morsel.

So far, so good.

When Anganil had accepted his presence, Cilarnen quickly mounted. The stallion held perfectly still, merely lifting one hind hoof and setting it down again.

Once they'd ridden away from camp, however, it was a different story. It was just as well that Cilarnen was—as he'd claimed—a good horseman—as Anganil was fresh, playful . . . and very, very bored.

After the third time the stallion plunged sidewise in feigned panic at a swirl of wind-drifted snow, Kellen said, "You'd better give him a run before he really starts playing up. Come on."

He spurred Firareth into a canter, then a gallop. Anganil was only too happy to follow.

Kellen figured they'd probably have time for a good gallop up to the end of the camp and back. In the distance, he could see others taking advantage of the rest and the comparatively good weather; there were teams of draft mules out, clearing a level practice field for the cavalry units to drill on later, and groups of Elves were even building the elaborate and mysterious snow-sculptures he'd seen back in Sentarshadeen after the first heavy snowfall.

Anganil overtook Firareth, and Kellen let him. Cilarnen still seemed to be in control, but Kellen could tell he was having to work for it.

Then he saw Shalkan.

Shalkan was pacing them, several hundred yards farther

out. The white unicorn was a ghost against the snow, running effortlessly along the top of it. Kellen waved, and Shalkan tossed his head in response.

Then, suddenly, Cilarnen saw Shalkan as well.

He stared, transfixed, at what was obviously the first unicorn he'd ever seen. For one moment, no part of his attention was on Anganil.

And Anganil knew it.

The stallion put on a burst of speed, then leaped into the air. He came down on his forehand, ducked his head, and kicked out hard with his hind legs.

Cilarnen went flying over his head into the snow. Anganil sprang sideways and began to run in good earnest.

Oh, no—

Kellen had wanted Cilarnen to take a fall—but not that hard a fall!

He checked Firareth and vaulted from the saddle, running to where Cilarnen lay sprawled in the snow. "Are you all right?" he demanded. *If he's dead—or hurt—Idalia will kill me. And I'll deserve it. Stupid, stupid, stupid—*

But Cilarnen seemed only to be breathless—and indignant.

"He threw me off!" Cilarnen said disgustedly, allowing Kellen to help him to his feet. He looked around, searching for Anganil. "And now he's bolted."

"He knew you weren't paying attention. Those are some of the war moves I told you about." Kellen helped him up, almost giddy with relief. "Don't worry. Shalkan will bring him back."

"That—was a unicorn," Cilarnen said, once he'd mounted up behind Kellen, and they were riding off in the direction Anganil had gone.

"Yes it was." Kellen smiled a little at the wonder in Cilarnen's voice. "His name is Shalkan, and he's my friend. There's a dragon here, too. His name is Ancaladar. You'll probably see him later."

Shalkan had herded Anganil in a wide circle, and now the destrier was running toward them, the unicorn at his heels. Kellen moved Firareth to block the young destrier's path.

Anganil, sensing that the game was up, stopped and stood quietly, switching his tail innocently.

"You have the oddest ideas of fun," Shalkan said, coming forward. "I suppose this is Cilarnen?"

"It can talk!" Cilarnen blurted.

Kellen groaned inwardly and closed his eyes. Poor Cilarnen. When Shalkan got done with him—

"Oh, my, yes," Shalkan said in his archest tones. "Quite as well as a human. Isn't that surprising? Of course, I've had a great deal more practice at talking than you seem to have. Why, I can form complete sentences and say exactly what I mean, for example."

"But— I mean— I didn't— That is—" Cilarnen stuttered.

Kellen ignored the byplay. He dismounted, walked over to Anganil, led the young stallion over to Firareth, and tied his reins firmly to Firareth's saddle. He didn't intend to spend the rest of the morning chasing Anganil through the snow if Anganil took it into his head to dash off again. Then he walked over to Shalkan.

"He doesn't know about unicorns because nobody teaches anything about them in the City—anything important, anyway," Kellen said, in a voice low enough that Cilarnen probably wouldn't hear. "Which you know already. And I haven't had time to explain everything to him yet."

Cilarnen clambered down from Firareth's back and came over to them. Apparently Shalkan was willing to permit his approach, for the unicorn stayed where he was.

Cilarnen was staring at Shalkan, oblivious to the falling snow. "Can I touch him?" he asked, and the note of raw longing in his voice would have melted a much harder heart than Kellen's.

"You have to ask Shalkan," Kellen said. "It's not my decision."

"May I?" Cilarnen asked, speaking directly to Shalkan now. "I didn't mean to insult you. It's just— You're so beautiful."

"He'll give you a honey-cake," Kellen said cunningly, rummaging in his tunic.

"Bribery," Shalkan scoffed, lowering his head and pawing at the snow—but apparently the combination of contrition, bribery, and flattery was sufficient. After crunching his way through the honey-cake held on Cilarnen's outstretched hand, Shalkan allowed himself to be touched. From the look on Cilarnen's face, he was willing to stand there forever, stroking the soft fur of Shalkan's neck.

"We need to get back," Kellen finally—reluctantly—said. He actually hated to tear Cilarnen away. The boy looked utterly smitten.

"Will I get to see you again?" Cilarnen said to Shalkan, sounding forlorn.

Kellen could tell that Shalkan was trying *very* hard not to laugh, but the unicorn's voice, when he answered, was admirably steady.

"Oh, have Kellen bring you up to the Unicorn Camp whenever he likes. You can meet the rest of us there." With that, Shalkan turned and trotted off.

Cilarnen turned to Kellen, his whole face a question.

"You didn't think Shalkan was the only one, did you?" Kellen said. "Come on."

He'd expected Cilarnen to ride back with him, but Cilarnen moved confidently toward Anganil.

"Cilarnen—"

"Yes, yes, yes. He's thrown me once, and now he'll see if he can do it again. I know." He looked over his shoulder at Kellen, with determination in the line of his jaw. "But you said I could try."

Yes, Idalia would kill him. And she'd skin him first. But how could he not give the boy a chance? He was learning.

He was learning faster than Kellen had, in some ways.

"Go ahead. Try not to get killed."

He waited, holding Anganil's headstall, until Cilarnen had mounted, and then handed him the reins.

The ride back went pretty much as Kellen had assumed it would—with one exception: Cilarnen was not thrown again. Once Anganil realized that this very entertaining spectacle was not to be allowed to repeat itself, he quieted down completely, and the two destriers trotted sedately side-by-side back to the horse-lines.

Cilarnen had only a little difficulty removing the unfamiliar tack, and soon they were on their way back to Kellen's pavilion again. And there was no doubt whatsoever that although meeting Shalkan must have been the high point of Cilarnen's life, riding the destrier had been the second highest. He was so full of wonder and ebullience that a little of it actually bubbled over and made Kellen's spirits rise.

"I've never ridden a horse like that before!" Cilarnen said excitedly.

"You've never *seen* a horse like that before," Kellen corrected him.

"Hyandur—" Cilarnen began.

"Rode a palfrey—a riding horse. Not a warhorse. Anything Elven-bred is beautiful," Kellen conceded, "but the destriers are special. Very, very special."

Kellen opened the flap of his tent and stepped inside, calling light into the lanterns to brighten the gloom. He noticed that Isinwen had already lit the brazier and stoked it high; it was actually warm in the tent.

And Isinwen had indeed been busy. There was a ewer and bowl waiting on the low table that had previously held the tea service, and piled on the clothes chest were Cilarnen's new clothes.

Not only was there a full outfit, including boots, gloves, and cloak—with, Kellen did not doubt, more to come—it all matched (at least as far as Kellen could tell), and since it looked turquoise in the light of Kellen's tent, it was probably blue.

Kellen picked up the gloves. Now here was something odd. There ought to be a pattern woven into the leggings, embroidered on the tunic, stamped into the leather of the gloves and boots. But there wasn't.

How, he wondered, had Isinwen managed that?

"Here you go," he said, gesturing at the clothing. "Get

dressed. You might even have time to get something to eat before we're supposed to be there, assuming your appetite's back."

Cilarnen had carried the tunic over to the doorway and was studying it in the light. "Blue," he said in disgust. "Like a Student."

"That's purely accident," Kellen said forcefully. "Isin-wen chose the color because he thought it would be becoming to you. The clothes are warm. You're not a Knight, so you're not stuck with the color. You can change it. You can ask for clothing to be made for you later in any color you like."

"To my House colors?"

"Maybe." Kellen tried to remember what they were, and couldn't. "Not if the Elves don't think they're suitable for your complexion though. And only Knights really have specific colors."

"Is that why everything you have is green?"

Here we go again. "It matches Shalkan's eyes. As you've probably noticed. Now, it would please me greatly if you would honor me by getting dressed. You'll be warmer, and you'll be appropriately garbed for the occasion."

Cilarnen pulled off his gloves and began to unlace his short cloak. "I suppose, since you're my friend, you're telling me the truth about the clothes," he said dubiously.

"I'm not your friend," Kellen said with simple bluntness. *Certainly not yet. Perhaps not ever.*

Cilarnen stopped. "Then . . . why did you give me An-ganil?"

Kellen thought hard—and honestly. "To teach you," he finally said.

Cilarnen removed his cloak and set it aside. For a few minutes he was occupied—in silence—with changing from old clothes to new, stopping for a quick wash in between. Isinwen had even been able to provide a belt with a couple of carrying-pouches, though Cilarnen's own Centaur-made knife would have to retain its own sheath until a new one could be made. It would look odd, but if he wore it toward the back, it would be hidden by the cloak.

When Cilarnen was dressed, he tucked his gloves through his belt in the fashion of Armethalieh, and smoothed his hand down the thick velvet. "You wanted to teach me that this is neither Armethalieh nor Stonehearth," he said, understanding in his voice.

"Yes," Kellen said. "Once more, you must begin again." *I hope you can.* He held out the cloak—hooded, ankle-length, and lined in ermine.

Cilarnen no longer looked like a rustic Wild Lands farmer. He looked elegant and patrician.

"Kellen," Cilarnen said in a troubled voice. "Remember that I told you I saw the *Thing* at Stonehearth?"

As if I've forgotten that for an instant.

"It looked human at first—when it spoke to me. It was wearing odd clothes, all white. Clothes I'd never seen before. Until now. Not exactly like these, but . . . similar."

It was dressed like an Elf? Kellen wasn't sure what that meant, but he was sure it was something meaningful . . . and bad.

"You'll need to draw what you saw for us, as exactly as you can. It may be important." He thought hard for a moment. "In fact, every tiny little detail you can remember might be critical."

Cilarnen nodded soberly.

Colors mattered to the Elves. White was the color of the Unformed—Anganil's tack had been white because he had no master.

It was also the color of the shrouds the Elves used to suspend their dead in the trees.

The color of Unmaking.

WHEN Kellen and Cilarnen arrived at Redhelwar's tent, the Senior Commanders and some others—Jermayan, Idalia,

Vestakia; representatives of the Centaur and High Reaches fighting forces; a few other Wildmages—were already there.

The honored guest arrives last, Kellen reminded himself. He hadn't expected quite so large an audience for Cilarnen's speech, but he suspected that rumors were already flying about the camp, and it would be just as well to be able to provide hard information in as many directions as possible as quickly as possible to keep those rumors from growing.

Small cups of tea were served; a token formality only.

"You have spoken with Cilarnen High-Mage of Armethalieh, Kellen," Redhelwar said, coming quickly to the point. "What have you learned?"

"I believe him indeed to be Cilarnen Volpiril," Kellen said carefully. Best to settle the obvious questions first. "Vestakia sensed no Taint in him, nor did Shalkan object to either his presence nor his touch. I would say . . . he is who he seems."

"And the reason for his presence here?" Redhelwar asked.

"In Stonehearth, one of *Them* spoke to him as if he were me." He looked at Cilarnen curiously. Why *had* Kardus brought Cilarnen to him? He'd never thought to ask.

"I had to tell someone," Cilarnen said. "Someone who could help. Kardus said to tell you."

"The Wild Magic gave Kardus the Task of bringing Cilarnen and his information to me," Kellen said, setting the pieces of the puzzle into a form the Elves would easily understand.

"From the look upon both your faces, the news that Cilarnen brought is of grave importance," Belepheriel said. "It would be good if you would share it with us."

"Tell them what *It* said to you," Kellen said.

Once more Cilarnen recited the words the Demon had spoken to him in Stonehearth. He might have dropped a bolt of lightning in their midst and gotten less reaction.

"A foothold in the human city!" Padredor exclaimed. "Impossible—they could not breach its wards any more than they can breach our own."

"Yet, if I ken these words aright, they *have* breached them," Adaerion pointed out. "Yet one does not properly understand what catspaws could they use in a place where everyone must be human and all magic but Mage-magic is banned."

"We have to find out," Kellen said. He looked at Idalia.

She shook her head. "I haven't had any luck Seeing the City since we fled the last Scouring Hunt. The Gods know I've tried, but . . . nothing. And putting that together with this news makes me very uneasy."

"There is another matter I would raise concerning Cilarnen," Kellen said, choosing his words with care. "I do not speak against his honor, yet it is a mystery. He is here because he was Banished, as I was, from Armethalieh. It is the custom of the High Mages to burn the Magegift from the minds of those they Banish. That they did not do it in my case was . . . an oversight." And the work of the Wild Magic, he did not doubt. "Yet Cilarnen's was not destroyed—only suppressed until the day of the battle at Stonehearth."

"Who was supposed to do it?" Idalia asked. "If we're looking for treasonous Mages, there's a place to start."

"It was Undermage Lord Anigrel," Cilarnen said.

"I suppose Master Anigrel could have been elevated," Kellen said doubtfully, "but he was Lycaelon's private secretary. You might as well expect Lycaelon himself to be plotting to overthrow the City."

"Could it have gone wrong?" Idalia asked. "Could he have tried to Burn it out and just . . . missed?"

Cilarnen shook his head. "I am no Mind-healer, my lady—one must study for years to become adept at that—but I know a little of the theory. To 'miss' would have killed me. To leave me whole, but without my Gift, that is as delicate a thing as—as taking the spice out of brewed tea. To simply put it to sleep, so I didn't even know it was there . . . that is more delicate work still. Yet—" He shook his head. "Yet I think, now, *that* is what was deliberately done."

"Could a Journeyman do it?" Kellen asked. That had been Anigrel's rank—and by the way the City worked, it would be for years to come.

Cilarnen shook his head again, smiling painfully. "It is not what I studied—*would* have studied. But Mindwork is only done by a Master Undermage . . . and work so delicate, I would say would require a Magister-Practimus—a full High Mage—at least."

"How delicate?" Kellen asked. "Is it just that you need a light touch, or a mind for details, or what, exactly?"

"I don't know! Kellen, I was only an Entered Apprentice! I'd barely begun my studies in the Art Magickal!" Cilarnen protested.

"You know more than anyone else here," Kellen said. "You're going to have to make your best guesses and tell us all you can."

"I'll tell you what I . . . know," Cilarnen said, hesitating over the last word. "You know the Mageborn swear oaths not to speak about the High Magick to the Commons, but don't worry that I'll hold anything back. I've already broken those oaths."

He looked miserable—no, more than that. Lost. Kellen didn't know what to say to comfort him.

"When you were Banished from your City, Cilarnen High Mage, your people took your name and your rank from you," Belepheriel said, with the gravity of a judge. "In doing that, they also took from you all your sworn oaths. In speaking now, you violate nothing, and may save many. It is a new way you must learn now, but this is a time of learning new ways."

"Thank you," Cilarnen said softly, bowing his head. Unconsciously he touched his chest, where his City-Talisman would have hung.

"It looks like Anigrel is where we need to start," Idalia said briskly. "And I *very* much want to see who's sitting on the High Council these days, if there's been a shift there. And who Lycaelon is now claiming as his son. The question is: how?"

"That is a matter to be settled among Wildmages," Redhelwar said firmly. "What my commanders and I must know is the extent of this 'foothold' *It* spoke of, so that we may determine what to do."

Idalia bowed. "We will bring you this information as quickly as we can, Redhelwar."

She and the other Wildmages left the pavilion.

⌣

KELLEN and Cilarnen remained behind.

Redhelwar regarded Kellen, brows raised.

Kellen bowed.

"You would speak," Redhelwar observed.

"I would," Kellen agreed. "You know it has long been in my mind that this campaign has been *Their* attempt to keep us from seeing what needs to be seen."

"And it is now in your mind that while we dally here, *They* strike first at Armethalieh," Redhelwar said.

"Not dally," Kellen said. "And not strike. I believe—I believe that this is a very different sort of warfare than *They* have ever practiced before. The Mageborn, I believe, remember *Them*, and fear *Them*, though they keep the fact a closely-guarded secret. I do not believe that a foothold could be taken by force. But . . . by seduction. As one of *Them* tried to seduce me at the Black Cairn. If it had worked—if I had believed *Its* lies—perhaps *I* would now be the agent you were all searching for in Armethalieh."

"No," Redhelwar said somberly, "for we would all be dead of drought and wildfire. But should Armethalieh fight for the Darkness instead of the Light . . . Go with Idalia, Kellen. See what Knight-Magery and High Magick can do to assist her."

Kellen bowed again and left, taking Cilarnen with him.

⌣

THEY caught up to the other Wildmages at the edge of the Mountainfolk camp.

"Redhelwar sent us to see what we could do to help," Kellen explained. "I can't think of a thing I can do," he added, shrugging.

"Not until we have some idea of what we're going to do," Idalia agreed. She turned her attention to Cilarnen.

"I know there *are* wards, but I've never worked on them," he said. "So I have no idea of how to get past them. The little ones, for things like keeping mice out of grain—I've helped with those."

"What about distance-seeing spells?" Idalia asked.

Cilarnen looked perfectly blank.

Why, Idalia, how could you ever imagine that any of the Mageborn would ever want to see anything that happened outside the City? Kellen thought mockingly. If such spells existed in the arsenal of the High Magick, they were undoubtedly restricted to the higher ranks of the Mageborn. Cilarnen wouldn't have begun to learn them for years—decades.

"Well, we'll get started. I want to try a few things—and have Jermayan and Ancaladar try them, too. Atroist and some of the Lost Lands Wildmages have arrived, and they know a number of ways of doing things I'm not familiar with. But I don't think we'll need your help yet. Join us here for dinner and I'll let you know how far we've gotten. Bring wine."

Kellen laughed shortly at the morose tone of Idalia's voice.

"Wine it is," he said. "Come on, Cilarnen, we'll go up to the Unicorn Camp and catch them up on the gossip. Shalkan will pin my ears back if I don't."

⟳

THEY stopped first at the dining tent to collect a cold lunch and some treats for the horses, and soon were riding up to the Unicorn Camp. Anganil behaved himself far better on this journey than he had on the last.

"So we don't have anything to do for the rest of the day?" Cilarnen asked.

"You may not," Kellen said. "When we get back, I'm going to see if the practice field is free. If it is, I'll take my troop out for a couple of hours of drill. You should see Artenel about getting some armor fitted—you may not be able to use a sword, but you'll still need armor."

"I *can* use a sword!" Cilarnen protested. "Master Kalos said I would have made a fine swordsman—I studied with him thrice a sennight."

"Reed-blade," Kellen said, struggling to keep his voice neutral. Cilarnen was right to be proud of his skill, but it was useless in war. "It is not the sort of sword we carry in the field."

"You think it's useless," Cilarnen said, stung.

"Pay attention to your mount. I did not say that. I have never studied reed-blade. The quickness and coordination: those skills will probably transfer to another weapon if you wish to learn one. But the swords we use take a great deal of strength, and learning any weapon takes time, and you are a Mage, not a Knight."

"You're both," Cilarnen pointed out. "And I'm not much of a Mage."

Leaf and Star, send me a Selken Trader! Kellen kept his voice patient. "I'm a particular kind of Wildmage, called a Knight-Mage. I'm very good at fighting, not as good at Wildmagery."

"It's nice to know there's *something* you're not good at," Cilarnen muttered.

Kellen wondered if Cilarnen had meant him to hear the remark. It was odd to think that Cilarnen must be just as off-balance and resentful as *he* was, now that their situations were reversed. Here, Kellen must seem to have all the advantages Cilarnen had once possessed, plus a higher rank than Cilarnen had ever held.

Well, the truth wouldn't hurt. "At the moment, you're the best High Mage in a thousand leagues. You are our only expert in High Magery. And as for Magecraft, who knows what the future may hold?"

"You can't believe the City would ever take me back?" Cilarnen said in disbelief.

"I believe I do not know—and neither do you," Kellen said firmly. "If there is one thing I've learned, it's that you should be very careful how you use the words 'never' and 'forever,' because you might have to eat them one day."

They reached the Unicorn Camp. In the distance, beyond the camp, Kellen could see plumes of snow arcing from the ground, as the remaining Unicorn Knights engaged in elaborate war games.

"They're practicing," Kellen said. "Let's go watch."

⌒

BEFORE he'd gotten his own command, he'd participated in a few of these games, but even a Knight-Mage's skill couldn't *quite* make up for years of practice, and he still hadn't entirely mastered the long Elven lance.

Both teams were armed with the lance. The object of the game was a small leather ring, to be picked up on the lance point, carried off, and defended.

There were, as far as Kellen could tell, no other rules.

He and Cilarnen stood well back from the edge of the field as the unicorns darted in and out among each other, springing like deer, as their riders vied strenuously for possession of the mostly-invisible object. Occasionally one unicorn would leap right over another, and woe to the rider who didn't duck in time.

"They ride them?" Cilarnen asked, sounding surprised.

"By mutual consent," Kellen said.

"Why are they all the way out here?" Cilarnen asked.

Kellen suspected the direction this conversation was going to go, but he really had no choice. There were things Cilarnen needed to know, and if he found out things Kellen would rather he *didn't* know in addition, well, that was a part of paying his price.

"Unicorns are creatures of magic. Magic has limitations as well as advantages. What did they teach you about unicorns in Armethalieh?"

Cilarnen frowned. "Their horn is proof against poison. That they share the nature of both the goat and the lion. And only virgins can tame them."

"Their horns purify just about anything. Their 'nature' is their own, and no one can actually 'tame' a unicorn. But only virgins can be around them," Kellen corrected. "Virgin meaning someone who is both chaste *and* celibate—and they can definitely tell."

"So that's why they're all this way from the rest of the camp?" Cilarnen said, accepting Kellen's explanation without a blink.

"That's right."

"Come to tell us what's going on?" Shalkan asked before Cilarnen could come up with any more questions. "Or is the game more interesting?"

"Oh, I'm sure they've come for a quiet chat," Gesade said.

Kellen looked over his shoulder. The two unicorns were standing behind them.

"Let's go back to the Unicorn Camp," he said to Cilarnen.

When they reached the edge, he swung down off Firareth and patted his shoulder.

"Drop Anganil's reins to the ground and tell him to stand," Kellen said to Cilarnen. "He won't wander."

Cilarnen looked dubious, but followed Kellen's suggestion.

They made their way to the center of camp. Kellen added more charcoal to the communal brazier.

The two unicorns waited expectantly. Gesade's ears flicked back and forth as she followed the sound of his movements. If Cilarnen noticed her blindness, he had the sense not to mention it.

Kellen told his part of the story, and encouraged Cilarnen to add his own, just as he had told it to Kellen early this morning.

"I hardly think that was fair," Gesade said when Cilarnen had finished. "You were *trying* to do the right thing."

"I didn't *think*," Cilarnen said, still sounding confused by his own actions. "My—my father would not have listened. The whole City knew that. But any of the Mageborn has the right of personal appeal to the Arch-Mage. It would have been a hideous scandal. I would certainly have been disowned. But . . . it would have been better."

"It wouldn't have worked," Kellen said flatly. "I don't say this because . . . " *Because he's a hidebound monster who tried to kill me twice.*

"Kellen, we all knew," Cilarnen said tactfully. "You and Lycaelon . . . didn't get on."

"Yes," Kellen said. "But . . . don't you see, Cilarnen? It's like war. Lycaelon was on one side. The other twelve members of the High Council were on the other. Those odds are not good for . . . winning. And we now know that *They* are involved somehow." A thought struck him. "I think that all of this might have been arranged to empty a Council seat. Your friends—did any of them have connections to the High Council?"

Cilarnen didn't even have to think. Unlike Kellen, he must have had the ranks and lineage of every one of the Mageborn committed to memory. "Jorade was the great-great-grandnephew of Lord Isas—and his heir. Geont was a Pentres, but the Pentreses are allied to the Breulins, and Lord Breulin sits upon the Council."

"So of the six of you, three had Council connections. What of Master Raellan?"

"He helped us a great deal—without him, we would never have found each other. But I'm sure he had no connection to the High Council. He was a Journeyman—of a minor house at best, perhaps even the son of a commoner like poor Tiedor. He never did give a family name, and we thought it would be tactless to ask."

But you trusted him with all your lives, because he was Mageborn. Kellen didn't ask what had happened to Master Raellen. It would be too cruel. Cilarnen didn't know what had happened to any of them. By now they were either dead, living somewhere in the City stripped of their Magegift and their memories, or—if they'd been incredibly lucky—simply didn't remember anything about the whole "conspiracy" at all.

"Kellen . . . you don't think . . . it all happened just so someone else could take a Council seat?" Cilarnen sounded horrified.

Kellen didn't answer. It seemed likely to him. In the normal course of things, there wouldn't have been a vacancy for years—even decades.

"If one of the Tainted is on the Council, *They* have more of a 'stranglehold' than a 'foothold,'" Gesade said, "assuming I understand how your High Council works."

"What does Redhelwar plan?" Shalkan asked.

"To see what Idalia and the others can come up with to see into the City," Kellen said. "And to make his plans depending on what they *do* see."

SCRYING was not the answer. Idalia and the others ruled that out quickly enough—even Jermayan, with Ancaladar's power to draw on, could not force the scrying bowl to show him Armethalieh.

"Flowers," Idalia said in rueful exasperation, looking at the image in the bowl. "Very nice, I don't think. I'm happy to know that spring will come, of course, but it isn't very helpful."

To send a spy into the City was impossible. To send anything but magic across the City-wards was impossible.

But they had to find the right spell.

It was Atroist who provided the first clue to the answer. The Lostlands Wildmages were accustomed to speaking to one another over far distances—Idalia and Jermayan had seen such a spell at work when Atroist spoke with Drothi.

"But it needs a focus at the other end," Atroist said. "And I do not think you will find one in your Golden City of Mages."

"Then combine it with a scrying spell—or parts of one, anyway," Tarik said. "That doesn't need a focus."

"But scrying is *un*focused," Idalia pointed out. "It shows

you what you need, not what you want—and this time, we need to see exactly what we want."

"Then blend in some Hunt Magic," Tarik suggested. "When you go hunting for deer, it's no use at all Calling hares."

"To see is well and good," Jermayan said, "but you do not need merely to See. You need also to Know. So this must be not just a spell of Seeing, but a spell of Knowing, such as Kellen uses. It does you no good to see if you do not understand what you see."

"There is a spell the Forest Wife teaches us," a Wildmage named Kavaaeri said slowly. She was one of the few female Wildmages to have come with the High Reaches folk. "We use it for herbs and mushrooms, so that we are sure of them before we use them. It is not a Knight-Mage spell . . . but it is a spell of Knowing."

The discussion went on.

AT dusk Kellen collected Cilarnen from the Centaur encampment and went to join the Wildmages.

He'd worried about whether Cilarnen would be able to stand the proximity of so many Wildmages—he suspected, from what Kardus had told him, that being around Wildmages for Cilarnen was like being around non-virgins for Shalkan.

"It's not too bad," Cilarnen said. "It's just . . . it feels as if something terrible is going to happen. But nothing ever does. I can stand it. As long as nobody casts a spell on me," he added darkly.

"We'd almost always ask your permission," Kellen assured him. "Unless you were unconscious, and it was for a healing—or to keep you from harming someone else."

"Well, I don't *ever* want a spell cast on me," Cilarnen said fervently. "To heal me or for anything else. If I'm going to hurt somebody, stop me some other way."

Kellen didn't answer. He wasn't about to make a promise he might not be able to keep.

⌒

THE Wildmages were gathered together in one of the great lodge-tents of the Mountainfolk, a structure large enough to accommodate several dozen people at once, and tall enough at its domed center for Kellen to stand comfortably upright.

Even Kardus was there, kneeling among the others and looking perfectly at ease, though Kellen wasn't sure how the Centaur had managed to negotiate the narrow doorway.

Both Kellen and Cilarnen were carrying rucksacks. Though wine was difficult to find in an Elven camp, with Vestakia's and Isinwen's help, Kellen had managed to assemble a number of bottles of things that more-or-less fit the definition, from mead to hard cider to Elven fruit cordials to some actual bottles of wine. He hoped Idalia appreciated the effort.

The lodge was filled with the good smells of roast meat and fresh bread—and the residue of enough magic to make him want to sneeze, though Cilarnen didn't seem to react to it. Looking around, Kellen saw a seat by Idalia and moved toward it. Cilarnen went to sit by Kardus.

"You look tired," Kellen said, folding himself easily into a cross-legged position beside his sister.

"A long day of battering my head against the merely difficult," Idalia said gloomily.

"We are to call hares and become mushrooms," Jermayan explained kindly. "Presuming Kindolhinadetil will grant us the loan of a mirror."

"Yes of course," Kellen said, with only a touch of irony. "That makes perfect sense." He opened the rucksack and passed Idalia one of the wine bottles.

"Spoiled fruit," Jermayan pronounced, regarding it.

Kellen grinned and offered him one of the cordials.

The food had been cooked elsewhere. Now the platters of

meat—roast mutton—and baskets of bread began to pass around. The meal was conducted in the style of the High Reaches, with several people sharing a communal platter.

As they ate, Idalia filled him in on what they'd accomplished that day.

"—so while we think we may have a spell that will allow us to see what's going on in the City, we aren't sure we have enough power to cast it," she finished.

There were three components to each spell of the Wild Magic: the power to cast the spell—always paid personally by the Wildmage—the power of the spell's work—which could be shared among many—and the Mageprice, which the Wildmage alone paid.

Idalia was saying that this spell was so powerful she didn't even have the power to cast it.

Kellen looked at Jermayan.

"Not even Ancaladar and I. I have spoken to him. And there is yet another difficulty, were I to be the one who cast this spell."

"One, we know they'll notice. It's only a matter of time. There'd probably be a little more time if a human were to cast it, instead of an Elf. Two, it's not just a spell of Seeing, but of Knowing—" Idalia said.

"Which means it would work best of all if somebody familiar with the City cast it," Kellen finished. "Because they'd already have some idea of what they were seeing, and wouldn't have to learn as much. That means you, me, or Cilarnen."

"That means me," Idalia corrected. "Cilarnen's not a Wildmage, and you're a Knight-Mage. I'd have the best chance of success—if I had the power to cast it."

"What about using a keystone?" Kellen said. "Like before?"

Idalia shook her head firmly. "We thought of that, and Drelech cast the talking stones to see if that would work. It needs to be a living source."

As the platters were cleared away, the discussion returned, once more, to the spell. Kellen could tell that the

Wildmages were now covering ground they had covered before, hoping for a solution.

He could see Cilarnen and Kardus talking quietly between themselves. Jermayan was watching them alertly, probably able to hear what was being said.

At last Cilarnen—who had obviously needed to be persuaded of something—made his way into the middle of the lodge and got to his feet.

The discussion stopped.

"I am unfamiliar with your . . . magic," he began hesitantly. "And I do not mean to offend. But Kardus tells me I must ask. Why do you not simply link your magic as the High Mages do?"

Kellen had rarely had the pleasure—if that was the word—of seeing his sister so completely nonplussed.

"Sit down over here," she said. "Explain."

Cilarnen darted an agonized glance at Kellen. Kellen did his best to look encouraging.

Cilarnen came and sat down in front of Idalia, doing his best to keep a respectable distance between them.

"In Armathalieh," Cilarnen said, obviously searching for just the right words, "the High Mages work together, sharing their power. It is part of every Mage's training to learn to meld the power each holds into a greater whole, for the good of the City. I had thought . . . " he faltered to a stop.

But it was something Wildmages never learned—never needed to learn. Because Wildmages were usually solitary creatures, who drew their power from themselves, from willing donors, and from paying their Mageprices.

"It's true," Kellen said, shrugging. "Anigrel told me. They may steal the citizens' personal power with the Talismans and use that instead of their own, but they still share the power among themselves when they do a Working. Somehow."

"Is that—" Cilarnen began, staring at Kellen.

Idalia interrupted him. "Do you know how this is done, Cilarnen? Can you tell me?"

"I know how to do it," Cilarnen said slowly. "I can tell you what the High Mages do—but I cannot do it with you! Not with a Wildmage!" His voice held unfeigned horror.

"I promise you, Cilarnen, if we figure this out, I will only practice on another Wildmage," Idalia said gently. "Jermayan, would Ancaladar consent to be a part of such a . . . sharing?"

"I do not know," Jermayan said. His voice was troubled. "First we must see if such a thing can be learned."

BUT before even that could be attempted, it had to be explained—and there they nearly came to grief, for Cilarnen was a High Mage of the Golden City . . . and High Magick and Wildmagery were nothing alike.

"Prayers to the Light? Fasting? Proper incense? Huntsman strike me if I do any such thing," a Wildmage named Kerleu growled, a few moments into Cilarnen's explanation.

"Nor am I going to wave my hands and babble to empty air like a mad thing," Cilarnen muttered under his breath.

"Patience, friends," Wirance said, his hands out in a placating gesture before things could grow more heated. "We will take what we can use—but we cannot do even that if you do not let the boy finish his explanation."

"Proper preparation. Proper intent," Kellen said, struggling to translate between the magic he only dimly remembered—and hadn't studied all that closely—and the one he knew. "Shielding?"

"Of course the working areas are shielded!" Cilarnen snapped. "Even you should remember that!"

Kellen held on to his temper with an effort. "What comes next?" he asked evenly.

Cilarnen explained.

And explained again.

And again.

"We'll try this again tomorrow," Idalia said with a sigh. "Maybe it will make more sense then. I don't know about anyone else, but I'm tired. Cilarnen, you've been very patient and you look like you could use a good night's sleep—and I know you can, Kellen."

And better to call a halt now, before tempers were well and truly lost, Kellen thought.

"Right. Come on, Cilarnen."

They were the first out of the lodge, but waited outside for Kardus.

"I'll see you back to your tent," Kellen said.

"You don't have to," Cilarnen said.

"Oh, but how else will I know where it is—so I can wake *you* up in the middle of the night?" Kellen said lightly. They walked a little to the side, out of the path of the emerging Wildmages.

"Why can't they understand it?" Cilarnen said in frustration. "It's so simple."

"It's a different kind of magic," Kellen said. "It's like—like trying to learn to play a lute when you've only ever played a trumpet. Wildmages generally work alone. It's even possible a Wildmage might not meet another Wildmage in his or her entire life."

Cilarnen shook his head, obviously finding the very concept unnatural.

"What you said back there—about the City Talismans—"

"It's why your spells don't work very well—and why the High Mages are so powerful," Kellen replied instantly, glad for the opening to let the boy know the truth about the Talismans. "Here, outside the City, the only thing that fuels your magic is your own personal power. Haven't you felt weak after casting a spell?"

"Yes, but—"

"That's why. You're only using your own power, not the power gathered from the whole City."

Kardus joined them—squirming less than gracefully out through the lodge's doorway, which had certainly not been designed for Centaurs—and the three of them began to walk toward Kardus and Cilarnen's tent.

"But— Then— I'm not ever going to be able to use most of the spells I know," Cilarnen said.

"Maybe," Kellen said. "Anigrel told me that everyone has the power that fuels Magery. Non-Mages have no use for it, so the Mages figured out a way to harvest and store it." His voice hardened. "They didn't ask permission, and they don't pay for what they take. That's wrong."

"No," Cilarnen said, slowly. "They *do* pay for it—with all the spells they do for the City. The power has to come from somewhere. You said so. The Mages work hard to keep the City running—*I* worked hard, when I was an Entered Apprentice. But . . . " Now he nodded. "You're right about one thing. They should still tell people what they're doing. The Commons have a right to know that *they're* helping the City, too."

It was a way of looking at the matter that Kellen hadn't considered before. And it was true that the City was a pleasant place to live—if you followed the rules.

"So you'd have the High Mages tell the people what they were doing?" he asked curiously. "What if someone didn't want to have his power harvested?"

He held his breath, waiting for Cilarnen's answer. Let it be the right one.

"It's just another tax—Light knows there are taxes enough," Cilarnen said, shrugging dismissively. "If they didn't want to pay this one, they'd have to leave, I suppose, because there's no way to live in the City without getting the benefit of the spells and it wouldn't be fair to everyone else to let them stay. A season mucking out stalls in one of the Delfier villages—like I did in Stonehearth—might convince them they'd rather pay the tax. Or they might like to farm, and not pay it. But either way, they'd know what was being taken, and whether or not they were willing to pay it. It's not *right* to take it without telling them."

Kellen let out his breath in a long sigh. The right answer indeed—and a number of ideas that would have the entire High Council in spinning fits if it ever heard them.

"There may be a solution to your problem of a power source. But we'll need to solve Idalia's first," Kellen said.

They'd reached the tent—and just in time. The snow, which had been falling in a thin powdery dust, began to thicken, and Kellen felt the sting of sleet.

"Sleep well," he said, and turned away.

⌒

KELLEN and his troop spent the following day with Vestakia at the further cavern as she attempted to communicate with the Crystal Spiders.

It was frustrating work—not because the gentle otherworldly creatures weren't willing to help, but because they were. Vestakia's mind was flooded with images and information she found it impossible to interpret.

"I *think*," she said, sitting up in the midst of a ring of softly glowing Spiders, "that they *do* sense their kindred in other caverns. And I *think* there is at least one more cavern of Shadowed Elves—if I am understanding anything they tell me! But, Kellen—if they never leave their caverns, how can they tell me *where* the cavern is?"

Kellen shook his head. There had to be a solution to that riddle, if they could only find it. "At least we know we need to keep looking."

"Maybe there's something, well, distinctive enough that someone could recognize it if I could describe it," Vestakia said. "But I'm getting a proper headache seeing the world through eight eyes instead of two!"

"Then you need to stop. Tell them you'll come back and talk with them again." *Maps. We need maps showing where all the caves beneath the Elven Lands are. Too bad there aren't any.*

Vestakia sighed and lay back down. The Crystal Spiders moved over her in a softly-glowing wave, and then retreated once she had spoken to them, moving quickly into the far depths of the cave. She rolled to her knees. Kellen turned away, and Isinwen moved forward to help her to her feet.

He mustn't think about her. Mustn't care if she was cold, or tired . . . because if he did, he'd never be able to stop. And he'd never stop with just thinking.

⌐

"I know what you're going to ask."

Jermayan waited.

The remains of Ancaladar's breakfast—Vestakia had brought the bullock up before she'd left for the cavern—was nothing more than a few smears of blood upon the snow; the dragon was a tidy eater. Keeping him fed had not precisely been a strain on the army's resources, but it had required careful planning. Still, a promise was a promise: Ancaladar had not had to hunt for himself since he had accepted Jermayan's Bond.

Last night, after the Wildmages' conclave, Jermayan had come here, to the place he and Ancaladar often shared. It was an ice-pavilion, similar to others he had built, but large enough to hold Ancaladar comfortably and shelter the dragon from the wind and the snow. There was even stabling for Valdien, for Ancaladar's "pavilion" was a certain distance from the camp, almost at the edge of the forest, to discourage idle sightseers.

Jermayan had explained everything that had taken place. Perhaps it was only an act of courtesy—Jermayan was still not entirely certain how much of his thoughts the dragon shared—but he found that talking matters over with his friend helped to clear his own mind.

He had asked for nothing.

"Ask, then." The dragon was coiled half-out of his pavilion, his sinuous neck curved about so that his jaw rested on the snow just before his foreclaws.

Jermayan swung down from Valdien's saddle and walked forward.

"Will you—will we—join in this link Idalia proposes? I do not yet understand how it may be done, but she seems to feel it can be learned. And Cilarnen is anxious to teach it."

"I could say no," Ancaladar said.

Jermayan knew that the dragon's greatest fear—bordering on paranoia—was to be *taken*—used as nothing more than a reservoir of magical power.

He knelt in the snow by Ancaladar's head.

"Beloved, I will let no one harm you. At least . . . it is a risk all will share equally. Every Wildmage. Without our power, I do not think it will succeed. And nothing can destroy our Bond."

"If I said no, you could force me," Ancaladar said, very softly. "You could take what you needed."

"But I would not," Jermayan said, reaching out to stroke Ancaladar's head. "I would only ask for your help. I would never take what you did not wish to give."

Ancaladar hesitated. Jermayan could feel the dragon's fear. And felt it begin to ebb.

"Yes," Ancaladar said at last. "We will share in the spells."

WHEN Kellen and his party reached the camp again, there was good news awaiting them.

"We've solved the problem—the first of them, anyway," Idalia said. There'd been a message waiting at the horse-lines for Kellen to come and see her, and he'd finally tracked her down in her tent.

He was surprised to see Cilarnen there as well. He was lying on Idalia's bedroll, a compress over his eyes.

Idalia shrugged, following Kellen's look. "Oh, he doesn't want any spells cast on him. But he doesn't have any objection to casting spells on someone else. So after we spent the morning getting nowhere, Kardus finally got the idea of asking him about the other spells he knew. He cast something called Knowing on Atroist—all with permission, of course—and put the spell directly into Atroist's mind. Atroist got a hideous headache and Cilarnen passed out. But then Atroist knew exactly how the High Mages perform the

Linking Spell, and was able to explain it to the rest of us. We're going to try it tonight, now that Kindolhinadetil's mirror has arrived. We don't need the link for that, but it's a good idea to practice it. And how was *your* day?"

"Less exciting," Kellen said, blinking at Idalia's matter-of-fact summary. If you had asked him two days ago just how likely this was—a High Mage casting a spell on a Wildmage!—he'd have assumed the questioner was mad to even think the idea. "Vestakia says the Crystal Spiders think there's at least one more cavern to clear, but she's having trouble finding out just where it is." He was still trying to wrap his mind about what she'd just told him so blithely. "Idalia, Cilarnen—Atroist—something could have gone wrong," he finished inadequately.

"They both knew the risks. We all discussed them before we tried it. They both agreed. It was probably more dangerous to Atroist, all things considered."

Considering, Kellen thought, that Cilarnen was a less than half-trained High Mage, it was entirely possible that he could have killed Atroist.

But this was war. And they had both known the risks.

"And it *did* work." Cilarnen's voice sounded faint, and very hoarse. He sat up with a stifled groan, running his fingers through his hair, and blinked owlishly at Kellen. There were dark shadows under his eyes, and he looked as if he'd just recovered from a high fever. "And I didn't kill anybody."

"No," Idalia said. "And you certainly put on quite a show."

Kellen wondered what it was Cilarnen had *done,* exactly.

"I don't think I could light a candle right now," Cilarnen said. He felt around himself, obviously searching for something.

"It's over here," Idalia said, indicating the table. "I had one of the Healers—not a Wildmage—bring it, after you dropped it. I didn't know if a Wildmage's handling it would make a difference."

"Neither do I." Cilarnen shrugged. "It's just a tool, but no one but one of the Mages would ever touch one in the City."

Kellen glanced over at the table. Lying on it was a crudely finished length of ashwood.

A Mageborn's Wand.

He shifted to spell-sight—it was truly second-nature now—and saw the residue of power eddying through the wood, fading slowly. The more it was used, the more attuned to its owner it would become—or so Mage-theory held.

"You'll want to finish that," he heard himself saying. "Artenel can loan you the tools, and give you the proper grade of silver for the caps. You'll need a belt-case, too."

"Just as if I were a proper Mage," Cilarnen said, a note of bitter humor in his voice. "Now all I lack is a dozen other tools, a library of spellbooks, and a lifetime of training."

" *'It is not meet to harvest the fruit before the seed is planted,'* " Kellen said, quoting Master Belesharon once more.

"In other words, the future will take care of itself," Idalia said. "And I wouldn't be too surprised to find that some of those things could come into our hands if we need them. Now, Kellen, we'll need your help with this spell—because I want you to be my anchor for the big one. For that, we'll need somebody keeping an eye on things in case . . . well, just in case. And no one better than a Knight-Mage. So you'll need the practice as well."

Kellen nodded. He wasn't looking forward to any of this—if someone was going to poke a stick into the hornet's nest, he'd much prefer it to be him rather than Idalia. But he had to admit that her logic was sound: a Wildmage would be better at a spell of pure Wildmagery than a Knight-Mage. And a Wildmage raised in Armethalieh would have the best chance of all.

"Lady Idalia, would it be permissible for me to watch?" Cilarnen asked. "Not if it is forbidden, of course," he added quickly.

"On the condition that you stop calling me 'Lady Idalia.' It's just 'Idalia.' And if you think you can walk that far," Idalia said. "Who knows? We might make a Wildmage of you yet," she added with a smile.

"The Eternal Light forfend," Cilarnen replied, but for the first time, it sounded as if he had a bit of a sense of humor about it. He got carefully to his feet and tucked his wand securely inside his tunic.

⌐

IT would have been impossible to gather the Wildmages together properly for this work in any of the structures within the camp except the main dining tent, and that would have inconvenienced far too many people, since they would need it for at least two days. So Jermayan and Ancaladar had once again created an ice-pavilion for the work, as they had for Atroist's Calling Spell—only this one was several times larger than that had been.

The ice-pavilion was circular, and glowed with Coldfire—an eerie sight in the dusk. Its polished surface—a faithful, though enormous, replica of a traditional Elven campaigning tent—was already crusted white with new-fallen snow.

Ancaladar was coiled around it. Kellen guessed from Cilarnen's lack of reaction that he'd already seen Ancaladar for the first time earlier today.

"Ah," the dragon said. "The young Mage who makes such lovely colors. Come to see what the Wildmages will do with the fruits of your wisdom?"

"Indeed I have," Cilarnen said. His voice shook only slightly—though with cold, weariness—or astonishment at conversing with a dragon—it was difficult to say. "But I think I can safely promise not to learn anything."

Ancaladar laughed. "Go inside before you freeze. And behold the wonders of Kindolhinadetil's mirror."

The three of them stepped inside. Some of the other Wildmages were already present. Jermayan had crafted a bench that ran all the way around the edge of the pavilion, and Cilarnen moved toward it quickly.

Idalia had seen the mirror before. Kellen hadn't. He stared.

It was a perfect oval as tall as he was, set in a wide stand-ing frame. The frame was of a light-colored fine-grained wood, intricately carved.

But it was hard to say with what. Each time Kellen was certain he had identified an object depicted in the frame and the base—fruit and flower, tree and bird—it seemed to change. Was that a deer? Or a wolf? Or was it a vine?

He gave up.

But then he looked directly *at* the mirror.

It was made of a single thick pane of flawless rock-crystal backed with Elvensilver, and the reflection it gave back was utterly perfect.

Kellen hadn't had much time for mirrors lately. There'd been none in the Wildwood, and he'd paid little attention to the small ones in the house in Sentarshadeen. Since then, well . . . he couldn't remember the last time he'd seen a mirror.

Was this him?

He faced a stranger. A man . . . and one he wouldn't want to face in battle, either. He towered over Cilarnen—even af-ter several moonturns working in Stonehearth's stables, you'd never mistake Cilarnen for anything but an Armethaliehan Mageborn. Kellen . . .

They'd call me a High Reaches barbarian trying to pass for an Elf, he thought with an inward grin. Well, if he wanted nothing to do with the City, the City had obviously returned the favor.

He turned away from the mirror.

"It's certainly impressive," he said.

"It will serve our needs," Jermayan said with a dismissive shrug.

"The rest of you have had all day to figure out this spell," Kellen said, as more Wildmages began to arrive. "Now you're going to have to explain it to me."

Twenty-six

Against All Odds

"Well, at heart it seems to be most like a Healing Spell that you stop in the middle," Idalia said. "And no actual Healing takes place. Everyone who uses magic has personal shields—with every gift comes an equal weakness. Wildmages can sense more of the world around them than non-Wildmages—without shields to block that out sometimes, we'd drown in all that information. Or be far more vulnerable to spells cast against us than non-Wildmages. Or just to the random influences of magical Otherfolk, even if they didn't mean to affect us. You don't have that problem as much as we do—"

"But then, I can't cast spells as well," Kellen finished.

"Right," Idalia said, pleased that he understood the matter so easily and seemed willing—so far—to go along with her plans. "A natural balance. So we need to drop those shields, blend our powers . . . and act as one."

She tried to sound confident and assured. She'd refused to accept Jermayan's betrothal pendant for fear that it would establish a deeper form of just such a link as she was proposing to forge now—allowing him to see into her mind, and perhaps glimpse her unpaid price in its fullness.

But that had been before so many things. His Bond with Ancaladar, for one. The discovery of precisely how much trouble they were all in, for another. She could just hope that with so many minds joined, all focused upon their task, the secret of her unpaid Mageprice would remain unshared.

"Tonight we charge the mirror with our shared energy," Idalia announced formally, once everyone had arrived. Even

Kardus was there—though the Centaur Wildmage had no innate magic, nor any ability to cast spells, he was as much a Wildmage as any of them. "Making it possibly the largest keystone any of us has ever seen. Tomorrow, in the light—at noon—we will work the spell, and see what we can see of Armethalieh. In addition to his mirror, Kindolhinadetil has sent *namanar* from Ysterialpoerin's Flower Forest— ghostwood—which we will need for the spell. I have spoken with Redhelwar. Tonight he will speak with the army, and see who will share in the price of the spell."

"Not the Healers," Wirance said. "They may be needed."

"And not all the army," Kellen said. "Even if they all volunteer. We could still be attacked."

"Agreed," Idalia said. "Kellen, you and Redhelwar make the disposition of the units that will *not* be involved. They'll need to be well away from here when the spell is cast. And now, let's get to work."

⟜

NORMALLY the charging of a keystone—even a big one— would have been simple, but for this, they needed a circle of protection as well. Idalia walked around outside the edge of the gathering, drawing a faint line on the snow floor of the pavilion with her walking staff. Then she returned to the center, and threw a handful of herbs on the waiting brazier.

Kellen felt the wall of protection go up around them, and a sudden sense of utter quiet descended upon him.

And more than that.

It was like that night at the battle for the farther cavern, when he had used his battle-sight to see every unit of the army at once. Only now it was the Wildmages around him that he sensed, and he realized that he could draw upon their power as easily as he could call upon his own.

But right now that was not his task. Kellen relaxed as much as he could, remembering what Idalia had said—that this was *like* a Healing. He concentrated on *not* concentrating, on being a vessel of power for another to draw from. He felt the magic shift and flow through him—his own, others'—strange, but not uncomfortable.

And then it was done.

Kindolhinadetil's mirror radiated power like a furnace, the clear crystal sheet of mirror glowing with an inward light to the senses of a Wildmage—or Knight-Mage.

"One more of that will be more than enough for me," Wirance said firmly, as soon as the shields had been dismissed. "Still, it will work."

"And I think it is something *we* shall do more of in the future," Atroist said, glancing at his fellow Lost Lands Wildmages. "With such strength to draw on, even the most difficult Healing could be made easy."

"To each fox his own hare," Wirance said agreeably.

The assembly began to disperse. Jermayan, Ancaladar, and Idalia would remain here tonight, to ensure that the mirror was not tampered with—for even the most benign of reasons.

Kellen took the opportunity to walk back with Atroist. He wanted to hear how the migration of the Lostlanders into the Wild Lands had gone.

"All came, as Drothi promised," Atroist said. "By the grace of the Good Goddess, it was as if the attention of the Dark Folk was turned elsewhere for that time, for if their creatures had harried us upon the way, we would not now be here. And the Firstlings met us far outside their own borders, with mules and wagons to speed the journey and see us safely through their own lands. Once we are settled in the west, the young men and the rest of the Wildmages will return to honor our bargain and join with the army . . . though it is not comfortable to hear that the Dark Folk have been seen in the Western Lands as well."

"I did not know it when I asked your aid," Kellen said. "I'm not certain how *They* manage it."

"Nevertheless, the west is a soft and pleasant land," Atroist said, "much in need of strong backs and hard work-

ers to make it bloom. The Springtide will be a glorious
sight."

If any of us lives to see it, Kellen thought.

⸺

HIS work that night was far from done, but fortunately the
spell of preparing the mirror had taken very little of his energy. He went from the ice-pavilion to Redhelwar's pavilion,
where he briefed the Army's General on Idalia's plans, and
the part the army would share in the spell.

For a healing, a physical link was needed between the
Wildmage and those who shared in the price. Fortunately
that wouldn't be necessary in this case—or Vestakia could
weave a cartload of blankets out of all the hair that would
have to be gathered.

"You say you would wish to withhold certain elements of
the army from sharing in the spell-price," Redhelwar said.
"It is . . . unlikely . . . that any will wish to refuse to pay the
price, so it will save time to make our dispositions now."

"The wounded will not participate, of course, nor will the
Healers," Kellen said. "I would wish to withhold a third of the
army and support troops—in case of attack, and to deal with
those matters which cannot be set aside, such as the care of
the horses. Those who participate . . . they could fight if they
had to, but they will be exhausted. Losses would be heavy."

"And we have had too many losses already. So."

Redhelwar brought out a thick—and much-amended—
scroll listing each unit by name, and they got to work.

⸺

WHEN their dispositions had been made, Redhelwar summoned his senior commanders, and Kellen had to explain the
entire matter again, albeit in a much shorter version this
time. Next, the senior commanders would brief their sub-
commanders, who would explain matters to their commands.

Tomorrow at the morning meal, Redhelwar would address the army. When those of his *komentaiia* who were to share in the price brought him their consent to participate in the Wildmage's spell, they would also bring the consent of every person serving under them. Redhelwar would consent to share the price of the spell, and in doing so, would bring with him the consent of all the others.

If there *were* an attack, it would deprive the army of its general, which was why Kellen had been careful to exclude two of the senior commanders from the price. But it was the only way: in magical terms, Redhelwar *was* the army, just as in Sentarshadeen, Andoreniel *was* the city. Only Redhelwar could properly give consent to participate on behalf of the entire army. Otherwise, the Wildmages themselves, and not proxies, would have to hear consent from each of the soldiers individually—and they'd still be listening a sennight from now!

But though Redhelwar would be the only one formally asked, all who participated in the spell would have been asked, and consented. That was the way it must be.

With that accomplished, Kellen had one last task before him. Tomorrow he would be acting as a Knight-Mage . . . which meant he must ask his troop to share in the price.

He gathered them together in a corner of the dining tent. Of the original thirty he had been given to command, there were less than a dozen left. The others were all new to him, added to his command since the battle of the farther cavern.

Briefly he explained to them what was to be done tomorrow, and the part they would be asked to play.

"And now I must ask: is there anyone here who will share in the price of the spell?"

The Elves exchanged glances.

"Foolish human," Ambanire—one of the new recruits—said. "We all will, of course."

The others nodded.

"Kellen, you know you don't have to ask," Isinwen said.

"No, actually," Kellen said. "I do. Trust me, that's the way

Wild Magic works. There is no such thing as implied consent. Isinwen, tomorrow you have command. I'll be busy. Afterward, you'll all be very . . . tired. I don't know more than that. So I suggest you all get a good night's sleep."

⌒

THERE was someone in his tent.

Kellen didn't need the footprints outside in the fresh snow to tell him so. He *knew*. And it didn't take a Knight-Mage's Gift to tell him who it was: even here in a war camp, the threshold of one's own dwelling was sacrosanct. No Elf would cross it without permission, even if its owner were not present. But a human—especially a young human entirely untutored in the courtesy that came so naturally to the Elves—

"What do you want, Cilarnen?" he said, stepping into the tent.

Cilarnen had left it dark; Kellen lit the lamps.

Cilarnen was sitting on the low stool that was the tent's only seating—probably to keep himself awake, for he had been half-dozing when Kellen arrived, and sat up with a jolt. Kellen could smell a faint unfamiliar medicinal smell in the air. Idalia's cordial? Well, exhaustion and strain could bring on a headache as well.

"I . . . I wanted to talk to you. Before tomorrow. Alone."

Kellen didn't want to talk. He wanted to sleep. But it must be something important—at least in Cilarnen's mind—to bring him here when he was obviously so desperately tired.

"You're here, it isn't tomorrow, and we're alone—as much as that's possible," Kellen said. He couldn't begin to imagine what Cilarnen wanted to see him about, but after all that Cilarnen had done to help make tomorrow's spell a success, he owed Cilarnen a hearing, no matter how much he'd rather be sleeping.

"Tomorrow . . . I want to be with the rest of you. With the Wildmages."

Kellen could not have been more stunned if Cilarnen had announced he suddenly wanted to *become* a Wildmage.

"*In* the Circle? Inside the Shields? With us?"

Cilarnen nodded.

"Why?" Kellen asked bluntly.

"Kellen, you said I was the smartest student at the Mage-College. I don't know if you were right or not, but I've been thinking, ever since, well, I finally saw you again. These *Things*—they're smart, too, aren't they?"

"As smart as we are," Kellen said grimly. "Maybe smarter."

"But the one in Stonehearth mistook me for you. And we look nothing alike, you know," Cilarnen said seriously. "So they're either stupid—or there's some reason for them to confuse the two of us. If you think like *Them*. Or see like *Them*."

Kellen waited. Cilarnen's reasoning made sense so far, though he didn't like where it was going.

"So—a reason. But I can't figure out what it is. I can't think like a . . . *That*. I can't even think like one of *you*. But Vestakia and Kardus both say I'm not Tainted with Dark Magery—Vestakia said she'd know, and that if she didn't, Shalkan would."

"That's true," Kellen said. "Whatever else we have to worry about, we don't have to worry about *that*."

Cilarnen smiled, though it clearly took an effort to do so.

"I think I'd rather die than be anything like the thing I saw at Stonehearth. It killed and it killed, and it . . . laughed. But you see, Kellen . . . maybe I'm supposed to be there tomorrow. Because you'll be there tomorrow. Maybe *It* saw something nobody else has seen—but not something bad. Maybe something it was afraid of. Something that could help."

It was possible, Kellen decided. All they really knew about Demons was that they were evil, terribly powerful, immortal, could assume any shape, and fueled their magic through the blood and pain of others. It was not impossible—in fact, it was highly likely—that they could sense things non-Demons couldn't. And he couldn't think like a Demon any more than Cilarnen could.

Oh, he could guess at their tactics. Imagine their strategy—some of the time. But truly think like one? No creature of the Light could manage that.

"Maybe you're right," Kellen said slowly. "Maybe your being there could help. Or maybe it will kill you."

Cilarnen looked directly at him, startled. This was obviously not what he'd expected to hear.

"Yes, I mean to scare you," Kellen said. "I want you to know exactly what you're asking for. This will be the most powerful spell any of us has ever attempted. A spell of the Wild Magic. You'll be right in the middle of it. We don't control the Wild Magic, not entirely; it works through us in its own way, though always for the Good. We're its tools, not the other way around. You might find yourself linked to several dozen Wildmages. If just being around us makes you uncomfortable, think what that would do. Think hard."

Kellen watched as Cilarnen pictured in his mind what Kellen had suggested. He could tell the boy was imagining something intolerably painful.

"I still want— I need—to be there. I've brought the message. My work—Kardus's Task—they're done. The Elves will take Tinsin back to Stonehearth. And Anganil will find another rider . . . if the Light forsakes me," Cilarnen said slowly. And if smiling had cost him an effort, there was no doubt in Kellen's mind that those words cost him every bit of courage and will that he had.

"Leaf and Star send that it doesn't," Kellen said. "Now go to bed. Here. It's too late and too cold for you to walk all the way back to the Centaur camp now—you'd probably fall asleep in the first snowdrift you found. Take the pallet. I've slept rougher than this before."

He opened his clothes chest and began pulling out his extra blankets and spare cloak. They'd make an adequate bed for the night, and his coldwarg-fur-lined cloak was warm enough to serve as a sleeping pallet in its own right.

"But—" Cilarnen began.

"No arguments. I'm saving all of mine for Idalia tomorrow," Kellen said.

Cilarnen was quickly asleep. Kellen lay awake a few moments longer, wondering if he were doing the right thing, then decided there was no point in worrying about it.

He slept.

⌐

THE funerals for the High Mages Perizel and Arance eclipsed in splendor even that of High Mage Vilmos two moonturns earlier, though they were held much more privately, in the Chapel of the Light at the Mage-College. At least Vilmos had died with dignity and honor—giving his all for the good of the City in a Great Working.

Perizel and Arance had been murdered.

It was impossible that the Commons should learn of it, of course—but every Mageborn in the Mage Quarter knew almost before the Magewardens had arrived at the houses of the deceased.

⌐

"THEY were poisoned, Lord Arch-Mage," Anigrel said, entering Lycaelon's office as Dawn Bells sounded its single lonely carillon. "We know how, but not by whom. My agents are questioning the servants—and the families."

"It seems that you were right, my son," Lycaelon said heavily, motioning for Anigrel to seat himself. "This monstrous conspiracy of Wildmages strikes at our very marrow. But *how* could they be poisoned?"

It seemed as if the Arch-Mage had aged a year for every sennight that had passed since the Banishings of early winter. In one sense, this was the time of his greatest triumph, since as far as Lycaelon Tavadon knew, the reins of power settled more firmly into his hands each day.

But apparently its emptiness ate at him like a wasting disease that owed nothing to any spell of Anigrel's. At the moment, Anigrel had no interest in hurrying his new father to reunion with the Light. He found the Arch-Mage too useful where he was: an enthusiastic partisan of Anigrel's policies, one whose purity of motive and loyalty to the City were unquestionable—and unquestioned.

"Lord Perizel is accustomed to take a cup of *kaffeyah* before he retires," Anigrel said, taking care to sound as if presenting the news pained him. "Lord Arance is fond of Ividion red—his servants say he generally takes wine in his library while looking over his collection of rare books. We did not find poison in either the glass or the cup. Nor would we . . . because we found traces of umbrastone. It would make any poison undetectable . . . Father."

"Light deliver us," Lycaelon groaned. He looked at Anigrel beseechingly.

"I will discover our enemies. I swear it. But until I do, I must ask you . . . do not fill those vacancies. We know that Arance and Perizel were good and loyal men. It is possible that we will not be able to say the same of any who put themselves forward to take their place."

"Yes." Lycaelon's eyes narrowed. "At a time like this, I must have no one about me whom I cannot trust. You are right, Anigrel. But . . . with only eight upon the Council, and you and I called so often to other duties, I fear the Great Workings will suffer. The City expects so much of us . . . "

"I have a plan that I hope will lift some of that burden from your shoulders," Anigrel said, lowering his eyes modestly.

He took a deep breath, forcing himself to remain calm. He was so very close now! For many years, against the possibility this day might come, he had been working upon an elaborate configuration of spells; tiny modifications of the City Wards. His changes would be undetectable to a casual inspection—but they would allow his Dark Lady and her kindred to send their magics through the City-Wards unhindered—and undetected.

And where spells could go, bodies could soon follow . . .

"Ah, my son, you are always thinking of the good of the City, even as you work yourself to exhaustion. You must share your thoughts with me," Lycaelon said eagerly.

Quickly Anigrel outlined his plan. All Mages of sufficient rank had always assisted in the Great Workings—why not dedicate specific groups of High Mages to specific tasks—weather spells, water purification spells, bell-setting, the City-Wards—freeing the more powerful and experienced Council Mages to lend their expertise to those unique and delicate problems that were sure to appear?

"Some of us could work with them at first, of course—to be sure everything runs properly. But other Mages often work in the Great Circles. It is in my mind to recruit from among their numbers. Those whom my Magewardens deem suitable, of course."

"It is an excellent plan," Lycaelon said. "The Council will approve it. It must. And, Anigrel . . . I hesitate to ask this of you, but you must lead the Circle that charges the City-Wards. I can trust no one but you with a task so vital to our welfare. You must choose the Mages for this Circle as well—and let as many of them be Magewardens as possible."

"It is a heavy burden you lay upon me, Father," Anigrel said gravely. "But I will try to bear it well—for the good of the City."

THE day of the Working dawned pale and overcast—and far too cold to snow. Kellen noted that fact almost automatically—and turned over and went back to sleep.

A few hours later he was roused—all the way from sleep this time—by the ringing of his bell-rope.

He was on his feet without being quite awake, sword in hand, wondering vaguely why he'd slept in his clothes. He unpegged the tent flap to find Kharren standing before him.

"Knight-Mage," she said courteously, "a last duty to discharge as *alakomentai* before you may leave your command to Isinwen. Adaerion gathers the first of the subcommanders in his pavilion in half an hour."

"I shall be there," Kellen promised, bowing.

He closed the tent flap again and glanced over at Cilarnen. Let him sleep as long as he could. Kellen added his own blankets to the ones already covering Cilarnen.

Kellen had just time to thrust his feet into his boots, comb his hair straight and tie it back—no time for braiding—and buckle on his weapons before running all the way to Adaerion's pavilion.

The day was just as cold as he'd suspected it would be.

In Adaerion's pavilion he, along with a dozen other subcommanders, gave his sworn oath, upon his honor, that he and all his command agreed to share in the price for the Work to come.

Afterward, Kellen felt both relieved and nervous. All the duties and responsibilities of the army had been lifted from him. All that remained was his service to the Wild Magic.

None of the Wildmages was certain of what would happen when the spell was cast. It could be as safe as a scrying spell—or as dangerous as the assault on the Black Cairn. There was no way to know except by doing.

What if this is a trap? Cilarnen is innocent—I truly believe that—but what if this is still a trap? The Demons have given us information before, knowing we would have no choice but to act upon it. If They *arranged for him to find out what he did,* They *would also know we would do everything in our power to investigate further. Making ourselves vulnerable . . .*

And just as with the discovery of the Shadowed Elves, there was no way to turn away from such a task. If what Cilarnen said was true—if there was any possibility that it was true—they had to know.

They had to do exactly what they were doing now.

Someday, Kellen vowed grimly, *we will no longer dance*

to your piping, Shadow Mountain. Someday WE will choose
the battlefield—and the battle. And we will win.

⌐

TWO hours before noon, Redhelwar addressed the army on
the drill field just outside the camp. He spoke slowly, pausing between each sentence, for his words must be relayed to
the edges of the command.

He spoke of simple things—the drought that was past, the
depth of the winter snows, the glory of the Springtide to
come. He did not speak of what the Wildmages were about
to do. He did not need to.

"We shall not go down to the Dark consenting," he said at
last. "We shall fight. Who will share with me in the price of
the spell?"

It was now that the senior and allied commanders were
to have come forward, bringing the oaths of their commands.

Instead, something unrehearsed, unplanned, and
unprecedented—especially in the lives of the Elves, who
lived by ritual and ceremony—happened.

The entire army—every Elf, every Centaur, every human
there—shouted out their consent, over and over again.

⌐

"LIGHT deliver us," Cilarnen said softly, listening to the
roar of the army. He and Kellen had remained behind to
watch; Kellen had wanted to hear Redhelwar's speech. They
were mounted on their destriers a few hundred yards from
where the army had gathered, for they would need to be inside the ice-pavilion before those who were sharing in the
spell-price surrounded it.

"Consent—asked and granted," Kellen said. "Without it
we are thieves, and the Wild Magic will turn against us.
Come on. It's time to go."

THEY rode Anganil and Firareth all the way to the pavilion—those of the army sharing in the price would follow on foot—and when they got there Kellen dismounted, looping his reins back over Firareth's saddle and motioning for Cilarnen to do the same.

"Home," he said to the destrier, pointing back at the camp and giving him an encouraging slap on the rump. "You, too," he said to Anganil.

Both animals trotted off toward the camp.

"They'll go where they're used to being fed," Kellen said, noting Cilarnen's look of disbelief. "The handlers will bring them in and take care of them. There's no magic involved. It's one of the commands they know."

"Like 'dump your rider in the snow'?" Cilarnen suggested, with a faint nervous smile.

"If we're both still alive tomorrow, maybe there will be time to start training you to make use of what Anganil knows," Kellen said absently. "I doubt you'll ever be a knight, but you have the makings of a fine rider."

They walked toward the pavilion, each occupied by his own sober thoughts.

The other Wildmages were already gathered here, though not all were yet inside. The Mountainfolk undoubtedly thought this was a fine calm day—even warm—and the Lostlanders were used to even harsher conditions. Some were gathered around a brazier, brewing their thick black tea and talking quietly. Others paced back and forth, their heavy furs dark against the snow.

It was the calm before battle.

Ancaladar was coiled around the pavilion, as immobile as if he'd decided to become a part of it. The dragon raised his head as they approached, his large golden eyes fixed on Cilarnen.

"This should be interesting," Ancaladar commented, lowering his head again.

They went inside. Idalia was standing near the mirror, talking intently to Jermayan. She looked up as Kellen entered.

And saw Cilarnen.

Last night Kellen had told Cilarnen he was saving all his arguments for Idalia. Now he wondered if arguing was going to be good enough. Idalia walked over to them.

"Good morning, Kellen. Have you decided to murder Cilarnen after all, or is there another reason he's here?" Her violet eyes flashed dangerously. She knew—they all knew—of Cilarnen's particular sensitivity to the Wild Magic. This was the last place he should be.

"He believes he has a good reason to stand in the Circle with us. I've heard his reasons, and I agree," Kellen said, matching bluntness with bluntness. "I've told him it may kill him. He has still chosen to come."

"Cilarnen—" Idalia began.

"Idalia," Kellen said gently. "No one is asking your permission."

Idalia stared at Kellen as if seeing him for the very first time.

Jermayan appeared at Idalia's side. Even in plain sight, even in a crowd of people, the Elven Mage could appear and disappear with a silent grace that owed nothing to magic.

"To know these reasons would make good hearing," Jermayan said quietly, putting a hand on Idalia's arm.

"It's a question," Kellen said to Cilarnen, when Cilarnen said nothing. Keyed-up as he was, Cilarnen might not have understood, and Jermayan was being very polite. "Answer it or not as you choose."

"I think . . . " Cilarnen faltered to a stop and started again. "The *Thing* in Stonehearth saw something in me. Something that made it confuse me with Kellen. I . . . *need* to be here. To help, if I can."

There was another silence. Idalia looked from Cilarnen to Kellen, and back again. At last she nodded—not permitting, but accepting. "As Kellen says, it's your choice."

"Stand where you like," Kellen said to Cilarnen. "I don't think it will matter."

"I'll want you in the center with me, Kellen," Idalia said. "Come on. I'll show you."

She took his arm and walked with him over to the space before Kindolhinadetil's mirror. Her stave leaned against it. There was now an iron brazier set before it—one of the largest the Elves possessed—filled with pieces of *namanar* wood. On a square of cloth beside it lay a small herb bundle that would also be needed.

"You've grown up, little brother. I'm glad," Idalia said.

"You always knew I would," Kellen pointed out. "And I've had good teachers, and better examples." Did she think he'd grown up because he'd argued with her? he wondered. Or because he hadn't?

"The best, I hope. Now. I'll stand here. You'll stand behind me. You'll see what I See—everyone will, I think, just like a regular scrying spell, but if this spell goes the way I think, I'm the only one who will Know whatever there is to know. But you should be able to sense how the spell is running, and . . . interfere, if it becomes necessary."

And hope the Wild Magic shows me what I need to do, Kellen thought soberly.

⭲

SOON all the Wildmages had moved into the pavilion, and the army had moved into position outside.

Redhelwar stepped through the opening, and bowed to Idalia.

Idalia returned the salute gravely.

"Today we will attempt to see beyond the wards of the City of a Thousand Bells, called Armethalieh, and know what takes place within her walls," Idalia announced formally. "Who will share with me the price of the Working?"

"The army and its allies will share in the price of the Working, Wildmage Idalia," Redhelwar said. "In token, I bring this."

He held out his hand. Resting upon the palm was a tiny

circlet: a band made of three strands of Redhelwar's hair, intricately braided into an endless ring.

"I accept your oath and your gift," Idalia said, taking the ring. "May the Gods of the Wild Magic favor us this day."

"Leaf and Star will that it be so," Redhelwar answered, bowing and retreating from the tent.

Idalia returned to the center and lit the brazier. As the ghostwood began to kindle, she took her staff and began to walk around the outer edge of the group of Wildmages, drawing a line in the beaten snow.

SHE refused to let herself think beyond each moment. There was one last reason why she was the only possible person to be the caster of this spell: all her prices were now paid, save for one. For any other, the Mageprice for a spell such as this would surely be heavy.

She returned to her place in the center of the circle, between Kellen and the brazier. He stood as calmly as if he were already in deep trance, as alertly as if he might be called upon to fight at any moment.

Waiting.

She'd said he'd grown up, and he had. Whatever past trouble there had been between him and Cilarnen, it was over now. He no longer needed her—he might still value her opinion, but he would never again depend on it instead of his own. The work of bringing him to adulthood—and vital work it had been—was done.

If disaster struck, those she loved—and who loved her—would survive.

Idalia knelt and took up the bundle of dried herbs and the ring of hair. She slipped her dagger from her belt and scored a long line down her palm, then clutched the herbs and hair in that hand tightly, moistening both with her blood.

Then she cast them onto the brazier of burning wood.

The smoke coiling upward changed color abruptly, and she felt the shimmer as the dome of protection rose around them all, expanding outward to enfold the army as well.

The Link formed, the Power of the assembled Wildmages joining together, becoming one, becoming hers. She felt the spell uncoil within her as she inhaled the smoke.

She reached out toward the mirror.

Show me what I need to See: Tell me what I need to Know.

It glowed bright as the moon, growing larger and larger until it was all there was.

⤶

SHE was in the City.

Not *now*—but *then*. What she saw was in the past. For a moment she was puzzled, then realized she must need to See this as well.

The Temple of the Light. An Adoption ceremony. The spell let her Know the meaning of everything she Saw, and so she knew that what she saw was Anigrel being adopted into House Tavadon, and that later this same day he would be appointed to the Mage Council and take Volpiril's seat.

She knew that Breulin and Isas had been forced to resign.

She knew that Anigrel was Cilarnen's Master Raellan.

There is no conspiracy. There never was. Anigrel started it all—

With dreamlike swiftness, the hours and days of Anigrel's life unfolded to her: the formation of the Magewardens and the Commons Wardens—the network of spies to inform upon the people of Armethalieh and sow terror among them. Every thread of unholy Darkness woven through the golden fabric of the City was spun from Anigrel's hands.

She watched as he murdered Lord Vilmos.

And she saw . . . she saw . . .

⤶

DEEP in the darkness of the World Without Sun, Savilla came out of her entrancement with a strangled cry of rage, though it was long before the proper time for her Rising.

Someone was tampering with her slave.

She *felt* it, through the soul-deep link she shared with her Mage-man.

The festering sickness of the Light approached him.

They will not!

⌐

WITH the fresh horrors of not one, but two murders to convince them—and not merely murders of Mageborn, but of members of the Mage Council itself—High Mage Anigrel's proposals for special, dedicated, highly secure groups of Mages to handle the routine magick of the City had passed by unanimous Council vote.

No one had suggested filling the empty Council seats. No one had dared. They were beginning to learn—slowly, but they were learning—that to disagree with any of Anigrel's proposals could well be seen as a sign of sympathy with the burgeoning Wildmage Menace.

And certainly there was no one better than the Chief Magewarden to see to the security of the City-Wards themselves.

Tonight his plans would bear their first fruits. Tonight he and highly loyal acolytes would begin to *change* the Wards surrounding the City. And soon . . .

Soon the City-wards would keep out only what Anigrel wanted kept out.

The Circle was assembled. The hour was correct. The braziers were lit, and the air was thick with the proper incense—a compound Anigrel had crafted *personally*. The nine Mages of the Points of the Light began to draw the elaborate sigils, chanting out the spell as they did so, while Anigrel and the remaining three sang the complex antiphon. The Great Sword warmed in his hands; soon it would be time to draw the first of the Seals . . .

⌒

IDALIA watched in sick horror. It was worse than she had imagined—worse than anyone had feared. Anigrel was the Demons' creature—had been for years. And now he'd managed to reach a position where he could strip away Armethalieh's defenses—and let the Demons in.

He was going to give them the City.

And all she could do was watch.

⌒

SAVILLA stood naked in her ivory chamber. The walls were spattered with blood, and the remains of half-a-dozen dismembered slaves lay scattered about, for she'd had no time to be neat or elegant. The obsidian bowl was filled to overflowing with hot fresh blood, and more pooled on the ebony table and ran down its legs to the floor.

Her Mage-man was doing his City-magic—that made everything much easier. She could touch what Overlooked him.

Wildmages.

Savilla's fury grew until it nearly choked her. How dare they meddle in her plans?

She bared her fangs in savage glee as she tested the power of their spell and followed it to its source. They'd worked so hard and so diligently to penetrate the human city's defenses.

But a breech for you is a breech for me, my darlings, Savilla purred to herself in sudden delight. In their desperation, they had made themselves vulnerable.

She struck with all her might.

⌒

KELLEN Saw all that Idalia Saw—they all did—but without the Knowing, it meant little to him. He let the images go, concentrating on feeling the currents of power that flowed through them all—through the ring of Wildmages into Idalia; from the army into the ring of Wildmages—searching constantly for anything out of place.

The spark that was Cilarnen was like a bright ember; different, apart, but not wrong.

Jermayan . . . another sort of difference. Not wrong.

Kellen ignored them both.

Then:

"No!"

Shouted—whispered—thought—he did not know which of these he did. But disaster—he sensed it—coming—already here—he didn't know which.

He reached out to Idalia. She had to end the spell.

He was too late.

Time seemed to slow. The surface of the mirror faded to darkness, and bowed outward as if its surface were not crystal, but oil. It reached for Idalia.

If it touched her, they would all die.

⌒

HE was sure they all felt they were doing something—even Kardus was staring into the mirror as if he could see something other than the reflections of Idalia and Kellen and everyone else here standing around in a circle. All Cilarnen knew was that the ice-pavilion was filled with smoke—very little of it was escaping through the smoke-hole in the roof—and it made him want to cough.

And that he'd never been so uncomfortable in his life.

It was like when he'd handled Wirance's Books—but worse.

It was like being terrified—only his mind wasn't terrified at all. His mind could see no reason for fear standing in a smoke-filled house made of ice.

But his heart was beating so hard that his entire body shook, and inside his gloves, his palms were slick with sweat.

And then he heard Kellen cry out.

CILARNEN flung Mageshield over Idalia at the exact moment Jermayan Cast his own shield. Kellen felt Cilarnen reach the end of his own power in seconds—

And felt Ancaladar bolster Cilarnen's power with his own.

"Freely given," Kellen heard. *"Freely given."*

Cilarnen's shield strengthened.

Held.

The two shields—one of High Magick, one of Elven Magery—sparked and boiled over each other, the emerald and purple refusing to blend.

They have to hold! Kellen felt as if the whole force of both forms of magic—neither his—was pouring through him, tearing him apart.

But the power of the Circle was his as well.

He drew upon it, forcing the two Shields together. His pain was a distant thing; he forced it still farther from his consciousness, focusing all his intent upon holding the two shields together. Now he could see them clasped in a faint blue tracery: his Will. The will of a Knight-Mage, which could not be turned aside from its purpose, save by death.

A bolt of pure Darkness struck their combined shield.

He heard Cilarnen scream; felt Jermayan's agony. Ancaladar bellowed in pain and outrage.

The shield held. And he held; though he felt as if every atom of his body was being torn asunder, he held, and held, and held, by will alone, and then as his will eroded, and he felt even that failing—

He was filled again with power, with a pure white power that held every color of magic there ever was within itself. And what little remained of his ability to think put a name to that power.

Shalkan.

This was why Shalkan held back from the other Workings, even when it was to heal one of his own kind. *This* was what Shalkan had been saving himself for, without knowing exactly what would be needed, only that it *would*. He fed the very essence of *unicorn* through the bond that tied him to Kellen, and into Kellen's Will, into Cilarnen, because Cilarnen was as virgin as Kellen, into the shield, so that all powers fused into one color that held all—

With a lightless flash and an earsplitting shriek of backlash, the Darkbolt recoiled upon itself.

The mirror . . . dissolved.

The Link was gone, and so was the Dome of Protection. The shields vanished beneath Kellen's grasp, and with them, his need to hold them. Suddenly alone in his own skin, Kellen tried to take a step, and went sprawling. Without the spell to concentrate on, all that was left was the pain: he felt drained—unnaturally drained—as if his body had given up more than it could safely give, and he *hurt* from the energies he had forced through himself.

Never be a High Mage . . . Kellen thought groggily.

He tried to get to his knees, but he was too sick and dizzy to move.

Cilarnen—Jermayan—I have to get up—

"Stay down. It's all right. I know what they want," someone—Idalia?—said. "I know what they're doing."

⟜

DARKNESS transmuted to Light fountained forth from the obsidian bowl, shattering it into a thousand razor shards that embedded themselves in the Demon Queen's flesh. Far worse than that was the backlash of her spell—Savilla had struck against the hated Enemy with all her might, and her own power had turned against her to strike her down. Drained of power, she lay insensible until Prince Zyperis found her.

It was he who carried her back to her resting chamber in secret, who drew the stone shards from her flesh and tenderly sucked each wound clean.

"Rest, darling Mama," he said lovingly. "Soon you will be strong again."

PRINCE Zyperis regarded his mother with every expression of tenderness—and why not? For the first time in his life, he had seen her helpless and vulnerable.

For now, it was their secret—and one Zyperis intended to share with no one else. But secrets were power among the Endarkened . . . and now he knew how Yethlenga had died: by the power of the Wild Magic and the High Magick combined.

It was a fearful thing to know that the puling creatures of the Light could slay them—they, who were meant to live forever, by the favor of He Who Is!

On the other hand, it was also . . . an opportunity.

He had not been ready to exploit it this time, nor had Queen Savilla been *quite* weak enough. But if he arranged matters properly—if he made sure that the Wildmages' pet High Mage flourished—

Then perhaps his beloved mother could meet with a timely accident the next time she faced the forces of the Light.

And there would be a new King in the World Without Sun.

THE cost of the spell to see into Armethalieh had been higher than any of them had imagined. No one had died, but that was as much as anyone could say. If there had been an attack in its aftermath, the army would have been slaughtered, for of those who had shared in the price, many had fainted where they stood, and the rest were too weak to as much as lift a sword. It would be sennights before the army was able to fight at full strength once more.

Those who had not shared in the spell-price—and it was

fortunate that so many had been exempted—found themselves occupied caring for those who had—helping the troops from the field around the ice-pavilion, and then returning to carry away the unconscious Wildmages and Cilarnen. Shalkan, too, had been found unconscious, guarded by the rest of the unicorn herd until a Healer could be brought to help him.

⌒

SOMEHOW the Demons—not the Mages—had seen the spell. And had managed to turn it against them. If Cilarnen had not been here—if Ancaladar had not granted him the power he had needed to use his magick—if he and Jermayan and Kellen had not somehow been able to fuse their powers and Shalkan had not added his own unique power to the lot . . .

She would be dead, and the Wildmages linked to her so mind-blasted that they might never have been able to serve the Wild Magic again. Cilarnen . . . she was not sure what would have happened to him. Nothing good.

If and if and if. But all had gone as the Wild Magic willed.

Their spell-shields had protected her—it was why she was still standing. And now—as soon as there was someone conscious to tell it to—she would be able to tell what she had learned.

Tears of fear and frustration gathered in Idalia's eyes as she thought of what she had seen in the mirror.

⌒

SHE was able to speak to Redhelwar that evening, though the Army's General was still confined to his bed. She summarized what she had learned through the spell.

"And soon the human City will be theirs, and all its Mages," Redhelwar said, his voice flat with exhaustion and grief. "As Kellen said: there was something *They* needed before *They* were willing to move openly."

"*They* don't have it yet," Idalia said. *And I pray to the Gods of the Wild Magic we can keep* Them *from getting it.*

⸺

IT was the next day before she dared to try to wake Kellen—even Jermayan, with Ancaladar's inexhaustible vitality to draw upon, still slept—but Kellen had to know what she knew as soon as possible.

They had to plan.

⸺

"DON'T wake him, Idalia," Isinwen begged as she entered Kellen's pavilion. The Elven Knight was sitting cross-legged beside the sleeping pallet, though he looked as if he ought to be in one himself. The pavilion was warm; obviously Isinwen was here to see that the brazier remained full and lit.

"I have to, Isinwen," Idalia said gently. "There are things he needs to know, and they cannot wait any longer."

"Then let me make tea first," Isinwen said resignedly, lighting the tea brazier.

When the tea was ready, Isinwen left.

No one can make you feel quite as guilty as a loyal servant, Idalia thought with an inward sigh. And Isinwen certainly seemed to have appointed himself to that position. She went over and knelt beside her sleeping brother.

⸺

IDALIA was calling him.

But he was so *tired* . . .

With an effort, Kellen forced himself to consciousness.

The mirror. The spell. The attack.

Idalia knows.

"Cilarnen—" he said, his voice a croak. "Shalkan."

"Alive," Idalia said. "They're all alive. I think he—they—will all be okay. They're still asleep. But I need you now."

Kellen tried to sit up. His body wouldn't obey, and that alarmed him enough to give him the strength to pull himself into a sitting position. Idalia steadied him and put a mug of tea into his hand.

Kellen took a deep breath, clearing his head, and gulped at the tea. It was hot, strong, and horribly sweet—just what he needed.

Exhaustion still dragged at him. But his mind was clearing quickly.

"*They* attacked us. Here."

"Yes," Idalia said. She shook her head in self-disgust. "Something I should have thought of, I suppose. We made a link to *Their* servant in the City. We expected an attack from the Mages, but . . . "

"But an opening is an opening, and *They* could use it just as well," Kellen finished. "But *Their* attack didn't work. Just like at Stonehearth—a Wildmage and a High Mage working together can hurt *Them*. Kill *Them*. I think . . . Idalia, I think that's what the High Magick was originally *for*."

"To help kill *Them*? It would be nice to think so. But I don't think knowing that is going to do us a lot of good now."

Kellen had finished his tea. Idalia refilled his mug, adding several more honey-disks.

"Idalia . . . I saw what you Saw. But I didn't understand it. Anigrel . . . he's on the Council now?"

"He's the one Cilarnen was told about in Stonehearth. Lycaelon has adopted him, made him a High Mage, and put him on the Council. He's the traitor—he has been for years. There's more—much more—but the main thing is this: he's changing the Wards of the City so that *Their* spells can pass through them."

His body might be exhausted, but Kellen's mind was fully

alert. It was the missing piece of the puzzle he'd searched for for so long.

"Once they can bespell the City, they can take the Wards down entirely and enter it in the flesh. But not . . . not just for prey. *They* could have stripped the Lost Land bare any time *They* liked if that was all they wanted. *They* want something more. Allies? But *They* are the ancient enemy of the Mageborn, too. Lycaelon would *never* . . . "

"He'll do what Anigrel tells him to," Idalia said grimly. "And Anigrel is telling him that *Wildmages* are the ones out to destroy his precious City—and have been for generations."

"*Xaqiue*," Kellen said. "We're the Wildmages, so we're the enemy—us, the Elves, the Allies. Idalia, it all makes sense now. *They* don't want to face us in the field. *They* never did. And if *They* destroy us . . . even Armethalieh might notice—and fight. But if *They* can get Armethalieh to do their fighting for *Them* . . . "

"Then Light destroys Light . . . and *They* destroy what's left," Idalia said despairingly.

"Now we know what *They* want," Kellen said. "And we know what we have to stop." And he felt a strange elation, as strong as Idalia's despair. "Knowledge is power, Idalia. And—I think—we've only begun to understand ours."

Epilogue

The first working had been accomplished successfully.

There had been a moment—just as he was about to inscribe the first of the seven Seals —when for a moment the Council chamber had vanished from Anigrel's sight, dissolved first in intolerable brightness and cold, and then in darkness and the scent of freshly-spilled blood.

But it had only been a moment. The web of the Working had held.

Of course Anigrel wondered about the cause. But none of the other Mages had sensed any disruption in the spell, and his own subsequent investigations had revealed nothing. Perhaps someone in the Mage Council had been attempting to Overlook the Working. Next time he would make doubly sure that any uninvited spectators received a more lasting greeting than they could imagine.

Each day, now, it would be safer to openly use those powers that were his true heritage.

He had waited impatiently for his Dark Lady to use her new freedom to contact him, and as the days passed and she did not, he grew close to despair. He *knew* his spells had not failed. How, then, had he displeased her?

At last the time came for him to make his own attempt. Even now, he dared not deviate from his schedule, lest his presumption displease her further. Besides, moondark was the time of greatest power for those spells he had learned under her tutelage.

At last the fortnight passed. He retreated to his rooms, filled the iron bowl with blood, and waited.

"You please me—and disappoint me," came the voice in his mind. Her touch was stronger than ever; he could almost feel her soft hands upon his flesh.

Anigrel dropped to his knees in confusion.

"I—I have done all you asked of me. I will do more!"

"Yes. You must do more—and quickly. Did you not notice, upon that night you worked to loosen the chains that bind your city against me, that the Wildmages struck at your life? It was only through my intervention that you still live. If I am to protect you further, those fetters must be loosed entirely. And you must convince the Arch-Mage to ally himself with us at once."

"But—" He'd known it was their ultimate goal. But it would not be an easy one to achieve. Another year—perhaps two—to soften Lycaelon's mind further—

"At once! I have indulged you for long enough—do this now, or face the ruin of all our hopes!"

Her fury was like a lash; Anigrel cringed from her displeasure even as he longed for the pain of her touch.

"Yes, Mistress—I swear to you I shall do this for you. Armethalieh shall be yours before the first flowers bloom."

"Much sooner, I hope . . . for your sake. My sweet Anigrel, do you not know how deeply I yearn to make you mine entirely? Do not make me wait much longer . . . "

"I swear to you, Mistress. The City shall be yours to do with as you will."

And I—I shall be yours as well.